Treasure Island

Kidnapped

The Black Arrow

R. L. Stevenson

TREASURE ISLAND

KIDNAPPED

THE BLACK ARROW

R. L. Stevenson

OCTOPUS

Robert Louis Stevenson was born in Scotland in 1850 and studied first engineering and then law. Ill health forced him to give up his legal practice and he turned to writing. He travelled through France and to America and finally settled in Samoa and published several books about his journeys. *Treasure Island* appeared as a serial for a boys' newspaper in 1881 and *Kidnapped* was published in 1886, to be followed by his celebrated work *The Strange Case of Dr Jekyll and Mr Hyde*. His reputation was now established and he continued to write prolifically after he had settled in the South Seas until his death in 1894.

This edition first published in Great Britain in 1978 by
Octopus Books Limited
59 Grosvenor Street London W1

© 1978 Illustrations Octopus Books Limited
Illustrated by Mark Thomas

ISBN 0 7064 07822

Printed in Czechoslovakia

50365

TREASURE ISLAND

TREASURE ISLAND

R. L. Stevenson

Contents

TO THE HESITATING PURCHASER

If sailor tales to sailor tunes,
　　Storm and adventure, heat and cold,
If schooners, islands, and maroons
　　And Buccaneers and buried Gold,
And all the old romance, retold
　　Exactly in the ancient way,
Can please, as me they pleased of old,
　　The wiser youngsters of to-day:

– So be it, and fall on! If not,
　　If studious youth no longer crave,
His ancient appetites forgot,
　　Kingston, or Ballantyne the brave,
Or Cooper of the wood and wave:
　　So be it, also! And may I
And all my pirates share the grave
　　Where these and their creations lie!

List of Illustrations

Foremast Hill

10
10

Strong tide here

6
1

Ye Spye glass Hill

2

14

7

Cape of ye Woods

4
5

Mizzenmast Hill

Haulbowline Head

12

North Inlet

Spring

Spye glass

Clean doing

South about W.B.

banks

15
6

15

Bulk of treasure here

Spring

Snow

White Rock

Skeleton Island

Foulground

12
10
6

12

A Scale of 3 English Miles

Treasure Island
Aug 1750 J.F.

Given by above J.F. & Mc JW Bones Maite of Ye Walrus
Savannah this twenty July 1754 W. B

Facsimile of Chart, latitude and
longitude struck out by J Hawkins

PART I THE OLD BUCCANEER

1 The Old Sea Dog at the 'Admiral Benbow'

Squire Trelawney, Dr. Livesey, and the rest of these gentlemen having asked me to write down the whole particulars about Treasure Island, from the beginning to the end, keeping nothing back but the bearings of the island, and that only because there is still treasure not yet lifted, I take up my pen in the year of grace 17—, and go back to the time when my father kept the 'Admiral Benbow' inn, and the brown old seaman, with the sabre cut, first took up his lodging under our roof.

I remember him as if it were yesterday, as he came plodding to the inn door, his sea-chest following behind him in a hand-barrow; a tall, strong, heavy, nut-brown man; his tarry pigtail falling over the shoulders of his soiled blue coat; his hands ragged and scarred, with black, broken nails; and the sabre cut across one cheek, a dirty, livid white. I remember him looking round the cove and whistling to himself as he did so, and then breaking out in that old sea-song that he sang so often afterwards:

> 'Fifteen men on the dead man's chest –
> Yo-ho-ho, and a bottle of rum!'

in the high old tottering voice that seemed to have been tuned and broken at the capstan bars. Then he rapped on the door with a bit of stick like a handspike that he carried, and when my father appeared, called roughly for a glass of rum. This, when it was brought to him, he drank slowly, like a connoisseur, lingering on the taste, and still looking about him at the cliffs and up at our signboard.

'This is a handy cove,' says he, at length; 'and a pleasant sittyated grog-shop. Much company, mate?'

My father told him no, very little company, the more was the pity.

'Well, then,' said he, 'this is the berth for me. Here you, matey,' he cried to the man who trundled the barrow; 'bring up alongside and help up my chest. I'll stay here a bit,' he continued. 'I'm a plain man;

rum and bacon and eggs is what I want, and that head up there for to watch ships off. What you mought call me? You mought call me captain. Oh, I see what you're at – there'; and he threw down three or four gold pieces on the threshold. 'You can tell me when I've worked through that,' says he, looking as fierce as a commander.

And, indeed, bad as his clothes were, and coarsely as he spoke, he had none of the appearance of a man who sailed before the mast; but seemed like a mate or skipper, accustomed to be obeyed or to strike. The man who came with the barrow told us the mail had set him down the morning before at the 'Royal George'; that he had inquired what inns there were along the coast, and hearing ours well spoken of, I suppose, and described as lonely, had chosen it from the others for his place of residence. And that was all we could learn of our guest.

He was a very silent man by custom. All day he hung round the cove, or upon the cliffs, with a brass telescope; all evening he sat in a corner of the parlour next the fire, and drank rum and water very strong. Mostly he would not speak when spoken to; only look up sudden and fierce, and blow through his nose like a fog-horn; and we and the people who came about our house soon learned to let him be. Every day, when he came back from his stroll, he would ask if any seafaring men had gone by along the road. At first we thought it was the want of company of his own kind that made him ask this question; but at last we began to see he was desirous to avoid them. When a seaman put up at the 'Admiral Benbow' (as now and then some did, making by the coast road for Bristol), he would look in at him through the curtained door before he entered the parlour; and he was always sure to be as silent as a mouse when any such was present. For me, at least, there was no secret about the matter; for I was, in a way, a sharer in his alarms. He had taken me aside one day, and promised me a silver fourpenny on the first of every month if I would only keep my 'weather-eye open for a seafaring man with one leg,' and let him know the moment he appeared. Often enough, when the first of the month came round, and I applied to him for my wage, he would only blow through his nose at me, and stare me down; but before the week was out he was sure to think better of it, bring me my fourpenny piece, and repeat his orders to look out for 'the seafaring man with one leg.'

How that personage haunted my dreams, I need scarcely tell you. On stormy nights, when the wind shook the four corners of the house, and the surf roared along the cove and up the cliffs, I would see him in a thousand forms, and with a thousand diabolical expressions. Now the leg would be cut off at the knee, now at the hip; now he was a monstrous kind of a creature who had never had but the one leg, and that in the middle of his body. To see him leap and run and pursue me over hedge and ditch was the worst of nightmares. And altogether I paid pretty dear for my monthly fourpenny piece, in the shape of these abominable fancies.

But though I was so terrified by the idea of the seafaring man with one leg, I was far less afraid of the captain himself than anybody else who knew him. There were nights when he took a deal more rum and water than his head would carry; and then he would sometimes sit and sing his wicked, old, wild sea-songs, minding nobody; but sometimes he would call for glasses round, and force all the trembling company to listen to his stories or bear a chorus to his singing. Often I have heard the house shaking with 'Yo-ho-ho, and a bottle of rum'; all the neighbours joining in for dear life, with the fear of death upon them, and each singing louder than the other, to avoid remark. For in these fits he was the most overriding companion ever known; he would slap his hand on the table for silence all round; he would fly up in a passion of anger at a question, or sometimes because none was put, and so he judged the company was not following his story. Nor would he allow any one to leave the inn till he had drunk himself sleepy and reeled off to bed.

His stories were what frightened people worst of all. Dreadful stories they were; about hanging, and walking the plank, and storms at sea, and the Dry Tortugas, and wild deeds and places on the Spanish Main. By his own account he must have lived his life among some of the wickedest men that God ever allowed upon the sea; and the language in which he told these stories shocked our plain country people almost as much as the crimes that he described. My father was always saying the inn would be ruined, for people would soon cease coming there to be tyrannized over and put down, and sent shivering to their beds; but I really believe his presence did us good. People were frightened at the time, but on looking back they rather liked it; it was a fine excitement in a quiet country life; and there was even a party of the younger men who pretended to admire him, calling him a 'true sea dog,' and a 'real old salt,' and such-like names, and saying there was the sort of man that made England terrible at sea.

In one way, indeed, he bade fair to ruin us; for he kept on staying week after week, and at last month after month, so that all the money had been long exhausted, and still my father never plucked up the heart to insist on having more. If ever he mentioned it, the captain blew through his nose so loudly, that you might say he roared, and stared my poor father out of the room. I have seen him wringing his hands after such a rebuff, and I am sure the annoyance and the terror he lived in must have greatly hastened his early and unhappy death.

All the time he lived with us the captain made no change whatever in his dress but to buy some stockings from a hawker. One of the cocks of his hat having fallen down, he let it hang from that day forth, though it was a great annoyance when it blew. I remember the appearance of his coat, which he patched himself upstairs in his room, and which, before the end, was nothing but patches. He never wrote or received a letter, and he never spoke with any but the neighbours, and with these, for the most part, only when drunk on rum. The great sea-chest none of us had ever seen open.

He was only once crossed, and that was towards the end, when my poor father was far gone in a decline that took him off. Dr. Livesey came late one afternoon to see the patient, took a bit of dinner from my mother, and went into the parlour to smoke a pipe until his horse should come down from the hamlet, for we had no stabling at the old 'Benbow.' I followed him in, and I remember observing the contrast the neat, bright doctor, with his powder as white as snow, and his bright, black eyes and pleasant manners, made with the coltish country folk, and above all, with that filthy, heavy, bleared scarecrow of a pirate of ours, sitting far gone in rum, with his arms on the table. Suddenly he – the captain, that is – began to pipe up his eternal song:

> 'Fifteen men on the dead man's chest –
>   Yo-ho-ho, and a bottle of rum!
> Drink and the devil had done for the rest –
>   Yo-ho-ho, and a bottle of rum!'

At first I had supposed 'the dead man's chest' to be that identical big box of his upstairs in the front room, and the thought had been mingled in my nightmares with that of the one-legged seafaring man. But by this time we had all long ceased to pay any particular notice to the song; it was new, that night, to nobody but Dr. Livesey, and on him I observed it did not produce an agreeable effect, for he looked up for a moment quite angrily before he went on with his talk to old

Taylor, the gardener, on a new cure for the rheumatics. In the meantime, the captain gradually brightened up at his own music, and at last flapped his hand upon the table before him in a way we all knew to mean – silence. The voices stopped at once, all but Dr. Livesey's; he went on as before, speaking clear and kind, and drawing briskly at his pipe between every word or two. The captain glared at him for a while, flapped his hand again, glared still harder, and at last broke out with a villainous, low oath: 'Silence, there, between decks!'

'Were you addressing me, sir?' says the doctor; and when the ruffian had told him, with another oath, that this was so, 'I have only one thing to say to you, sir,' replies the doctor, 'that if you keep on drinking rum, the world will soon be quit of a very dirty scoundrel!'

The old fellow's fury was awful. He sprang to his feet, drew and opened a sailor's clasp-knife, and, balancing it open on the palm of his hand, threatened to pin the doctor to the wall.

The doctor never so much as moved. He spoke to him, as before, over his shoulder, and in the same tone of voice; rather high, so that all the room might hear, but perfectly calm and steady:

'If you do not put that knife this instant in your pocket, I promise, upon my honour, you shall hang at next assizes.'

Then followed a battle of looks between them; but the captain soon knuckled under, put up his weapon, and resumed his seat, grumbling like a beaten dog.

'And now, sir,' continued the doctor, 'since I now know there's such a fellow in my district, you may count I'll have an eye upon you day and night. I'm not a doctor only; I'm a magistrate; and if I catch a breath of complaint against you, if it's only for a piece of incivility like to-night's, I'll take effectual means to have you hunted down and routed out of this. Let that suffice.'

Soon after Dr. Livesey's horse came to the door, and he rode away; but the captain held his peace that evening, and for many evenings to come.

2 Black Dog Appears and Disappears

It was not very long after this that there occurred the first of the mysterious events that rid us at last of the captain, though not, as you will see, of his affairs. It was a bitter cold winter, with long, hard frosts and heavy gales; and it was plain from the first that my poor father was little likely to see the spring. He sank daily, and my mother and I had all the inn upon our hands; and were kept busy enough, without paying much regard to our unpleasant guest.

It was one January morning, very early – a pinching, frosty morning – the cove all grey with hoar-frost, the ripple lapping softly on the stones, the sun still low and only touching the hill-tops and shining far to seaward. The captain had risen earlier than usual, and set out down the beach, his cutlass swinging under the broad skirts of the old blue coat, his brass telescope under his arm, his hat tilted back upon his head. I remember his breath hanging like smoke in his wake as he strode off, and the last sound I heard of him, as he turned the big rock, was a loud snort of indignation, as though his mind was still running upon Dr. Livesey.

Well, mother was upstairs with father; and I was laying the breakfast table against the captain's return, when the parlour door opened, and a man stepped in on whom I had never set my eyes before. He was a pale, tallowy creature, wanting two fingers of the left hand; and, though he wore a cutlass, he did not look much like a fighter. I had always my eye open for seafaring men, with one leg or two, and I remember this one puzzled me. He was not sailorly, and yet he had a smack of the sea about him too.

I asked him what was for his service, and he said he would take rum; but as I was going out of the room to fetch it he sat down upon a table and motioned me to draw near. I paused where I was with my napkin in my hand.

'Come here, sonny,' says he. 'Come nearer here.'

I took a step nearer.

'Is this here table for my mate Bill?' he asked, with a kind of leer.

I told him I did not know his mate Bill; and this was for a person who stayed in our house, whom we called the captain.

'Well,' said he, 'my mate Bill would be called the captain, as like as not. He has a cut on one cheek, and a mighty pleasant way with him, particularly in drink, has my mate Bill. We'll put it, for argument like, that your captain has a cut on one cheek – and we'll put it, if you like, that that cheek's the right one. Ah, well! I told you. Now, is my mate Bill in this here house?'

I told him he was out walking.

'Which way, sonny? Which way is he gone?'

And when I had pointed out the rock and told him how the captain was likely to return, and how soon, and answered a few other questions, 'Ah,' said he, 'this'll be as good as drink to my mate Bill.'

The expression of his face as he said these words was not at all pleasant, and I had my own reasons for thinking that the stranger was mistaken, even supposing he meant what he said. But it was no affair of mine, I thought; and, besides, it was difficult to know what to do. The stranger kept hanging about just outside the inn door, peering round the corner like a cat waiting for a mouse. Once I stepped out myself into the road, but he immediately called me back, and, as I did not obey quick enough for his fancy, a most horrible change came over his tallowy face and he ordered me in, with an oath that made me jump. As soon as I was back again he returned to his former manner, half fawning, half sneering, patted me on the shoulder, told me I was a good boy, and he had taken quite a fancy to me. 'I have a son of my own,' said he, 'as like you as two blocks, and he's all the pride of my 'art. But the great thing for boys is discipline, sonny – discipline. Now, if you had sailed along of Bill, you wouldn't have stood there to be spoke to twice – not you. That was never Bill's way, nor the way of sich as sailed with him. And here, sure enough, is my mate Bill, with a spy-glass under his arm, bless his old 'art to be sure. You and me'll just go back into the parlour, sonny, and get behind the door, and we'll give Bill a little surprise – bless his 'art, I say again.'

So saying, the stranger backed along with me into the parlour, and put me behind him in the corner, so that we were both hidden by the open door. I was very uneasy and alarmed, as you may fancy, and it rather added to my fears to observe that the stranger was certainly frightened himself. He cleared the hilt of his cutlass and loosened the blade in the sheath; and all the time we were waiting there he kept swallowing as if he felt what we used to call a lump in the throat.

At last in strode the captain, slammed the door behind him, without looking to the right or left, and marched straight across the room to where his breakfast awaited him.

'Bill,' said the stranger, in a voice that I thought he had tried to make bold and big.

The captain spun round on his heel and fronted us; all the brown had gone out of his face, and even his nose was blue; he had the look of a man who sees a ghost, or the evil one, or something worse, if anything can be; and, upon my word, I felt sorry to see him, all in a moment, turn so old and sick.

'Come, Bill, you know me; you know an old shipmate, Bill, surely,' said the stranger.

The captain made a sort of gasp.

'Black Dog!' said he.

'And who else?' returned the other, getting more at his ease. 'Black Dog as ever was, come for to see his old shipmate, Billy, at the "Admiral Benbow" inn. Ah, Bill, Bill, we have seen a sight of times, us two, since I lost them two talons,' holding up his mutilated hand.

'Now look here,' said the captain; 'you've run me down; here I am; well, then, speak up: what is it?'

'That's you, Bill,' returned Black Dog, 'you're in the right of it, Billy. I'll have a glass of rum from this dear child here, as I've took such a liking to; and we'll sit down, if you please, and talk square, like old shipmates.'

When I returned with the rum, they were already seated on either side of the captain's breakfast table – Black Dog next to the door, and sitting sideways, so as to have one eye on his old shipmate, and one, as I thought, on his retreat.

He bade me go, and leave the door wide open. 'None of your keyholes for me, sonny,' he said; and I left them together, and retired into the bar.

For a long time, though I certainly did my best to listen, I could hear nothing but a low gabbling; but at last the voices began to grow higher, and I could pick up a word or two, mostly oaths, from the captain.

'No, no, no, no; and an end of it!' he cried once. And again: 'If it comes to swinging, swing all, say I.'

Then all of a sudden there was a tremendous explosion of oaths and other noises – the chair and table went over in a lump, a clash of steel followed, and then a cry of pain, and the next instant I saw Black Dog in full flight, and the captain hotly pursuing, both with drawn cutlasses, and the former streaming blood from the left shoulder. Just at the door, the captain aimed at the fugitive one last tremendous cut, which would certainly have split him to the chine had it not been intercepted by our big signboard of Admiral Benbow. You may see the notch on the lower side of the frame to this day.

That blow was the last of the battle. Once out upon the road, Black Dog, in spite of his wound, showed a wonderful clean pair of heels, and disappeared over the edge of the hill in half a minute. The captain, for his part, stood staring at the signboard like a bewildered man. Then he passed his hand over his eyes several times, and at last turned back into the house.

'Jim,' says he, 'rum'; and as he spoke, he reeled a little, and caught himself with one hand against the wall.

'Are you hurt?' cried I.

'Rum,' he repeated. 'I must get away from here. Rum! rum!'

I ran to fetch it; but I was quite unsteadied by all that had fallen out, and I broke one glass and fouled the tap, and while I was still getting in my own way, I heard a loud fall in the parlour, and, running in, beheld the captain lying full length upon the floor. At the same instant my mother, alarmed by the cries and fighting, came running downstairs to help me. Between us we raised his head. He was breathing very loud and hard; but his eyes were closed, and his face a horrible colour.

'Dear, deary me!' cried my mother, 'what a disgrace upon the house! And your poor father sick!'

In the meantime, we had no idea what to do to help the captain, nor any other thought but that he had got his death-hurt in the scuffle with the stranger. I got the rum, to be sure, and tried to put it down his throat; but his teeth were tightly shut, and his jaws as strong as iron. It was a happy relief for us when the door opened and Dr. Livesey came in, on his visit to my father.

'Oh, doctor,' we cried, 'what shall we do? Where is he wounded?'

'Wounded? A fiddle-stick's end!' said the doctor. 'No more wounded than you or I. The man has had a stroke, as I warned him.

'The Captain aimed . . . one last tremendous cut'

Now, Mrs. Hawkins, just you run upstairs to your husband, and tell him, if possible, nothing about it. For my part, I must do my best to save this fellow's trebly worthless life; and Jim here will get me a basin.'

When I got back with the basin, the doctor had already ripped up the captain's sleeve, and exposed his great sinewy arm. It was tattooed in several places: 'Here's luck,' 'A fair wind,' and 'Billy Bones his fancy,' were very neatly and clearly executed on the forearm; and up near the shoulder there was a sketch of a gallows and a man hanging from it – done, as I thought, with great spirit.

'Prophetic,' said the doctor, touching this picture with his finger. 'And now, Master Billy Bones, if that be your name, we'll have a look at the colour of your blood. Jim,' he said, 'are you afraid of blood?'

'No, sir,' said I.

'Well, then,' said he, 'you hold the basin'; and with that he took his lancet and opened a vein.

A great deal of blood was taken before the captain opened his eyes and looked mistily about him. First he recognized the doctor with an unmistakable frown; then his glance fell upon me, and he looked relieved. But suddenly his colour changed, and he tried to raise himself, crying:

'Where's Black Dog?'

'There's no Black Dog here,' said the doctor, 'except what you have on your own back. You have been drinking rum; you have had a stroke, precisely as I told you; and I have just, very much against my own will, dragged you head foremost out of the grave. Now, Mr. Bones——'

'That's not my name,' he interrupted.

'Much I care,' returned the doctor. 'It's the name of a buccaneer of my acquaintance; and I call you by it for the sake of shortness, and what I have to say to you is this: one glass of rum won't kill you, but if you take one you'll take another and another, and I stake my wig if you don't break off short, you'll die – do you understand that? – die, and go to your own place, like the man in the Bible. Come, now, make an effort. I'll help you to your bed for once.'

Between us, with much trouble, we managed to hoist him upstairs, and laid him on his bed, where his head fell back on the pillow, as if he were almost fainting.

'Now, mind you,' said the doctor,' I clear my conscience – the name of rum for you is death.'

And with that he went off to see my father, taking me with him by the arm.

'This is nothing,' he said, as soon as he had closed the door. 'I have drawn blood enough to keep him quiet a while; he should lie for a week where he is – that is the best thing for him and you; but another stroke would settle him.'

3 The Black Spot

About noon I stopped at the captain's door with some cooling drinks and medicines. He was lying very much as we had left him, only a little higher, and he seemed both weak and excited.

'Jim,' he said, 'you're the only one here that's worth anything; and you know I've been always good to you. Never a month but I've given you a silver fourpenny for yourself. And now you see, mate, I'm pretty low, and deserted by all; and Jim, you'll bring me one noggin of rum, now, won't you, matey?'

'The doctor——' I began.

But he broke in cursing the doctor, in a feeble voice, but heartily. 'Doctors is all swabs,' he said; 'and that doctor there, why, what do he know about seafaring men? I been in places hot as pitch, and mates dropping round with Yellow Jack, and the blessed land a-heaving like the sea with earthquakes – what do the doctor know of lands like that? – and I lived on rum, I tell you. It's been meat and drink, and man and wife, to me; and if I'm not to have my rum now I'm a poor old hulk on a lee-shore, my blood'll be on you, Jim, and that doctor swab'; and he ran on again for a while with curses. 'Look, Jim, how my fingers fidget,' he continued, in the pleading tone. 'I can't keep 'em still, not I. I haven't had a drop this blessed day. That doctor's a fool, I tell you. If I don't have a drain o' rum, Jim, I'll have the horrors; I seen some on 'em already. I seen old Flint in the corner there, behind you; as plain as print, I seen him; and if I get the horrors, I'm a man that has lived rough, and I'll raise Cain. Your doctor hisself said one glass wouldn't hurt me. I'll give you a golden guinea for a noggin, Jim.'

He was growing more and more excited, and this alarmed me for my father, who was very low that day, and needed quiet; besides, I was reassured by the doctor's words, now quoted to me, and rather offended by the offer of a bribe.

'I want none of your money,' said I, 'but what you owe my father.

I'll get you one glass, and no more.'

When I brought it to him, he seized it greedily, and drank it out.

'Ay, ay,' said he, 'that's some better, sure enough. And now, matey, did that doctor say how long I was to lie here in this old berth?'

'A week at least,' said I.

'Thunder!' he cried. 'A week! I can't do that: they'd have the black spot on me by then. The lubbers is going about to get the wind of me this blessed moment; lubbers as couldn't keep what they got, and want to nail what is another's. Is that seamanly behaviour, now, I want to know? But I'm a saving soul. I never wasted good money of mine, nor lost it neither; and I'll trick 'em again. I'm not afraid on 'em. I'll shake out another reef, matey, and daddle 'em again.'

As he was thus speaking, he had risen from bed with great difficulty, holding to my shoulder with a grip that almost made me cry out, and moving his legs like so much dead weight. His words, spirited as they were in meaning, contrasted sadly with the weakness of the voice in which they were uttered. He paused when he had got into a sitting position on the edge.

'That doctor's done me,' he murmured. 'My ears is singing. Lay me back.'

Before I could do much to help him he had fallen back again to his former place, where he lay for a while silent.

'Jim,' he said, at length, 'you saw that seafaring man to-day?'

'Black Dog?' I asked.

'Ah! Black Dog,' says he. '*He*'s a bad 'un; but there's worse that put him on. Now, if I can't get away nohow, and they tip me the black spot, mind you, it's my old sea-chest they're after; you get on a horse – you can, can't you? Well, then, you get on a horse, and go to – well, yes, I will! – to that eternal doctor swab, and tell him to pipe all hands – magistrates and sich – and he'll lay 'em aboard at the "Admiral Benbow" – all old Flint's crew, man and boy, all on 'em that's left. I was first mate, I was, old Flint's first mate, and I'm the on'y one as knows the place. He gave it me to Savannah, when he lay a-dying, like as if I was to now, you see. But you won't peach unless they get the black spot on me, or unless you see that Black Dog again, or a seafaring man with one leg, Jim – him above all.'

'But what is the black spot, captain?' I asked.

'That's a summons, mate. I'll tell you if they get that. But you keep your weather-eye open, Jim, and I'll share with you equals, upon my honour.'

He wandered a little longer, his voice growing weaker; but soon after I had given him his medicine, which he took like a child, with the remark: 'If ever a seaman wanted drugs, it's me,' he fell at last into a heavy, swoon-like sleep, in which I left him. What I should have done had all gone well I do not know. Probably I should have told the whole story to the doctor; for I was in mortal fear lest the captain should repent of his confessions and make an end of me. But as things fell out, my poor father died quite suddenly that evening, which put all other matters on one side. Our natural distress, the visits of the neighbours, the arranging of the funeral, and all the work of the inn to be carried on in the meanwhile, kept me so busy that I had scarcely time to think of the captain, far less to be afraid of him.

He got downstairs next morning, to be sure, and had his meals as usual, though he ate little, and had more, I am afraid, than his usual supply of rum, for he helped himself out of the bar, scowling and blowing through his nose, and no one dared to cross him. On the night before the funeral he was as drunk as ever; and it was shocking, in that house of mourning, to hear him singing away at his ugly old sea-song; but, weak as he was, we were all in the fear of death for him, and the doctor was suddenly taken up with a case many miles away, and was never near the house after my father's death. I have said the captain was weak; and indeed he seemed rather to grow weaker than regain his strength. He clambered up and down stairs, and went from the parlour to the bar and back again, and sometimes put his nose out of doors to smell the sea, holding on to the walls as he went for support, and breathing hard and fast like a man on a steep mountain. He never particularly addressed me, and it is my belief he had as good as forgotten his confidences; but his temper was more flighty, and, allowing for his bodily weakness, more violent than ever. He had an alarming way now when he was drunk of drawing his cutlass and laying it bare before him on the table. But, with all that, he minded people less, and seemed shut up in his own thoughts and rather wandering. Once, for instance, to our extreme wonder, he piped up to a different air, a kind of country love-song, that he must have learned in his youth before he had begun to follow the sea.

So things passed until, the day after the funeral, and about three o'clock of a bitter, foggy, frosty afternoon, I was standing at the door for a moment, full of sad thoughts about my father, when I saw someone drawing slowly near along the road. He was plainly blind, for he tapped before him with a stick, and wore a great green shade over his eyes and nose; and he was hunched, as if with age or weakness, and wore a huge old tattered sea-cloak with a hood, that made him appear positively deformed. I never saw in my life a more dreadful-looking figure. He stopped a little from the inn, and, raising his voice in an odd sing-song, addressed the air in front of him:

'Will any kind friend inform a poor blind man, who has lost the precious sight of his eyes in the gracious defence of his native country, England, and God bless King George! – where or in what part of this country he may now be?'

'You are at the "Admiral Benbow," Black Hill Cove, my good man,' said I.

'I hear a voice,' said he – 'a young voice. Will you give me your hand, my kind young friend, and lead me in?'

I held out my hand, and the horrible, soft-spoken, eyeless creature gripped it in a moment like a vice. I was so much startled that I struggled to withdraw; but the blind man pulled me close up to him with a single action of his arm.

'Now, boy,' he said, 'take me in to the captain.'

'Sir,' said I, 'upon my word I dare not.'

'Oh,' he sneered, that's it! Take me in straight, or I'll break your arm.'

And he gave it, as he spoke, a wrench that made me cry out.

'Sir,' I said, 'it is for yourself I mean. The captain is not what he used to be. He sits with a drawn cutlass. Another gentleman——'

'Come, now, march,' interrupted he; and I never heard a voice so cruel, and cold, and ugly as that blind man's. It cowed me more than the pain, and I began to obey him at once, walking straight in at the door and towards the parlour where our sick old buccaneer was sitting, dazed with rum. The blind man clung close to me, holding me in one iron fist, and leaning almost more of his weight on me than I could carry. 'Lead me straight up to him, and when I'm in view, cry out: "Here's a friend for you, Bill." If you don't, I'll do this'; and with that he gave me a twitch that I thought would have made me faint. Between this and that, I was so utterly terrified of the blind beggar that I forgot my terror of the captain, and as I opened the parlour door, cried out the words he had ordered in a trembling voice.

The poor captain raised his eyes, and at one look the rum went out of him, and left him staring sober. The expression of his face was not so much of terror as of mortal sickness. He made a movement to rise, but I do not believe he had enough force left in his body.

'Now, Bill, sit where you are,' said the beggar. 'If I can't see, I can hear a finger stirring. Business is business. Hold out your left hand. Boy, take his left hand by the wrist, and bring it near to my right.'

We both obeyed him to the letter, and I saw him pass something from the hollow of the hand that held his stick into the palm of the captain's, which closed upon it instantly.

'And now that's done,' said the blind man; and at the words he suddenly left hold of me, and, with incredible accuracy and nimbleness, skipped out of the parlour and into the road, where, as I still stood motionless, I could hear his stick go tap-tap-tapping into the distance.

It was some time before either I or the captain seemed to gather our sense; but at length, and about at the same moment, I released his wrist, which I was still holding, and he drew in his hand and looked sharply into the palm.

'Ten o'clock!' he cried. 'Six hours. We'll do them yet'; and he sprang to his feet.

Even as he did so, he reeled, put his hand to his throat, stood swaying for a moment, and then, with a peculiar sound, fell from his whole height face foremost to the floor.

I ran to him at once, calling to my mother. But haste was all in vain. The captain had been struck dead by thundering apoplexy. It is a curious thing to understand, for I had certainly never liked the man, though of late I had begun to pity him, but as soon as I saw that he was dead, I burst into a flood of tears. It was the second death I had known, and the sorrow of the first was still fresh in my heart.

4 The Sea-Chest

I lost no time, of course, in telling my mother all that I knew, and perhaps should have told her long before, and we saw ourselves at once in a difficult and dangerous position. Some of the man's money – if he had any – was certainly due to us; but it was not likely that our captain's shipmates, above all the two specimens seen by me, Black Dog and the blind beggar, would be inclined to give up their booty in payment of the dead man's debts. The captain's order to mount at once and ride for Dr. Livesey would have left my mother alone and unprotected, which was not to be thought of. Indeed, it seemed impossible for either of us to remain much longer in the house: the fall of coals in the kitchen grate, the very ticking of the clock, filled us with alarms. The neighbourhood, to our ears, seemed haunted by approaching footsteps; and what between the dead body of the captain on the parlour floor, and the thought of that detestable blind beggar hovering near at hand, and ready to return, there were moments when, as the saying goes, I jumped in my skin for terror. Something must speedily be resolved upon; and it occurred to us at last to go forth together and seek help in the neighbouring hamlet. No sooner said than done. Bareheaded as we were, we ran out at once in the gathering evening and the frosty fog.

The hamlet lay not many hundred yards away though out of view, on the other side of the next cove; and what greatly encouraged me, it was in an opposite direction from that whence the blind man had made his appearance, and whither he had presumably returned. We were not many minutes on the road, though we sometimes stopped to lay hold of each other and hearken. But there was no unusual sound – nothing but the low wash of the ripple and the croaking of the crows in the wood.

It was already candle-light when we reached the hamlet, and I shall never forget how much I was cheered to see the yellow shine

in doors and windows; but that, as it proved, was the best of the help
we were likely to get in that quarter. For – you would have thought
men would have been ashamed of themselves – no soul would consent
to return with us to the 'Admiral Benbow.' The more we told of our
troubles, the more – man, woman, and child – they clung to the shelter
of their houses. The name of Captain Flint, though it was strange to
me, was well enough known to some there, and carried a great weight
of terror. Some of the men who had been to field-work on the far side
of the 'Admiral Benbow' remembered, besides, to have seen several
strangers on the road, and, taking them to be smugglers, to have bolted
away; and one at least had seen a little lugger in what we called Kitt's
Hole. For that matter, any one who was a comrade of the captain's was
enough to frighten them to death. And the short and the long of the
matter was, that while we could get several who were willing enough to
ride to Dr. Livesey's, which lay in another direction, not one would
help us to defend the inn.

They say cowardice is infectious; but then argument is, on the
other hand, a great emboldener; and so when each had said his say, my
mother made them a speech. She would not, she declared, lose money
that belonged to her fatherless boy; 'if none of the rest of you dare,' she
said, 'Jim and I dare. Back we will go, the way we came, and small
thanks to you big, hulking, chicken-hearted men. We'll have that chest
open, if we die for it. And I'll thank you for that bag, Mrs. Crossley, to
bring back our lawful money in.'

Of course, I said I would go with my mother; and of course they all
cried out at our foolhardiness; but even then not a man would go along
with us. All they would do was to give me a loaded pistol, lest we were
attacked; and to promise to have horses ready saddled, in case we were
pursued on our return; while one lad was to ride forward to the
doctor's in search of armed assistance.

My heart was beating finely when we two set forth in the cold
night upon this dangerous venture. A full moon was beginning to rise
and peered redly through the upper edges of the fog, and this increased
our haste, for it was plain, before we came forth again, that all would be
as bright as day, and our departure exposed to the eyes of any
watchers. We slipped along the hedges, noiseless and swift, nor did we
see or hear anything to increase our terrors, till, to our huge relief, the
door of the 'Admiral Benbow' had closed behind us.

I slipped the bolt at once, and we stood and panted for a moment in the dark, alone in the house with the dead captain's body. Then my mother got a candle in the bar, and, holding each other's hands, we advanced into the parlour. He lay as we had left him, on his back, with his eyes open, and one arm stretched out.

'Draw down the blind, Jim,' whispered my mother; 'they might come and watch outside. And now,' said she, when I had done so, 'we have to get the key off *that*; and who's to touch it, I should like to know!' and she gave a kind of sob as she said the words.

I went down on my knees at once. On the floor close to his hand there was a little round of paper, blackened on the one side. I could not doubt that this was the *black spot*; and taking it up, I found written on the other side, in a very good, clear hand, this short message: 'You have till ten to-night.'

'He had till ten, mother,' said I; and just as I said it, our old clock began striking. This sudden noise startled us shockingly; but the news was good, for it was only six.

'Now, Jim,' she said, 'that key.'

I felt in his pockets, one after another. A few small coins, a thimble, and some thread and big needles, a piece of pigtail tobacco bitten away at the end, his gully with the crooked handle, a pocket compass, and a tinder-box, were all that they contained, and I began to despair.

'Perhaps it's round his neck,' suggested my mother.

Overcoming a strong repugnance, I tore open his shirt at the neck, and there, sure enough, hanging to a bit of tarry string, which I cut with his own gully, we found the key. At this triumph we were filled with hope, and hurried upstairs, without delay, to the little room where he had slept so long, and where his box had stood since the day of his arrival.

It was like any other seaman's chest on the outside, the initial 'B.' burned on the top of it with a hot iron, and the corners somewhat smashed and broken as by long, rough usage.

'Give me the key,' said my mother; and though the lock was very stiff, she had turned it and thrown back the lid in a twinkling.

A strong smell of tobacco and tar rose from the interior, but nothing was to be seen on the top except a suit of very good clothes, carefully brushed and folded. They had never been worn, my mother said. Under that, the miscellany began – a quadrant, a tin cannikin, several sticks of tobacco, two brace of very handsome pistols, a piece of bar silver, an old Spanish watch and some other trinkets of little value and mostly of foreign make, a pair of compasses mounted with brass, and five or six curious West Indian shells. It has often set me thinking since that he should have carried about these shells with him in his wandering, guilty, and hunted life.

In the meantime we had found nothing of any value but the silver and the trinkets, and neither of these were in our way. Underneath there was an old boat-cloak, whitened with sea salt on many a harbour bar. My mother pulled it up with impatience, and there lay before us, the last things in the chest, a bundle tied up in oil-cloth, and looking like papers, and a canvas bag, that gave forth, at a touch, the jingle of gold.

'I'll show these rogues that I'm an honest woman,' said my mother. I'll have my dues, and not a farthing over. Hold Mrs. Crossley's bag.' And she began to count over the amount of the captain's score from the sailor's bag into the one that I was holding.

It was a long, difficult business, for the coins were of all countries and sizes – doubloons, and louis-d'ors, and guineas, and pieces of eight, and I know not what besides, all shaken together at random. The guineas, too, were about the scarcest, and it was with these only that my mother knew how to make her count.

When we were about half-way through, I suddenly put my hand upon her arm; for I had heard in the silent, frosty air, a sound that brought my heart into my mouth – the tap-tapping of the blind man's stick upon the frozen road. It drew nearer and nearer, while we sat holding our breath. Then it struck sharp on the inn door, and then we could hear the handle being turned, and the bolt rattling as the wretched being tried to enter; and then there was a long time of silence both within and without. At last the tapping recommenced, and, to our indescribable joy and gratitude, died slowly away again until it ceased to be heard.

'Mother,' said I, 'take the whole and let's be going'; for I was sure the bolted door must have seemed suspicious, and would bring the whole hornets' nest about our ears; though how thankful I was that I had bolted it, none could tell who had never met that terrible blind man.

But my mother, frightened as she was, would not consent to take a fraction more than was due to her, and was obstinately unwilling to be content with less. It was not yet seven, she said, by a long way;

she knew her rights and she would have them; and she was still arguing with me, when a little low whistle sounded a good way off upon the hill. That was enough, and more than enough, for both of us.

'I'll take what I have,' she said, jumping to her feet.

'And I'll take this to square the count,' said I, picking up the oilskin packet.

Next moment we were both groping downstairs, leaving the candle by the empty chest; and the next we had opened the door and were in full retreat. We had not started a moment too soon. The fog was rapidly dispersing; already the moon shone quite clear on the high ground on either side; and it was only in the exact bottom of the dell and round the tavern door that a thin veil still hung unbroken to conceal the first steps of our escape. Far less than half-way to the hamlet, very little beyond the bottom of the hill, we must come forth into the moonlight. Nor was this all; for the sound of several footsteps running came already to our ears, and as we looked back in their direction, a light tossing to and fro and still rapidly advancing, showed that one of the newcomers carried a lantern.

'My dear,' said my mother suddenly, 'take the money and run on. I am going to faint.'

This was certainly the end for both of us, I thought. How I cursed the cowardice of the neighbours; how I blamed my poor mother for her honesty and her greed, for her past foolhardiness and present weakness!

We were just at the little bridge, by good fortune; and I helped her, tottering as she was, to the edge of the bank, where, sure enough, she gave a sigh and fell on my shoulder. I do not know how I found the strength to do it at all, and I am afraid it was roughly done; but I managed to drag her down the bank and a little way under the arch. Farther I could not move her, for the bridge was too low to let me do more than crawl below it. So there we had to stay – my mother almost entirely exposed, and both of us within earshot of the inn.

5 The Last of the Blind Man

My curiosity, in a sense, was stronger than my fear; for I could not remain where I was, but crept back to the bank again, whence, sheltering my head behind a bush of broom, I might command the road before our door. I was scarcely in position ere my enemies began to arrive, seven or eight of them, running hard, their feet beating out of time along the road, and the man with the lantern some paces in front. Three men ran together, hand in hand; and I made out, even through the mist, that the middle man of this trio was the blind beggar. The next moment his voice showed me that I was right.

'Down with the door!' he cried.

'Ay, ay, sir!' answered two or three; and a rush was made upon the 'Admiral Benbow,' the lantern-bearer following; and then I could see them pause, and hear speeches passed in a lower key, as if they were surprised to find the door open. But the pause was brief, for the blind man again issued his commands. His voice sounded louder and higher, as if he were afire with eagerness and rage.

'In, in, in!' he shouted, and cursed them for their delay.

Four or five of them obeyed at once, two remaining on the road with the formidable beggar. There was a pause, then a cry of surprise, and then a voice shouting from the house:

'Bill's dead!'

But the blind man swore at them again for their delay.

'Search him, some of you shirking lubbers, and the rest of you aloft and get the chest,' he cried.

I could hear their feet rattling up our old stairs, so that the house must have shook with it. Promptly afterwards, fresh sounds of astonishment arose; the window of the captain's room was thrown open with a slam and a jingle of broken glass, and a man leaned out into the moonlight, head and shoulders, and addressed the blind beggar on the road below him.

'Pew,' he cried, 'they've been before us. Someone's turned the chest out alow and aloft.'

'Is it there?' roared Pew.

'The money's there.'

The blind man cursed the money.

'Flint's fist, I mean,' he cried.

'We don't see it here nohow,' returned the man.

'Here, you below there, is it on Bill?' cried the blind man again.

At that, another fellow, probably he who had remained below to search the captain's body, came to the door of the inn. 'Bill's been overhauled a'ready,' said he, 'nothin' left.'

'It's these people of the inn – it's that boy. I wish I had put his eyes out!' cried the blind man, Pew. 'They were here no time ago – they had the door bolted when I tried it. Scatter, lads, and find 'em.'

'Sure enough, they left their glim here,' said the fellow from the window.

'Scatter and find 'em! Rout the house out!' reiterated Pew, striking with his stick upon the road.

Then there followed a great to-do through all our old inn, heavy feet pounding to and fro, furniture thrown over, doors kicked in, until the very rocks re-echoed, and the men came out again, one after another, on the road, and declared that we were nowhere to be found. And just then the same whistle that had alarmed my mother and myself over the dead captain's money was once more clearly audible through the night, but this time twice repeated. I had thought it to be the blind man's trumpet, so to speak, summoning his crew to the assault; but I now found that it was a signal from the hillside towards the hamlet, and, from its effect upon the buccaneers, a signal to warn them of approaching danger.

'There's Dirk again,' said one. 'Twice! We'll have to budge, mates.'

'Budge, you skulk!' cried Pew. 'Dirk was a fool and a coward from the first – you wouldn't mind him. They must be close by; they can't be far; you have your hands on it. Scatter and look for them, dogs! Oh, shiver my soul,' he cried, 'if I had eyes!'

This appeal seemed to produce some effect, for two of the fellows began to look here and there among the lumber, but half-heartedly, I thought, and with half an eye to their own danger all the time, while the rest stood irresolute on the road.

'You have your hands on thousands, you fools, and you hang a leg! You'd be as rich as kings if you could find it, and you know it's here, and you stand there malingering. There wasn't one of you dared face Bill, and I did – a blind man! And I'm to lose my chance for you! I'm to be a poor, crawling beggar, sponging for rum, when I might be rolling in a coach! If you had the pluck of a weevil in a biscuit you would catch them still.'

'Hang it, Pew, we've got the doubloons!' grumbled one.

'They might have hid the blessed thing,' said another. 'Take the Georges, Pew, and don't stand here squalling.'

Squalling was the word for it, Pew's anger rose so high at these objections; till at last, his passion completely taking the upper hand, he struck at them right and left in his blindness, and his stick sounded heavily on more than one.

These, in their turn, cursed back at the blind miscreant, threatening him in horrid terms, and tried in vain to catch the stick and wrest it from his grasp.

This quarrel was the saving for us; for while it was still raging, another sound came from the top of the hill on the side of the hamlet – the tramp of horses galloping. Almost at the same time, a pistol shot, flash and report, came from the hedge-side. And that was plainly the last signal of danger; for the buccaneers turned at once and ran, separating in every direction, one seaward along the cove, one slant across the hill, and so on, so that in half a minute not a sign of them remained but Pew. Him they had deserted, whether in sheer panic or out of revenge for his ill words and blows, I know not; but there he remained behind, tapping up and down the road in a frenzy, and groping and calling for his comrades. Finally he took the wrong turn, and ran a few steps past me, towards the hamlet, crying:

'Johnny, Black Dog, Dirk,' and other names, 'you won't leave old Pew, mates – not old Pew!'

Just then the noise of horses topped the rise, and four or five riders came in sight in the moonlight, and swept at full gallop down the slope.

At this Pew saw his error, turned with a scream, and ran straight for the ditch, into which he rolled. But he was on his feet again in a second, and made another dash, now utterly bewildered, right under the nearest of the coming horses.

The rider tried to save him, but in vain. Down went Pew with a cry that rang high into the night; and the four hoofs trampled and spurned him and passed by. He fell on his side, then gently collapsed upon his face, and moved no more.

I leaped to my feet and hailed the riders. They were pulling up at any rate, horrified at the accident; and I soon saw what they were. One, tailing out behind the rest, was a lad that had gone from the hamlet to Dr. Livesey's; the rest were revenue officers, whom he had met by the way, and with whom he had had the intelligence to return at once. Some news of the lugger in Kitt's Hole had found its way to Supervisor Dance, and set him forth that night in our direction, and to that circumstance my mother and I owed our preservation from death.

Pew was dead, stone dead. As for my mother, when we had carried her up to the hamlet, a little cold water and salts and that soon brought her back again, and she was none the worse for her terror, though she still continued to deplore the balance of the money. In the meantime, the supervisor rode on, as fast as he could, to Kitt's Hole; but his men had to dismount and grope down the dingle, leading, and sometimes supporting, their horses, and in continual fear of ambushes; so it was no great matter for surprise that when they got down to the Hole the lugger was already under way, though still close in. He hailed her. A voice replied, telling him to keep out of the moonlight, or he would get some lead in him, and at the same time a bullet whistled close by his arm. Soon after, the lugger doubled the point and disappeared. Mr. Dance stood there, as he said, 'like a fish out of water,' and all he could do was to dispatch a man to B—— to warn the cutter. 'And that,' said he, 'is just about as good as nothing. They've got off clean, and there's an end. Only,' he added, 'I'm glad I trod on Master Pew's corns'; for by this time he had heard my story.

I went back with him to the 'Admiral Benbow,' and you cannot imagine a house in such a state of smash; the very clock had been thrown down by these fellows in their furious hunt after my mother and myself; and though nothing had actually been taken away except the captain's money-bag and a little silver from the till, I could see at once that we were ruined. Mr. Dance could make nothing of the scene.

'They got the money, you say? Well then, Hawkins, what in fortune were they after? More money, I suppose?'

'No, sir; not money, I think,' replied I. 'In fact, sir, I believe I have the thing in my breast-pocket; and, to tell you the truth, I should like to get it put in safety.'

'To be sure, boy; quite right,' said he. 'I'll take it, if you like.'

'I thought, perhaps, Dr. Livesey——' I began

'Perfectly right,' he interrupted very cheerily, 'perfectly right – a gentleman and a magistrate. And, now I come to think of it, I might as well ride round there myself and report to him or squire. Master Pew's dead, when all's done; not that I regret it, but he's dead, you see, and people will make it out against an officer of His Majesty's revenue, if make it out they can. Now, I'll tell you, Hawkins: if you like, I'll take you along.'

I thanked him heartily for the offer, and we walked back to the hamlet where the horses were. By the time I had told mother of my purpose they were all in the saddle.

'Dogger,' said Mr. Dance, 'you have a good horse; take up this lad behind you.'

As soon as I was mounted, holding on to Dogger's belt, the supervisor gave the word, and the party struck out at a bouncing trot on the road to Dr. Livesey's house.

6 The Captain's Papers

We rode hard all the way, till we drew up before Dr. Livesey's door. The house was all dark to the front.

Mr. Dance told me to jump down and knock, and Dogger gave me a stirrup to descend by. The door was opened almost at once by the maid.

'Is Dr. Livesey in?' I asked.

No, she said; he had come home in the afternoon, but had gone up to the Hall to dine and pass the evening with the squire.

'So there we go, boys,' said Mr. Dance.

This time, as the distance was short, I did not mount, but ran with Dogger's stirrup-leather to the lodge gates, and up the long, leafless, moonlit avenue to where the white line of the Hall buildings looked on either hand on great old gardens. Here Mr. Dance dismounted, and, taking me along with him, was admitted at a word into the house.

The servant led us down a matted passage, and showed us at the end into a great library, all lined with bookcases and busts upon the top of them, where the squire and Dr. Livesey sat, pipe in hand, on either side of a bright fire.

I had never seen the squire so near at hand. He was a tall man, over six feet high, and broad in proportion, and he had a bluff, rough-and-ready face, all roughened and reddened and lined in his long travels. His eyebrows were very black, and moved readily, and this gave him a look of some temper, not bad, you would say, but quick and high.

'Come in, Mr. Dance,' says he, very stately and condescending.

'Good evening, Dance,' says the doctor, with a nod. 'And good evening to you, friend Jim. What good wind brings you here?'

The supervisor stood up straight and stiff, and told his story like a lesson; and you should have seen how the two gentlemen leaned forward and looked at each other, and forgot to smoke in their surprise and interest. When they heard how my mother went back to the inn,

Dr. Livesey fairly slapped his thigh, and the squire cried 'Bravo!' and broke his long pipe against the grate. Long before it was done, Mr. Trelawney (that, you will remember, was the squire's name) had got up from his seat, and was striding about the room, and the doctor, as if to hear the better, had taken off his powdered wig, and sat there, looking very strange indeed with his own close-cropped, black poll.

At last Mr. Dance finished the story.

'Mr. Dance,' said the squire, 'you are a very noble fellow. And as for riding down that black, atrocious miscreant, I regard it as an act of virtue, sir, like stamping on a cockroach. This lad Hawkins is a trump, I perceive. Hawkins, will you ring that bell? Mr. Dance must have some ale.'

'And so, Jim,' said the doctor, 'you have the thing that they were after, have you?'

'Here it is, sir,' said I, and gave him the oilskin packet.

The doctor looked it all over, as if his fingers were itching to open it; but, instead of doing that, he put it quietly in the pocket of his coat.

'Squire,' said he, 'when Dance has had his ale he must, of course, be off on His Majesty's service; but I mean to keep Jim Hawkins here to sleep at my house, and, with your permission, I propose we should have up the cold pie, and let him sup.'

'As you will, Livesey,' said the squire; 'Hawkins has earned better than cold pie.'

So a big pigeon pie was brought in and put on a side table, and I made a hearty supper, for I was as hungry as a hawk, while Mr. Dance was further complimented, and at last dismissed.

'And now, squire,' said the doctor.

'And now, Livesey,' said the squire, in the same breath.

'One at a time, one at a time,' laughed Dr. Livesey. 'You have heard of this Flint, I suppose?'

'Heard of him!' cried the squire. 'Heard of him, you say! He was the bloodthirstiest buccaneer that sailed. Blackbeard was a child to Flint. The Spaniards were so prodigiously afraid of him, that, I tell you, sir, I was sometimes proud he was an Englishman. I've seen his topsails with these eyes, off Trinidad, and the cowardly son of a rum-puncheon that I sailed with put back – put back, sir, into Port of Spain.'

'Well, I've heard of him myself, in England,' said the doctor. 'But the point is, had he money?'

'The squire and I were both peering over his shoulder'

'Money!' cried the squire. 'Have you heard the story? What were these villains after but money? What do they care for but money? For what would they risk their rascal carcasses but money?'

'That we shall soon know,' replied the doctor. 'But you are so confoundedly hot-headed and exclamatory that I cannot get a word in. What I want to know is this: Supposing that I have here in my pocket some clue to where Flint buried his treasure, will that treasure amount to much?'

'Amount, sir!' cried the squire. 'It will amount to this; if we have the clue you talk about, I fit out a ship in Bristol dock, and take you and Hawkins here along, and I'll have that treasure if I search a year.'

'Very well,' said the doctor. 'Now, then, if Jim is agreeable, we'll open the packet'; and he laid it before him on the table.

The bundle was sewn together, and the doctor had to get out his instrument case and cut the stitches with his medical scissors. It contained two things – a book and a sealed paper.

'First of all we'll try the book,' observed the doctor.

The squire and I were both peering over his shoulder as he opened it, for Dr. Livesey had kindly motioned me to come round from the side table, where I had been eating, to enjoy the sport of the search. On the first page there were only some scraps of writing, such as a man with a pen in his hand might make for idleness or practice. One was the same as the tattoo mark: 'Billy Bones his fancy'; then there was 'Mr. W. Bones, mate.' 'No more rum.' 'Off Palm Key he got itt'; and some other snatches, mostly single words and unintelligible. I could not help wondering who it was that had 'got itt,' and what 'itt' was that he got. A knife in his back as like as not.

'Not much instruction there,' said Dr. Livesey, as he passed on.

The next ten or twelve pages were filled with a curious series of entries. There was a date at one end of the line and at the other a sum of money, as in common account books; but instead of explanatory writing, only a varying number of crosses between the two. On the 12th of June 1745, for instance, a sum of seventy pounds had plainly become due to someone, and there was nothing but six crosses to explain the cause. In a few cases, to be sure, the name of a place would be added, as 'Offe Caraccas'; or a mere entry of latitude and longitude, as '62° 17′ 20″, 19° 2′ 40″.'

The record lasted over nearly twenty years, the amount of the separate entries growing larger as time went on, and at the end a grand total had been made out after five or six wrong additions, and these words appended: 'Bones, his pile.'

'I can't make head or tail of this,' said Dr. Livesey.

'The thing is as clear as noonday,' cried the squire. 'This is the black-hearted hound's account book. These crosses stand for the names of ships or towns that they sank or plundered. The sums are the scoundrel's share, and where he feared an ambiguity, you see he added something clearer. "Offe Caraccas," now; you see, here was some unhappy vessel boarded off that coast. God help the poor souls that˙ manned her – coral long ago.'

'Right!' said the doctor. 'See what it is to be a traveller. Right! And the amounts increase, you see, as he rose in rank.'

There was little else in the volume but a few bearings of places noted in the blank leaves towards the end, and a table for reducing French, English, and Spanish moneys to a common value.

'Thrifty man!' cried the doctor. 'He wasn't the one to be cheated.'

'And now,' said the squire, 'for the other.'

The paper had been sealed in several places with a thimble, by way of seal; the very thimble, perhaps, that I had found in the captain's pocket. The doctor opened the seals with great care, and there fell out the map of an island, with latitude and longitude, soundings, names of hills, and bays and inlets, and every particular that would be needed to bring a ship to a safe anchorage upon its shores. It was about nine miles long and five across, shaped, you might say, like a fat dragon standing up, and had two fine landlocked harbours, and a hill in the centre part marked 'The Spy-glass.' There were several additions of a later date; but, above all, three crosses of red ink – two on the north part of the island, one in the south-west, and, beside this last, in the same red ink, and in a small neat hand, very different from the captain's tottery characters, these words: 'Bulk of treasure here.'

Over on the back the same hand had written this further information:

Tall tree, Spy-glass Shoulder, bearing a point to the N. of N.N.E.

Skeleton Island E.S.E. and by E.

Ten feet.

The bar silver is in the north cache; you can find it by the trend of the east hummock, ten fathoms south of the black crag with the face on it.

The arms are easy found, in the sand hill, N. point of north inlet cape, bearing E. and a quarter N.   J. F.

That was all; but brief as it was, and, to me, incomprehensible, it filled the squire and Dr. Livesey with delight.

'Livesey,' said the squire, 'you will give up this wretched practice at once. To-morrow I start for Bristol. In three weeks' time – three weeks! – two weeks – ten days – we'll have the best ship, sir, and the choicest crew in England. Hawkins shall come as cabin-boy. You'll make a famous cabin-boy, Hawkins. You, Livesey, are ship's doctor; I am admiral. We'll take Redruth, Joyce, and Hunter. We'll have favourable winds, a quick passage, and not the least difficulty in finding the spot, and money to eat – to roll in – to play duck and drake with ever after.'

'Trelawney,' said the doctor, 'I'll go with you; and, I'll go bail for it, so will Jim, and be a credit to the undertaking. There's only one man I'm afraid of.'

'And who's that?' cried the squire. 'Name the dog, sir!'

'You,' replied the doctor; 'for you cannot hold your tongue. We are not the only men who know of this paper. These fellows who attacked the inn to-night – bold, desperate blades, for sure – and the rest who stayed aboard that lugger, and more, I dare say, not far off, are, one and all, through thick and thin, bound that they'll get that money. We must none of us go alone till we get to sea. Jim and I shall stick together in the meanwhile; you'll take Joyce and Hunter when you ride to Bristol, and, from first to last, not one of us must breathe a word of what we've found.'

'Livesey,' returned the squire, 'you are always in the right of it. I'll be as silent as the grave.'

PART 2 THE SEA COOK

1 I Go To Bristol

It was longer than the squire imagined ere we were ready for the sea, and none of our first plans – not even Dr. Livesey's, of keeping me beside him – could be carried out as we intended. The doctor had to go to London for a physician to take charge of his practice; the squire was hard at work at Bristol; and I lived on at the Hall under the charge of old Redruth, the gamekeeper, almost a prisoner, but full of sea-dreams and the most charming anticipations of strange islands and adventures. I brooded by the hour together over the map, all the details of which I well remembered. Sitting by the fire in the housekeeper's room, I approached that island, in my fancy, from every possible direction; I explored every acre of its surface; I climbed a thousand times to that tall hill they call the Spy-glass, and from the top enjoyed the most wonderful and changing prospects. Sometimes the isle was thick with savages, with whom we fought; sometimes full of dangerous animals that hunted us; but in all my fancies nothing occurred to me so strange and tragic as our actual adventures.

So the weeks passed on – till one fine day there came a letter addressed to Dr. Livesey, with this addition: 'To be opened, in the case of his absence, by Tom Redruth, or young Hawkins.' Obeying this order we found, or rather I found – for the gamekeeper was a poor hand at reading anything but print – the following important news:

Old Anchor Inn, Bristol, March 1, 17—.

DEAR LIVESEY,—As I do not know whether you are at the Hall or still in London, I send this in double to both places.

The ship is bought and fitted. She lies at anchor, ready for sea. You never imagined a sweeter schooner – a child might sail her – two hundred tons; name, *Hispaniola.*

I got her through my old friend, Blandly, who has proved himself throughout the most surprising trump. The admirable fellow literally slaved in my interest, and, I may say, did every one in Bristol, as soon as they got wind of the port we sailed for – treasure, I mean.

'Redruth,' said I, interrupting the letter, 'Dr. Livesey will not like that. The squire has been talking, after all.'

'Well, who's a better right?' growled the gamekeeper. 'A pretty rum go if squire ain't to talk for Dr. Livesey, I should think.'

At that I gave up all attempt at commentary, and read straight on:

Blandly himself found the *Hispaniola*, and by the most admirable management got her for the merest trifle. There is a class of men in Bristol monstrously prejudiced against Blandly. They go the length of declaring that this honest creature would do anything for money, that the *Hispaniola* belonged to him, and that he sold it me absurdly high – the most transparent calumnies. None of them dare, however, to deny the merits of the ship.

So far there was not a hitch. The workpeople, to be sure – riggers and what not – were most annoyingly slow; but time cured that. It was the crew that troubled me.

I wished a round score of men – in case of natives, buccaneers, or the odious French – and I had the worry of the deuce itself to find so much as half a dozen, till the most remarkable stroke of fortune brought me the very man that I required.

I was standing on the dock, when, by the merest accident, I fell in talk with him. I found he was an old sailor, kept a public-house, knew all the seafaring men in Bristol, had lost his health ashore, and wanted a good berth as cook to get to sea again. He had hobbled down there that morning, he said, to get a smell of the salt.

I was monstrously touched – so would you have been – and, out of pure pity, I engaged him on the spot to be ship's cook. Long John Silver, he is called, and has lost a leg; but that I regarded as a recommendation, since he lost it in his country's service under the immortal Hawke. He has no pension, Livesey. Imagine the abominable age we live in!

Well, sir, I thought I had only found a cook, but it was a crew I had discovered. Between Silver and myself we got together in a few days a company of the toughest old salts imaginable – not pretty to look at, but fellows, by their faces, of the most indomitable spirit. I declare we could fight a frigate.

Long John even got rid of two out of the six or seven I had already engaged. He showed me in a moment that they were just the sort of fresh-water swabs we had to fear ·in an adventure of importance.

I am in the most magnificent health and spirits, eating like a bull, sleeping like a tree, yet I shall not enjoy a moment till I hear my old tarpaulins tramping round the capstan. Seaward ho! Hang the treasure! It's the glory of the sea that has turned my head. So now, Livesey, come post; do not lose an hour, if you respect me.

Let young Hawkins go at once to see his mother, with Redruth for a guard; and then both come full speed to Bristol.

JOHN TRELAWNEY.

Postscript. I did not tell you that Blandly, who, by the way, is to send a consort after us if we don't turn up by the end of August, had found an admirable fellow for sailing master – a stiff man, which I regret, but in all other respects, a treasure. Long John Silver unearthed a very competent man for a mate, a man named Arrow. I have a boatswain who pipes, Livesey; so things shall go man-o'-war fashion on board the good ship *Hispaniola*.

I forgot to tell you that Silver is a man of substance; I know of my own knowledge that he has a banker's account, which has never been overdrawn. He leaves his wife to manage the inn; and as she is a woman of colour, a pair of old bachelors like you and I may be excused for guessing that it is the wife, quite as much as the health, that sends him back to roving.   J.T.

PPS. Hawkins may stay one night with his mother.   J.T.

You can fancy the excitement into which that letter put me. I was half beside myself with glee; and if ever I despised a man, it was old Tom Redruth, who could do nothing but grumble and lament. Any of the under-gamekeepers would gladly have changed places with him; but such was not the squire's pleasure, and the squire's pleasure was like law among them all. Nobody but old Redruth would have dared so much as even to grumble.

The next morning he and I set out on foot for the 'Admiral Benbow,' and there I found my mother in good health and spirits. The captain, who had so long been a cause of so much discomfort, was gone where the wicked cease from troubling. The squire had had everything repaired, and the public rooms and the sign repainted, and had added some furniture – above all, a beautiful armchair for mother in the bar. He had found her a boy as an apprentice also, so that she should not want help while I was gone.

It was on seeing that boy that I understood, for the first time, my situation. I had thought up to that moment of the adventures before me, not at all of the home that I was leaving; and now at sight of this clumsy stranger, who was to stay here in my place beside my mother, I had my first attack of tears. I am afraid I led that boy a dog's life; for as he was new to the work, I had a hundred opportunities of setting him right and putting him down, and I was not slow to profit by them.

The night passed, and the next day, after dinner, Redruth and I were afoot again, and on the road. I said good-bye to mother and the cove where I had lived since I was born, and the dear old 'Admiral Benbow' – since he was repainted, no longer quite so dear. One of my last thoughts was of the captain, who had so often strode along the beach with his cocked hat, his sabre-cut cheek, and his old brass telescope. Next moment we had turned the corner and my home was out of sight.

The mail picked us up about dusk at the 'Royal George' on the heath. I was wedged in between Redruth and a stout old gentleman, and in spite of the swift motion and the cold night air, I must have dozed a great deal from the very first, and then slept like a log, up hill and down dale through stage after stage; for when I was awakened at last, it was by a punch in the ribs, and I opened my eyes, to find that we were standing still before a large building in a city street, and that the day had already broken a long time.

'Where are we?' I asked.

'Bristol,' said Tom. 'Get down.'

Mr. Trelawney had taken up his residence at an inn far down the docks, to superintend the work upon the schooner. Thither we had now to walk, and our way, to my great delight, lay along the quays and beside the great multitude of ships of all sizes and rigs and nations. In one, sailors were singing at their work; in another, there were men aloft, high over my head, hanging to threads that seemed no thicker than a spider's. Though I had lived by the shore all my life, I seemed never to have been near the sea till then. The smell of tar and salt was something new. I saw the most wonderful figureheads, that had all been far over the ocean. I saw, besides, many old sailors, with rings in their ears, and whiskers curled in ringlets, and tarry pigtails, and their swaggering, clumsy sea-walk; and if I had seen as many kings or archbishops I could not have been more delighted.

And I was going to sea myself; to sea in a schooner, with a piping boatswain, and pig-tailed singing seamen; to sea, bound for an unknown island, and to seek for buried treasures!

While I was still in this delightful dream, we came suddenly in front of a large inn, and met Squire Trelawney, all dressed out like a sea-officer, in stout blue cloth, coming out of the door with a smile on his face, and a capital imitation of a sailor's walk.

'Here you are,' he cried, 'and the doctor came last night from London. Bravo! the ship's company complete!'

'Oh, sir,' cried I, 'when do we sail?'

'Sail!' says he. 'We sail to-morrow!'

2 At the Sign of the 'Spy-Glass'

When I had done breakfasting the squire gave me a note addressed to John Silver, at the sign of the 'Spy-glass,' and told me I should easily find the place by following the line of the docks, and keeping a bright look-out for a little tavern with a large brass telescope for sign. I set off, overjoyed at this opportunity to see some more of the ships and seamen, and picked my way among a great crowd of people and carts and bales, for the dock was now at its busiest, until I found the tavern in question.

It was a bright enough little place of entertainment. The sign was newly painted; the windows had neat red curtains; the floor was cleanly sanded. There was a street on either side, and an open door on both, which made the large, low room pretty clear to see in, in spite of clouds of tobacco smoke.

The customers were mostly seafaring men; and they talked so loudly that I hung at the door, almost afraid to enter.

As I was waiting, a man came out of a side-room, and, at a glance, I was sure he must be Long John. His left leg was cut off close by the hip, and under the left shoulder he carried a crutch, which he managed with wonderful dexterity, hopping about upon it like a bird. He was very tall and strong, with a face as big as a ham – plain and pale, but intelligent and smiling. Indeed, he seemed in the most cheerful spirits, whistling as he moved about among the tables, with a merry word or a slap on the shoulder for the more favoured of his guests.

Now, to tell you the truth, from the very first mention of Long John in Squire Trelawney's letter, I had taken a fear in my mind that he might prove to be the very one-legged sailor whom I had watched for so long at the old 'Benbow.' But one look at the man before me was enough. I had seen the captain, and Black Dog, and the blind man Pew, and I thought I knew what a buccaneer was like a very different creature, according to me, from this clean and pleasant-tempered landlord.

'"Oh," I cried, "Stop him! It's Black Dog"'

I plucked up courage at once, crossed the threshold, and walked right up to the man where he stood, propped on his crutch, talking to a customer.

'Mr. Silver, sir?' I asked, holding out the note.

'Yes, my lad,' said he; 'such is my name, to be sure. And who may you be?' And then as he saw the squire's letter, he seemed to me to give something almost like a start.

'Oh!' said he, quite loud, and offering his hand, 'I see. You are our new cabin-boy; pleased I am to see you.'

And he took my hand in his large firm grasp.

Just then one of the customers at the far side rose suddenly and made for the door. It was close by him, and he was out in the street in a moment. But his hurry had attracted my notice, and I recognized him at a glance. It was the tallow-faced man, wanting two fingers, who had come first to the 'Admiral Benbow.'

'Oh,' I cried, 'stop him! it's Black Dog!'

'I don't care two coppers who he is,' cried Silver. 'But he hasn't paid his score. Harry, run and catch him.'

One of the others who was nearest the door leaped up, and started in pursuit.

'If he were Admiral Hawke he shall pay his score,' cried Silver; and then, relinquishing my hand – 'Who did you say he was?' he asked. 'Black what?'

'Dog, sir,' said I. 'Has Mr. Trelawney not told you of the buccaneers? He was one of them.'

'So?' cried Silver. 'In my house! Ben, run and help Harry. One of those swabs, was he? Was that you drinking with him, Morgan? Step up here.'

The man whom he called Morgan – an old, grey-haired, mahogany-faced sailor – came forward pretty sheepishly, rolling his quid.

'Now, Morgan,' said Long John, very sternly; 'you never clapped your eyes on that Black – Black Dog before, did you, now?'

'Not I, sir,' said Morgan, with a salute.

'You didn't know his name, did you?'

'No, sir.'

'By the powers, Tom Morgan, it's as good for you!' exclaimed the landlord. 'If you had been mixed up with the like of that, you would never have put another foot in my house, you may lay to that. And what was he saying to you?'

'I don't rightly know, sir,' answered Morgan.

'Do you call that a head on your shoulders, or a blessed dead-eye?' cried Long John. 'Don't rightly know, don't you! Perhaps you don't happen to rightly know who you was speaking to, perhaps? Come, now, what was he jawing – v'yages, cap'ns, ships? Pipe up! What was it?'

'We was a-talkin' of keel-hauling,' answered Morgan.

'Keel-hauling, was you? and a mighty suitable thing, too, and you may lay to that. Get back to your place for a lubber, Tom.'

And then, as Morgan rolled back to his seat, Silver added to me in a confidential whisper, that was very flattering, as I thought:

'He's quite an honest man, Tom Morgan, on'y stupid. And now,' he ran on again aloud, 'let's see – Black Dog? No, I don't know the name, not I. Yet I kind of think I've – yes, I've seen the swab. He used to come here with a blind beggar, he used.'

'That he did, you may be sure,' said I. 'I knew that blind man, too. His name was Pew.'

'It was!' cried Silver, now quite excited. 'Pew! That were his name for certain. Ah, he looked a shark, he did! If we run down this Black Dog, now, there'll be news for Cap'n Trelawney! Ben's a good runner; few seamen run better than Ben. He should run him down, hand over hand, by the powers. He talked o' keel-hauling, did he? *I*'ll keel-haul him!'

All the time he was jerking out these phrases he was stumping up and down the tavern on his crutch, slapping tables with his hand, and giving such a show of excitement as would have convinced an Old Bailey judge or a Bow Street runner. My suspicions had been thoroughly reawakened on finding Black Dog at the 'Spy-glass,' and I watched the cook narrowly. But he was too deep, and too ready, and too clever for me, and by the time the two men had come back out of breath, and confessed that they had lost the track in a crowd, and been scolded like thieves, I would have gone bail for the innocence of Long John Silver.

'See here, now, Hawkins,' said he, 'here's a blessed hard thing on a man like me, now, ain't it? There's Cap'n Trelawney – what's he to think? Here I have this confounded son of a Dutchman sitting in my own house, drinking of my own rum! Here you comes and tells me of it plain; and here I let him give us all the slip before my blessed deadlights! Now, Hawkins, you do me justice with the cap'n. You're a lad, you are, but you're as smart as paint. I see that when you first came in. Now, here it is: What could I do, with this old timber I hobble on? When I was an A.B. master mariner I'd have come up alongside of him, hand over hand, and broached him to in a brace of old shakes, I would; but now——'

And then, all of a sudden, he stopped, and his jaw dropped as though he had remembered something.

'The score!' he burst out. 'Three goes o' rum! Why, shiver my timbers, if I hadn't forgotten my score!'

And, falling on a bench, he laughed until the tears ran down his cheeks. I could not help joining; and we laughed together, peal after peal, until the tavern rang again.

'Why, what a precious old sea-calf I am!' he said, at last, wiping his cheeks. 'You and me should get on well, Hawkins, for I'll take my davy I should be rated ship's boy. But, come now, stand by to go about. This won't do. Dooty is dooty, messmates. I'll put on my old cocked hat, and step along of you to Cap'n Trelawney, and report this here affair. For, mind you, it's serious, young Hawkins; and neither you nor me's come out of it with what I should make so bold as to call credit. Nor you neither, says you; not smart – none of the pair of us smart. But dash my buttons! that was a good 'un about my score.'

And he began to laugh again, and that so heartily, that though I did not see the joke as he did, I was again obliged to join him in his mirth.

On our little walk along the quays, he made himself the most interesting companion, telling me about the different ships that we passed by, their rig, tonnage, and nationality, explaining the work that was going forward – how one was discharging, another taking in cargo, and a third making ready for sea; and every now and then telling me some little anecdote of ships or seamen, or repeating a nautical phrase till I had learned it perfectly. I began to see that here was one of the best of possible shipmates.

When we got to the inn, the squire and Dr. Livesey were seated together, finishing a quart of ale with a toast in it, before they should go aboard the schooner on a visit of inspection.

Long John told the story from first to last, with a great deal of spirit and the most perfect truth. 'That was how it were, now, weren't it, Hawkins?' he would say, now and again, and I could always bear him entirely out.

The two gentlemen regretted that Black Dog had got away; but we all agreed there was nothing to be done, and after he had been complimented, Long John took up his crutch and departed.

'All hands aboard by four this afternoon,' shouted the squire after him.

'Ay, ay, sir,' cried the cook, in the passage.

'Well, squire,' said Dr. Livesey, 'I don't put much faith in your discoveries, as a general thing; but I will say this, John Silver suits me.'

'The man's a perfect trump,' declared the squire.

'And now,' added the doctor, 'Jim may come on board with us, may he not?'

'To be sure he may,' says squire. 'Take your hat, Hawkins, and we'll see the ship.'

3 Powder and Arms

The *Hispaniola* lay some way out, and we went under the figureheads and round the sterns of many other ships, and their cables sometimes grated underneath our keel, and sometimes swung above us. At last, however, we got alongside, and were met and saluted as we stepped aboard by the mate, Mr. Arrow, a brown old sailor, with earrings in his ears and a squint. He and the squire were very thick and friendly, but I soon observed that things were not the same between Mr. Trelawney and the captain.

This last was a sharp-looking man, who seemed angry with everything on board, and was soon to tell us why, for we had hardly got down into the cabin when a sailor followed us.

'Captain Smollet, sir, axing to speak with you,' said he.

'I am always at the captain's orders. Show him in,' said the squire.

The captain, who was close behind his messenger, entered at once, and shut the door behind him.

'Well, Captain Smollett, what have you to say? All well, I hope; all shipshape and seaworthy?'

'Well, sir,' said the captain, 'better speak plain, I believe, even at the risk of offence. I don't like this cruise; I don't like the men; and I don't like my officer. That's short and sweet.'

'Perhaps, sir, you don't like the ship?' inquired the squire, very angry, as I could see.

'I can't speak as to that, sir, not having seen her tried,' said the captain. 'She seems a clever craft; more I can't say.'

'Possibly, sir, you may not like your employer, either?' says the squire.

But here Dr. Livesey cut in.

'Stay a bit,' said he, 'stay a bit. No use of such questions as that but to produce ill feeling. The captain has said too much or he has said too little, and I'm bound to say that I require an explanation of his words.

You don't, you say, like the cruise. Now, why?'

'I was engaged, sir, on what we call sealed orders, to sail this ship for that gentleman where he should bid me,' said the captain. 'So far so good. But now I find that every man before the mast knows more than I do. I don't call that fair, now, do you?'

'No,' said Dr. Livesey, 'I don't.'

'Next,' said the captain, 'I learn we are going after treasure – hear it from my own hands, mind you. Now, treasure is ticklish work; I don't like treasure voyages on any account; and I don't like them, above all, when they are secret, and when (begging your pardon, Mr. Trelawney) the secret has been told to the parrot.'

'Silver's parrot?' asked the squire.

'It's a way of speaking,' said the captain. 'Blabbed, I mean. It's my belief neither of you gentlemen know what you are about; but I'll tell you my way of it – life or death, and a close run.'

'That is all clear, and, I dare say, true enough,' replied Dr. Livesey. 'We take the risk; but we are not so ignorant as you believe us. Next, you say you don't like the crew. Are they not good seamen?'

'I don't like them, sir,' returned Captain Smollett. 'And I think I should have had the choosing of my own hands, if you go to that.'

'Perhaps you should,' replied the doctor. 'My friend should, perhaps, have taken you along with him; but the slight, if there be one, was unintentional. And you don't like Mr. Arrow?'

'I don't, sir. I believe he's a good seaman; but he's too free with the crew to be a good officer. A mate should keep himself to himself – shouldn't drink with the men before the mast!'

'Do you mean he drinks?' cried the squire.

'No, sir,' replied the captain; 'only that he's too familiar.'

'Well, now, and the short and long of it, captain?' asked the doctor. 'Tell us what you want.'

'Well, gentlemen, are you determined to go on this cruise?'

'Like iron,' answered the squire.

'Very good,' said the captain. 'Then, as you've heard me very patiently, saying things that I could not prove, hear me a few words more. They are putting the powder and the arms in the fore-hold. Now, you have a good place under the cabin; why not put them there? – first point. Then you are bringing four of your own people with you, and they tell me some of them are to be berthed forward. Why not give them the berths here beside the cabin? – second point.'

'Any more?' asked Mr. Trelawney.

'One more,' said the captain. 'There's been too much blabbing already.'

'Far too much,' agreed the doctor.

'I'll tell you what I've heard myself,' continued Captain Smollett: 'that you have a map of an island; that there's crosses on the map to show where treasure is; and that the island lies——' And then he named the latitude and longitude exactly.

'I never told that,' cried the squire, 'to a soul!'

The hands know it, sir,' returned the captain.

'Livesey, that must have been you or Hawkins,' cried the squire.

'It doesn't much matter who it was,' replied the doctor. And I could see that neither he nor the captain paid much regard to Mr. Trelawney's protestations. Neither did I, to be sure, he was so loose a talker; yet in this case I believe he was really right, and that nobody had told the situation of the island.

'Well, gentlemen,' continued the captain, 'I don't know who has this map; but I make it a point, it shall be kept secret even from me and Mr. Arrow. Otherwise I would ask you to let me resign.'

'I see,' said the doctor. 'You wish us to keep this matter dark, and to make a garrison of the stern part of the ship, manned with my friend's own people, and provided with all the arms and powder on board. In other words, you fear a mutiny.'

'Sir,' said Captain Smollett, 'with no intention to take offence, I deny your right to put words into my mouth. No captain, sir, would be justified in going to sea at all if he had ground enough to say that. As for Mr. Arrow, I believe him thoroughly honest; some of the men are the same; all may be for what I know. But I am responsible for the ship's safety and the life of every man Jack aboard of her. I see things going, as I think, not quite right. And I ask you to take certain precautions, or let me resign my berth. And that's all.'

'Captain Smollett,' began the doctor, with a smile, 'did you ever hear the fable of the mountain and the mouse? You'll excuse me, I dare say, but you remind me of that fable. When you came in here I'll stake my wig that you meant more than this.'

'Doctor,' said the captain, 'you are smart. When I came in here I meant to get discharged. I had no thought that Mr. Trelawney would hear a word.'

'No more I would,' cried the squire. 'Had Livesey not been here I should have seen you to the deuce. As it is, I have heard you. I will do as you desire; but I think the worse of you.'

'That's as you please, sir,' said the captain. 'You'll find I do my duty.'

And with that he took his leave.

'Trelawney,' said the doctor, 'contrary to all my notions, I believe you have managed to get two honest men on board with you – that man and John Silver.'

'Silver, if you like,' cried the squire; 'but as for that intolerable humbug, I declare I think his conduct unmanly, unsailorly, and downright un-English.'

'Well,' says the doctor, 'we shall see.'

When we came on deck, the men had begun already to take out the arms and powder, yo-ho-ing at their work, while the captain and Mr. Arrow stood by superintending.

The new arrangement was quite to my liking. The whole schooner had been overhauled; six berths had been made astern, out of what had been the after-part of the main hold; and this set of cabins was only joined to the galley and forecastle by a sparred passage on the port side. It had been originally meant that the captain, Mr. Arrow, Hunter, Joyce, the doctor, and the squire, were to occupy these six berths. Now, Redruth and I were to get two of them, and Mr. Arrow and the captain were to sleep on deck in the companion, which had been enlarged on each side till you might almost have called it a round-house. Very low it was still, of course; but there was room to swing two hammocks, and even the mate seemed pleased with the arrangement. Even he, perhaps, had been doubtful as to the crew, but that is only guess; for, as you shall hear, we had not long the benefit of his opinion.

We were all hard at work, changing the powder and the berths, when the last man or two, and Long John along with them, came off in a shore-boat.

The cook came up the side like a monkey for cleverness, and, as soon as he saw what was doing, 'So ho, mates!' says he, 'what's this?'

'We're a-changing of the powder Jack,' answers one.

'Why, by the powers,' cried Long John, 'if we do, we'll miss the morning tide!'

'My orders!' said the captain shortly. 'You may go below, my man. Hands will want supper.'

'Ay, ay, sir,' answered the cook; and, touching his forelock, he disappeared at once in the direction of his galley.

'That's a good man, captain,' said the doctor.

'Very likely, sir,' replied Captain Smollett. 'Easy with that, men – easy,' he ran on, to the fellows who were shifting the powder; and then suddenly observing me examining the swivel we carried amidships, a long brass nine – 'Here, you ship's boy,' he cried out, 'out o' that! Off with you to the cook and get some work.'

And then as I was hurrying off I heard him say, quite loudly, to the doctor:

'I'll have no favourites on my ship.'

I assure you I was quite of the squire's way of thinking, and hated the captain deeply.

4 The Voyage

All that night we were in a great bustle getting things stowed in their place, and boatfuls of the squire's friends, Mr. Blandly and the like, coming off to wish him a good voyage and a safe return. We never had a night at the 'Admiral Benbow' when I had half the work; and I was dog-tired when, a little before dawn, the boatswain sounded his pipe, and the crew began to man the capstan-bars. I might have been twice as weary, yet I would not have left the deck; all was so new and interesting to me – the brief commands, the shrill note of the whistle, the men bustling to their places in the glimmer of the ship's lanterns.

'Now, Barbecue, tip us a stave,' cried one voice.

'The old one,' cried another.

'Ay, ay, mates,' said Long John, who was standing by, with his crutch under his arm, and at once broke out in the air and words I knew so well:

> 'Fifteen men on the dead man's chest—'

And then the whole crew bore chorus:

> 'Yo-ho-ho, and a bottle of rum!'

And at the third 'ho!' drove the bars before them with a will.

Even at that exciting moment it carried me back to the old 'Admiral Benbow' in a second; and I seemed to hear the voice of the captain piping in the chorus. But soon the anchor was short up; soon it was hanging dripping at the bows; soon the sails began to draw, and the land and shipping to flit by on either side; and before I could lie down to snatch an hour of slumber the *Hispaniola* had begun her voyage to the Isle of Treasure.

I am not going to relate that voyage in detail. It was fairly prosperous. The ship proved to be a good ship, the crew were capable seamen, and the captain thoroughly understood his business. But before we came the length of Treasure Island, two or three things had happened which require to be known.

Mr. Arrow, first of all, turned out even worse than the captain had feared. He had no command among the men, and people did what they pleased with him. But that was by no means the worst of it; for after a day or two at sea he began to appear on deck with hazy eye, red cheeks, stuttering tongue, and other marks of drunkenness. Time after time he was ordered below in disgrace. Sometimes he fell and cut himself; sometimes he lay all day long in his little bunk at one side of the companion; sometimes for a day or two he would be almost sober and attend to his work at least passably.

In the meantime, we could never make out where he got the drink. That was the ship's mystery. Watch him as we pleased, we could do nothing to solve it; and when we asked him to his face, he would only laugh, if he were drunk, and if he were sober, deny solemnly that he ever tasted anything but water.

He was not only useless as an officer, and a bad influence amongst the men, but it was plain that at this rate he must soon kill himself outright; so nobody was much surprised nor very sorry when one dark night, with a head sea, he disappeared entirely and was seen no more.

'Overboard!' said the captain. 'Well, gentlemen, that saves the trouble of putting him in irons.'

But there we were, without a mate; and it was necessary, of course, to advance one of the men. The boatswain, Job Anderson, was the likeliest man aboard, and, though he kept his old title, he served in a way as mate. Mr. Trelawney had followed the sea, and his knowledge made him very useful, for he often took a watch himself in easy weather. And the coxswain, Israel Hands, was a careful, wily, old, experienced seaman, who could be trusted at a pinch with almost anything.

He was a great confidant of Long John Silver, and so the mention of his name leads me on to speak of our ship's cook, Barbecue, as the men called him.

Aboard ship he carried his crutch by a lanyard round his neck, to have both hands as free as possible. It was something to see him wedge the foot of the crutch against a bulkhead, and, propped against it, yielding to every movement of the ship, get on with his cooking like someone safe ashore. Still more strange was it to see him in the heaviest of weather cross the deck. He had a line or two rigged up to help him across the widest spaces – Long John's earrings, they were called; and he would hand himself from one place to another, now using the crutch, now trailing it alongside by the lanyard, as quickly as another man could walk. Yet some of the men who had sailed with him before expressed their pity to see him so reduced.

'He's no common man, Barbecue,' said the coxswain to me. 'He had good schooling in his young days, and can speak like a book when so minded; and brave – a lion's nothing alongside of Long John! I seen him grapple four, and knock their heads together – him unarmed.'

All the crew respected and even obeyed him. He had a way of talking to each, and doing everybody some particular service. To me he was unweariedly kind; and always glad to see me in the galley, which he kept as clean as a new pin; the dishes hanging up burnished, and his parrot in a cage in one corner.'

'Come away, Hawkins,' he would say; 'come and have a yarn with John. Nobody more welcome than yourself, my son. Sit you down, and hear the news. Here's Cap'n Flint – I calls my parrot Cap'n Flint, after the famous buccaneer – here's Cap'n Flint predicting success to our v'yage. Wasn't you, Cap'n?'

And the parrot would say, with great rapidity: 'Pieces of eight! pieces of eight! pieces of eight!' till you wondered that it was not out of breath, or till John threw his handkerchief over the cage.

'Now, that bird,' he would say, 'is, may be, two hundred years old, Hawkins – they lives for ever mostly; and if anybody's seen more wickedness, it must be the devil himself. She's sailed with England, the great Cap'n England, the pirate. She's been at Madagascar, and at Malabar, and Surinam, and Providence, and Portobello. She was at the fishing up of the wrecked Plate ships. It's there she learned "Pieces of eight," and little wonder; three hundred and fifty thousand of 'em, Hawkins! She was at the boarding of the *Viceroy of the Indies* out of Goa, she was; and to look at her you would think she was a babby. But you smelt powder – didn't you, Cap'n?'

'Stand by to go about,' the parrot would scream.

'Ah, she's a handsome craft, she is,' the cook would say, and give her sugar from his pocket, and then the bird would peck at the bars and swear straight on, passing belief for wickedness. 'There,' John would add, 'you can't touch pitch and not be mucked, lad. Here's this poor old innocent bird o' mine swearing blue fire, and none the wiser, you may lay to that. She would swear the same, in a manner of speaking, before chaplain.' And John would touch his forelock with a solemn way he had, that made me think he was the best of men.

In the meantime, squire and Captain Smollett were still on pretty distant terms with one another. The squire made no bones about the matter; he despised the captain. The captain, on his part, never spoke but when he was spoken to, and then sharp and short and dry, and not a word wasted. He owned, when driven into a corner, that he seemed to have been wrong about the crew, that some of them were as brisk as he wanted to see, and all had behaved fairly well. As for the ship, he had taken a downright fancy to her. 'She'll lie a point nearer the wind than a man has a right to expect of his own married wife, sir. But,' he would add, 'all I say is we're not home again, and I don't like the cruise.'

The squire, at this, would turn away and march up and down the deck, chin in air.

'A trifle more of that man,' he would say, 'and I should explode.'

We had some heavy weather, which only proved the qualities of the *Hispaniola*. Every man on board seemed well content, and they must have been hard to please if they had been otherwise; for it is my belief there was never a ship's company so spoiled since Noah put to sea. Double grog was going on the least excuse; there was duff on odd days, as, for instance, if the squire heard it was any man's birthday; and always a barrel of apples standing broached in the waist, for any one to help himself that had a fancy.

'Never knew good come of it, yet,' the captain said to Dr. Livesey. 'Spoil foc's'le hands, make devils. That's my belief.'

But good did come of the apple barrel, as you shall hear; for if it had not been for that, we should have had no note of warning, and might all have perished by the hand of treachery.

This was how it came about.

We had run up the trades to get the wind of the island we were after – I am not allowed to be more plain – and now we were running down for it with a bright look-out day and night. It was about the last day of our outward voyage, by the largest computation; some time that night, or, at latest, before noon of the morrow, we should sight the Treasure Island. We were heading S.S.W., and had a steady breeze abeam and a quiet sea. The *Hispaniola* rolled steadily, dipping her bowsprit now and then with a whiff of spray. All was drawing alow and aloft; every one was in the bravest spirits; because we were now so near an end of the first part of our adventure.

Now, just after sundown, when all my work was over, and I was on my way to my berth, it occurred to me that I should like an apple. I ran on deck. The watch was all forward looking out for the island. The man at the helm was watching the luff of the sail, and whistling away gently to himself; and that was the only sound excepting the swish of the sea against the bows and around the sides of the ship.

In I got bodily into the apple barrel, and found there was scarce an apple left; but sitting down there in the dark, what with the sound of the waters and the rocking movement of the ship, I had either fallen asleep, or was on the point of doing so,'when a heavy man sat down with rather a clash close by. The barrel shook as he leaned his shoulder against it, and I was just about to jump up when the man began to speak. It was Silver's voice, and, before I had heard a dozen words, I would not have shown myself for all the world, but lay there, trembling and listening, in the extreme of fear and curiosity; for from these dozen words I understood that the lives of all the honest men aboard depended upon me alone.

5 What I Heard in the Apple Barrel

'No, not I,' said Silver. 'Flint was cap'n; I was quartermaster, along of my timber leg. The same broadside I lost my leg, old Pew lost his deadlights. It was a master surgeon, him that ampytated me – out of college and all – Latin by the bucket, and what not; but he was hanged like a dog, and sun-dried like the rest, at Corso Castle. That was Roberts's men, that was, and comed of changing names to their ships – *Royal Fortune* and so on. Now, what a ship was christened, so let her stay, I says. So it was with the *Cassandra*, as brought us all safe home from Malabar, after England took the *Viceroy of the Indies*; so it was with the old *Walrus*, Flint's old ship, as I've seen a-muck with the red blood and fit to sink with gold.'

'Ah!' cried another voice, that of the youngest hand on board, and evidently full of admiration, 'he was the flower of the flock, was Flint!'

'Davis was a man, too, by all accounts,' said Silver. 'I never sailed along of him; first with England, then with Flint, that's my story; and now here on my own account, in a manner of speaking. I laid by nine hundred safe, from England, and two thousand after Flint. That ain't bad for a man before the mast – all safe in bank. 'Tain't earning now, it's saving does it, you may lay to that. Where's all England's men now? I dunno. Where's Flint's? Why, most on 'em aboard here, and glad to get the duff – been begging before that, some on 'em. Old Pew, as had lost his sight, and might have thought shame, spends twelve hundred pound in a year, like a lord in Parliament. Where is he now? Well, he's dead now and under hatches; but for two year before that, shiver my timbers! the man was starving. He begged, and he stole, and he cut throats, and starved at that, by the powers!'

'Well, it ain't much use, after all,' said the young seaman.

''Tain't much use for fools, you may lay to it – that, nor nothing,' cried Silver. 'But now, you look here: you're young, you are, but you're as smart as paint. I see that when I set my eyes on you, and I'll talk to you like a man.'

You may imagine how I felt when I heard this abominable old rogue addressing another in the very same words of flattery as he had used to myself. I think, if I had been able, that I would have killed him through the barrel. Meantime, he ran on, little supposing he was overheard.

'Here it is about gentlemen of fortune. They lives rough, and they risk swinging, but they eat and drink like fighting-cocks, and when a cruise is done, why it's hundreds of pounds instead of hundreds of farthings in their pockets. Now, the most goes for rum and a good fling, and to sea again in their shirts. But that's not the course I lay. I puts it all away, some here, some there, and none too much anywheres, by reason of suspicion. I'm fifty, mark you; once back from this cruise, I set up gentleman in earnest. Time enough, too, says you. Ah, but I've lived easy in the meantime; never denied myself o' nothing heart desires, and slep' soft and ate dainty all my days, but when at sea. And how did I begin? Before the mast, like you!'

'Well,' said the other, 'but all the other money's gone now, ain't it? You daren't show face in Bristol after this.'

'Why, where might you suppose it was?' asked Silver, derisively.

'At Bristol, in banks and places,' answered his companion.

'It were,' said the cook; 'it were when we weighed anchor. But my old missus has it all by now. And the "Spy-glass" is sold, lease and goodwill and rigging; and the old girl's off to meet me. I would tell you where, for I trust you; but it 'ud make jealousy among the mates.'

'And can you trust your missus?' asked the other.

'Gentlemen of fortune,' returned the cook, 'usually trust little among themselves, and right they are, you may lay to it. But I have a way with me, I have. When a mate brings a slip on his cable – one as knows me, I mean – it won't be in the same world with old John. There was some that was feared of Pew, and some that was feared of Flint; and Flint his own self was feared of me. Feared he was, and proud. They was the roughest crew afloat, was Flint's; the devil himself would have been feared to go to sea with them. Well, now, I tell you, I'm not a boasting man, and you seen yourself how easy I keep company; but when I was quartermaster, *lambs* wasn't the word for Flint's old buccaneers. Ah, you may be sure of yourself in old John's ship.'

'Well, I tell you now,' replied the lad, 'I didn't half a quarter like the job till I had this talk with you, John; but there's my hand on it now.'

'And a brave lad you were, and smart, too,' answered Silver, shaking hands so heartily that all the barrel shook, 'and a finer figurehead for a gentleman of fortune I never clapped my eyes on.'

By this time I had begun to understand the meaning of their terms. By a 'gentleman of fortune' they plainly meant neither more nor less than a common pirate, and the little scene that I had overheard was the last act in the corruption of one of the honest hands – perhaps of the last one left aboard. But on this point I was soon to be relieved, for Silver giving a little whistle, a third man strolled up and sat down by the party.

'Dick's square,' said Silver.

'Oh, I know'd Dick was square,' returned the voice of the coxswain, Israel Hands. 'He's no fool, is Dick.' And he turned his quid and spat. 'But look here,' he went on, 'here's what I want to know, Barbecue: how long are we a-going to stand off and on like a blessed bum-boat? I've had a'most enough o' Cap'n Smollett; he's hazed me long enough, by thunder! I want to go into that cabin, I do. I want their pickles and wines, and that.'

'Israel,' said Silver, 'your head ain't much account, nor ever was. But you're able to hear, I reckon; leastways, your ears is big enough. Now, here's what I say: you'll berth forward, and you'll live hard, and you'll speak soft, and you'll keep sober, till I give the word; and you may lay to that, my son.'

'Well, I don't say no, do I?' growled the coxswain. 'What I say is, when? That's what I say.'

'When! by the powers!' cried Silver. 'Well, now, if you want to know, I'll tell you when. The last moment I can manage; and that's when. Here's a first-rate seaman, Cap'n Smollett, sails the blessed ship for us. Here's this squire and doctor with a map and such – I don't know where it is, do I? No more do you, says you. Well, then, I mean this squire and doctor shall find the stuff, and help us to get it aboard, by the powers. Then we'll see. If I was sure of you all, sons of double Dutchmen, I'd have Cap'n Smollett navigate us half-way back again before I struck.'

'Why, we're all seamen aboard here, I should think,' said the lad Dick.

'We're all foc's'le hands, you mean,' snapped Silver. 'We can steer a course, but who's to set one? That's what all you gentlemen split on, first and last. If I had my way, I'd have Cap'n Smollett work us back into the trades at least; then we'd have no blessed miscalculations and a spoonful of water a day. But I know the sort you are. I'll finish with 'em at the island, as soon's the blunt's on board, and a pity it is. But you're never happy till you're drunk. Split my sides, I've a sick heart to sail with the likes of you!'

'Easy all, Long John,' cried Israel. 'Who's acrossin' of you?'

'Why, how many tall ships, think ye, now, have I seen laid aboard? and how many brisk lads drying in the sun at Execution Dock?' cried Silver, 'and all for this same hurry and hurry and hurry. You hear me? I seen a thing or two at sea, I have. If you would on'y lay your course, and a p'int to windward, you would ride in carriages, you would. But not you! I know you. You'll have your mouthful of rum to-morrow, and go hang.'

'Everybody know'd you was a kind of a chapling, John; but there's others as could hand and steer as well as you,' said Israel. 'They liked a bit o' fun, they did. They wasn't so high and dry, nohow, but took their fling, like jolly companions every one.'

'So?' says Silver. 'Well, and where are they now? Pew was that sort, and he died a beggar-man. Flint was, and he died of rum at Savannah. Ah, they was a sweet crew, they was! on'y, where are they?'

'But,' asked Dick, 'when we do lay 'em athwart, what are we to do with 'em, anyhow?'

'There's the man for me!' cried the cook, admiringly. 'That's what I call business. Well, what would you think? Put 'em ashore like maroons? That would have been England's way. Or cut 'em down like that much pork? That would have been Flint's or Billy Bones's.'

'Billy was the man for that,' said Israel. ' "Dead men don't bite," says he. Well, he's dead now hisself; he knows the long and short on it now; and if ever a rough hand come to port, it was Billy.'

'Right you are,' said Silver, 'rough and ready. But mark you here: I'm an easy man – I'm quite the gentleman, says you; but this time it's serious. Dooty is dooty, mates. I give my vote – death. When I'm in Parlyment, and riding in my coach, I don't want none of these sea-lawyers in the cabin a-coming home, unlooked for, like the devil at prayers. Wait is what I say; but when the time comes, why let her rip!'

'John,' cries the coxswain, 'you're a man!'

'You'll say so, Israel, when you see,' said Silver. 'Only one thing I claim – I claim Trelawney. I'll wring his calf's head off his body with these hands. Dick!' he added, breaking off, 'you just jump up, like a sweet lad, and get me an apple, to wet my pipe like.'

You may fancy the terror I was in! I should have leaped out and run for it, if I had found the strength; but my limbs and heart alike misgave me. I heard Dick begin to rise, and then someone seemingly stopped him, and the voice of Hands exclaimed:

'Oh, stow that! Don't you get sucking of that bilge, John. Let's have a go of the rum.'

'Dick,' said Silver, 'I trust you. I've a gauge on the keg, mind. There's the key; you fill a pannikin and bring it up.'

Terrified as I was, I could not help thinking to myself that this must have been how Mr. Arrow got the strong waters that destroyed him.

Dick was gone but a little while, and during his absence Israel spoke straight on in the cook's ear. It was but a word or two that I could catch, and yet I gathered some important news; for, besides other scraps that tended to the same purpose, this whole clause was audible: 'Not another man of them'll jine.' Hence there were still faithful men on board.

When Dick returned, one after another of the trio took the pannikin and drank – one 'To luck'; another with a 'Here's to old Flint'; and Silver himself saying, in a kind of song: 'Here's to ourselves, and hold your luff, plenty of prizes and plenty of duff.'

Just then a sort of brightness fell upon me in the barrel, and, looking up, I found the moon had risen, and was silvering the mizzen-top and shining white on the luff of the foresail; and almost at the same time the voice of the look-out shouted: 'Land ho!'

6 Council of War

There was a great rush of feet across the deck. I could hear people tumbling up from the cabin and the foc's'le; and, slipping in an instant outside my barrel, I dived behind the foresail, made a double towards the stern, and came out upon the open deck in time to join Hunter and Dr. Livesey in the rush for the weather bow.

There all hands were already congregated. A belt of fog had lifted almost simultaneously with the appearance of the moon. Away to the south-west of us we saw two low hills, about a couple of miles apart, and rising behind one of them a third and higher hill, whose peak was still buried in the fog. All three seemed sharp and conical in figure.

So much I saw, almost in a dream, for I had not yet recovered from my horrid fear of a minute or two before. And then I heard the voice of Captain Smollett issuing orders. The *Hispaniola* was laid a couple of points nearer the wind, and now sailed a course that would just clear the island on the east.

'And now, men,' said the captain, when all was sheeted home, 'has any one of you ever seen that land ahead?'

'I have, sir,' said Silver. 'I've watered there with a trader I was cook in.'

'The anchorage is on the south, behind an islet, I fancy?' asked the captain.

'Yes, sir; Skeleton Island they calls it. It were a main place for pirates once, and a hand we had on board knowed all their names for it. That hill to the nor'ard they calls the Fore-mast Hill; there are three hills in a row running south'ard – fore, main, and mizzen, sir. But the main – that's the big 'un with the cloud on it – they usually calls the Spy-glass, by reason of a look-out they kept when they was in the anchorage cleaning; for it's there they cleaned their ships, sir, asking your pardon.'

'I have a chart here,' says Captain Smollett. 'See if that's the place.'

Long John's eyes burned in his head as he took the chart; but by the fresh look of the paper, I knew he was doomed to disappointment. This was not the map we found in Billy Bones's chest, but an accurate copy, complete in all things – names and heights and soundings – with the single exception of the red crosses and the written notes. Sharp as must have been his annoyance, Silver had the strength of mind to hide it.

'Yes, sir,' said he, 'this is the spot to be sure; and very prettily drawed out. Who might have done that, I wonder? The pirates were too ignorant, I reckon. Ay, here it is: "Capt. Kidd's Anchorage" – just the name my shipmate called it. There's a strong current runs along the south, and then away nor'ard up the west coast. Right you was, sir,' says he, 'to haul your wind and keep the weather of the island. Leastways, if such was your intention as to enter and careen, and there ain't no better place for that in these waters.'

'Thank you, my man,' says Captain Smollett. 'I'll ask you, later on, to give us a help. You may go.'

I was surprised at the coolness with which John avowed his knowledge of the island; and I own I was half frightened when I saw him drawing nearer to myself. He did not know, to be sure, that I had overheard his council from the apple barrel, and yet I had, by this time, taken such a horror of his cruelty, duplicity, and power, that I could scarce conceal a shudder when he laid his hand upon my arm.

'Ah,' says he, 'this is a sweet spot, this island – a sweet spot for a lad to get ashore on. You'll bathe, and you'll climb trees, and you'll hunt goats, you will; and you'll get aloft on them hills like a goat yourself. Why, it makes me young again. I was going to forget my timber leg, I was. It's a pleasant thing to be young, and have ten toes, and you may lay to that. When you want to go a bit of exploring, you must ask old John, and he'll put up a snack for you to take along.'

And clapping me in the friendliest way upon the shoulder, he hobbled off forward and went below.

Captain Smollett, the squire, and Dr. Livesey, were talking together on the quarter-deck, and anxious as I was to tell them my story, I durst not interrupt them openly. While I was still casting about in my thoughts to find some probable excuse, Dr. Livesey called me to his side. He had left his pipe below, and being a slave to tobacco, had meant that I should fetch it; but as soon as I was near enough to speak and not to be overheard, I broke out immediately: 'Doctor, let me speak. Get the captain and squire down to the cabin, and then make some pretence to send for me. I have terrible news.'

The doctor changed countenance a little, but next moment he was master of himself.

'Thank you, Jim,' said he, quite loudly, 'that was all I wanted to know,' as if he had asked me a question.

And with that he turned on his heel and rejoined the other two. They spoke together for a little, and though none of them started, or raised his voice, or so much as whistled, it was plain enough that Dr. Livesey had communicated my request; for the next thing that I heard was the captain giving an order to Job Anderson, and all hands were piped on deck.

'My lads,' said Captain Smollett, 'I've a word to say to you. This land that we have sighted is the place we have been sailing to. Mr. Trelawney, being a very open-handed gentleman, as we all know, has just asked me a word or two, and as I was able to tell him that every man on board had done his duty, alow and aloft, as I never ask to see it done better, why, he and I and the doctor are going below to the cabin to drink *your* health and luck, and you'll have grog served out for you to drink *our* health and luck. I'll tell you what I think of this: I think it handsome. And if you think as I do, you'll give a good sea cheer for the gentleman that does it.'

The cheer followed – that was a matter of course; but it rang out so full and hearty, that I confess I could hardly believe these same men were plotting for our blood.

'One more cheer for Cap'n Smollett,' cried Long John, when the first had subsided.

And this also was given with a will.

On the top of that the three gentlemen went below, and not long after, word was sent forward that Jim Hawkins was wanted in the cabin.

I found them all three seated round the table, a bottle of Spanish wine and some raisins before them, and the doctor smoking away, with his wig on his lap, and that, I knew, was a sign that he was agitated. The stern window was open, for it was a warm night, and you could see the moon shining behind on the ship's wake.

'Now, Hawkins,' said the squire, 'you have something to say. Speak up.'

I did as I was bid, and, as short as I could make it, told the whole details of Silver's conversation. Nobody interrupted me till I was done, nor did any one of the three of them make so much as a movement, but they kept their eyes upon my face from first to last.

'Jim,' said Dr. Livesey, 'take a seat.'

And they made me sit down at table beside them, poured me out a glass of wine, filled my hands with raisins, and all three, one after the other, and each with a bow, drank my good health, and their service to me, for my luck and courage.

'Now, captain,' said the squire, 'you were right, and I was wrong. I own myself an ass, and I await your orders.'

'No more an ass than I, sir,' returned the captain. 'I never heard of a crew that meant to mutiny but what showed signs before, for any man that had an eye in his head to see the mischief and take steps according. But this crew,' he added, 'beats me.'

'Captain,' said the doctor, 'with your permission, that's Silver. A very remarkable man.'

'He'd look remarkably well from a yard-arm, sir,' returned the captain. 'But this is talk; this don't lead to anything. I see three or four points, and with Mr. Trelawney's permission, I'll name them.'

'You, sir, are the captain. It is for you to speak,' says Mr. Trelawney, grandly.

'First point,' began Mr. Smollett. 'We must go on, because we can't turn back. If I gave the word to go about, they would rise at once. Second point, we have time before us – at least, until this treasure's found. Third point, there are faithful hands. Now, sir, it's got to come to blows sooner or later; and what I propose is, to take time by the forelock, as the saying is, and come to blows some fine day when they least expect it. We can count, I take it, on your own home servants, Mr. Trelawney?'

'As upon myself,' declared the squire.

'Three,' reckoned the captain, 'ourselves make seven, counting Hawkins, here. Now, about the honest hands?'

'Most likely Trelawney's own men,' said the doctor; 'those he had picked up for himself, before he lit on Silver.'

'Nay,' replied the squire, 'Hands was one of mine.'

'I did think I could have trusted Hands,' added the captain.

'And to think that they're all Englishmen!' broke out the squire. 'Sir, I could find it in my heart to blow the ship up.'

'Well, gentlemen,' said the captain, 'the best that I can say is not much. We must lay to, if you please, and keep a bright look-out. It's trying on a man, I know. It would be pleasanter to come to blows. But there's no help for it till we know our men. Lay to, and whistle for a wind, that's my view.

'Jim here,' said the doctor, 'can help us more than any one. The men are not shy with him, and Jim is a noticing lad.'

'Hawkins, I put prodigious faith in you,' added the squire.

I began to feel pretty desperate at this, for I felt altogether helpless; and yet, by an odd train of circumstances, it was indeed through me that safety came. In the meantime, talk as we pleased, there were only seven out of the twenty-six on whom we knew we could rely; and out of these seven one was a boy, so that the grown men on our side were six to their nineteen.

1 How I Began My Shore Adventure

The appearance of the island when I came on deck next morning was altogether changed. Although the breeze had now utterly failed, we had made a great deal of way during the night, and were now lying becalmed about half a mile to the south-east of the low eastern coast. Grey-coloured woods covered a large part of the surface. This even tint was indeed broken up by streaks of yellow sandbreak in the lower lands, and by many tall trees of the pine family, out-topping the others – some singly, some in clumps; but the general colouring was uniform and sad. The hills ran up clear above the vegetation in spires of naked rock. All were strangely shaped, and the Spy-glass, which was by three or four hundred feet the tallest on the island, was likewise the strangest in configuration, running up sheer from almost every side, and then suddenly cut off at the top like a pedestal to put a statue on.

The *Hispaniola* was rolling scuppers under in the ocean swell. The booms were tearing at the blocks, the rudder was banging to and fro, and the whole ship creaking, groaning, and jumping like a manufactory. I had to cling tight to the backstay, and the world turned giddily before my eyes; for though I was a good enough sailor when there was way on, this standing still and being rolled about like a bottle was a thing I never learned to stand without a qualm or so, above all in the morning, on an empty stomach.

Perhaps it was this – perhaps it was the look of the island with its grey, melancholy woods, and wild stone spires, and the surf that we could both see and hear foaming and thundering on the steep beach – at least, although the sun shone bright and hot, and the shore birds were fishing and crying all around us, and you would have thought any one would have been glad to get to land after being so long at sea, my heart sank, as the saying is, into my boots; and from that first look onward, I hated the very thought of Treasure Island.

We had a dreary morning's work before us, for there was no sign of any wind, and the boats had to be got out and manned, and the ship warped three or four miles round the corner of the island, and up the narrow passage to the haven behind Skeleton Island. I volunteered for one of the boats, where I had, of course, no business. The heat was sweltering, and the men grumbled fiercely over their work. Anderson was in command of my boat, and instead of keeping the crew in order, he grumbled as loud as the worst.

'Well,' he said, with an oath, 'it's not for ever.'

I thought this was a very bad sign; for, up to that day, the men had gone briskly and willingly about their business; but the very sight of the island had relaxed the cords of discipline.

All the way in, Long John stood by the steersman and conned the ship. He knew the passage like the palm of his hand; and though the man in the chains got everywhere more water than was down in the chart, John never hesitated once.

'There's a strong scour with the ebb,' he said, 'and this here passage has been dug out, in a manner of speaking, with a spade.'

We brought up just where the anchor was in the chart, about a third of a mile from either shore, the mainland on one side and Skeleton Island on the other. The bottom was clean sand. The plunge of our anchor sent up clouds of birds wheeling and crying over the woods; but in less than a minute they were down again, and all was once more silent.

The place was entirely land-locked, buried in woods, the trees coming right down to high-water mark, the shores mostly flat, and the hill-tops standing round at a distance in a sort of amphitheatre, one here, one there. Two little rivers, or, rather, two swamps, emptied out into this pond, as you might call it; and the foliage round that part of the shore had a kind of poisonous brightness. From the ship, we could see nothing of the house or stockade, for they were quite buried among trees; and if it had not been for the chart on the companion, we might have been the first that had ever anchored there since the island arose out of the seas.

There was not a breath of air moving, nor a sound but that of the surf booming half a mile away along the beaches and against the rocks outside. A peculiar stagnant smell hung over the anchorage – a smell of sodden leaves and rotting tree trunks. I observed the doctor sniffing and sniffing, like someone tasting a bad egg.

'I don't know about treasure,' he said, 'but I'll stake my wig there's fever here.'

If the conduct of the men had been alarming in the boat, it became truly threatening when they had come aboard. They lay about the deck growling together in talk. The slightest order was received with a black look, and grudgingly and carelessly obeyed. Even the honest hands must have caught the infection, for there was not one man aboard to mend another. Mutiny, it was plain, hung over us like a thunder-cloud.

And it was not only we of the cabin party who perceived the danger. Long John was hard at work going from group to group, spending himself in good advice, and as for example no man could have shown a better. He fairly outstripped himself in willingness and civility; he was all smiles to every one. If an order were given, John would be on his crutch in an instant, with the cheeriest 'Ay, ay, sir!' in the world; and when there was nothing else to do, he kept up one song after another, as if to conceal the discontent of the rest.

Of all the gloomy features of that gloomy afternoon, this obvious anxiety on the part of Long John appeared the worst.

We held a council in the cabin.

'Sir,' said the captain, 'if I risk another order, the whole ship'll come about our ears by the run. You see, sir, here it is. I get a rough answer, do I not? Well, if I speak back, pikes will be going in two shakes; if I don't, Silver will see there's something under that, and the game's up. Now, we've only one man to rely on.'

'And who is that?' asked the squire.

'Silver, sir,' returned the captain; 'he's as anxious as you and I to smother things up. This is a tiff; he'd soon talk 'em out of it if he had the chance, and what I propose to do is to give him the chance. Let's allow the men an afternoon ashore. If they all go, why, we'll fight the ship. If they none of them go, well, then, we hold the cabin, and God defend the right. If some go, you mark my words, sir, Silver'll bring 'em aboard again as mild as lambs.'

It was so decided; loaded pistols were served out to all the sure men; Hunter, Joyce, and Redruth were taken into our confidence, and received the news with less surprise and a better spirit than we had looked for, and then the captain went on deck and addressed the crew.

'My lads,' said he, 'we've had a hot day, and are all tired and out of sorts. A turn ashore'll hurt nobody – the boats are still in the water; you can take the gigs, and as many as please can go ashore for the afternoon. I'll fire a gun half an hour before sundown.'

I believe the silly fellows must have thought they would break their shins over treasure as soon as they were landed; for they all came out of their sulks in a moment, and gave a cheer that started the echo in a far-away hill, and sent the birds once more flying and squalling round the anchorage.

The captain was too bright to be in the way. He whipped out of sight in a moment, leaving Silver to arrange the party, and I fancy it was as well he did so. Had he been on deck, he could no longer so much as have pretended not to understand the situation. It was as plain as day. Silver was the captain, and a mighty rebellious crew he had of it. The honest hands – and I was soon to see it proved that there were such on board – must have been very stupid fellows. Or, rather, I suppose the truth was this, that all hands were disaffected by the example of the ringleaders – only some more, some less; and a few, being good fellows in the main, could neither be led nor driven any further. It is one thing to be idle and skulk, and quite another to take a ship and murder a number of innocent men.

At last, however, the party was made up. Six fellows were to stay on board, and the remaining thirteen, including Silver, began to embark.

Then it was that there came into my head the first of the mad notions that contributed so much to save our lives. If six men were left by Silver, it was plain our party could not take and fight the ship; and since only six were left, it was equally plain that the cabin party had no present need of my assistance. It occurred to me at once to go ashore. In a jiffy I had slipped over the side, and curled up in the foresheets of the nearest boat, and almost at the same moment she shoved off.

No one took notice of me, only the bow oar saying: 'Is that you, Jim? Keep your head down.' But Silver, from the other boat, looked sharply over and called out to know if that were me; and from that moment I began to regret what I had done.

The crews raced for the beach; but the boat I was in, having some start, and being at once the lighter and the better manned, shot far ahead of her consort, and the bow had struck among the shore-side trees, and I had caught a branch and swung myself out, and plunged into the nearest thicket, while Silver and the rest were still a hundred yards behind.

'Jim, Jim!' I heard him shouting.

But you may suppose I paid no heed; jumping, ducking, and breaking through, I ran straight before my nose, till I could run no longer.

2 The First Blow

I was so pleased at having given the slip to Long John, that I began to enjoy myself and look round me with some interest on the strange land that I was in.

I had crossed a marshy tract full of willows, bulrushes, and odd, outlandish, swampy trees; and I had now come out upon the skirts of an open piece of undulating, sandy country, about a mile long, dotted with a few pines, and a great number of contorted trees, not unlike the oak in growth, but pale in the foliage, like willows. On the far side of the open stood one of the hills, with two quaint, craggy peaks, shining vividly in the sun.

I now felt for the first time the joy of exploration. The isle was uninhabited; my shipmates I had left behind, and nothing lived in front of me but dumb brutes and fowls. I turned hither and thither among the trees. Here and there were flowering plants, unknown to me; here and there I saw snakes, and one raised his head from a ledge of rock and hissed at me with a noise not unlike the spinning of a top. Little did I suppose that he was a deadly enemy, and that the noise was the famous rattle.

Then I came to a long thicket of these oak-like trees – live, or evergreen, oaks, I heard afterwards they should be called – which grew low along the sand like brambles, the boughs curiously twisted, the foliage compact, like thatch. The thicket stretched down from the top of one of the sandy knolls, spreading and growing taller as it went, until it reached the margin of the broad, reedy fen, through which the nearest of the little rivers soaked its way into the anchorage. The marsh was steaming in the strong sun, and the outline of the Spy-glass trembled through the haze.

All at once there began to go a sort of bustle among the bulrushes; a wild duck flew up with a quack, another followed, and soon over the whole surface of the marsh a great cloud of birds hung screaming and circling in the air. I judged at once that some of my shipmates must be drawing near along the borders of the fen. Nor was I deceived; for soon I heard the very distant and low tones of a human voice, which, as I continued to give ear, grew steadily louder and nearer.

This put me in a great fear, and I crawled under cover of the nearest live oak, and squatted there, hearkening, as silent as a mouse.

Another voice answered; and then the first voice, which I now recognized to be Silver's, once more took up the story, and ran on for a long while in a stream, only now and again interrupted by the other. By the sound they must have been talking earnestly, and almost fiercely; but no distinct word came to my hearing.

At last the speakers seemed to have paused, and perhaps to have sat down; for not only did they cease to draw any nearer, but the birds themselves began to grow more quiet, and to settle again to their places in the swamp.

And now I began to feel that I was neglecting my business; that since I had been so foolhardy as to come ashore with these desperadoes, the least I could do was to overhear them at their councils; and that my plain and obvious duty was to draw as close as I could manage, under the favourable ambush of the crouching trees.

I could tell the direction of the speakers pretty exactly, not only by the sound of their voices, but by the behaviour of the few birds that still hung in alarm above the heads of the intruders.

Crawling on all-fours, I made steadily but slowly towards them; till at last, raising my head to an aperture among the leaves, I could see clear down into a little green dell beside the marsh, and closely set about with trees, where Long John Silver and another of the crew stood face to face in conversation.

The sun beat full upon them. Silver had thrown his hat beside him on the ground, and his great smooth, blond face, all shining with heat, was lifted to the other man's in a kind of appeal.

'Mate,' he was saying, 'it's because I thinks gold dust of you – gold dust, and you may lay to that! If I hadn't took to you like pitch, do you think I'd have been here a-warning of you? All's up – you can't make nor mend; it's to save your neck that I'm a-speaking, and if one of the wild 'uns knew it, where 'ud I be, Tom – now, tell me, where 'ud I be?'

'Silver,' said the other man – and I observed he was not only red in the face, but spoke as hoarse as a crow, and his voice shook, too, like a taut rope – 'Silver,' says he, 'you're old, and you're honest, or has the name for it; and you've money, too, which lots of poor sailors hasn't; and you're brave, or I'm mistook. And will you tell me you'll let yourself be led away with that kind of a mess of swabs? not you! As sure as God sees me, I'd sooner lose my hand. If I turn agin my dooty——'

And then all of a sudden he was interrupted by a noise. I had found one of the honest hands – well, here, at that same moment, came news of another. Far away out in the marsh there arose, all of a sudden, a sound like the cry of anger, then another on the back of it; and then one horrid, long-drawn scream. The rocks of the Spy-glass re-echoed it a score of times; the whole troop of marsh-birds rose again, darkening heaven, with a simultaneous whirr; and long after that death-yell was still ringing in my brain, silence had re-established its empire, and only the rustle of the re-descending birds and the boom of the distant surges disturbed the languor of the afternoon.

Tom had leaped at the sound, like a horse at the spur; but Silver had not winked an eye. He stood where he was, resting lightly on his crutch, watching his companion like a snake about to spring.

'John!' said the sailor, stretching out his hand.

'Hands off!' cried Silver, leaping back a yard, as it seemed to me, with the speed and security of a trained gymnast.

'Hands off, if you like, John Silver,' said the other. 'It's a black conscience that can make you feared of me. But, in heaven's name, tell me what was that?'

'That?' returned Silver, smiling away, but warier than ever, his eye a mere pin-point in his big face, but gleaming like a crumb of glass. 'That? O, I reckon that'll be Alan.'

And at this poor Tom flashed out like a hero.

'Alan!' he cried. 'Then rest his soul for a true seaman! And as for you, John Silver, long you've been a mate of mine, but you're mate of mine no more. If I die like a dog, I'll die in my dooty. You've killed Alan, have you? Kill me, too, if you can. But I defies you.'

And with that, this brave fellow turned his back directly on the cook, and set off walking for the beach. But he was not destined to go far. With a cry, John seized the branch of a tree, whipped the crutch out of his armpit, and sent that uncouth missile hurtling through the air. It struck poor Tom, point foremost, and with stunning violence, right between the shoulders in the middle of his back. His hands flew up, he gave a sort of gasp, and fell.

Whether he were injured much or little, none could ever tell. Like

'With a cry, John seized the branch of a tree'

enough, to judge from the sound, his back was broken on the spot. But he had no time given him to recover. Silver, agile as a monkey, even without leg or crutch, was on the top of him next moment, and had twice buried his knife up to the hilt in that defenceless body. From my place of ambush, I could hear him pant aloud as he struck the blows.

I do not know what it rightly is to faint, but I do know that for the next little while the whole world swam away from before me in a whirling mist; Silver and the birds and the tall Spy-glass hill-top going round and round and topsy-turvy before my eyes, and all manner of bells ringing and distant voices shouting in my ear.

When I came again to myself, the monster had pulled himself together, his crutch under his arm, his hat upon his head. Just before him Tom lay motionless upon the sward; but the murderer minded him not a whit, cleansing his blood-stained knife the while upon a wisp of grass. Everything else was unchanged, the sun still shining mercilessly on the steaming marsh and the tall pinnacle of the mountain, and I could scarce persuade myself that murder had been actually done, and a human life cruelly cut short a moment since, before my eyes.

But now John put his hand into his pocket, brought out a whistle, and blew upon it several modulated blasts, that rang far across the heated air. I could not tell, of course, the meaning of the signal; but it instantly awoke my fears. More men would be coming. I might be discovered. They had already slain two of the honest people; after Tom and Alan, might not I come next?

Instantly I began to extricate myself and crawl back again, with what speed and silence I could manage, to the more open portion of the wood. As I did so, I could hear hails coming and going between the old buccaneer and his comrades, and this sound of danger lent me wings. As soon as I was clear of the thicket, I ran as I never ran before, scarce minding the direction of my flight, so long as it led me from the murderers; and as I ran, fear grew and grew upon me, until it turned into a kind of frenzy.

Indeed, could any one be more entirely lost than I? When the gun fired, how should I dare to go down to the boats among those fiends, still smoking from their crime? Would not the first of them who saw me wring my neck like a snipe's? Would not my absence itself be an evidence to them of my alarm, and therefore of my fatal knowledge? It was all over, I thought. Good-bye to the *Hispaniola*; good-bye to the squire, the doctor, and the captain! There was nothing left for me but death by starvation, or death by the hands of the mutineers.

All this while, as I say, I was still running, and, without taking any notice, I had drawn near to the foot of the little hill with the two peaks, and had got into a part of the island where the live oaks grew more widely apart, and seemed more like forest trees in their bearing and dimensions. Mingled with these were a few scattered pines, some fifty, some nearer seventy, feet high. The air, too, smelt more freshly than down beside the marsh.

And here a fresh alarm brought me to a standstill with a thumping heart.

3 The Man of the Island

From the side of the hill, which was here steep and stony, a spout of gravel was dislodged and fell rattling and bounding through the trees. My eyes turned instinctively in that direction, and I saw a figure leap with great rapidity behind the trunk of a pine. What it was, whether bear or monkey, I could in no wise tell. It seemed dark and shaggy; more I knew not. But the terror of this new apparition brought me to a stand.

I was now, it seemed, cut off upon both sides; behind me the murderers, before me this lurking nondescript. And immediately I began to prefer the dangers that I knew to those I knew not. Silver himself appeared less terrible in contrast with this creature of the woods, and I turned on my heel, and, looking sharply behind me over my shoulder, began to retrace my steps in the direction of the boats.

Instantly the figure reappeared, and, making a wide circuit, began to head me off. I was tired, at any rate; but had I been as fresh as when I rose, I could see it was in vain for me to contend in speed with such an adversary. From trunk to trunk the creature flitted like a deer, running manlike on two legs, but unlike any man that I had ever seen, stooping almost double as it ran. Yet a man it was, I could no longer be in doubt about that.

I began to recall what I had heard of cannibals. I was within an ace of calling for help. But the mere fact that he was a man, however wild, had somewhat reassured me, and my fear of Silver began to revive in proportion. I stood still, therefore, and cast about for some method of escape; and as I was so thinking, the recollection of my pistol flashed into my mind. As soon as I remembered I was not defenceless, courage glowed again in my heart; and I set my face resolutely for this man of the island, and walked briskly towards him.

He was concealed by this time, behind another tree trunk; but he must have been watching me closely, for as soon as I began to move in his direction he reappeared and took a step to meet me. Then he hesitated, drew back, came forward again, and at last, to my wonder and confusion, threw himself on his knees, and held out his clasped hands in supplication.

At that I once more stopped.

'Who are you?' I asked.

'Ben Gunn,' he answered, and his voice sounded hoarse and awkward, like a rusty lock. 'I'm poor Ben Gunn, I am; and I haven't spoke with a Christian these three years.'

I could now see that he was a white man like myself, and that his features were even pleasing. His skin, wherever it was exposed, was burnt by the sun; even his lips were black; and his fair eyes looked quite startling in so dark a face. Of all the beggar-men that I had seen or fancied, he was the chief for raggedness. He was clothed with tatters of old ship's canvas and old sea cloth; and this extraordinary patchwork was all held together by a system of the most various and incongruous fastenings, brass buttons, bits of stick, and loops of tarry gaskin. About his waist he wore an old brass-buckled leather belt, which was the one thing solid in his whole accoutrement.

'Three years!' I cried. 'Were you shipwrecked?'

'Nay, mate,' said he – 'marooned.'

I had heard the word, and I knew it stood for a horrible kind of punishment common enough among the buccaneers, in which the offender is put ashore with a little powder and shot, and left behind on some desolate and distant island.

'Marooned three years agone,' he continued, 'and lived on goats since then, and berries, and oysters. Wherever a man is, says I, a man can do for himself. But, mate, my heart is sore for Christian diet. You mightn't happen to have a piece of cheese about you, now? No? Well, many's the long night I've dreamed of cheese – toasted, mostly – and woke up again, and here I were.'

'If ever I can get aboard again,' said I, 'you shall have cheese by the stone.'

All this time he had been feeling the stuff of my jacket, smoothing my hands, looking at my boots, and generally, in the intervals of his speech, showing a childish pleasure in the presence of a fellow creature. But at my last words he perked up into a kind of startled shyness.

'If ever you can get aboard again, says you?' he repeated. 'Why, now, who's to hinder you?'

'Not you, I know,' was my reply.

'And right you was,' he cried. 'Now you – what do you call yourself, mate?'

'Jim,' I told him.

'Jim, Jim,' says he, quite pleased apparently. 'Well, now, Jim, I've lived that rough as you'd be ashamed to hear of. Now, for instance, you wouldn't think I had had a pious mother – to look at me?' he asked.

'Why, no, not in particular,' I answered.

'Ah, well,' said he, 'but I had – *re*markable pious. And I was a civil, pious boy, and could rattle off my catechism that fast, as you couldn't tell one word from another. And here's what it come to, Jim, and it begun with chuck-farthen on the blessed grave-stones! That's what it begun with, but it went further'n that; and so my mother told me, and predicked the whole, she did, the pious woman! But it were Providence that put me here. I've thought it all out in this here lonely island, and I'm back on piety. You don't catch me tasting rum so much; but just a thimbleful for luck, of course, the first chance I have. I'm bound I'll be good, and I see the way to. And, Jim' – looking all round him, and lowering his voice to a whisper – 'I'm rich.'

I now felt sure that the poor fellow had gone crazy in his solitude, and I suppose I must have shown the feeling in my face; for he repeated the statement hotly:

'Rich! rich! I says. And I'll tell you what: I'll make a man of you, Jim. Ah, Jim, you'll bless your stars, you will, you was the first that found me!'

And at this there came suddenly a lowering shadow over his face, and he tightened his grasp upon my hand, and raised a forefinger threateningly before my eyes.

'Now, Jim, you tell me true; that ain't Flint's ship?' he asked.

At this I had a happy inspiration. I began to believe that I had found an ally, and I answered him at once.

'It's not Flint's ship, and Flint is dead; but I'll tell you true, as you ask me – there are some of Flint's hands aboard; worse luck for the rest of us.'

'Not a man – with one – leg?' he gasped.

'Silver?' I asked.

'Ah, Silver!' says he; 'that were his name.'

'He's the cook; and the ringleader, too.'

He was still holding me by the wrist, and at that he gave it quite a wring.

'If you was sent by Long John,' he said, 'I'm as good as pork, and I know it. But where was you, do you suppose?'

I had made my mind up in a moment, and by way of answer told him the whole story of our voyage, and the predicament in which we found ourselves. He heard me with the keenest interest, and when I had done he patted me on the head.

'You're a good lad, Jim,' he said, 'and you're all in a clove-hitch, ain't you? Well, you just put your trust in Ben Gunn – Ben Gunn's the man to do it. Would you think it likely, now, that your squire would prove a liberal-minded one in case of help – him being in a clove-hitch, as you remark?'

I told him the squire was the most liberal of men.

'Ay, but you see,' returned Ben Gunn, 'I didn't mean giving me a gate to keep, and a shuit of livery clothes, and such; that's not my mark, Jim. What I mean is, would he be likely to come down to the toon of, say one thousand pounds out of money that's as good as a man's own already?'

'I am sure he would,' said I. 'As it was, all hands were to share.'

'*And* a passage home?' he added, with a look of great shrewdness.

'Why,' I cried, 'the squire's a gentleman. And, besides, if we got rid of the others, we should want you to help work the vessel home.'

'Ah,' said he, 'so you would.' And he seemed very much relieved.

'Now, I'll tell you what,' he went on. 'So much I'll tell you, and no more. I were in Flint's ship when he buried the treasure; he and six along – six strong seamen. They was ashore nigh on a week, and us standing off and on in the old *Walrus*. One fine day up went the signal, and here come Flint by himself in a little boat, and his head done up in a blue scarf. The sun was getting up, and mortal white he looked about the cutwater. But, there he was, you mind, and the six all dead – dead and buried. How he done it, not a man aboard us could make out. It was battle, murder, and sudden death, leastways – him against six. Billy Bones was the mate; Long John, he was quartermaster; and they asked him where the treasure was. "Ah," says he, "you can go ashore, if you like, and stay," he says: "But as for the ship, she'll beat up for more, by thunder!" That's what he said.

'Well, I was in another ship three years back, and we sighted this island. "Boys," said I, "here's Flint's treasure; let's land and find it."

The cap'n was displeased at that; but my messmates were all of a mind, and landed. Twelve days they looked for it, and every day they had the worse word for me, until one fine morning all hands went aboard. "As for you, Benjamin Gunn," says they, "here's a musket," they says, "and a spade, and pickaxe. You can stay here, and find Flint's money for yourself," they says.

'Well, Jim, three years have I been here, and not a bite of Christian diet from that day to this. But now, you look here; look at me. Do I look like a man before the mast? No, says you. Nor I weren't neither, I says.'

With that he winked and pinched me hard.

'Just you mention them words to your squire, Jim,' he went on: 'Nor he weren't, neither – that's the words. Three years he were the man of this island, light and dark, fair and rain; and sometimes he would, maybe, think upon a prayer (says you), and sometimes he would, maybe, think of his old mother, so be as she's alive (you'll say); but the most part of Gunn's time (this is what you'll say) – the most part of his time was took up with another matter. And then you'll give him a nip, like I do.'

And he pinched me again in the most confidential manner.

'Then,' he continued – 'then you'll up, and you'll say this: Gunn is a good man (you'll say), and he puts a precious sight more confidence – a precious sight, mind that – in a gen'leman born than in these gen'lemen of fortune, having been one hisself.'

'Well,' I said, 'I don't understand one word that you've been saying. But that's neither here nor there; for how am I to get on board?'

'Ah,' said he, 'that's the hitch, for sure. Well, there's my boat, that I made with my two hands. I keep her under the white rock. If the worst come to the worst, we might try that after dark. Hi!' he broke out, 'what's that?'

For just then, although the sun had still an hour or two to run, all the echoes of the island awoke and bellowed to the thunder of a cannon.

'They have begun to fight!' I cried. 'Follow me.'

And I began to run towards the anchorage, my terrors all forgotten; while, close at my side, the marooned man in his goatskins trotted easily and lightly.

'Left, left,' says he; 'keep to your left hand, mate Jim! Under the trees with you! Theer's where I killed my first goat. They don't come down here now; they're all mastheaded on them mountings for the fear of Benjamin Gunn. Ah! and there's the cetemery' – cemetery he must have meant. 'You see the mounds? I come here and prayed, nows and thens, when I thought maybe a Sunday would be about doo. It weren't quite a chapel, but it seemed more solemn like; and then, says you, Ben Gunn was short-handed – no chapling, nor so much as a Bible and a flag, you says.'

So he kept talking as I ran, neither expecting nor receiving any answer.

The cannon-shot was followed, after a considerable interval, by a volley of small arms.

Another pause, and then, not a quarter of a mile in front of me, I beheld the Union Jack flutter in the air above a wood.

1 Narrative continued by the Doctor:
How the Ship was Abandoned

It was about half-past one – three bells in the sea phrase – that the two boats went ashore from the *Hispaniola*. The captain, the squire, and I were talking matters over in the cabin. Had there been a breath of wind we should have fallen on the six mutineers who were left aboard with us, slipped our cable, and away to sea. But the wind was wanting; and, to complete our helplessness, down came Hunter with the news that Jim Hawkins had slipped into a boat and was gone ashore with the rest.

It never occurred to us to doubt Jim Hawkins; but we were alarmed for his safety. With the men in the temper they were in, it seemed an even chance if we should see the lad again. We ran on deck. The pitch was bubbling in the seams; the hasty stench of the place turned me sick; if ever a man smelt fever and dysentery, it was in that abominable anchorage. The six scoundrels were sitting grumbling under a sail in the forecastle; ashore we could see the gigs made fast, and a man sitting in each, hard by where the river runs in. One of them was whistling *Lillibullero*.

Waiting was a strain; and it was decided that Hunter and I should go ashore with the jolly-boat, in quest of information. The gigs had leaned to their right; but Hunter and I pulled straight in, in the direction of the stockade upon the chart. The two who were left guarding their boats seemed in a bustle at our appearance; *Lillibullero* stopped off, and I could see the pair discussing what they ought to do. Had they gone and told Silver, all might have turned out differently; but they had their orders, I suppose, and decided to sit quietly where they were and hark back again to *Lillibullero*.

There was a slight bend in the coast, and I steered so as to put it between us; even before we landed we had thus lost sight of the gigs. I jumped out, and came as near running as I durst, with a big silk handkerchief under my hat for coolness' sake, and a brace of pistols ready primed for safety.

I had not gone a hundred yards when I came on the stockade.

This was how it was: a spring of clear water rose almost at the top of a knoll. Well, on the knoll, and enclosing the spring, they had clapped a stout log-house, fit to hold two-score people on a pinch, and loopholed for musketry on every side. All round this they had cleared a wide space, and then the thing was completed by a paling six feet high, without door or opening, too strong to pull down without time and labour, and too open to shelter the besiegers. The people in the log-house had them in every way; they stood quiet in shelter and shot the others like partridges. All they wanted was a good watch and food; for, short of a complete surprise, they might have held the place against a regiment.

What particularly took my fancy was the spring. For, though we had a good enough place of it in the cabin of the *Hispaniola*, with plenty of arms and ammunition, and things to eat, and excellent wines, there had been one thing overlooked – we had no water. I was thinking this over, when there came ringing over the island the cry of a man at the point of death. I was not new to violent death – I have served His Royal Highness the Duke of Cumberland, and got a wound myself at Fontenoy – but I know my pulse went dot and carry one. 'Jim Hawkins is gone,' was my first thought.

It is something to have been an old soldier, but more still to have been a doctor. There is no time to dilly-dally in our work. And so now I made up my mind instantly, and with no time lost returned to the shore, and jumped on board the jolly-boat.

By good fortune Hunter pulled a good oar. We made the water fly; and the boat was soon alongside, and I aboard the schooner.

I found them all shaken, as was natural. The squire was sitting down, as white as a sheet, thinking of the harm he had led us to, the good soul! and one of the six forecastle hands was little better.

'There's a man,' says Captain Smollett, nodding towards him, 'new to this work. He came nigh-hand fainting, doctor, when he heard the cry. Another touch of the rudder and that man would join us.'

I told my plan to the captain, and between us we settled on the details of its accomplishment.

We put old Redruth in the gallery between the cabin and the forecastle, with three or four loaded muskets and a mattress for protection. Hunter brought the boat round under the stern-port, and Joyce and I set to work loading her with powder tins, muskets, bags of biscuits, kegs of pork, a cask of cognac, and my invaluable medicine chest.

In the meantime, the squire and the captain stayed on deck, and the latter hailed the coxswain, who was the principal man aboard.

'Mr. Hands,' he said, 'here are two of us with a brace of pistols each. If any one of you six make a signal of any description, that man's dead.'

They were a good deal taken aback; and, after a little consultation, one and all tumbled down the fore companion, thinking, no doubt, to take us on the rear. But when they saw Redruth waiting for them in the sparred gallery, they went about-ship at once, and a head popped out again on deck.

'Down, dog!' cries the captain.

And the head popped back again; and we heard no more, for the time, of these six very faint-hearted seamen.

By this time, tumbling things in as they came, we had the jolly-boat loaded as much as we dared. Joyce and I got out through the stern-port, and we made for shore again, as fast as oars could take us.

This second trip fairly aroused the watchers along shore. *Lillibullero* was dropped again; and just before we lost sight of them behind the little point, one of them whipped ashore and disappeared. I had half a mind to change my plan and destroy their boats, but I feared that Silver and the others might be close at hand, and all might very well be lost by trying for too much.

We had soon touched land in the same place as before, and set to provision the blockhouse. All three made the first journey, heavily laden, and tossed our stores over the palisade. Then, leaving Joyce to guard them – one man, to be sure, but with half a dozen muskets – Hunter and I returned to the jolly-boat, and loaded ourselves once more. So we proceeded without pausing to take breath, till the whole cargo was bestowed, when the two servants took up their position in the blockhouse, and I, with all my power, sculled back to the *Hispaniola*.

That we should have risked a second boat-load seems more daring than it really was. They had the advantage of numbers, of course, but we had the advantage of arms. Not one of them ashore had a musket, and before they could get within range for pistol shooting, we flattered ourselves we should be able to give a good account of a half-dozen at least.

The squire was waiting for me at the stern window, all his faintness gone from him. He caught the painter and made it fast, and we fell to loading the boat for our very lives. Pork, powder, and biscuit was the cargo, with only a musket and a cutlass apiece for squire and me and Redruth and the captain. The rest of the arms and powder we dropped overboard in two fathoms and a half of water, so that we could see the bright steel shining far below us in the sun, on the clean, sandy bottom.

By this time the tide was beginning to ebb, and the ship was swinging round to her anchor. Voices were heard faintly halloaing in the direction of the two gigs; and though this reassured us for Joyce and Hunter, who were well to the eastward, it warned our party to be off.

Redruth retreated from his place in the gallery, and dropped into the boat, which we then brought round to the ship's counter, to be handier for Captain Smollett.

'Now, men,' said he, 'do you hear me?'

There was no answer from the forecastle.

'It's to you, Abraham Grey – it's to you I am speaking.'

Still no reply.

'Gray,' resumed Mr. Smollett, a little louder, 'I am leaving this ship, and I order you to follow your captain. I know you are a good man at bottom, and I dare say not one of the lot of you's as bad as he makes out. I have my watch here in my hand; I give you thirty seconds to join me in.'

There was a pause.

'Come, my fine fellow,' continued the captain, 'don't hang so long in stays. I'm risking my life and the lives of these good gentlemen every second.'

There was a sudden scuffle, a sound of blows, and out burst Abraham Gray with a knife-cut on the side of the cheek, and came running to the captain, like a dog to the whistle.

'I'm with you, sir,' said he.

And the next moment he and the captain had dropped aboard of us, and we had shoved off and given way.

We were clear out of the ship; but not yet ashore in our stockade.

2 Narrative continued by the Doctor: The Jolly-boat's Last Trip

This fifth trip was quite different from any of the others. In the first place, the little gallipot of a boat that we were in was gravely overloaded. Five grown men, and three of them – Trelawney, Redruth, and the captain – over six feet high, was already more than she was meant to carry. Add to that the powder, pork, and bread-bags. The gunwale was lipping astern. Several times we shipped a little water, and my breeches and the tails of my coat were all soaking wet before we had gone a hundred yards.

The captain made us trim the boat, and we got her to lie a little more evenly. All the same, we were afraid to breathe.

In the second place, the ebb was now making – a strong rippling current running westward, through the basin, and then south'ard and seaward down the straits by which we had entered in the morning. Even the ripples were a danger to our overloaded craft; but the worst of it was that we were swept out of our true course, and away from our proper landing-place behind the point. If we let the current have its way we should come ashore beside the gigs, where the pirates might appear at any moment.

'I cannot keep her head for the stockade, sir,' said I to the captain. I was steering, while he and Redruth, two fresh men, were at the oars. 'The tide keeps washing her down. Could you pull a little stronger?'

'Not without swamping the boat,' said he. 'You must bear up, sir, if you please bear up until you see you're gaining.'

I tried, and found by experiment that the tide kept sweeping us westward until I had laid her head due east, or just about right angles to the way we ought to go.

'We'll never get ashore at this rate,' said I.

'If it's the only course that we can lie, sir, we must even lie it,' returned the captain. 'We must keep upstream. You see, sir,' he went on, 'if once we dropped to leeward of the landing-place, it's hard to say where we should get ashore, besides the chance of being boarded by the gigs; whereas, the way we go the current must slacken, and then we can dodge back along the shore.'

'The current's less a'ready, sir,' said the man Gray, who was sitting in the fore-sheets; 'you can ease her off a bit.'

'Thank you, my man,' said I, quite as if nothing had happened: for we had all quietly made up our minds to treat him like one of ourselves.

Suddenly the captain spoke up again, and I thought his voice was a little changed.

'The gun!' said he.

'I have thought of that,' said I, for I made sure he was thinking of a bombardment of the fort. 'They could never get the gun ashore, and if they did, they could never haul it through the woods.'

'Look astern, doctor,' replied the captain.

We had entirely forgotten the long nine; and there, to our horror, were the five rogues busy about her, getting off her jacket, as they called the stout tarpaulin cover under which she sailed. Not only that, but it flashed into my mind at the same moment that the round-shot and the powder for the gun had been left behind, and a stroke with an axe would put it all into the possession of the evil ones aboard.

'Israel was Flint's gunner,' said Gray, hoarsely.

At any risk, we put the boat's head direct for the landing-place. By this time we had got so far out of the run of the current that we kept steerage way even at our necessarily gentle rate of rowing, and I could keep her steady for the goal. But the worst of it was, that with the course I now held, we turned our broadside instead of our stern to the *Hispaniola*, and offered a target like a barn door.

I could hear, as well as see, that brandy-faced rascal, Israel Hands, plumping down a round-shot on the deck.

'Who's the best shot?' asked the captain.

'Mr. Trelawney, out and away,' said I.

'Mr. Trelawney, will you please pick me off one of these men, sir? – Hands, if possible,' said the captain.

Trelawney was as cool as steel. He looked to the priming of his gun.

'Now,' cried the captain, 'easy with that gun, sir, or you'll swamp the boat. All hands stand by to trim her when he aims.'

The squire raised his gun, the rowing ceased, and we leaned over to the other side to keep the balance, and all was so nicely contrived that we did not ship a drop.

They had the gun, by this time, slewed round upon the swivel, and Hands, who was at the muzzle with the rammer, was, in consequence, the most exposed. However, we had no luck; for just as Trelawney fired, down he stooped, the ball whistled over him, and it was one of the other four who fell.

The cry he gave was echoed, not only by his companions on board, but by a great number of voices from the shore, and looking in that direction I saw the other pirates trooping out from among the trees and tumbling into their places in the boats.

'Here come the gigs, sir,' said I.

'Give way then,' cried the captain. 'We musn't mind if we swamp her now. If we can't get ashore, all's up.'

'Only one of the gigs is being manned, sir,' I added, 'the crew of the other most likely going round by shore to cut us off.'

'They'll have a hot run, sir,' returned the captain. 'Jack ashore, you know. It's not them I mind; it's the round-shot. Carpet bowls! My lady's maid couldn't miss. Tell us, squire, when you see the match, and we'll hold water.'

In the meanwhile we had been making headway at a good pace for a boat so overloaded, and we had shipped but little water in the process. We were now close in; thirty or forty strokes and we should beach her; for the ebb had already disclosed a narrow belt of sand below the clustering trees. The gig was no longer to be feared; the little point had already concealed it from our eyes. The ebb-tide, which had so cruelly delayed us, was now making reparation, and delaying our assailants. The one source of danger was the gun.

'If I durst,' said the captain, 'I'd stop and pick off another man.'

But it was plain that they meant nothing should delay their shot. They had never so much as looked at their fallen comrade, though he was not dead, and I could see him trying to crawl away.

'Ready!' cried the squire.

'Hold!' cried the captain, quick as an echo.

And he and Redruth backed with a great heave that sent her stern bodily under water. The report fell in at the same instant of time. This was the first that Jim heard, the sound of the squire's shot not having reached him. Where the ball passed, not one of us precisely knew; but I fancy it must have been over our heads, and that the wind of it may have contributed to our disaster.

At any rate the boat sank by the stern, quite gently, in three feet of water, leaving the captain and myself, facing each other, on our feet. The other three took complete headers, and came up again, drenched and bubbling.

So far there was no great harm. No lives were lost, and we could wade ashore in safety. But there were all our stores at the bottom, and, to make things worse, only two guns out of five remained in a state for service. Mine I had snatched from my knees and held over my head, by a sort of instinct. As for the captain, he had carried his over his shoulder by a bandoleer, and, like a wise man, lock uppermost. The other three had gone down with the boat.

To add to our concern we heard voices already drawing near us in the woods along shore; and we had not only the danger of being cut off from the stockade in our half-crippled state, but the fear before us whether, if Hunter and Joyce were attacked by half a dozen, they would have the sense and conduct to stand firm. Hunter was steady, that we knew; Joyce was a doubtful case – a pleasant, polite man for a valet, and to brush one's clothes, but not entirely fitted for a man of war.

With all this in our minds, we waded ashore as fast as we could, leaving behind us the poor jolly-boat, and a good half of all our powder and provisions.

3 Narrative continued by the Doctor:
End of the First Day's Fighting

We made our best speed across the strip of wood that now divided us from the stockade; and at every step we took the voices of the buccaneers rang nearer. Soon we could hear their footfalls as they ran, and the cracking of the branches as they breasted across a bit of thicket.

I began to see we should have a brush for it in earnest, and looked to my priming.

'Captain,' said I, 'Trelawney is the dead shot. Give him your gun; his own is useless.'

They exchanged guns, and Trelawney, silent and cool as he had been since the beginning of the bustle, hung a moment on his heel to see that all was fit for service. At the same time, observing Gray to be unarmed, I handed him my cutlass. It did all our hearts good to see him spit in his hand, knit his brows, and make the blade sing through the air. It was plain from every line of his body that our new hand was worth his salt.

Forty paces further we came to the edge of the wood and saw the stockade in front of us. We struck the enclosure about the middle of the south side, and, almost at the same time, seven mutineers – Job Anderson, the boatswain, at their head – appeared in full cry at the south-western corner.

They paused, as if taken aback; and before they recovered, not only the squire and I, but Hunter and Joyce from the blockhouse, had time to fire. The four shots came in rather a scattering volley; but they did the business; one of the enemy actually fell, and the rest, without hesitation, turned and plunged into the trees.

After reloading, we walked down the outside of the palisade to see to the fallen enemy. He was stone dead – shot through the heart.

We began to rejoice over our good success, when just at that moment a pistol cracked in the bush, a ball whistled close past my ear, and poor Tom Redruth stumbled, and fell his length on the ground.

Both the squire and I returned the shot; but as we had nothing to aim at, it is probable we only wasted powder. Then we reloaded, and turned our attention to poor Tom.

The captain and Gray were already examining him; and I saw with half an eye that all was over.

I believe the readiness of our return volley had scattered the mutineers once more, for we were suffered without further molestation to get the poor old gamekeeper hoisted over the stockade, and carried, groaning and bleeding, into the log-house.

Poor old fellow, he had not uttered one word of surprise, complaint, fear, or even acquiescence, from the very beginning of our troubles till now, when we had laid him down in the log-house to die. He had lain like a Trojan behind his mattress in the gallery; he had followed every order silently, doggedly, and well; he was the oldest of our party by a score of years; and now, sullen, old serviceable servant, it was he that was to die.

The squire dropped down beside him on his knees and kissed his hand, crying like a child.

'Be I going, doctor?' he asked.

'Tom, my man,' said I, 'you're going home.'

'I wish I had had a lick at them with the gun first,' he replied.

'Tom,' said the squire, 'say you forgive me, won't you?'

'Would that be respectful-like, from me to you, squire?' was the answer. 'Howsoever, so be it, amen!'

After a little while of silence, he said he thought somebody might read a prayer. 'It's the custom, sir,' he added, apologetically. And not long after, without another word, he passed away.

In the meantime the captain, whom I had observed to be wonderfully swollen about the chest and pockets, had turned out a great many various stores – the British colours, a Bible, a coil of stoutish rope, pen, ink, the log-book, and pounds of tobacco. He had found a longish fir-tree lying felled and cleared in the enclosure, and with the help of Hunter, he had set it up at the corner of the log-house where the trunks crossed and made an angle. Then, climbing on the roof, he had with his own hand bent and run up the colours.

This seemed mightily to relieve him. He re-entered the log-house, and set about counting up the stores, as if nothing else existed. But he had an eye on Tom's passage for all that; and as soon as all was over, came forward with another flag, and reverently spread it on the body.

'Don't you take on, sir,' he said, shaking the squire's hand. 'All's well with him; no fear for a hand that's been shot down in his duty to captain and owner. It mayn't be good divinity, but it's a fact.'

Then he pulled me aside.

'Dr. Livesey,' he said, 'in how many weeks do you and squire expect the consort?'

I told him it was a question, not of weeks, but of months; that if we were not back by the end of August, Blandly was to send to find us; but neither sooner nor later. 'You can calculate for yourself,' I said.

'Why, yes,' returned the captain, scratching his head, 'and making a large allowance, sir, for all the gifts of Providence, I should say we were pretty close hauled.'

'How do you mean?' I asked.

'It's a pity, sir, we lost that second load. That's what I mean,' replied the captain. 'As for powder and shot, we'll do. But the rations are short, very short – so short, Dr. Livesey, that we're, perhaps, as well without that extra mouth.'

And he pointed to the dead body under the flag.

Just then, with a roar and a whistle, a round-shot passed high above the roof of the log-house and plumped far beyond us in the wood.

'Oho!' said the captain. 'Blaze away! You've little enough powder already, my lads.'

At the second trial, the aim was better, and the ball descended inside the stockade, scattering a cloud of sand, but doing no further damage.

'Captain,' said the squire, 'the house is quite invisible from the ship. It must be the flag they are aiming at. Would it not be wiser to take it in?'

'Strike my colours!' cried the captain. 'No, sir, not I'; and, as soon as he had said the words, I think we all agreed with him. For it was not only a piece of stout, seamanly, good feeling; it was good policy besides, and showed our enemies that we despised their cannonade.

All through the evening they kept thundering away. Ball after ball flew over or fell short, or kicked up the sand in the enclosure; but they had to fire so high that the shot fell dead and buried itself in the soft sand. We had no ricochet to fear; and though one popped in through the roof of the log-house and out again through the floor, we soon got used to that sort of horse-play, and minded it no more than cricket.

'There is one thing good about all this,' observed the captain: 'the wood in front of us is likely clear. The ebb has made a good while; our stores should be uncovered. Volunteers to go and bring in pork.'

Gray and Hunter were the first to come forward. Well armed, they stole out of the stockade; but it proved a useless mission. The mutineers were bolder than we fancied, or they put more trust in Israel's gunnery. For four or five of them were busy carrying off our stores, and wading out with them to one of the gigs that lay close by, pulling an oar or so to hold her steady against the current. Silver was in the stern-sheets in command; and every man of them was now provided with a musket from some secret magazine of their own.

The captain sat down to his log, and here is the beginning of the entry:

Alexander Smollett, master; David Livesey, ship's doctor; Abraham Gray, carpenter's mate; John Trelawney, owner; John Hunter and Richard Joyce, owner's servants, landsmen – being all that is left faithful of the ship's company – with stores for ten days at short rations, came ashore this day, and flew British colours on the log-house in Treasure Island. Thomas Redruth, owner's servant, landsman, shot by the mutineers; James Hawkins, cabin-boy——

And at the same time I was wondering over poor Jim Hawkins's fate.

A hail on the land side.

'Somebody hailing us,' said Hunter, who was on guard.

'Doctor! squire! captain! Hullo, Hunter, is that you?' came the cries.

And I ran to the door in time to see Jim Hawkins, safe and sound, come climbing over the stockade.

4 Narrative Resumed by Jim Hawkins: The Garrison in the Stockade

As soon as Ben Gunn saw the colours he came to a halt, stopped me by the arm, and sat down.

'Now,' said he 'there's your friends, sure enough.'

'Far more likely it's the mutineers,' I answered.

'That!' he cried. 'Why, in a place like this, where nobody puts in but gen'lemen of fortune, Silver would fly the Jolly Roger, you don't make no doubt of that. No; that's your friends. There's been blows, too, and I reckon your friends has had the best of it; and here they are ashore in the old stockade, as was made years and years ago by Flint. Ah, he was the man to have a head-piece, was Flint! Barring rum, his match were never seen. He were afraid of none, not he; on'y Silver – Silver was that genteel.'

'Well,' said I, 'that may be so, and so be it; all the more reason that I should hurry on and join my friends.'

'Nay, mate,' returned Ben, 'not you. You're a good boy, or I'm mistook; but you're on'y a boy, all told. Now, Ben Gunn is fly. Rum wouldn't bring me there, where you're going – not rum wouldn't, till I see your born gen'leman, and gets it on his word of honour. And you won't forget my words: "A precious sight (that's what you'll say), a precious sight more confidence" – and then nips him.'

And he pinched me the third time with the same air of cleverness.

'And when Ben Gunn is wanted, you know where to find him, Jim. Just wheer you found him to-day. And him that comes is to have a white thing in his hand: and he's to come alone. Oh! and you'll say this: "Ben Gunn," says you, "has reasons of his own."'

'Well,' said I, 'I believe I understand. You have something to propose, and you wish to see the squire or the doctor; and you're to be found where I found you. Is that all?'

'And when? says you,' he added. 'Why, from about noon observation to about six bells.'

'A cannon ball came tearing through the trees'

'Good,' said I, 'and now may I go?'

'You won't forget?' he inquired, anxiously. 'Precious sight, and reasons of his own, says you. Reasons of his own; that's the mainstay; as between man and man. Well, then,' – still holding me – 'I reckon you can go, Jim. And, Jim, if you was to see Silver, you wouldn't go for to sell Ben Gunn? wild horses wouldn't draw it from you? No, says you. And if them pirates camp ashore, Jim, what would you say but there'd be widders in the morning?'

He was interrupted by a loud report, and a cannon ball came tearing through the trees and pitched in the sand, not a hundred yards from where we two were talking. The next moment each of us had taken to his heels in a different direction.

For a good hour to come frequent reports shook the island, and balls kept crashing through the woods. I moved from hiding-place to hiding-place, always pursued, or so it seemed to me, by these terrifying missiles. But towards the end of the bombardment, though still I durst not venture in the direction of the stockade, where the balls fell oftenest, I had begun, in a manner, to pluck up my heart again; and after a long detour to the east, crept down among the shore-side trees.

The sun had just set, the sea breeze was rustling and tumbling in the woods, and ruffling the grey surface of the anchorage; the tide, too, was far out, and great tracts of sand lay uncovered; the air, after the heat of the day, chilled me through my jacket.

The *Hispaniola* still lay where she had anchored; but, sure enough, there was the Jolly Roger – the black flag of piracy – flying from her peak. Even as I looked, there came another red flash and another report, that sent the echoes clattering, and one more round-shot whistled through the air. It was the last of the cannonade.

I lay for some time, watching the bustle which succeeded the attack. Men were demolishing something with axes on the beach near the stockade; the poor jolly-boat, I afterwards discovered. Away, near the mouth of the river, a great fire was glowing among the trees, and between that point and the ship one of the gigs kept coming and going, the men, whom I had seen so gloomy, shouting at the oars like children. But there was a sound in their voices which suggested rum.

At length I thought I might return towards the stockade. I was pretty far down on the low, sandy spit that encloses the anchorage to the east, and is joined at half-water to Skeleton Island; and now, as I rose to my feet, I saw, some distance further down the spit, and rising from among low bushes, an isolated rock, pretty high, and peculiarly white in colour. It occurred to me that this might be the white rock of which Ben Gunn had spoken, and that some day or other a boat might be wanted, and I should know where to look for one.

Then I skirted among the woods until I had regained the rear, or shoreward side, of the stockade, and was soon warmly welcomed by the faithful party.

I had soon told my story, and began to look about me. The log-house was made of unsquared trunks of pine – roof, walls, and floor. The latter stood in several places as much as a foot or a foot and a half above the surface of the sand. There was porch at the door, and under this porch the little spring welled up into an artificial basin of a rather odd kind – no other than a great ship's kettle of iron, with the bottom knocked out, and sunk 'to her bearings,' as the captain said, among the sand.

Little had been left beside the framework of the house; but in one corner there was a stone slab laid down by way of hearth, and an old rusty iron basket to contain the fire.

The slopes of the knoll and all the inside of the stockade had been cleared of timber to build the house, and we could see by the stumps what a fine and lofty grove had been destroyed. Most of the soil had been washed away or buried in drift after the removal of the trees; only where the streamlet ran down from the kettle a thick bed of moss and some ferns and little creeping bushes were still green among the sand. Very close around the stockade – too close for defence, they said – the wood still flourished high and dense, all of fir on the land side, but towards the sea with a large admixture of live oaks.

The cold evening breeze, of which I have spoken, whistled through every chink of the rude building, and sprinkled the floor with a continual rain of fine sand. There was sand in our eyes, sand in our teeth, sand in our suppers, sand dancing in the spring at the bottom of the kettle, for all the world like porridge beginning to boil. Our chimney was a square hole in the roof: it was but a little part of the smoke that found its way out, and the rest eddied about the house, and kept us coughing and piping the eye.

Add to this that Gray, the new man, had his face tied up in a bandage for a cut he had got in breaking away from the mutineers; and that poor old Tom Redruth, still unburied, lay along the wall, stiff and stark, under the Union Jack.

If we had been allowed to sit idle, we should all have fallen in the blues, but Captain Smollett was never the man for that. All hands were called up before him, and he divided us into watches. The doctor, and Gray, and I, for one; the squire, Hunter, and Joyce upon the other. Tired as we all were, two were sent out for firewood; two more were set to dig a grave for Redruth; the doctor was named cook; I was put sentry at the door; and the captain himself went from one to another, keeping up our spirits, and lending a hand wherever it was wanted.

From time to time the doctor came to the door for a little air and to rest his eyes, which were almost smoked out of his head; and whenever he did so, he had a word for me.

'That man Smollett,' he said once, 'is a better man than I am. And when I say that it means a deal, Jim.'

Another time he came and was silent for a while. Then he put his head on one side, and looked at me.

'Is this Ben Gunn a man?' he asked.

'I do not know, sir,' said I. 'I am not very sure whether he's sane.'

'If there's any doubt about the matter, he is,' returned the doctor. 'A man who has been three years biting his nails on a desert island, Jim, can't expect to appear as sane as you or me. It doesn't lie in human nature. Was it cheese you said he had a fancy for?'

'Yes, sir, cheese,' I answered.

'Well, Jim,' says he, 'just see the good that comes of being dainty in your food. You've seen my snuff-box, haven't you? And you never saw me take snuff; the reason being that in my snuff-box I carry a piece of Parmesan cheese – a cheese made in Italy, very nutritious. Well, that's for Ben Gunn!'

Before supper was eaten we buried old Tom in the sand, and stood round him for a while bare-headed in the breeze. A good deal of firewood had been got in, but not enough for the captain's fancy; and he shook his head over it, and told us we 'must get back to this to-morrow rather livelier.' Then, when we had eaten our pork, and each had a good stiff glass of brandy grog, the three chiefs got together in a corner to discuss our prospects.

It appears they were at their wits' end what to do, the stores being so low that we must have been starved into surrender long before help came. But our best hope, it was decided, was to kill off the buccaneers until they either hauled down their flag or ran away with the *Hispaniola*. From nineteen they were already reduced to fifteen, two others were wounded, and one, at least – the man shot beside the gun – severely wounded, if he were not dead. Every time we had a crack at them, we were to take it, saving our own lives, with the extremest care. And, besides that, we had two able allies – rum and the climate.

As for the first, though we were about half a mile away, we could hear them roaring and singing late into the night; and as for the second, the doctor staked his wig that, camped where they were in the marsh and unprovided with remedies, the half of them would be on their backs before a week.

'So,' he added, 'if we are not all shot down first they'll be glad to be packing in the schooner. It's always a ship, and they can get to buccaneering again, I suppose.'

'First ship that ever I lost,' said Captain Smollett.

I was dead tired, as you may fancy; and when I got to sleep, which was not till after a great deal of tossing, I slept like a log of wood.

The rest had long been up, and had already breakfasted and increased the pile of firewood by about half as much again, when I was awakened by a bustle and the sound of voices.

'Flag of truce!' I heard someone say; and then, immediately after, with a cry of surprise: 'Silver himself!'

And, at that, up I jumped, and, rubbing my eyes, ran to a loophole in the wall.

5 Silver's Embassy

Sure enough, there were two men just outside the stockade, one of them waving a white cloth; the other, no less a person than Silver himself, standing placidly by.

It was still quite early, and the coldest morning that I think I ever was abroad in; a chill that pierced into the marrow. The sky was bright and cloudless overhead, and the tops of the trees shone rosily in the sun. But where Silver stood with his lieutenant all was still in shadow, and they waded knee deep in a low, white vapour, and had crawled during the night out of the morass. The chill and the vapour taken together told a poor tale of the island. It was plainly a damp, feverish, unhealthy spot.

'Keep indoors, men,' said the captain. 'Ten to one this is a trick.'

Then he hailed the buccaneer.

'Who goes? Stand, or we fire.'

'Flag of truce,' cried Silver.

The captain was in the porch, keeping himself carefully out of the way of a treacherous shot should any be intended. He turned and spoke to us:

'Doctor's watch on the look-out. Dr. Livesey, take the north side, if you please; Jim, the east; Gray, west. The watch below, all hands to load muskets. Lively, men, and careful.'

And then he turned again to the mutineers.

'And what do you want with your flag of truce?' he cried.

This time it was the other man who replied.

'Cap'n Silver, sir, to come on board and make terms,' he shouted.

'Cap'n Silver! Don't know him. Who's he?' cried the captain. And we could hear him adding to himself: 'Cap'n, is it? My heart, and here's promotion!'

Long John answered for himself.

'Me, sir. These poor lads have chosen me cap'n, after your

desertion, sir' – laying a particular emphasis upon the word 'desertion.' 'We're willing to submit, if we can come to terms, and no bones about it. All I ask is your word, Cap'n Smollett, to let me safe and sound out of this here stockade, and one minute to get out o' shot before a gun is fired.'

'My man,' said Captain Smollett, 'I have not the slightest desire to talk to you. If you wish to talk to me, you can come, that's all. If there's any treachery, it'll be on your side, and the Lord help you.'

'That's enough, cap'n,' shouted Long John, cheerily. 'A word from you's enough. I know a gentleman, and you may lay to that.'

We could see the man who carried the flag of truce attempting to hold Silver back. Nor was that wonderful, seeing how cavalier had been the captain's answer. But Silver laughed at him aloud, and slapped him on the back, as if the idea of alarm had been absurd. Then he advanced to the stockade, threw over his crutch, got a leg up, and with great vigour and skill succeeded in surmounting the fence and dropping safely to the other side.

I will confess that I was far too much taken up with what was going on to be of the slightest use as sentry; indeed, I had already deserted my eastern loophole, and crept up behind the captain, who had now seated himself on the threshold, with his elbows on his knees, his head in his hands, and his eyes fixed on the water, as it bubbled out of the old iron kettle in the sand. He was whistling to himself: *Come, Lasses and Lads.*

Silver had terrible hard work getting up the knoll. What with the steepness of the incline, the thick tree stumps, and the soft sand, he and his crutch were as helpless as a ship in stays. But he stuck to it like a man in silence, and at last arrived before the captain, whom he saluted in the handsomest style. He was tricked out in his best; an immense blue coat, thick with brass buttons, hung as low as to his knees, and a fine laced hat was set on the back of his head.

'Here you are, my man,' said the captain, raising his head. 'You had better sit down.'

'You ain't a-going to let me inside, cap'n?' complained Long John. 'It's a main cold morning, to be sure, sir, to sit outside upon the sand.'

'Why, Silver,' said the captain, 'if you had pleased to be an honest man, you might have been sitting in your galley. It's your own doing. You're either my ship's cook – and then you were treated handsome – or Cap'n Silver, a common mutineer and pirate, and then you can go hang!'

'Well, well, cap'n,' returned the sea cook, sitting down as he was bidden on the sand, 'you'll have to give me a hand up again, that's all. A sweet pretty place you have of it here. Ah, there's Jim! The top of the morning to you, Jim. Doctor, here's my service. Why, there you all are together like a happy family, in a manner of speaking.'

'If you have anything to say, my man, better say it,' said the captain.

'Right you were, Cap'n Smollett,' replied Silver. 'Dooty is dooty, to be sure. Well, now, you look here, that was a good lay of yours last night. I don't deny it was a good lay. Some of you pretty handy with a hand-spike-end. And I'll not deny neither but what some of my people was shook – maybe all was shook; maybe I was shook myself; maybe that's why I'm here for terms. But you mark me, cap'n, it won't do twice, by thunder! We'll have to do sentry-go, and ease off a point or so on the rum. Maybe you think we were all a sheet in the wind's eye. But I'll tell you I was sober; I was on'y dog tired; and if I'd awoke a second sooner I'd a' caught you at the act, I would. He wasn't dead when I got round to him, not he.'

'Well?' says Captain Smollett, as cool as can be.

All that Silver said was a riddle to him, but you would never have guessed it from his tone. As for me, I began to have an inkling. Ben Gunn's last words came back to my mind. I began to suppose that he had paid the buccaneers a visit while they all lay drunk together round their fire, and I reckoned up with glee that we had only fourteen enemies to deal with.

'Well, here it is,' said Silver. 'We want that treasure, and we'll have it – that's our point! You would just as soon save your lives, I reckon; and that's yours. You have a chart, haven't you?'

'That's as may be,' replied the captain.

'Oh, well, you have, I know that,' returned Long John. 'You needn't be so husky with a man; there ain't a particle of service in that, and you may lay to it. What I mean is, we want your chart. Now, I never meant you no harm, myself.'

'That won't do with me, my man,' interrupted the captain. 'We know exactly what you meant to do, and we don't care; for now, you see, you can't do it.'

And the captain looked at him calmly, and proceeded to fill a pipe.

'If Abe Gray——' Silver broke out.

'Avast there!' cried Mr. Smollett. 'Gray told me nothing, and I asked him nothing; and what's more, I would see you and him and this whole island blown clean out of the water into blazes first. So there's my mind for you, my man, on that.'

This little whiff of temper seemed to cool Silver down. He had been growing nettled before, but now he pulled himself together.

'Like enough,' said he. 'I would set no limits to what gentlemen might consider shipshape, or might not, as the case were. And, seein' as how you are about to take a pipe, cap'n, I'll make so free as do likewise.'

And he filled a pipe and lighted it; and the two men sat silently smoking for quite a while, now looking each other in the face, now stopping their tobacco, now leaning forward to spit. It was as good as the play to see them.

'Now,' resumed Silver, 'here it is. You give us the chart to get the treasure by, and drop shooting poor seamen, and stoving of their heads in while asleep. You do that, and we'll offer you a choice. Either you come aboard along of us, once the treasure's shipped, and then I'll give you my affy-davy, upon my word of honour, to clap you somewhere safe ashore. Or, if that ain't to your fancy, some of my hands being rough, and having old scores, on account of hazing, then you can stay here, you can. We'll divide stores with you, man for man; and I'll give my affy-davy, as before, to speak the first ship I sight, and send 'em here to pick you up. Now you'll own that's talking. Handsomer you couldn't look to get, not you. And I hope' – raising his voice – 'that all hands in this here blockhouse will overhaul my words, for what is spoke to one is spoke to all.'

Captain Smollett rose from his seat, and knocked out the ashes of his pipe in the palm of his left hand.

'Is that all?' he asked.

'Every last word, by thunder!' answered John. 'Refuse that, and you've seen the last of me but musketballs.'

'Very good,' said the captain. 'Now you'll hear me. If you'll come up one by one, unarmed, I'll engage to clap you all in irons, and take you home to a fair trial in England. If you won't, my name is Alexander Smollett, I've flown my sovereign's colours, and I'll see you all to Davy Jones. You can't find the treasure. You can't sail the ship – there's not a man among you fit to sail the ship. You can't fight us – Gray, there, got away from five of you. Your ship's in irons, Master Silver; you're on a lee shore, and so you'll find. I stand here and tell you so; and they're the last good words you'll get from me, for, in the name of heaven, I'll put a bullet in your back when next I meet you. Tramp, my lad. Bundle out of this, please, hand over hand and double quick.'

Silver's face was a picture; his eyes started in his head with wrath. He shook the fire out of his pipe.

'Give me a hand up!' he cried.

'Not I,' returned the captain.

'Who'll give me a hand up?' he roared.

Not a man among us moved. Growling the foulest imprecations, he crawled along the sand till he got hold of the porch and could hoist himself again upon his crutch. Then he spat into the spring.

'There,' he cried, 'that's what I think of ye. Before an hour's out, I'll stove in your old blockhouse like a rum-puncheon. Laugh, by thunder, laugh! Before an hour's out, ye'll laugh upon the other side. Them that die'll be the lucky ones.'

And with a dreadful oath he stumbled off, ploughed down the sand, was helped across the stockade, after four or five failures, by the man with the flag of truce, and disappeared in an instant afterwards among the trees.

6 The Attack

As soon as Silver disappeared, the captain, who had been closely watching him, turned towards the interior of the house, and found not a man of us at his post but Gray. It was the first time we had ever seen him angry.

'Quarters!' he roared. And then, as we all slunk back to our places, 'Gray,' he said, 'I'll put your name in the log; you've stood by your duty like a seaman. Mr. Trelawney, I'm surprised at you, sir. Doctor, I thought you had worn the king's coat! If that was how you served at Fontenoy, sir, you'd have been better in your berth.'

The doctor's watch were all back at their loopholes, the rest were busy, loading the spare muskets, and every one with a red face, you may be certain, and a flea in his ear, as the saying is.

The captain looked on for a while in silence. Then he spoke.

'My lads,' said he, 'I've given Silver a broadside. I pitched it in red-hot on purpose; and before the hour's out, as he said, we shall be boarded. We're outnumbered, I needn't tell you that, but we fight in shelter; and, a minute ago, I should have said we fought with discipline. I've no manner of doubt that we can drub them, if you choose.'

Then he went the rounds, and saw, as he said, that all was clear.

On the two short sides of the house, east and west, there were only two loopholes; on the south side where the porch was, two again; and on the north side, five. There was a round score of muskets for the seven of us; the firewood had been built into four piles – tables, you might say – one about the middle of each side, and on each of these tables some ammunition and four loaded muskets were laid ready to the hand of the defenders. In the middle, the cutlasses lay ranged.

'Toss out the fire,' said the captain; 'the chill is past, and we mustn't have smoke in our eyes.'

The iron fire basket was carried bodily out by Mr. Trelawney, and the embers smothered among sand.

'Hawkins hasn't had his breakfast. Hawkins, help yourself, and back to your post to eat it,' continued Captain Smollett. 'Lively, now, my lad; you'll want it before you've done. Hunter, serve out a round of brandy to all hands.'

And while this was going on, the captain completed, in his own mind, the plan of the defence.

'Doctor, you will take the door,' he resumed. 'See, and don't expose yourself; keep within, and fire through the porch. Hunter, take the east side, there. Joyce, you stand by the west, my man. **Mr.** Trelawney, you are the best shot – you and Gray will take this long north side, with the five loopholes; it's there the danger is. If they can get up to it, and fire in upon as through our own ports, things would begin to look dirty. Hawkins, neither you nor I are much account at the shooting; we'll stand by to load and bear a hand.'

As the captain had said, the chill was past. As soon as the sun had climbed above our girdle of trees, it fell with all its force upon the clearing, and drank up the vapours at a draught. Soon the sand was baking and the resin melting in the logs of the blockhouse. Jackets and coats were flung aside; shirts blown open at the neck, and rolled up to the shoulders; and we stood there, each at his post, in a fever of heat and anxiety.

An hour passed away.

'Hang them!' said the captain. 'This is as dull as the doldrums. Gray, whistle for a wind.'

And just at that moment came the first news of the attack.

'If you please, sir,' said Joyce, 'if I see any one am I to fire?'

'I told you so!' cried the captain.

'Thank you, sir,' returned Joyce, with the same quiet civility.

Nothing followed for a time; but the remark had set us all on the alert, straining ears and eyes – the musketeers with their pieces balanced in their hands, the captain out in the middle of the blockhouse, with his mouth very tight and a frown on his face.

So some seconds passed, till suddenly Joyce whipped up his musket and fired. The report had scarcely died away ere it was repeated and repeated from without in a scattering volley, shot behind shot, like a string of geese, from every side of the enclosure. Several bullets struck the log-house, but not one entered; and, as the smoke cleared away and vanished, the stockade and the woods around it looked as quiet and empty as before. Not a bough waved, not the gleam of a musket-barrel betrayed the presence of our foes.

'Did you hit your man?' asked the captain.

'No, sir,' replied Joyce. 'I believe not, sir.'

'Next best thing to tell the truth,' muttered Captain Smollett. 'Load his gun, Hawkins. How many should you say there were on your side, doctor?'

'I know precisely,' said Dr. Livesey. 'Three shots were fired on this side. I saw the three flashes – two close together – one further to the west.'

'Three!' repeated the captain. 'And how many on yours, Mr. Trelawney?'

But this was not so easily answered. There had come many from the north – seven, by the squire's computation; eight or nine, according to Gray. From the east and west only a single shot had been fired. It was plain, therefore, that the attack would be developed from the north, and that on the other three sides we were only to be annoyed by a show of hostilities. But Captain Smollett made no change in his arrangements. If the mutineers succeeded in crossing the blockade, he argued, they would take possession of any unprotected loophole, and shoot us down like rats in our own stronghold.

Nor had we much time left to us for thought. Suddenly, with a loud huzza, a little cloud of pirates leaped from the woods on the north side, and ran straight on the stockade. At the same moment, the fire was once more opened from the woods, and a rifle-ball sang through the doorway, and knocked the doctor's musket into bits.

The boarders swarmed over the fence like monkeys. Squire and Gray fired again and yet again; three men fell, one forwards into the enclosure, two back on the outside. But of these, one was evidently more frightened than hurt, for he was on his feet again in a crack, and instantly disappeared among the trees.

Two had bit the dust, one had fled, four had made good their footing inside our defences; while from the shelter of the woods seven or eight men, each evidently supplied with several muskets, kept up a hot though useless fire on the log-house.

The four who had boarded made straight before them for the building, shouting as they ran, and the men among the trees shouted back to encourage them. Several shots were fired; but, such was the hurry of the marksmen, that not one appears to have taken effect. In a moment, the four pirates had swarmed up the mound and were upon us.

The head of Job Anderson, the boatswain, appeared at the middle loophole.

'At 'em, all hands – all hands!' he roared, in a voice of thunder.

At the same moment, another pirate grasped Hunter's musket by the muzzle, wrenched it from his hands, plucked it through the loophole, and, with one stunning blow, laid the poor fellow senseless on the floor. Meanwhile a third, running unharmed all round the house, appeared suddenly in the doorway, and fell with his cutlass on the doctor.

Our position was utterly reversed. A moment since, we were firing, under cover, at an exposed enemy; now it was we who lay uncovered, and could not return a blow.

The log-house was full of smoke, to which we owed our comparative safety. Cries and confusion, the flashes and reports of pistol shots, and one loud groan, rang in my ears.

'Out, lads, out, and fight 'em in the open! Cutlasses!' cried the captain.

I snatched a cutlass from the pile, and someone, at the same time snatching another, gave me a cut across the knuckles which I hardly felt. I dashed out of the door into the clear sunlight. Someone was close behind, I knew not whom. Right in front, the doctor was pursuing his assailant down the hill, and, just as my eyes fell upon him, beat down his guard, and sent him sprawling on his back, with a great slash across the face.

'Round the house, lads! round the house!' cried the captain; and even in the hurly-burly I perceived a change in his voice.

Mechanically I obeyed, turned eastwards, and with my cutlass raised, ran round the corner of the house. Next moment I was face to face with Anderson. He roared aloud, and his hanger went up above his head, flashing in the sunlight. I had not time to be afraid; but, as the blow still hung impending, leaped in a trice upon one side, and missing my foot in the soft sand, rolled headlong down the slope.

When I had first sallied from the door, the other mutineers had been already swarming up the palisade to make an end of us. One man, in a red night-cap, with his cutlass in his mouth, had even got upon the top and thrown a leg across. Well, so short had been the interval, that when I found my feet again all was in the same posture, the fellow with the red night-cap still half-way over, another still just showing his head above the top of the stockade. And yet, in this breath of time, the fight was over, and the victory was ours.

Gray, following close behind me, had cut down the big boatswain ere he had time to recover from his lost blow. Another had been shot at a loophole in the very act of firing into the house, and now lay in agony, the pistol still smoking in his hand. A third, as I had seen, the doctor had disposed of at a blow. Of the four who had scaled the palisade, one only remained unaccounted for, and he, having left his cutlass on the field, was now clambering out again with the fear of death upon him.

'Fire – fire from the house!' cried the doctor. 'And you, lads, back into cover.'

But his words were unheeded, no shot was fired, and the last boarder made good his escape, and disappeared with the rest into the wood. In three seconds nothing remained of the attacking party but the five who had fallen, four on the inside, and one on the outside, of the palisade.

The doctor and Gray and I ran full speed for shelter. The survivors would soon be back where they had left their muskets, and at any moment the fire might recommence.

The house was by this time somewhat cleared of smoke, and we saw at a glance the price we had paid for victory. Hunter lay beside his loophole, stunned; Joyce by his, shot through the head, never to move again; while right in the centre, the squire was supporting the captain, one as pale as the other.

'The captain's wounded,' said Mr. Trelawney.

'Have they run?' asked Mr. Smollett.

'All that could, you may be bound,' returned the doctor; 'but there's five of them will never run again.'

'Five!' cried the captain. 'Come, that's better. Five against three leaves us four to nine. That's better odds than we had at starting. We were seven to nineteen then, or thought we were, and that's as bad to bear.'[1]

---

[1] The mutineers were soon only eight in number, for the man shot by Mr. Trelawney on board the schooner died that same evening of his wound. But this was, of course, not known till after by the faithful party.

1 How I Began My Sea Adventure

There was no return of the mutineers – not so much as another shot out of the woods. They had 'got their rations for that day,' as the captain put it, and we had the place to ourselves and a quiet time to overhaul the wounded and get dinner. Squire and I cooked outside in spite of the danger, and even outside we could hardly tell what we were at, for horror of the loud groans that reached us from the doctor's patients.

Out of the eight men who had fallen in the action, only three still breathed – that one of the pirates who had been shot at the loophole, Hunter, and Captain Smollett; and of these the first two were as good as dead; the mutineer, indeed, died under the doctor's knife, and Hunter, do what we could, never recovered consciousness in this world. He lingered all day, breathing loudly like the old buccaneer at home in his apoplectic fit; but the bones of his chest had been crushed by the blow and his skull fractured in falling, and some time in the following night, without sign or sound, he went to his Maker.

As for the captain, his wounds were grievous indeed, but not dangerous. No organ was fatally injured. Anderson's ball – for it was Job that shot him first – had broken his shoulder-blade and touched the lung, not badly; the second had only torn and displaced some muscles in the calf. He was sure to recover, the doctor said, but, in the meantime and for weeks to come, he must not walk nor move his arm, nor so much as speak when he could help it.

My own accidental cut across the knuckles was a fleabite. Dr. Livesey patched it up with plaster, and pulled my ears for me into the bargain.

After dinner the squire and the doctor sat by the captain's side a while in consultation; and when they had talked to their heart's content, it being then a little past noon, the doctor took up his hat and pistols, girt on a cutlass, put the chart in his pocket, and, with a musket

over his shoulder, crossed the palisade on the north side, and set off
briskly through the trees.

Gray and I were sitting together at the far end of the blockhouse,
to be out of earshot of our officers consulting; and Gray took his pipe
out of his mouth and fairly forgot to put it back again, so thunderstruck
he was at this occurrence.

'Why, in the name of Davy Jones,' said he, 'is Dr. Livesey mad?'

'Why, no,' says I. 'He's about the last of this crew for that, I take
it!'

'Well, shipmate,' said Gray, 'mad he may not be; but if *he*'s not,
you mark my words, *I* am.'

'I take it,' replied I, 'the doctor has his idea; and if I am right, he's
going now to see Ben Gunn.'

I was right, as appeared later; but, in the meantime, the house
being stifling hot, and the little patch of sand inside the palisade ablaze
with midday sun, I began to get another thought into my head, which
was not by any means so right. What I began to do was to envy the
doctor, walking in the cool shadow of the woods, with the birds about
him, and the pleasant smell of the pines, while I sat grilling, with my
clothes stuck to the hot resin, and so much blood about me, and so
many poor dead bodies lying all around, that I took a disgust of the
place that was almost as strong as fear.

All the time I was washing out the blockhouse, and then washing
up the things from dinner, this disgust and envy kept growing stronger
and stronger, till at last, being near a bread-bag, and no one then
observing me, I took the first step towards my escapade, and filled both
pockets of my coat with biscuit.

I was a fool, if you like, and certainly I was going to do a foolish,
over-bold act; but I was determined to do it with all the precautions in
my power. These biscuits, should anything befall me, would keep me,
at least, from starving till far on in the next day.

The next thing I laid hold of was a brace of pistols, and as I already
had a powder-horn and bullets, I felt myself well supplied with arms.

As for the scheme I had in my head, it was not a bad one in itself. I
was to go down the sandy spit that divides the anchorage on the east
from the open sea, find the white rock I had observed last evening, and
ascertain whether it was there or not that Ben Gunn had hidden his
boat; a thing quite worth doing, as I still believe. But as I was certain I
should not be allowed to leave the enclosure, my only plan was to take

French leave, and slip out when nobody was watching; and that was so bad a way of doing it as made the thing itself wrong. But I was only a boy, and I had made my mind up.

Well, as things at last fell out, I found an admirable opportunity. The squire and Gray were busy helping the captain with his bandages; the coast was clear; I made a bolt for it over the stockade and into the thickest of the trees, and before my absence was observed I was out of cry of my companions.

This was my second folly, far worse than my first, as I left but two sound men to guard the house; but, like the first, it was a help towards saving all of us.

I took my way straight for the east coast of the island, for I was determined to go down the sea side of the spit to avoid all chance of observation from the anchorage. It was already late in the afternoon, although still warm and sunny. As I continued to thread the tall woods I could hear from far before me not only the continuous thunder of the surf, but a certain tossing of foliage and grinding of boughs which showed me the sea breeze had set in higher than usual. Soon cool draughts of air began to reach me; and a few steps further I came forth into the open borders of the grove, and saw the sea lying blue and sunny to the horizon, and the surf tumbling and tossing its foam along the beach.

I have never seen the sea quiet round Treasure Island. The sun might blaze overhead, the air be without a breath, the surface smooth and blue, but still these great rollers would be running along all the external coast, thundering and thundering by day and night; and I scarce believe there is one spot in the island where a man would be out of earshot of their noise.

I walked along beside the surf with great enjoyment, till, thinking I was not got far enough to the south, I took the cover of some thick bushes and crept warily up to the ridge of the spit.

Behind me was the sea, in front the anchorage. The sea breeze, as though it had the sooner blown itself out by its unusual violence, was already at an end; it had been succeeded by light, variable airs from the south and south-east, carrying great banks of fog; and the anchorage, under lee of Skeleton Island, lay still and leaden as when first we entered it. The *Hispaniola*, in that unbroken mirror, was exactly portrayed from the truck to the water-line, the Jolly Roger hanging from her peak.

Alongside lay one of the gigs, Silver in the stern-sheets – him I could always recognize – while a couple of men were leaning over the stern bulwarks, one of them with a red cap – the very rogue that I had seen some hours before stride-legs upon the palisade. Apparently they were talking and laughing, though at that distance – upwards of a mile – I could, of course, hear no word of what was said. All at once, there began the most horrid, unearthly screaming, which at first startled me badly, though I had soon remembered the voice of Captain Flint, and even thought I could make out the bird by her bright plumage as she sat perched upon her master's wrist.

Soon after the jolly-boat shoved off and pulled for shore, and the man with the red cap and his comrade went below by the cabin companion.

Just about the same time the sun had gone down behind the Spy-glass, and as the fog was collecting rapidly, it began to grow dark in earnest. I saw I must lose no time if I were to find the boat that evening.

The white rock, visible enough above the brush, was still some eighth of a mile further down the spit, and it took me a goodish while to get up with it, crawling, often on all-fours, among the scrub. Night had almost come when I laid my hand on its rough sides. Right below it there was an exceedingly small hollow of green turf, hidden by banks and a thick underwood about knee-deep, that grew there very plentifully; and in the centre of the dell, sure enough, a little tent of goat-skins, like what the gipsies carry about with them in England.

I dropped into the hollow, lifted the side of the tent, and there was Ben Gunn's boat – home-made if ever anything was home-made; a rude, lop-sided framework of tough wood, and stretched upon that a covering of goat-skin, with the hair inside. The thing was extremely small, even for me, and I can hardly imagine that it could have floated with a full-sized man. There was one thwart, set as low as possible, a kind of stretcher in the bows, and a double paddle for propulsion.

I had not then seen a coracle, such as the ancient Britons made, but I have seen one since, and I can give you no fairer idea of Ben Gunn's boat than by saying it was like the first and the worst coracle ever made by man. But the great advantage of the coracle it certainly possessed, for it was exceedingly light and portable.

Well, now that I had found the boat, you would have thought I had had enough of truantry for once; but, in the meantime, I had taken another notion, and become so obstinately fond of it, that I would have carried it out, I believe, in the teeth of Captain Smollett himself. This was to slip out under cover of the night, cut the *Hispaniola* adrift, and let her go ashore where she fancied. I had quite made up my mind that the mutineers, after their repulse of the morning, had nothing nearer their hearts than to up anchor and away to sea; this, I thought, it would be a fine thing to prevent; and now that I had seen how they left their watchmen unprovided with a boat, I thought it might be done with little risk.

Down I sat to wait for darkness, and made a hearty meal of biscuit. It was a night out of ten thousand for my purpose. The fog had now buried all heaven. As the last rays of daylight dwindled and disappeared, absolute blackness settled down on Treasure Island. And when at last I shouldered the coracle, and groped my way stumblingly out of the hollow where I had supped, there were but two points visible on the whole anchorage.

One was the great fire on shore, by which the defeated pirates lay carousing in the swamp. The other, a mere blur of light upon the darkness, indicated the position of the anchored ship. She had swung round to the ebb – her bow was now towards me – the only lights on board were in the cabin; and what I saw was merely a reflection on the fog of the strong rays that flowed from the stern window.

The ebb had already run some time, and I had to wade through a long belt of swampy sand, where I sank several times above the ankle, before I came to the edge of the retreating water, and wading a little way in, with some strength and dexterity, set my coracle, keel downwards, on the surface.

2 The Ebb-tide Runs

The coracle – as I had ample reason to know before I was done with her – was a very safe boat for a person of my height and weight, both buoyant and clever in a seaway; but she was the most cross-grained, lop-sided craft to manage. Do as you please, she always made more leeway than anything else, and turning round and round was the manœuvre she was best at. Even Ben Gunn himself has admitted that she was 'queer to handle till you knew her way.'

Certainly I did not know her way. She turned in every direction but the one I was bound to go; the most part of the time we were broadside on, and I am very sure I never should have made the ship at all but for the tide. By good fortune, paddle as I pleased, the tide was still sweeping me down; and there lay the *Hispaniola* right in the fairway, hardly to be missed.

First she loomed before me like a blot of something yet blacker than darkness, then her spars and hull began to take shape, and the next moment, as it seemed (for the further I went, the brisker grew the current of the ebb), I was alongside of her hawser, and had laid hold.

The hawser was as taut as a bowstring – so strong she pulled upon her anchor. All round the hull, in the blackness, the rippling current bubbled and chattered like a little mountain stream. One cut with my sea-gully, and the *Hispaniola* would go humming down the tide.

So far so good; but it next occurred to my recollection that a taut hawser, suddenly cut, is a thing as dangerous as a kicking horse. Ten to one, if I were so foolhardy as to cut the *Hispaniola* from her anchor, I and the coracle would be knocked clean out of the water.

This brought me to a full stop, and if fortune had not again particularly favoured me, I should have had to abandon my design. But the light airs which had begun blowing from the south-east and south had hauled round after nightfall into the south-west. Just while I was meditating, a puff came, caught the *Hispaniola*, and forced her up into the current; and to my great joy, I felt the hawser slacken in my grasp, and the hand by which I held it dip for a second under water.

With that I made my mind up, took out my gully, opened it with my teeth, and cut one strand after another, till the vessel only swung by two. Then I lay quiet, waiting to sever these last when the strain should be once more lightened by a breath of wind.

All this time I had heard the sound of loud voices from the cabin; but, to say truth, my mind had been so entirely taken up with other thoughts that I had scarcely given ear. Now, however, when I had nothing else to do, I began to pay more heed.

One I recognized for the coxswain's, Israel Hands, that had been Flint's gunner in former days. The other was, of course, my friend of the red night-cap. Both men were plainly the worse of drink, and they were still drinking; for, even while I was listening, one of them, with a drunken cry, opened the stern window and threw out something, which I divined to be an empty bottle. But they were not only tipsy; it was plain that they were furiously angry. Oaths flew like hailstones, and every now and then there came forth such an explosion as I thought was sure to end in blows. But each time the quarrel passed off, and the voices grumbled lower for a while, until the next crisis came, and, in its turn, passed away without result.

On shore, I could see the glow of the great camp fire burning warmly through the shore-side trees. Someone was singing, a dull, old, droning sailors' song, with a droop and a quaver at the end of every verse, and seemingly no end to it at all but the patience of the singer. I had heard it on the voyage more than once, and remembered these words:

> But one man of her crew alive,
> What put to sea with seventy-five.

And I thought it was a ditty rather too dolefully appropriate for a company that had met such cruel losses in the morning. But, indeed, from what I saw, all these buccaneers were as callous as the sea they sailed on.

At last the breeze came; the schooner sidled and drew nearer in the dark; I felt the hawser slacken once more, and with a good, tough effort, cut the last fibres through.

The breeze had but little action on the coracle, and I was almost instantly swept against the bows of the *Hispaniola*. At the same time

'One glance, however, was sufficient'

the schooner began to turn upon her heel, spinning slowly, end for end, across the current.

I wrought like a fiend, for I expected every moment to be swamped; and since I found I could not push the coracle directly off, I now shoved straight astern. At length I was clear of my dangerous neighbour; and just as I gave the last impulsion, my hands came across a light cord that was trailing overboard across the stern bulwarks. Instantly I grasped it.

Why I should have done so I can hardly say. It was at first mere instinct; but once I had it in my hands, and found it fast, curiosity began to get the upper hand, and I determined I should have one look through the cabin window.

I pulled in hand over hand on the cord, and, when I judged myself near enough, rose at infinite risk to about half my height, and thus commanded the roof and a slice of the interior of the cabin.

By this time the schooner and her little consort were gliding pretty swiftly through the water; indeed, we had already fetched up level with the camp fire. The ship was talking, as sailors say, loudly, treading the innumerable ripples with an incessant weltering splash; and until I got my eye above the window-sill I could not comprehend why the watchmen had taken no alarm. One glance, however, was sufficient; and it was only one glance that I durst take from that unsteady skiff. It showed me Hands and his companion locked together in deadly wrestle, each with a hand upon the other's throat.

I dropped upon the thwart again, none too soon, for I was near overboard. I could see nothing for the moment but these two furious, encrimsoned faces, swaying together under the smoky lamp; and I shut my eyes to let them grow once more familiar with the darkness.

The endless ballad had come to an end at last, and the whole diminished company about the camp fire had broken into the chorus I had heard so often:

> 'Fifteen men on the dead man's chest –
> Yo-ho-ho, and a bottle of rum!
> Drink and the devil had done for the rest –
> Yo-ho-ho, and a bottle of rum!'

I was just thinking how busy drink and the devil were at that very moment in the cabin of the *Hispaniola*, when I was surprised by a sudden lurch of the coracle. At the same moment she yawed sharply and seemed to change her course. The speed in the meantime had strangely increased.

I opened my eyes at once. All round me were little ripples, combing over with a sharp, bristling sound and slightly phosphorescent. The *Hispaniola* herself, a few yards in whose wake I was still being whirled along, seemed to stagger in her course, and I saw her spars toss a little against the blackness of the night; nay, as I looked longer, I made sure she also was wheeling to the southward.

I glanced over my shoulder, and my heart jumped against my ribs. There, right behind me, was the glow of the camp fire. The current had turned at right angles, sweeping round along with it the tall schooner and the little dancing coracle; ever quickening, ever bubbling higher, ever muttering louder, it went spinning through the narrows for the open sea.

Suddenly the schooner in front of me gave a violent yaw, turning, perhaps, through twenty degrees; and almost at the same moment one shout followed another from on board; I could hear feet pounding on the companion ladder; and I knew that the two drunkards had at last been interrupted in their quarrel and awakened to a sense of their disaster.

I lay down flat in the bottom of that wretched skiff, and devoutly recommended my spirit to its Maker. At the end of the straits, I made sure we must fall into some bar of raging breakers, where all my troubles would be ended speedily; and though I could, perhaps, bear to die, I could not bear to look upon my fate as it approached.

So I must have lain for hours, continually beaten to and fro upon the billows, now and again wetted with flying sprays, and never ceasing to expect death at the next plunge. Gradually weariness grew upon me; a numbness, an occasional stupor, fell upon my mind even in the midst of my terrors; until sleep at last supervened, and in my sea-tossed coracle I lay and dreamed of home and the old 'Admiral Benbow.'

3 The Cruise of the Coracle

It was broad day when I awoke, and found myself tossing at the south-west end of Treasure Island. The sun was up, but was still hid from me behind the great bulk of the Spy-glass, which on this side descended almost to the sea in formidable cliffs.

Haulbowline Head and Mizzen-mast Hill were at my elbow; the hill bare and dark, the head bound with cliffs forty or fifty feet high, and fringed with great masses of fallen rock. I was scarce a quarter of a mile to seaward, and it was my first thought to paddle in and land.

That notion was soon given over. Among the fallen rocks the breakers spouted and bellowed; loud reverberations, heavy sprays flying and falling, succeeded one another from second to second; and I saw myself, if I ventured nearer, dashed to death upon the rough shore or spending my strength in vain to scale the beetling crags.

Nor was that all; for crawling together on flat tables of rock, or letting themselves drop into the sea with loud reports, I beheld huge slimy monsters – soft snails, as it were, of incredible bigness – two or three score of them together, making the rocks to echo with their barkings.

I have understood since that they were sea-lions, and entirely harmless. But the look of them, added to the difficulty of the shore and the high running of the surf, was more than enough to disgust me of that landing-place. I felt willing rather to starve at sea than to confront such perils.

In the meantime I had a better chance, as I supposed, before me. North of Haulbowline Head, the land runs in a long way, leaving, at low tide, a long stretch of yellow sand. To the north of that, again, there comes another cape – Cape of the Woods, as it was marked upon the chart – buried in tall green pines, which descended to the margin of the sea.

I remembered what Silver had said about the current that sets northwards along the whole west coast of Treasure Island; and seeing from my position that I was already under its influence, I preferred to leave Haulbowline Head behind me, and reserve my strength for an attempt to land upon the kindlier-looking Cape of the Woods.

There was a great, smooth swell upon the sea. The wind blowing steady and gentle from the south, there was no contrariety between that and the current, and the billows rose and fell unbroken.

Had it been otherwise, I must long ago have perished; but as it was, it is surprising how easily and securely my little and light boat could ride. Often, as I still lay at the bottom, and kept no more than an eye above the gunwale, I would see a big blue summit heaving close above me; yet the coracle would but bounce a little, dance as if on springs, and subside on the other side into the trough as lightly as a bird.

I began after a little to grow very bold, and sat up to try my skill at paddling. But even a small change in the disposition of the weight will produce violent changes in the behaviour of a coracle. And I had hardly moved before the boat, giving up at once her gentle dancing movement, ran straight down a slope of water so steep that it made me giddy, and struck her nose, with a spout of spray, deep into the side of the next wave.

I was drenched and terrified, and fell instantly back into my old position, whereupon the coracle seemed to find her head again, and led me as softly as before among the billows. It was plain she was not to be interfered with, and at that rate, since I could in no way influence her course, what hope had I left of reaching land?

I began to be horribly frightened, but I kept my head, for all that. First, moving with all care, I gradually baled out the coracle with my sea-cap; then getting my eye once more above the gunwale, I set myself to study how it was she managed to slip so quietly through the rollers.

I found each wave, instead of the big, smooth, glossy mountain it looks from shore, or from a vessel's deck, was for all the world like any range of hills on the dry land, full of peaks and smooth places and valleys. The coracle, left to herself, turning from side to side, threaded, so to speak, her way through these lower parts, and avoided the steep slopes and higher, toppling summits of the wave.

'Well, now,' thought I to myself, 'it is plain I must lie where I am, and not disturb the balance; but it is plain, also, that I can put the paddle over the side, and from time to time, in smooth places, give her a shove or two towards land.' No sooner thought upon than done. There I lay on my elbows, in the most trying attitude, and every now and again gave a weak stroke or two to turn her head to shore.'

It was very tiring and slow work, yet I did visibly gain ground; and, as we drew near the Cape of the Woods, though I saw I must infallibly miss that point, I had still made some hundred yards of easting. I was, indeed, close in. I could see the cool, green tree-tops swaying together in the breeze, and I felt sure I should make the next promontory without fail.

It was high time, for I now began to be tortured with thirst. The glow of the sun from above, its thousandfold reflection from the waves, the sea-water that fell and dried upon me, caking my very lips with salt, combined to make my throat burn and my brain ache. The sight of the trees so near at hand had almost made me sick with longing; but the current had soon carried me past the point; and, as the next reach of sea opened out, I beheld a sight that changed the nature of my thoughts.

Right in front of me, not half a mile away, I beheld the *Hispaniola* under sail. I made sure, of course, that I should be taken; but I was so distressed for want of water that I scarce knew whether to be glad or sorry at the thought; and, long before I had come to a conclusion, surprise had taken entire possession of my mind, and I could do nothing but stare and wonder.

The *Hispaniola* was under her main-sail and two jibs, and the beautiful white canvas shone in the sun like snow or silver. When I first sighted her, all her sails were drawing; she was lying a course about north-west; and I presumed the men on board were going round the island on their way back to the anchorage. Presently she began to fetch more and more to the westward, so that I thought they had sighted me and were going about in chase. At last, however, she fell right into the wind's eye, was taken dead aback, and stood there awhile helpless, with her sails shivering.

'Clumsy fellows,' said I; 'they must still be drunk as owls.' And I thought how Captain Smollett would have set them skipping.

Meanwhile, the schooner gradually fell off, and filled again upon another tack, sailed swiftly for a minute or so, and brought up once more dead in the wind's eye. Again and again was this repeated. To and fro, up and down, north, south, east, and west, the *Hispaniola* sailed by swoops and dashes, and at each repetition ended as she had begun, with idly flapping canvas. It became plain to me that nobody was steering. And, if so, where were the men? Either they were dead drunk, or had deserted her, I thought, and perhaps if I could get on board, I might return the vessel to her captain.

The current was bearing coracle and schooner southward at an equal rate. As for the latter's sailing, it was so wild and intermittent, and she hung each time so long in irons, that she certainly gained nothing, if she did not even lose. If only I dared to sit up and paddle, I made sure that I could overhaul her. The scheme had an air of adventure that inspired me, and the thought of the water-breaker beside the fore companion doubled my growing courage.

Up I got, was welcomed almost instantly by another cloud of spray, but this time stuck to my purpose; and set myself, with all my strength and caution, to paddle after the unsteered *Hispaniola*. Once I shipped a sea so heavy that I had to stop and bale, with my heart fluttering like a bird; but gradually I got into the way of the thing, and guided my coracle among the waves, with only now and then a blow upon her bows and a dash of foam in my face.

I was now gaining rapidly on the schooner; I could see the brass glisten on the tiller as it banged about; and still no soul appeared upon her decks. I could not choose but suppose she was deserted. If not, the men were lying drunk below, where I might batten them down, perhaps, and do what I chose with the ship.

For some time she had been doing the worst thing possible for me – standing still. She headed nearly due south, yawing, of course, all the time. Each time she fell off her sails partly filled, and these brought her, in a moment, right to the wind again. I have said this was the worst thing possible for me; for, helpless as she looked in this situation, with the canvas cracking like cannon, and the blocks trundling and banging on the deck, she still continued to run away from me, not only with the speed of the current, but by the whole amount of her leeway, which was naturally great.

But now, at last, I had my chance. The breeze fell, for some seconds, very low, and the current gradually turning her, the *Hispaniola* revolved slowly round her centre, and at last presented me her stern, with the cabin window still gaping open, and the lamp over the table still burning on into the day. The main-sail hung drooped like a banner. She was stock-still, but for the current.

For the last little while I had even lost; but now redoubling my efforts, I began once more to overhaul the chase.

I was not a hundred yards from her when the wind came again in a clap; she filled on the port tack, and was off again, stooping and skimming like a swallow.

My first impulse was one of despair, but my second was towards joy. Round she came, till she was broadside on to me – round still till she had covered a half, and then two-thirds, and then three-quarters of the distance that separated us. I could see the waves boiling white under her forefoot. Immensely tall she looked to me from my low station in the coracle.

And then, of a sudden, I began to comprehend. I had scarce time to think – scarce time to act and save myself. I was on the summit of one swell when the schooner came swooping over the next. The bowsprit was over my head. I sprang to my feet, and leaped, stamping the coracle under water. With one hand I caught the jib-boom, while my foot was lodged between the stay and the brace; and as I still clung there panting, a dull blow told me that the schooner had charged down upon and struck the coracle, and that I was left without retreat on the *Hispaniola*.

4 I Strike the Jolly Roger

I had scarce gained a position on the bowsprit, when the flying jib flapped and filled upon the other tack, with a report like a gun. The schooner trembled to her keel under the reverse; but next moment, the other sails still drawing, the jib flapped back again, and hung idle.

This had nearly tossed me off into the sea; and now I lost no time, crawled back along the bowsprit, and tumbled head foremost on the deck.

I was on the lee side of the forecastle, and the main-sail, which was still drawing, concealed from me a certain portion of the after-deck. Not a soul was to be seen. The planks, which had not been swabbed since the mutiny, bore the print of many feet; and an empty bottle, broken by the neck, tumbled to and fro like a live thing in the scuppers.

Suddenly the *Hispaniola* came right into the wind. The jibs behind me cracked aloud; the rudder slammed to; the whole ship gave a sickening heave and shudder, and at the same moment the main-boom swung inboard, the sheet groaning in the blocks, and showed me the lee after-deck.

There were the two watchmen, sure enough; Redcap on his back, as stiff as a handspike, with his arms stretched out like those of a crucifix, and his teeth showing through his open lips; Israel Hands propped against the bulwarks, his chin on his chest, his hands lying open before him on the deck, his face as white, under its tan, as a tallow candle.

For a while the ship kept bucking and sidling like a vicious horse, the sails filling, now on one tack, now on another, and the boom swinging to and fro till the mast groaned aloud under the strain. Now and again, too, there would come a cloud of light sprays over the bulwark, and a heavy blow of the ship's bows against the swell; so much heavier weather was made of it by this great rigged ship than by my home-made, lop-sided coracle, now gone to the bottom of the sea.

At every jump of the schooner, Red-cap slipped to and fro; but – what was ghastly to behold – neither his attitude nor his fixed teeth-disclosing grin was anyway disturbed by this rough usage. At every jump, too, Hands appeared still more to sink into himself and settle down upon the deck, his feet sliding ever the further out, and the whole body canting towards the stern, so that his face became, little by little, hid from me; and at last I could see nothing beyond his ear and the frayed ringlet of one whisker.

At the same time, I observed, around both of them, splashes of dark blood upon the planks, and began to feel sure that they had killed each other in their drunken wrath.

While I was thus looking and wondering, in a calm moment, when the ship was still, Israel Hands turned partly round, and, with a low moan, writhed himself back to the position in which I had seen him first. The moan, which told of pain and deadly weakness, and the way in which his jaw hung open, went right to my heart. But when I remembered the talk I had overheard from the apple barrel, all pity left me.

I walked aft until I reached the main-mast.

'Come aboard, Mr. Hands,' I said ironically.

He rolled his eyes round heavily; but he was too far gone to express surprise. All he could do was to utter one word: 'Brandy.'

It occurred to me there was no time to lose; and dodging the boom as it once more lurched across the deck, I slipped aft, and down the companion-stairs into the cabin.

It was such a scene of confusion as you can hardly fancy. All the lock-fast places had been broken open in quest of the chart. The floor was thick with mud, where ruffians had sat down to drink or consult after wading in the marshes round their camp. The bulkheads, all painted in clear white, and beaded round with gilt, bore a pattern of dirty hands. Dozens of empty bottles clinked together in corners to the rolling of the ship. One of the doctor's medical books lay open on the table, half of the leaves gutted out, I suppose, for pipe-lights. In the midst of all this the lamp still cast a smoky glow, obscure and brown as umber.

I went into the cellar; all the barrels were gone, and of the bottles a most surprising number had been drunk out and thrown away. Certainly, since the mutiny began, not a man of them could ever have been sober.

Foraging about, I found a bottle with some brandy left, for Hands; and for myself I routed out some biscuit, some pickled fruits, a great bunch of raisins, and a piece of cheese. With these I came on deck, put down my own stock behind the rudder-head, and well out of the coxswain's reach, went forward to the water-breaker, and had a good deep drink of water, and then, and not till then, gave Hands the brandy.

He must have drunk a gill before he took the bottle from his mouth.

'Ay,' said he, 'by thunder, but I wanted some o' that!'

I had sat down already in my own corner and begun to eat.

'Much hurt?' I asked him.

He grunted, or rather I might say, he barked.

'If that doctor was aboard,' he said, 'I'd be right enough in a couple of turns; but I don't have no manner of luck, you see, and that's what's the matter with me. As for that swab, he's good and dead, he is,' he added, indicating the man with the red cap. 'He warn't no seaman, anyhow. And where mought you have come from?'

'Well,' said I, 'I've come aboard to take possession of this ship, Mr. Hands; and you'll please regard me as your captain until further notice.'

He looked at me sourly enough, but said nothing. Some of the colour had come back into this cheeks, though he still looked very sick, and still continued to slip out and settle down as the ship banged about.

'By the by,' I continued, 'I can't have these colours, Mr. Hands; and, by your leave, I'll strike 'em. Better none than these.'

And, again dodging the boom, I ran to the colour lines, handed down their cursed black flag, and chucked it overboard.

'God save the king!' said I, waving my cap; 'and there's an end to Captain Silver!'

He watched me keenly and slyly, his chin all the while on his breast.

'I reckon,' he said at last – 'I reckon, Cap'n Hawkins, you'll kind of want to get ashore, now. S'pose we talks.'

'Why, yes,' says I, 'with all my heart, Mr. Hands. Say on.' And I went back to my meal with a good appetite.

'This man,' he began, nodding feebly at the corpse – 'O'Brien were his name – a rank Irelander – this man and me got the canvas on her, meaning for to sail her back. Well, *he*'s dead now, he is – as dead as bilge; and who's to sail this ship, I don't see. Without I gives you a hint, you ain't that man, as far's I can tell. Now, look here, you gives me food and drink, and a old scarf or ankecher to tie my wound up, you do; and I'll tell you how to sail her; and that's about square all round, I take it.'

'I'll tell you one thing,' says I: 'I'm not going back to Captain Kidd's anchorage. I mean to get into North Inlet, and beach her quietly there.'

'To be sure you did,' he cried. 'Why, I ain't sich an infernal lubber, after all. I can see, can't I? I've tried my fling, I have, and I've lost, and it's you has the wind of me. North Inlet? Why, I haven't no ch'ice, not I! I'd help you sail her up to Execution Dock, by thunder! so I would.'

Well, as it seemed to me, there was some sense in this. We struck our bargain on the spot. In three minutes I had the *Hispaniola* sailing easily before the wind along the coast of Treasure Island, with good hopes of turning the northern point ere noon, and beating down again as far as North Inlet before high water, when we might beach her safely, and wait till the subsiding tide permitted us to land.

Then I lashed the tiller and went below to my own chest, where I got a soft silk handkerchief of my mother's. With this, and with my aid, Hands bound up the great bleeding stab he had received in the thigh, and after he had eaten a little and had a swallow or two more of the brandy, he began to pick up visibly, sat straighter up, spoke louder and clearer, and looked in every way another man.

The breeze served us admirably. We skimmed before it like a bird, the coast of the island flashing by, and the view changing every minute. Soon we were past the high lands and bowling beside low, sandy country, sparsely dotted with dwarf pines, and soon we were beyond that again, and had turned the corner of the rocky hill that ends the island on the north.

I was greatly elated with my new command, and pleased with the bright, sunshiny weather and these different prospects of the coast. I had now plenty of water and good things to eat, and my conscience, which had smitten me hard for my desertion, was quieted by the great conquest I had made. I should, I think, have had nothing left me to desire but for the eyes of the coxswain as they followed me derisively about the deck, and the odd smile that appeared continually on his

face. It was a smile that had in it something both of pain and weakness
– a haggard, old man's smile; but there was, besides that, a grain of
derision, a shadow of treachery, in his expression as he craftily
watched, and watched, and watched me at my work.

5 Israel Hands

The wind, serving us to a desire, now hauled into the west. We could run so much the easier from the north-east corner of the island to the mouth of the North Inlet. Only, as we had no power to anchor, and dared not beach her till the tide had flowed a good deal further, time hung on our hands. The coxswain told me how to lay the ship to; after a good many trials I succeeded, and we both sat in silence over another meal.

'Cap'n,' said he, at length, with that same uncomfortable smile, 'here's my old shipmate, O'Brien; s'pose you was to heave him overboard. I ain't partic'ler as a rule, and I don't take no blame for settling his hash; but I don't reckon him ornamental, now, do you?'

'I'm not strong enough, and I don't like the job; and there he lies, for me,' said I.

'This here's an unlucky ship – this *Hispaniola* Jim,' he went on, blinking. 'There's a power of men been killed in this *Hispaniola* – a sight o' poor seamen dead and gone since you and me took ship to Bristol. I never seen sich dirty luck, not I. There was this here O'Brien, now – he's dead, ain't he? Well, now, I'm no scholar, and you're a lad as can read and figure; and to put it straight, do you take it as a dead man is dead for good, or do he come alive again?'

'You can kill the body, Mr. Hands, but not the spirit; you must know that already,' I replied. 'O'Brien there is in another world, and maybe watching us.'

'Ah!' says he. 'Well, that's unfort'nate – appears as if killing parties was a waste of time. Howsomever, sperrits don't reckon for much, by what I've seen. I'll chance it with the sperrits, Jim. And now, you've spoke up free, and I'll take it kind if you'd step down into that there cabin and get me a – well, a – shiver my timbers! I can't hit the name on 't; well, you get me a bottle of wine, Jim – this here brandy's too strong for my head.'

Now, the coxswain's hesitation seemed to be unnatural; and as for the notion of his preferring wine to brandy, I entirely disbelieved it. The whole story was a pretext. He wanted me to leave the deck – so much was plain; but with what purpose I could in no way imagine. His eyes never met mine; they kept wandering to and fro, up and down, now with a look to the sky, now with a flitting glance upon the dead O'Brien. All the time he kept smiling, and putting his tongue out in the most guilty, embarrassed manner, so that a child could have told that he was bent on some deception. I was prompt with my answer, however, for I saw where my advantage lay; and that with a fellow so densely stupid I could easily conceal my suspicions to the end.

'Some wine?' I said. 'Far better. Will you have white or red?'

'Well, I reckon it's about the blessed same to me, shipmate,' he replied; 'so it's strong, and plenty of it, what's the odds?

'All right,' I answered. 'I'll bring you port, Mr. Hands. But I'll have to dig for it.'

With that I scuttled down the companion with all the noise I could, slipped off my shoes, ran quietly along the sparred gallery, mounted the forecastle ladder, and popped my head out of the fore companion. I knew he would not expect to see me there; yet I took every precaution possible; and certainly the worst of my suspicions proved too true.

He had risen from his position to his hands and knees; and, though his leg obviously hurt him pretty sharply when he moved – for I could hear him stifle a groan – yet it was at a good, rattling rate that he trailed himself across the deck. In half a minute he had reached the port scuppers, and picked out of a coil of rope a long knife, or rather a short dirk, discoloured to the hilt with blood. He looked upon it for a moment, thrusting forth his under-jaw, tried the point upon his hand, and then, hastily concealing it in the bosom of his jacket, trundled back again into his old place against the bulwark.

This was all that I required to know. Israel could move about; he was now armed; and if he had been at so much trouble to get rid of me, it was plain that I was meant to be the victim. What he would do afterwards – whether he would try to crawl right across the island from North Inlet to the camp among the swamps, or whether he would fire Long Tom, trusting that his own comrades might come first to help him, was, of course, more than I could say.

Yet I felt sure that I could trust him in one point, since in that our interests jumped together, and that was in the disposition of the schooner. We both desired to have her stranded safe enough, in a sheltered place, and so that, when the time came, she could be got off again with as little labour and danger as might be; and until that was done I considered that my life would certainly be spared.

While I was thus turning the business over in my mind, I had not been idle with my body. I had stolen back to the cabin, slipped once more into my shoes, and laid my hand at random on a bottle of wine, and now, with this for an excuse, I made my reappearance on the deck.

Hands lay as I had left him, all fallen through in a bundle, and with his eyelids lowered, as though he were too weak to bear the light. He looked up, however, at my coming, knocked the neck off the bottle, like a man who had done the same thing often, and took a good swig with his favourite toast of 'Here's luck!' Then he lay quiet for a little, and then, pulling out a stick of tobacco, begged me to cut him a quid.

'Cut me a junk o' that,' says he, 'for I haven't no knife, and hardly strength enough, so be as I had. Ah, Jim, Jim, I reckon I've missed stays! Cut me a quid, as'll likely be the last, lad; for I'm for my long home, and no mistake.'

'Well,' said I, 'I'll cut you some tobacco; but if I was you and thought myself so badly, I would go to my prayers, like a Christian man.'

'Why?' said he. 'Now, you tell me why.'

'Why?' I cried. 'You were asking me just now about the dead. You've broken your trust; you've lived in sin and lies and blood; there's a man you killed lying at your feet this moment; and you ask me why! For God's mercy, Mr. Hands, that's why.'

I spoke with a little heat, thinking of the bloody dirk he had hidden in his pocket, and designed, in his ill thoughts, to end me with. He, for his part, took a great draught of the wine, and spoke with the most unusual solemnity.

'For thirty years,' he said, 'I've sailed the seas, and seen good and bad, better and worse, fair weather and foul, provisions running out, knives going, and what not. Well, now I tell you, I never seen good come o' goodness yet. Him as strikes first is my fancy; dead men don't bite; them's my views – amen, so be it. And now, you look here,' he added, suddenly changing his tone, 'we've had about enough of this foolery. The tide's made good enough by now. You just take my orders, Cap'n Hawkins, and we'll sail slap in and be done with it.'

All told, we had scarce two miles to run; but the navigation was delicate, the entrance to this northern anchorage was not only narrow and shoal, but lay east and west, so that the schooner must be nicely handled to be got in. I think I was a good, prompt subaltern, and I am very sure that Hands was an excellent pilot; for we went about and about, and dodged in, shaving the banks, with a certainty and a neatness that were a pleasure to behold.

Scarcely had we passed the heads before the land closed around us. The shores of North Inlet were as thickly wooded as those of the southern anchorage; but the space was longer and narrower, and more like, what in truth it was, the estuary of a river. Right before us, at the southern end, we saw the wreck of a ship in the last stages of dilapidation. It had been a great vessel of three masts, but had lain so long exposed to the injuries of the weather, that it was hung about with great webs of dripping seaweed, and on the deck of it shore bushes had taken root, and now flourished thick with flowers. It was a sad sight, but it showed us that the anchorage was calm.

'Now,' said Hands, 'look there; there's a pet bit for to beach a ship in. Fine flat sand, never a catspaw, trees all around of it, and flowers a-blowing like a garding on that old ship.'

'And once beached,' I inquired, 'how shall we get her off again?'

'Why, so,' he replied; 'you take a line ashore there on the other side at low water: take a turn about one o' them big pines; bring it back, take a turn round the capstan, and lie-to for the tide. Come high water, all hands take a pull upon line, and off she comes as sweet as natur'. And now, boy, you stand by. We're near the bit now, and she's too much way on her. Starboard a little – so – steady – starboard – larboard a little – steady – steady!'

So he issued his commands, which I breathlessly obeyed; till, all of a sudden, he cried: 'Now, my hearty, luff!' And I put the helm hard up, and the *Hispaniola* swung round rapidly, and ran stem on for the low wooded shore.

The excitement of these last manœuvres had somewhat interfered with the watch I had kept hitherto, sharply enough, upon the coxswain. Even then I was still so much interested, waiting for the ship to touch, that I had quite forgot the peril that hung over my head, and stood craning over the starboard bulwarks and watching the ripples spreading wide before the bows. I might have fallen without a struggle for my life, had not a sudden disquietude seized upon me, and made me turn my head. Perhaps I had heard a creak, or seen his shadow moving with the tail of my eye; perhaps it was an instinct like a cat's; but, sure enough, when I looked round, there was Hands, already half-way towards me, with the dirk in his right hand.

We must both have cried out aloud when our eyes met; but while mine was the shrill cry of terror, his was a roar of fury like a charging bull's. At the same instant he threw himself forward, and I leapt sideways towards the bows. As I did so, I left hold of the tiller, which sprang sharp to leeward; and I think this saved my life, for it struck Hands across the chest, and stopped him, for the moment, dead.

Before he could recover, I was safe out of the corner where he had me trapped, with all the deck to dodge about. Just forward of the mainmast I stopped, drew a pistol from my pocket, took a cool aim, though he had already turned and was once more coming directly after me, and drew the trigger. The hammer fell, but there followed neither flash nor sound; the priming was useless with sea water. I cursed myself for my neglect. Why had not I, long before, reprimed and reloaded my only weapons? Then I should not have been, as now, a mere fleeing sheep before this butcher.

Wounded as he was, it was wonderful how fast he could move, his grizzled hair tumbling over his face, and his face itself as red as a red ensign with his haste and fury. I had no time to try my other pistol, nor, indeed, much inclination, for I was sure it would be useless. One thing I saw plainly: I must not simply retreat before him, or he would speedily hold me boxed into the bows, as a moment since he had so nearly boxed me in the stern. Once so caught, and nine or ten inches of the blood-stained dirk would be my last experience on this side of eternity. I placed my palms against the mainmast, which was of a goodish bigness, and waited, every nerve upon the stretch.

Seeing that I meant to dodge, he also paused; and a moment or two passed in feints on his part, and corresponding movements upon mine. It was such a game as I had often played at home about the rocks of Black Hill Cove; but never before, you may be sure, with such a wildly beating heart as now. Still, as I say, it was a boy's game, and I thought I could hold my own at it, against an elderly seaman with a wounded thigh. Indeed, my courage had begun to rise so high, that I allowed myself a few darting thoughts on what would be the end of the affair; and while I saw certainly that I could spin it out for long, I saw no hope of any ultimate escape.

Well, while things stood thus, suddenly the *Hispaniola* struck, staggered, ground for an instant in the sand, and then, swift as a blow, canted over to the port side, till the deck stood at an angle of forty-five degrees, and about a puncheon of water splashed into the scupper holes, and lay, in a pool, between the deck and bulwark.

We were both of us capsized in a second, and both of us rolled, almost together, into the scuppers; the dead Red-cap, with his arms still spread out, tumbling stiffly after us. So near were we, indeed, that my head came againt the coxswain's foot with a crack that made my teeth rattle. Blow and all, I was the first afoot again; for Hands had got involved with the dead body. The sudden canting of the ship had made the deck no place for running on; I had to find some new way of escape, and that upon the instant, for my foe was almost touching me. Quick as thought I sprang into the mizzen shrouds, rattled up hand over hand, and did not draw a breath till I was seated on the cross-trees.

I had been saved by being prompt; the dirk had struck not half a foot below me, as I pursued my upward flight; and there stood Israel Hands with his mouth open and his face upturned to mine, a perfect statue of surprise and disappointment.

Now that I had a moment to myself, I lost no time in changing the priming of my pistol, and then, having one ready for service, and to make assurance doubly sure, I proceeded to draw the load of the other, and recharge it afresh from the beginning.

My new employment struck Hands all of a heap; he began to see the dice going against him; and after an obvious hesitation, he also hauled himself heavily into the shrouds, and, with the dirk in his teeth, began slowly and painfully to mount. It cost him no end of time and groans to haul his wounded leg behind him; and I had quietly finished my arrangements before he was much more than a third of the way up. Then, with a pistol in either hand, I addressed him.

'One more step, Mr. Hands,' said I, 'and I'll blow your brains out! Dead men don't bite, you know,' I added, with a chuckle.

He stopped instantly. I could see by the working of his face that he was trying to think, and the process was so slow and laborious that, in my new-found security, I laughed aloud. At last, with a swallow or two, he spoke, his face still wearing the same expression of extreme perplexity. In order to speak he had to take the dagger from his mouth, but in all else he remained unmoved.

'Jim,' says he, 'I reckon we're fouled, you and me, and we'll have to sign articles. I'd have had you but for that there lurch; but I don't have no luck, not I; and I reckon I'll have to strike, which comes hard, you see, for a master mariner, to a ship's younker like you, Jim.'

I was drinking in his words and smiling away, as conceited as a cock upon a wall, when, all in a breath, back went his right hand over his shoulder. Something sang like an arrow through the air; I felt a blow and then a sharp pang, and there I was pinned by the shoulder to the mast. In the horrid pain and surprise of the moment – I scarce can say it was by my own volition, and I am sure it was without a conscious aim – both my pistols went off, and both escaped out of my hands. They did not fall alone; with a choked cry, the coxswain loosed his grasp upon the shrouds, and plunged head first into the water.

6 'Pieces of Eight'

Owing to the cant of the vessel, the masts hung far out over the water, and from my perch on the cross-trees I had nothing below me but the surface of the bay. Hands, who was not so far up, was, in consequence, nearer to the ship, and fell between me and the bulwarks. He rose once to the surface in a lather of foam and blood, and then sank again for good. As the water settled I could see him lying huddled together on the clean, bright sand in the shadow of the vessel's sides. A fish or two whipped past his body. Sometimes, by the quivering of the water, he appeared to move a little, as if he were trying to rise. But he was dead enough, for all that, being both shot and drowned, and was food for fish in the very place where he had designed my slaughter.

I was no sooner certain of this than I began to feel sick, faint, and terrified. The hot blood was running over my back and chest. The dirk, where it had pinned my shoulder to the mast, seemed to burn like a hot iron; yet it was not so much these real sufferings that distressed me, for these, it seemed to me, I could bear without a murmur; it was the horror I had upon my mind of falling from the cross-trees into that still green water, beside the body of the coxswain.

I clung with both hands till my nails ached, and I shut my eyes as if to cover up the peril. Gradually my mind came back again, my pulses quieted down to a more natural time, and I was once more in possession of myself.

It was my first thought to pluck forth the dirk; but either it stuck too hard or my nerve failed me; and I desisted with a violent shudder. Oddly enough, that very shudder did the business. The knife, in fact, had come the nearest in the world to missing me altogether; it held me by a mere pinch of skin, and this the shudder tore away. The blood ran down the faster, to be sure; but I was my own master again, and only tacked to the mast by my coat and shirt.

These last I broke through with a sudden jerk, and then regained the deck by the starboard shrouds. For nothing in the world would I have again ventured, shaken as I was, upon the overhanging port shrouds, from which Israel had so lately fallen.

I went below, and did what I could for my wound; it pained me a good deal, and still bled freely; but it was neither deep nor dangerous, nor did it greatly gall me when I used my arm. Then I looked around me, and as the ship was now, in a sense, my own, I began to think of clearing it from its last passenger – the dead man, O'Brien.

He had pitched, as I have said, against the bulwarks, where he lay like some horrible, ungainly sort of puppet; life-sized, indeed, but how different from life's colour or life's comeliness! In that position, I could easily have my way with him; and as the habit of tragical adventures had worn off almost all my terror for the dead, I took him by the waist as if he had been a sack of bran, and, with one good heave, tumbled him overboard. He went in with a sounding plunge; the red cap came off, and remained floating on the surface; and as soon as the splash subsided, I could see him and Israel lying side by side, both wavering with the tremulous movement of the water. O'Brien, though still quite a young man, was very bald. There he lay, with that bald head across the knees of the man who had killed him, and the quick fishes steering to and fro over both.

I was now alone upon the ship; the tide had just turned. The sun was within so few degrees of setting that already the shadow of the pines upon the western shore began to reach right across the anchorage, and fall in patterns on the deck. The evening breeze had sprung up, and though it was well warded off by the hill with the two peaks upon the east, the cordage had begun to sing a little softly to itself and the idle sails to rattle to and fro.

I began to see a danger to the ship. The jibs I speedily doused and brought tumbling to the deck; but the mainsail was a harder matter. Of course, when the schooner canted over, the boom had swung outboard, and the cap of it and a foot or two of sail hung even under water. I thought this made it still more dangerous; yet the strain was so heavy that I half feared to meddle. At last, I got my knife and cut the halyards. The peak dropped instantly, a great belly of loose canvas floated broad upon the water; and since, pull as I liked, I could not budge the downhaul, that was the extent of what I could accomplish. For the rest, the *Hispaniola* must trust to luck, like myself.

By this time the whole anchorage had fallen into shadow – the last rays, I remember, falling through a glade of the wood, and shining bright as jewels, on the flowery mantle of the wreck. It began to be chill; the tide was rapidly fleeting seaward, the schooner settling more and more on her beam-ends.

I scrambled forward and looked over. It seemed shallow enough, and holding the cut hawser in both hands for a last security, I let myself drop softly overboard. The water scarcely reached my waist; the sand was firm and covered with ripple marks, and I waded ashore in great spirits, leaving the *Hispaniola* on her side, with her main-sail trailing wide upon the surface of the bay. About the same time the sun went fairly down, and the breeze whistled low in the dusk among the tossing pines.

At least, and at last, I was off the sea, nor had I returned thence empty-handed. There lay the schooner, clear at last from buccaneers and ready for our own men to board and get to sea again. I had nothing nearer my fancy than to get home to the stockade and boast of my achievements. Possibly I might be blamed a bit for my truantry, but the recapture of the *Hispaniola* was a clenching answer, and I hoped that even Captain Smollett would confess I had not lost my time.

So thinking, and in famous spirits, I began to set my face homeward for the blockhouse and my companions. I remembered that the most easterly of the rivers which drain into Captain Kidd's anchorage ran from the two-peaked hill upon my left; and I bent my course in that direction that I might pass the stream while it was small. The wood was pretty open, and keeping along the lower spurs, I had soon turned the corner of the hill, and not long after waded to the mid-calf across the water-course.

This brought me near to where I had encountered Ben Gunn, the maroon; and I walked more circumspectly, keeping an eye on every side. The dusk had come nigh hand completely, and, as I opened out the cleft between the two peaks, I became aware of a wavering glow against the sky, where, as I judged, the man of the island was cooking his supper before a roaring fire. And yet I wondered, in my heart, that he should show himself so careless. For if I could see this radiance, might it not reach the eyes of Silver himself where he camped upon the shore among the marshes?

Gradually the night fell blacker; it was all I could do to guide myself even roughly towards my destination; the double hill behind me and the Spy-glass on my right hand loomed faint and fainter; the stars were few and pale; and in the low ground where I wandered I kept tripping among bushes and rolling into sandy pits.

Suddenly a kind of brightness fell about me. I looked up; a pale glimmer of moonbeams had alighted on the summit of the Spy-glass, and soon after I saw something broad and silvery moving low down behind the trees, and knew the moon had risen.

With this to help me, I passed rapidly over what remained to me of my journey; and, sometimes walking, sometimes running, impatiently drew near to the stockade. Yet, as I began to thread the grove that lies before it, I was not so thoughtless but that I slacked my pace and went a trifle warily. It would have been a poor end of my adventures to get shot down by my own party in mistake.

The moon was climbing higher and higher; its light began to fall here and there in masses through the more open districts of the wood; and right in front of me a glow of a different colour appeared among the trees. It was red and hot, and now and again it was a little darkened – as it were the embers of a bonfire smouldering.

For the life of me, I could not think what it might be.

At last I came right down upon the borders of the clearing. The western end was already steeped in moonshine; the rest, and the blockhouse itself, still lay in a black shadow, chequered with long, silvery streaks of light. On the other side of the house an immense fire had burned itself into clear embers and shed a steady, red reverberation, contrasted strongly with the mellow paleness of the moon. There was not a soul stirring, nor a sound beside the noises of the breeze.

I stopped, with much wonder in my heart, and perhaps a little terror also. It had not been our way to build great fires; we were, indeed, by the captain's orders, somewhat niggardly of firewood; and I began to fear that something had gone wrong while I was absent.

I stole round by the eastern end, keeping close in shadow, and at a convenient place, where the darkness was thickest, crossed the palisade.

To make assurance surer, I got upon my hands and knees, and crawled, without a sound, towards the corner of the house. As I drew nearer, my heart was suddenly and greatly lightened. It is not a pleasant noise in itself, and I have often complained of it at other times; but just then it was like music to hear my friends snoring together so loud and peaceful in their sleep. The sea-cry of the watch, that beautiful 'All's well,' never fell more reassuringly on my ear.

In the meantime, there was no doubt of one thing; they kept an infamous bad watch. If it had been Silver and his lads that were now creeping in on them, not a soul would have seen daybreak. That was what it was, thought I, to have the captain wounded; and again I blamed myself sharply for leaving them in that danger with so few to mount guard.

By this time I had got to the door and stood up. All was dark within, so that I could distinguish nothing by the eye. As for sounds, there was the steady drone of the snorers, and a small occasional noise, a flickering or pecking that I could in no way account for.

With my arms before me I walked steadily in. I should lie down in my own place (I thought, with a silent chuckle) and enjoy their faces when they found me in the morning.

My foot struck something yielding – it was a sleeper's leg; and he turned and groaned, but without awaking.

And then, all of a sudden, a shrill voice broke forth out of the darkness:

'Pieces of eight! pieces of eight! pieces of eight! pieces of eight! pieces of eight!' and so forth, without pause or change, like the clacking of a tiny mill.

Silver's green parrot, Captain Flint! It was she whom I had heard pecking at a piece of bark; it was she, keeping better watch than any human being, who thus announced my arrival with her wearisome refrain.

I had no time left me to recover. At the sharp, clipping tone of the parrot, the sleepers awoke and sprang up; and with a mighty oath, the voice of Silver cried:

'Who goes?'

I turned to run, struck violently against one person, recoiled, and ran full into the arms of a second, who, for his part, closed upon and held me tight.

'Bring a torch, Dick,' said Silver, when my capture was thus assured.

And one of the men left the log-house and presently returned with a lighted brand.

PART 6. CAPTAIN SILVER

1 In The Enemy's Camp

The red glare of the torch, lighting up the interior of the blockhouse,
showed me the worst of my apprehensions realized. The pirates were
in possession of the house and stores; there was the cask of cognac,
there were the pork and bread, as before; and, what tenfold increased
my horror, not a sign of any prisoner. I could only judge that all had
perished, and my heart smote me sorely that I had not been there to
perish with them.

There were six of the buccaneers, all told; not another man was
left alive. Five of them were on their feet, flushed and swollen,
suddenly called out of the first sleep of drunkenness. The sixth had
only risen upon his elbow: he was deadly pale, and the blood-stained
bandage round his head told that he had recently been wounded, and
still more recently dressed. I remembered the man who had been shot
and had run back among the woods in the great attack, and doubted
not that this was he.

The parrot sat, preening her plumage, on Long John's shoulder.
He himself, I thought, looked somewhat paler and more stern than I
was used to. He still wore the fine broadcloth suit in which he had
fulfilled his mission, but it was bitterly the worse for wear, daubed
with clay and torn with the sharp briers of the wood.

'So,' said he, 'here's Jim Hawkins, shiver my timbers! dropped in,
like, eh? Well, come, I take that friendly.'

And thereupon he sat down across the brandy cask, and began to
fill a pipe.

'Give me a loan of the link, Dick', said he; and then, when he had a
good light, 'That'll do, lad,' he added; 'stick the glim in the wood heap;
and you, gentlemen, bring yourselves to! – you needn't stand up for
Mr. Hawkins; *he*'ll excuse you, you may lay to that. And so, Jim' –
stopping the tobacco – 'here you were, and quite a pleasant surprise for
poor old John. I see you were smart when first I set my eyes on you;

'"So," said he, "here's Jim Hawkins, shiver my timbers!"'

but this here gets away from me clean, it do.'

To all this, as may be well supposed, I made no answer. They had set me with my back against the wall; and I stood there, looking Silver in the face, pluckily enough, I hope, to all outward appearance, but with black despair in my heart.

Silver took a whiff or two of his pipe, with great composure, and then ran on again.

'Now, you see, Jim, so be as you *are* here,' says he, 'I'll give you a piece of my mind. I've always liked you, I have, for a lad of spirit, and the picter of my own self when I was young and handsome. I always wanted you to jine and take your share, and die a gentleman, and now, my cock, you've got to. Cap'n Smollett's a fine seaman, as I'll own up to any day, but stiff on discipline. "Dooty is dooty," says he, and right he is. Just you keep clear of the cap'n. The doctor himself is gone dead again you – "ungrateful scamp" was what he said; and the short and the long of the whole story is about here: you can't go back to your own lot, for they won't have you; and without you start a third ship's company all by yourself, which might be lonely, you'll have to jine with Cap'n Silver.'

So far so good. My friends, then, were still alive, and though I partly believed the truth of Silver's statement, that the cabin party were incensed at me for my desertion, I was more relieved than distressed by what I heard.

'I don't say nothing as to your being in our hands,' continued Silver, 'though there you are, and you may lay to it. I'm all for argyment; I never seen good come out o' threatening. If you like the service, well, you'll jine; and if you don't, Jim, why, you're free to answer no – free and welcome, shipmate; and if fairer can be said by mortal seaman, shiver my sides!'

'Am I to answer, then?' I asked, with a very tremulous voice. Through all this sneering talk, I was made to feel the threat of death that overhung me, and my cheeks burned and my heart beat painfully in my breast.

'Lad,' said Silver, 'no one's a-pressing of you. Take your bearings. None of us won't hurry you, mate; time goes so pleasant in your company, you see.'

'Well,' says I, growing a bit bolder, 'if I'm to choose, I declare I have a right to know what's what, and why you're here, and where my friends are.'

'Wot's wot?' repeated one of the buccaneers, in a deep growl. 'Ah, he'd be a lucky one as knowed that!'

'You'll, perhaps, batten down your hatches till you're spoke, my friend,' cried Silver truculently to this speaker. And then, in his first gracious tones, he replied to me: 'Yesterday morning, Mr. Hawkins,' said he, 'in the dogwatch, down came Dr. Livesey with a flag of truce. Says he: "Cap'n Silver, you're sold out. Ship's gone." Well, maybe we'd been taking a glass, and a song to help it round. I won't say no. Leastways none of us had looked out. We looked out, and, by thunder! the old ship was gone. I never seen a pack of fools look fishier; and you may lay to that, if I tells you that looked the fishiest. "Well," says the doctor, "let's bargain." We bargained, him and I, and here we are: stores, brandy, blockhouse, the firewood you was thoughtful enough to cut, and in a manner of speaking, the whole blessed boat from cross-trees to kelson. As for them, they've tramped; I don't know wheres they are.'

He drew again quietly at his pipe.

'And lest you should take it into that head of yours,' he went on, 'that you was included in the treaty, here's the last word that was said: "How many are you," says I, "to leave?" "Four," says he – "four, and one of us wounded. As for that boy, I don't know where he is, confound him," says he, "nor I don't much care. We're about sick of him." These was his words.'

'Is that all?' I asked.

'Well, it's all that you're to hear, my son,' returned Silver.

'And now I am to choose?'

'And now you are to choose, and you may lay to that,' said Silver.

'Well,' said I, 'I am not such a fool but I know pretty well what I have to look for. Let the worst come to the worst, it's little I care. I've seen too many die since I fell in with you. But there's a thing or two I have to tell you,' I said, and by this time I was quite excited; 'and the first is this: here you are in a bad way: ship lost, treasure lost, men lost; your whole business gone to wreck; and if you want to know who did it – it was I! I was in the apple barrel the night we sighted land, and I heard you, John, and you, Dick Johnson, and Hands, who is now at the bottom of the sea, and told every word you said before the hour was out. And as for the schooner, it was I who cut her cable, and it was I that killed the men you had aboard of her, and it was I who brought her where you'll never see her more, not one of you. The laugh's on my side; I've had the top of this business from the first; I no more fear you than I fear a fly. Kill me, if you please, or spare me. But one thing I'll say, and no more; if you spare me, bygones are bygones, and when you fellows are in court for piracy, I'll save you all I can. It is for you to choose. Kill another and do yourselves no good, or spare me and keep a witness to save you from the gallows.'

I stopped, for, I tell you, I was out of breath, and, to my wonder, not a man of them moved, but all sat staring at me like as many sheep. And while they were still staring, I broke out again:

'And now, Mr. Silver,' I said, 'I believe you're the best man here, and if things go the worst, I'll take it kind of you to let the doctor know the way I took it.'

'I'll bear it in mind,' said Silver, with an accent so curious that I could not, for the life of me, decide whether he were laughing at my request, or had been favourably affected by my courage.

'I'll put one to that,' cried the old mahogany-faced seaman – Morgan by name – whom I had seen in Long John's public-house upon the quays of Bristol. 'It was him that knowed Black Dog.'

'Well, and see here,' added the sea-cook. 'I'll put another again to that, by thunder! for it was this same boy that faked the chart from Billy Bones. First and last, we've split upon Jim Hawkins!'

'Then here goes!' said Morgan, with an oath.

And he sprang up, drawing his knife as if he had been twenty.

'Avast there!' cried Silver. 'Who are you, Tom Morgan? Maybe you thought you was cap'n here, perhaps. By the powers, but I'll teach you better! Cross me, and you'll go where many a good man's gone before you, first and last, these thirty years back – some to the yard-arm, shiver my sides! and some by the board, and all to feed the fishes. There's never a man looked me between the eyes and seen a good day a'terwards, Tom Morgan, you may lay to that.'

Morgan paused; but a hoarse murmur rose from the others.

'Tom's right,' said one.

'I stood hazing long enough from one,' added another. 'I'll be hanged if I'll be hazed by you, John Silver.'

'Did any of you gentlemen want to have it out with *me*?' roared Silver, bending far forward from his position on the keg, with his pipe still glowing in his right hand. 'Put a name on what you're at; you ain't dumb, I reckon. Him that wants shall get it. Have I lived this many years, and a son of a rum puncheon cock his hat athwart my hawse at the latter end of it? You know the way; you're all gentlemen o' fortune, by your account. Well, I'm ready. Take a cutlass, him that dares, and I'll see the colour of his inside, crutch and all, before that pipe's empty.'

Not a man stirred; not a man answered.

'That's your sort, is it?' he added, returning his pipe to his mouth. 'Well, you're a gay lot to look at, anyway. Not much worth to fight, you ain't. P'r'aps you can understand King George's English. I'm cap'n here by 'lection. I'm cap'n here because I'm the best man by a long sea-mile. You won't fight as gentlemen o' fortune should; then, by thunder, you'll obey, and you may lay to it! I like that boy, now; I never seen a better boy than that. He's more a man than any pair of rats of you in this here house, and what I say is this: let me see him that'll lay a hand on him – that's what I say, and you may lay to it.'

There was a long pause after this. I stood straight up against the wall, my heart still going like a sledge-hammer, but with a ray of hope now shining in my bosom. Silver leant back against the wall, his arms crossed, his pipe in the corner of his mouth, as calm as though he had been in church; yet his eye kept wandering furtively, and he kept the tail of it on his unruly followers. They, on their part, drew gradually together towards the far end of the blockhouse, and the low hiss of their whispering sounded in my ear continuously like a stream. One after another they would look up, and the red light of the torch would fall for a second on their nervous faces; but it was not towards me, it was towards Silver that they turned their eyes.

'You seem to have a lot to say,' remarked Silver, spitting far into the air. 'Pipe up and let me hear it, or lay to.'

'Ax your pardon, sir,' returned one of the men; 'you're pretty free with some of the rules; maybe you'll kindly keep an eye upon the rest. This crew's dissatisfied; this crew don't vally bullying a marlin-spike; this crew has its rights like other crews, I'll make so free as that; and by your own rules, I take it we can talk together. I ax your pardon, sir, acknowledging you for to be capting at this present; but I claim my right, and steps outside for a council.'

And with an elaborate sea-salute, this fellow, a long, ill-looking, yellow-eyed man of five-and-thirty, stepped coolly towards the door and disappeared out of the house. One after another, the rest followed his example; each making a salute as he passed; each adding some apology. 'According to rules,' said one. 'Fo'c's'le council,' said

Morgan. And so with one remark or another, all marched out, and left Silver and me alone with the torch.

The sea-cook instantly removed his pipe.

'Now, look you here, Jim Hawkins,' he said, in a steady whisper, that was no more than audible, 'you're within half a plank of death, and, what's a long sight worse, of torture. They're going to throw me off. But, you mark, I stand by you through thick and thin. I didn't mean to; no, not till you spoke up. I was about desperate to lose that much blunt, and be hanged into the bargain. But I see you was the right sort. I says to myself: You stand by Hawkins, John, and Hawkins'll stand by you. You're his last card, and, by the living thunder, John, he's yours! Back to back, says I. You save your witness, and he'll save your neck!'

I began to dimly understand.

'You mean all's lost?' I asked.

'Ay, by gum, I do!' he answered. 'Ship gone, neck gone – that's the size of it. Once I looked into that bay, Jim Hawkins, and seen no schooner – well, I'm tough, but I gave out. As for that lot and their council, mark me, they're outright fools and cowards. I'll save your life – if so be as I can – from them. But, see here, Jim – tit for tat – you save Long John from swinging.'

I was bewildered; it seemed a thing so hopeless he was asking – he, the old buccaneer, the ringleader throughout.

'What I can do, that I'll do,' I said.

'It's a bargain!' cried Long John. 'You speak up plucky, and, by thunder! I've a chance.'

He hobbled to the torch, where it stood propped among the firewood, and took a fresh light to his pipe.

'Understand me, Jim,' he said, returning. 'I've a head on my shoulders, I have. I'm on squire's side now. I know you've got that ship safe somewheres. How you done it, I don't know, but safe it is. I guess Hands and O'Brien turned soft. I never much believed in neither of *them*. Now you mark me. I ask no questions, nor I won't let others. I know when a game's up, I do; and I know a lad that's staunch. Ah, you that's young – you and me might have done a power of good together!'

He drew some cognac from the cask into a tin cannikin.

'Will you taste, messmate?' he asked; and when I had refused: 'Well, I'll take a drain myself, Jim,' said he. 'I need a caulker, for there's trouble on hand. And, talking o' trouble, why did that doctor give me the chart, Jim?'

My face expressed a wonder so unaffected that he saw the needlessness of further questions.

'Ah, well, he did, though,' said he. 'And there's something under that, no doubt – something, surely, under that, Jim – bad or good.'

And he took another swallow of the brandy, shaking his great fair head like a man who looks forward to the worst.

2 The Black Spot Again

The council of the buccaneers had lasted some time when one of them re-entered the house, and with a repetition of the same salute, which had in my eyes an ironical air, begged for a moment's loan of the torch. Silver briefly agreed; and this emissary retired again, leaving us together in the dark.

'There's a breeze coming, Jim,' said Silver, who had, by this time, adopted quite a friendly and familiar tone.

I turned to the loophole nearest me and looked out. The embers of the great fire had so far burned themselves out, and now glowed so low and duskily, that I understood why these conspirators desired a torch. About half-way down the slope to the stockade, they were collected in a group; one held the light; another was on his knees in their midst, and I saw the blade of an open knife shine in his hand with varying colours, in the moon and torchlight. The rest were all somewhat stooping, as though watching the manœuvres of this last. I could just make out that he had a book as well as a knife in his hand; and was still wondering how anything so incongruous had come in their possession, when the kneeling figure rose once more to his feet, and the whole party began to move together towards the house.

'Here they come,' said I; and I returned to my former position, for it seemed beneath my dignity that they should find me watching them.

'Well, let 'em come, lad – let 'em come,' said Silver, cheerily. 'I've still a shot in my locker.'

The door opened, and the five men, standing huddled together just inside, pushed one of their number forward. In any other circumstances it would have been comical to see his slow advance, hesitating as he set down each foot, but holding his closed right hand in front of him.

'Step up, lad,' cried Silver. 'I won't eat you. Hand it over, lubber. I know the rules, I do; I won't hurt a depytation.'

Thus encouraged, the buccaneer stepped forth more briskly, and having passed something to Silver, from hand to hand, slipped yet more smartly back again to his companions.

The sea-cook looked at what had been given him.

'The black spot! I thought so,' he observed. 'Where might you have got the paper? Why, hillo! look here, now: this ain't lucky! You've gone and cut this out of a Bible. What fool's cut a Bible?'

'Ah, there!' said Morgan – 'there! Wot did I say? No good'll come o' that, I said.'

'Well, you've about fixed it now among you,' continued Silver. 'You'll all swing now, I reckon. What soft-headed lubber had a Bible?'

'It was Dick,' said one.

'Dick, was it? Then Dick can get to prayers,' said Silver. 'He's seen his slice of luck, has Dick, and you may lay to that.'

But here the long man with the yellow eyes struck in.

'Belay that talk, John Silver,' he said. 'This crew has tipped you the black spot in full council, as in dooty bound; just you turn it over, as in dooty bound, and see what's wrote there. Then you can talk.'

'Thanky, George,' replied the sea-cook. 'You always was brisk for business, and has the rules by heart, George, as I'm pleased to see. Well, what is it, anyway? Ah! "Deposed" – that's it, is it? Very pretty wrote, to be sure; like print, I swear. Your hand o' write, George? Why, you was gettin' quite a leadin' man in this here crew. You'll be cap'n next, I shouldn't wonder. Just oblige me with that torch again, will you? this pipe don't draw.'

'Come, now,' said George, 'you don't fool this crew no more. You're a funny man, by your account; but you're over now, and you'll maybe step down off that barrel and help vote.'

'I thought you said you knowed the rules,' returned Silver, contemptuously. 'Leastways, if you don't, I do; and I wait here – and I'm still your cap'n, mind – till you outs with your grievances, and I reply; in the meantime, your black spot ain't worth a biscuit. After that, we'll see.'

'Oh,' replied George, 'you don't be under no kind of apprehension; we're all square, we are. First, you've made a hash of this cruise – you'll be a bold man to say no to that. Second, you let the enemy out o' this here trap for nothing. Why did they want out? I dunno; but it's pretty plain they wanted it. Third, you wouldn't let us go at them upon the march. Oh, we see through you, John Silver; you want to play booty, that's what's wrong with you. And then, fourth, there's this here boy.'

'Is that all?' asked Silver quietly.

'Enough, too,' retorted George. 'We'll all swing and sun-dry for your bungling.'

'Well, now, look here, I'll answer these four p'ints; one after another I'll answer 'em. I made a hash o' this cruise, did I? Well, now, you all know what I wanted; and you all know, if that had been done, that we'd 'a' been aboard the *Hispaniola* this night as ever was, every man of us alive, and fit, and full of good plum-duff, and the treasure in the hold of her, by thunder! Well, who crossed me? Who forced my hand, as was the lawful cap'n? Who tipped me the black spot the day we landed, and began this dance? Ah, it's a fine dance – I'm with you there – and looks mighty like a hornpipe in a rope's end at Execution Dock by London town, it does. But who done it? Why, it was Anderson, and Hands, and you, George Merry! And you're the last above board of that same meddling crew; and you have the Davy Jones's insolence to up and stand for cap'n over me – you, that sank the lot of us! By the powers; but this tops the stiffest yarn to nothing.'

Silver paused, and I could see by the faces of George and his late comrades that these words had not been said in vain.

'That's for number one,' cried the accused, wiping the sweat from his brow, for he had been talking with a vehemence that shook the house. 'Why, I give you my word, I'm sick to speak to you. You've neither sense nor memory, and I leave it to fancy where your mothers was that let you come to sea. Sea! Gentlemen o' fortune! I reckon tailors is your trade.'

'Go on, John,' said Morgan. 'Speak up to the others.'

'Ah, the others!' returned John. 'They're a nice lot, ain't they? You say this cruise is bungled. Ah! by gum, if you could understand how bad it's bungled, you would see! We're that near the gibbet that my neck's stiff with thinking on it. You've seen 'em, maybe, hanged in chains, birds about 'em, seamen p'inting 'em out as they go down with the tide. "Who's that?" says one. "That! Why, that's John Silver. I knowed him well," says another. And you can hear the chains a-jangle as you go about and reach for the other buoy. Now that's about where we are, every mother's son of us, thanks to him, and Hands, and Anderson, and other ruination fools of you. And if you want to know about number four, and that boy, why, shiver my timbers! isn't he a hostage? Are we a-going to waste a hostage? No, not us; he might be our last chance, and I shouldn't wonder. Kill that boy? not me, mates! And number three? Ah, well, there's a deal to say to number three. Maybe you don't count it nothing to have a real college doctor come to see you every day – you, John, with your head broke – or you, George Merry, that had the ague shakes upon you not six hours agone, and has your eyes the colour of lemon-peel to this same moment on the clock? And maybe, perhaps, you didn't know there was a consort coming, either? But there is; and not so long till then; and we'll see who'll be glad to have a hostage when it comes to that. And as for number two, and why I made a bargain – well, you came crawling on your knees to me to make it – on your knees you came, you was that downhearted – and you'd have starved, too, if I hadn't – but that's a trifle! you look there – that's why!'

And he cast down upon the floor a paper that I instantly recognized – none other than the chart on yellow paper, with the three red crosses, that I had found in the oilcloth at the bottom of the captain's chest. Why the doctor had given it to him was more than I could fancy.

But if it were inexplicable to me, the appearance of the chart was incredible to the surviving mutineers. They leaped upon it like cats upon a mouse. It went from hand to hand, one tearing it from another; and by the oaths and the cries and the childish laughter with which they accompanied their examination, you would have thought, not only they were fingering the very gold, but were at sea with it, besides, in safety.

'Yes,' said one, 'that's Flint, sure enough. J. F., and a score below with a clove hitch to it; so he done ever.'

'Mighty pretty,' said George. 'But how are are we to get away with it, and us no ship?'

Silver suddenly sprang up, and supporting himself with a hand against the wall: 'Now I give you warning, George,' he cried. 'One more word of your sauce, and I'll call you down and fight you. How? Why, how do I know? You had ought to tell me that – you and the rest, that lost me my schooner, with your interference, burn you! But not you, you can't; you hain't got the invention of a cockroach. But civil you can speak, and shall, George Merry, you may lay to that.'

'That's fair enow,' said the old man Morgan.

'Fair! I reckon so,' said the sea-cook. 'You lost the ship; I found the treasure. Who's the better man at that? And now I resign, by thunder! Elect whom you please to be your cap'n now; I'm done with it.'

'Silver!' they cried. 'Barbecue for ever! Barbecue for cap'n!'

'So that's the toon, is it?' cried the cook. 'George, I reckon you'll have to wait another turn, friend! and lucky for you as I'm not a revengeful man. But that was never my way. And now, shipmates, this black spot? 'Tain't much good now, is it? Dick's crossed his luck and spoiled his Bible, and that's about all.'

'It'll do to kiss the book on still, won't it?' growled Dick, who was evidently uneasy at the curse he had brought upon himself.

A Bible with bit cut out!' returned Silver derisively. 'Not it. It don't bind no more'n a ballad-book.'

'Don't it, though?' cried Dick, with a sort of joy. 'Well, I reckon that's worth having, too.'

'Here, Jim – here's a cur'osity for you,' said Silver; and he tossed me the paper.

It was a round about the size of a crown piece. One side was blank, for it had been the last leaf; the other contained a verse or two of Revelation – these words among the rest, which struck sharply home upon my mind: 'Without are dogs and murderers.' The printed side had been blackened with wood ash, which already began to come off and soil my fingers; on the blank side had been written with the same material the one word 'Depposed.' I have that curiosity beside me at this moment; but not a trace of writing now remains beyond a single scratch, such as a man might make with his thumb-nail.

That was the end of the night's business. Soon after, with a drink all round, we lay down to sleep, and the outside of Silver's vengeance was to put George Merry up for sentinel and threaten him with death if he should prove unfaithful.

It was long ere I could close an eye, and Heaven knows I had matter enough for thought in the man whom I had slain that afternoon, in my own most perilous position, and, above all, in the remarkable game that I saw Silver now engaged upon – keeping the mutineers together with one hand, and grasping, with the other, after every means, possible and impossible, to make his peace and save his miserable life. He himself slept peacefully, and snored aloud; yet my heart was sore for him, wicked as he was, to think on the dark perils that environed, and the shameful gibbet that awaited him.

3 On Parole

I was wakened – indeed, we were all wakened, for I could see even the sentinel shake himself together from where he had fallen against the door-post – by a clear, hearty voice hailing us from the margin of the wood:

'Blockhouse, ahoy!' it cried. 'Here's the doctor.'

And the doctor it was. Although I was glad to hear the sound, yet my gladness was not without admixture. I remembered with confusion my insubordinate and stealthy conduct; and when I saw where it had brought me – among what companions and surrounded by what dangers – I felt ashamed to look him in the face.

He must have risen in the dark, for the day had hardly come; and when I ran to a loophole and looked out, I saw him standing, like Silver once before, up to the mid-leg in creeping vapour.

'You, doctor! Top o' the morning to you, sir!' cried Silver, broad awake and beaming with good nature in a moment. 'Bright and early, to be sure; and it's the early bird, as the saying goes, that gets the rations. George, shake up your timbers, son, and help Dr. Livesey over the ship's side. All a-doin' well, your patients was – all well and merry.'

So he pattered on, standing on the hill-top, with his crutch under his elbow, and one hand upon the side of the log-house – quite the old John in voice, manner, and expression.

'We've quite a surprise for you, too, sir,' he continued. 'We've a little stranger here – he! he! A noo boarder and lodger, sir, and looking fit and taut as a fiddle; slep' like a supercargo, he did, right alongside of John – stem to stem we was, all night.'

Dr. Livesey was by this time across the stockade and pretty near the cook; and I could hear the alteration in his voice as he said:

'Not Jim?'

'The very same as ever was,' says Silver.

The doctor stopped outright, although he did not speak, and it was some seconds before he seemed able to move on.

'Well, well,' he said, at last, 'duty first and pleasure afterwards, as you might have said yourself, Silver. Let us overhaul these patients of yours.'

A moment afterwards he had entered the blockhouse, and, with one grim nod to me, proceeded with his work among the sick. He seemed under no apprehension, though he must have known that his life, among these treacherous demons, depended on a hair; and he rattled on to his patients as if he were paying an ordinary professional visit in a quiet English family. His manner, I suppose, reacted on the men; for they behaved to him as if nothing had occurred – as if he were still ship's doctor, and they still faithful hands before the mast.

'You're doing well, my friend,' he said to the fellow with the bandaged head; 'and if ever any person had a close shave, it was you; your head must be as hard as iron. Well, George, how goes it? You're a pretty colour, certainly; why, your liver, man, is upside down. Did you take that medicine? Did he take that medicine, men?'

'Ay, ay, sir, he took it, sure enough,' returned Morgan.

'Because, you see, since I am mutineers' doctor, or prison doctor, as I prefer to call it,' says Dr. Livesey, in his pleasantest way, 'I make it a point of honour not to lose a man for King George (God bless him!) and the gallows.'

The rogues looked at each other, but swallowed the home-thrust in silence.

'Dick don't feel well, sir,' said one.

'Don't he?' replied the doctor. 'Well, step up here, Dick, and let me see your tongue. No, I should be surprised if he did! the man's tongue is fit to frighten the French. Another fever.'

'Ah, there,' said Morgan, 'that comed of sp'iling Bibles.'

'That comed – as you call it – of being arrant asses,' retorted the doctor, 'and not having sense enough to know honest air from poison, and the dry land from a vile, pestiferous slough. I think it most probable – though, of course, it's only an opinion – that you'll all have the deuce to pay before you get that malaria out of your systems. Camp in a bog, would you? Silver, I'm surprised at you. You're less of a fool than many, take you all round; but you don't appear to me to have the rudiments of a notion of the rules of health.'

'Well,' he added, after he had dosed them round, and they had taken his prescriptions, with really laughable humility, more like charity school-children than blood-guilty mutineers and pirates – 'well, that's done for to-day. And now I should wish to have a talk with that boy, please.'

And he nodded his head in my direction carelessly.

George Merry was at the door, spitting and spluttering over some bad-tasting medicine; but at the first word of the doctor's proposal he swung round with a deep flush and cried 'No!' and swore.

Silver struck the barrel with his open hand.

'Si-lence!' he roared, and looked about him positively like a lion. 'Doctor,' he went on, in his usual tones, 'I was a-thinking of that, knowing as how you had a fancy for the boy. We're all humbly grateful for your kindness, and, as you see, puts faith in you, and takes the drugs down like that much grog. And I take it, I've found a way as'll suit all. Hawkins, will you give me your word of honour as a young gentleman – for a young gentleman you are, although poor born – your word of honour not to slip your cable?'

I readily gave the pledge required.

'Then, doctor,' said Silver, 'you just step outside o' that stockade, and once you're there, I'll bring the boy down on the inside, and I reckon you can yarn through the spars. Good day to you, sir, and all our dooties to the squire and Cap'n Smollett.'

The explosion of disapproval, which nothing but Silver's black looks had restrained, broke out immediately the doctor had left the house. Silver was roundly accused of playing double – of trying to make a separate peace for himself – of sacrificing the interests of his accomplices and victims; and, in one word, of the identical, exact thing that he was doing. It seemed to me so obvious, in this case, that I could not imagine how he was to turn their anger. But he was twice the man the rest were; and his last night's victory had given him a huge proponderance on their minds. He called them all the fools and dolts you can imagine, said it was necessary I should talk to the doctor, fluttered the chart in their faces, asked them if they could afford to break the treaty the very day they were bound a-treasure-hunting.

'No, by thunder!' he cried, 'it's us must break the treaty when the time comes; and till then I'll gammon that doctor, if I have to ile his boots with brandy.'

And then he bade them get the fire lit, and stalked out upon his crutch, with his hand on my shoulder, leaving them in a disarray, and silenced by his volubility rather than convinced.

'Slow, lad, slow,' he said. 'They might round upon us in a twinkle of an eye, if we was seen to hurry.'

Very deliberately, then, did we advance across the sand to where the doctor awaited us on the other side of the stockade, and as soon as we were within easy speaking distance, Silver stopped.

'You'll make a note of this here also, doctor,' says he, 'and the boy'll tell you how I saved his life, and were deposed for it, too, and you may lay to that. Doctor, when a man's steering as near the wind as me – playing chuck-farthing with the last breath in his body, like – you wouldn't think it too much, mayhap, to give him one good word? You'll please bear in mind it's not my life only now – it's that boy's into the bargain; and you'll speak me fair, doctor, and give me a bit o' hope to go on, for the sake of mercy.'

Silver was a changed man, once he was out there and had his back to his friends and the blockhouse; his cheeks seemed to have fallen in, his voice trembled; never was a soul more dead in earnest.

'Why, John, you're not afraid?' asked Dr. Livesey.

'Doctor, I'm no coward! no, not I – not *so* much!' and he snapped his fingers. 'If I was I wouldn't say it. But I'll own up fairly, I've the shakes upon me for the gallows. You're a good man and a true; I never seen a better man! And you'll not forget what I done good, not any more than you'll forget the bad, I know. And I step aside – see here – and leave you and Jim alone. And you'll put that down for me, too, for it's a long stretch, is that!'

So saying, he stepped back a little way, till he was out of earshot, and there sat down upon a tree-stump and began to whistle; spinning round now and again upon his seat so as to command a sight, sometimes of me and the doctor, and sometimes of his unruly ruffians as they went to and fro in the sand, between the fire – which they were busy rekindling – and the house, from which they brought forth pork and bread to make the breakfast.

'So, Jim,' said the doctor sadly, 'here you are. As you have brewed, so shall you drink, my boy. Heaven knows, I cannot find it in my heart to blame you; but this much I will say, be it kind or unkind; when Captain Smollett was well, you dared not have gone off, and when he was ill, and couldn't help it, by George, it was downright cowardly!'

I will own that I here began to weep. 'Doctor,' I said, 'you might spare me. I have blamed myself enough; my life's forfeit anyway, and I should have been dead by now, if Silver hadn't stood for me; and, doctor, believe this, I can die – and I dare say I deserve it – but what I fear is torture. If they come to torture me——'

'Jim,' the doctor interrupted, and his voice was quite changed, 'Jim, I can't have this. Whip over, and we'll run for it.'

'Doctor,' said I, 'I passed my word.'

'I know, I know,' he cried. 'We can't help that, Jim, now. I'll take it on my shoulders, holus bolus, blame and shame, my boy; but stay here, I cannot let you. Jump! One jump and you're out, and we'll run for it like antelopes.'

'No,' I replied, 'you know right well you wouldn't do the thing yourself; neither you, nor squire, nor captain; and no more will I. Silver trusted me; I passed my word, and back I go. But, doctor, you did not let me finish. If they come to torture me, I might let slip a word of where the ship is; for I got the ship, part by luck and part by risking, and she lies in North Inlet, on the southern beach, and just below high water. At half-tide she must be high and dry.'

'The ship!' exclaimed the doctor.

Rapidly I described to him my adventures, and he heard me out in silence.

'There is a kind of fate in this,' he observed, when I had done. 'Every step, it's you that saves our lives; and do you suppose by any chance that we are going to let you lose yours? That would be a poor return, my boy. You found out the plot; you found Ben Gunn – the best deed that ever you did, or will do, though you live to ninety. Oh, by Jupiter, and talking of Ben Gunn! why, this is the mischief in person. Silver!' he cried, 'Silver! – I'll give you a piece of advice,' he continued as the cook drew near again; 'don't you be in any great hurry after that treasure.'

'Why, sir, I do my possible, which that ain't,' said Silver. 'I can only, asking your pardon, save my life and the boy's by seeking for that treasure; and you may lay to that.'

'Well, Silver,' replied the doctor, 'if that is so, I'll go one step further: look out for squalls when you find it.'

'Sir,' said Silver, 'as between man and man, that's too much and too little. What you're after, why you left the blockhouse, why you given me that there chart, I don't know, now, do I? and yet I done your bidding with my eyes shut and never a word of hope! But, no, this here's too much. If you won't tell me what you mean plain out, just say so, and I'll leave the helm.'

'No,' said the doctor, musingly, 'I've no right to say more; it's not my secret, you see, Silver, or, I give you my word, I'd tell it you. But I'll go as far with you as I dare go, and a step beyond; for I'll have my wig sorted by the captain, or I'm mistaken. And, first, I'll give you a bit of hope: Silver, if we both get alive out of this wolf-trap, I'll do my best to save you, short of perjury.'

Silver's face was radiant. 'You couldn't say more, I'm sure, sir, not if you was my mother,' he cried.

'Well, that's my first concession,' added the doctor. 'My second is a piece of advice: Keep the boy close beside you, and when you need help, halloo. I'm off to seek it for you, and that itself will show you if I speak at random. Good-bye, Jim.'

And Dr. Livesey shook hands with me through the stockade, nodded to Silver, and set off at a brisk pace into the wood.

4 The Treasure Hunt – Flint's Pointer

'Jim,' said Silver, when we were alone, 'if I saved your life, you saved mine; and I'll not forget it. I seen the doctor waving you to run for it – with the tail of my eye, I did; and I seen you say no, as plain as hearing. Jim, that's one to you. This is the first glint of hope I had since the attack failed, and I owe it you. And now, Jim, we're to go in for this here treasure-hunting, with sealed orders, too, and I don't like it; and you and me must stick close, back to back like, and we'll save our necks in spite o' fate and fortune.'

Just then a man hailed us from the fire that breakfast was ready, and we were soon seated here and there about the sand over biscuit and fried junk. They had lit a fire fit to roast an ox; and it was now grown so hot that they could only approach it from the windward, and even there not without precaution. In the same wasteful spirit, they had cooked, I suppose, three times more than we could eat; and one of them, with an empty laugh, threw what was left into the fire, which blazed and roared again over this unusual fuel. I never in my life saw men so careless of the morrow; hand to mouth is the only word that can describe their way of doing; and what with wasted food and sleeping sentries, though they were bold enough for a brush and be done with it, I could see their entire unfitness for anything like a prolonged campaign.

Even Silver, eating away, with Captain Flint upon his shoulder, had not a word of blame for their recklessness. And this the more surprised me, for I thought he had never shown himself so cunning as he did then.

'Ay, mates,' said he, 'it's lucky you have Barbecue to think for you with this here head. I got what I wanted, I did. Sure enough, they have the ship. Where they have it, I don't know yet; but once we hit the treasure, we'll have to jump about and find out. And then, mates, us that has the boats, I reckon, has the upper hand.'

Thus he kept running on, with his mouth full of the hot bacon; thus he restored their hope and confidence, and, I more than suspect, repaired his own at the same time.

'As for hostage,' he continued, 'that's his last talk, I guess, with them he loves so dear. I've got my piece o' news, and thanky to him for that; but it's over and done. I'll take him in a line when we go treasure-hunting, for we'll keep him like so much gold, in case of accidents, you mark, and in the meantime. Once we got the ship and treasure both, and off to sea like jolly companions, why, then, we'll talk Mr. Hawkins over, we will, and we'll give him his share, to 'ie sure, for all his kindness.'

It was no wonder the men were in a good humour now. For my part, I was horribly cast down. Should the scheme he had now sketched prove feasible, Silver, already doubly a traitor, would not hesitate to adopt it. He had still a foot in either camp, and there was no doubt he would prefer wealth and freedom with the pirates to a bare escape from hanging, which was the best he had to hope on our side.

Nay, and even if things so fell out that he was forced to keep his faith with Dr. Livesey, even then what danger lay before us! What a moment that would be when the suspicions of his followers turned to certainty, and he and I should have to fight for dear life – he, a cripple, and I, a boy – against five strong and active seamen!

Add to this double apprehension, the mystery that still hung over the behaviour of my friends; their unexplained desertion of the stockade; their inexplicable cession of the chart; or, harder still to understand, the doctor's last warning to Silver: 'Look out for squalls when you find it'; and you will readily believe how little taste I found in my breakfast, and with how uneasy a heart I set forth behind my captors on the quest for treasure.

We made a curious figure, had any one been there to see us; all in soiled sailor clothes, and all but me armed to the teeth. Silver had two guns slung about him – one before and one behind – besides the great cutlass at his waist, and a pistol in each pocket of his square-tailed coat. To complete his strange appearance, Captain Flint sat perched upon his shoulder and gabbling odds and ends of purposeless sea-talk. I had a line about my waist, and followed obediently after the sea-cook, who held the loose end of the rope, now in his free hand, now between his powerful teeth. For all the world, I was led like a dancing bear.

The other men were variously burthened; some carrying picks and shovels – for that had been the very first necessary they brought ashore from the *Hispaniola* – others laden with pork, bread, and brandy for the midday meal. All the stores, I observed, came from our stock; and I could see the truth of Silver's words the night before. Had he not struck a bargain with the doctor, he and his mutineers, deserted by the ship, must have been driven to subsist on clear water and the proceeds of their hunting. Water would have been little to their taste; a sailor is not usually a good shot; and besides all that, when they were so short of eatables, it was not likely they would be very flush of powder.

Well, thus equipped, we all set out – even the fellow with the broken head, who should certainly have kept in shadow – and straggled, one after another, to the beach, where the two gigs awaited us. Even these bore trace of the drunken folly of the pirates, one in a broken thwart, and both in their muddied and unbaled condition. Both were to be carried along with us, for the sake of safety; and so, with our numbers divided between them, we set forth upon the bosom of the anchorage.

As we pulled over, there was some discussion on the chart. The red cross was, of course, far too large to be a guide; and the terms of the note on the back, as you will hear, admitted of some ambiguity. They ran, the reader may remember, thus:

Tall tree, Spy-glass Shoulder, bearing a point to the N. of N.N.E.
Skeleton Island E.S.E. and by E.
Ten feet.

A tall tree was thus the principal mark. Now, right before us, the anchorage was bounded by a plateau from two to three hundred feet high, adjoining on the north the sloping southern shoulder of the Spyglass, and rising again towards the south into the rough cliffy eminence called the Mizzen-mast Hill. The top of the plateau was dotted thickly with pine trees of varying heights. Every here and there, one of a different species rose forty or fifty feet clear above its neighbours, and which of these was the particular 'tall tree' of Captain Flint could only be decided on the spot, and by the readings of the compass.

Yet, although that was the case, every man on board the boats had picked a favourite of his own ere we were half-way over, Long John alone shrugging his shoulders and bidding them wait till they were there.

We pulled easily, by Silver's directions, not to weary the hands prematurely; and, after quite a long passage, landed at the mouth of the second river – that which runs down a woody cleft of the Spy-glass. Thence, bending to our left, we began to ascend the slope towards the plateau.

At the first outset, heavy, miry ground and a matted, marish vegetation greatly delayed our progress; but by little and little the hill began to steepen and become stony under foot, and the wood to change its character and to grow in a more open order. It was, indeed, a most pleasant portion of the island that we were now approaching. A heavy-scented broom and many flowering shrubs had almost taken the place of grass. Thickets of green nutmeg trees were dotted here and there with the red columns and the broad shadow of the pines; and the first mingled their spice with the aroma of the others. The air, besides, was fresh and stirring, and this, under the sheer sunbeams, was a wonderful refreshment to our senses.

The party spread itself abroad, in a fan shape, shouting and leaping to and fro. About the centre, and a good way behind the rest, Silver and I followed – I tethered by my rope, he ploughing, with deep pants, among the sliding gravel. From time to time, indeed, I had to lend him a hand, or he must have missed his footing and fallen backward down the hill.

We had thus proceeded for about half a mile, and were approaching the brow of the plateau, when the man upon the farthest left began to cry aloud, as if in terror. Shout after shout came from him, and the others began to run in his direction.

'He can't 'a' found the treasure,' said old Morgan, hurrying past us from the right, 'for that's clean a-top.'

Indeed, as we found when we also reached the spot, it was something very different. At the foot of a pretty big pine, and involved in a green creeper, which had even partly lifted some of the smaller bones, a human skeleton lay, with a few shreds of clothing, on the ground. I believe a chill struck for a moment to every heart.

'He was a seaman,' said George Merry, who, bolder than the rest, had gone up close, and was examining the rags of clothing. 'Leastways, this is good sea-cloth.'

'Ay, ay,' said Silver, 'like enough; you wouldn't look to find a bishop here, I reckon. But what sort of a way is that for bones to lie? 'Tain't in natur'.'

Indeed, on a second glance, it seemed impossible to fancy that the body was in a natural position. But for some disarray (the work, perhaps, of the birds that had fed upon him, or of the slow-growing creeper that had gradually enveloped his remains) the man lay perfectly straight – his feet pointing in one direction, his hands, raised above his head like a diver's, pointing directly in the opposite.

'I've taken a notion into my old numskull,' observed Silver. 'Here's the compass; there's the tip-top p'int o' Skeleton Island, stickin' out like a tooth. Just take a bearing, will you, along the line of them bones.'

It was done. The body pointed straight in the direction of the island, and the compass read duly E.S.E. and by E.

'I thought so,' cried the cook; 'this here is a p'inter. Right up there is our line for the Pole Star and the jolly dollars. But, by thunder! if it don't make me cold inside to think of Flint. This is one of *his* jokes, and no mistake. Him and these six was alone here; he killed 'em, every man; and this one he hauled here and laid down by compass, shiver my timbers! They're long bones, and the hair's been yellow. Ay, that would be Allardyce. You mind Allardyce, Tom Morgan?'

'Ay, ay,' returned Morgan, 'I mind him; he owed me money, he did, and took my knife ashore with him.'

'Speaking of knives,' said another, 'why don't we find his'n lying round? Flint warn't the man to pick a seaman's pocket; and the birds, I guess, would leave it be.'

'By the powers, and that's true!' cried Silver.

'There ain't a thing left here,' said Merry, still feeling round among the bones, 'not a copper doit nor a baccy-box. It don't look nat'ral to me.'

'No, by gum, it don't,' agreed Silver; 'not nat'ral, nor not nice, says you. Great guns! messmates, but if Flint was living, this would be a hot spot for you and me. Six they were, and six we are; and bones is what they are now.'

'I saw him dead with these here deadlights,' said Morgan. 'Billy took me in. There he laid, with penny-pieces on his eyes.'

'Dead – ay, sure enough he's dead and gone below,' said the fellow with the bandage; 'but if ever sperrit walked, it would be Flint's. Dear heart, but he died bad, did Flint!'

'Ay, that he did,' observed another; 'now he raged, and now he hollered for the rum, and now he sang. *Fifteen Men* were his only song, mates; and I tell you true, I never rightly liked to hear it since. It was main hot, and the windy was open, and I hear that old song comin' out as clear as clear — and the death-haul on the man already.'

'Come, come,' said Silver, 'stow this talk. He's dead, and he don't walk, that I know; leastways, he won't walk by day, and you may lay to that. Care killed a cat. Fetch ahead for the doubloons.'

We started, certainly; but in spite of the hot sun and the staring daylight, the pirates no longer ran separate and shouting through the wood, but kept side by side and spoke with bated breath. The terror of the dead buccaneer had fallen on their spirits.

5 The Treasure Hunt – the Voice Among the Trees

Partly from the damping influence of this alarm, partly to rest Silver and the sick folk, the whole party sat down as soon as they had gained the brow of the ascent.

The plateau being somewhat tilted towards the west, this spot on which we had paused commanded a wide prospect on either hand. Before us, over the tree-tops, we beheld the Cape of the Woods fringed with surf; behind, we not only looked down upon the anchorage and Skeleton Island, but saw – clear across the spit and the eastern lowlands – a great field of open sea upon the east. Sheer above us rose the Spy-glass, here dotted with single pines, there black with precipices. There was no sound but that of the distant breakers, mounting from all round, and the chirp of countless insects in the brush. Not a man, not a sail upon the sea; the very largeness of the view increased the sense of solitude.

Silver, as he sat, took certain bearings with his compass.

'There are three "tall trees," ' said he, 'about in the right line from Skeleton Island. "Spy-glass Shoulder," I take it, means that lower p'int there. It's child's play to find the stuff now. I've half a mind to dine first.'

'I don't feel sharp,' growled Morgan. 'Thinkin' o' Flint – I think it were – has done me.'

'Ah, well, my son, you praise your stars he's dead,' said Silver.

'He were an ugly devil,' cried a third pirate, with a shudder; 'that blue in the face, too!'

'That was how the rum took him,' added Merry. 'Blue! well, I reckon he was blue. That's a true word.'

Ever since they had found the skeleton and got upon this train of thought, they had spoken lower and lower, and they had almost got to whispering by now, so that the sound of their talk hardly interrupted the silence of the wood. All of a sudden, out of the middle of the trees in front of us, a thin, high, trembling voice struck up the well-known air and words:

> 'Fifteen men on the dead man's chest –
> Yo-ho-ho, and a bottle of rum!'

I never have seen men more dreadfully affected than the pirates. The colour went from their six faces like enchantment; some leaped to their feet, some clawed hold of others; Morgan grovelled on the ground.

'It's Flint, by ——!' cried Merry.

The song had stopped as suddenly as it began – broken off, you would have said, in the middle of a note, as though someone had laid his hand upon the singer's mouth. Coming so far through the clear, sunny atmosphere among the green tree-tops, I thought it had sounded airily and sweetly; and the effect on my companions was the stranger.

'Come,' said Silver, struggling with his ashen lips to get the word out, 'this won't do. Stand by to go about. This is a rum start, and I can't name the voice, but it's someone skylarking – someone that's flesh and blood, and you may lay to that.'

His courage had come back as he spoke, and some of the colour to his face along with it. Already the others had begun to lend an ear to this encouragement, and were coming a little to themselves, when the same voice broke out again – not this time singing, but in a faint distant hail, that echoed yet fainter among the clefts of the Spy-glass.

'Darby M'Graw,' it wailed – for that is the word that best describes the sound – 'Darby M'Graw! Darby M'Graw!' again and again and again; and then rising a little higher, and with an oath that I leave out: 'Fetch aft the rum, Darby!'

The buccaneers remained rooted to the ground, their eyes starting from their heads. Long after the voice had died away, they still stared in silence, dreadfully, before them.

'That fixes it!' gasped one. 'Let's go.'

'They was his last words,' moaned Morgan, 'his last words above board.'

Dick had his Bible out, and was praying volubly. He had been well brought up, had Dick, before he came to sea and fell among bad companions.

Still, Silver was unconquered. I could hear his teeth rattle in his head, but he had not yet surrendered.

'Nobody in this here island ever heard of Darby,' he muttered, 'not one but us that's here.' And then, making a great effort, 'Shipmates,' he cried, 'I'm here to get that stuff, and I'll not be beat by man nor devil. I never was feared of Flint in his life, and, by the powers, I'll face him dead. There's seven hundred thousand pound not a quarter of a mile from here. When did ever a gentleman o' fortune show his stern to that much dollars, for a boozy old seaman with a blue mug – and him dead, too?'

But there was no sign of reawakening courage in his followers; rather, indeed, of growing terror at the irreverence of his words.

'Belay there, John!' said Merry. 'Don't you cross a sperrit.'

And the rest were all too terrified to reply. They would have run away severally had they dared; but fear kept them together, and kept them close by John, as if his daring helped them. He, on his part, had pretty well fought his weakness down.

'Sperrit? Well, maybe,' he said. 'But there's one thing not clear to me. There was an echo. Now, no man ever seen a sperrit with a shadow; well, then, what's he doing with an echo to him, I should like to know? That ain't in natur', surely?'

This argument seemed weak enough to me. But you can never tell what will affect the superstitious, and, to my wonder, George Merry was greatly relieved.

'Well, that's so,' he said. 'You've a head upon your shoulders, John, and no mistake. 'Bout ship, mates! this here crew is on a wrong tack, I do believe. And come to think on it, it was like Flint's voice, I grant you, but not just so clear-away like it, after all. It was liker somebody else's voice, now – it was liker——'

'By the powers, Ben Gunn!' roared Silver.

'Ay, and so it were,' cried Morgan, springing on his knees. 'Ben Gunn it were!'

'It don't make much odds, do it, now?' asked Dick. 'Ben Gunn's not here in the body, any more'n Flint.'

But the older hands greeted this remark with scorn.

'Why, nobody minds Ben Gunn,' cried Merry; 'dead or alive, nobody minds him.'

It was extraordinary how their spirits had returned, and how the natural colour had revived in their faces. Soon they were chatting together, with intervals of listening; and not long after, hearing no further sound, they shouldered the tools and set forth again, Merry walking first with Silver's compass to keep them on the right line with Skeleton Island. He had said the truth: dead or alive, nobody minded Ben Gunn.

Dick alone still held his Bible, and looked around him as he went, with fearful glances; but he found no sympathy, and Silver even joked him on his precautions.

'I told you,' said he— 'I told you, you had sp'iled your Bible. If it ain't no good to swear by, what do you suppose a sperrit would give for it? Not that!' and he snapped his big fingers, halting a moment on his crutch.

But Dick was not to be comforted; indeed, it was soon plain to me that the lad was falling sick; hastened by heat, exhaustion, and the shock of his alarm, the fever, predicted by Dr. Livesey, was evidently growing swiftly higher.

It was fine open walking here, upon the summit; our way lay a little downhill, for, as I have said, the plateau tilted towards the west. The pines, great and small, grew wide apart: and even between the clumps of nutmeg and azalea, wide open spaces baked in the hot sunshine. Striking, as we did, pretty near north-west across the island, we drew, on the one hand, ever nearer under the shoulders of the Spy-glass, and on the other, looked ever wider over that western bay where I had once tossed and trembled in the coracle.

The first of the tall trees was reached, and, by the bearing, proved the wrong one. So with the second. The third rose nearly two hundred feet into the air above a clump of underwood; a giant of a vegetable, with a red column as big as a cottage, and a wide shadow around in which a company could have manœuvred. It was conspicuous far to sea both on the east and west, and might have been entered as a sailing mark upon the chart.

But it was not its size that now impressed my companions; it was the knowledge that seven hundred thousand pounds in gold lay somewhere buried below its spreading shadow. The thought of the money, as they drew nearer, swallowed up their previous terrors. Their eyes burned in their heads; their feet grew speedier and lighter; their whole soul was bound up in that fortune, that whole lifetime of extravagance and pleasure, that lay waiting there for each of them.

Silver hobbled, grunting, on his crutch; his nostrils stood out and quivered; he cursed like a madman when the flies settled on his hot and shiny countenance; he plucked furiously at the line that held me to him, and, from time to time, turned his eyes upon me with a deadly look. Certainly he took no pains to hide his thoughts; and certainly I read them like print. In the immediate nearness of the gold, all else had been forgotten; his promise and the doctor's warning were both things of the past; and I could not doubt that he hoped to seize upon the treasure, find and board the *Hispaniola* under cover of night, cut every honest throat about that island, and sail away as he had at first intended, laden with crimes and riches.

Shaken as I was with these alarms, it was hard for me to keep up with the rapid pace of the treasure-hunters. Now and again I stumbled; and it was then that Silver plucked so roughly at the rope and launched at me his murderous glances. Dick, who had dropped behind us, and now brought up the rear, was babbling to himself both prayers and curses, as his fever kept rising. This also added to my wretchedness, and, to crown all, I was haunted by the thought of the tragedy that had once been acted on that plateau, when that ungodly buccaneer with the blue face – he who died at Savannah, singing and shouting for drink – had there, with his own hand, cut down his six accomplices. This grove, that was now so peaceful, must then have rung with cries, I thought; and even with the thought I could believe I heard it ringing still.

We were now at the margin of the thicket.

'Huzza, mates, all together!' shouted Merry; and the foremost broke into a run.

And suddenly, not ten yards further, we beheld them stop. A low cry arose. Silver doubled his pace, digging away with the foot of his crutch like one possessed; and next moment he and I had come also to a dead halt.

Before us was a great excavation, not very recent, for the sides had fallen in and grass had sprouted on the bottom. In this were the shaft of a pick broken in two and the boards of several packing-cases strewn around. On one of these boards I saw, branded with a hot iron, the name *Walrus* – the name of Flint's ship.

All was clear to probation. The cache had been found and rifled; the seven hundred thousand pounds were gone!

6 The Fall of a Chieftain

There never was such an overturn in this world. Each of these six men was as though he had been struck. But with Silver the blow passed almost instantly. Every thought of his soul had been set full-stretch, like a racer, on that money; well, he was brought up in a single second, dead; and he kept his head, found his temper, and changed his plan before the others had had time to realize the disappointment.

'Jim,' he whispered, 'take that, and stand by for trouble.'

And he passed me a double-barrelled pistol.

At the same time he began quietly moving northward, and in a few steps had put the hollow between us two and the other five. Then he looked at me and nodded, as much as to say, 'Here is a narrow corner,' as, indeed, I thought it was. His looks were now quite friendly; and I was so revolted at these constant changes, that I could not forbear whispering: 'So you've changed sides again.'

There was no time left for him to answer in. The buccaneers, with oaths and cries, began to leap, one after another, into the pit, and to dig with their fingers, throwing the boards aside as they did so. Morgan found a piece of gold. He held it up with a perfect spout of oaths. It was a two-guinea piece, and it went from hand to hand among them for a quarter of a minute.

'Two guineas!' roared Merry, shaking it at Silver. 'That's your seven hundred thousand pounds, is it? You're the man for bargains, ain't you? You're him that never bungled nothing, you wooden-headed lubber!'

'Dig away, boys,' said Silver, with the coolest insolence; 'you'll find some pig-nuts and I shouldn't wonder.'

'Pig-nuts!' repeated Merry, in a scream. 'Mates, do you hear that? I tell you, now, that man there knew it all along. Look in the face of him, and you'll see it wrote there.'

'Ah, Merry,' remarked Silver, 'standing for cap'n again? You're a

'Silver never moved; he watched them, upright'

pushing lad, to be sure.'

But this time every one was entirely in Merry's favour. They began to scramble out of the excavation, darting furious glances behind them. One thing I observed, which looked well for us: they all got out upon the opposite side from Silver.

Well, there we stood, two on one side, five on the other, the pit between us, and nobody screwed up high enough to offer the first blow. Silver never moved; he watched them, very upright on his crutch, and looked as cool as ever I saw him. He was brave, and no mistake.

At last, Merry seemed to think a speech might help matters.

'Mates,' says he, 'there's two of them alone there; one's the old cripple that brought us all here and blundered us down to this; the other's that cub that I mean to have the heart of. Now, mates——'

He was raising his arm and his voice, and plainly meant to lead a charge. But just then – crack! crack! crack! – three musket shots flashed out of the thicket. Merry tumbled head foremost into the excavation; the man with the bandage spun round like a teetotum, and fell all his length upon his side, where he lay, dead but still twitching; and the other three turned and ran for it with all their might.

Before you could wink, Long John had fired two barrels of a pistol into the struggling Merry; and as the man rolled up his eyes at him in the last agony, 'George,' said he, 'I reckon I settled you.'

At the same moment the doctor, Gray, and Ben Gunn joined us, with smoking muskets, from among the nutmeg trees.

'Forward!' cried the doctor. 'Double quick, my lads. We must head 'em off the boats.'

And we set off, at a great pace, sometimes plunging through the bushes to the chest.

I tell you, but Silver was anxious to keep up with us. The work that man went through, leaping on his crutch till the muscles of his chest were fit to burst, was work no sound man ever equalled; and so thinks the doctor. As it was, he was already thirty yards behind us, and on the verge of strangling, when we reached the brow of the slope.

'Doctor,' he hailed, 'see there! no hurry!'

Sure enough there was no hurry. In a more open part of the plateau, we could see the three survivors still running in the same direction as they had started, right for Mizzen-mast Hill. We were already between them and the boats; and so we four sat down to breathe, while Long John, mopping his face, came slowly up with us.

'Thank ye kindly, doctor,' says he. 'You came in in about the nick, I guess, for me and Hawkins. And so it's you, Ben Gunn!' he added. 'Well, you're a nice one, to be sure.'

'I'm Ben Gunn, I am,' replied the maroon, wriggling like an eel in his embarrassment. 'And,' he added, after a long pause, 'how do, Mr. Silver? Pretty well, I thank ye, says you.'

'Ben, Ben,' murmured Silver, 'to think as you've done me!'

The doctor sent back Gray for one of the pickaxes, deserted, in their flight, by the mutineers; and then as we proceeded leisurely downhill to where the boats were lying, related, in a few words, what had taken place. It was a story that profoundly interested Silver; and Ben Gunn, the half-idiot maroon, was the hero from beginning to end.

Ben, in his long, lonely wanderings about the island, had found the skeleton – it was he that had rifled it; he had found the treasure; he had dug it up (it was the shaft of his pickaxe that lay broken in the excavation); he had carried it on his back, in many weary journeys, from the foot of the tall pine to a cave he had on the two-pointed hill at the north-east angle of the island, and there it had lain stored in safety since two months before the arrival of the *Hispaniola*.

When the doctor had wormed this secret from him, on the afternoon of the attack, and when, next morning, he saw the anchorage deserted, he had gone to Silver, given him the chart, which was now useless – given him the stores, for Ben Gunn's cave was well supplied with goats' meat salted by himself – given anything and everything to get a chance of moving in safety from the stockade to the two-pointed hill, there to be clear of malaria and keep a guard upon the money.

'As for you, Jim,' he said, 'it went against my heart, but I did what I thought best for those who had stood by their duty; and if you were not one of these, whose fault was it?'

That morning, finding that I was to be involved in the horrid disappointment he had prepared for the mutineers, he had run all the way to the cave, and, leaving squire to guard the captain, had taken Gray and the maroon, and started, making the diagonal across the island, to be at hand beside the pine. Soon, however, he saw that our party had the start of him; and Ben Gunn, being fleet of foot, had been dispatched in front to do his best alone. Then it had occurred to him to work upon the superstitions of his former shipmates; and he was so far successful that Gray and the doctor had come up and were already ambushed before the arrival of the treasure-hunters.

'Ah,' said Silver, 'it were fortunate for me that I had Hawkins here. You would have let old John be cut to bits, and never given it a thought, doctor.'

'Not a thought,' replied Dr. Livesey, cheerily.

And by this time we had reached the gigs. The doctor, with the pickaxe, demolished one of them, and then we all got aboard the other and set out to go round by sea for North Inlet.

This was a run of eight or nine miles. Silver, though he was almost killed already with fatigue, was set to an oar, like the rest of us, and we were soon skimming swiftly over a smooth sea. Soon we passed out of the straits and doubled the south-east corner of the island, round which, four days ago, we had towed the *Hispaniola*.

As we passed the two-pointed hill, we could see the black mouth of Ben Gunn's cave, and a figure standing by it, leaning on a musket. It was the squire; and we waved a handkerchief and gave him three cheers, in which the voice of Silver joined as heartily as any.

Three miles further, just inside the mouth of North Inlet, what should we meet but the *Hispaniola*, cruising by herself? The last flood had lifted her; and had there been much wind, or a strong tide current, as in the southern anchorage, we should never have found her more, or found her stranded beyond help. As it was, there was little amiss, beyond the wreck of the main-sail. Another anchor was got ready, and dropped in a fathom and a half of water. We all pulled round again to Rum Cove, the nearest point for Ben Gunn's treasure house; and then Gray, single-handed, returned with the gig to the *Hispaniola*, where he was to pass the night on guard.

A gentle slope ran up from the beach to the entrance of the cave. At the top, the squire met us. To me he was cordial and kind, saying nothing of my escapade, either in the way of blame or praise. At Silver's polite salute he somewhat flushed.

'John Silver,' he said, 'you're a prodigious villain and impostor – a monstrous impostor, sir. I am told I am not to prosecute you. Well, then, I will not. But the dead men, sir, hang about your neck like mill-stones.'

'Thank you kindly, sir,' replied Long John, again saluting.

'I dare you to thank me!' cried the squire. 'It is a gross dereliction of my duty. Stand back!'

And thereupon we all entered the cave. It was a large airy place, with a little spring and a pool of clear water, overhung with ferns. The floor was sand. Before a big fire lay Captain Smollett; and in a far corner, only duskily flickered over by the blaze, I beheld great heaps of coin and quadrilaterals built of bars of gold. That was Flint's treasure that we had come so far to seek, and that had cost already the lives of seventeen men from the *Hispaniola*. How many it had cost in the amassing, what blood and sorrow, what good ships scuttled on the deep, what brave men walking the plank blindfold, what shot of cannon, what shame and lies and cruelty, perhaps no man alive could tell. Yet there were still three upon that island – Silver, and old Morgan, and Ben Gunn – who had each taken his share in these crimes, as each had hoped in vain to share in the reward.

'Come in, Jim,' said the captain. 'You're a good boy in your line, Jim; but I don't think you and me'll go to sea again. You're too much of the born favourite for me. Is that you, John Silver? What brings you here, man?'

'Come back to my dooty, sir,' returned Silver.

'Ah!' said the captain; and that was all he said.

What a supper I had of it that night, with all my friends around me; and what a meal it was, with Ben Gunn's salted goat, and some delicacies and a bottle of old wine from the *Hispaniola*. Never, I am sure, were people gayer or happier. And there was Silver, sitting back almost out of the firelight, but eating heartily, prompt to spring forward when anything was wanted, even joining quietly in our laughter – the same bland, polite, obsequious seaman of the voyage out.

7 And Last

The next morning we fell early to work, for the transportation of this great mass of gold near a mile by land to the beach, and thence three miles by boat to the *Hispaniola*, was a considerable task for so small a number of workmen. The three fellows still abroad upon the island did not greatly trouble us; a single sentry on the shoulder of the hill was sufficient to ensure us against any sudden onslaught, and we thought, besides, they had had more than enough of fighting.

Therefore the work was pushed on briskly. Gray and Ben Gunn came and went with the boat, while the rest, during their absences, piled treasure on the beach. Two of the bars, slung in a rope's-end, made a good load for a grown man – one that he was glad to walk slowly with. For my part, as I was not much use at carrying, I was kept busy all day in the cave, packing the minted money into bread-bags.

It was a strange collection, like Billy Bones's hoard for the diversity of coinage, but so much larger and so much more varied that I think I never had more pleasure than in sorting them. English, French, Spanish, Portuguese, Georges and Louises, doubloons and double guineas and moidores and sequins, the pictures of all the kings of Europe for the last hundred years, strange Oriental pieces stamped with what looked like wisps of string or bits of spider's web, round pieces and square pieces, and pieces bored through the middle, as if to wear them round your neck – nearly every variety of money in the world must, I think, have found a place in that collection; and for number, I am sure they were like autumn leaves, so that my back ached with stooping and my fingers with sorting them out.

Day after day this work went on; by every evening a fortune had been stowed aboard, but there was another fortune waiting for the morrow; and all this time we heard nothing of the three surviving mutineers.

At last – I think it was on the third night – the doctor and I were

strolling on the shoulder of the hill where it overlooks the lowlands of
the isle, when, from out the thick darkness below, the wind brought us
a noise between shrieking and singing. It was only a snatch that
reached our ears, followed by the former silence. 'Heaven forgive
them,' said the doctor; ' 'tis the mutineers!'

'All drunk, sir,' struck in the voice of Silver from behind us.

Silver, I should say, was allowed his entire liberty, and, in spite of
daily rebuffs, seemed to regard himself once more as quite a privileged
and friendly dependant. Indeed, it was remarkable how well he bore
these slights, and with what unwearying politeness he kept on trying to
ingratiate himself with all. Yet, I think, none treated him better than a
dog; unless it was Ben Gunn, who was still terribly afraid of his old
quartermaster, or myself, who had really something to thank him for;
although for that matter, I suppose, I had reason to think even worse of
him than anybody else, for I had seen him meditating a fresh treachery
upon the plateau. Accordingly, it was pretty gruffly that the doctor
answered him.

'Drunk or raving,' said he.

'Right you were, sir,' replied Silver; 'and precious little odds
which, to you and me.'

'I suppose you would hardly ask me to call you a humane man,'
returned the doctor with a sneer, 'and so my feelings may surprise you,
Master Silver. But if I were sure they were raving – as I am morally
certain one, at least, of them is down with fever – I should leave this
camp, and, at whatever risk to my own carcass, take them the
assistance of my skill.'

'Ask your pardon, sir, you would be very wrong,' quoth Silver.
'You would lose your precious life, and you may lay to that. I'm on
your side now, hand and glove; and I shouldn't wish for to see the
party weakened, let alone yourself, seeing as I know what I owes you.
But these men down there, they couldn't keep their word – no, not
supposing they wished to; and what's more, they couldn't believe as
you could.'

'No,' said the doctor. 'You're the man to keep your word, we know
that.'

Well, that was about the last news we had of the three pirates.
Only once we heard a gunshot a great way off, and supposed them to be
hunting. A council was held, and it was decided that we must desert
them on the island – to the huge glee, I must say, of Ben Gunn, and

with the strong approval of Gray. We left a good stock of powder and shot, the bulk of the salt goat, a few medicines, and some other necessaries, tools, clothing, a spare sail, a fathom or two of rope, and, by the particular desire of the doctor, a handsome present of tobacco.

That was about our last doing on the island. Before that, we had got the treasure stowed, and had shipped enough water and the remainder of the goat meat, in case of any distress; and at last, one fine morning, we weighed anchor, which was about all that we could manage, and stood out of North Inlet; the same colours flying that the captain had flown and fought under at the palisade.

The three fellows must have been watching us closer than we thought for, as we soon had proved. For, coming through the narrows, we had to lie very near the southern point, and there we saw all three of them kneeling together on a spit of sand, with their arms raised in supplication. It went to all our hearts, I think, to leave them in that wretched state; but we could not risk another mutiny; and to take them home for the gibbet would have been a cruel sort of kindness. The doctor hailed them and told them of the stores we had left, and where they were to find them. But they continued to call us by name, and appeal to us, for God's sake, to be merciful, and not leave them to die in such a place.

At last, seeing the ship still bore on her course, and was now swiftly drawing out of earshot, one of them – I know not which it was – leapt to his feet with a hoarse cry, whipped his musket to his shoulder, and sent a shot whistling over Silver's head and through the main-sail.

After that, we kept under cover of the bulwarks, and when next I looked out they had disappeared from the spit, and the spit itself had almost melted out of sight in the growing distance. That was, at least, the end of that; and before noon, to my inexpressible joy, the highest rock of Treasure Island had sunk into the blue round of sea.

We were so short of men that every one on board had to bear a hand – only the captain lying on a mattress in the stern and giving his orders; for, though greatly recovered, he was still in want of quiet. We laid her head for the nearest port in Spanish America, for we could not risk the voyage home without fresh hands; and as it was, what with baffling winds and a couple of fresh gales, we were all worn out before we reached it.

It was just at sundown when we cast anchor in a most beautiful land-locked gulf, and were immediately surrounded by shore boats full of Negroes, and Mexican Indians, and half-bloods, selling fruits and vegetables, and offering to dive for bits of money. The sight of so many good-humoured faces (especially the blacks), the taste of the tropical fruits, and above all, the lights that began to shine in the town, made a most charming contrast to our dark and bloody sojourn on the island; and the doctor and the squire, taking me along with them, went ashore to pass the early part of the night. Here they met the captain of an English man-of-war, fell in talk with him, went on board his ship, and, in short, had so agreeable a time, that day was breaking when we came alongside the *Hispaniola*.

Ben Gunn was on deck alone, and, as soon as we came on board, he began, with wonderful contortions, to make us a confession. Silver was gone. The maroon had connived at his escape in a shore boat some hours ago, and he now assured us he had only done so to preserve our lives, which would certainly have been forfeit if 'that man with the one leg had stayed aboard.' But this was not all. The sea-cook had not gone empty-handed. He had cut through a bulkhead unobserved, and had removed one of the sacks of coin, worth, perhaps, three or four hundred guineas, to help him on his further wanderings.

I think we were all pleased to be so cheaply quit of him.

Well, to make a long story short, we got a few hands on board, made a good cruise home, and the *Hispaniola* reached Bristol just as Mr. Blandly was beginning to think of fitting out her consort. Five men only of those who had sailed returned with her. 'Drink and the devil had done for the rest,' with a vengeance; although, to be sure, we were not quite in so bad a case as that other ship they sang about:

'With one man of her crew alive,
What put to sea with seventy-five.'

All of us had an ample share of the treasure, and used it wisely or foolishly, according to our natures. Captain Smollett is now retired from the sea. Gray not only saved his money, but, being suddenly smit with a desire to rise, also studied his profession; and he is now mate and part owner of a fine full-rigged ship; married besides, and the father of a family. As for Ben Gunn, he got a thousand pounds, which he spent or lost in three weeks, or, to be more exact, in nineteen days, for he was back begging on the twentieth. Then he was given a lodge to keep, exactly as he had feared upon the island; and he still lives, a great favourite, though something of a butt, with the country boys, and a notable singer in church on Sundays and saints' days.

Of Silver we have heard no more. That formidable seafaring man with one leg has at last gone clean out of my life; but I dare say he met his old Negress, and perhaps still lives in comfort with her and Captain Flint. It is to be hoped so, I suppose, for his chances of comfort in another world are very small.

The bar silver and the arms still lie, for all that I know, where Flint buried them; and certainly they shall lie there for me. Oxen and wain-ropes would not bring me back again to that accursed island; and the worst dreams that ever I have are when I hear the surf booming about its coasts, or start upright in bed, with the sharp voice of Captain Flint still ringing in my ears: 'Pieces of eight! pieces of eight!'

KIDNAPPED

KIDNAPPED

being the memoirs of David Balfour

in the year 1751

How he was Kidnapped and Cast away; his sufferings
in a Desert Isle; his journey in the Wild Highlands; his
Aquaintance with Alan Breck Stewart and other
notorious Highland Jacobites; with all that he suffered
at the hands of his Uncle, EBENEZER BALFOUR OF
SHAWS, falsely so-called: Written by Himself, and
now set forth.

R. L. Stevenson

Contents

List of Illustrations

Dedication

My Dear Charles Baxter,

If you ever read this tale, you will likely ask yourself more questions than I should care to answer: as for instance how the Appin murder has come to fall in the year 1751, how the Torran rocks have crept so near to Earraid, or why the printed trial is silent as to all that touches David Balfour. These are nuts beyond my ability to crack. But if you tried me on the point of Alan's guilt or innocence, I think I could defend the reading of the text. To this day you will find the tradition of Appin clear in Alan's favour. If you inquire, you may even hear that the descendants of "the other man" who fired the shot are in the country to this day. But that other man's name, inquire as you please, you shall not hear; for the Highlander values a secret for itself and for the congenial exercise of keeping it. I might go on for long to justify one point and own another indefensible; it is more honest to confess at once how little I am touched by the desire of accuracy. This is no furniture for the scholar's library, but a book for the winter evening school-room when the tasks are over and the hour for bed draws near; and honest Alan, who was a grim old fire-eater in his day, has in this new avatar no more desperate purpose than to steal some young gentleman's attention from his Ovid, carry him awhile into the Highlands and the last century, and pack him to bed with some engaging images to mingle with his dreams.

As for you, my dear Charles, I do not even ask you to like the tale. But perhaps when he is older, your son will; he may then be pleased to find his father's name on the fly-leaf; and in the meanwhile it pleases me to set it there, in memory of many days that were happy and some (now perhaps as pleasant to remember) that were sad. If it is strange for me to look back from a distance both in time and space on these bygone adventures of our youth, it must be stranger for you who tread the same streets – who may to-morrow open the door of the old Speculative, where we begin to rank with Scott and Robert Emmet and the beloved and inglorious Macbean – or may pass the corner of the close where that great society, the L. J. R., held its meetings and drank its beer, sitting in the seats of Burns and his companions. I think I see you, moving there by plain daylight, beholding with your natural eyes those places that have now become for your companion a part of the scenery of dreams. How, in the intervals of present business, the past must echo in your memory! Let it not echo often without some kind thoughts of your friend.

R. L. S.

Skerryvore, Bournemouth.

1   I set off upon my Journey to the House of Shaws

I will begin the story of my adventures with a certain morning early in the month of June, the year of grace 1751, when I took the key for the last time out of the door of my father's house. The sun began to shine upon the summit of the hills as I went down the road; and by the time I had come as far as the manse, the blackbirds were whistling in the garden lilacs, and the mist that hung around the valley in the time of the dawn was beginning to arise and die away.

Mr. Campbell, the minister of Essendean, was waiting for me by the garden gate, good man! He asked me if I had breakfasted; and hearing that I lacked for nothing, he took my hand in both of his and clapped it kindly under his arm.

'Well, Davie, lad,' said he, 'I will go with you as far as the ford, to set you on the way.'

And we began to walk forward in silence.

'Are ye sorry to leave Essendean?' said he, after a while.

'Why, sir,' said I, 'if I knew where I was going, or what was likely to become of me, I would tell you candidly. Essendean is a good place indeed, and I have been very happy there; but then I have never been anywhere else. My father and mother, since they are both dead, I shall be no nearer to in Essendean than in the Kingdom of Hungary; and, to speak truth, if I thought I had a chance to better myself where I was going, I would go with a good will.'

'Ay?' said Mr. Campbell. 'Very well, Davie. Then it behoves me to tell your fortune; or so far as I may. When your mother was gone, and your father (the worthy, Christian man) began to sicken for his end, he gave me in charge a certain letter, which he said was your inheritance. "So soon," says he, "as I am gone, and the house is redd up and the gear disposed of" (all which, Davie, hath been done), "give my boy this letter into his hand, and start him off to the house of Shaws, not far from Cramond. That is the place I came from," he said, "and it's where it befits that my boy should return. He is a steady lad," your father said, "and a canny goer; and I doubt not he will come safe, and be well liked where he goes." '

'The house of Shaws!' I cried. 'What had my poor father to do with the house of Shaws?'

'Nay,' said Mr. Campbell, 'who can tell that for surety? But the name of that family, Davie boy, is the name you bear – Balfours of Shaws: an ancient, honest, reputable house, peradventure in these latter days decayed. Your father, too, was a man of learning as befitted his position; no man more plausibly conducted school; nor had he the manner or the speech of a common dominie; but (as ye will yourself remember) I took aye a pleasure to have him to the manse to meet the gentry; and those of my own house, Campbell of Kilrennet, Campbell of Dunswire, Campbell of Minch, and others, all well-kenned gentlemen, had pleasure in his society. Lastly, to put all the elements of this affair before you, here is the testamentary letter itself, superscrived by the own hand of our departed brother.'

He gave me the letter, which was addressed in these words: 'To the hands of Ebenezer Balfour, Esq., of Shaws, in his house of Shaws, these will be delivered by my son, David Balfour.' My heart was beating hard at this great prospect now suddenly opening before a lad of sixteen years of age, the son of a poor country dominie in the Forest of Ettrick.

'Mr. Campbell,' I stammered, 'and if you were in my shoes, would you go?'

'Of a surety,' said the minister, 'that would I, and without pause. A pretty lad like you should get to Cramond (which is near in by Edinburgh) in two days of walk. If the worst came to the worst, and your high relations (as I cannot but suppose them to be somewhat of your blood) should put you to the door, ye can but walk the two days back again and risp at the manse door. But I would rather hope that ye shall be well received, as your poor father forecast for you, and for anything that I ken, come to be a great man in time. And here, Davie, laddie', he resumed, 'it lies near upon my conscience to improve this parting, and set you on the right guard against the dangers of the world.'

Here he cast about for a comfortable seat, lighted on a big boulder under a birch by the trackside, sate down upon it with a very long, serious upper lip, and, the sun now shining in upon us between two peaks, put his pocket-handkerchief over his cocked hat to shelter him. There, then, with uplifted forefinger, he first put me on my guard against a considerable number of heresies, to which I had no temptation, and urged upon me to be instant in my prayers and reading of the Bible. That done, he drew a picture of the great house that I was bound to, and how I should conduct myself with its inhabitants.

'Be soople, Davie, in things immaterial,' said he. 'Bear ye this in mind, that, though gentle born, ye have had a country rearing. Dinnae shame us, Davie, dinnae shame us! In yon great, muckle house, with all these domestics, upper and under, show yourself as nice, as circumspect, as quick at the conception, and as slow of speech as any. As for the laird – remember he's the laird; I say no more: honour to whom honour. It's a pleasure to obey a laird; or should be, to the young.'

'Well, sir,' said I, 'it may be; and I'll promise you I'll try to make it so.'

'Why, very well said,' replied Mr. Campbell heartily. 'And now to come to the material, or (to make a quibble) to the immaterial. I have here a little packet which contains four things.' He tugged it, as he spoke, and with some difficulty, from the skirt pocket of his coat. 'Of these four things, the first is your legal due: the little pickle money for your father's books and plenishing, which I have bought (as I have explained from the first) in the design of re-selling at a profit to the incoming dominie. The other three are gifties that Mrs. Campbell and myself would be blithe of your acceptance. The first, which is round, will likely please ye best at the first off-go; but, O Davie, laddie, it's but a drop of water in the sea; it'll help you but a step, and vanish like the morning. The second, which is flat and square and written upon, will stand by you through life, like a good staff for the road, and a good pillow to your head in sickness. And as for the last, which is cubical, that'll see you, it's my prayerful wish, into a better land.'

With that he got upon his feet, took off his hat, and prayed a little while aloud, and in affecting terms, for a young man setting out into the world; then suddenly took me in his arms and embraced me very hard; then held me at arm's length, looking at me with his face all working with sorrow; and then whipped about, and crying goodbye to me, set off backward by the way that we had come at a sort of jogging run. It might have been laughable to another; but I was in no mind to laugh. I watched him as long as he was in sight; and he never stopped hurrying, nor once looked back. Then it came in upon my mind that this was all his sorrow at my departure; and my conscience smote me hard and fast, because I, for my part, was overjoyed to get away out of that quiet countryside, and go to a great, busy house, among rich and respected gentlefolk of my own name and blood.

'Davie, Davie,' I thought, 'was ever seen such black ingratitude? Can you forget old favours and old friends at the mere whistle of a name? Fie, fie; think shame!

And I sat down on the boulder the good man had just left, and opened the parcel to see the nature of my gifts. That which he had called cubical, I had never had much doubt of; sure enough it was a little Bible, to carry in a plaid-neuk. That which he had called round, I found to be a shilling piece; and the third, which was to help me so wonderfully both in health and sickness all the days of my life, was a little piece of coarse yellow paper, written upon thus in red ink:

TO MAKE LILLY OF THE VALLEY WATER. Take the flowers of lilly of the valley and distil them in sack, and drink a spoonful or two as there is occasion. It restores speech to those that have the dumb palsey. It is good against the Gout; it comforts the heart and strengthens the memory; and the flowers, put into a Glasse close stopt, and set into ane hill of ants for a month, then take it out, and you will find a liquor which comes from the flowers, which keep in a vial; it is good, ill or well, and whether man or woman.

And then, in the minister's own hand, was added:

Likewise for sprains, rub it in; and for the cholic, a great spoonful in the hour.

To be sure, I laughed over this; but it was rather tremulous laughter; and I was glad to get my bundle on my staff's end and set out over the ford and up the hill upon the farther side; till, just as I came on the green drove-road running wide through the heather, I took my last look of Kirk Essendean, the trees about the manse and the big rowans in the kirkyard where my father and my mother lay.

2 I come to my Journey's End

On the forenoon of the second day, coming to the top of a hill, I saw all the country fall away before me down to the sea; and in the midst of this descent, on a long ridge, the city of Edinburgh smoking like a kiln. There was a flag upon the castle, and ships moving or lying anchored in the firth; both of which, for as far away as they were, I could distinguish clearly; and both brought my country heart into my mouth.

Presently after, I came by a house where a shepherd lived, and got a rough direction for the neighbourhood of Cramond; and so, from one to another, worked my way to the westward of the capital by Colinton, till I came out upon the Glasgow road. And there, to my great pleasure and wonder, I beheld a regiment marching to the fifes, every foot in time; an old red-faced general on a grey horse at the one end, and at the other the company of Grenadiers, with their Pope's-hats. The pride of life seemed to mount into my brain at the sight of the red coats and the hearing of that merry music.

A little farther on, and I was told I was in Cramond parish, and began to substitute in my inquiries the name of the house of Shaws. It was a word that seemed to surprise those of whom I sought my way. At first I thought the plainness of my appearance, in my country habit, and that all dusty from the road, consorted ill with the greatness of the place to which I was bound. But after two, or maybe three, had given me the same look and the same answer, I began to take it in my head there was something strange about the Shaws itself.

The better to set this fear at rest, I changed the form of my inquiries; and spying an honest fellow coming along a lane on the shaft of his cart, I asked him if he had ever heard tell of a house they called the house of Shaws.

He stopped his cart and looked at me, like the others.

'Ay,' said he. 'What for?'

'It's a great house?' I asked.

'Doubtless,' says he. 'The house is a big, muckle house.'

'Ay,' said I, 'but the folk that are in it?'

'Folk?' cried he. 'Are ye daft? There's nae folk there – to call folk.'

'What?' says I; 'not Mr. Ebenezer?'

'Ou, ay,' says the man; 'there's the laird, to be sure, if it's him you're wanting. What'll like be your business, mannie?'

'I was led to think that I would get a situation,' I said, looking as modest as I could.

'What?' cries the carter, in so sharp a note that his very horse started; and then, 'Well, mannie,' he added, 'it's nane of my affairs; but ye seem a decent-spoken lad; and if ye'll take a word from me, ye'll keep clear of the Shaws.'

The next person I came across was a dapper little man in a beautiful white wig, whom I saw to be a barber on his rounds; and knowing well that barbers were great gossips, I asked him plainly what sort of a man was Mr. Balfour of the Shaws.

'Hoot, hoot, hoot,' said the barber, 'nae kind of a man, nae kind of a man at all'; and began to ask me very shrewdly what my business was; but I was more than a match for him at that, and he went on to his next customer no wiser than he came.

I cannot well describe the blow this dealt to my illusions. The more indistinct the accusations were, the less I liked them, for they left the wider field to fancy. What kind of a great house was this, that all the parish should start and stare to be asked the way to it? or what sort of a gentleman, that his ill fame should be thus current on the wayside? If an hour's walking would have brought me back to Essendean, I had left my adventure then and there, and returned to Mr. Campbell's. But when I had come so far a way already, mere shame would not suffer me to desist till I had put the matter to the touch of proof; I was bound, out of mere self-respect, to carry it through; and little as I liked the sound of what I heard, and slow as I began to travel, I still kept asking my way and still kept advancing.

It was drawing on to sundown when I met a stout, dark, sour-looking woman coming trudging down a hill; and she, when I had put my usual question, turned sharp about, accompanied me back to the summit she had just left, and pointed to a great bulk of building standing very bare upon a green in the bottom of the next valley. The country was pleasant round about, running in low hills, pleasantly watered and wooded, and the crops, to my eyes, wonderfully good; but the house itself appeared to be a kind of ruin; no road led up to it; no smoke arose from any of the chimneys; nor was there any semblance of a garden. My heart sank. 'That!' I cried.

The woman's face lit up with a malignant anger. 'That is the house of Shaws!' she cried. 'Blood built it; blood stopped the building of it; blood shall bring it down. See here!' she cried again – 'I spit upon the ground, and crack my thumb at it! Black be its fall! If ye see the laird, tell him what ye hear; tell him this makes the twelve hunner and nineteen time that Jennet Clouston has called down the curse on him and his house, byre and stable, man, guest, and master, wife, miss, or bairn – black, black be their fall!'

And the woman, whose voice had risen to a kind of eldritch sing-song, turned with a skip, and was gone. I stood where she left me, with my hair on end. In those days folk still believed in witches and trembled at a curse; and this one, falling so pat, like a wayside omen, to arrest me ere I carried out my purpose, took the pith out of my legs.

I sat me down and stared at the house of Shaws. The more I looked, the pleasanter that countryside appeared; being all set with hawthorn bushes full of flowers; the fields dotted with sheep; a fine flight of rooks in the sky; and every sign of a kind soil and climate; and yet the barrack in the midst of it went sore against my fancy.

Country folk went by from the fields as I sat there on the side of the ditch, but I lacked the spirit to give them a goode'en. At last the sun went down, and then, right up against the yellow sky, I saw a scroll of smoke go mounting, not much thicker, as it seemed to me, than the smoke of a candle; but still there it was, and meant a fire, and warmth, and cookery, and some living inhabitant that must have lit it; and this comforted my heart wonderfully – more, I feel sure, than a whole flask of the lily of the valley water that Mrs. Campbell set so great a store by.

So I set forward by a little faint track in the grass that led in my direction. It was very faint indeed to be the only way to a place of habitation; yet I saw no other. Presently it brought me to stone uprights, with an unroofed lodge beside them, and coats of arms upon the top. A main entrance it was plainly meant to be, but never finished; instead of gates of wrought iron, a pair of hurdles were tied across with a straw rope; and as there were no park walls nor any sign of avenue, the track that I was following passed on the right hand of the pillars, and went wandering on toward the house.

'"It's loaded," said a voice'

The nearer I got to that, the drearier it appeared. It seemed like the one wing of a house that had never been finished. What should have been the inner end stood open on the upper floors, and showed against the sky with steps and stairs of uncompleted masonry. Many of the windows were unglazed, and bats flew in and out like doves out of a dovecote.

The night had begun to fall as I got close; and in three of the lower windows, which were very high up and narrow, and well barred, the changing light of a little fire began to glimmer.

Was this the palace I had been coming to? Was it within these walls that I was to seek new friends and begin great fortunes? Why, in my father's house on Essen-Waterside, the fire and the bright lights would show a mile away, and the door open to a beggar's knock!

I came forward cautiously, and giving ear as I came, heard someone rattling with dishes, and a little dry, eager cough that came in fits; but there was no sound of speech, and not a dog barked.

The door, as well as I could see it in the dim light, was a great piece of wood all studded with nails; and I lifted my hand with a faint heart under my jacket, and knocked once. Then I stood and waited. The house had fallen into a dead silence; a whole minute passed away, and nothing stirred but the bats overhead. I knocked again, and hearkened again. By this time my ears had grown so accustomed to the quiet, that I could hear the ticking of the clock inside as it slowly counted out the seconds; but whoever was in that house kept deadly still, and must have held his breath.

I was in two minds whether to run away; but anger got the upper hand, and I began instead to rain kicks and buffets on the door, and to shout out loud for Mr. Balfour. I was in full career, when I heard the cough right overhead, and jumping back and looking up, beheld a man's head in a tall night-cap, and the bell mouth of a blunderbuss, at one of the first-storey windows.

'It's loaded,' said a voice.

'I have come here with a letter,' I said, 'to Mr. Ebenezer Balfour of Shaws. Is he here?'

'From whom is it?' asked the man with the blunderbuss.

'That is neither here nor there,' said I, for I was growing very wroth.

'Well,' was the reply, 'ye can put it down upon the doorstep, and be off with ye.'

'I will do no such thing,' I cried. 'I will deliver it into Mr. Balfour's hands, as it was meant I should. It is a letter of introduction.'

'A what?' cried the voice sharply.

I repeated what I had said.

'Who are ye, yourself?' was the next question, after a considerable pause.

'I am not ashamed of my name,' said I. 'They call me David Balfour.'

At that, I made sure the man started, for I heard the blunderbuss rattle on the window-sill; and it was after quite a long pause, and with a curious change of voice, that the next question followed:

'Is your father dead?'

I was so much surprised at this that I could find no voice to answer, but stood staring.

'Ay,' the man resumed, 'he'll be dead, no doubt; and that'll be what brings ye chapping to my door.' Another pause, and then defiantly, 'Well, man,' he said, 'I'll let ye in'; and he disappeared from the window.

3   I make Acquaintance of my Uncle

Presently there came a great rattling of chains and bolts, and the door was cautiously opened and shut to again behind me as soon as I had passed.

'Go into the kitchen and touch naething,' said the voice; and while the person of the house set himself to replacing the defences of the door, I groped my way forward and entered the kitchen.

The fire had burned up fairly bright, and showed me the barest room I think I ever put my eyes on. Half a dozen dishes stood upon the shelves; the table was laid for supper with a bowl of porridge, a horn spoon, and a cup of small beer. Besides what I have named, there was not another thing in that great, stone-vaulted, empty chamber but lockfast chests arranged along the wall, and a corner cupboard with a padlock.

As soon as the last chain was up, the man rejoined me. He was a mean, stooping, narrow-shouldered, clay-faced creature; and his age might have been anything between fifty and seventy. His night-cap was of flannel, and so was the night-gown that he wore, instead of coat and waistcoat, over his ragged shirt. He was long unshaved; but what most distressed and even daunted me, he would neither take his eyes away from me nor look me fairly in the face. What he was, whether by trade or birth, was more than I could fathom; but he seemed most like an old, unprofitable serving-man, who should have been left in charge of that big house upon board wages.

'Are ye sharp-set?' he asked, glancing at about the level of my knee. 'Ye can eat that drop parritch?'

I said I feared it was his own supper.

'Oh,' said he, 'I can do fine wanting it. I'll take the ale, though, for it slockens[1] my cough.' He drank the cup about half out, still keeping an eye upon me as he drank; and then suddenly held out his hand. 'Let's see the letter,' said he.

I told him the letter was for Mr. Balfour; not for him.

'And who do ye think I am?' says he. 'Give me Alexander's letter!'

'You know my father's dame?'

'It would be strange if I didnae,' he returned, 'for he was my born brother; and little as ye seem to like either me or my house, or my good parritch, I'm your born uncle, Davie, my man, and you my born nephew. So give us the letter, and sit down and fill your kyte.'

If I had been some years younger, what with shame, weariness, and disappointment, I believe I had burst into tears. As it was, I could find no words, neither black nor white, but handed him the letter, and sat down to the porridge with as little appetite for meat as ever a young man had.

Meanwhile my uncle, stooping over the fire, turned the letter over and over in his hands.

'Do ye ken what's in it?' he asked suddenly.

'You see for yourself, sir,' said I, 'that the seal has not been broken.'

'Ay,' said he, 'but what brought you here?'

'To give the letter,' said I.

'No,' says he cunningly, 'but ye'll have had some hopes, nae doubt?'

'I confess, sir,' said I, 'when I was told that I had kinsfolk well to do, I did indeed indulge the hope that they might help me in my life. But I am no beggar; I look for no favours at your hands, and I want none that are not freely given. For as poor as I appear, I have friends of my own that will be blithe to help me.'

'Hoot-toot!' said Uncle Ebenezer, 'dinnae fly up in the snuff at me. We'll agree fine yet. And, Davie, my man, if you're done with that bit parritch, I could just take a sup of it myself. Ay,' he continued, as soon as he had ousted me from the stool and spoon, 'they're fine, halesome food – they're grand food, parritch.' He murmured a little grace to himself and fell to. 'Your father was very fond of his meat, I mind; he was a hearty, if not a great eater; but as for me, I could never do mair than pyke at food.' He took a pull at the small beer, which probably reminded him of hospitable duties, for his next speech ran thus: 'If ye're dry, ye'll find water behind the door.'

'To this I returned no answer, standing stiffly on my two feet, and looking down upon my uncle with a mighty angry heart. He, on his part, continued to eat like a man under some pressure of time, and to throw out little darting glances now at my shoes and now at my home-spun stockings. Once only, when he had ventured to look a little higher, our eyes met; and no thief taken with a hand in a man's pocket could have shown more lively signals of distress. This set me in a muse, whether his timidity arose from too long a disuse of any human company; and whether perhaps, upon a little trial, it might pass off, and my uncle change into an altogether different man. From this I was awakened by his sharp voice.

'Your father's been long dead?' he asked.

'Three weeks, sir,' said I.

'He was a secret man, Alexander – a secret, silent man,' he continued. 'He never said muckle when he was young. He'll never have spoken muckle of me?'

'I never knew, sir, till you told it me yourself, that he had any brother.'

'Dear me, dear me!' said Ebenezer. 'Nor of Shaws, I dare say?'

'Not so much as the name, sir,' said I.

'To think o' that!' said he. 'A strange nature of a man!' For all that, he seemed singularly satisfied, but whether with himself, or me, or with this conduct of my father's, was more than I could read. Certainly, however, he seemed to be outgrowing that distaste, or ill will, that he had conceived at first against my person; for presently he jumped up, came across the room behind me, and hit me a smack upon the shoulder. 'We'll agree fine yet!' he cried. 'I'm just as glad I let you in. And now come awa' to your bed.'

To my surprise, he lit no lamp or candle, but set forth into the dark passage, groped his way, breathing deeply, up a flight of steps, and paused before a door, which he unlocked. I was close upon his heels, having stumbled after him as best I might; and he bade me go in, for that was my chamber. I did as he bid, but paused after a few steps, and begged a light to go to bed with.

'Hoot-toot!' said Uncle Ebenezer, 'there's a fine moon.'

'Neither moon nor star, sir, and pit-mirk,'[2] said I. 'I cannae see the bed.'

'Hoot-toot! hoot-toot,' said he. 'Lights in a house is a thing I dinnae agree with. I'm unco feared of fires. Good night to ye, Davie, my man.' And before I had time to add a further protest, he pulled the door to, and I heard him lock me in from the outside.

I did not know whether to laugh or cry. The room was as cold as a well, and the bed, when I had found my way to it, as damp as a peat-hag; but by good fortune I had caught up my bundle and my plaid, and rolling myself in the latter, I lay down upon the floor under lee of the big bedstead, and fell speedily asleep.

With the first peep of day I opened my eyes, to find myself in a great chamber, hung with stamped leather, furnished with fine embroidered furniture, and lit by three fair windows. Ten years ago, or perhaps twenty, it must have been as pleasant a room to lie down or to awake in, as a man could wish: but damp, dirt, disuse, and the mice and spiders had done their worst since then. Many of the window-panes, besides, were broken; and indeed this was so common a feature in that house, that I believe my uncle must at some time have stood a siege from his indignant neighbours – perhaps with Jennet Clouston at their head.

Meanwhile the sun was shining outside; and being very cold in that miserable room, I knocked and shouted till my jailer came and let me out. He carried me to the back of the house, where was a draw-well, and told me to 'wash my face there, if I wanted'; and when that was done, I made the best of my own way back to the kitchen, where he had lit the fire and was making the porridge. The table was laid with two bowls and two horn spoons, but the same single measure of small beer. Perhaps my eye rested on this particular with some surprise, and perhaps my uncle observed it; for he spoke up as if in answer to my thought, asking me if I would like to drink ale – for so he called it.

I told him such was my habit, but not to put himself about.

'Na, na,' said he; 'I'll deny you nothing in reason.'

He fetched another cup from the shelf; and then, to my great surprise, instead of drawing more beer, he poured an accurate half from one cup to the other. There was a kind of nobleness in this that took my breath away; if my uncle was certainly a miser, he was one of that thorough breed that goes near to make the vice respectable.

When we had made an end of our meal, my Uncle Ebenezer unlocked a drawer, and drew out of it a clay pipe and a lump of tobacco, from which he cut one fill before he locked it up again. Then he sat down in the sun at one of the windows and silently smoked. From time to time his eyes came coasting round to me, and he shot out one of his questions. Once it was, 'And your mother?' 'And when I had told him that she, too, was dead, 'Ay, she was a bonnie lassie!' Then, after another long pause, 'Whae were these friends o' yours?'

I told him they were different gentlemen of the name of Campbell;

though, indeed, there was only one, and that the minister, that had ever taken the least note of me; but I began to think my uncle made too light of my position, and finding myself all alone with him, I did not wish him to suppose me helpless.

He seemed to turn this over in his mind; and then, 'Davie, my man,' said he, 'ye've come to the right bit when ye came to your Uncle Ebenezer. I've a great notion of the family, and I mean to do the right by you; but while I'm taking a bit think to mysel' of what's the best thing to put you to – whether the law, or the meenistry, or maybe the army, whilk is what boys are fondest of – I wouldnae like the Balfours to be humbled before a wheen Hieland Campbells, and I'll ask you to keep your tongue within your teeth. Nae letters; nae messages; no kind of word to onybody; or else – there's my door.'

'Uncle Ebenezer,' said I, 'I've no manner of reason to suppose you mean anything but well by me. For all that, I would have you to know that I have a pride of my own. It was by no will of mine that I came seeking you; and if you show me your door again, I'll take you at the word.'

He seemed grievously put out. 'Hoots-toots' said he, 'ca' cannie, man – ca' cannie! Bide a day or two. I'm nae warlock to find a fortune for you in the bottom of a parritch bowl; but just you give me a day or two, and say naething to naebody, and as sure as sure, I'll do the right by you.'

'Very well,' said I, 'enough said. If you want to help me, there's no doubt but I'll be glad of it, and none but I'll be grateful.'

It seemed to me (too soon, I dare say) that I was getting the upper hand of my uncle; and I began next to say that I must have the bed and bedclothes aired and put to sundry; for nothing would make me sleep in such a pickle.

'Is this my house, or yours?' said he, in his keen voice, and then all of a sudden broke off. 'Na, na,' said he, 'I dinnae mean that. What's mine is yours, Davie, my man, and what's yours is mine. Blood's thicker than water; and there's naebody but you and me that ought the name.' And then on he rambled about the family, and its ancient greatness, and his father that began to enlarge the house, and himself that stopped the building as a sinful waste; and this put it in my head to give him Jennet Clouston's message.

'The limmer!' he cried. 'Twelve hunner and fifteen – that's every day since I had the limmer roupit!³ Dod, Davie, I'll have her roasted on red peats before I'm by with it! A witch – a proclaimed witch! I'll aff and see the session clerk.'

And with that he opened a chest, and got out a very old and well-preserved blue coat and waistcoat, and a good enough beaver hat, both without lace. These he threw on anyway, and taking a staff from the cupboard, locked all up again, and was for setting out, when a thought arrested him.

'I cannae leave you by yoursel' in the house,' said he. 'I'll have to lock you out.'

'The blood came into my face. 'If you lock me out,' I said, 'it'll be the last you see of me in friendship.'

He turned very pale, and sucked his mouth in. 'This is no the way,' he said, looking wickedly at a corner of the floor – 'this is no the way to win my favour, David.'

'Sir,' says I, 'with a proper reverence for your age and our common blood, I do not value your favour at a boddle's purchase. I was brought up to have a good conceit of myself; and if you were all the uncle, and all the family I had in the world ten times over, I wouldn't buy your liking at such prices.'

Uncle Ebenezer went and looked out of the window for a while. I could see him all trembling and twitching, like a man with palsy. But when he turned round he had a smile upon his face.

'Well, well,' said he, 'we must bear and forbear. I'll no go; that's all that's to be said of it.'

'Uncle Ebenezer,' I said, 'I can make nothing out of this. You use me like a thief; you hate to have me in this house; you let me see it, every word and every minute; it's not possible that you can like me; and as for me, I've spoken to you as I never thought to speak to any man. Why do you seek to keep me, then? Let me gang back – let me gang back to the friends I have and that like me!'

'Na, na; na, na,' he said very earnestly. 'I like you fine; we'll agree fine yet; and for the honour of the house I couldnae let you leave the way ye came. Bide here quiet, there's a good lad; just you bide here quiet a bittie, and ye'll find that we agree.'

'Well, sir,' said I, after I had thought the matter out in silence, 'I'll stay awhile. It's more just I should be helped by my own blood than strangers; and if we don't agree, I'll do my best it shall be through no fault of mine.'

---

1 Moistens.   2 Dark as the pit.   3 Sold up.

4 I run a Great Danger in the House of Shaws

For a day that was begun so ill, the day passed fairly well. We had the porridge cold again at noon, and hot porridge at night; porridge and small beer was my uncle's diet. He spoke but little, and that in the same way as before, shooting a question at me after a long silence; and when I sought to lead him in talk about my future, slipped out of it again. In a room next door to the kitchen, where he suffered me to go, I found a great number of books, both Latin and English, in which I took great pleasure all the afternoon. Indeed, the time passed so lightly in this good company that I began to be almost reconciled to my residence at Shaws; and nothing but the sight of my uncle, and his eyes playing hide and seek with mine, reviving the force of my distrust.

One thing I discovered which put me in some doubt. This was an entry on the fly-leaf of a chap-book (one of Patrick Walker's) plainly written by my father's hand and thus conceived: 'To my brother Ebenezer on his fifth birthday.' Now, what puzzled me was this: That, as my father was, of course, the younger brother, he must either have made some strange error, or he must have written, before he was yet five, an excellent, clear, manly hand of writing.

I tried to get this out of my head; but though I took down many interesting authors, old and new, history, poetry, and story-book, this notion of my father's hand of writing stuck to me; and when at length I went into the kitchen, and sat down once more to porridge and small beer, the first thing I said to Uncle Ebenezer was to ask him if my father had not been very quick at his book.

'Alexander! No him!' was the reply. 'I was far quicker mysel'; I was a clever chappie when I was young. Why, I could read as soon as he could.'

This puzzled me yet more: and a thought coming into my head, I asked if he and my father had been twins.

He jumped upon his stool, and the horn spoon fell out of his hand upon the floor. 'What gars ye ask that?' he said, and caught me by the breast of the jacket, and looked this time straight into my eyes; his own, which were little and light and bright like a bird's, blinking and winking strangely.

'What do you mean?' I asked very calmly, for I was far stronger than he, and not easily frightened. 'Take your hand from my jacket. This is no way to behave.'

My uncle seemed to make a great effort upon himself. 'Dod man, David', he said 'ye shouldnae speak to me about your father. That's where the mistake is.' He sat awhile and shook, blinking in his plate: 'He was all the brother that ever I had,' he added, but with no heart in his voice; and then he caught up his spoon and fell to supper again, but still shaking.

Now this last passage, this laying of hands upon my person and sudden profession of love for my dead father, went so clean beyond my comprehension that it put me into both fear and hope. On the one hand, I began to think my uncle was perhaps insane and might be dangerous; on the other there came up into my mind (quite unbidden by me and even discouraged) a story like some ballad I had heard folks singing, of a poor lad that was a rightful heir and a wicked kinsman that tried to keep him from his own. For why should my uncle play a part with a relative that came, almost a beggar, to his door, unless in his heart he had some cause to fear him?

With this notion, all unacknowledged, but nevertheless getting firmly settled in my head, I now began to imitate his covert looks; so that we sat at table like a cat and a mouse, each stealthily observing the other. Not another word had he to say to me, black or white, but was busy turning something secretly over in his mind; and the longer we sat and the more I looked at him the more certain I became that the something was unfriendly to myself.

When he had cleared the platter, he got out a single pipeful of tobacco, just as in the morning, turned round a stool into the chimney corner, and sat awhile smoking, with his back to me.

'Davie,' he said at length, 'I've been thinking'; then he paused and said it again. 'There's a wee bit siller that I half promised ye before ye were born,' he continued; 'promised it to your father. O, naething legal, ye understand; just gentlemen daffing at their wine. Well, I keepit that bit money separate – it was a great expense, but a promise is a promise – and it has grown by now to be a matter of just precisely –

just exactly' – and here he paused and stumbled – 'of just exactly forty pounds!' This last he rapped out with a sidelong glance over his shoulder; and the next moment added, almost with a scream 'Scots!'

The pound Scots being the same thing as an English shilling, the difference made by this second thought was considerable; I could see, besides, that the whole story was a lie, invented with some end which it puzzled me to guess; and I made no attempt to conceal the tone of raillery in which I answered:

'O, think again, sir! Pounds sterling, I believe!'

'That's what I said,' returned my uncle: 'pounds sterling! And if you'll step out-by to the door a minute, just to see what kind of a night it is, I'll get it out to ye and call ye in again.'

I did his will, smiling to myself in my contempt that he should think I was so easily to be deceived. It was a dark night, with a few stars low down; and as I stood just outside the door, I heard a hollow moaning of wind far off among the hills. I said to myself there was something thundery and changeful in the weather, and little knew of what a vast importance that should prove to me before the evening passed.

When I was called in again, my uncle counted out into my hand seven and thirty golden guinea pieces; the rest was in his hand, in small gold and silver; but his heart failed him there and he crammed the change into his pocket.

'There,' said he, 'that'll show you! I'm a queer man, and strange wi' strangers; but my word is my bond, and there's the proof of it.'

Now, my uncle seemed so miserly that I was struck dumb by this sudden generosity, and could find no words in which to thank him.

'No a word!' said he. 'Nae thanks; I want nae thanks. I do my duty; I'm no saying that everybody would have done it; but for my part (though I'm a careful body, too) it's a pleasure to me to do the right by my brother's son; and it's a pleasure to me to think that now we'll agree as such near friends should.'

I spoke him in return as handsomely as I was able; but all the while I was wondering what would come next, and why he had parted with his precious guineas; for as to the reason he had given, a baby would have refused it.

Presently he looked towards me sideways.

'And see here,' says he, 'tit for tat.'

I told him I was ready to prove my gratitude in any reasonable degree, and then waited, looking for some monstrous demand. And yet, when at last he plucked up courage to speak, it was only to tell me (very properly, as I thought) that he was growing old and a little broken, and that he would expect me to help him with the house and the bit garden.

I answered, and expressed my readiness to serve.

'Well,' he said, 'let's begin.' He pulled out of his pocket a rusty key. 'There,' says he, 'there's the key of the stair-tower at the far end of the house. Ye can only win into it from the outside, for that part of the house is no finished. Gang ye in there, and up the stairs, and bring me down the chest that's at the top. There's papers in't,' he added.

'Can I have a light, sir?' said I.

'Na,' said he, very cunningly. 'Nae lights in my house.'

'Very well, sir,' said I. 'Are the stairs good?'

'They're grand,' said he; and then as I was going, 'Keep to the wall,' he added; 'there's nae banisters. But the stairs are grand under foot.'

Out I went into the night. The wind was still moaning in the distance though never a breath of it came near the house of Shaws. It had fallen blacker than ever; and I was glad to feel along the wall, till I came the length of the stair-tower door at the far end of the unfinished wing. I had got the key into the keyhole and had just turned it, when all upon a sudden, without sound or wind or thunder, the whole sky lighted up with wild fire and went black again. I had to put my hand over my eyes to get back to the colour of the darkness; and indeed I was already half blinded when I stepped into the tower.

It was so dark inside, it seemed a body could scarce breathe; but I pushed out with foot and hand, and presently struck the wall with the one, and the lowermost round of the stair with the other. The wall, by the touch, was of fine hewn stone; the steps too, though somewhat steep and narrow, were of polished mason work, and regular and solid under foot. Minding my uncle's word about the banisters, I kept close to the tower side, and felt my way in the pitch darkness with a beating heart.

The house of Shaws stood some five full storeys high, not counting lofts. Well, as I advanced, it seemed to me the stair grew airier and a thought more lightsome; and I was wondering what might be the cause of this change, when a second blink of the summer lightning came and went. If I did not cry out, it was because fear had me by the throat; and if I did not fall, it was more by Heaven's mercy than my own strength. It was not only that the flash shone in on every side through breaches in the wall, so that I seemed to be clambering aloft upon an open scaffold, but the same passing brightness showed me the steps were of unequal length, and that one of my feet rested that moment within two inches of the well.

This was the grand stair! I thought; and with the thought a gust of a kind of angry courage came into my heart. My uncle had sent me here, certainly to run great risks, perhaps to die. I swore I would settle that 'perhaps,' if I should break my neck for it; got me down upon my hands and knees; and as slowly as a snail, feeling before me every inch, and testing the solidity of every stone, I continued to ascend the stair. The darkness, by contrast with the flash, appeared to have redoubled; nor was that all, for my ears were now troubled and my mind confounded by a great stir of bats in the top part of the tower, and the foul beasts, flying downwards, sometimes beat about my face and body.

The tower, I should have said, was square; and in every corner the step was made of a great stone of a different shape, to join the flights. Well, I had come close to one of these turns, when, feeling forward as usual, my hand slipped upon an edge and found nothing but emptiness beyond it. The stair had been carried no higher: to set a stranger mounting it in the darkness was to send him straight to his death; and (although, thanks to the lightning and my own precautions, I was safe enough) the mere thought of the peril in which I might have stood, and the dreadful height I might have fallen from, brought out the sweat upon my body and relaxed my joints.

But I knew what I wanted now, and turned and groped my way down again with a wonderful anger in my heart. About half-way down, the wind sprang up in a clap and shook the tower, and died again; the rain followed; and before I had reached the ground level it fell in buckets. I put out my head into the storm, and looked along towards the kitchen. The door, which I had shut behind me when I left, now stood open, and shed a little glimmer of light; and I thought I could see a figure standing in the rain, quite still, like a man hearkening. And then there came a blinding flash, which showed me my uncle plainly, just where I had fancied him to stand; and hard upon the heels of it a great tow-row of thunder.

Now, whether my uncle thought the crash to be the sound of my fall, or whether he heard in it God's voice denouncing murder, I will leave you to guess. Certain it is, at least, that he was seized on by a kind of panic fear, and that he ran into the house and left the door open behind him. I followed as softly as I could, and coming unheard into the kitchen, stood and watched him.

He had found time to open the corner cupboard and bring out a great case-bottle of aqua-vitae, and now sat with his back towards me at the table. Ever and again he would be seized with a fit of deadly shuddering and groan aloud, and carrying the bottle to his lips, drink down the raw spirits by the mouthful.

I stepped forward, came close behind him where he sat, and suddenly clapped my two hands down upon his shoulders – 'Ah!' cried I.

My uncle gave a kind of broken cry like a sheep's bleat, flung up his arms, and tumbled to the floor like a dead man. I was somewhat shocked at this; but I had myself to look to first of all, and did not hesitate to let him lie as he had fallen. The keys were hanging in the cupboard; and it was my design to furnish myself with arms before my uncle should come again to his senses and the power of devising evil. In the cupboard were a few bottles, some apparently of medicine; a great many bills and other papers, which I should willingly enough have rummaged, had I had the time; and a few necessaries that were nothing to my purpose. Thence I turned to the chests. The first was full of meal; the second of money-bags and papers tied into sheaves; in the third, with many other things (and these for the most part clothes), I found a rusty, ugly-looking Highland dirk without the scabbard. This, then, I concealed inside my waistcoat, and turned to my uncle.

He lay as he had fallen, all huddled, with one knee up and one arm sprawling abroad; his face had a strange colour of blue, and he seemed to have ceased breathing. Fear came on me that he was dead; then I got water and dashed it in his face; and with that he seemed to come a little to himself, working his mouth and fluttering his eyelids. At last he looked up and saw me, and there came into his eyes a terror that was not of this world.

'Come, come,' said I, 'sit up.'

'Are ye alive?' he sobbed. 'O man, are ye alive?'

'That am I,' said I. 'Small thanks to you!'

He had begun to seek for his breath with deep sighs. 'The blue phial,' said he – 'in the aumry – the blue phial.' His breath came slower still.

I ran to the cupboard, and, sure enough, found there a blue phial of medicine, with the dose written on it on a paper, and this I administered to him with what speed I might.

'It's the trouble,' said he, reviving a little; 'I have a trouble, Davie. It's the heart.'

I set him on a chair and looked at him. It is true I felt some pity for a man that looked so sick, but I was full besides of righteous anger; and I numbered over before him the points on which I wanted explanation: Why he lied to me at every word; why he feared that I should leave him; why he disliked it to be hinted that he and my father were twins – 'Is that because it is true?' I asked; why he had given me money to which I was convinced I had no claim; and, last of all, why he had tried to kill me. He heard me all through in silence; and then, in a broken voice, begged me to let him go to bed.

'I'll tell ye the morn,' he said; 'as sure as death I will.'

And so weak was he that I could do nothing but consent. I locked him into his room, however, and pocketed the key; and then returning to the kitchen, made up such a blaze as had not shone there for many a long year, and, wrapping myself in my plaid, lay down upon the chests and fell asleep.

5　I go to the Queen's Ferry

Much rain fell in the night; and the next morning there blew a bitter wintry wind out of the north-west, driving scattered clouds. For all that, and before the sun began to peep or the last of the stars had vanished, I made my way to the side of the burn, and had a plunge in a deep whirling pool. All aglow from my bath, I sat down once more beside the fire, which I replenished, and began gravely to consider my position.

There was now no doubt about my uncle's enmity; there was no doubt I carried my life in my hand, and he would leave no stone unturned that he might compass my destruction. But I was young and spirited, and like most lads that have been country-bred, I had a great opinion of my shrewdness. I had come to his door no better than a beggar and little more than a child; he had met me with treachery and violence; it would be a fine consummation to take the upper hand, and drive him like a herd of sheep.

I sat there nursing my knee and smiling at the fire; and I saw myself in fancy smell out his secrets one after another, and grow to be that man's king and ruler. The warlock of Essendean, they say, had made a mirror in which men could read the future; it must have been of other stuff than burning coal; for in all the shapes and pictures that I sat and gazed at there was never a ship, never a seaman with a hairy cap, never a big bludgeon for my silly head, or the least sign of all those tribulations that were ripe to fall on me.

Presently, all swollen with conceit, I went upstairs and gave my prisoner his liberty. He gave me good morning civilly; and I gave the same to him, smiling down upon him from the heights of my sufficiency. Soon we were set to breakfast, as it might have been the day before.

'Well, sir' said I, with a jeering tone, 'have you nothing more to say to me?' And then, as he made no articulate reply, 'It will be time, I think, to understand each other,' I continued. 'You took me for a country Johnnie Raw, with no more mother-wit or courage than a porridge-stick. I took you for a good man, or no worse than others at the least. It seems we were both wrong. What cause you have to fear me, to cheat me, and to attempt my life———'

He murmured something about a jest, and that he liked a bit of fun; and then, seeing me smile, changed his tone, and assured me he would make all clear as soon as we had breakfasted. I saw by his face that he had no lie ready for me, though he was hard at work preparing one; and I think I was about to tell him so, when we were interrupted by a knocking at the door.

Bidding my uncle sit where he was, I went to open it, and found on the doorstep a half-grown boy in sea-clothes. He had no sooner seen me than he began to dance some steps of the sea-hornpipe (which I had never before heard of, far less seen), snapping his fingers in the air and footing it right cleverly. For all that, he was blue with the cold; and there was something in his face, a look between tears and laughter, that was highly pathetic and consisted ill with this gaiety of manner.

'What cheer, mate?' says he, with a cracked voice.

I asked him soberly to name his pleasure.

'O, pleasure!' says he; and then began to sing:

> 'For it's my delight, of a shiny night,
> In the season of the year.'

'Well,' said I, 'if you have no business at all, I will even be so unmannerly as to shut you out.'

'Stay, brother!' he cried. 'Have you no fun about you? or do you want to get me thrashed? I've brought a letter from old Heasy-oasy to Mr. Belflower.' He showed me a letter as he spoke. 'And I say, mate,' he added, 'I'm mortal hungry.'

'Well,' said I, 'come into the house, and you shall have a bite if I go empty for it.'

With that I brought him in and set him down to my own place, where he fell-to greedily on the remains of breakfast, winking to me between whiles, and making many faces, which I think the poor soul considered manly. Meanwhile, my uncle had read the letter and sat thinking; then, suddenly, he got to his feet with a great air of liveliness, and pulled me apart into the farthest corner of the room.

'Read that,' said he, and put the letter in my hand.

Here it is, lying before me as I write:

The Hawes Inn, at the Queen's Ferry.
Sir, – I lie here with my hawser up and down, and send my cabin-boy to informe. If you have any further commands for over-seas, to-day will be the last occasion, as the wind will serve us well out of the firth. I will not seek to deny that I have had crosses with your doer,[1] Mr Rankeillor; of which, if not speedily redd up, you may looke to see some losses follow. I have drawn a bill upon you, as per margin, and am, sir, your most obedt., humble servant,
ELIAS HOSEASON.

'You see, Davie,' resumed my uncle, as soon as he saw that I had done, 'I have a venture with this man Hoseason, the captain of a trading brig, the *Covenant*, of Dysart. Now, if you and me was to walk over with yon lad, I could see the captain at the Hawes, or maybe on board the *Covenant* if there was papers to be signed; and so far from a loss of time, we can jog on to the lawyer, Mr. Rankeillor's. After a' that's come and gone, ye would be sweir[2] to believe me upon my naked word; but ye'll believe Rankeillor. He's factor to half the gentry in these parts; an auld man, forby: highly respeckit; and he kenned your father.'

I stood awhile and thought. I was going to some place of shipping, which was doubtless populous, and where my uncle durst attempt no violence, and, indeed, even the society of the cabin-boy so far protected me. Once there, I believed I could force on the visit to the lawyer, even if my uncle were now insincere in proposing it; and, perhaps, in the bottom of my heart, I wished a nearer view of the sea and ships. You are to remember I had lived all my life in the inland hills, and just two days before had my first sight of the firth lying like a blue floor, and the sailed ships moving on the face of it, no bigger than toys. One thing with another, I made up my mind.

'Very well,' says I, 'let us go to the Ferry.'

My uncle got into his hat and coat, and buckled an old rusty cutlass on; and then we trod the fire out, locked the door, and set forth upon our walk.

The wind, being in that cold quarter the north-west, blew nearly in our faces as we went. It was the month of June; the grass was all white with daisies and the trees with blossom; but, to judge by our blue nails and aching wrists, the time might have been winter and the whiteness a December frost.

Uncle Ebenezer trudged in the ditch, jogging from side to side like an old ploughman coming home from work. He never said a word the whole way; and I was thrown for talk on the cabin-boy. He told me his name was Ransome, and that he had followed the sea since he was nine, but could not say how old he was, as he had lost his reckoning. He showed me tattoo marks, baring his breast in the teeth of the wind and in spite of my remonstrances, for I thought it was enough to kill him; he swore horribly whenever he remembered, but more like a silly schoolboy than a man; and boasted of many wild and bad things that he had done: stealthy thefts, false accusations, ay, and even murder; but all with such a dearth of likelihood in the details, and such a weak and crazy swagger in the delivery, as disposed me rather to pity than to believe him.

I asked him of the brig (which he declared was the finest ship that sailed) and of Captain Hoseason, in whose praises he was equally loud. Heasy-oasy (for so he still named the skipper) was a man, by his account, that minded for nothing either in heaven or earth; one that, as people said, would 'crack on all sail into the day of judgment'; rough, fierce, unscrupulous, and brutal; and all this my poor cabin-boy had taught himself to admire as something seamanlike and manly. He would only admit one flaw in his idol. 'He ain't no seaman,' he admitted. 'That's Mr. Shuan that navigates the brig; he's the finest seaman in the trade, only for drink; and I tell you I believe it! Why, look 'ere'; and turning down his stocking he showed me a great, raw, red wound that made my blood run cold. 'He done that – Mr. Shuan done it,' he said, with an air of pride.

'What!' I cried, 'do you take such savage usage at his hands? Why, you are no slave, to be so handled!'

'No,' said the poor moon-calf, changing his tune at once, 'and so he'll find. See 'ere'; and he showed me a great case-knife, which he told me was stolen. 'Oh,' says he, 'let me see him try; I dare him to; I'll do for him! Oh, he ain't the first!' And he confirmed it with a poor, silly, ugly oath.

I have never felt such pity for anyone in this wide world as I felt for that half-witted creature; and it began to come over me that the brig *Covenant* (for all her pious name) was little better than a hell upon the seas.

'Have you no friends?' said I.

He said he had a father in some English seaport, I forget which. 'He was a fine man, too,' he said; 'but he's dead.'

'In Heaven's name,' cried I, 'can you find no reputable life on shore?'

'Oh, no,' says he, winking and looking very sly; 'they would put me to a trade. I know a trick worth two of that I do!'

I asked him what trade could be so dreadful as the one he followed, where he ran the continual peril of his life, not alone from wind and sea, but by the horrid cruelty of those who were his masters. He said it was very true; and then began to praise the life, and tell what a pleasure it was to get on shore with money in his pocket, and spend it like a man, and buy apples, and swagger, and surprise what he called stick-in-the-mud boys. 'And then it's not all as bad as that,' says he; 'there's worse off than me: there's the twenty-pounders. O, laws! you should see them taking on. Why, I've seen a man as old as you, I dessay' – (to him I seemed old) – 'ah, and he had a beard, too – well, and as soon as we cleared out of the river, and he had the drug out of his head – my! how he cried and carried on! I made a fine fool of him, I tell you! And then there's little uns, too; oh, little by me! I tell you, I keep them in order. When we carry little uns, I have a rope's end of my own to wallop 'em.' And so he ran on, until it came in on me that what he meant by twenty-pounders were those unhappy criminals who were sent overseas to slavery in North America, or the still more unhappy innocents who were kidnapped or trepanned (as the word went) for private interest or vengeance.

Just then we came to the top of the hill, and looked down on the Ferry and the Hope. The Firth of Forth (as is very well known) narrows at this point to the width of a good-sized river, which makes a convenient ferry going north, and turns the upper reach into a landlocked haven for all manner of ships. Right in the midst of the narrows lies an islet with some ruins; on the south shore they have built a pier for the service of the Ferry: and at the end of the pier, on the other side of the road, and backed against a pretty garden of holly-trees and hawthorns, I could see the building which they called the Hawes Inn.

The town of Queensferry lies farther west, and the neighbourhood of the inn looked pretty lonely at that time of day, for the boat had just gone north with passengers. A skiff, however, lay beside the pier, with some seamen sleeping on the thwarts; this, as Ransome told me, was the brig's boat waiting for the captain; and about half a mile off, and all alone in the anchorage, he showed me the *Covenant* herself. There was a sea-going bustle on board; yards were swinging into place; and as the wind blew from that quarter, I could hear the song of the sailors as they pulled upon the ropes. After all I had listened to upon the way, I looked at that ship with an extreme abhorrence; and from the bottom of my heart I pitied all poor souls that were condemned to sail in her.

We had all three pulled up on the brow of the hill: and now I marched across the road and addressed my uncle. 'I think it right to tell you, sir,' says I, 'there's nothing that will bring me on board that *Covenant*.'

He seemed to waken from a dream. 'Eh?' he said. 'What's that?'

I told him over again.

'Well, well,' he said, 'we'll have to please ye, I suppose. But what are we standing here for? It's perishing cold; and if I'm no mistaken, they're busking the *Covenant* for sea.'

1 Agent
2 Unwilling

6 What befell at the Queen's Ferry

As soon as we came to the inn, Ransome led us up the stair to a small room, with a bed in it, and heated like an oven by a great fire of coal. At a table hard by the chimney, a tall, dark, sober-looking man sat writing. In spite of the heat of the room, he wore a thick sea-jacket, buttoned to the neck, and a tall hairy cap drawn down over his ears; yet I never saw any man, not even a judge upon the bench, look cooler, or more studious and self-possessed, than this ship-captain.

He got to his feet at once, and coming forward, offered his large hand to Ebenezer. 'I am proud to see you, Mr. Balfour,' said he, in a fine deep voice, 'and glad that ye are here in time. The wind's fair, and the tide upon the turn; we'll see the old coal-bucket burning on the Isle of May before to-night.'

'Captain Hoseason,' returned my uncle, 'you keep your room unco hot.'

'It's a habit I have, Mr. Balfour,' said the skipper. 'I'm a coldrife man by my nature; I have a cold blood, sir. There's neither fur, nor flannel – no, sir, nor hot rum, will warm up what they call the temperature. Sir, it's the same with most men that have been carbonadoed, as they call it, in the tropic seas.'

'Well, well, captain,' replied my uncle, 'we must all be the way we're made.'

But it chanced that this fancy of the captain's had a great share in my misfortunes. For though I had promised myself not to let my kinsman out of sight, I was both so impatient for a nearer look of the sea, and so sickened by the closeness of the room, that when he told me to 'run downstairs and play myself awhile,' I was fool enough to take him at his word.

Away I went, therefore, leaving the two men sitting down to a bottle and a great mass of papers; and crossing the road in front of the inn, walked down upon the beach. With the wind in that quarter, only little wavelets, not much bigger than I had seen upon a lake, beat upon the shore. But the weeds were new to me – some green, some brown and long, and some with little bladders that crackled between my fingers. Even so far up the firth, the smell of the sea-water was exceedingly salt and stirring; the *Covenant*, besides, was beginning to shake out her sails, which hung upon the yards in clusters; and the spirit of all that I beheld put me in thoughts of far voyages and foreign places.

I looked, too, at the seamen with the skiff – big brown fellows, some in shirts, some with jackets, some with coloured handkerchiefs about their throats, one with a brace of pistols stuck into his pockets, two or three with knotty bludgeons, and all with their case-knives. I passed the time of day with one that looked less desperate than his fellows, and asked him of the sailing of the brig. He said they would get under way as soon as the ebb set, and expressed his gladness to be out of a port where there were no taverns and fiddlers; but all with such horrifying oaths, that I made haste to get away from him.

This threw me back on Ransome, who seemed the least wicked of that gang, and who soon came out of the inn and ran to me, crying for a bowl of punch. I told him I would give him no such thing, for neither he nor I was of an age for such indulgences. 'But a glass of ale you may have, and welcome,' said I. He mopped and mowed at me, and called me names; but he was glad to get the ale, for all that; and presently we were set down at a table in the front room of the inn, and both eating and drinking with a good appetite.

Here it occurred to me that, as the landlord was a man of that county, I might do well to make a friend of him. I offered him a share, as was much the custom in those days; but he was far too great a man to sit with such poor customers as Ransome and myself, and he was leaving the room, when I called him back to ask if he knew Mr. Rankeillor.

'Hoot, ay,' says he, 'and a very honest man. And, oh, by the way,' says he, 'was it you that came in with Ebenezer?' And when I had told him yes, 'Ye'll be no friend of his?' he asked, meaning, in the Scottish way, that I would be no relative.

I told him no, none.

'I thought not,' said he, 'and yet ye have a kind of gliff[1] of Mr. Alexander.'

I said it seemed that Ebenezer was ill seen in the country.

'Nae doubt,' said the landlord. 'He's a wicked auld man, and there's many would like to see him girnning in a tow:[2] Jennet Clouston and mony mair that he has harried out of house and hame. And yet he was ance a fine young fellow, too. But that was before the sough[3] gaed abroad about Mr. Alexander; that was like the death of him.'

'And what was it?' I asked.

'Ou, just that he had killed him,' said the landlord. 'Did ye never hear that?'

'And what would he kill him for?' said I.

'And what for, but just to get the place,' said he.

'The place?' said I. 'The Shaws?'

'Nae other place that I ken,' said he.

'Ay, man?' said I. 'Is that so? 'Was my – was Alexander the eldest son?'

'Deed was he,' said the landlord. 'What else would he have killed him for?'

And with that he went away, as he had been impatient to do from the beginning.

Of course I had guessed it a long while ago; but it is one thing to guess, another to know; and I sat stunned with my good fortune, and could scarce grow to believe that the same poor lad who had trudged in the dust from Ettrick Forest not two days ago was now one of the rich of the earth, and had a house and broad lands, and if he but knew how to ride, might mount his horse to-morrow. All these pleasant things, and a thousand others, crowded into my mind, as I sat staring before me out of the inn window, and paying no heed to what I saw; only I remember that my eye lighted on Captain Hoseason down on the pier among his seamen, and speaking with some authority. And presently he came marching back towards the house, with no mark of a sailor's clumsiness, but carrying his fine, tall figure with a manly bearing, and still with the same sober, grave expression on his face. I wondered if it was possible that Ransome's stories could be true, and half disbelieved them; they fitted so ill with the man's looks. But indeed, he was neither so good as I supposed him nor quite so bad as Ransome did; for, in fact, he was two men, and left the better one behind as soon as he set foot on board his vessel.

The next thing, I heard my uncle calling me, and found the pair in the road together. It was the captain who addressed me, and that with an air (very flattering to a young lad) of grave equality.

'Sir,' said he, 'Mr. Balfour tells me great things of you; and for my own part, I like your looks. I wish I was for longer here, that we might make the better friends; but we'll make the most of what we have. Ye shall come on board my brig for half an hour, till the ebb sets, and drink a bowl with me.'

Now, I longed to see the inside of a ship more than words can tell; but I was not going to put myself in jeopardy, and I told him my uncle and I had an appointment with a lawyer.

'Ay, ay,' said he, 'he passed me word of that. But, ye see, the boat'll set ye ashore at the town pier, and that's but a penny stonecast from Rankeillor's house.' And here he suddenly leaned down and whispered in my ear: 'Take care of the old tod;[4] he means mischief. Come aboard till I can get a word with ye.' And then, passing his arm through mine, he continued aloud, as he set off towards his boat: 'But come, what can I bring ye from the Carolinas? Any friend of Mr. Balfour's can command. A roll of tobacco? Indian featherwork? a skin of a wild beast? a stone pipe? the mocking-bird that mews for all the world like a cat? the cardinal bird that is as red as blood? – take your pick and say your pleasure.'

By this time we were at the boat-side, and he was handing me in. I did not dream of hanging back; I thought (the poor fool) that I had found a good friend and helper, and I was rejoiced to see the ship. As soon as we were all set in our places, the boat was thrust off from the pier and began to move over the waters; and what with my pleasure in this new movement and my surprise at our low position, and the appearance of the shores, and the growing bigness of the brig as we drew near to it, I could hardly understand what the captain said, and must have answered him at random.

As soon as we were alongside (where I sat fairly gaping at the ship's height, the strong humming of the tide against its sides, and the pleasant cries of the seamen at their work) Hoseason, declaring that he and I must be the first aboard, ordered a tackle to be sent down from the main-yard. In this I was whipped into the air and set down again on the deck, where the captain stood ready waiting for me, and instantly slipped back his arm under mine. There I stood some while, a little dizzy with the unsteadiness of all around me, perhaps a little afraid, and yet vastly pleased with these strange sights; the captain meanwhile pointing out the strangest, and telling me their names and uses.

'But where is my uncle?' said I, suddenly.

'Ay,' said Hoseason, with a sudden grimness, 'that's the point.'

I felt I was lost. With all my strength, I plucked myself clear of him, and ran to the bulwarks. Sure enough, there was the boat pulling for the town, with my uncle sitting in the stern. I gave a piercing cry – 'Help, help! Murder!' – so that both sides of the anchorage rang with it, and my uncle turned round where he was sitting, and showed me a face full of cruelty and terror.

It was the last I saw. Already strong hands had been plucking me back from the ship's side; and now a thunderbolt seemed to strike me; I saw a great flash of fire, and fell senseless.

1 Look
2 Rope
3 Report
4 Fox

7 I go to Sea in the Brig *Covenant* of Dysart

I came to myself in darkness, in great pain, bound hand and foot, and deafened by many unfamiliar noises. There sounded in my ears a roaring of water as of a huge mill-dam, the thrashing of heavy sprays, the thundering of the sails, and the shrill cries of seamen. The whole world now heaved giddily up, and now rushed giddily downward; and so sick and hurt was I in body, and my mind so much confounded, that it took me a long while, chasing my thoughts up and down, and ever stunned again by a fresh stab of pain, to realize that I must be lying somewhere bound in the belly of that unlucky ship, and that the wind must have strengthened to a gale. With the clear perception of my plight, there fell upon me a blackness of despair, a horror of remorse at my own folly, and a passion of anger at my uncle, that once more bereft me of my senses.

When I returned again to life, the same uproar, the same confused and violent movements, shook and deafened me; and presently, to my other pains and distresses, there was added the sickness of an unused landsman on the sea. In that time of my adventurous youth I suffered many hardships; but none that was so crushing to my mind and body, or lit by so few hopes, as these first few hours on board the brig.

I heard a gun fire, and supposed the storm had proved too strong for us, and we were firing signals of distress. The thought of deliverance, even by death in the deep sea, was welcome to me. Yet it was no such matter; but (as I was afterwards told) a common habit of the captain's, which I here set down to show that even the worst man may have his kindlier sides. We were then passing, it appeared, within some miles of Dysart, where the brig was built, and where old Mrs. Hoseason, the captain's mother, had come some years before to live; and whether outward or inward bound, the *Covenant* was never suffered to go by that place by day without a gun fired and colours shown.

I had no measure of time; day and night were alike in that ill-smelling cavern of the ship's bowels where I lay; and the misery of my situation drew out the hours to double. How long, therefore, I lay waiting to hear the ship split upon some rock, or to feel her reel head foremost into the depths of the sea, I have not the means of computation. But sleep at length stole from me the consciousness of sorrow.

I was wakened by the light of a hand-lantern shining in my face. A small man of about thirty, with green eyes and a tangle of fair hair, stood looking down at me.

'Well,' said he, 'how goes it?'

I answered by a sob; and my visitor then felt my pulse and temples, and set himself to wash and dress the wound upon my scalp.

'Ay,' said he, 'a sore dunt.¹ What, man? Cheer up! The world's no done; you've made a bad start of it, but you'll make a better. Have you had any meat?'

I said I could not look at it; and thereupon he gave me some brandy and water in a tin pannikin, and left me once more to myself.

The next time he came to see me, I was lying betwixt sleep and waking, my eyes wide open in the darkness, the sickness quite departed, but succeeded by a horrid giddiness and swimming that was almost worse to bear. I ached, besides, in every limb, and the cords that bound me seemed to be of fire. The smell of the hole in which I lay seemed to have become a part of me; and during the long interval since his last visit I had suffered tortures of fear, now from the scurrying of the ship's rats, that sometimes pattered on my very face, and now from the dismal imaginings that haunt the bed of fever.

The glimmer of the lantern, as a trap opened, shone in like the heaven's sunlight; and though it only showed me the strong, dark beams of the ship that was my prison, I could have cried aloud for gladness. The man with the green eyes was the first to descend the ladder, and I noticed that he came somewhat unsteadily. He was followed by the captain. Neither said a word; but the first set to and examined me, and dressed my wound as before, while Hoseason looked me in the face with an odd, black look.

'Now, sir, you see for yourself,' said the first; 'a high fever, no appetite, no light, no meat; you see for yourself what that means.'

'I am no conjurer, Mr. Riach,' said the captain.

'Give me leave, sir,' said Riach; 'you've a good head upon your shoulders, and a good Scotch tongue to ask with; but I will leave you no manner of excuse; I want that boy taken out of this hole and put in the forecastle.'

'What ye may want, sir, is a matter of concern to nobody but yoursel',' returned the captain; 'but I can tell ye that which is to be. Here he is; here he shall bide.'

'Admitting that you have been paid in a proportion,' said the other, 'I will crave leave humbly to say that I have not. Paid I am, and none too much, to be the second officer of this old tub; and you ken very well if I do my best to earn it. But I was paid for nothing more.'

'If ye could hold back your hand from the tin-pan, Mr. Riach, I would have no complaint to make of ye,' returned the skipper; 'and instead of asking riddles, I make bold to say that ye would keep your breath to cool your porridge. We'll be required on deck,' he added, in a sharper note, and set one foot upon the ladder.

But Mr. Riach caught him by the sleeve.

'Admitting that you have been paid to do a murder——' he began.

Hoseason turned upon him with a flash.

'What's that?' he cried. 'What kind of talk is that?'

'It seems it is the talk that you can understand,' said Mr. Riach, looking him steadily in the face.

'Mr. Riach, I have sailed with ye three cruises,' replied the captain. 'In all that time, sir, ye should have learned to know me; I'm a stiff man, and a dour man; but for what ye say the now – fie, fie! – it comes from a bad heart and a black conscience. If ye say the lad will die——'

'Ay, will he!' said Mr. Riach.

'Well, sir, is not that enough?' said Hoseason. 'Flit him where ye please!'

Thereupon the captain ascended the ladder; and I, who had lain silent throughout this strange conversation, beheld Mr. Riach turn after him and bow as low as to his knees in what was plainly a spirit of derision. Even in my then state of sickness I perceived two things: that the mate was touched with liquor, as the captain hinted, and that (drunk or sober) he was like to prove a valuable friend.

Five minutes afterwards my bonds were cut, I was hoisted on a man's back, carried up to the forecastle, and laid in a bunk on some sea-blankets; where the first thing that I did was to lose my senses.

It was a blessed thing indeed to open my eyes again upon the daylight, and to find myself in the society of men. The forecastle was a

'*Hoseason turned upon him with a flash*'

roomy place enough, set all about with berths, in which the men of the watch below were seated smoking, or lying down asleep. The day being calm and the wind fair, the scuttle was open, and not only the good daylight, but from time to time (as the ship rolled) a dusty beam of sunlight shone in, and dazzled and delighted me. I had no sooner moved, moreover, than one of the men brought me a drink of something healing which Mr. Riach had prepared, and bade me lie still and I should soon be well again. There were no bones broken, he explained: 'A clour² on the head was naething. Man,' said he, 'it was me that gave it ye!'

Here I lay for the space of many days a close prisoner, and not only got my health again, but came to know my companions. They were a rough lot indeed, as sailors mostly are; being men rooted out of all the kindly parts of life, and condemned to toss together on the rough seas, with masters no less cruel. There were some among them that had sailed with the pirates and seen things it would be a shame even to speak of; some were men that had run from the king's ships, and went with a halter round their necks, of which they made no secret; and all, as the saying goes, were 'at a word and a blow' with their best friends. Yet I had not been many days shut up with them before I began to be ashamed of my first judgment, when I had drawn away from them at the Ferry pier, as though they had been unclean beasts. No class of man is altogether bad; but each has his own faults and virtues; and these shipmates of mine were no exception to the rule. Rough they were, sure enough; and bad, I suppose; but they had many virtues. They were kind when it occurred to them, simple even beyond the simplicity of a country lad like me, and had some glimmerings of honesty.

There was one man, of maybe forty, that would sit on my berthside for hours and tell me of his wife and child. He was a fisher that had lost his boat, and thus been driven to the deep-sea voyaging. Well, it is years ago now; but I have never forgotten him. His wife (who was 'young by him,' as he often told me) waited in vain to see her man return; he would never again make the fire for her in the morning, nor yet keep the bairn when she was sick. Indeed, many of these poor fellows (as the event proved) were upon their last cruise; the deep seas and cannibal fish received them; and it is a thankless business to speak ill of the dead.

Among other good deeds that they did, they returned my money, which had been shared among them; and though it was about a third short, I was very glad to get it, and hoped great good from it in the land I was going to. The ship was bound for the Carolinas; and you must not suppose that I was going to that place merely as an exile. The trade was even then much depressed; since that, and with the rebellion of the colonies and the formation of the United States, it has, of course, come to an end; but in these days of my youth, white men were still sold into slavery on the plantations, and that was the destiny to which my wicked uncle had condemned me.

The cabin-boy Ransome (from whom I had first heard of these atrocities) came in at times from the round-house, where he berthed and served, now nursing a bruised limb in silent agony, now raving against the cruelty of Mr. Shuan. It made my heart bleed; but the men had a great respect for the chief mate, who was, as they said, 'the only seaman of the whole jing-bang, and none such a bad man when he was sober.' Indeed, I found there was a strange peculiarity about our two mates: that Mr. Riach was sullen, unkind, and harsh when he was sober, and Mr. Shuan would not hurt a fly except when he was drinking. I asked about the captain; but I was told drink made no difference upon that man of iron.

I did my best in the small time allowed me to make something like a man, or rather I should say something like a boy, of the poor creature, Ransome. But his mind was scarce truly human. He could remember nothing of the time before he came to sea; only that his father had made clocks, and had a starling in the parlour, which could whistle 'The North Countrie'; all else had been blotted out in these years of hardship and cruelties. He had a strange notion of the dry land, picked up from sailors' stories: that it was a place where lads were put to some kind of slavery called a trade, and where apprentices were continually lashed and clapped into foul prisons. In a town, he thought every second person a decoy, and every third house a place in which seamen would be drugged and murdered. To be sure, I could tell him how kindly I had myself been used upon that dry land he was so much afraid of, and how well fed and carefully taught both by my friends and my parents: and if he had been recently hurt, he would weep bitterly and swear to run away; but if he was in his usual crackbrain humour, or (still more) if he had had a glass of spirits in the round-house, he would deride the notion.

It was Mr. Riach (Heaven forgive him!) who gave the boy drink;

and it was, doubtless, kindly meant; but besides that it was ruin to his health, it was the pitifullest thing in life to see this unhappy, unfriended creature staggering, and dancing, and talking he knew not what. Some of the men laughed, but not all; others would grow as black as thunder (thinking, perhaps, of their own childhood or their own children) and bid him stop that nonsense, and think what he was doing. As for me, I felt ashamed to look at him, and the poor child still comes about me in my dreams.

All this time, you should know, the *Covenant* was meeting continual head-winds and tumbling up and down against head-seas, so that the scuttle was almost constantly shut, and the forecastle lighted only by a swinging lantern on a beam. There was constant labour for all hands; the sails had to be made and shortened every hour; the strain told on the men's temper; there was a growl of quarrelling all day long from berth to berth; and as I was never allowed to set my foot on deck, you can picture to yourselves how weary of my life I grew to be, and how impatient for a change.

And a change I was to get, as you shall hear; but I must first tell of a conversation I had with Mr. Riach, which put a little heart in me to bear my troubles. Getting him in a favourable stage of drink (for indeed he never looked near me when he was sober) I pledged him to secrecy, and told him my whole story.

He declared it was like a ballad; that he would do his best to help me; that I should have paper, pen, and ink, and write one line to Mr. Campbell and another to Mr. Rankeillor; and that if I had told the truth, ten to one he would be able (with their help) to pull me through and set me in my rights.

'And in the meantime,' says he, 'keep your heart up. You're not the only one, I'll tell you that. There's many a man hoeing tobacco overseas that should be mounting his horse at his own door at home; many and many! And life is all a variorum, at the best. Look at me: I'm a laird's son and more than half a doctor, and here I am, man-Jack to Hoseason!'

I thought it would be civil to ask him for his story.

He whistled loud.

'Never had one,' said he. 'I liked fun, that's all.' And he skipped out of the forecastle.

1 Stroke.   2 Blow.

8 The Round-House

One night, about twelve o'clock, a man of Mr. Riach's watch (which was on deck) came down for his jacket; and instantly there began to go a whisper about the forecastle that 'Shuan had done for him at last.' There was no need of a name; we all knew who was meant; but we had scarce time to get the idea rightly in our heads, far less to speak of it, when the scuttle was again flung open, and Captain Hoseason came down the ladder. He looked sharply round the bunks in the tossing light of the lantern; and then, walking up to me, he addressed me, to my surprise, in tones of kindness.

'My man,' said he, 'we want ye to serve in the round-house. You and Ransome are to change berths. Run away aft with ye.'

Even as he spoke, two seamen appeared in the scuttle, carrying Ransome in their arms; and the ship at that moment giving a great sheer into the sea, and the lantern swinging, the light fell direct on the boy's face. It was as white as wax, and had a look upon it like a dreadful smile. The blood in me ran cold, and I drew in my breath as if I had been struck.

'Run away aft; run away aft with ye!' cried Hoseason.

And at that I brushed by the sailors and the boy (who neither spoke nor moved), and ran up the ladder on deck.

The brig was sheering swiftly and giddily through a long cresting swell. She was on the starboard tack, and on the left hand, under the arched foot of the foresail, I could see the sunset still quite bright. This, at such an hour of the night, surprised me greatly; but I was too ignorant to draw the true conclusion – that we were going north-about round Scotland, and were now on the high sea between the Orkney and Shetland Islands, having avoided the dangerous currents of the Pentland Firth. For my part, who had been so long shut in the dark and knew nothing of head-winds, I thought we might be half-way or more across the Atlantic. And indeed (beyond that I wondered a little at the lateness of the sunset light) I gave no heed to it, and pushed on across the decks, running between the seas, catching at ropes, and only saved from going overboard by one of the hands on deck, who had been always kind to me.

The round-house, for which I was bound, and where I was now to sleep and serve, stood some six feet above the decks, and considering the size of the brig, was of good dimensions. Inside were a fixed table and bench, and two berths, one for the captain and the other for the two mates, turn and turn about. It was all fitted with lockers from top to bottom, so as to stow away the officers' belongings and a part of the ship's stores; there was a second store-room underneath, which you entered by a hatchway in the middle of the deck; indeed, all the best of the meat and drink and the whole of the powder were collected in this place; and all the firearms, except the two pieces of brass ordnance, were set in a rack in the aftermost wall of the round-house. The most of the cutlasses were in another place.

A small window with a shutter on each side, and a skylight in the roof, gave it light by day; and after dark there was a lamp always burning. It was burning when I entered, not brightly, but enough to show Mr. Shuan sitting at the table, with the brandy bottle and a tin pannikin in front of him. He was a tall man, strongly made and very black; and he stared before him on the table like one stupid.

He took no notice of my coming in; nor did he move when the captain followed and leant on the berth beside me, looking darkly at the mate. I stood in great fear of Hoseason, and had my reasons for it; but something told me I need not be afraid of him just then; and I whispered in his ear, 'How is he?' He shook his head like one that does not know and does not wish to think, and his face was very stern.

Presently Mr. Riach came in. He gave the captain a glance that meant the boy was dead as plain as speaking, and took his place like the rest of us; so that we all three stood without a word, staring down at Mr. Shuan, and Mr. Shuan (on his side) sat without a word, looking hard upon the table.

All of a sudden he put out his hand to take the bottle; and at that Mr. Riach started forward and caught it away from him, rather by surprise than violence, crying out, with an oath, that there had been too much of this work altogether, and that a judgment would fall upon the ship. And as he spoke (the weather sliding-doors standing open) he tossed the bottle into the sea.

Mr. Shuan was on his feet in a trice; he still looked dazed, but he meant murder, ay, and would have done it, for the second time that night, had not the captain stepped in between him and his victim.

'Sit down!' roars the captain. 'Ye sot and swine, do ye know what ye've done? Ye've murdered the boy!'

Mr. Shuan seemed to understand; for he sat down again, and put up his hand to his brow.

'Well,' he said, 'he brought me a dirty pannikin!'

At that word, the captain and I and Mr. Riach all looked at each other for a second with a kind of frightened look; and then Hoseason walked up to his chief officer, took him by the shoulder, led him across to his bunk, and bade him lie down and go to sleep, as you might speak to a bad child. The murderer cried a little, but he took off his sea-boots and obeyed.

'Ah!' cried Mr. Riach, with a dreadful voice, 'ye should have interfered long syne. It's too late now.'

'Mr. Riach,' said the captain, 'this night's work must never be kennt in Dysart. The boy went overboard, sir; that's what the story is; and I would give five pounds out of my pocket it was true!' He turned to the table. 'What made ye throw the good bottle away?' he added. 'There was nae sense in that, sir. Here, David, draw me another. They're in the bottom locker,' and he tossed me a key. 'Ye'll need a glass yourself, sir,' he added to Riach. 'Yon was an ugly thing to see.'

So the pair sat down and hob-a-nobbed; and while they did so, the murderer, who had been lying and whimpering in his berth, raised himself upon his elbow and looked at them and at me.

That was the first night of my new duties; and in the course of the day I had got well into the run of them. I had to serve at the meals, which the captain took at regular hours, sitting down with the officer who was off duty; all the day through I would be running with a dram to one or other of my three masters; and at night I slept on a blanket thrown on the deck boards at the aftermost end of the round-house, and right in the draught of the two doors. It was a hard and a cold bed; nor was I suffered to sleep without interruption; for someone would be always coming in from deck to get a dram, and when a fresh watch was to be set, two and sometimes all three would sit down and brew a bowl together. How they kept their health I know not, any more than how I kept my own.

And yet in other ways it was an easy service. There was no cloth to

lay; the meals were either of oatmeal porridge or salt junk, except twice
a week, when there was duff: and though I was clumsy enough and (not
being firm on my sea-legs) sometimes fell with what I was bringing
them, both Mr. Riach and the captain were singularly patient. I could
not but fancy they were making up leeway with their consciences, and
that they would scarce have been so good with me if they had not been
worse with Ransome.

As for Mr. Shuan, the drink, or his crime, or the two together, had
certainly troubled his mind. I cannot say I ever saw him in his proper
wits. He never grew used to my being there, stared at me continually
(sometimes, I could have thought, with terror), and more than once
drew back from my hand when I was serving him. I was pretty sure
from the first that he had no clear mind of what he had done, and on
my second day in the round-house I had the proof of it. We were alone,
and he had been staring at me a long time, when, all at once, up he got,
as pale as death, and came close up to me, to my great terror. But I had
no cause to be afraid of him.

'You were not here before?' he asked.

'No, sir,' said I.

'There was another boy?' he asked again; and when I had
answered him, 'Ah!' says he, 'I thought that,' and went and sat down,
without another word, except to call for brandy.

You may think it strange, but for all the horror I had, I was still
sorry for him. He was a married man, with a wife in Leith; but whether
or no he had a family, I have now forgotten; I hope not.

Altogether it was no very hard life for the time it lasted, which (as
you are to hear) was not long. I was as well fed as the best of them; even
their pickles, which were the great dainty, I was allowed my share of;
and had I liked, I might have been drunk from morning to night, like
Mr. Shuan. I had company, too, and good company of its sort. Mr.
Riach, who had been to the college, spoke to me like a friend when he
was not sulking, and told me many curious things, and some that were
informing; and even the captain, though he kept me at the stick's end
the most part of the time, would sometimes unbuckle a bit and tell me
of the fine countries he had visited.

The shadow of poor Ransome, to be sure, lay on all four of us, and
on me and Mr. Shuan, in particular, most heavily. And then I had
another trouble of my own. Here I was, doing dirty work for three men
that I looked down upon, and one of whom, at least, should have hung

upon a gallows; that was for the present; and as for the future, I could only see myself slaving alongside of Negroes in the tobacco fields. Mr. Riach, perhaps from caution, would never suffer me to say another word about my story; the captain, whom I tried to approach, rebuffed me like a dog and would not hear a word; and as the days came and went, my heart sank lower and lower, till I was even glad of the work which kept me from thinking.

9 The Man with the Belt of Gold

More than a week went by, in which the ill luck that had hitherto pursued the *Covenant* upon this voyage grew yet more strongly marked. Some days she made a little way; others, she was driven actually back. At last we were beaten so far to the south that we tossed and tacked to and fro the whole of the ninth day, within sight of Cape Wrath and the wild rocky coast on either hand of it. There followed on that a council of the officers, and some decision which I did not rightly understand, seeing only the result: that we had made a fair wind of a foul one and were running south.

The tenth afternoon there was a falling swell and a thick, wet, white fog that hid one end of the brig from the other. All afternoon, when I went on deck, I saw men and officers listening hard over the bulwarks – 'for breakers,' they said; and though I did not so much as understand the word, I felt danger in the air, and was excited.

Maybe about ten at night, I was serving Mr. Riach and the captain at their supper, when the ship struck something with a great sound, and we heard voices singing out. My two masters leaped to their feet.

'She's struck!' said Mr. Riach.

'No, sir,' said the captain. 'We've only run a boat down.'

And they hurried out.

The captain was in the right of it. We had run down a boat in the fog, and she had parted in the midst and gone to the bottom with all her crew but one. This man (as I heard afterwards) had been sitting in the stern as a passenger, while the rest were on the benches rowing. At the moment of the blow, the stern had been thrown into the air, and the man (having his hands free, and for all he was encumbered with a frieze overcoat that came below his knees) had leaped up and caught hold of the brig's bowsprit. It showed he had luck and much agility and unusual strength, that he should have thus saved himself from such a pass. And yet, when the captain brought him into the round-house, and I set eyes on him for the first time, he looked as cool as I did.

He was smallish in stature, but well set and as nimble as a goat; his face was of a good open expression, but sunburnt very dark, and heavily freckled and pitted with the smallpox; his eyes were unusually light and had a kind of dancing madness in them, that was both engaging and alarming; and when he took off his greatcoat, he laid a pair of fine silver-mounted pistols on the table, and I saw that he was belted with a great sword. His manners, besides, were elegant, and he pledged the captain handsomely. Altogether I thought of him, at the first sight, that here was a man I would rather call my friend than my enemy.

The captain, too, was taking his observations, but rather of the man's clothes than his person. And to be sure, as soon as he had taken off the greatcoat, he showed forth mighty fine for the round-house of a merchant brig: having a hat with feathers, a red waistcoat, breeches of black plush, and a blue coat with silver buttons and handsome silver lace; costly clothes, though somewhat spoiled with the fog and being slept in.

'I'm vexed, sir, about the boat,' says the captain.

'There are some pretty men gone to the bottom,' said the stranger, 'that I would rather see on the dry land again than half a score of boats.'

'Friends of yours?' said Hoseason.

'You have none such friends in your country,' was the reply. 'They would have died for me like dogs.'

'Well, sir,' said the captain, still watching him, 'there are more men in the world than boats to put them in.'

'And that's true, too,' cried the other, 'and ye seem to be a gentleman of great penetration.'

'I have been in France, sir,' says the captain, so that it was plain he meant more by the words than showed upon the face of them.

'Well, sir,' says the other, 'and so has many a pretty man, for the matter of that.'

'No doubt, sir,' says the captain, 'and fine coats.'

'Oho!' says the stranger, 'is that how the wind sets?' And he laid his hand quickly on his pistols.

'Don't be hasty,' said the captain. 'Don't do a mischief before ye see the need for it. Ye've a French soldier's coat upon your back and a Scotch tongue in your head, to be sure; but so has many an honest fellow in these days, and I dare say none the worse of it.'

'So?' said the gentleman in the fine coat: 'are ye of the honest party?' (meaning, Was he a Jacobite? for each side, in these sort of civil broils, takes the name of honesty for its own).

'Why, sir,' replied the captain, 'I am a true-blue Protestant, and I thank God for it.' (It was the first word of any religion I had ever heard from him, but I learnt afterwards he was a great church-goer while on shore.) 'But for all that,' says he, 'I can be sorry to see another man with his back to the wall.'

'Can ye so, indeed?' asked the Jacobite. 'Well, sir, to be quite plain with ye, I am one of those honest gentlemen that were in trouble about the years forty-five and six; and (to be still quite plain with ye) if I got into the hands of any of the red-coated gentry, it's like it would go hard with me. Now, sir, I was for France; and there was a French ship cruising here to pick me up; but she gave us the go-by in the fog – as I wish from the heart that ye had done yoursel'! And the best that I can say is this: If ye can set me ashore where I was going, I have that upon me will reward you highly for your trouble.'

'In France?' says the captain. 'No, sir; that I cannot do. But where ye come from – we might talk of that.'

And then, unhappily, he observed me standing in my corner, and packed me off to the galley to get supper for the gentleman. I lost no time, I promise you; and when I came back into the round-house, I found the gentleman had taken a money-belt from about his waist, and poured out a guinea or two upon the table. The captain was looking at the guineas, and then at the belt, and then at the gentleman's face; and I thought he seemed excited.

'Half of it,' he cried, 'and I'm your man!'

The other swept back the guineas into the belt, and put it on again under his waistcoat. 'I have told ye, sir,' said he, 'that not one doit of it belongs to me. It belongs to my chieftain' – and here he touched his hat – 'and while I would be but a silly messenger to grudge some of it that the rest might come safe, I should show myself a hound indeed if I bought my own carcass any too dear. Thirty guineas on the seaside, or sixty if ye set me on the Linnhe Loch. Take it, if ye will; if not, ye can do your worst.'

'Ay,' said Hoseason. 'And if I give ye over to the soldiers?'

'Ye would make a fool's bargain,' said the other. 'My chief, let me tell you, sir, is forfeited, like every honest man in Scotland. His estate is in the hands of the man they call King George; and it is his officers that collect the rents, or try to collect them. But for the honour of Scotland, the poor tenant bodies take a thought upon their chief lying in exile; and this money is a part of that very rent for which King George is looking. Now, sir, ye seem to me to be a man that understands things: bring this money within the reach of Government, and how much of it'll come to you?'

'Little enough, to be sure,' said Hoseason; and then, 'If they knew,' he added drily. 'But I think, if I was to try, that I could hold my tongue about it.'

'Ah, but I'll begowk¹ ye there!' cried the gentleman. 'Play me false, and I'll play you cunning. If a hand's laid upon me, they shall ken what money it is.'

'Well,' returned the captain, 'what must be must. Sixty guineas, and done. Here's my hand upon it.'

'And here's mine,' said the other.

And thereupon the captain went out (rather hurriedly, I thought), and left me alone in the round-house with the stranger.

At that period (so soon after the forty-five) there were many exiled gentlemen coming back at the peril of their lives, either to see their friends or to collect a little money; and as for the Highland chiefs that had been forfeited, it was a common matter of talk how their tenants would stint themselves to send them money, and their clansmen outface the soldiery to get it in, and run the gauntlet of our great navy to carry it across. All this I had, of course, heard tell of; and now I had a man under my eyes whose life was forfeit on all these counts and upon one more, for he was not only a rebel and a smuggler of rents, but had taken service with King Louis of France. And as if all this were not enough, he had a belt full of golden guineas round his loins. Whatever my opinions, I could not look on such a man without a lively interest.

'And so you're a Jacobite?' said I, as I set meat before him.

'Ay,' said he, beginning to eat. 'And you, by your long face, should be a Whig?'²

Betwixt and between,' said I, not to annoy him; for indeed I was as good a Whig as Mr. Campbell could make me.

'And that's naething,' said he. 'But I'm saying, Mr. Betwixt-and-Between,' he added, 'this bottle of yours is dry; and it's hard if I'm to pay sixty guineas and be grudged a dram upon the back of it.'

'I'll go and ask for the key,' said I, and stepped on deck.

The fog was as close as ever, but the swell almost down. They had laid the brig to, not knowing precisely where they were, and the wind (what little there was of it) not serving well for their true course. Some of the hands were still hearkening for breakers; but the captain and the two officers were in the waist with their heads together. It struck me (I don't know why) that they were after no good; and the first word I heard, as I drew softly near, more than confirmed me.

It was Mr. Riach, crying out as if upon a sudden thought:

'Couldn't we wile him out of the round-house?'

'He's better where he is,' returned Hoseason; 'he hasn't room to use his sword.'

'Well, that's true,' said Riach; 'but he's hard to come at.'

'Hut!' said Hoseason. 'We can get the man in talk, one upon each side, and pin him by the two arms; or if that'll not hold, sir, we can make a run by both the doors and get him under hand before he has the time to draw.'

At this hearing, I was seized with both fear and anger at these treacherous, greedy, bloody men that I sailed with. My first mind was to run away; my second was bolder.

'Captain,' said I, 'the gentleman is seeking a dram, and the bottle's out. Will you give me the key?'

They all started and turned about.

'Why, here's our chance to get the firearms!' Riach cried; and then to me: 'Hark ye, David,' he said, 'do ye ken where the pistols are?'

'Ay, ay,' put in Hoseason. 'David kens; David's a good lad. Ye see, David my man, yon wild Hielandman is a danger to the ship, besides being a rank foe to King George, God bless him!'

I had never been so be-Davided since I came on board; but I said Yes, as if all I heard were quite natural.

'The trouble is,' resumed the captain, 'that all our firelocks, great and little, are in the round-house under this man's nose; likewise the powder. Now, if I, or one of the officers, was to go in and take them, he would fall to thinking. But a lad like you, David, might snap up a horn and a pistol or two without remark. And if ye can do it cleverly, I'll bear it in mind when it'll be good for you to have friends; and that's when we come to Carolina.'

Here Mr. Riach whispered him a little.

'Very right, sir,' said the captain; and then to myself: 'And see here, David, yon man has a beltful of gold, and I give you my word that you shall have your fingers in it.'

I told him I would do as he wished, though indeed I had scarce breath to speak with; and upon that he gave me the key of the spirit locker, and I began to go slowly back to the round-house. What was I to do? They were dogs and thieves; they had stolen me from my own country; they had killed poor Ransome; and was I to hold the candle to another murder? But then, upon the other hand, there was the fear of death very plain before me; for what could a boy and a man, if they were as brave as lions, against a whole ship's company?

I was still arguing it back and forth, and getting no great clearness, when I came into the round-house and saw the Jacobite eating his supper under the lamp; and at that my mind was made up all in a moment. I have no credit by it; it was by no choice of mine, but as if by compulsion, that I walked right up to the table and put my hand on his shoulder.

'Do ye want to be killed?' said I.

He sprang to his feet, and looked a question at me as clear as if he had spoken.

'Oh!' cried I, 'they're all murderers here; it's a ship full of them! They've murdered a boy already. Now it's you.'

'Ay, ay,' said he; 'but they haven't got me yet.' And then looking at me curiously, 'Will ye stand with me?'

'That will I!' said I. 'I am no thief, nor yet murderer. I'll stand by you.'

'Why, then,' said he, 'what's your name?'

'David Balfour,' said I; and then thinking that a man with so fine a coat must like fine people, I added for the first time, 'of Shaws.'

It never occurred to him to doubt me, for a Highlander is used to see great gentlefolk in great poverty; but as he had no estate of his own, my words nettled a very childish vanity he had.

'My name is Stewart,' he said, drawing himself up. 'Alan Breck, they call me. A king's name is good enough for me, though I bear it plain and have the name of no farm-midden to clap to the hind-end of it.'

And having administered this rebuke, as though it were something of a chief importance, he turned to examine our defences.

The round-house was built very strong, to support the breaching of the seas. Of its five apertures, only the skylight and the two doors were large enough for the passage of a man. The doors, besides, could be drawn close: they were of stout oak, and ran in grooves, and were fitted with hooks to keep them either shut or open, as the need arose. The one that was already shut I secured in this fashion; but when I was proceeding to slide to the other, Alan stopped me.

'David,' said he – 'for I cannae bring to mind the name of your landed estate, and so will make so bold as to call you David – that door, being open, is the best part of my defences.'

'It would be yet better shut,' says I.

'Not so, David,' says he. 'Ye see, I have but one face; but so long as that door is open and my face to it, the best part of my enemies will be in front of me, where I would aye wish to find them.'

Then he gave me from the rack a cutlass (of which there were a few besides the firearms), choosing it with great care, shaking his head and saying he had never in all his life seen poorer weapons; and next he set me down to the table with a powder-horn, a bag of bullets and all the pistols, which he bade me charge.

'And that will be better work, let me tell you,' said he, 'for a gentleman of decent birth, than scraping plates and raxing[3] drams to a wheen tarry sailors.'

Thereupon he stood up in the midst with his face to the door, and drawing his great sword, made trial of the room he had to wield it in.

'I must stick to the point,' he said, shaking his head; 'and that's a pity, too. It doesn't set my genius, which is all for the upper guard. And now,' said he, 'do you keep on charging the pistols, and give heed to me.'

I told him I would listen closely. My chest was tight, my mouth dry, the light dark to my eyes; the thought of the numbers that were soon to leap in upon us kept my heart in a flutter; and the sea which I heard washing round the brig, and where I thought my dead body would be cast ere morning, ran in my mind strangely.

'First of all,' said he, 'how many are against us?'

I reckoned them up; and such was the hurry of my mind, I had to cast the numbers twice. 'Fifteen,' said I.

Alan whistled. 'Well,' said he, 'that can't be cured. And now follow me. It is my part to keep this door, where I look for the main battle. In that, ye have no hand. And mind and dinnae fire to this side unless they get me down; for I would rather have ten foes in front of me than one friend like you cracking pistols at my back.'

I told him, indeed I was no great shot.

'And that's very bravely said,' he cried in a great admiration of my candour. 'There's many a pretty gentleman that wouldnae dare to say it.'

'But then, sir, said I, 'there is the door behind you, which they may perhaps break in.'

'Ay,' said he, 'and that is a part of your work. No sooner the pistols charged, than ye must climb up into yon bed where ye're handy at the window; and if they lift hand against the door, ye're to shoot. But that's not all. Let's make a bit of a soldier of ye, David. What else have ye to guard?'

'There's the skylight,' said I. 'But indeed, Mr. Stewart, I would need to have eyes upon both sides to keep the two of them; for when my face is at the one, my back is to the other.'

'And that's very true,' said Alan. 'But have ye no ears to your head?'

'To be sure!' cried I. 'I must hear the bursting of the glass!'

'Ye have some rudiments of sense,' said Alan grimly.

1 Befool.
2 Whig or Whigamore was the cant name for those who were loyal to King George.
3 Reaching.

10 The Siege of the Round-House

But now our time of truce was come to an end. Those on deck had waited for my coming till they grew impatient; and scarce had Alan spoken, when the captain showed his face in the open door.

'Stand!' cried Alan, and pointed his sword at him.

The captain stood, indeed; but he neither winced nor drew back a foot.

'A naked sword?' says he. 'This is a strange return for hospitality.'

'Do ye see me?' said Alan. 'I am come of kings; I bear a king's name. My badge is the oak. Do ye see my sword? It has slashed the heads off mair Whigamores than you have toes upon your feet. Call up your vermin to your back, sir, and fall on! The sooner the clash begins the sooner ye'll taste this steel throughout your vitals.'

The captain said nothing to Alan, but he looked over at me with an ugly look. 'David,' said he, 'I'll mind this'; and the sound of his voice went through me with a jar.

Next moment he was gone.

'And now,' said Alan, 'let your hand keep your head, for the grip is coming.'

Alan drew a dirk, which he held in his left hand in case they should run in under his sword. I, on my part, clambered up into the berth with an armful of pistols and something of a heavy heart, and set open the window where I was to watch. It was a small part of the deck that I could overlook, but enough for our purpose. The sea had gone down, and the wind was steady and kept the sails quiet; so that there was a great stillness in the ship, in which I made sure I heard the sound of muttering voices. A little after, and there came a clash of steel upon the deck, by which I knew they were dealing out the cutlasses and one had been let fall: and after that, silence again.

I do not know if I was what you call afraid; but my heart beat like a bird's, both quick and little; and there was a dimness came before my eyes which I continually rubbed away, and which continually returned. As for hope, I had none; but only a darkness of despair and a sort of anger against all the world that made me long to sell my life as dear as I was able. I tried to pray, I remember, but that same hurry of my mind, like a man running, would not suffer me to think upon the words; and my chief wish was to have the thing begin and be done with it.

It came all of a sudden when it did, with a rush of feet and a roar, and then a shout from Alan, and a sound of blows and someone crying out as if hurt. I looked back over my shoulder, and saw Mr. Shuan in the doorway, crossing blades with Alan.

'That's him that killed the boy!' I cried.

'Look to your window!' said Alan; and as I turned back to my place, I saw him pass the sword through the mate's body.

It was none too soon for me to look to my own part; for my head was scarce back at the window, before five men, carrying a spare yard for a battering-ram, ran past me and took post to drive the door in. I had never fired with a pistol in my life, and not often with a gun; far less against a fellow creature. But it was now or never; and just as they swang the yard, I cried out, 'Take that!' and shot into their midst.

I must have hit one of them, for he sang out and gave back a step, and the rest stopped as if a little disconcerted. Before they had time to recover, I sent another ball over their heads; and at my third shot (which went as wide as the second) the whole party threw down the yard and ran for it.

Then I looked round again into the deck-house. The whole place was full of the smoke of my own firing, just as my ears seemed to be burst with the noise of the shots. But there was Alan, standing as before; only now his sword was running blood to the hilt, and himself so swelled with triumph and fallen into so fine an attitude, that he looked to be invincible. Right before him on the floor was Mr. Shuan, on his hands and knees; the blood was pouring from his mouth, and he was sinking slowly lower, with a terrible, white face; and just as I looked, some of those from behind caught hold of him by the heels and dragged him bodily out of the round-house. I believe he died as they were doing it.

'There's one of your Whigs for ye!' cried Alan; and then turning to me, he asked if I had done much execution.

I told him I had winged one, and thought it was the captain.

'And I've settled two,' says he. 'No, there's not enough blood let; they'll be back again. To your watch, David. This was but a dram before meat.'

I settled back to my place, recharging the three pistols I had fired, and keeping watch with both eye and ear.

Our enemies were disputing not far off upon the deck, and that so loudly that I could hear a word or two above the washing of the seas.

'It was Shuan bauchled[1] it,' I heard one say.

And another answered him with a 'Wheesht, man! He's paid the piper.'

After that the voices fell again into the same muttering as before. Only now, one person spoke most of the time, as though laying down a plan, and first one and then another answered him briefly, like men taking orders. By this, I made sure they were coming on again, and told Alan.

'It's what we have to pray for,' said he. 'Unless we can give them a good distaste of us, and done with it, there'll be nae sleep for either you or me. But this time, mind, they'll be in earnest.'

By this, my pistols were ready, and there was nothing to do but listen and wait. While the brush lasted, I had not the time to think if I was frighted; but now, when all was still again, my mind ran upon nothing else. The thought of the sharp swords and the cold steel was strong in me; and presently, when I began to hear stealthy steps and a brushing of men's clothes against the round-house wall, and knew they were taking their places in the dark, I could have found it in my mind to cry out aloud.

All this was upon Alan's side; and I had begun to think my share of the fight was at an end, when I heard someone drop softly on the roof above me.

Then there came a single call on the sea-pipe, and that was the signal. A knot of them made one rush of it, cutlass in hand, against the door; and at the same moment, the glass of the skylight was dashed in a thousand pieces, and a man leaped through and landed on the floor. Before he got his feet, I had clapped a pistol to his back, and might have shot him, too; only at the touch of him (and him alive) my whole flesh misgave me, and I could no more pull the trigger than I could have flown.

He had dropped his cutlass as he jumped, and when he felt the pistol, whipped straight round and laid hold of me, roaring out an

'Alan . . . ran upon the others like a bull, . . .'

oath; and at that either my courage came again, or I grew so much afraid as came to the same thing; for I gave a shriek and shot him in the midst of the body. He gave the most horrible, ugly groan, and fell to the floor. The foot of a second fellow, whose legs were dangling through the skylight, struck me at the same time upon the head; and at that I snatched another pistol and shot this one through the thigh, so that he slipped through and tumbled in a lump on his companion's body. There was no talk of missing, any more than there was time to aim; I clapped the muzzle to the very place and fired.

I might have stood and stared at them for long, but I heard Alan shout as if for help, and that brought me to my senses.

He had kept the door so long; but one of the seamen, while he was engaged with others, had run in under his guard and caught him about the body. Alan was dirking him with his left hand, but the fellow clung like a leech. Another had broken in and had his cutlass raised. The door was thronged with their faces. I thought we were lost, and catching up my cutlass, fell on them in flank.

But I had not time to be of help. The wrestler dropped at last; and Alan, leaping back to get his distance, ran upon the others like a bull, roaring as he went. They broke before him like water, turning, and running, and falling one against another in their haste. The sword in his hands flashed like quicksilver into the huddle of our fleeing enemies; and at every flash there came the scream of a man hurt. I was still thinking we were lost, when lo! they were all gone, and Alan was driving them along the deck as a sheep-dog chases sheep.

Yet he was no sooner out than he was back again, being as cautious as he was brave; and meanwhile the seamen continued running and crying out as if he was still behind them; and we heard them tumble one upon another into the forecastle, and clap-to the hatch upon the top.

The round-house was like a shambles; three were dead inside, another lay in his death agony across the threshold; and there were Alan and I victorious and unhurt.

He came up to me with open arms. 'Come to my arms!' he cried, and embraced and kissed me hard upon both cheeks. 'David,' said he, 'I love you like a brother. And oh, man,' he cried in a kind of ecstasy, 'am I no a bonny fighter?'

Thereupon he turned to the four enemies, passed his sword clean through each of them, and tumbled them out of doors one after the other. As he did so, he kept humming and singing and whistling to himself, like a man trying to recall an air; only what *he* was trying was to make one. All the while, the flush was in his face, and his eyes were as bright as a five-year-old child's with a new toy. And presently he sat down upon the table, sword in hand; the air that he was making all the time began to run a little clearer, and then clearer still; and then out he burst with a great voice into a Gaelic song.

I have translated it here, not in verse (of which I have no skill) but at least in the King's English. He sang it often afterwards, and the thing became popular; so that I have heard it, and had it explained to me, many's the time.

> This is the song of the sword of Alan:
> The smith made it,
> The fire set it;
> Now it shines in the hand of Alan Breck.
>
> Their eyes were many and bright,
> Swift were they to behold,
> Many the hands they guided:
> The sword was alone.
>
> The dun deer troop over the hill,
> They are many, the hill is one:
> The dun deer vanish,
> The hill remains.
>
> Come to me from the hills of heather
> Come from the isles of the sea.
> O far-beholding eagles,
> Here is your meat.

Now this song which he made (both words and music) in the hour of our victory is something less than just to me, who stood beside him in the tussle. Mr. Shuan and five more were either killed outright or thoroughly disabled; but of these, two fell by my hand, the two that came by the skylight. Four more were hurt, and of that number, one (and he not the least important) got his hurt from me. So that, altogether, I did my fair share both of the killing and the wounding, and might have claimed a place in Alan's verses. But poets (as a very wise man once told me) have to think upon their rhymes; and in good prose talk, Alan always did me more than justice.

In the meanwhile, I was innocent of any wrong being done me. For not only I knew no word of the Gaelic; but what with the long suspense of the waiting, and the scurry and strain of our two spirts of fighting, and more than all, the horror I had of some of my own share in it, the thing was no sooner over than I was glad to stagger to a seat. There was a tightness on my chest that I could hardly breathe; the thought of the two men I had shot sat upon me like a nightmare; and all upon a sudden, and before I had a guess of what was coming, I began to sob and cry like any child.

Alan clapped my shoulder, and said I was a brave lad and wanted nothing but a sleep.

'I'll take the first watch,' said he. 'Ye've done well by me, David, first and last; and I wouldn't lose you for all Appin – no, nor for Breadalbane.'

So he made up my bed on the floor; and took the first spell, pistol in hand and sword on knee, three hours by the captain's watch upon the wall. Then he roused me up, and I took my turn of three hours; before the end of which it was broad day, and a very quiet morning, with a smooth, rolling sea that tossed the ship and made the blood run to and fro on the round-house floor, and a heavy rain that drummed upon the roof. All my watch there was nothing stirring; and by the banging of the helm, I knew they had even no one at the tiller. Indeed (as I learned afterwards) they were so many of them hurt or dead, and the rest in so ill a temper, that Mr. Riach and the captain had to take turn and turn like Alan and me, or the brig might have gone ashore and nobody the wiser. It was a mercy the night had fallen so still, for the wind had gone down as soon as the rain began. Even as it was, I judged by the wailing of a great number of gulls that went crying and fishing round the ship, that she must have drifted pretty near the coast or one of the islands of the Hebrides; and at last, looking out of the door of the round-house, I saw the great stone hills of Skye on the right hand, and, a little more astern, the strange Isle of Rum.

1 Bungled.

11 The Captain Knuckles Under

Alan and I sat down to breakfast about six of the clock. The floor was covered with broken glass and in a horrid mess of blood, which took away my hunger. In all other ways we were in a situation not only agreeable but merry; having ousted the officers from their own cabin, and having at command all the drink in the ship – both wine and spirits – and all the dainty part of what was eatable, such as the pickles and the fine sort of biscuit. This, of itself, was enough to set us in good humour; but the richest part of it was this, that the two thirstiest men that ever came out of Scotland (Mr. Shuan being dead) were now shut in the fore-part of the ship and condemned to what they hated most – cold water.

'And depend upon it,' Alan said, 'we shall hear more of them ere long. Ye may keep a man from the fighting, but never from his bottle.'

We made good company for each other. Alan, indeed, expressed himself most lovingly; and taking a knife from the table, cut me off one of the silver buttons from his coat.

'I had them,' says he, 'from my father, Duncan Stewart; and now give ye one of them to be a keepsake for last night's work. And wherever ye go and show that button, the friends of Alan Breck will come around you.'

He said this as if he had been Charlemagne, and commanded armies; and indeed, much as I admired his courage, I was always in danger of smiling at his vanity; in danger, I say, for had I not kept my countenance, I would be afraid to think what a quarrel might have followed.

As soon as we were through with our meal, he rummaged in the captain's locker till he found a clothes-brush; and then taking off his coat, began to visit his suit and brush away the stains, with such care and labour as I supposed to have been only usual with women. To be sure, he had no other; and, besides (as he said), it belonged to a King and so behoved to be royally looked after.

For all that, when I saw what care he took to pluck out the threads where the button had been cut away, I put a higher value on his gift.

He was still so engaged when we were hailed by Mr. Riach from the deck, asking for a parley; and I, climbing through the skylight and sitting on the edge of it, pistol in hand and with a bold front, though inwardly in fear of broken glass, hailed him back again and bade him speak out. He came to the edge of the round-house, and stood on a coil of rope, so that his chin was on a level with the roof; and we looked at each other awhile in silence. Mr. Riach, as I do not think he had been very forward in the battle, so he had got off with nothing worse than a blow upon the cheek: but he looked out of heart and very weary, having been all night afoot, either standing watch or doctoring the wounded.

'This is a bad job,' said he at last, shaking his head.

'It was none of our choosing,' said I.

'The captain,' says he, 'would like to speak with your friend. They might speak at the window.'

'And how do we know what treachery he means?' cried I.

'He means none, David,' returned Mr. Riach, 'and if he did, I'll tell ye the honest truth, we couldnae get the men to follow.'

'Is that so?' said I.

'I'll tell ye more than that,' said he. 'It's not only the men; it's me, I'm frich'ened, Davie.' And he smiled across at me. 'No,' he continued, 'what we want is to be shut of him.'

Thereupon I consulted with Alan, and the parley was agreed to and parole given upon either side; but this was not the whole of Mr. Riach's business, and he now begged me for a dram with such instancy and such reminders of his former kindness, that at last I handed him a pannikin with about a gill of brandy. He drank a part, and then carried the rest down upon the deck, to share it (I suppose) with his superior.

A little after, the captain came (as was agreed) to one of the windows, and stood there in the rain, with his arm in a sling, and looking stern and pale, and so old that my heart smote me for having fired upon him.

Alan at once held a pistol to his face.

'Put that thing up!' said the captain. 'Have I not passed my word, sir? or do ye seek to affront me?'

'Captain,' says Alan, 'I doubt your word is a breakable. Last night ye haggled and argle-bargled like an apple-wife; and then passed me your word, and gave me your hand to back it; and ye ken very well what was the upshot. Be damned to your word!' says he.

'Well, well, sir,' said the captain, 'ye'll get little good by swearing.' (And truly that was a fault of which the captain was quite free.) 'But we have other things to speak,' he continued bitterly. 'Ye've made a sore hash of my brig; I haven't hands enough left to work her; and my first officer (whom I could ill spare) has got your sword throughout his vitals, and passed without speech. There is nothing left me, sir, but to put back into the port of Glasgow after hands; and there (by your leave) ye will find them that are better able to talk to you.'

'Ay?' said Alan; 'and faith, I'll have a talk with them mysel'! Unless there's naebody speaks English in that town, I have a bonny tale for them. Fifteen tarry sailors upon the one side, and a man and a halfling boy upon the other! Oh, man, it's peetiful!'

Hoseason flushed red.

'No,' continued Alan, 'that'll no do. Ye'll just have to set me ashore as we agreed.'

'Ay,' said Hoseason, 'but my first officer is dead – ye ken best how. There's none of the rest of us acquaint with this coast, sir; and it's one very dangerous to ships.'

'I give ye your choice,' says Alan. 'Set me on dry ground in Appin, or Ardgour, or in Morven, or Arisaig, or Morar; or, in brief, where ye please, within thirty miles of my own country; except in a country of the Campbells. That's a broad target. If ye miss that, ye must be as feckless at the sailoring as I have found ye at the fighting. Why, my poor country people in their bit cobles¹ pass from island to island in all weathers – ay, and by night too, for the matter of that.'

'A coble's not a ship, sir,' said the captain. 'It has nae draught of water.'

'Well, then, to Glasgow, if ye list!' says Alan. 'We'll have the laugh of ye at the least.'

'My mind runs little upon laughing,' said the captain. 'But all this will cost money, sir.'

'Well, sir,' says Alan, 'I am nae weathercock. Thirty guineas, if ye land me on the sea side; and sixty, if ye put me in the Linnhe Loch.'

'But see, sir, where we lie, we are but a few hours' sail from Ardnamurchan,' said Hoseason. 'Give me sixty, and I'll set ye there.'

'And I'm to wear my brogues and run jeopardy of the redcoats to please you?' cries Alan. 'No, sir; if ye want sixty guineas, earn them, and set me in my own country.'

'It's to risk the brig, sir,' said the captain, 'and your own lives along with her.'

'Take it or want it,' says Alan.

'Could ye pilot us at all?' asked the captain, who was frowning to himself.

'Well, it's doubtful,' said Alan. 'I'm more of a fighting man (as ye have seen for yoursel') than a sailorman. But I have been often enough picked up and set down upon this coast, and should ken something of the lie of it.'

The captain shook his head, still frowning.

'If I had lost less money on this unchancy cruise,' says he, 'I would see you in a rope's-end before I risked my brig, sir. But be it as ye will. As soon as I get a slant of wind (and there's some coming, or I'm the more mistaken) I'll put it in hand. But there's one thing more. We may meet in with a king's ship and she may lay us aboard, sir, with no blame of mine: they keep the cruisers thick upon this coast, ye ken who for. Now, sir, if that was to befall, ye might leave the money.'

'Captain,' says Alan, 'if ye see a pennant, it shall be your part to run away. And now, as I hear you're a little short of brandy in the fore-part, I'll offer ye a change: a bottle of brandy against two buckets of water.'

That was the last clause of the treaty, and was duly executed on both sides; so that Alan and I could at last wash out the round-house and be quit of the memorials of those whom we had slain, and the captain and Mr. Riach could be happy again in their own way, the name of which was drink.

---

1 Coble: a small boat used in fishing.

12 I Hear of the Red Fox

Before we had done cleaning out the round-house, a breeze sprang up from a little to the east of north. This blew off the rain and brought out the sun.

And here I must explain; and the reader would do well to look at a map. On the day when the fog fell and we ran down Alan's boat, we had been running through the Little Minch. At dawn after the battle, we lay becalmed to the east of the Isle of Canna or between that and Isle Eriska in the chain of the Long Island. Now to get from there to the Linnhe Loch, the straight course was through the narrows of the Sound of Mull. But the captain had no chart; he was afraid to trust his brig so deep among the islands; and the wind serving well, he preferred to go by west of Tiree and come up under the southern coast of the great Isle of Mull.

All day the breeze held in the same point, and rather freshened than died down; and towards afternoon, a swell began to set in from round the outer Hebrides. Our course, to go round about the inner isles, was to the west of south, so that at first we had this swell upon our beam, and were much rolled about. But after nightfall, when we had turned the end of Tiree and began to head more to the east, the sea came right astern.

Meanwhile, the early part of the day, before the swell came up, was very pleasant; sailing, as we were, in a bright sunshine and with many mountainous islands upon different sides. Alan and I sat in the round-house with the doors open on each side (the wind being straight astern), and smoked a pipe or two of the captain's fine tobacco. It was at this time we heard each other's stories, which was the more important to me, as I gained some knowledge of that wild Highland country on which I was so soon to land. In those days, so close on the back of the great rebellion, it was needful a man should know what he was doing when he went upon the heather.

It was I that showed the example, telling him all my misfortune; which he heard with great good nature. Only, when I came to mention that good friend of mine, Mr. Campbell the minister, Alan fired up and cried out that he hated all that were of that name.

'Why,' said I, 'he is a man you should be proud to give your hand to.'

'I know nothing I would help a Campbell to,' says he, 'unless it was a leaden bullet. I would hunt all of that name like blackcocks. If I lay dying, I would crawl upon my knees to my chamber window for a shot at one.'

'Why, Alan,' I cried, 'what ails ye at the Campbells?'

'Well,' says he, 'ye ken very well that I am an Appin Stewart, and the Campbells have long harried and wasted those of my name; ay, and got lands of us by treachery – but never with the sword,' he cried loudly, and with the word brought down his fist upon the table. But I paid the less attention to this, for I knew it was usually said by those who have the underhand. 'There's more than that,' he continued, 'and all in the same story: lying words, lying papers, tricks fit for a pedlar, and the show of what's legal over all, to make a man the more angry.'

'You that are so wasteful of your buttons,' said I, 'I can hardly think you would be a good judge of business.'

'Ah!' says he, falling again to smiling, 'I got my wastefulness from the same man I got the buttons from; and that was my poor father, Duncan Stewart, grace be to him! He was the prettiest man of his kindred; and the best swordsman in the Hielands, David, and that is the same as to say, in all the world. I should ken, for it was him that taught me. He was in the Black Watch, when first it was mustered; and, like other gentleman privates, had a gillie at his back to carry his firelock for him on the march. Well, the King, it appears, was wishful to see Hieland swordsmanship; and my father and three more were chosen out and sent to London town, to let him see it at the best. So they were had into the palace and showed the whole art of the sword for two hours at a stretch, before King George and Queen Caroline, and the Butcher Cumberland, and many more of whom I havenae mind. And when they were through, the King (for all he was a rank usurper) spoke them fair and gave each man three guineas in his hand. Now, as they were going out of the palace, they had a porter's lodge to go by; and it came in on my father, as he was perhaps the first private Hieland gentleman that had ever gone by that door, it was right he should give the poor porter a proper notion of their quality. So he gives the King's three guineas into the man's hand, as if it was his common custom; the three others that came behind him did the same; and there they were on the street, never a penny the better for their pains. Some say it was one that was the first to fee the King's porter; and some say it was another; but the truth of it is that it was Duncan Stewart, as I am willing to prove with either sword or pistol. And that was the father that I had, God rest him!'

'I think he was not the man to leave you rich,' said I.

'And that's true,' said Alan. 'He left me my breeks to cover me. and little besides. And that was how I came to enlist, which was a black spot upon my character at the best of times, and would still be a sore job for me if I fell among the redcoats.'

'What,' cried I, 'were you in the English army?'

'That was I,' said Alan. 'But I deserted to the right side at Prestonpans – and that's some comfort.'

I could scarcely share this view: holding desertion under arms for an unpardonable fault in honour. But for all I was so young, I was wiser than say my thought. 'Dear, dear,' says I, 'the punishment is death.'

'Ay,' said he, 'if they got hands on me, it would be a short shrift and a lang tow for Alan! But I have the King of France's commission in my pocket, which would aye be some protection.'

'I misdoubt it much,' said I.

'I have doubts mysel',' said Alan dryly.

'And, good heaven, man,' cried I, 'you that are a condemned rebel, and a deserter, and a man of the French King's – what tempts ye back into this country? It's a braving of Providence.'

'Tut!' says Alan, 'I have been back every year since forty-six!'

'And what brings ye, man?' cried I.

'Well, ye see, I weary for my friends and country,' said he. 'France is a braw place, nae doubt; but I weary for the heather and the deer. And then I have bit things that I attend to. Whiles I pick up a few lads to serve the King of France: recruits, ye see; and that's aye a little money. But the heart of the matter is the business of my chief, Ardshiel.'

'I thought they called your chief Appin,' said I.

'Ay, but Ardshiel is the captain of the clan,' said he, which scarcely cleared my mind. 'Ye see, David, he that was all his life so great a man, and come of the blood and bearing the name of kings, is now brought down to live in a French town like a poor and private person. He that had four hundred swords at his whistle, I have seen, with these eyes of mine, buying butter in the market-place, and taking it home in a kale-leaf. This is not only a pain but a disgrace to us of his family and clan. There are the bairns forby, the children and the hope of Appin, that must be learned their letters and how to hold a sword, in that far country. Now the tenants of Appin have to pay a rent to King George, but their hearts are staunch, they are true to their chief; and what with love and a bit of pressure, and maybe a threat or two, the poor folk scrape up a second rent for Ardshiel. Well, David, I'm the hand that carries it.' And he struck the belt about his body so that the guineas rang.

'Do they pay both?' cried I.

'Ay, David, both,' says he.

'What! two rents?' I repeated.

'Ay, David,' said he. 'I told a different tale to yon captain man; but this is the truth of it. And it's wonderful to me how little pressure is needed. But that's the handiwork of my good kinsman and my father's friend, James of the Glens; James Stewart, that is: Ardshiel's half-brother. He it is that gets the money in, and does the management.'

This was the first time I heard the name of that James Stewart who was afterwards so famous at the time of his hanging. But I took little heed at the moment, for all my mind was occupied with the generosity of these poor Highlanders.

'I call it noble,' I cried. 'I'm a Whig, or little better; but I call it noble.'

'Ay,' said he, 'ye're a Whig, but ye're a gentleman; and that's what does it. Now, if ye were one of the cursed race of Campbell, ye would gnash your teeth to hear tell of it. If ye were the Red Fox' . . . And at that name his teeth shut together, and he ceased speaking. I have seen many a grim face, but never a grimmer than Alan's when he had named the Red Fox.

'And who is the Red Fox?' I asked, daunted, but still curious.

'Who is he?' cried Alan. 'Well, and I'll tell you that. When the men of the clans were broken at Culloden, and the good cause went down, and the horses rode over the fetlocks in the best blood of the north, Ardshiel had to flee like a poor deer upon the mountains – he and his lady and his bairns. A sair job we had of it before we got him shipped;

and while he still lay in the heather, the English rogues, that couldnae come at his life, were striking at his rights. They stripped him of his powers; they stripped him of his lands; they plucked the weapons from the hands of his clansmen, that had borne arms for thirty centuries; ay, and the very clothes off their backs – so that it's now a sin to wear a tartan plaid, and a man may be cast into a jail if he has but a kilt about his legs. One thing they couldnae kill. That was the love the clansmen bore their chief. These guineas are the proof of it. And now, in there steps a man, a Campbell, red-headed Colin of Glenure——'

'Is that him you call the Red Fox?' said I.

'Will ye bring me his brush?' cries Alan fiercely. 'Ay, that's the man. In he steps, and gets papers from King George, to be so-called King's factor on the lands of Appin. And at first he sings small, and is hail-fellow-well-met with Sheamus – that's James of the Glens, my chieftain's agent. But by and by, that came to his ears that I have just told you; how the poor commons of Appin, the farmers and the crofters and boumen, were wringing their very plaids to get a second rent, and send it overseas for Ardshiel and his poor bairns. What was it ye called it, when I told ye?'

'I called it noble, Alan,' said I.

'And you little better than a common Whig!' cried Alan. 'But when it came to Colin Roy, the black Campbell blood in him ran wild. He sat gnashing his teeth at the wine table. What! should a Stewart get a bite of bread, and him not able to prevent it? Ah! Red Fox, if ever I hold you at a gun's end, the Lord have pity upon ye!' (Alan stopped to swallow down his anger.) 'Well, David, what does he do? He declares all the farms to let. And, thinks he, in his black heart, "I'll soon get other tenants that'll overbid these Stewarts, and Maccolls, and Macrobs" (for these are all names in my clan, David), "and then," thinks he, "Ardshiel will have to hold his bonnet on a French roadside."'

'Well,' said I, 'what followed?'

Alan laid down his pipe, which he had long since suffered to go out, and set his two hands upon his knees.

'Ay,' said he, 'ye'll never guess that! For these same Stewarts, and Maccolls, and Macrobs (that had two rents to pay, one to King George by stark force, and one to Ardshiel by natural kindness) offered him a better price than any Campbell in all broad Scotland; and far he sent seeking them – as far as to the sides of Clyde and the cross of

Edinburgh – seeking, and fleeching, and begging them to come, where there was a Stewart to be starved and a red-headed hound of a Campbell to be pleasured!'

'Well, Alan,' said I, 'that is a strange story, and a fine one, too. And Whig as I may be, I am glad the man was beaten.'

'Him beaten?' echoed Alan. 'It's little ye ken of Campbells, and less of the Red Fox. Him beaten? No: nor will be, till his blood's on the hillside! But if the day comes, David man, that I can find time and leisure for a bit of hunting, there grows not enough heather in all Scotland to hide him from my vengeance!'

'Man Alan,' said I, 'ye are neither very wise nor very Christian to blow off so many words of anger. They will do the man ye call the Fox no harm, and yourself no good. Tell me your tale plainly out. What did he next?'

'And that's a good observe, David,' said Alan. 'Troth and indeed, they will do him no harm; the more's the pity! And barring that about Christianity (of which my opinion is quite otherwise, or I would be nae Christian), I am much of your mind.'

'Opinion here or opinion there,' said I, 'it's a kent thing that Christianity forbids revenge.'

'Ay,' said he, 'it's well seen it was a Campbell taught ye! It would be a convenient world for them and their sort, if there was no such a thing as a lad and a gun behind a heather bush! But that's nothing to the point. This is what he did.'

'Ay,' said I, 'come to that.'

'Well, David,' said he, 'since he couldnae be rid of the loyal commons by fair means, he swore he would be rid of them by foul. Ardshiel was to starve; that was the thing he aimed at. And since them that fed him in his exile wouldnae be bought out – right or wrong, he would drive them out. Therefore he sent for lawyers, and papers, and redcoats to stand at his back. And the kindly folk of that country must all pack and tramp, every father's son out of his father's house, and out of the place where he was bred and fed, and played when he was a callant. And who are to succeed them? Bare-leggit beggars! King George is to whistle for his rents; he maun dow with less; he can spread his butter thinner: what cares Red Colin? If he can hurt Ardshiel, he has his wish; if he can pluck the meat from my chieftain's table, and the bit toys out of his children's hands, he will gang hame singing to Glenure!'

'Let me have a word,' said I. 'Be sure, if they take less rents, be sure Government has a finger in the pie. It's not this Campbell's fault, man – it's his orders. And if ye killed this Colin to-morrow, what better would ye be? There would be another factor in his shoes, as fast as spur can drive.'

'Ye're a good lad in a fight,' said Alan; 'but, man! ye have Whig blood in ye!'

He spoke kindly enough, but there was so much anger under his contempt that I thought it was wise to change the conversation. I expressed my wonder how, with the Highlands covered with troops, and guarded like a city in a siege, a man in his situation could come and go without arrest.

'It's easier than ye would think' said Alan. 'A bare hillside (ye see) is like all one road; if there's a sentry at one place, ye just go by another. And then heather's a great help. And everywhere there are friends' houses and friends' byres and haystacks. And besides, when folk talk of a country covered with troops, it's but a kind of a byword at the best. A soldier covers nae mair of it than his bootsoles. I have fished a water with a sentry on the other side of the brae, and killed a fine trout; and I have sat in a heather bush within six feet of another, and learned a real bonny tune from his whistling. This was it,' said he, and whistled me the air.

'And then, besides,' he continued, 'it's no sae bad now as it was in forty-six. The Hielands are what they call pacified. Small wonder, with never a gun or a sword left from Cantyre to Cape Wrath, but what tenty¹ folk have hidden in their thatch! But what I would like to ken, David, is just how long? Not long, ye would think, with men like Ardshiel in exile and men like the Red Fox sitting birling the wine and oppressing the poor at home. But it's a kittle thing to decide what folk'll bear, and what they will not. Or why would Red Colin be riding his horse all over my poor country of Appin, and never a pretty lad to put a bullet in him?'

'And with this Alan fell into a muse, and for a long time sate very sad and silent.

I will add the rest of what I have to say about my friend, that he was skilled in all kinds of music, but principally pipe-music; was a well-considered poet in his own tongue; had read several books both in French and English; was a dead shot, a good angler, and an excellent fencer with the small-sword as well as with his own particular weapon.

For his faults, they were on his face, and I now knew them all. But the worst of them, his childish propensity to take offence and to pick quarrels, he greatly laid aside in my case, out of regard for the battle of the round-house. But whether it was because I had done well myself, or because I had been a witness of his own much greater prowess, is more than I can tell. For though he had a great taste for courage in other men, yet he admired it most in Alan Breck.

1 Careful.

13 The Loss of the Brig

It was already late at night, and as dark as it ever would be at that season of the year (and that is to say, it was still pretty bright), when Hoseason clapped his head into the round-house door.

'Here,' said he, 'come out and see if ye can pilot.'

'Is this one of your tricks?' asked Alan.

'Do I look like tricks?' cried the captain. 'I have other things to think of – my brig's in danger!'

By the concerned look of his face, and, above all, by the sharp tones in which he spoke of his brig, it was plain to both of us he was in deadly earnest; and so Alan and I, with no great fear of treachery, stepped on deck.

The sky was clear; it blew hard, and was bitter cold; a great deal of daylight lingered; and the moon, which was nearly full, shone brightly. The brig was close hauled, so as to round the south-west corner of the Island of Mull, the hills of which (and Ben More above them all, with a wisp of mist upon the top of it) lay full upon the larboard bow. Though it was no good point of sailing for the *Covenant*, she tore through the seas at a great rate, pitching and straining, and pursued by the westerly swell.

Altogether it was no such ill night to keep the seas in; and I had begun to wonder what it was that sat so heavily upon the captain, when the brig rising suddenly on the top of a high swell, he pointed and cried to us to look. Away on the lee bow, a thing like a fountain rose out of the moonlit sea, and immediately after we heard a low sound of roaring.

'What do ye call that?' asked the captain gloomily.

'The sea breaking on a reef,' said Alan. 'And now ye ken where it is; and what better would ye have?'

'Ay,' said Hoseason, 'if it was the only one.'

And sure enough, just as he spoke there came a second fountain farther to the south.

'There!' said Hoseason. 'Ye see for yourself. If I had kent of these reefs, if I had had a chart, or if Shuan had been spared, it's not sixty guineas, no, nor six hundred, would have made me risk my brig in sic a stoneyard! But you, sir, that was to pilot us, have ye never a word?'

'I'm thinking,' said Alan, 'these'll be what they call the Torran Rocks.'

'Are there many of them?' says the captain.

'Truly, sir, I am nae pilot,' said Alan; 'but it sticks in my mind there are ten miles of them.'

'Mr. Riach and the captain looked at each other.

'There's a way through them, I suppose?' said the captain.

'Doubtless,' said Alan, 'but where? But it somehow runs in my mind once more that it is clearer under the land.'

'So?' said Hoseason. 'We'll have to haul our wind then, Mr. Riach; we'll have to come as near in about the end of Mull as we can take her, sir; and even then we'll have the land to kep the wind off us, and that stoneyard on our lee. Well, we're in for it now, and may as well crack on.'

With that he gave an order to the steersman, and sent Riach to the foretop. There were only five men on deck, counting the officers; these were all that were fit (or, at least, both fit and willing) for their work; and two of these were hurt. So, as I say, it fell to Mr. Riach to go aloft, and he sat there looking out and hailing the deck with news of all he saw.

'The sea to the south is thick,' he cried; and then, after a while, 'it does seem clearer in by the land.'

'Well, sir,' said Hoseason to Alan, 'we'll try your way of it. But I think I might as well trust to a blind fiddler. Pray God you're right.'

'Pray God I am!' says Alan to me. 'But where did I hear it? Well, well, it will be as it must.'

As we got nearer to the turn of the land the reefs began to be sown here and there on our very path; and Mr. Riach sometimes cried down to us to change the course. Sometimes, indeed, none too soon; for one reef was so close on the brig's weather-board that when a sea burst upon it the lighter sprays fell upon her deck and wetted us like rain.

The brightness of the night showed us these perils as clearly as by day, which was, perhaps, the more alarming. It showed me, too, the face of the captain as he stood by the steersman, now on one foot, now on the other, and sometimes blowing in his hands, but listening and looking and as steady as steel. Neither he nor Mr. Riach had shown well in the fighting; but I saw they were brave in their own trade, and admired them all the more because I found Alan very white.

'Ochone, David,' says he, 'this is no the kind of death I fancy!'

'What, Alan!' I cried, 'you're not afraid?'

'No,' said he, wetting his lips, 'but you'll allow yourself, it's a cold ending.'

By this time, now and then sheering to one side or the other to avoid a reef, but still hugging the wind and the land, we had got round Iona and begun to come alongside Mull. The tide at the tail of the land ran very strong, and threw the brig about. Two hands were put to the helm, and Hoseason himself would sometimes lend a help; and it was strange to see three strong men throw their weight upon the tiller, and it (like a living thing) struggle against and drive them back. This would have been the greater danger had not the sea been for some while free of obstacles. Mr. Riach, besides, announced from the top that he saw clear water ahead.

'Ye were right,' said Hoseason to Alan. 'Ye have saved the brig, sir; I'll mind that when we come to clear accounts.' And I believe he not only meant what he said but would have done it; so high a place did the *Covenant* hold in his affections.

But this is matter only for conjecture, things having gone otherwise than he forecast.

'Keep her away a point,' sings out Mr. Riach. 'Reef to windward!'

And just at the same time the tide caught the brig, and threw the wind out of her sails. She came round into the wind like a top, and the next moment struck the reef with such a dunch as threw us all flat upon the deck, and came near to shake Mr. Riach from his place upon the mast.

I was on my feet in a minute. The reef on which we had struck was close in under the south-west end of Mull, off a little isle they called Earraid, which lay low and black upon the larboard. Sometimes the swell broke clean over us; sometimes it only ground the poor brig upon the reef, so that we could hear her beat herself to pieces; and what with the great noise of the sails, and the singing of the wind, and the flying of the spray in the moonlight, and the sense of danger, I think my head must have been partly turned, for I could scarcely understand the things I saw.

Presently I observed Mr. Riach and the seamen busy round the skiff, and still in the same blank, ran over to assist them; and as soon as I set my hand to work, my mind came clear again. It was no very easy task, for the skiff lay amidships and was full of hamper, and the breaking of the heavier seas continually forced us to give over and hold on; but we all wrought like horses while we could.

Meanwhile such of the wounded as could move came clambering out of the fore-scuttle and began to help; while the rest that lay helpless in their bunks harrowed me with screaming and begging to be saved.

The captain took no part. It seemed he was struck stupid. He stood holding by the shrouds, talking to himself and groaning out aloud whenever the ship hammered on the rock. His brig was like wife and child to him; he had looked on, day by day, at the mishandling of poor Ransome; but when it came to the brig, he seemed to suffer along with her.

All the time of our working at the boat, I remember only one thing: that I asked Alan, looking across at the shore, what country it was; and he answered, it was the worst possible for him, for it was a land of the Campbells.

We had one of the wounded men told off to keep a watch upon the seas and cry us warning. Well, we had the boat about ready to be launched, when this man sang out pretty shrill: 'For God's sake, hold on!' We knew by his tone that it was something more than ordinary; and sure enough, there followed a sea so huge that it lifted the brig right up and canted her over on her beam. Whether the cry came too late, or my hold was too weak, I know not; but at the sudden tilting of the ship I was cast clean over the bulwarks into the sea.

I went down, and drank my fill, and then came up, and got a blink of the moon, and then down again. They say a man sinks the third time for good. I cannot be made like other folk, then; for I would not like to write how often I went down, or how often I came up again. All the while, I was being hurled along, and beaten upon and choked, and then swallowed whole; and the thing was so distracting to my wits, that I was neither sorry nor afraid.

Presently, I found I was holding to a spar, which helped me somewhat. And then all of a sudden I was in quiet water, and began to come to myself.

It was the spare yard I had got hold of, and I was amazed to see how far I had travelled from the brig. I hailed her, indeed; but it was plain she was already out of cry. She was still holding together; but whether or not they had yet launched the boat, I was too far off and too low down to see.

While I was hailing the brig, I spied a tract of water lying between us where no great waves came, but which yet boiled white all over and bristled in the moon with rings and bubbles. Sometimes the whole tract swung to one side, like the tail of a live serpent; sometimes, for a glimpse, it all would disappear and then boil up again. What it was I had no guess, which for the time increased my fear of it; but I now know it must have been the roost or tide race, which had carried me away so fast and tumbled me about so cruelly, and at last, as if tired of that play, had flung out me and the spare yard upon its landward margin.

I now lay quite becalmed, and began to feel that a man can die of cold as well as of drowning. The shores of Earraid were close in; I could see in the moonlight the dots of heather and sparkling of the mica on the rocks.

'Well,' thought I to myself, 'if I cannot get as far as that, it's strange!'

I had no skill of swimming, Essen Water being small in our neighbourhood; but when I laid hold upon the yard with both arms, and kicked out with both feet, I soon began to find that I was moving. Hard work it was, and mortally slow; but in about an hour of kicking and splashing, I had got well in between the points of a sandy bay surrounded by low hills.

The sea was here quite quiet; there was no sound of any surf; the moon shone clear; and I thought in my heart I had never seen a place so desert and desolate. But it was dry land; and when at last it grew so shallow that I could leave the yard and wade ashore upon my feet, I cannot tell if I was more tired or more grateful. Both at least I was; tired as I never was before that night; and grateful to God as I trust I have been often, though never with more cause.

14 The Islet

With my stepping ashore I began the most unhappy part of my adventures. It was half past twelve in the morning, and though the wind was broken by the land it was a cold night. I dared not sit down (for I thought I should have frozen), but took off my shoes and walked to and fro upon the sand, barefoot, and beating my breast with infinite weariness. There was no sound of man or cattle; not a cock crew, though it was about the hour of their first waking; only the surf broke outside in the distance, which put me in mind of my perils and those of my friend. To walk by the sea at that hour of the morning, and in a place so desert-like and lonesome, struck me with a kind of fear.

As soon as the day began to break, I put on my shoes and climbed a hill – the ruggedest scramble I ever undertook – falling, the whole way, between big blocks of granite, or leaping from one to another. When I got to the top the dawn was come. There was no sign of the brig, which must have lifted from the reef and sunk. The boat, too, was nowhere to be seen. There was never a sail upon the ocean; and in what I could see of the land was neither house nor man.

I was afraid to think what had befallen my shipmates, and afraid to look longer at so empty a scene. What with my wet clothes and weariness, and my belly that now began to ache with hunger, I had enough to trouble me without that. So I set off eastward along the south coast, hoping to find a house where I might warm myself, and perhaps get news of those I had lost. And at the worst, I considered the sun would soon rise and dry my clothes.

After a little, my way was stopped by a creek or inlet of the sea, which seemed to run pretty deep into the land; and as I had no means to get across, I must needs change my direction to go about the end of it. It was still the roughest kind of walking; indeed the whole, not only of Earraid, but of the neighbouring part of Mull (which they call the Ross), is nothing but a jumble of granite rocks with heather in among.

At first the creek kept narrowing as I had looked to see; but presently to my surprise it began to widen out again. At this I scratched my head, but had still no notion of the truth; until at last I came to a rising ground, and it burst upon me all in a moment that I was cast upon a little barren isle, and cut off on every side by the salt seas.

Instead of the sun rising to dry me, it came on to rain, with a thick mist; so that my case was lamentable.

I stood in the rain, and shivered, and wondered what to do, till it occurred to me that perhaps the creek was fordable. Back I went to the narrowest point and waded in. But not three yards from shore I plumped in head over ears; and if ever I was heard of more, it was rather by God's grace than my own prudence. I was no wetter (for that could hardly be), but I was all the colder for this mishap; and having lost another hope was the more unhappy.

And now, all at once, the yard came in my head. What had carried me through the roost would surely serve me to cross the little quiet creek in safety. With that I set off, undaunted, across the top of the isle, to fetch and carry it back. It was a weary tramp in all ways, and if hope had not buoyed me up, I must have cast myself down and given up. Whether with the sea salt, or because I was growing fevered, I was distressed with thirst, and had to stop, as I went, and drink the peaty water out of the hags.

I came to the bay at last, more dead than alive; and at the first glance, I thought the yard was something farther out than when I left it. In I went for the third time into the sea. The sand was smooth and firm, and shelved gradually down, so that I could wade out till the water was almost to my neck and the little waves splashed into my face. But at that depth my feet began to leave me and I durst venture in no farther. As for the yard, I saw it bobbing very quietly some twenty feet in front of me.

I had borne up well until this last disappointment; but at that I came ashore, and flung myself down upon the sands and wept.

The time I spent upon the island is still so horrible a thought to me, that I must pass it lightly over. In all the books I have read of people cast away, they had either their pockets full of tools, or a chest of things would be thrown upon the beach along with them, as if on purpose. My case was very different. I had nothing in my pockets but money and Alan's silver button; and being inland bred, I was as much short of knowledge as of means.

I knew indeed that shell-fish were counted good to eat; and among the rocks of the isle I found a great plenty of limpets, which at first I could scarcely strike from their places, not knowing quickness to be needful. There were, besides, some of the little shells that we call buckies; I think periwinkle is the English name. Of these two I made my whole diet, devouring them cold and raw as I found them; and so hungry was I, that at first they seemed to me delicious.

Perhaps they were out of season, or perhaps there was something wrong in the sea about my island. But at least I had no sooner eaten my first meal than I was seized with giddiness and retching, and lay for a long time no better than dead. A second trial of the same food (indeed I had no other) did better with me, and revived my strength. But as long as I was on the island, I never knew what to expect when I had eaten; sometimes all was well, and sometimes I was thrown into a miserable sickness; nor could I ever distinguish what particular fish it was that hurt me.

All day it streamed rain; the island ran like a sop, there was no dry spot to be found; and when I lay down that night, between two boulders that made a kind of roof, my feet were in a bog.

The second day I crossed the island to all sides. There was no one part of it better than another; it was all desolate and rocky; nothing living on it but game birds which I lacked the means to kill, and the gulls which haunted the outlying rocks in a prodigious number. But the creek, or straits, that cut off the isle from the mainland of the Ross, opened out on the north into a bay, and the bay again opened into the Sound of Iona; and it was the neighbourhood of this place that I chose to be my home; though if I had thought upon the very name of home in such a spot, I must have burst out weeping.

I had good reasons for my choice. There was in this part of the isle a little hut of a house like a pig's hut, where fishers used to sleep when they came there upon their business; but the turf roof of it had fallen entirely in, so that the hut was of no use to me, and gave me less shelter than my rocks. What was more important, the shell-fish on which I lived grew there in great plenty; when the tide was out I could gather a peck at a time: and this was doubtless a convenience. But the other reason went deeper. I had become in no way used to the horrid solitude of the isle, but still looked round me on all sides (like a man that was hunted), between fear and hope that I might see some human creature coming. Now, from a little up the hillside over the bay, I could catch a sight of the great, ancient church and the roofs of the people's houses in Iona. And on the other hand, over the low country of the Ross, I saw smoke go up, morning and evening, as if from a homestead in a hollow of the land.

I used to watch this smoke, when I was wet and cold, and had my head half turned with loneliness; and think of the fireside and the company, till my heart burned. It was the same with the roofs of Iona. Altogether, this sight I had of men's homes and comfortable lives, although it put a point on my own sufferings, yet it kept hope alive, and helped me to eat my raw shell-fish (which had soon grown to be a disgust) and saved me from the sense of horror I had whenever I was quite alone with dead rocks, and fowls, and the rain, and the cold sea.

I say it kept hope alive, and indeed it seemed impossible that I should be left to die on the shores of my own country, and within view of a church tower and the smoke of men's houses. But the second day passed; and though as long as the light lasted I kept a bright look-out for boats on the Sound or men passing on the Ross, no help came near me. It still rained, and I turned in to sleep, as wet as ever, and with a cruel sore throat, but a little comforted, perhaps, by having said good night to my next neighbours, the people of Iona.

Charles the Second declared a man could stay outdoors more days in the year in the climate of England than in any other. This was very like a king, with a palace at his back and changes of dry clothes. But he must have had better luck on his flight from Worcester than I had on that miserable isle. It was the height of the summer; yet it rained for more than twenty-four hours, and did not clear until the afternoon of the third day.

This was the day of incidents. In the morning I saw a red deer, a buck with a fine spread of antlers, standing in the rain on the top of the island; but he had scarce seen me rise from under my rock, before he trotted off upon the other side. I supposed he must have swum the straits; though what should bring any creature to Earraid was more than I could fancy.

A little after, as I was jumping about after my limpets, I was startled by a guinea-piece, which fell upon a rock in front of me and glanced off into the sea. When the sailors gave me my money again, they kept back not only about a third of the whole sum, but my father's leather purse; so that from that day out I carried my gold loose in a pocket with a button. I now saw there must be a hole, and clapped my hand to the place in a great hurry. But this was to lock the stable door after the steed was stolen. I had left the shore at Queensferry with near on fifty pounds; now I found no more than two guinea-pieces and a silver shilling.

It is true I picked up a third guinea a little after, where it lay shining on a piece of turf. That made a fortune of three pounds and four shillings, English money, for a lad, the rightful heir of an estate, and now starving on an isle at the extreme end of the wild Highlands.

This state of my affairs dashed me still further; and indeed my plight on that third morning was truly pitiful. My clothes were beginning to rot; my stockings in particular were quite worn through, so that my shanks went naked; my hands had grown quite soft with the continual soaking; my throat was very sore, my strength had much abated, and my heart so turned against the horrid stuff I was condemned to eat, that the very sight of it came near to sicken me.

And yet the worst was not yet come.

There is a pretty high rock on the north-west of Earraid, which (because it had a flat top and overlooked the Sound) I was much in the habit of frequenting; not that ever I stayed in one place, save when asleep, my misery giving me no rest. Indeed, I wore myself down with continual and aimless goings and comings in the rain.

As soon, however, as the sun came out, I lay down on the top of that rock to dry myself. The comfort of the sunshine is a thing I cannot tell. It set me thinking hopefully of my deliverance, of which I had begun to despair; and I scanned the sea and the Ross with a fresh interest. On the south of my rock, a part of the island jutted out and hid the open ocean, so that a boat could thus come quite near me upon that side and I be none the wiser.

Well, all of a sudden, a coble with a brown sail and a pair of fishers aboard of it came flying round that corner of the isle, bound for Iona. I shouted out, and then fell on my knees on the rock and reached up my hands and prayed to them. They were near enough to hear – I could even see the colour of their hair; and there was no doubt but they observed me, for they cried out in the Gaelic tongue, and laughed. But the boat never turned aside, and flew on, right before my eyes, for Iona.

I could not believe such wickedness, and ran along the shore from rock to rock, crying on them piteously: even after they were out of reach of my voice, I still cried and waved to them; and when they were

'*I ran along the shore from rock to rock, crying on them piteously*'

quite gone, I thought my heart would have burst. All the time of my troubles I wept only twice. Once, when I could reach the yard, and now, the second time, when these fishers turned a deaf ear to my cries. But this time I wept and roared like a wicked child, tearing up the turf with my nails and grinding my face in the earth. If a wish would kill men, those two fishers would never have seen morning, and I should likely have died upon the island.

When I was a little over my anger, I must eat again, but with such loathing of the mess as I could now scarce control. Sure enough, I should have done as well to fast, for my fishes poisoned me again. I had all my first pains; my throat was so sore I could scarce swallow; I had a fit of strong shuddering, which clucked my teeth together; and there came on me that dreadful sense of illness, which we have no name for either in Scotch or English. I thought I should have died, and made my peace with God, forgiving all men, even my uncle and the fishers; and as soon as I had thus made up my mind to the worst, clearness came upon me: I observed the night was falling dry; my clothes were dried a good deal, truly; I was in a better case than ever before since I had landed on the isle; and so I got to sleep at last, with a thought of gratitude.

The next day (which was the fourth of this horrible life of mine) I found my bodily strength run very low. But the sun shone, the air was sweet, and what I managed to eat of the shell-fish agreed well with me and revived my courage.

I was scarce back on my rock (where I went always the first thing after I had eaten) before I observed a boat coming down the Sound, and with her head, as I thought, in my direction.

I began at once to hope and fear exceedingly; for I thought these men might have thought better of their cruelty and be coming back to my assistance. But another disappointment, such as yesterday's, was more than I could bear. I turned my back, accordingly, upon the sea, and did not look again till I had counted many hundreds. The boat was still heading for the island. The next time I counted the full thousand, as slowly as I could, my heart beating so as to hurt me. And then it was out of all question. She was coming straight to Earraid!

I could no longer hold myself back, but ran to the sea side and out, from one rock to another, as far as I could go. It is a marvel I was not drowned; for when I was brought to a stand at last, my legs shook under me, and my mouth was so dry, I must wet it with the sea-water before I was able to shout.

All this time the boat was coming on; and now I was able to perceive it was the same boat and the same two men as yesterday. This I knew by their hair, which the one had a bright yellow and the other black. But now there was a third man along with them, who looked to be of a better class.

As soon as they were come within easy speech, they let down their sail and lay quiet. In spite of my supplications, they drew no nearer in, and what frightened me most of all, the new man tee-hee'd with laughter as he talked and looked at me.

Then he stood up in the boat and addressed me a long while, speaking fast and with many wavings of his hand. I told him I had no Gaelic; and at this he became very angry, and I began to suspect he thought he was talking English. Listening very close, I caught the word 'whateffer' several times; but all the rest was Gaelic and might have been Greek and Hebrew for me.

'Whatever,' said I, to show him I had caught a word.

'Yes, yes – yes, yes,' says he, and then he looked at the other men, as much as to say, 'I told you I spoke English,' and began again as hard as ever in the Gaelic.

This time I picked out another word, 'tide.' Then I had a flash of hope. I remembered he was always waving his hand towards the mainland of the Ross.

'Do you mean when the tide is out——?' I cried, and could not finish.

'Yes, yes,' said he. 'Tide.'

At that I turned tail upon their boat (where my adviser had once more begun to tee-hee with laughter), leaped back the way I had come, from one stone to another, and set off running across the isle as I had never run before. In about half an hour I came out upon the shores of the creek; and, sure enough, it was shrunk into a little trickle of water, through which I dashed, not above my knees, and landed with a shout on the main island.

A sea-bred boy would not have stayed a day on Earraid; which is only what they call a tidal islet, and, except in the bottom of the neaps, can be entered and left twice in every twenty-four hours, either dryshod, or at the most by wading. Even I (I say), if I had sat down to think, instead of raging at my fate, must have soon guessed the secret, and got free. It was no wonder the fishers had not understood me. The wonder was rather that they had ever guessed my pitiful illusion, and taken the trouble to come back. I had starved with cold and hunger on that island for close upon one hundred hours. But for the fishers, I might have left my bones there in pure folly. And even as it was, I had paid for it pretty dear, not only in past sufferings, but in my present case; being clothed like a beggar-man, scarce able to walk, and in great pain of my sore throat.

I have seen wicked men and fools, a great many of both; and I believe they both get paid in the end; but the fools first.

15 The Lad with the Silver Button:
Through the Isle of Mull

The Ross of Mull, which I had now got upon, was rugged and trackless, like the isle I had just left; being all bog, and brier, and big stone. There may be roads for them that know that country well; but for my part I had no better guide than my own nose, and no other landmark than Ben More.

I aimed as well as I could for the smoke I had seen so often from the island; and with all my great weariness and the difficulty of the way, came upon the house in the bottom of a little hollow about five or six at night. It was low and longish, roofed with turf and built of unmortared stones, and on a mound in front of it an old gentleman sat smoking his pipe in the sun.

With what little English he had, he gave me to understand that my shipmates had got safe ashore, and had broken bread in that very house on the day after.

'Was there one,' I asked, 'dressed like a gentleman?'

He said they all wore rough greatcoats; but, to be sure, the first of them, the one that came alone, wore breeches and stockings, while the rest had sailors' trousers.

'Ah,' said I, 'and he would have a feathered hat?'

He told me, no, that he was bare-headed like myself.

At first I thought Alan might have lost his hat; and then the rain came in my mind, and I judged it more likely he had it out of harm's way under his greatcoat. This set me smiling, partly because my friend was safe, partly to think of his vanity in dress.

And then the old gentleman clapped his hand to his brow, and cried out that I must be the lad with the silver button.

'Why, yes!' said I, in some wonder.

'Well, then,' said the old gentleman, 'I have a word for you, that you are to follow your friend to his country, by Torosay.'

He then asked how I fared, and I told him my tale. A

south-country man would certainly have laughed; but this old gentleman (I call him so because of his manners, for his clothes were dropping off his back) heard me all through with nothing but gravity and pity. When I had done, he took me by the hand, led me into his hut (it was no better) and presented me before his wife, as if she had been the Queen and I a duke.

The good woman set oat-bread before me and a cold grouse, patting my shoulder and smiling to me all the time, for she had no English; and the old gentleman (not to be behind) brewed me a strong punch out of their country spirit. All the while I was eating, and after that when I was drinking the punch, I could scarce come to believe in my good fortune; and the house, though it was thick with the peat smoke and as full of holes as a colander, seemed like a palace.

The punch threw me in a strong sweat and a deep slumber; the good people let me lie; and it was near noon of the next day before I took the road, my throat already easier and my spirits quite restored by good fare and good news. The old gentleman, although I pressed him hard, would take no money, and gave me an old bonnet for my head: though I am free to own I was no sooner out of view of the house than I very jealously washed this gift of his in a wayside fountain.

Thought I to myself: 'If these are the wild Highlanders, I could wish my own folk wilder.'

I not only started late, but I must have wandered nearly half the time. True, I met plenty of people, grubbing in little miserable fields that would not keep a cat, or herding little kine about the bigness of asses. The Highland dress being forbidden by law since the rebellion, and the people condemned to the Lowland habit, which they much disliked, it was strange to see the variety of their array. Some went bare, only for a hanging cloak or greatcoat, and carried their trousers on their backs like a useless burthen; some had made an imitation of the tartan with little parti-coloured stripes patched together like an old wife's quilt; others, again, still wore the Highland philabeg, but by putting a few stitches between the legs, transformed it into a pair of trousers like a Dutchman's. All those makeshifts were condemned and punished, for the law was harshly applied, in hopes to break up the clan spirit; but in that out-of-the-way, sea-bound isle there were few to make remarks and fewer to tell tales.

They seemed in great poverty; which was no doubt natural, now that rapine was put down, and the chiefs kept no longer an open house;

and the roads (even such a wandering country by-track as the one I followed) were infested with beggars. And here again I marked a difference from my own part of the country. For our Lowland beggars – even the gownsmen themselves, who beg by patent – had a louting, flattering way with them, and if you gave them a plack and asked change, would very civilly return you a boddle. But these Highland beggars stood on their dignity, asked alms only to buy snuff (by their account) and would give no change.

To be sure, this was no concern of mine, except in so far as it entertained me by the way. What was much more to the purpose, few had any English, and these few (unless they were of the brotherhood of beggars) not very anxious to place it at my service. I knew Torosay to be my destination, and repeated the name to them and pointed; but instead of simply pointing in reply, they would give me a screed of the Gaelic that set me foolish; so it was small wonder if I went out of my road as often as I stayed in it.

At last, about eight at night, and already very weary, I came to a lone house, where I asked admittance, and was refused, until I bethought me of the power of money in so poor a country, and held up one of my guineas in my finger and thumb. Thereupon, the man of the house, who had hitherto pretended to have no English, and driven me from his door by signals, suddenly began to speak as clearly as was needful, and agreed for five shillings to give me a night's lodging and guide me the next day to Torosay.

I slept uneasily that night, fearing I should be robbed; but I might have spared myself the pain; for my host was no robber, only miserably poor and a great cheat. He was not alone in his poverty; for the next morning, we must go five miles about to the house of what he called a rich man to have one of my guineas changed. This was perhaps a rich man for Mull; he would have scarce been thought so in the south; for it took all he had – the whole house was turned upside-down, and a neighbour brought under contribution, before he could scrape together twenty shillings in silver. The odd shilling he kept for himself, protesting he could ill afford to have so great a sum of money lying 'locked up.' For all that he was very courteous and well spoken, made us both sit down with his family to dinner, and brewed punch in a fine china bowl, over which my rascal guide grew so merry that he refused to start.

I was for getting angry, and appealed to the rich man (Hector

Maclean was his name) who had been a witness to our bargain and to my payment of the five shillings. But Maclean had taken his share of the punch, and vowed that no gentleman should leave his table after the bowl was brewed; so there was nothing for it but to sit and hear Jacobite toasts and Gaelic songs, till all were tipsy and staggered off to the bed or the barn for their night's rest.

Next day (the fourth of my travels) we were up before five upon the clock; but my rascal guide got to the bottle at once, and it was three hours before I had him clear of the house, and then (as you shall hear) only for a worse disappointment.

As long as we went down a heathery valley that lay before Mr. Maclean's house, all went well; only my guide looked constantly over his shoulder, and when I asked him the cause, only grinned at me. No sooner, however, had we crossed the back of a hill, and got out of sight of the house windows, than he told me Torosay lay right in front, and that a hill-top (which he pointed out) was my best landmark.

'I care very little for that,' said I, 'since you are going with me.'

The impudent cheat answered me in the Gaelic that he had no English.

'My fine fellow,' I said, 'I know very well your English comes and goes. Tell me what will bring it back? Is it more money you wish?'

'Five shillings mair,' said he, 'and hersel' will bring ye there.'

I reflected awhile and then offered him two, which he accepted greedily, and insisted on having in his hands at once—'for luck,' as he said, but I think it was rather for my misfortune.

The two shillings carried him not quite as many miles; at the end of which distance he sat down upon the wayside and took off his brogues from his feet, like a man about to rest.

I was now red hot. 'Ha!' said I, 'have you no more English?'

He said impudently, 'No.'

At that I boiled over, and lifted my hand to strike him; and he, drawing a knife from his rags, squatted back and grinned at me like a wild cat. At that, forgetting everything but my anger, I ran in upon him, put aside his knife with my left, and struck him in the mouth with the right. I was a strong lad and very angry, and he but a little man; and he went down before me heavily. By good luck, his knife flew out of his hand as he fell.

I picked up both that and his brogues, wished him a good morning, and set off upon my way, leaving him barefoot and disarmed.

I chuckled to myself as I went, being sure I was done with that rogue, for a variety of reasons. First, he knew he could have no more of my money; next, the brogues were worth in that country only a few pence; and, lastly, the knife, which was really a dagger, it was against the law for him to carry.

In about half an hour of walk I overtook a great, ragged man, moving pretty fast but feeling before him with a staff. He was quite blind, and told me he was a catechist, which should have put me at my ease. But his face went against me; it seemed dark and dangerous and secret; and presently, as we began to go on alongside, I saw the steel butt of a pistol sticking from under the flap of his coat pocket. To carry such a thing meant a fine of fifteen pounds sterling upon a first offence, and transportation to the colonies upon a second. Nor could I quite see why a religious teacher should go armed, or what a blind man could be doing with a pistol.

I told him about my guide, for I was proud of what I had done, and my vanity for once got the heels of my prudence. At the mention of the five shillings he cried out so loud that I made up my mind I should say nothing of the other two, and was glad he could not see my blushes.

'Was it too much?' I asked, a little faltering.

'Too much!' cries he. 'Why, I will guide you to Torosay myself for a dram of brandy. And give you the great pleasure of my company (me that is a man of some learning) in the bargain.'

I said I did not see how a blind man could be a guide: but at that he laughed aloud, and said his stick was eyes enough for an eagle.

'In the Isle of Mull at least,' says he, 'where I know every stone and heather bush by mark of head. See now,' he said, striking right and left, as if to make sure, 'down there a burn is running; and at the head of it there stands a bit of a small hill with a stone cocked upon the top of that; and it's hard at the foot of the hill that the way runs by to Torosay; and the way here, being for droves, is plainly trodden, and will show grassy through the heather.'

I had to own he was right in every feature, and told my wonder.

'Ha!' says he, 'that's nothing. Would ye believe me now, that before the Act came out, and when there were weepons in this country, I could shoot? Ay, could I!' cries he, and then with a leer: 'If ye had such a thing as a pistol here to try with, I would show ye how it's done.'

I told him I had nothing of the sort, and gave him a wider berth. If he had known, his pistol stuck at that time quite plainly out of his pocket, and I could see the sun twinkle on the steel of the butt. But by the better luck for me, he knew nothing, thought all was covered, and lied on in the dark.

He then began to question me cunningly, where I came from, whether I was rich, whether I could change a five-shilling piece for him (which he declared he had that moment in his sporran), and all the time he kept edging up to me and I avoiding him. We were now upon a sort of green cattle track which crossed the hills towards Torosay, and we kept changing sides upon that like dancers in a reel. I had so plainly the upper hand that my spirits rose, and indeed I took a pleasure in this game of blind-man's-buff; but the catechist grew angrier and angrier, and at last began to swear in Gaelic and to strike for my legs with his staff.

Then I told him that, sure enough, I had a pistol in my pocket as well as he, and if he did not strike across the hill due south I would even blow his brains out.

He became at once very polite; and after trying to soften me for some time, but quite in vain, he cursed me once more in the Gaelic and took himself off. I watched him striding along, through bog and brier, tapping with his stick, until he turned the end of a hill and disappeared in the next hollow. Then I struck on again for Torosay, much better pleased to be alone than to travel with that man of learning. This was an unlucky day; and these two, of whom I had just rid myself, one after the other, were the two worst men I met with in the Highlands.

At Torosay, on the Sound of Mull, and looking over to the mainland of Morven, there was an inn with an innkeeper who was a Maclean, it appeared, of a very high family; for to keep an inn is thought even more genteel in the Highlands than it is with us, perhaps as partaking of hospitality, or perhaps because the trade is idle and drunken. He spoke good English, and finding me to be something of a scholar, tried me first in French, where he easily beat me, and then in the Latin, in which I don't know which of us did best. This pleasant rivalry put us at once upon friendly terms; and I sat up and drank punch with him (or to be more correct, sat up and watched him drink it), until he was so tipsy that he wept upon my shoulder.

I tried him, as if by accident, with a sight of Alan's button; but it was plain he had never seen or heard of it. Indeed, he bore some grudge against the family and friends of Ardshiel, and before he was drunk he read me a lampoon, in very good Latin, but with a very ill meaning, which he had made in elegiac verses upon a person of that house.

When I told him of my catechist, he shook his head, and said I was lucky to have got clear off. 'That is a very dangerous man,' he said; 'Duncan Mackiegh is his name; he can shoot by the ear at several yards, and has been often accused of highway robberies, and once of murder.'

'The cream of it is,' says I, 'that he called himself a catechist.'

'And why should he not?'says he, 'when that is what he is. It was Maclean of Duart gave it to him because he was blind. But, perhaps it was a peety,' says my host, 'for he is always on the road, going from one place to another to hear the young folk say their religion; and, doubtless, that is a great temptation to the poor man.'

At last, when my landlord could drink no more, he showed me to a bed, and I lay down in very good spirits; having travelled the greater part of that big and crooked Island of Mull, from Earraid to Torosay, fifty miles as the crow flies, and (with my wanderings) much nearer a hundred, in four days and with little fatigue. Indeed I was by far in better heart and health of body at the end of that long tramp than I had been at the beginning.

16 The Lad with the Silver Button: Across Morven

There is a regular ferry from Torosay to Kinlochaline on the mainland. Both shores of the Sound are in the country of the strong clan of the Macleans, and the people that passed the ferry with me were almost all of that clan. The skipper of the boat, on the other hand, was called Neil Roy Macrob; and since Macrob was one of the names of Alan's clansmen, and Alan himself had sent me to the ferry, I was eager to come to private speech of Neil Roy.

In the crowded boat this was of course impossible, and the passage was a very slow affair. There was no wind, and as the boat was wretchedly equipped, we could pull but two oars on one side, and one on the other. The men gave way, however, with a good will, the passengers taking spells to help them, and the whole company giving the time in Gaelic boat songs. And what with the songs, and the sea air, and the good nature and spirit of all concerned, and the bright weather, the passage was a pretty thing to have seen.

But there was one melancholy part. In the mouth of Loch Aline we found a great seagoing ship at anchor; and this I supposed at first to be one of the King's cruisers which were kept along the coast, both summer and winter to prevent communication with the French. As we got a little nearer, it became plain she was a ship of merchandise; and what still puzzled me, not only her decks, but the sea-beach also, were quite black with people, and skiffs were continually plying to and fro between them. Yet nearer, and there began to come to our ears a great sound of mourning, the people on board and those on the shore crying and lamenting one to another so as to pierce the heart.

Then I understood this was an emigrant ship bound for the American colonies.

We put the ferry-boat alongside, and the exiles leaned over the bulwarks, weeping and reaching out their hands to my fellow passengers, among whom they counted some near friends. How long this might have gone on I do not know, for they seemed to have no sense of time; but at last the captain of the ship, who seemed near beside himself (and no great wonder) in the midst of this crying and confusion, came to the side and begged us to depart.

Thereupon Neil sheered off; and the chief singer in our boat struck into a melancholy air, which was presently taken up both by the emigrants and their friends upon the beach, so that it sounded from all sides like a lament for the dying. I saw the tears run down the cheeks of the men and women in the boat, even as they bent at the oars; and the circumstances and the music of the song (which is one called 'Lochaber no more') were highly affecting even to myself.

At Kinlochaline I got Neil Roy upon one side on the beach, and said I made sure he was one of Appin's men.

'And what for no?' said he.

'I am seeking somebody,' said I; 'and it comes in my mind that you will have news of him. Alan Breck Stewart is his name.' And very foolishly, instead of showing him the button, I sought to pass a shilling in his hand.

At this he drew back. 'I am very much affronted,' he said; 'and this is not the way that one shentleman should behave to another at all. The man you ask for is in France; but if he was in my sporran,' says he, 'and your belly full of shillings, I would not hurt a hair upon his body.'

I saw I had gone the wrong way to work, and without wasting time upon apologies, showed him the button lying in the hollow of my palm.

'Aweel, aweel,' said Neil; 'and I think ye might have begun with that end of the stick, whatever! But if ye are the lad with the silver button, all is well, and I have the word to see that ye come safe. But if ye will pardon me to speak plainly,' says he, 'there is a name that you should never take into your mouth, and that is the name of Alan Breck; and there is a thing that ye would never do, and that is to offer your dirty money to a Hieland shentleman.'

It was not very easy to apologize; for I could scarce tell him (what was the truth) that I had never dreamed he would set up to be a gentleman until he told me so. Neil on his part had no wish to prolong his dealings with me, only to fulfil his orders and be done with it; and he made haste to give me my route. This was to lie the night in Kinlochaline in the public inn; to cross Morven the next day to Ardgour, and lie the night in the house of one John of the Claymore, who was warned that I might come; the third day, to be set across one loch at Corran and another at Balachulish, and then ask my way to the house of James of the Glens, at Aucharn in Duror of Appin. There was a good deal of ferrying, as you hear; the sea in all this part running deep into the mountains and winding about their roots. It makes the country strong to hold and difficult to travel, but full of prodigious wild and dreadful prospects.

I had some other advice from Neil: to speak with no one by the way, to avoid Whigs, Campbells, and the 'red soldiers'; to leave the road and lie in a bush if I saw any of the latter coming, 'for it was never chancy to meet in with them'; and in brief, to conduct myself like a robber or a Jacobite agent, as perhaps Neil thought me.

The inn at Kinlochaline was the most beggarly vile place that ever pigs were styed in, full of smoke, vermin, and silent Highlanders. I was not only discontented with my lodging, but with myself for my mismanagement of Neil, and thought I could hardly be worse off. But very wrongly, as I was soon to see; for I had not been half an hour at the inn (standing in the door most of the time, to ease my eyes from the peat smoke) when a thunderstorm came close by, the springs broke in a little hill on which the inn stood, and one end of the house became a running water. Places of public entertainment were bad enough all over Scotland in those days; yet it was a wonder to myself, when I had to go from the fireside to the bed in which I slept, wading over the shoes.

Early in my next day's journey I overtook a little, stout, solemn man, walking very slowly with his toes turned out, sometimes reading in a book and sometimes marking the place with his finger, and dressed decently and plainly in something of a clerical style.

This I found to be another catechist, but of a different order from the blind man of Mull: being indeed one of those sent out by the Edinburgh Society for Propagating Christian Knowledge, to evangelize the more savage places of the Highlands. His name was Henderland; he spoke with the broad south-country tongue, which I was beginning to weary for the sound of; and besides common countryship, we soon found we had a more particular bond of interest. For my good friend, the minister of Essendean, had translated into Gaelic in his by-time a number of hymns and pious books, which Henderland used in his work, and held in great esteem. Indeed, it was one of these he was carrying and reading when we met.

We fell in company at once, our ways lying together as far as to Kingairloch. As we went, he stopped and spoke with all the wayfarers and workers that we met or passed; and though of course I could not tell what they discoursed about, yet I judged Mr. Henderland must be well liked in the countryside, for I observed many of them to bring out their mulls and share a pinch of snuff with him.

I told him as far in my affairs as I judged wise; as far that is, as they were none of Alan's; and gave Balachulish as the place I was travelling to, to meet a friend; for I thought Aucharn, or even Duror, would be too particular, and might put him on the scent.

On his part, he told me much of his work and the people he worked among, the hiding priests and Jacobites, the Disarming Act, the dress, and many other curiosities of the time and place. He seemed moderate; blaming Parliament in several points, and especially because they had framed the Act more severely against those who wore the dress than against those who carried weapons.

This moderation put it in my mind to question him of the Red Fox and the Appin tenants; questions which, I thought, would seem natural enough in the mouth of one travelling to that country.

He said it was a bad business. 'It's wonderful,' said he, 'where the tenants find the money, for their life is mere starvation. (Ye don't carry such a thing as snuff, do ye, Mr. Balfour? No. Well, I'm better wanting it.) But these tenants (as I was saying) are doubtless partly driven to it. James Stewart in Duror (that's him they call James of the Glens) is half-brother to Ardshiel, the captain of the clan; and he is a man much looked up to, and drives very hard. And then there's one they call Alan Breck——'

'Ah!' cried I, 'what of him?'

'What of the wind that bloweth where it listeth?' said Henderland. 'He's here and awa'; here to-day and gone to-morrow: a fair heather-cat. He might be glowering at the two of us out of yon whin-bush, and I wouldnae wonder! Ye'll no carry such a thing as snuff, will ye?'

I told him no, and that he had asked the same thing more than once.

'It's highly possible,' said he, sighing. 'But it seems strange ye shouldnae carry it. However, as I was saying, this Alan Breck is a bold, desperate customer, and well kent to be James's right hand. He life is forfeit already; he would boggle at naething; and maybe, if a tenant body was to hang back he would get a dirk in his wame.'

'You make a poor story of it all, Mr. Henderland,' said I. 'If it is all fear upon both sides, I care to hear no more of it.'

'Na,' said Mr. Henderland, 'but there's love too, and self-denial that should put the like of you and me to shame. There's something fine about it; no perhaps Christian, but humanly fine. Even Alan Breck, by all that I hear, is a chicld to be respected. There's many a lying sneck-draw sits close in kirk in our part of the country, and stands well in the world's eye, and maybe is a far worse man, Mr. Balfour, than yon misguided shedder of man's blood. Ay, ay, we might take a lesson by them. Ye'll perhaps think I've been too long in the Hielands?' he added, smiling to me.

I told him not at all; that I had seen much to admire among the Highlanders; and if he came to that, Mr. Campbell himself was a Highlander.

'Ay,' said he, 'that's true. It's a fine blood.'

'And what is the King's agent about?' I asked.

'Colin Campbell?' says Henderland. 'Putting his head in a bees' byke!'

'He is to turn the tenants out by force, I hear?' said I.

'Yes,' says he, 'but the business has gone back and forth, as folk say. First, James of the Glens rode to Edinburgh, and got some lawyer (a Stewart, nae doubt – they all hing together like bats in a steeple) and had the proceedings stayed. And then Colin Campbell cam' in again, and had the upper hand before the Barons of Exchequer. And now they tell me the first of the tenants are to flit to-morrow. It's to begin at Duror under James's very windows, which doesnae seem wise by my humble way of it.'

'Do you think they'll fight?' I asked.

'Well,' says Henderland, 'they're disarmed – or supposed to be – for there's still a good deal of cold iron lying by in quiet places. And then Colin Campbell has the sogers coming. But for all that, if I was his lady wife, I wouldnae be well pleased till I got home again. They're queer customers, the Appin Stewarts.'

I asked if they were worse than their neighbours.

'No they,' said he. 'And that's the worst part of it. For if Colin Roy can get his business done in Appin, he has it all to begin again in the next country, which they call Mamore, and which is one of the countries of the Camerons. He's King's Factor upon both, and from both he has to drive out the tenants; and indeed, Mr. Balfour (to be open with ye), it's my belief that if he escapes the one lot, he'll get his death by the other.'

So we continued talking and walking the great part of the day; until, at last, Mr. Henderland, after expressing his delight in my company, and satisfaction at meeting with a friend of Mr. Campbell's ('whom,' says he, 'I will make bold to call that sweet singer of our covenanted Zion'), proposed that I should make a short stage, and lie the night in his house a little beyond Kingairloch. To say truth, I was overjoyed; for I had no great desire for John of the Claymore, and since my double misadventure, first with the guide and next with the gentleman skipper, I stood in some fear of any Highland stranger. Accordingly we shook hands upon the bargain, and came in the afternoon to a small house, standing alone by the shore of the Linnhe Loch. The sun was already gone from the desert mountains of Ardgour upon the hither side, but shone on those of Appin on the farther; the loch lay as still as a lake, only the gulls were crying round the sides of it; and the whole place seemed solemn and uncouth.

We had no sooner come to the door of Mr. Henderland's dwelling, than to my great surprise (for I was now used to the politeness of the Highlanders) he burst rudely past me, dashed into the room, caught up a jar and a small horn spoon, and began ladling snuff into his nose in most excessive quantities. Then he had a hearty fit of sneezing, and looked round upon me with a rather silly smile.

'It's a vow I took,' says he. 'I took a vow upon me that I wouldnae carry it. Doubtless it's a great privation; but when I think upon the martyrs, not only to the Scottish Covenant but to other points of Christianity, I think shame to mind it.'

As soon as we had eaten (and porridge and whey was the best of the good man's diet) he took a grave face and said he had a duty to perform by Mr. Campbell, and that was to inquire into my state of mind towards God. I was inclined to smile at him since the business of the snuff; but he had not spoken long before he brought the tears into my eyes. There are two things that men should never weary of, goodness and humility; we get none too much of them in this rough world among cold, proud people; but Mr. Henderland had their very speech upon his tongue. And though I was a good deal puffed up with my adventures and with having come off, as the saying is, with flying colours; yet he soon had me on my knees beside a simple, poor old man, and both proud and glad to be there.

Before we went to bed he offered me sixpence to help me on my way, out of a scanty store he kept in the turf wall of his house; at which excess of goodness I knew not what to do. But at last he was so earnest with me, that I thought it the more mannerly part to let him have his way, and so left him poorer than myself.

17 The Death of the Red Fox

The next day Mr. Henderland found for me a man who had a boat of his own and was to cross the Linnhe Loch that afternoon into Appin, fishing. Him he prevailed on to take me, for he was one of his flock; and in this way I saved a long day's travel and the price of the two public ferries I must otherwise have passed.

It was near noon before we set out; a dark day with clouds, and the sun shining upon little patches. The sea was here very deep and still, and had scarce a wave upon it; so that I must put the water to my lips before I could believe it to be truly salt. The mountains on either side were high, rough, and barren, very black and gloomy in the shadow of the clouds, but all silver-laced with little water-courses where the sun shone upon them. It seemed a hard country, this of Appin, for people to care as much about as Alan did.

There was but one thing to mention. A little after we had started, the sun shone upon a little moving clump of scarlet close in along the waterside to the north. It was much of the same red as soldiers' coats; every now and then, too, there came little sparks and lightnings, as though the sun had struck upon bright steel.

I asked my boatman what it should be; and he answered he supposed it was some of the red soldiers coming from Fort William into Appin, against the poor tenantry of the country. Well, it was a sad sight to me; and whether it was because of my thoughts of Alan, or from something prophetic in my bosom, although this was but the second time I had seen King George's troops, I had no good will to them.

At last we came so near the point of land at the entering in of Loch Leven that I begged to be set on shore. My boatman (who was an honest fellow and mindful of his promise to the catechist) would fain have carried me on to Balachulish; but as this was to take me farther from my secret destination, I insisted, and was set on shore at last under the wood of Lettermore (or Lettervore, for I have heard it both ways) in Alan's country of Appin.

This was a wood of birches, growing on a steep, craggy side of a mountain that overhung the loch. It had many openings and ferny dells; and a road or bridle track ran north and south through the midst of it, by the edge of which, where was a spring, I sat down to eat some oat-bread of Mr. Henderland's, and think upon my situation.

Here I was not only troubled by a cloud of stinging midges, but far more by the doubts of my mind. What I ought to do, why I was going to join myself with an outlaw and a would-be murderer like Alan, whether I should not be acting more like a man of sense to tramp back to the south country direct, by my own guidance and at my own charges, and what Mr. Campbell or even Mr. Henderland would think of me if they should ever learn my folly and presumption: these were the doubts that now began to come in on me stronger than ever.

As I was so sitting and thinking, a sound of men and horses came to me through the wood; and presently after, at a turning of the road, I saw four travellers come into view. The way was in this part so rough and narrow that they came single and led their horses by the reins. The first was a great red-headed gentleman, of an imperious and flushed face, who carried his hat in his hand and fanned himself, for he was in a breathing heat. The second, by his decent black garb and white whig, I correctly took to be a lawyer. The third was a servant, and wore some part of his clothes in tartan, which showed that his master was of a Highland family, and either an outlaw or else in singular good odour with the Government, since the wearing of tartan was against the Act. If I had been better versed in these things, I would have known the tartan to be of the Argyle (or Campbell) colours. This servant had a good-sized portmanteau strapped on his horse, and a net of lemons (to brew punch with) hanging at the saddle-bow; as was often enough the custom with luxurious travellers in that part of the country.

As for the fourth, who brought up the tail, I had seen his like before, and knew him at once to be a sherriff's officer.

I had no sooner seen these people coming than I made up my mind (for no reason that I can tell) to go through with my adventure; and when the first came alongside of me, I rose up from the bracken and asked him the way to Aucharn.

He stopped and looked at me, as I thought, a little oddly; and then, turning to the lawyer, 'Mungo,' said he, 'there's many a man would think this more of a warning than two pyats. Here am I on my road to Duror on the job ye ken; and here is a young lad starts up out of the bracken, and speers if I am on the way to Aucharn.'

'Glenure,' said the other, 'this is an ill subject for jesting.'

These two had now drawn close up and were gazing at me, while the two followers had halted about a stone-cast in the rear.

'And what seek ye in Aucharn?' said Colin Roy Campbell of Glenure; him they call the Red Fox; for he it was that I stopped.

'The man that lives there,' said I.

'James of the Glens,' says Glenure musingly; and then to the lawyer: 'Is he gathering his people, think ye?'

'Anyway,' says the lawyer, 'we shall do better to bide where we are, and let the soldiers rally us.'

'If you are concerned for me,' said I, 'I am neither of his people nor yours, but an honest subject of King George, owing no man and fearing no man.'

'Why, very well said,' replies the Factor. 'But if I may make so bold as ask, what does this honest man so far from his country? and why does he come seeking the brother of Ardshiel? I have power here, I must tell you. I am King's Factor upon several of these estates, and have twelve files of soldiers at my back.'

'I have heard a waif word in the country,' said I, a little nettled, 'that you were a hard man to drive.'

He still kept looking at me, as if in doubt.

'Well,' said he, at last, 'your tongue is bold; but I am no unfriend to plainness. If ye had asked me the way to the door of James Stewart on any other day but this, I would have set ye right and bidden ye God-speed. But to-day – eh, Mungo?' And he turned again to look at the lawyer.

But just as he turned there came the shot of a firelock from higher up the hill; and with the very sound of it Glenure fell upon the road.

'Oh, I am dead!' he cried, several times over.

The lawyer had caught him up and held him in his arms, the servant standing over and clasping his hands. And now the wounded man looked from one to another with scared eyes, and there was a change in his voice that went to the heart.

'Take care of yourselves,' says he. 'I am dead.'

He tried to open his clothes as if to look for the wound, but his fingers slipped on the buttons. With that he gave a great sigh, his head rolled on his shoulder, and he passed away.

The lawyer said never a word, but his face was as sharp as a pen and as white as the dead man's; the servant broke out into a great noise of crying and weeping, like a child; and I, on my side, stood staring at them in a kind of horror. The sherriff's officer had run back at the first sound of the shot, to hasten the coming of the soldiers.

At last the lawyer laid down the dead man in his blood upon the road, and got to his own feet with a kind of stagger.

I believe it was his movement that brought me to my senses; for he had no sooner done so than I began to scramble up the hill, crying out, 'The murderer! the murderer!'

So little a time had elapsed, that when I got to the top of the first steepness, and could see some part of the open mountain, the murderer was still moving away at no great distance. He was a big man, in a black coat, with metal buttons, and carried a long fowling-piece.

'Here!' I cried, 'I see him!'

At that the murderer gave a little, quick look over his shoulder, and began to run. The next moment he was lost in the fringe of birches; then he came out again on the upper side, where I could see him climbing like a jackanapes, for that part was again very steep; and then he dipped behind a shoulder, and I saw him no more.

All this time I had been running on my side, and had got a good way up, when a voice cried upon me to stand.

I was at the edge of the upper wood, and so now, when I halted and looked back, I saw all the open part of the hill below me.

The lawyer and the sherriff's officer were standing just above the road, crying and waving on me to come back; and on their left, the redcoats, musket in hand, were beginning to struggle singly out of the lower wood.

'Why should I come back?' I cried. 'Come you on.'

'Ten pounds if ye take that lad!' cried the lawyer. 'He's an accomplice. He was posted here to hold us in talk.'

At that word (which I could hear quite plainly, though it was to the soldiers and not to me that he was crying it) my heart came to my mouth with quite a new kind of terror. Indeed, it is one thing to stand the danger of your life, and quite another to run the peril of both life and character. The thing, besides, had come so suddenly, like thunder out of a clear sky, that I was all amazed and helpless.

The soldiers began to spread, some of them to run, and others to put up their pieces and cover me; and still I stood.

'Jouk[1] in here among the trees,' said a voice, close by.

Indeed, I scarce knew what I was doing, but I obeyed; and as I did so, I heard the firelocks bang and the balls whistle in the birches.

Just inside the shelter of the trees I found Alan Breck standing, with a fishing-rod. He gave me no salutation; indeed it was no time for civilities; only 'Come!' says he, and set off running along the side of the mountain towards Balachulish; and I, like a sheep, to follow him.

Now we ran among the birches; now stooping behind low humps upon the mountainside; now crawling on all-fours among the heather. The pace was deadly; my heart seemed bursting against my ribs; and I had neither time to think nor breath to speak with. Only I remember seeing with wonder that Alan every now and then would straighten himself to his full height and look back; and every time he did so, there came a great far-away cheering and crying of the soldiers.

Quarter of an hour later, Alan stopped, clapped down flat in the heather, and turned to me.

'Now,' said he, 'it's earnest. Do as I do, for your life.'

And at the same speed, but now with infinitely more precaution, we traced back again across the mountainside by the same way that we had come, only perhaps higher; till at last Alan threw himself down in the upper wood of Lettermore, where I had found him at the first, and lay, with his face in the bracken, panting like a dog.

My own sides so ached, my head so swam, my tongue so hung out of my mouth with heat and dryness, that I lay beside him like one dead.

1 Duck.

18 I talk with Alan in the Wood of Lettermore

Alan was the first to come round. He rose, went to the border of the wood, peered out a little, and then returned and sat down.

'Well,' said he, 'yon was a hot burst, David.'

I said nothing, nor so much as lifted my face. I had seen murder done, and a great, ruddy, jovial gentleman struck out of life in a moment; the pity of that sight was still sore within me, and yet that was but a part of my concern. Here was murder done upon the man Alan hated; here was Alan skulking in the trees and running from the troops; and whether his was the hand that fired or only the head that ordered, signified but little. By my way of it, my only friend in that wild country was blood-guilty in the first degree; I held him in horror; I could not look upon his face; I would have rather lain alone in the rain on my cold isle, than in that warm wood beside a murderer.

'Are ye still wearied?' he asked again.

'No,' said I, still with my face in the bracken; 'no, I am not wearied now, and I can speak. You and me must twine,'[1] I said. 'I liked you very well, Alan, but your ways are not mine, and they're not God's; and the short and the long of it is just that we must twine.'

'I will hardly twine from ye, David, without some kind of reason for the same,' said Alan, mighty gravely. 'If ye ken anything against my reputation, it's the least thing that ye should do, for old acquaintance' sake, to let me hear the name of it; and if ye have only taken a distaste to my society, it will be proper for me to judge if I'm insulted.'

'Alan,' said I, 'what is the sense of this? Ye ken very well yon Campbell-man lies in his blood upon the road.'

He was silent for a little; then he says he, 'Did ever ye hear tell of the story of the Man and the Good People?' – by which he meant the fairies.

'No,' said I, 'nor do I want to hear it.'

'With your permission, Mr. Balfour, I will tell it you, whatever,' says Alan. 'The man, ye should ken, was cast upon a rock in the sea, where it appears the Good People were in use to come and rest as they went through to Ireland. The name of this rock is called Skerryvore, and it's not far from where we suffered shipwreck. Well, it seems the man cried so sore, if he could just see his little bairn before he died! that at last the king of the Good People took peety upon him, and sent one flying that brought back the bairn in a poke² and laid it down beside the man where he lay sleeping. So when the man woke, there was a poke beside him and something into the inside of it that moved. Well, it seems he was one of these gentry that think aye the worst of things; and for greater security, he stuck his dirk throughout that poke before he opened it, and there was the bairn dead. I am thinking to myself, Mr. Balfour, that you and the man are very much alike.'

'Do you mean you had no hand in it?' cried I, sitting up.

'I will tell you first of all, Mr. Balfour of Shaws, as one friend to another,' said Alan, 'that if I were going to kill a gentleman, it would not be in my own country, to bring trouble to my clan; and I would not go wanting sword and gun, and with a long fishing-rod upon my back.'

'Well,' said I, 'that's true!'

'And now,' continued Alan, taking out his dirk and laying his hand upon it in a certain manner, 'I swear upon the Holy Iron I had neither art nor part, act nor thought in it.'

'I thank God for that!' cried I, and offered him my hand.

He did not appear to see it.

'And here is a great deal of work about a Campbell!' said he. 'They are not so scarce, that I ken!'

'At least,' said I, 'you cannot justly blame me, for you know very well what you told me in the brig. But the temptation and the act are different, I thank God again for that. We may all be tempted; but to take a life in cold blood Alan!' And I could say no more for the moment. 'And do you know who did it?' I added. 'Do you know that man in the black coat?'

'I have nae clear mind about his coat,' said Alan cunningly; 'but it sticks in my head it was blue.'

'Blue or black, did ye know him!' said I.

'I couldnae just conscientiously swear to him,' says Alan. 'He gaed very close by me, to be sure, but it's a strange thing that I should just have been tying my brogues.'

'Can you swear that you didn't know him, Alan?' I cried, half angered, half in a mind to laugh at his evasions.

'Not yet,' says he; 'but I've a grand memory for forgetting, David.'

'And yet there was one thing I saw clearly,' said I; 'and that was, that you exposed yourself and me to draw the soldiers.'

'It's very likely,' said Alan; 'and so would any gentleman. You and me were innocent of that transaction.'

'The better reason, since we were falsely suspected, that we should get clear,' I cried. 'The innocent should surely come before the guilty.'

'Why, David,' said he, 'the innocent have aye a chance to get assoiled in court; but for the lad that shot the bullet, I think the best place for him will be the heather. Them that havenae dipped their hands in any little difficulty, should be very mindful of the case of them that have. And that is the good Christianity. For if it was the other way round about, and the lad whom I couldnae just clearly see had been in our shoes, and we in his (as might very well have been), I think we would be a good deal obliged to him oursel's if he would draw the soldiers.'

When it came to this, I gave Alan up. But he looked so innocent all the time, and was in such clear good faith in what he said, and so ready to sacrifice himself for what he deemed his duty, that my mouth was closed. Mr. Henderland's words came back to me: that we ourselves might take a lesson by these wild Highlanders. Well, here I had taken mine. Alan's morals were all tail-first; but he was ready to give his life for them, such as they were.

'Alan,' said I, 'I'll not say it's the good Christianity as I understand it, but it's good enough. And here I offer ye my hand for the second time.'

Whereupon he gave me both of his, saying surely I had cast a spell upon him, for he could forgive me anything. Then he grew very grave, and said we had not much time to throw away, but must both flee that country; he, because he was a deserter, and the whole of Appin would now be searched like a chamber, and everyone obliged to give a good account of himself; and I, because I was certainly involved in the murder.

'Oh!' says I, willing to give him a little lesson, 'I have no fear of the justice of my country.'

'As if this was your country!' said he. 'Or as if ye would be tried here, in a country of Stewarts!'

'It's all Scotland,' said I.

'Man, I whiles wonder at ye,' said Alan. 'This is a Campbell that's been killed. Well, it'll be tried in Inverara, the Campbells' head place; with fifteen Campbells in the jury-box, and the biggest Campbell of all (and that's the Duke) sitting cocking on the bench. Justice, David? The same justice, by all the world, as Glenure found a while ago at the roadside.'

This frighted me a little, I confess, and would have frighted me more if I had known how nearly exact were Alan's predictions; indeed it was but in one point that he exaggerated, there being but eleven Campbells on the jury; though as the other four were equally in the Duke's dependence, it mattered less than might appear. Still I cried out that he was unjust to the Duke of Argyle, who (for all he was a Whig) was yet a wise and honest nobleman.

'Hoot!' said Alan, 'the man's a Whig, nae doubt; but I would never deny he was a good chieftain to his clan. And what would the clan think if there was a Campbell shot, and naebody hanged, and their own chief the Justice General? But I have often observed,' says Alan, 'that you Low-country bodies have no clear idea of what's right and wrong.'

At this I did at last laugh out aloud; when to my surprise Alan joined in, and laughed as merrily as myself.

'Na, na,' said he, 'we're in the Hielands, David: and when I tell ye to run, take my word and run. Nae doubt it's a hard thing to skulk and starve in the heather, but it's harder yet to lie shackled in a redcoat prison.'

I asked him whither we should flee; and as he told me 'to the Lowlands,' I was a little better inclined to go with him; for, indeed, I was growing impatient to get back and have the upper hand of my uncle. Alan made so sure there would be no question of justice in the matter, that I began to be afraid he might be right. Of all deaths, I would truly like least to die by the gallows; and the picture of that uncanny instrument came into my head with extraordinary clearness (as I had once seen it engraved at the top of a pedlar's ballad) and took away my appetite for courts of justice.

'I'll chance it, Alan,' said I. 'I'll go with you.'

'But mind you,' said Alan, 'it's no small thing. Ye maun lie bare and hard, and brook many an empty belly. Your bed shall be the moorcock's, and your life shall be like the hunted deer's, and ye shall sleep with your hand upon your weapons. Ay, man, ye shall taigle many a weary foot, or we get clear! I tell ye this at the start, for it's a life that I ken well. But if ye ask what other chance ye have, I answer: Nane. Either take to the heather with me, or else hang.'

'And that's a choice very easily made,' said I; and we shook hands upon it.

'And now let's take another keek at the redcoats,' says Alan, and he led me to the north-eastern fringe of the wood.

Looking out between the trees, we could see a great side of mountain, running down exceeding steep into the waters of the loch. It was a rough part, all hanging stone, and heather, and bit scrogs of birchwood; and away at the far end towards Balachulish, little wee red soldiers were dipping up and down over hill and howe, and growing smaller every minute. There was no cheering now, for I think they had other uses for what breath was left them; but they still stuck to the trail, and doubtless thought that we were close in front of them.

Alan watched them, smiling to himself.

'Ay,' said he, 'they'll be gey weary before they've got to the end of that employ! And so you and me, David, can sit down and eat a bite, and breathe a bit longer, and take a dram from my bottle. Then we'll strike for Aucharn, the house of my kinsman, James of the Glens, where I must get my clothes, and my arms, and money to carry us along; and then, David, we'll cry "Forth, Fortune!" and take a cast among the heather.'

So we sat again and ate and drank, in a place whence we could see the sun going down into a field of great, wild and houseless mountains, such as I was now condemned to wander in with my companion. Partly as we so sat and partly afterwards, on the way to Aucharn, each of us narrated his adventure; and I shall here set down so much of Alan's as seems either curious or needful.

It appears he ran to the bulwarks as soon as the wave was passed: saw me, and lost me, and saw me again, as I tumbled in the roost; and at last had one glimpse of me clinging on the yard. It was this that put in some hope I would maybe get to land after all, and made him leave those clues and messages which had brought me (for my sins) to that unlucky country of Appin.

In the meanwhile, those still on the brig had got the skiff launched, and one or two were on board of her already, when there came a second wave greater than the first, and heaved the brig out of her place, and would certainly have sent her to the bottom, had she not struck and caught on some projection of the reef. When she had struck first, it had been bows-on, so that the stern had hitherto been lowest. But now her stern was thrown in the air, and the bows plunged under the sea; and with that, the water began to pour into the fore-scuttle like the pouring of a mill-dam.

It took the colour out of Alan's face even to tell what followed. For there were still two men lying impotent in their bunks; and these, seeing the water pour in and thinking the ship had foundered, began to cry out aloud, and that with such harrowing cries that all who were on deck tumbled one after another into the skiff and fell to their oars. They were not two hundred yards away when there came a third great sea; and at that the brig lifted clean over the reef; her canvas filled for a moment, and she seemed to sail in chase of them, but settling all the while; and presently she drew down and down, as if a hand was drawing her; and the sea closed over the *Covenant* of Dysart.

Never a word they spoke as they pulled ashore, being stunned with the horror of that screaming; but they had scarce set foot upon the beach when Hoseason woke up, as if out of a muse, and bade them lay hands upon Alan. They hung back indeed, having little taste for the employment; but Hoseason was like a fiend, crying that Alan was alone, that he had a great sum about him, that he had been the means of losing the brig and drowning all their comrades, and that here was both revenge and wealth upon a single cast. I was seven against one; in that part of the shore there was no rock that Alan could set his back to; and the sailors, began to spread out and come behind him.

'And then,' said Alan, 'the little man with the red head – I havenae mind of the name that he is called.'

'Riach,' said I.

'Ay,' said Alan, 'Riach! Well, it was him that took up the clubs for me, asked the men if they werenae feared of a judgment, and, says he, "Dod, I'll put my back to the Hielandman's mysel'." That's none such an entirely bad little man, yon little man with the red head,' said Alan. 'He has some spunks of decency.'

'Well,' said I, 'he was kind to me in his way.'

'And so he was Alan,' said he; 'and by my troth, I found his way a very good one! But ye see, David, the loss of the ship and the cries of these poor lads sat very ill upon the man; and I'm thinking that would be the cause of it.'

'Well, I would think so,' says I; 'for he was as keen as any of the rest at the beginning. But how did Hoseason take it?'

'It sticks in my mind that he would take it very ill,' says Alan. 'But the little man cried to me to run, and indeed I thought it was a good observe, and ran. The last that I saw they were all in a knot upon the beach, like folk that were not agreeing very well together.'

'What do you mean by that?' said I.

'Well, the fists were going,' said Alan; 'and I saw one man go down like a pair of breeks.² But I thought it would be better no to wait. Ye see there's a strip of Campbells in that end of Mull, which is no good company for a gentleman like me. If it hadnae been for that I would have waited and looked for ye mysel', let alone giving a hand to the little man.' (It was droll how Alan dwelt on Mr. Riach's stature, for, to say the truth, the one was not smaller than the other.) 'So,' says he, continuing, 'I set my best foot forward, and whenever I met in with anyone I cried out there was a wreck ashore. Man, they didnae stop to fash with me! Ye should have seen them linking for the beach! And when they got there they found they had had the pleasure of a run,¹ which is aye good for a Campbell. I'm thinking it was a judgment on the clan that the brig went down in the lump and didnae break. But it was a very lucky thing for you, that same; for if any wreck had come ashore they would have hunted high and low, and would soon have found ye.'

1 Part.
2 Bag.

19   The House of Fear

Night fell as we were walking and the clouds, which had broken up in the afternoon, settled in and thickened, so that it fell, for the season of the year, extremely dark. The way we went was over rough mountainsides; and though Alan pushed on with an assured manner, I could by no means see how he directed himself.

At last, about half past ten of the clock, we came to the top of a brae, and saw lights below us. It seemed a house door stood open and let out a beam of fire- and candle-light; and all round the house and steading five or six persons were moving hurriedly about, each carrying a lighted brand.

'James must have tint his wits,' said Alan. 'If this was the soldiers instead of you and me, he would be in a bonny mess. But I dare say he'll have a sentry on the road, and he would ken well enough no soldiers would find the way that we came.'

Hereupon he whistled three times in a particular manner. It was strange to see how, at the first sound of it, all the moving torches came to a stand, as if the bearers were affrighted; and how, at the third, the bustle began again as before.

Having thus set folks' minds at rest, we came down the brae, and were met at the yard gate (for this place was like a well-doing farm) by a tall, handsome man of more than fifty, who cried out to Alan in the Gaelic.

'James Stewart,' said Alan, 'I will ask ye to speak in Scotch, for here is a young gentleman with me that has nane of the other. This is him,' he added, putting his arm through mine, 'a young gentleman of the Lowlands, and a laird in his country, too, but I'm thinking it will be the better for his health if we give his name the go-by.'

James of the Glens turned to me for a moment, and greeted me courteously enough; the next he had turned to Alan.

'This has been a dreadful accident,' he cried. 'It will bring trouble on the country.' And he wrung his hands.

'Hoots!' said Alan, 'ye must take the sour with the sweet, man. Colin Roy is dead, and be thankful for that!'

'Ay,' said James, 'and by my troth, I wish he was alive again! It's all very fine to blow and boast beforehand; but now it's done, Alan; and who's to bear the wyte[1] of it? The accident fell out in Appin – mind ye that, Alan; it's Appin that must pay; and I am a man that has a family.'

While this was going on I looked about me at the servants. Some were on ladders, digging in the thatch of the house or the farm buildings, from which they brought out guns, swords, and different weapons of war; others carried them away; and by the sound of mattock blows from somewhere farther down the brae, I suppose they buried them. Though they were all so busy, there prevailed no kind of order in their efforts; men struggled together for the same gun and ran into each other with their burning torches; and James was continually turning about from his talk with Alan, to cry out orders which were apparently never understood. The faces in the torch-light were like those of people over-borne with hurry and panic; and though none spoke above his breath, their speech sounded both anxious and angry.

It was about this time that a lassie came out of the house carrying a pack or bundle; and it has often made me smile to think how Alan's instinct awoke at the mere sight of it.

'What's that the lassie has?' he asked.

'We're just setting the house in order, Alan,' said James, in his frightened and somewhat fawning way. 'They'll search Appin with candles, and we must have all things straight. We're digging the bit guns and swords into the moss, ye see; and these, I am thinking, will be your ain French clothes.'

'Bury my French clothes!' cried Alan. 'Troth, no!' And he laid hold upon the packet and retired into the barn to shift himself, recommending me in the meanwhile to his kinsman.

James carried me accordingly into the kitchen, and sat down with me at table, smiling and talking at first in a very hospitable manner. But presently the gloom returned upon him; he sat frowning and biting his fingers; only remembered me from time to time; and then gave me but a word or two and a poor smile, and back into his private terrors. His wife sat by the fire and wept, with her face in her hands; his eldest son was crouched upon the floor, running over a great mass of papers and now and again setting one alight and burning it to the bitter end; all the while a servant lass with a red face was rummaging about the room, in a blind hurry of fear, and whimpering as she went: and every now and again one of the men would thrust in his face from the yard and cry for orders.

At last James could keep his seat no longer, and begged my permission to be so unmannerly as walk about. 'I am but poor company altogether, sir,' says he, 'but I can think of nothing but this dreadful accident, and the trouble it is like to bring upon quite innocent persons.'

A little after he observed his son burning a paper which he thought should have been kept; and at that his excitement burst out so that it was painful to witness. He struck the lad repeatedly.

'Are you going gyte?'[2] he cried. 'Do you wish to hang your father?' and forgetful of my presence, carried on at him a long time together in the Gaelic, the young man answering nothing only the wife, at the name of hanging, throwing her apron over her face and sobbing out louder than before.

This was all wretched for a stranger like myself to hear and see and I was right glad when Alan returned, looking like himself in his fine French clothes, though (to be sure) they were now grown almost too battered and withered to deserve the name of fine. I was then taken out in my turn by another of the sons, and given that change of clothing of which I had stood so long in need, and a pair of Highland brogues made of deer-leather, rather strange at first, but after a little practice very easy to the feet.

By the time I came back Alan must have told his story; for it seemed understood that I was to fly with him, and they were all busy upon our equipment. They gave us each a sword and pistols, though I professed my inability to use the former; and with these, and some ammunition, a bag of oatmeal, an iron pan, and a bottle of right French brandy, we were ready for the heather. Money, indeed, was lacking. I had about two guineas left; Alan's belt having been dispatched by another hand, that trusty messenger had no more than seventeen pence to his whole fortune; and as for James, it appears he had brought himself so low with journeys to Edinburgh and legal expenses on behalf of the tenants, that he could only scrape together three and fivepence halfpenny, the most of it in coppers.

'This'll no do,' said Alan.

'Ye must find a safe bit somewhere near by,' said James, 'and get word sent to me. Ye see, ye'll have to get this business prettily off, Alan. This is no time to be stayed for a guinea or two. They're sure to get wind of ye, sure to seek ye, and by my way of it, sure to lay on ye the wyte of this day's accident. If it falls on you, it falls on me that am your near kinsman and harboured ye while ye were in the country. And if it comes on me ——' He paused, and bit his fingers, with a white face. 'It would be a painful thing for our friends if I was to hang,' said he.

'It would be an ill day for Appin,' says Alan.

'It's a day that sticks in my throat,' said James. 'Oh, man, man, man – man Alan you and me have spoken like two fools!' he cried, sticking his hand upon the wall so that the house rang again.

'Well, and that's true, too,' said Alan; 'and my friend from the Lowlands here' (nodding at me) 'gave me good word upon that head, if I would only have listened to him.'

'But see here,' said James, returning to his former manner. 'if they lay me by the heels, Alan, it's then that you'll be needing the money. For with all that I have said and that you have said, it will look very black against the two of us; do ye mark that? Well, follow me out, and ye'll see that I'll have to get a paper out against ye mysel'; I'll have to offer a reward for ye; ay, will I! It's a sore thing to do between such near friends; but if I get the dirdum³ of this dreadful accident, I'll have to fend for myself, man. Do ye see that?'

He spoke with a pleading earnestness, taking Alan by the breast of the coat.

'Ay,' said Alan, 'I see that.'

'And ye'll have to be clear of the country, Alan – ay, and clear of Scotland – you and your friend from the Lowlands too. For I'll have to paper your friend from the Lowlands. Ye see that, Alan – say that ye see that!'

I thought Alan flushed a bit. 'This is unco hard on me that brought him here, James,' said he, throwing his head back. 'It's like making me a traitor!'

'Now, Alan, man!' cried James. 'Look things in the face! He'll be prepared anyway; Mungo Campbell'll be sure to paper him; what matters if I paper him too? And then, Alan, I am a man that has a family.' And then, after a little pause on both sides: 'And, Alan, it'll be a jury of Campbells,' said he.

'There's one thing,' said Alan musingly, 'that naebody kens his name.'

'Nor yet they shallnae, Alan! There's my hand on that,' cried James, for all the world as if he had really known my name and was foregoing some advantage. 'But just the habit he was in, and what he looked like, and his age, and the like? I couldnae well do less.'

'I wonder at your father's son,' cried Alan sternly. 'Would ye sell the lad with a gift? Would ye change his clothes and then betray him?'

'No, no, Alan,' said James. 'No, no; the habit he took off – the habit Mungo saw him in.' But I thought he seemed crestfallen; indeed, he was clutching at every straw, and all the time, I dare say, saw the faces of his hereditary foes on the bench, and in the jury-box, and the gallows in the background.

'Well, sir,' says Alan, turning to me, 'what say ye to that? Ye are here under the safeguard of my honour; and it's my part to see nothing done but what shall please you.'

'I have but one word to say,' said I; 'for to all this dispute I am a perfect stranger. But the plain common sense is to set the blame where it belongs, and that is on the man that fired the shot. Paper him, as ye call it, set the hunt on him; and let honest, innocent folk show their faces in safety.'

But at this both Alan and James cried out in horror; bidding me hold my tongue, for that was not to be thought of; and asking me what the Camerons would think? (which confirmed me, it must have been a Cameron from Mamore that did the act) and if I did not see that the lad might be caught? 'Ye havenae surely thought of that?' said they, with such innocent earnestness, that my hands dropped at my side and I despaired of argument.

'Very well, then,' said I, 'paper me, if you please, paper Alan, paper King George! We're all three innocent, and that seems to be what's wanted. But at least, sir,' said I to James, recovering from my little fit of annoyance, 'I am Alan's friend, and if I can be helpful to friends of his, I will not stumble at the risk.'

I thought it best to put a fair face on my consent, for I saw Alan troubled; and besides (thinks I to myself), as soon as my back is turned, they will paper me, as they call it, whether I consent or not. But in this I saw I was wrong; for I had no sooner said the words, than Mrs. Stewart leaped out of her chair, came running over to us, and wept first upon my neck and them on Alan's, blessing God for our goodness to her family.

'As for you, Alan, it was no more than your bounden duty,' she said. 'But for this lad that has come here and seen us at our worst, and seen the goodman fleeching like a suitor, him that by rights should give his commands like any king – as for you, my lad,' she says, 'my heart is wae not to have your name, but I have your face; and as long as my heart beats under my bosom, I will keep it and think of it, and bless it.' And with that she kissed me, and burst once more into such sobbing, that I stood abashed.

'Hoot, hoot,' said Alan, looking mighty silly. 'The day comes unco soon in this month of July; and to-morrow there'll be a fine to-do in Appin, a fine riding of dragoons, and crying of "Cruachan!"[4] and running of redcoats; and it behoves you and me to be the sooner gone.'

Thereupon we said farewell, and set out again, bending somewhat eastward, in a fine, mild, dark night, and over much the same broken country as before.

1 Blame.
2 Mad, crazy.
3 Blame.
4 The rallying-word of the Campbells.

20 The Flight in the Heather: The Rocks

Sometimes we walked, sometimes ran; and as it drew on to morning, walked ever the less and ran the more. Though, upon its face, that country appeared to be a desert, yet there were huts and houses of the people, of which we must have passed more than twenty, hidden in quiet places of the hills. When we came to one of these, Alan would leave me in the way, and go himself and rap upon the side of the house and speak awhile at the window with some sleeper awakened. This was to pass the news; which, in that country, was so much of a duty that Alan must pause to attend to it even while fleeing for his life; and so well attended to by others, that in more than half of the houses where we called they had heard already of the murder. In the others, as well as I could make out (standing back at a distance and hearing a strange tongue), the news was received with more of consternation than surprise.

For all our hurry, day began to come in while we were still far from any shelter. It found us in a prodigious valley strewn with rocks and where ran a foaming river. Wild mountains stood around it; there grew there neither grass nor trees; and I have sometimes thought since then that it may have been the valley called Glencoe, where the massacre was in the time of King William. But for the details of our itinerary, I am all to seek; our way lying now by short cuts, now by great detours; our pace being so hurried, our time of journeying usually by night; and the names of such places as I asked and heard being in the Gaelic tongue and the more easily forgotten.

The first peep of morning, then, showed us this horrible place, and I could see Alan knit his brow.

'This is no fit place for you and me,' he said. 'This is a place they're bound to watch.'

And with that he ran harder than ever down to the water side, in a part where the river was split in two among three rocks. It went through with a horrid thundering that made my belly quake; and there hung over the lynn a little mist of spray. Alan looked neither to the right nor to the left, but jumped clean upon the middle rock and fell there on his hands and knees to check himself, for that rock was small and he might have pitched over on the far side. I had scarce time to measure the distance or to understand the peril before I had followed him, and he had caught and stopped me.

So there we stood, side by side upon a small rock slippery with spray, a far broader leap in front of us, and the river dinning upon all sides. When I saw where I was, there came on me a deadly sickness of fear, and I put my hand over my eyes. Alan took me and shook me; I saw he was speaking, but the roaring of the falls and the trouble of my mind prevented me from hearing; only I saw his face was red with anger, and that he stamped upon the rock. The same look showed me the water raging by, and the mist hanging in the air: and with that I covered my eyes again and shuddered.

The next minute Alan had set the brandy bottle to my lips, and forced me to drink about a gill, which sent the blood into my head again. Then putting his hands to his mouth, and his mouth to my ear, he shouted, 'Hang or drown!' and turning his back upon me, leaped over the farther branch of the stream, and landed safe.

I was now alone upon the rock, which gave me the more room; the brandy was singing in my ears; I had this good example fresh before me, and just wit enough to see that if I did not leap at once, I should never leap at all. I bent low on my knees and flung myself forth, with that kind of anger of despair that has sometimes stood me in stead of courage. Sure enough, it was but my hands that reached the full length; these slipped, caught again, slipped again; and I was sliddering back into the lynn, when Alan seized me, first by the hair, then by the collar, and with a great strain dragged me into safety.

Never a word he said, but set off running again for his life, and I must stagger to my feet and run after him. 'I had been weary before, but now I was sick and bruised, and partly drunken with the brandy; I kept stumbling as I ran, I had a stitch that came near to overmaster me; and when at last Alan paused under a great rock that stood there among a number of others, it was none too soon for David Balfour.

A great rock I have said; but by rights it was two rocks leaning together at the top, both some twenty feet high, and at the first sight inaccessible. Even Alan (though you may say he had as good as four

'When I saw where I was, there came upon me a deadly sickness of fear'

hands) failed twice in an attempt to climb them; and it was only at the third trial, and then by standing on my shoulders and leaping up with such force as I thought must have broken my collar-bone, that he secured a lodgement. Once there, he let down his leathern girdle, and with the aid of that and a pair of shallow footholds in the rock, I scrambled up beside him.

Then I saw why we had come there; for the two rocks, being both somewhat hollow on the top and sloping one to the other, made a kind of dish or saucer, where as many as three or four men might have lain hidden.

All this while Alan had not said a word, and had run and climbed with such a savage, silent frenzy of hurry, that I knew he was in mortal fear of some miscarriage. Even now we were on the rock he said nothing, nor so much as relaxed the frowning look upon his face; but clapped flat down, and keeping only one eye above the edge of our place of shelter, scouted all round the compass. The dawn had come quite clear; we could see the stony sides of the valley, and its bottom, which was bestrewed with rocks, and the river, which went from one side to another, and made white falls; but nowhere the smoke of a house, nor any living creature but some eagles screaming round a cliff.

Then at last Alan smiled.

'Ay,' said he, 'now we have a chance'; and then looking at me with some amusement, 'Ye're no very gleg¹ at the jumping,' said he.

At this I suppose I coloured with mortification, for he added at once, 'Hoots! small blame to ye! To be feared of a thing and yet to do it is what makes the prettiest kind of a man. And then there was water there, and water's a thing that dauntons even me. No, no,' said Alan, 'it's no you that's to blame, it's me.'

I asked him why.

'Why,' said he, 'I have proved myself a gomeral this night. For first of all I take a wrong road, and that in my own country of Appin; so that the day has caught us where we should never have been; and thanks to that, we lie here in some danger and mair discomfort. And next (which is the worst of the two, for a man that has been so much among the heather as myself), I have come wanting a water-bottle, and here we lie for a long summer's day with naething but neat spirit. Ye may think that a small matter: but before it comes night, David, ye'll give me news of it.'

I was anxious to redeem my character, and offered, if he would pour out the brandy, to run down and fill the bottle at the river.

'I wouldnae waste the good spirit either,' says he. 'It's been a good friend to you this night; or in my poor opinion, ye would still be cocking on yon stone. And what's mair,' says he, 'ye may have observed (you that's a man of so much penetration) that Alan Breck Stewart was perhaps walking quicker than his ordinar'.'

'You!' I cried, 'you were running fit to burst.'

'Was I so?' said he. 'Well, then, ye may depend upon it, there was nae time to be lost. And now here is enough said; gang you to your sleep, lad, and I'll watch.'

Accordingly, I lay down to sleep; a little peaty earth had drifted in between the top of the two rocks, and some bracken grew there, to be a bed to me; the last thing I heard was still the crying of the eagles.

I dare say it would be nine in the morning when I was roughly awakened, and found Alan's hand pressed upon my mouth.

'Wheesht!' he whispered. 'Ye were snoring.'

'Well,' said I, surprised at his anxious and dark face, 'and why not?'

He peered over the edge of the rock, and signed to me to do the like.

It was now high day, cloudless, and very hot. The valley was as clear as in a picture. About half a mile up the water was a camp of redcoats; a big fire blazed in their midst, at which some were cooking; and near by, on the top of a rock about as high as ours, there stood a sentry, with the sun sparkling on his arms. All the way down along the riverside were posted other sentries; here near together, there widelier scattered; some planted like the first, on places of command, some on the ground level and marching and counter-marching so as to meet half-way. Higher up the glen, where the ground was more open, the chain of posts was continued by horse-soldiers, whom we could see in the distance riding to and fro. Lower down, the infantry continued; but as the stream was suddenly swelled by the confluence of a considerable burn, they were more widely set, and only watched the fords and stepping-stones.

I took but one look at them and ducked again into my place. It was strange indeed to see this valley, which had lain so solitary in the hour of dawn, bristling with arms and dotted with the red coats and breeches.

'Ye see,' said Alan, 'this was what I was afraid of, Davie: that they would watch the burnside. They began to come in about two hours ago, and, man! but ye're a grand hand at the sleeping! We're in a narrow place. If they get up the sides of the hill they could easy spy us with a glass; but if they'll only keep in the foot of the valley, we'll do yet. The posts are thinner down the water: and, come night, we'll try our hand at getting by them.'

'And what are we to do till night?' I asked.

'Lie here,' says he, 'and birstle.'

That one good Scotch word, 'birstle,' was indeed the most of the story of the day that we had now to pass. You are to remember that we lay on the bare top of a rock, like scones upon a girdle; the sun beat upon us cruelly; the rock grew so heated, a man could scarce endure the touch of it; and the little patch of earth and fern, which kept cooler, was only large enough for one at a time. We took turn about to lie on the naked rock, which was indeed like the position of that saint that was martyred on a gridiron; and it ran in my mind how strange it was, that in the same climate and at only a few days' distance, I should have suffered so cruelly, first from cold upon my island and now from heat upon this rock.

All the while we had no water, only raw brandy for a drink, which was worse than nothing; but we kept the bottle as cool as we could, burying it in the earth, and got some relief by bathing our breasts and temples.

The soldiers kept stirring all day in the bottom of the valley, now changing guard, now in patrolling parties hunting among the rocks. These lay round in so great a number, that to look for men among them was like looking for a needle in a bottle of hay and being so hopeless a task, it was gone about with the less care. Yet we could see the soldiers pike their bayonets among the heather, which sent a cold thrill into my vitals; and they would sometimes hang about our rock, so that we scarce dared to breathe.

It was in this way that I first heard the right English speech; one fellow as he went by actually clapping his hand upon the sunny face of the rock on which we lay, and plucking it off again with an oath. 'I tell you it's 'ot,' says he; and I was amazed at the clipping tones and the odd sing-song in which he spoke, and no less at that strange trick of dropping out the letter 'h.' To be sure, I had heard Ransome; but he had taken his ways from all sorts of people and spoke so imperfectly at the best, that I set down the most of it to childishness. My surprise was all the greater to hear that manner of speaking in the mouth of a grown man; and indeed I have never grown used to it; nor yet altogether with the English grammar, as perhaps a very critical eye might here and there spy out even in these memoirs.

The tediousness and pain of these hours upon the rock grew only the greater as the day went on; the rock getting still the hotter, and the sun fiercer. There were giddiness, and sickness, and sharp pangs like rheumatism to be supported. I minded then, and have often minded since, on the lines in our Scotch psalm:

> The moon by night thee shall not smite,
> Nor yet the sun by day;

and indeed it was only by God's blessing that we were neither of us sun-smitten.

At last, about two, it was beyond men's bearing, and there was now temptation to resist, as well as pain to thole. For the sun being now got a little into the west, there came a patch of shade on the east side of our rock, which was the side sheltered from the soldiers.

'As well one death as another,' said Alan, and slipped over the edge and dropped on the ground on the shadowy side.

I followed him at once, and instantly fell all my length, so weak was I and so giddy with that long exposure. Here, then, we lay for an hour or two, aching from head to foot, as weak as water, and lying quite naked to the eye of any soldier who should have strolled that way. None came, however, all passing by on the other side; so that our rock continued to be our shield even in this new position.

Presently we began again to get a little strength; and as the soldiers were now lying closer along the riverside, Alan proposed that we should try a start. I was by this time afraid of but one thing in the world; and that was to be set back upon the rock; anything else was welcome to me; so we got ourselves at once in marching order, and began to slip from rock to rock one after the other, now crawling flat on our bellies in the shade, now making a run for it, heart in mouth.

The soldiers, having searched this side of the valley after a fashion, and being perhaps somewhat sleepy with the sultriness of the afternoon, had now laid by much of their vigilance, and stood dozing at their posts or only kept a look-out along the banks of the river; so that in this way, keeping down the valley and at the same time towards the mountains, we drew steadily away from their neighbourhood. But the business was the most wearing I had ever taken part in. A man had need of a hundred eyes in every part of him, to keep concealed in that uneven country and within cry of so many and scattered sentries. When we must pass an open place, quickness was not all, but a swift judgment not only of the lie of the whole country, but of the solidity of every stone on which we must set foot; for the afternoon was now fallen so breathless that the rolling of a pebble sounded abroad like a pistol shot, and would start the echo calling among the hills and cliffs.

By sundown we had made some distance, even by our slow rate of progress, though to be sure the sentry on the rock was still plainly in our view. But now we came on something that put all fears out of season; and that was a deep rushing burn, that tore down, in that part, to join the glen river. At the sight of this we cast ourselves on the ground and plunged head and shoulders in the water; and I cannot tell which was the more pleasant, the great shock as the cool stream went over us, or the greed with which we drank of it.

We lay there (for the banks hid us), drank again and again, bathed our chests, let our wrists trail in the running water till they ached with the chill; and at last, being wonderfully renewed, we got out the meal-bag and made drammach in the iron pan. This, though it is but cold water mingled with oatmeal, yet makes a good enough dish for a hungry man; and where there are no means of making fire, or (as in our case) good reason for not making one, it is the chief stand-by of those who have taken to the heather.

As soon as the shadow of the night had fallen, we set forth again, at first with the same caution, but presently with more boldness, standing our full height and stepping out at a good pace of walking. The way was very intricate, lying up the steep sides of mountains and along the brows of cliffs; clouds had come in with the sunset, and the night was dark and cool; so that I walked without much fatigue, but in continual fear of falling and rolling down the mountains, and with no guess at our direction.

The moon rose at last and found us still on the road; it was in its last quarter, and was long beset with clouds; but after a while shone out and showed me many dark heads of mountains, and was reflected far underneath us on the narrow arm of a sea-loch.

At this sight we both paused: I struck with wonder to find myself so high and walking (as it seemed to me) upon clouds: Alan to make sure of his direction.

Seemingly he was well pleased, and he must certainly have judged us out of earshot of all our enemies; for throughout the rest of our night march he beguiled the way with whistling of many tunes, warlike, merry, plaintive; reel tunes that made the foot go faster; tunes of my own south country that made me fain to be home from my adventures; and all these, on the great, dark, desert mountains, making company upon the way.

1 Brisk.

21 The Flight in the Heather: The Heugh of Corrynakiegh

Early as day comes in the beginning of July, it was still dark when we reached our destination, a cleft in the head of a great mountain, with a water running through the midst, and upon the one hand a shallow cave in a rock. Birches grew there in a thin, pretty wood, which a little farther on was changed into a wood of pines. The burn was full of trout; the wood of cushat-doves; on the open side of the mountain beyond, whaups would be always whistling, and cuckoos were plentiful. From the mouth of the cleft we looked down upon a part of Mamore, and on the sea-loch that divides that country from Appin; and this from so great a height as made it my continual wonder and pleasure to sit and behold them.

The name of the cleft was the Heugh of Corrynakiegh; and although from its height and being so near upon the sea it was often beset with clouds, yet it was on the whole a pleasant place, and the five days we lived in it went happily.

We slept in the cave, making our bed of heather bushes which we cut for that purpose, and covering ourselves with Alan's greatcoat. There was a low concealed place, in a turning of the glen, where we were so bold as to make fire: so that we could warm ourselves when the clouds set in, cook hot porridge, and grill the little trouts that we caught with our hands under the stones and overhanging banks of the burn. This was indeed our chief pleasure and business; and not only to save our meal against worse times, but with a rivalry that much amused us, we spent a great part of our days at the waterside, stripped to the waist and groping about or (as they say) guddling for these fish. The largest we got might have been a quarter of a pound; but they were of good flesh and flavour, and when broiled upon the coals, lacked only a little salt to be delicious.

In any by-time Alan must teach me to use my sword, for my ignorance had much distressed him; and I think besides, as I had sometimes the upper hand of him in the fishing, he was not sorry to turn to an exercise where he had so much the upper hand of me. He made it somewhat more of a pain than need have been, for he stormed at me all through the lessons in a very violent manner of scolding, and would push me so close that I made sure he must run me through the body. I was often tempted to turn tail, but held my ground for all that, and got some profit of my lessons; if it was but to stand on guard with an assured countenance, which is often all that is required. So, though I could never in the least please my master, I was not altogether displeased with myself.

In the meanwhile, you are not to suppose that we neglected our chief business, which was to get away.

'It will be many a long day,' Alan said to me on our first morning, 'before the redcoats think upon seeking Corrynakiegh; so now we must get word sent to James, and he must find the siller for us.'

'And how shall we send that word?' says I. 'We are here in a desert place, which yet we dare not leave; and unless ye get the fowls of the air to be your messengers, I see not what we shall be able to do.'

'Ay?' said Alan. 'Ye're a man of small contrivance, David.'

Thereupon he fell in a muse, looking in the embers of the fire; and presently, getting a piece of wood, he fashioned it in a cross, the four ends of which he blackened on the coals. Then he looked at me a little shyly.

'Could ye lend me my button?' says he. 'It seems a strange thing to ask a gift again, but I own I am laith to cut another.'

I gave him the button; whereupon he strung it on a strip of his greatcoat which he had used to bind the cross; and tying in a little sprig of birch and another of fir, he looked upon his work with satisfaction.

'Now,' said he, 'there is a little clachan' (what is called a hamlet in the English) 'not very far from Corrynakiegh, and it has the name of Koalisnacoan. There, there are living many friends of mine whom I could trust with my life, and some that I am no just so sure of. Ye see, David, there will be money set upon our heads; James himsel' is to set money on them; and as for the Campbells, they would never spare siller where there was a Stewart to be hurt. If it was otherwise, I would go down to Koalisnacoan whatever, and trust my life into these people's hands as lightly as I would trust another with my glove.'

'But being so?' said I.

'Being so,' said he, 'I would as lief they didnae see me. There's bad folk everywhere, and what's far worse, weak ones. So when it comes dark again, I will steal down into that clachan, and set this that I have been making in the window of a good friend of mine, John Breck Maccoll, a bouman[1] of Appin's.'

'With all my heart,' says I; 'and if he finds it, what is he to think?'

'Well,' says Alan. 'I wish he was a man of more penetration, for by my troth I am afraid he will make little enough of it! But this is what I have in my mind. This cross is something in the nature of the crosstarrie, or fiery cross, which is the signal of gathering in our clans; yet he will know well enough the clan is not to rise, for there it is standing in his window, and no word with it. So he will say to himsel', *The clan is not to rise, but there is something.* Then he will see my button, and that was Duncan Stewart's. And then he will say to himsel', *The son of Duncan is in the heather, and has need of me.*'

'Well,' said I, 'it may be. But even supposing so, there is a good deal of heather between here and the Forth.'

'And that is a very true word,' says Alan. 'But then John Breck will see the sprig of birch and the sprig of pine; and he will say to himsel' (if he is a man of any penetration at all, which I misdoubt), *Alan will be lying in a wood which is both of pines and birches.* Then he will think to himsel', *That is not so very rife hereabout*; and then he will come and give us a look up in Corrynakiegh. And if he does not, David, the devil may fly away with him, for what I care; for he will no be worth the salt to his porridge.'

'Eh, man,' said I, drolling with him a little, 'you're very ingenious! But would it not be simpler for you to write him a few words in black and white?'

'And that is an excellent observe, Mr. Balfour of Shaws,' says Alan, drolling with me; 'and it would certainly be much simpler for me to write to him, but it would be a sore job for John Breck to read it. He would have to go to the school for two-three years; and it's possible we might be wearied waiting on him.'

So that night Alan carried down his fiery cross and set it in the bouman's window. He was troubled when he came back; for the dogs had barked and the folk run out from their houses; and he thought he had heard a clatter of arms and seen a redcoat come to one of the doors. On all accounts we lay the next day in the borders of the wood and kept a close look-out, so that if it was John Breck that came we might be ready to guide him, and if it was the redcoats we should have time to get away.

About noon a man was to be spied straggling up the open side of the mountain in the sun, and looking round him as he came from under his hand. No sooner had Alan seen him than he whistled; the man turned and came a little towards us; then Alan would give another 'peep!' and the man would come still nearer; and so by the sound of whistling, he was guided to the spot where we lay.

He was a ragged, wild, bearded man, about forty, grossly disfigured with the smallpox, and looked both dull and savage. Although his English was very bad and broken, yet Alan (according to his very handsome use, whenever I was by) would suffer him to speak no Gaelic. Perhaps the strange language made him appear more backward than he really was; but I thought he had little goodwill to serve us, and what he had was the child of terror.

Alan would have had him carry a message to James; but the bouman would hear of no message. 'She was forget it,' he said in his screaming voice; and would either have a letter or wash his hands of us.

I thought Alan would be gravelled at that, for we lacked the means of writing in that desert. But he was a man of more resources than I knew; searched the wood until he found the quill of a cushat-dove, which he shaped into a pen; made himself a kind of ink with gunpowder from his horn and water from the running stream; and tearing a corner from his pocket, like a talisman to keep him from the gallows), he sat down and wrote as follows:

DEAR KINSMAN, Please send the money by the bearer to the place he kens of. Your affectionate cousin,   A. S.

This he entrusted to the bouman, who promised to make what manner of speed he best could, and carried it off with him down the hill.

He was three full days gone, but about five in the evening of the third we heard a whistling in the wood, which Alan answered; and presently the bouman came up the waterside, looking for us right and left. He seemed less sulky than before, and indeed he was no doubt well pleased to have got to the end of such a dangerous commission.

He gave us the news of the country; that it was alive with redcoats: that arms were being found, and poor folk brought in trouble daily; and that James and some of his servants were already clapped in prison at Fort William, under strong suspicion of complicity. It seemed it was noised on all sides that Alan Breck had fired the shot; and there was a bill issued for both him and me, with one hundred pounds reward.

This was all as bad as could be; and the little note the bouman had carried us from Mrs. Stewart was of a miserable sadness. In it she besought Alan not to let himself be captured, assuring him, if he fell in the hands of the troops, both he and James were no better than dead men. The money she had sent was all that she could beg or borrow, and she prayed Heaven we could be doing with it. Lastly, she said, she enclosed us one of the bills in which we were described.

This we looked upon with great curiosity and not a little fear, partly as a man may look in a mirror, partly as he might look into the barrel of an enemy's gun to judge if it be truly aimed. Alan was advertised as 'a small, pock-marked, active man of thirty-five or thereby, dressed in a feathered hat, a French side-coat of blue with silver buttons, and lace a great deal tarnished, a red waistcoat and breeches of black shag'; and I as 'a tall strong lad of about eighteen, wearing an old blue coat, very ragged, an old Highland bonnet, a long homespun waistcoat, blue breeches; his legs bare, low-country shoes, wanting the toes; speaks like a Lowlander, and has no beard.'

Alan was well enough pleased to see his finery so fully remembered and set down; only when he came to the word tarnish, he looked upon his lace like one a little mortified. As for myself, I thought I cut a miserable figure in the bill; and yet was well enough pleased too, for since I had changed these rags, the description had ceased to be a danger and become a source of safety.

'Alan,' said I, 'you should change your clothes.'

'Na, troth!' said Alan, 'I have nae others. A fine sight I would be, if I went back to France in a bonnet!'

This put a second reflection in my mind: that if I were to separate from Alan and his telltale clothes I should be safe against arrest, and might go openly about my business. Nor was this all; for suppose I was arrested when I was alone, there was little against me; but suppose I was taken in company with the reputed murderer, my case would begin to be grave. For generosity's sake I dare not speak my mind upon this head; but I thought of it none the less.

I thought of it all the more, too, when the bouman brought out a green purse with four guineas in gold, and the best part of another in small change. True, it was more than I had. But then Alan, with less than five guineas, had to get as far as France; I, with my less than two, not beyond Queensferry; so that, taking things in their proportion, Alan's society was not only a peril to my life, but a burden on my purse.

But there was no thought of the sort in the honest head of my companion. He believed he was serving, helping, and protecting me. And what could I do but hold my peace, and chafe, and take my chance of it?

'It's little enough,' said Alan, putting the purse in his pocket, 'but it'll do my business. And now, John Breck, if ye will hand me over my button, this gentleman and me will be for taking the road.'

But the bouman, after feeling about in a hairy purse that hung in front of him in the Highland manner (though he wore otherwise the Lowland habit, with sea-trousers), began to roll his eyes strangely, and at last said, 'Her nainsel will loss it,' meaning he thought he had lost it.

'What!' cried Alan, 'you will lose my button, that was my father's before me? Now I will tell you what is in my mind, John Breck: it is in my mind this is the worst day's work that ever ye did since ye were born.'

And as Alan spoke, he set his hands on his knees and looked at the bouman with a smiling mouth, and that dancing light in his eyes that meant mischief to his enemies.

Perhaps the bouman was honest enough; perhaps he had meant to cheat and then, finding himself alone with two of us in a desert place, cast back to honesty as being safer; at least, and all at once, he seemed to find that button and handed it to Alan.

'Well, and it is a good thing for the honour of the Maccolls,' said Alan, and then to me, 'Here is my button back again, and I thank you for parting with it, which is of a piece with all your friendships to me.' Then he took the warmest parting of the bouman. 'For,' says he, 'ye have done very well by me, and set your neck at a venture, and I will always give you the name of a good man.'

Lastly, the bouman took himself off by one way; and Alan and I (getting our chattels together) struck into another to resume our flight.

---

1 A bouman is a tenant who takes stock from the landlord and shares with him the increase.

More than eleven hours of incessant, hard travelling brought us early in the morning to the end of a range of mountains. In front of us there lay a piece of low, broken, desert land, which we must now cross. The sun was not long up, and shone straight in our eyes; a little, thin mist went up from the face of the moorland like a smoke; so that (as Alan said) there might have been twenty squadron of dragoons there and we none the wiser.

We sat down, therefore, in a howe of the hillside till the mist should have risen, and made ourselves a dish of drammach, and held a council of war.

'David,' said Alan, 'this is the kittle bit. Shall we lie here till it comes night, or shall we risk it and stave on ahead?'

'Well,' said I, 'I am tired indeed, but I could walk as far again, if that was all.'

'Ay, but it isnae,' said Alan, 'nor yet the half. This is how we stand: Appin's fair death to us. To the south it's all Campbells, and no to be thought of. To the north; well, there's no muckle to be gained by going north; neither for you, that wants to get to Queensferry, nor yet for me, that wants to get to France. Well, then, we'll can strike east.'

'East be it!' says I quite cheerily; but I was thinking in to myself: 'Oh, man, if you would only take one point of the compass, and let me take any other, it would be the best for both of us.'

'Well, then, east, ye see, we have the muirs,' said Alan. 'Once there, David, it's mere pitch-and-toss. Out on yon bald, naked, flat place, where can a body turn to? Let the redcoats come over a hill, they can spy you miles away; and the sorrow's in their horses' heels, they would soon ride you down. It's no good place, David; and I'm free to say, it's worse by daylight than by dark.'

'Alan,' said I, 'hear my way of it. Appin's death for us; we have none too much money, nor yet meal; the longer they seek, the nearer they may guess where we are; it's all a risk; and I give my word to go ahead until we drop.'

Alan was delighted. 'There are whiles,' said he, 'when ye are altogether too canny and Whiggish to be company for a gentleman like me; but there come other whiles when ye show yoursel' a mettle spark; and it's then, David, that I love ye like a brother.'

The mist rose and died away, and showed us that country lying as waste as the sea; only the moorfowl and the peewees crying upon it, and far over to the east a herd of deer, moving like dots. Much of it was red with heather; much of the rest broken up with bogs and hags and peaty pools; some had been burnt in a heath fire; and in another place there was quite a forest of dead firs, standing like skeletons. A wearier-looking desert man never saw; but at least it was clear of troops, which was our point.

We went down accordingly into the waste, and began to make our toilsome and devious travel towards the eastern verge. There were the tops of mountains all round (you are to remember) from whence we might be spied at any moment; so it behoved us to keep in the hollow parts of the moor, and when these turned aside from our direction to move upon its naked face with infinite care. Sometimes, for half an hour together, we must crawl from one heather bush to another, as hunters do when they are hard upon the deer. It was clear day again, with a blazing sun; the water in the brandy bottle was soon gone; and altogether, if I had guessed what it would be to crawl half the time upon my belly and to walk much of the rest stooping nearly to the knees, I should certainly have held back from such a killing enterprise.

Toiling and resting and toiling again, we wore away the morning; and about noon lay down in a thick bush of heather to sleep. Alan took the first watch; and it seemed to me I scarce closed my eyes before I was shaken up to take the second. We had no clock to go by; and Alan stuck a sprig of heath in the ground to serve instead; so that as soon as the shadow of the bush should fall so far to the east, I might know to rouse him. But I was by this time so weary that I could have slept twelve hours at a stretch; I had the taste of sleep in my throat; my joints slept even when my mind was waking; the hot smell of the heather, and the drone of the wild bees, were like possets to me; and every now and again I would give a jump and find I had been dozing.

The last time I woke I seemed to come back from farther away, and thought the sun had taken a great start in the heavens. I looked at

'My head was nearly turned with fear and shame'

the sprig of heath, and at that I could have cried aloud: for I saw I had betrayed my trust. My head was nearly turned with fear and shame; and at what I saw, when I looked out around me on the moor, my heart was like dying in my body. For sure enough, a body of horse-soldiers had come down during my sleep, and were drawing near to us from the south-east, spread out in the shape of a fan and riding their horses to and fro in the deep parts of the heather.

When I waked Alan, he glanced first at the soldiers, then at the mark and the position of the sun, and knitted his brows with a sudden, quick look, both ugly and anxious, which was all the reproach I had of him.

'What are we to do now?' I asked.

'We'll have to play at being hares,' said he. 'Do ye see yon mountain?' pointing to one on the north-eastern sky.

'Ay,' said I.

'Well, then,' says he, 'let us strike for that. Its name is Ben Alder; it is a wild, desert mountain full of hills and hollows, and if we can win to it before the morn, we may do yet.'

'But, Alan,' cried I, 'that will take us across the very coming of the soldiers!'

'I ken that fine,' said he; 'but if we are driven back on Appin, we are two dead men. So now, David man, be brisk!'

With that he began to run forward on his hands and knees with an incredible quickness, as though it were his natural way of going. All the time, too, he kept winding in and out in the lower parts of the moorland where we were the best concealed. Some of these had been burned or at least scathed with fire; and there rose in our faces (which were close to the ground) a blinding, choking dust as fine as smoke. The water was long out; and this posture of running on the hands and knees brings an overmastering weakness and weariness, so that the joints ache and the wrists faint under your weight.

Now and then, indeed, where was a big bush of heather we lay awhile, and panted, and putting aside the leaves, looked back at the dragoons. They had not spied us, for they held straight on; a half-troop, I think, covering about two miles of ground, and beating it mighty thoroughly as they went. I had awakened just in time; a little later, and we must have fled in front of them, instead of escaping on one side. Even as it was, the least misfortune might betray us; and now and again, when a grouse rose out of the heather with a clap of wings, we lay as still as the dead and were afraid to breathe.

The aching and faintness of my body, the labouring of my heart, the soreness of my hands, and the smarting of my throat and eyes in the continual smoke of dust and ashes, had soon grown to be so unbearable that I would gladly have given up. Nothing but the fear of Alan lent me enough of a false kind of courage to continue. As for himself (and you are to bear in mind that he was cumbered with a greatcoat), he had first turned crimson, but as time went on the redness began to be mingled with patches of white; his breath cried and whistled as it came; and his voice, when he whispered his observations in my ear during our halts, sounded like nothing human. Yet he seemed in no way dashed in spirits, nor did he at all abate in his activity; so that I was driven to marvel at the man's endurance.

At length, in the first gloaming of the night, we heard a trumpet sound, and looking back from among the heather, saw the troop beginning to collect. A little after, they had built a fire and camped for the night, about the middle of the waste.

At this I begged and besought that we lie down and sleep.

'There shall be no sleep the night!' said Alan. 'From now on, these weary dragoons of yours will keep the crown of the muirland, and none will get out of Appin but winged fowls. We got through in the nick of time, and shall we jeopard what we've gained? Na, na, when the day comes, it shall find you and me in a fast place on Ben Alder.'

'Alan,' I said, 'it's not the want of will: it's the strength that I want. If I could, I would: but as sure as I'm alive I cannot.

'Very well, then,' said Alan. 'I'll carry ye.'

I looked to see if he were jesting; but no, the little man was in dead earnest; and the sight of so much resolution shamed me.

'Lead away!' said I. 'I'll follow.'

He gave me one look as much as to say, 'Well done, David!' and off he set again at top speed.

It grew cooler and even a little darker (but not much) with the coming of night. The sky was cloudless; it was still early in July, and pretty far north; in the darkest part of that night you would have needed pretty good eyes to read, but for all that, I have often seen it darker in a winter midday. Heavy dew fell and drenched the moor like rain; and this refreshed me for a while. When we stopped to breathe, and I had time to see all about me, the clearness and sweetness of the night, the shapes of the hills like things asleep, and the fire dwindling away behind us like a bright spot in the midst of the moor, anger would come upon me in a clap that I must still drag myself in agony and eat the dust like a worm.

By what I read in books, I think few that have held a pen were ever really wearied, or they would write of it more strongly. I had no care of my life, neither past nor future, and I scarce remembered there was such a lad as David Balfour; I did not think of myself, but just of each fresh step which I was sure would be my last, with despair — and of Alan, who was the cause of it, with hatred. Alan was in the right trade as a soldier; this is the officer's part to make men continue to do things, they know not wherefore, and when, if the choice was offered, they would lie down where they were and be killed. And I dare say I would have made a good enough private; for in these last hours it never occurred to me that I had any choice but just to obey as long as I was able, and die obeying.

Day began to come in, after years, I thought; and by that time we were past the greatest danger, and could walk upon our feet like men, instead of crawling like brutes. But, dear heart have mercy! what a pair we must have made, going double like old grandfathers, stumbling like babes, and as white as dead folk. Never a word passed between us; each set his mouth and kept his eyes in front of him, and lifted up his foot and set it down again, like people lifting weights at a country play;[1] all the while with the moorfowl crying 'peep!' in the heather, and the light coming slowly clearer in the east.

I say Alan did as I did. Not that ever I looked at him, for I had enough ado to keep my feet; but because it is plain he must have been stupid with weariness as myself, and looked as little where we were going, or we should not have walked into an ambush like blind men.

It fell in this way. We were going down a heathery brae, Alan leading and I following a pace or two behind, like a fiddler and his wife; when upon a sudden the heather gave a rustle, three or four ragged men leaped out, and the next moment we were lying on our backs, each with a dirk at his throat.

I don't think I cared; the pain of this rough handling was quite swallowed up by the pains of which I was already full; and I was too glad to have stopped walking to mind about a dirk. I lay looking up in the face of the man that held me; and I mind his face was black with the sun and his eyes very light, but I was not afraid of him. I heard Alan and another whispering in the Gaelic; and what they said was all one to me.

Then the dirks were put up, our weapons were taken away, and we were set face to face, sitting in the heather.

'They are Cluny's men,' said Alan. 'We couldnae have fallen better. We're just to bide here with these, which are his out-sentries, till they can get word to the chief of my arrival.'

Now Cluny Macpherson, the chief of the clan Vourich, had been one of the leaders of the great rebellion six years before; there was a price on his life; and I had supposed him long ago in France, with the rest of the heads of that desperate party. Even tired as I was, the surprise of what I heard half wakened me.

'What,' I cried, 'is Cluny still here?'

'Ay, is he so!' said Alan. 'Still in his own country and kept by his own clan. King George can do no more.'

I think I would have asked further, but Alan gave me the put-off. 'I am rather wearied,' he said, 'and I would like fine to get a sleep.' And without more words, he rolled on his face in a deep heather bush, and seemed to sleep at once.

There was no such thing possible for me. You have heard grasshoppers whirring in the grass in the summer-time? Well, I had no sooner closed my eyes, than my body, and above all my head, belly, and wrists, seemed to be filled with whirring grasshoppers; and I must open my eyes again at once, and tumble and toss, and sit up and lie down; and look at the sky which dazzled me, or at Cluny's wild and dirty sentries, peering out over the top of the brae and chattering to each other in the Gaelic.

That was all the rest I had, until the messenger returned; when, as it appeared that Cluny would be glad to receive us, we must get once more upon our feet and set forward. Alan was in excellent good spirits, much refreshed by his sleep, very hungry, and looking pleasantly forward to a dram and a dish of hot collops, of which, it seems, the messenger had brought him word. For my part, it made me sick to hear of eating. I had been dead-heavy before, and now I felt a kind of dreadful lightness, which would not suffer me to walk. I drifted like a gossamer; the ground seemed to me a cloud, the hills a feather-weight, the air to have a current, like a running burn, which carried me to and fro. With all that, a sort of horror of despair sat on my mind, so that I could have wept at my own helplessness.

I saw Alan knitting his brows at me, and supposed it was in anger; and that gave me a pang of light-headed fear, like what a child may have. I remember, too, that I was smiling, and could not stop smiling, hard as I tried; for I thought it was out of place at such a time. But my good companion had nothing in his mind but kindness; and the next moment two of the gillies had me by the arms, and I began to be carried forward with great swiftness (or so it appeared to me, although I dare say it was slowly enough in truth) through a labyrinth of dreary glens and hollows and into the heart of that dismal mountain of Ben Alder.

1 Village fair.

23 Cluny's Cage

We came at last to the foot of an exceedingly steep wood, which scrambled up a craggy hillside, and was crowned by a naked precipice.

'It's here,' said one of the guides, and we struck uphill.

The trees clung upon the slope, like sailors on the shrouds of a ship; and their trunks were like the rounds of a ladder, by which we mounted.

Quite at the top, and just before the rocky face of the cliff sprang above the foliage, we found that strange house which was known in the country as 'Cluny's Cage.' The trunks of several trees had been wattled across, the intervals strengthened with stakes, and the ground behind this barricade levelled up with earth to make the floor. A tree, which grew out from the hillside, was the living centre-beam of the roof. The walls were of wattle and covered with moss. The whole house had something of an egg-shape; and it half hung, half stood in that steep, hillside thicket, like a wasps' nest in a green hawthorn.

Within, it was large enough to shelter five or six persons with some comfort. A projection of the cliff had been cunningly employed to be the fire-place; and the smoke rising against the face of the rock, and being not dissimilar in colour, readily escaped notice from below.

This was but one of Cluny's hiding-places; he had caves, besides, and underground chambers in several parts of his country; and following the reports of his scouts, he moved from one to another as the soldiers drew near or moved away. By this manner of living, and thanks to the affection of his clan, he had not only stayed all this time in safety, while so many others had fled or been taken and slain; but stayed four or five years longer, and only went to France at last by the express command of his master. There he soon died; and it is strange to reflect that he may have regretted his Cage upon Ben Alder.

When we came to the door he was seated by his rock chimney, watching a gillie about some cookery. He was mighty plainly habited, with a knitted nightcap drawn over his ears, and smoked a foul cutty pipe. For all that he had the manners of a king, and it was quite a sight to see him rise out of his place to welcome us.

'Well, Mr. Stewart, come awa', sir!' said he, 'and bring in your friend that as yet I dinna ken the name of.'

'And how is yourself, Cluny?' said Alan. 'I hope ye do brawly, sir. And I am proud to see ye, and to present to ye my friend the Laird of Shaws, Mr. David Balfour.'

Alan never referred to my estate without a touch of a sneer, when we were alone; but with strangers, he rang the words out like a herald.

'Step in by, the both of ye, gentlemen,' says Cluny. 'I make ye welcome to my house, which is a queer, rude place for certain, but one where I have entertained a royal personage, Mr. Stewart – ye doubtless ken the personage I have in my eye. We'll take a dram for luck, and as soon as this handless man of mine has the collops ready, we'll dine and take a hand at the cartes as gentlemen should. My life is a bit driegh,' says he, pouring out the brandy; 'I see little company, and sit and twirl my thumbs, and mind upon a great day that is gone by, and weary for another great day that we all hope will be upon the road. And so here's a toast to ye: The Restoration!'

Thereupon we all touched glasses and drank. I am sure I wished no ill to King George; and if he had been there himself in proper person, it's like he would have done as I did. No sooner had I taken out the dram than I felt hugely better, and could look and listen, still a little mistily perhaps, but no longer with the same groundless horror and distress of mind.

It was certainly a strange place, and we had a strange host. In his long hiding, Cluny had grown to have all manner of precise habits, like those of an old maid. He had a particular place, where no one else must sit; the Cage was arranged in a particular way, which none must disturb; cookery was one of his chief fancies, and even while he was greeting us in, he kept an eye to the collops.

It appears, he sometimes visited or received visits from his wife and one or two of his nearest friends, under the cover of night; but for the more part lived quite alone, and communicated only with his sentinels and the gillies that waited on him in the Cage. The first thing in the morning, one of them, who was a barber, came and shaved him, and gave him the news of the country, of which he was immoderately greedy. There was no end to his questions; he put them as earnestly as a child; and at some of the answers laughed out of all bounds of reason, and would break out again laughing at the mere memory, hours after the barber was gone.

To be sure, there might have been a purpose in his questions; for though he was thus sequestered, and like the other landed gentlemen of Scotland, stripped by the late Act of Parliament of legal powers, he still exercised a patriarchal justice in his clan. Disputes were brought to him in his hiding-hole to be decided; and the men of his country, who would have snapped their fingers at the Court of Session, laid aside revenge and paid down money at the bare word of this forfeited and hunted outlaw. When he was angered, which was often enough, he gave his commands and breathed threats of punishment like any king; and his gillies trembled and crouched away from him like children before a hasty father. With each of them, as he entered, he ceremoniously shook hands, both parties touching their bonnets at the same time in a military manner. Altogether, I had a fair chance to see some of the inner workings of a Highland clan; and this with a proscribed, fugitive chief; his country conquered; the troops riding upon all sides in quest of him, sometimes within a mile of where he lay; and when the least of the ragged fellows whom he rated and threatened could have made a fortune by betraying him.

On that first day, as soon as the collops were ready Cluny gave them with his own hand a squeeze of a lemon (for he was well supplied with luxuries) and bade us draw in to our meal.

'They,' said he, meaning the collops, 'are such as I gave His Royal Highness in this very house; bating the lemon juice, for at that time we were glad to get the meat and never fashed for kitchen.[1] Indeed, there were mair dragoons than lemons in my country in the year forty-six.'

I do not know if the collops were truly very good, but my heart rose against the sight of them, and I could eat but little. All the while Cluny entertained us with stories of Prince Charlie's stay in the Cage, giving us the very words of the speakers, and rising from his place to show us where they stood. By these, I gathered the Prince was a gracious, spirited boy, like the son of a race of polite kings, but not so wise as Solomon. I gathered, too, that while he was in the Cage he was often drunk; so the fault that has since, by all accounts, made such a wreck of him, had even then begun to show itself.

We were no sooner done eating than Cluny brought out an old, thumbed, greasy pack of cards, such as you may find in a mean inn;

and his eyes brightened in his face as he proposed that we should fall to playing.

Now this was one of the things I had been brought up to eschew like disgrace; it being held by my father neither the part of a Christian nor yet of a gentleman to set his own livelihood and fish for that of others on the cast of painted pasteboard. To be sure, I might have pleaded my fatigue, which was excuse enough; but I thought it behoved that I should bear testimony. I must have got very red in the face, but I spoke steadily, and told them I had no call to be a judge of others, but for my own part, it was a matter in which I had no clearness.

Cluny stopped mingling the cards. 'What in deil's name is this?' says he. 'What kind of Whiggish, canting talk is this, for the house of Cluny Macpherson?'

'I will put my hand in the fire for Mr. Balfour,' says Alan. 'He is an honest and a mettle gentleman, and I would have ye bear in mind who says it. I bear a king's name,' says he, cocking his hat; 'and I and any that I call friend are company for the best. But the gentleman is tired, and should sleep; if he has no mind to the cartes, it will never hinder you and me. And I'm fit and willing, sir, to play ye any game that ye can name.'

'Sir,' says Cluny,'in this poor house of mine I would have you to ken that any gentleman may follow his pleasure. If your friend would like to stand on his head, he is welcome. And if either he, or you, or any other man, is not preceesely satisfied, I will be proud to step outside with him.'

I had no will that these two friends should cut their throats for my sake.

'Sir,' said I, 'I am very wearied, as Alan says; and what's more, as you are a man that likely has sons of your own, I may tell you it was a promise to my father.'

'Say nay mair, say nae muir,' said Cluny, and pointed me to a bed of heather in a corner of the Cage. For all that he was displeased enough, looked at me askance, and grumbled when he looked. And indeed it must be owned that both my scruples and the words in which I declared them, smacked somewhat of the Covenanter, and were little in their place among wild Highland Jacobites.

What with the brandy and the venison, a strange heaviness had come over me; and I had scarce lain down upon the bed before I fell into a kind of trance, in which I continued almost the whole of the time of our stay in the Cage. Sometimes I was broad awake and understood what passed; sometimes I only heard voices, or men snoring, like the voice of a silly river; and the plaids upon the wall dwindled down and swelled out again, like firelight shadows on the roof. I must sometimes have spoken or cried out, for I remember I was now and then amazed at being answered; yet I was conscious of no particular nightmare, only of a general black, abiding horror – a horror of the place I was in, and the bed I lay in, and the plaids on the wall, and the voices, and the fire, and myself.

The barber-gillie, who was a doctor too, was ...lled into prescribe for me; but as he spoke in the Gaelic, I understood not a word of his opinion, and was too sick even to ask for a translation. I knew well enough I was ill, and that was all I cared about.

I paid little heed while I lay in this poor pass. But Alan and Cluny were most of the time at the cards, and I am clear that Alan must have begun by winning; for I remember sitting up, and seeing them hard at it, and a great glittering pile of as much as sixty or a hundred guineas on the table. It looked strange enough to see all this wealth in a nest upon a cliffside, wattled about growing trees. And even then, I thought it seemed deep water for Alan to be riding, who had no better battle-horse than a green purse and a matter of five pounds.

The luck, it seems, changed on the second day. About noon I was wakened as usual for dinner, and as usual refused to eat, and was given a dram with some bitter infusion which the barber had prescribed. The sun was shining in at the open door of the Cage, and this dazzled and offended me. Cluny sat at the table, biting the pack of cards. Alan had stooped over the bed, and had his face close to my eyes; to which, troubled as they were with the fever, it seemed of the most shocking bigness.

He asked me for a loan of my money.

'What for?' said I.

'Oh, just for a loan,' said he.

'But why?' I repeated. 'I don't see.'

'Hut, David!' said Alan, 'ye wouldnae grudge me

I would though, if I had had my senses. But all

was to get his face away, and I handed him m

On the morning of the third day, whe

hours in the Cage, I awoke with a gre

weary indeed, but seeing things of the right size and with their honest everyday appearance. I had a mind to eat, moreover, rose from bed of my own movement, and as soon as we had breakfasted, stepped to the entry of the Cage and sat down outside in the top of the wood. It was a grey day with a cool, mild air: and I sat in a dream all morning, only disturbed by the passing by of Cluny's scouts and servants coming with provisions and reports; for as the coast was at that time clear, you might almost say he held court openly.

When I returned, he and Alan had laid the cards aside, and were questioning a gillie; and the chief turned about and spoke to me in the Gaelic.

'I have no Gaelic, sir,' said I.

Now since the card question, everything I said or did had the power of annoying Cluny. 'Your name has more sense than yourself, then,' said he angrily, 'for it's good Gaelic. But the point is this. My scout reports all clear in the south, and the question is, have ye the strength to go?'

I saw cards on the table, but no gold; only a heap of little written papers, and these all on Cluny's side. Alan, besides, had an odd look, like a man not very well content; and I began to have a strong misgiving.

'I do not know if I am well as I should be,' said I, looking at Alan; 'but the little money we have has a long way to carry us.'

Alan took his under-lip into his mouth, and looked upon the ground.

'David,' says he at last, 'I've lost it; there's the naked truth.'

'My money too?' said I.

'Your money too,' says Alan, with a groan. 'Ye shouldnae have given it me. I'm daft when I get to the cartes.'

'Hoot-toot! hoot-toot!' said Cluny. 'It was all daffing; it's all nonsense. Of course you'll have your money back again, and the double of it, if ye'll make so free with me. It would be a singular thing for me to keep it. It's not to be supposed that I would be any hindrance to gentlemen in your situation; that would be a singular thing!' cries he, and began to pull gold out of his pocket with a mighty red face.

Alan said nothing, only looked on the ground.

'Will you step to the door with me, sir?' said I.

Cluny said he would be very glad, and followed me readily enough, but he looked flustered and put out.

'And now, sir,' says I, 'I must first acknowledge your generosity.'

'Nonsensical nonsense!' cries Cluny. 'Where's the generosity? This is just a most unfortunate affair; but what would ye have me do – boxed up in this beeskep of a cage of mine – but just set my friends to the cartes, when I can get them? And if they lose, of course, it's not to be supposed——' And here he came to a pause.

'Yes,' said I, 'if they lose, you give them back their money; and if they win, they carry away yours in their pouches! I have said before that I grant your generosity; but to me, sir, it's a very painful thing to be placed in this position.'

There was a little silence, in which Cluny seemed always as if he was about to speak, but said nothing. All the time he grew redder and redder in the face.

'I am a young man,' said I, 'and I ask your advice. Advise me as you would your son. My friend fairly lost this money, after having fairly gained a far greater sum of yours; can I accept it back again? Would that be the right part for me to play? Whatever I do, you can see for yourself it must be hard upon a man of any pride.'

'It's rather hard on me, too, Mr. Balfour,' said Cluny, 'and ye give me very much the look of a man that has entrapped poor people to their hurt. I wouldnae have my friends come to any house of mine to accepts affronts; no ,' he cried, with a sudden heat of anger, 'nor yet to give them!'

'And so you see, sir,' said I, 'there is something to be said upon my side; and this gambling is a very poor employ for gentlefolks. But I am still waiting your opinion.'

I am sure if ever Cluny hated any man it was David Balfour. He looked me all over with a warlike eye, and I saw the challenge at his lips. But either my youth disarmed him, or perhaps his own sense of justice. Certainly it was a mortifying matter for all concerned, and not least for Cluny; the more credit that he took it as he did.

'Mr. Balfour,' said he, 'I think you are too nice and covenanting, but for all that you have the spirit of a very pretty gentleman. Upon my honest word, ye may take this money – it's what I would tell my son – and here's my hand along with it!'

1 Condiment.

24   The Flight in the Heather: The Quarrel

Alan and I were put across Loch Errocht under cloud of night, and went down its eastern shore to another hiding-place near the head of Loch Rannoch, whither we were led by one of the gillies from the Cage. This fellow carried all our luggage and Alan's greatcoat in the bargain, trotting along under the burthen, far less than the half of which used to weigh me to the ground, like a stout hill pony with a feather; yet he was a man that, in plain contest, I could have broken on my knee.

Doubtless it was a great relief to walk disencumbered; and perhaps without that relief, and the consequent sense of liberty and lightness, I could not have walked at all. I was but new risen from a bed of sickness; and there was nothing in the state of our affairs to hearten me for much exertion; travelling, as we did, over the most dismal deserts in Scotland, under a cloudy heaven, and with divided hearts among the travellers.

For long we said nothing; marching alongside or one behind the other, each with a set countenance; I, angry and proud, and drawing what strength I had from these two violent and sinful feelings: Alan, angry and ashamed, ashamed that he had lost my money, angry that I. should take it so ill.

The thought of a separation ran always the stronger in my mind; and the more I approved of it, the more ashamed I grew of my approval. It would be a fine, handsome, generous thing, indeed, for Alan to turn round and say to me: 'Go, I am in the most danger, and my company only increases yours.' But for me to turn to the friend who certainly loved me, and say to him: 'You are in great danger, I am in but little; your friendship is a burden; go, take your risks and bear your hardships alone' – no, that was impossible; and even to think of it privily to myself made my cheeks to burn.

And yet Alan had behaved like a child, and (what is worse) a treacherous child. Wheedling my money from me while I lay half conscious was scarce better than theft; and yet here he was trudging by my side, without a penny to his name, and by what I could see, quite blithe to sponge upon the money he had driven me to beg. True, I was ready to share it with him; but it made me rage to see him count upon my readiness.

These were the two things uppermost in my mind; and I could open my mouth upon neither without black ungenerosity. So I did the next worst, and said nothing, nor so much as looked once at my companion, save with the tail of my eye.

At last, upon the other side of Loch Ericht, going over a smooth, rushy place, where the walking was easy, he could bear it no longer, and came close to me.

'David,' says he, 'this is no way for two friends to take a small accident. I have to say that I'm sorry; and so that's said. And now if you have anything, ye'd better say it.'

'Oh,' says I, 'I have nothing.'

He seemed disconcerted; at which I was meanly pleased.

'No,' said he, with rather a trembling voice, 'but when I say I was to blame?'

'Why, of course, ye were to blame,' said I coolly; 'and you will bear me out that I have never reproached you.'

'Never,' says he; 'but ye ken very well that ye've done worse. Are we to part? Ye said so once before. Are ye to say it again? There's hills and heather enough between here and the seas, David; and I will own I'm no very keen to stay where I'm no wanted.'

This pierced me like a sword, and seemed to lay bare my private disloyalty.

'Alan Breck!' I cried; and then: 'Do you think I am one to turn my back on you in your chief need? You dursn't say it to my face. My whole conduct's there to give the lie to it. It's true, I fell asleep upon the muir; but that was from weariness, and you do wrong to cast it up to me——'

'Which is what I never did,' said Alan.

'But aside from that,' I continued, 'what have I done that you should even me to dogs by such a supposition? I never yet failed a friend, and it's not likely I'll begin with you. There are things between us that I can never forget, even if you can.'

'I will only say this to ye, David,' said Alan very quietly, 'that I have long been owing ye my life, and now I owe ye money. Ye should try to make that burden light for me.'

This ought to have touched me, and in a manner it did, but the wrong manner. I felt I was behaving badly, and was now not only angry with Alan, but angry with myself in the bargain; and it made me the more cruel.

'You asked me to speak,' said I. 'Well, then, I will. You own yourself that you have done me a disservice; I have had to swallow an affront: I have never reproached you, I never named the thing till you did. And now you blame me,' cried I, 'because I cannae laugh and sing as if I was glad to be affronted. The next thing will be that I'm to go down upon my knees and thank you for it! Ye should think more of others, Alan Breck. If ye thought more of others, ye would perhaps speak less about yourself; and when a friend that likes you very well has passed over an offence without a word, you would be blithe to let it lie, instead of making it a stick to break his back with. By your own way of it, it was you that was to blame; then it shouldnae be you to seek the quarrel.'

'Aweel,' said Alan, 'say nae mair.'

And we fell back into our former silence, and came to our journey's end, and supped, and lay down to sleep, without another word.

The gillie put us across Loch Rannoch in the dusk of the next day, and gave us his opinion as to our best route. This was to get us up at once into the tops of the mountains; to round by a circuit, turning the heads of Glen Lyon, Glen Lochay, and Glen Dochart, and come down upon the Lowlands by Kippen and the upper waters of the Forth. Alan was little pleased with a route which led us through the country of his blood foes, the Glenorchy Campbells. He objected that by turning to the east we should come almost at once among the Athole Stewarts, a race of his own name and lineage although following a different chief, and come besides by a far easier and swifter way to the place whither we were bound. But the gillie, who was indeed the chief man of Cluny's scouts, had good reasons to give him on all hands, naming the force of troops in every district, and alleging finally (as well as I could understand) that we should nowhere be so little troubled as in a country of the Campbells.

Alan gave way at last, but with only half a heart. 'It's one of the dowiest countries in Scotland,' said he. 'There's naething there that I ken, but heath, and crows, and Campbells. But I see that ye're a man of some penetration; and be it as ye please!'

We set forth accordingly by this itinerary; and for the best part of three nights travelled on eerie mountains and among the well-heads of wild rivers; often buried in mist, almost continually blown and rained upon, and not once cheered by any glimpse of sunshine. By day, we lay and slept in the drenching heather; by night, incessantly clambered upon breakneck hills and among rude crags. We often wandered; we were often so involved in fog that we must lie quiet till it lightened. A fire was never to be thought of. Our food was only drammach and a portion of cold meat that we had carried from the Cage; and as for drink, Heaven knows we had no want of water.

This was a dreadful time, rendered the more dreadful by the gloom of the weather and the country. I was never warm; my teeth chattered in my head; I was troubled with a very sore throat, such as I had on the isle; I had a painful stitch in my side, which never left me; and when I slept in my wet bed, with rain beating above and the mud oozing below me, it was to live over again in fancy the worst part of my adventures – to see the tower of Shaws lit by lightning, Ransome carried below on the men's backs, Shuan dying on the round-house floor, or Colin Campbell grasping at the bosom of his coat. From such broken slumbers I would be aroused in the gloaming, to sit up in the same puddle where I had slept, and sup cold drammach; the rain driving sharp in my face or running down my back in icy trickles; the mist enfolding us like as in a gloomy chamber – or, perhaps, if the wind blew, falling suddenly apart and showing us the gulf of some dark valley where the streams were crying aloud.

The sound of an infinite number of rivers came up from all round. In this steady rain the springs of the mountain were broken up; every glen gushed water like a cistern; every stream was in high spate, and had filled and over-flowed its channel. During our night tramps, it was solemn to hear the voice of them below in the valleys, now booming like thunder, now with an angry cry. I would well understand the story of the Water Kelpie, that demon of the streams, who is fabled to keep wailing and roaring at the ford until the coming of the doomed traveller. Alan I saw believed it, or half believed it; and when the cry of the river rose more than usually sharp, I was little surprised (though, of course, I would still be shocked) to see him cross himself in the manner of the Catholics.

During all these horrid wanderings we had no familiarity, scarcely even that of speech. The truth is that I was sickening for my grave, which is my best excuse. But besides that I was of an unforgiving disposition from my birth, slow to take offence, slower to forget it, and now incensed both against my companion and myself. For the best part of two days he was unweariedly kind; silent, indeed, but always ready to help, and always hoping (as I could very well see) that my displeasure would blow by. For the same length of time I stayed in myself, nursing my anger, roughly refusing his services, and passing him over with my eyes as if he had been a bush or a stone.

The second night, or rather the peep of the third day, found us upon a very open hill, so that we could not follow our usual plan and lie down immediately to eat and sleep. Before we had reached a place of shelter, the grey had come pretty clear, for though it still rained, the clouds ran higher; and Alan, looking in my face, showed some marks of concern.

'Ye had better let me take your pack,' said he, for perhaps the ninth time since we had parted from the scout beside Loch Rannoch.

'I do very well, I thank you,' said I, as cold as ice.

Alan flushed darkly. 'I'll not offer it again,' he said. 'I'm not a patient man, David.'

'I never said you were,' said I, which was exactly the rude silly speech of a boy of ten.

Alan made no answer at the time, but his conduct answered for him. Henceforth, it is to be thought, he quite forgave himself for the affair at Cluny's; cocked his hat again, walked jauntily, whistled airs, and looked at me upon one side with a provoking smile.

The third night we were to pass through the western end of the country of Balquhidder. It came clear and cold, with a touch in the air like frost, and a northerly wind that blew the clouds away and made the stars bright. The streams were full, of course, and still made a great noise among the hills; but I observed that Alan thought no more upon the Kelpie, and was in high good spirits. As for me, the change of weather came too late; I had lain in the mire so long that (as the Bible has it) my very clothes 'abhorred me'; I was dead weary, deadly sick and full of pains and shiverings; the chill of the wind went through me, and the sound of it confused my ears. In this poor state I had to bear from my companion something in the nature of a persecution. He spoke a good deal, and never without a taunt. 'Whig' was the best name he had to give me. 'Here,' he would say, 'here's a dub for ye to jump, my Whiggie! I ken you're a fine jumper!' And so on; all the time with a gibing voice and face.

I knew it was my own doing, and no one else's; but I was too miserable to repent. I felt I could drag myself but little farther; pretty soon, I must lie down and die on these wet mountains like a sheep or a fox, and my bones must whiten there like the bones of a beast. My head was light, perhaps; but I began to love the prospect, I began to glory in the thought of such a death, alone in the desert, with the wild eagles besieging my last moments. Alan would repent then, I thought; he would remember, when I was dead, how much he owed me, and the remembrance would be torture. So I went like a sick, silly, and bad-hearted schoolboy, feeding my anger against a fellow man, when I would have been better on my knees, crying on God for mercy. And at each of Alan's taunts I hugged myself. 'Ah!' thinks I to myself, 'I have a better taunt in readiness; when I lie down and die, you will feel it like a buffet in your face; ah, what a revenge! ah, how you will regret your ingratitude and cruelty!'

All the while I was growing worse and worse. Once I had fallen, my legs simply doubling under me, and this had struck Alan for the moment; but I was afoot so briskly, and set off again with such a natural manner, that he soon forgot the incident. Flushes of heat went over me, and then spasms of shuddering. The stitch in my side was hardly bearable. At last I began to feel that I could trail myself no farther: and with that, there came to me all at once the wish to have it out with Alan, let my anger blaze, and be done with my life in a more sudden manner. He had just called me 'Whig.' I stopped.

'Mr. Stewart,' said I, in a voice that quivered like a fiddle-string, 'you are older than I am, and should know your manners. Do you think it either very wise or very witty to cast my politics in my teeth? I thought, where folk differed, it was the part of gentlemen to differ civilly; and if I did not, I may tell you I could find a better taunt than some of yours.'

Alan had stopped opposite to me, his hat cocked, his hands in his breeches pockets, his head a little on one side. He listened, smiling evilly, as I could see by the starlight; and when I had done he began to whistle a Jacobite air. It was the air made in mockery of General Cope's defeat at Prestonpans:

Hey, Johnnie Cope, are ye waukin' yet?
And are your drums a-beatin, yet?

'"It's the bare truth," he said, and drew his sword'

And it came in my mind that Alan, on the day of that battle, had been engaged upon the royal side.

'Why do ye take that air, Mr. Stewart?' said I. 'Is that to remind me you have been beaten on both sides?'

The air stopped on Alan's lips. 'David!' said he.

'But it's time these manners ceased,' I continued; 'and I mean you shall henceforth speak civilly of my King and my good friends the Campbells.'

'I am a Stewart——' began Alan.

'Oh,' says I, 'I ken ye bear a king's name. But you are to remember, since I have been in the Highlands, I have seen a good many of those that bear it; and the best I can say of them is this, that they would be none the worse of washing.'

'Do you know that you insult me?' said Alan very low.

'I am sorry for that,' said I, 'for I am not done; and if you distaste the sermon I doubt the pirliecue[1] will please you as little. You have been chased in the field by the grown men of my party; it seems a poor kind of pleasure to outface a boy. Both the Campbells and the Whigs have beaten you; you have run before them like a hare. It behoves you to speak of them as your betters.'

Alan stood quite still, the tails of his greatcoat clapping behind him in the wind.

'This is a pity,' he said at last, 'There are things said that cannot be passed over.'

'I never asked you to,' said I. 'I am as ready as yourself.'

'Ready?' said he.

'Ready,' I repeated. 'I am no blower and boaster like some that I could name. Come on!' And drawing my sword, I fell on guard as Alan himself had taught me.

'David!' he cried. 'Are ye daft? I cannae draw upon ye, David. It's fair murder.'

'That was your look-out when you insulted me,' said I.

'It's the truth!' cried Alan, and he stood for a moment, wringing his mouth in his hand like a man in sore perplexity. 'It's the bare truth,' he said, and drew his sword. But before I could touch his blade with mine, he had thrown it from him and fallen to the ground. 'Na, na,' he kept saying, 'na, na – I cannae, I cannae.'

At this the last of my anger oozed all out of me; and I found myself only sick, and sorry, and blank, and wondering at myself. I would have given the world to take back what I had said; but a word once spoken, who can recapture it? I minded me of all Alan's kindness and courage in the past, how he had helped and cheered and borne with me in our evil days; and then recalled my own insults, and saw that I had lost for ever that doughty friend. At the same time, the sickness that hung upon me seemed to redouble and the pang in my side was like a sword for sharpness. I have thought I must have swooned where I stood.

This it was that gave me a thought. No apology could blot out what I had said; it was needless to think of one, none could cover the offence; but where an apology was vain, a mere cry for help might bring Alan back to my side. I put my pride away from me. 'Alan!' I said; 'if you cannae help me, I must just die here.'

He started up sitting, and looked at me.

'It's true,' said I. 'I'm by with it. Oh, let me get into the bield of a house – I'll can die there easier.' I had no need to pretend; whether I choose or not I spoke in a weeping voice that would have melted a heart of stone.

'Can ye walk?' asked Alan.

'No,' said I, 'not without help. This last hour my legs have been fainting under me; I've a stitch in my side like a red-hot iron; I cannae breathe right. If I die, ye'll can forgive me, Alan? In my heart, I liked ye fine – even when I was the angriest.'

Wheesht, wheesht!' cried Alan. 'Dinna say that! David man, ye ken——' He shut his mouth upon a sob. 'Let me get my arm about ye,' he continued; 'that's the way! Now lean upon me hard. Gude kens where there's a house! We're in Balwhidder, too; there should be no want of houses, no, nor friends' houses here. Do ye gang easier so, Davie?'

'Ay,' said I, 'I can be doing this way'; and I pressed his arm with my hand.

Again he came near sobbing. 'Davie,' said he, 'I'm no a right man at all; I have neither sense nor kindness; I couldnae remember ye were just a bairn, I couldnae see ye were dying on your feet; Davie, ye'll have to try and forgive me.'

'Oh, man, let's say no more about it!' said I. 'We're neither one of us to mend the other – that's the truth! We must just bear and forbear, man Alan. Oh, but my stitch is sore! Is there nae house?'

'I'll find a house to ye, David,' he said stoutly. 'We'll follow down the burn, where there's bound to be houses. My poor man, will ye no be better on my back?'

'Oh, Alan,' says I, 'and me a good twelve inches taller?'

'Ye're no such a thing,' cried Alan, with a start. 'There may be a trifling matter of an inch or two; I'm no saying I'm just exactly what ye would call a tall man, whatever; and I dare say,' he added, his voice tailing off in a laughable manner, 'now when I come to think of it, I dare say ye'll be just about right. Ay, it'll be a foot, or near hand; or may be even mair.'

It was sweet and laughable to hear Alan eat his words up in the fear of some fresh quarrel. I could have laughed, had not my stitch caught me so hard; but if I had laughed, I think I must have wept too.

'Alan!' cried I, 'what makes ye so good to me? What makes ye care for such a thankless fellow?'

'Deed, and I don't know,' said Alan. 'or just precisely what I thought I liked about ye, was that ye never quarrelled: and now I like ye better!'

1 A second sermon.

25 In Balquhidder

At the door of the first house we came to, Alan knocked, which was no very safe enterprise in such a part of the Highlands as the Braes of Balquhidder. No great clan held rule there; it was filled and disputed by small septs, and broken remnants, and what they call 'chiefless folk,' driven into the wild country about the springs of Forth and Teith by the advance of the Campbells. Here were Stewarts and Maclarens, which came to the same thing, for the Maclarens followed Alan's chief in war, and made but one clan with Appin. Here, too, were many of that old, proscribed, nameless, red-handed clan of the Macgregors. They had always been ill considered, and now worse than ever, having credit with no side or party in the whole country of Scotland. Their chief, Macgregor of Macgregor, was in exile; the more immediate leader of that part of them about Balquhidder, James More, Rob Roy's eldest son, lay waiting his trial in Edinburgh Castle; they were in ill blood with Highlander and Lowlander, with the Grahames, the Maclarens, and the Stewarts; and Alan, who took up the quarrel of any friend, however distant, was extremely wishful to avoid them.

Chance served us very well; for it was a household of Mclarens that we found, where Alan was not only welcome for his name's sake, but known by reputation. Here then I was got to bed without delay, and a doctor fetched, who found me in a sorry plight. But whether because he was a very good doctor, or I a very young, strong man, I lay bed-ridden for no more than a week, and before a month I was able to take the road again with a good heart.

All this time Alan would not leave me though I often pressed him, and indeed his foolhardiness in staying was a common subject of outcry with the two or three friends that were let into the secret. He hid by day in a hole of the braes under a little wood; and at night, when the coast was clear, would come into the house to visit me. I need not say if I was pleased to see him; Mrs. Maclaren, our hostess, thought nothing good enough for such a guest; and as Duncan Dhu (which was the name of our host) had a pair of pipes in his house, and was much a lover of music, the time of my recovery was quite a festival, and we commonly turned night into day.

The soldiers let us be; although once a party of two companies and some dragoons went by in the bottom of the valley, where I could see them through the window as I lay in bed. What was much more astonishing, no magistrate came near me, and there was no question put of whence I came or whither I was going; and in that time of excitement, I was as free of all inquiry as though I had lain in a desert. Yet my presence was known before I left to all the people in Balquhidder and the adjacent parts; many coming about the house on visits and these (after the custom of the country) spreading the news among their neighbours. The bills, too, had now been printed. There was one pinned near the foot of my bed, where I could read my own not very flattering portrait and, in larger characters, the amount of the blood money that had been set upon my life. Duncan Dhu and the rest that knew that I had come there in Alan's company, could have entertained no doubt of who I was; and many others must have had their guess. For though I had changed my clothes, I could not change my age or person, and Lowland boys of eighteen were not so rife in these parts of the world, and above all about that time, that they could fail to put one thing with another and connect me with the bill. So it was, at least. Other folk keep a secret among two or three near friends, and somehow it leaks out; but among these clansmen, it is told to a whole countryside, and they will keep it for a century.

There was but one thing happened worth narrating; and that is the visit I had of Robin Oig, one of the sons of the notorious Rob Roy. He was sought upon all sides on a charge of carrying a young woman from Balfron and marrying her (as was alleged) by force; yet he stepped about Balquhidder like a gentleman in his own walled policy. It was he who had shot James Maclaren at the plough stilts, a quarrel never satisfied; yet he walked into the house of his blood enemies as a rider[1] might into a public inn.

Duncan had time to pass me word of who it was; and we looked at one another in concern. You should understand, it was then close upon the time of Alan's coming; the two were little likely to agree; and yet if we sent word or sought to make a signal, it was sure to arouse suspicion in a man under so dark a cloud as the Macgregor.

He came in with a great show of civility, but like a man among inferiors; took off his bonnet to Mrs. Maclaren, but clapped it on his head again to speak to Duncan; and having thus set himself (as he would have thought) in a proper light, came to my bedside and bowed.

'I am given to know, sir,' says he, 'that your name is Balfour.'

'They call me David Balfour,' said I, 'at your service.'

'I would give ye my name in return, sir,' he replied, 'but it's one somewhat blown upon of late days; and it'll perhaps suffice if I tell ye that I am own brother to James More Drummond or Macgregor, of whom ye will scarce have failed to hear.'

'No, sir,' said I, a little alarmed; 'nor yet of your father, Macgregor-Campbell.' And I sat up and bowed in bed; for I thought best to compliment him, in case he was proud of having had an outlaw to his father.

He bowed in return. 'But what I am to say, sir,' he went on, 'is this. In the year '45, my brother raised a part of the "Gregara," and marched six companies to strike a stroke for the good side; and the surgeon that marched with our clan and cured my brothers leg when it was broken in the bush at Prestonpans, was a gentleman of the same name precisely as yourself. He was brother Balfour of Baith; and if you are in any reasonable degree of nearness one of that gentleman's kin, I have come to put myself and my people at your command.'

You are to remember that I knew no more of my descent than any cadger's dog; my uncle, to be sure, had prated of some of our high connections, but nothing to the present purpose; and there was nothing left me but that bitter disgrace of owning that I could not tell.

Robin told me shortly he was sorry he had put himself about, turned his back upon me without a sign of salutation; and as he went towards the door, I could hear him telling Duncan that I was 'only some kinless loon that didn't know his own father.' Angry as I was at these words, and ashamed of my own ignorance, I could scarce keep from smiling that a man who was under the lash of the law (and was indeed hanged some three years later) should be so nice as to the descent of his acquaintances.

Just in the door he met Alan coming in; and the two drew back and looked at each other like strange dogs. They were neither of them big men, but they seemed fairly to swell out with pride. Each wore a sword, and by a movement of his haunch, thrust clear the hilt of it, so that it might be the more readily grasped and the blade drawn.

'Mr. Stewart, I am thinking,' says Robin.

'Troth, Mr. Macgregor, it's not a name to be ashamed of,' answered Alan.

'I did not know ye were in my country, sir,' says Robin.

'It sticks in my mind that I am in the country of my friends the Maclarens,' says Alan.

'That's a kittle point,' returned the other. 'There may be two words to say to that. But I think I will have heard that you are a man of your sword?'

'Unless ye were born deaf, Mr. Macgregor, ye will have heard a good deal more than that,' says Alan. 'I am not the only man that can draw steel in Appin; and when my kinsman and captain, Ardshiel, had a talk with a gentleman of your name, not so many years back, I could never hear that the Macgregor had the best of it.'

'Do ye mean my father, sir?' says Robin.

'Well, I wouldnae wonder,' said Alan. 'The gentleman I have in my mind had the ill taste to clap Campbell to his name.'

'My father was an old man,' returned Robin. 'The match was unequal. You and me would make a better pair, sir.'

'I was thinking that,' said Alan.

I was half out of bed, and Duncan had been hanging at the elbow of these fighting cocks, ready to intervene upon the least occasion. But when that word was uttered, it was a case of now or never; and Duncan, with something of a white face to be sure, thrust himself between.

'Gentlemen,' said he, 'I will have been thinking of a very different matter whateffer. Here are my pipes, and here are you two gentlemen who are baith acclaimed pipers. It's an auld dispute which one of ye's the best. Here will be a braw chance to settle it.'

'Why, sir,' said Alan, still addressing Robin, from whom indeed he had not so much as shifted his eyes, nor yet Robin from him, 'why, sir,' says Alan, 'I think I will have heard some sough[2] of the sort. Have ye music, as folk say? Are ye a bit of a piper?'

'I can pipe like a Macrimmon!' cries Robin.

'And that is a very bold word,' quoth Alan.

'I have made bolder words good before now,' returned Robin, 'and that against better adversaries.'

'It's easy to try that,' says Alan.

Duncan Dhu made haste to bring out the pair of pipes that was his principal possession, and to set before his guests a mutton-ham and a bottle of that drink which they call Athole brose, and which is made of old whisky, strained honey, and sweet cream, slowly beaten together in the right order and proportion. The two enemies were still on the very breach of a quarrel; but down they sat, one upon each side of the peat fire, with a mighty show of politeness. Maclaren pressed them to taste his mutton-ham and 'the wife's brose,' reminding them the wife was out of Athole and had a name far and wide for her skill in that confection. But Robin put aside these hospitalities as bad for the breath.

'I would have ye to remark, sir,' said Alan, 'that I havenae broken bread for near ten hours, which will be worse for the breath than any brose in Scotland.'

'I will take no advantages, Mr. Stewart,' replied Robin. 'Eat and drink; I'll follow you.'

Each ate a small portion of the ham and drank a glass of the brose to Mrs. Maclaren; and then after a great number of civilities, Robin took the pipes and played a little spring in a very ranting manner.

'Ay, ye can blow,' said Alan; and taking the instrument from his rival, he first played the same spring in a manner identical with Robin's; and then wandered into variations, which, as he went on, he decorated with a perfect flight of grace-notes, such as pipers love, and call the 'warblers.'

I had been pleased with Robin's playing; Alan's ravished me.

'That's no very bad, Mr. Stewart,' said the rival, 'but ye show a poor device in your warblers.'

'Me!' cried Alan, the blood starting to his face. 'I give ye the lie.'

'Do ye own yourself beaten at the pipes, then,' said Robin, 'that ye seek to change them for the sword?'

'And that's very well said, Mr. Macgregor,' returned Alan; 'and in the meantime' (laying a strong accent on the word) 'I take back the lie. I appeal to Duncan.'

'Indeed, ye need appeal to naebody,' said Robin. 'Ye're a far better judge than any Maclaren in Balquhidder: for it's a God's truth that you're a very creditable piper for a Stewart. Hand me the pipes.'

Alan did as he asked; and Robin proceeded to imitate and correct some part of Alan's variations, which it seemed that he remembered perfectly.

'Ay, ye have music,' said Alan gloomily.

'And now be the judge yourself, Mr. Stewart,' said Robin; and taking up the variations from the beginning, he worked them throughout to so new a purpose, with such ingenuity and sentiment, and with so odd a fancy and so quick a knack in the grace-notes, that I was amazed to hear him.

As for Alan, his face grew dark and hot, and he sat and gnawed his fingers, like a man under some deep affront. 'Enough!' he cried. 'Ye can blow the pipes – make the most of that.' And he made as if to rise.

But Robin only held out his hand as if to ask for silence, and struck into the slow measure of a pibroch. It was a fine piece of music in itself and nobly played; but it seems, besides, it was a piece peculiar to the Appin Stewarts and chief favourite with Alan. The first notes were scarce out, before there came a change in his face; when the time quickened, he seemed to grow restless in his seat; and long before that piece was at an end, the last signs of his anger died from him, and he had no thought but for the music.

'Robin Oig,' he said, when he had done, 'ye are a great piper. I am not fit to blow in the same kingdom with ye. Body of me! ye have mair music in your sporran than I have in my head! And though it still sticks in my mind that I could maybe show ye another of it with the cold steel, I warn ye beforehand – it'll no be fair! It would go against my heart to haggle a man that can blow the pipes as you can!'

Thereupon that quarrel was made up; all night long the brose was going and the pipes changing hands; and the day had come pretty bright, and the three men were none the better for what they had been taking, before Robin as much as thought upon the road.

It was the last I saw of him, for I was in the Low Countries at the University of Leyden when he stood trial, and was hanged in the Grassmarket. And I have told this at so great length, partly because it was the last incident of any note that befell me on the wrong side of the Highland Line, and partly because (as the man came to be hanged) it's in a manner history.

1 Commercial traveller.
2 Rumour.

26 End of the Flight: We pass the Forth

The month, as I have said, was not yet out, but it was already far through August, and beautiful warm weather, with every sign of an early and great harvest, when I was pronounced able for my journey. Our money was now run to so low an ebb that we must think first of all on speed; for if we came not soon to Mr. Rankeillor's, or if when we came there he should fail to help me, we must surely starve. In Alan's view, besides, the hunt must have now greatly slackened; and the line of the Forth and even Stirling Bridge, which is the main pass over that river, would be watched with little interest.

'It's a chief principle in military affairs,' said he, 'to go where ye are least expected. Forth is our trouble; ye ken the saying, "Forth bridles the wild Hielandman." Well, if we seek to creep round about the head of that river and come down by Kippen or Balfron, it's just precisely there that they'll be looking to lay hands on us. But if we stave on straight to the auld Brig of Stirling, I'll lay my sword they let us pass unchallenged.'

The first night, accordingly, we pushed to the house of a Maclaren in Strathire, a friend of Duncan's, where we slept the twenty-first of the month, and whence we set forth again about the fall of night to make another easy stage. The twenty-second we lay in a heather bush on a hillside in Uam Var, within view of a herd of deer, the happiest ten hours of sleep in a fine, breathing sunshine and on bone-dry ground that I have ever tasted. That night we struck Allan Water, and followed it down; and coming to the edge of the hills saw the whole Carse of Stirling underfoot, as flat as a pancake, with the town and castle on a hill in the midst of it, and the moon shining on the Links of Forth.

'Now,' said Alan, 'I kenna if ye care, but ye're in your own land again. We passed the Hieland Line in the first hour; and now if we could but pass yon crooked water, we might cast our bonnets in the air.'

In Allan Water, near by where it falls into the Forth, we found a little sandy islet, overgrown with burdock, butterbur, and the like low plants, that would just cover us if we lay flat. Here it was we made our camp, within plain view of Stirling Castle, whence we could hear the drums beat as some part of the garrison paraded. Shearers worked all day in a field on one side of the river, and we could hear the stones going on the hooks and the voices and even the words of the men talking. It behoved to lie close and keep silent. But the sand of the little isle was sun-warm, the green plants gave us shelter for our heads, we had food and drink in plenty; and to crown all, we were within sight of safety.

As soon as the shearers quit their work and the dusk began to fall, we waded ashore and struck for the Bridge of Stirling, keeping to the fields and under the field fences.

The bridge is close under the castle hill, an old, high, narrow bridge with pinnacles along the parapet; and you may conceive with how much interest I looked upon it, not only as a place famous in history, but as the very doors of salvation to Alan and myself. The moon was not yet up when we came there; a few lights shone along the front of the fortress, and lower down a few lighted windows in the town; but it was all mighty still, and there seemed to be no guard upon the passage.

I was for pushing straight across; but Alan was more wary.

'It looks unco quiet,' said he; 'but for all that we'll lie down here cannily behind a dike, and make sure.'

So we lay for a quarter of an hour, whiles whispering, whiles lying still and hearing nothing earthly but the washing of the water on the piers. At last there came by an old, hobbling woman with a crutch stick; who first stopped a little, close to where we lay, and bemoaned herself and the long way she had travelled; and then set forth again up the steep spring of the bridge. The woman was so little, and the night still so dark, that we soon lost sight of her; only heard the sound of her steps, and her stick, and a cough that she had by fits, draw slowly farther away.

'She's bound to be across now,' I whispered.

'Na,' said Alan, 'her foot still sounds boss[1] upon the bridge.'

And just then – 'Who goes?' cried a voice, and we heard the butt of a musket rattle on the stones. I must suppose the sentry had been sleeping, so that had we tried, we might have passed unseen; but he was awake now, and the chance forfeited.

'This'll never do,' said Alan. 'This'll never, never do for us, David.'

And without another word, he began to crawl away through the fields; and a little after, being well out of eyeshot, got to his feet again, and struck along a road that led to the eastward. I could not conceive what he was doing; and indeed I was so sharply cut by the disappointment, that I was little likely to be pleased with anything. A moment back and I had seen myself knocking at Mr. Rankeillor's door to claim my inheritance, like a hero in a ballad; and here was I back again, a wandering, hunted blackguard, on the wrong side of the Forth.

'Well?' said I.

'Well,' said Alan, 'what would ye have? They're none such fools as I took them for. We have still the Forth to pass, Davie – weary fall the rains that fed and the hillsides that guided it!'

'And why go east? said I.

'Ou, just upon the chance!' said he. 'If we cannae pass the river, we'll have to see what we can do for the firth.'

'There are fords upon the river, and none upon the firth,' said I.

'To be sure there are fords, and a bridge forbye,' quoth Alan; 'and of what service, when they are watched?'

'Well,' said I, 'but a river can be swum.'

'By them that have the skill of it,' returned he; 'but I have yet to hear that either you or me is much of a hand at that exercise; and for my own part, I swim like a stone.'

'I'm not up to you in talking back, Alan,' I said; 'but I can see we're making bad worse. If it's hard to pass a river, it stands to reason it must be worse to pass a sea.'

'But there's such a thing as a boat,' says Alan, 'or I'm the more deceived.'

Ay, and such a thing as money,' says I. 'But for us that have neither one nor other, they might just as well not have been invented.'

'Ye think so?' said Alan.

'I do that,' said I.

'David,' says he, ye're a man of small invention and less faith. But let me set my wits upon the hone, and if I cannae beg; borrow, nor yet steal a boat, I'll make one!'

'I think I see ye!' said I. 'And what's more than all that: if ye pass a bridge, it can tell no tales; but if we pass the firth, there's the boat on the wrong side – somebody must have brought it – the countryside will all be in a bizz——'

'Man!' cried Alan, 'if I make a boat, I'll make a body to take it back again! So deave me with no more of your nonsense, but walk (for that's what you've got to do)   and let Alan think for ye.'

All night, then, we walked through the north side of the Carse under the high line of the Ochil mountains; and by Alloa and Clackmannan and Culross, all of which we avoided: and about ten in the morning, mighty hungry and tired, came to the little clachan of Limekilns. This is a place that sits near in by the waterside, and looks across the Hope to the town of Queensferry. Smoke went up from both of these, and from other villages and farms upon all hands. The fields were being reaped; two ships lay anchored, and boats were coming and going on the Hope. It was altogether a right pleasant sight to me; and I could not take my fill of gazing at these comfortable, green, cultivated hills and the busy people both of the field and sea.

For all that, there was Mr. Rankeillor's house on the south shore, where I had no doubt wealth awaited me; and here I was upon the north, clad in poor enough attire of an outlandish fashion, with three silver shillings left to me of all my fortune, a price set upon my head, and an outlawed man for my sole company.

'Oh, Alan!' said I, 'to think of it! Over there, there's all that heart could want waiting me; and the birds go over, and the boats go over – all that please can go, but just me only! Oh, man, but it's a heart-break!'

In Limekilns we entered a small change-house, which we only knew to be a public by the wand over the door, and bought some bread and cheese from a good-looking lass that was the servant. This we carried with us in a bundle, meaning to sit and eat it in a bush of wood on the seashore, that we saw some third part of a mile in front. As we went, I kept looking across the water and sighing to myself; and though I took no heed of it, Alan had fallen into a muse. At last he stopped in the way.

'Did ye take heed of the lass we bought this of? says he, tapping on the bread and cheese.

'To be sure,' said I, 'and a bonny lass she was.'

'Ye thought that?' cries he. 'Man David, that's good news.'

'In the name of all that's wonderful, why so?' says I. 'What good can that do?'

'Well,' said Alan, with one of his droll looks, 'I was rather in hopes it would maybe get us that boat.'

'If it were the other way about, it would be liker it,' said I.

'That's all that you ken, ye see,' said Alan. 'I don't want the lass to fall in love with ye, I want her to be sorry for ye, David; to which end there is no manner of need that she should take you for a beauty. Let me see' (looking me curiously over). 'I wish ye were a wee thing paler; but apart from that ye'll do fine for my purpose – ye have a fine hang-dog, rag-and-tatter, clappermaclaw kind of a look to ye, as if ye had stolen the coat from a potato-bogle. Come; right about, and back to the change-house for that boat of ours.'

I followed him, laughing.

'David Balfour,' said he, 'ye're a very funny gentleman by your way of it, and this is a very funny employ for ye, no doubt. For all that, if ye have any affection for my neck (to say nothing of your own) ye will perhaps be kind enough to take this matter responsibly. I am going to do a bit of play-acting, the bottom ground of which is just exactly as serious as the gallows for the pair of us. So bear it, if ye please, in mind, and conduct yourself according.'

'Well, well,' said I, 'have it as you will.'

As we got near the clachan, he made me take his arm and hang upon it like one almost helpless with weariness; and by the time he pushed open the change-house door, he seemed to be half carrying me. The maid appeared surprised (as well she might be) at our speedy return; but Alan had no words to spare for her in explanation, helped me to a chair, called for a tass of brandy with which he fed me in little sips, and then breaking up the bread and cheese helped me to eat it like a nursery-lass; the whole with that grave, concerned, affectionate countenance, that might have imposed upon a judge. It was small wonder if the maid were taken with the picture we presented, of a poor, sick, over-wrought lad and his most tender comrade. She drew quite near, and stood leaning with her back on the next table.

'What's like wrong with him?' said she at last.

Alan turned upon her, to my great wonder, with a kind of fury. 'Wrong!' cries he. 'He's walked more hundreds of miles than he has hairs upon his chin, and slept oftener in wet heather than dry sheets. Wrong, quo' she! Wrong enough, I would think! Wrong indeed!' and he kept grumbling to himself as he fed me, like a man ill pleased.

'He's young for the like of that,' said the maid.

'Ower young,' said Alan, with his back to her.

'He would be better riding,' says she.

'And where could I get a horse to him?' cried Alan, turning on her with the same appearance of fury. 'Would ye have me steal?'

I thought this roughness would have sent her off in dudgeon, as indeed it closed her mouth for the time. But my companion knew very well what he was doing; and for as simple as he was in some things of life, he had a great fund of roguishness in such affairs as these.

'Ye neednae tell me,' she said at last – ye're gentry.'

'Well,' said Alan, softened a little (I believe against his will) by this artless comment, 'and suppose we were? Did ever you hear that gentrice put money in folk's pockets?'

She sighed at this, as if she were herself some disinherited great lady. 'No,' says she, 'that's true indeed.'

I was all this while chafing at the part I played, and sitting tongue-tied between shame and merriment; but somehow at this I could hold in no longer, and bade Alan let me be, for I was better already. My voice stuck in my throat, for I ever hated to take part in lies; but my very embarrassment helped on the plot, for the lass no doubt set down my husky voice to sickness and fatigue.

'Has he nae friends?' said she, in a tearful voice.

'That has he so!' cried Alan, 'if we could but win to them! – friends and rich friends, beds to lie in, food to eat, doctors to see him – and there he must tramp in the dubs and sleep in the heather like a beggarman.'

'And why that?' says the lass.

'My dear,' says Alan, 'I cannae very safely say; but I'll tell ye what I'll do instead,' says he, 'I'll whistle ye a bit tune.' And with that he leaned pretty far over the table, and in a mere breath of a whistle, but with a wonderful pretty sentiment, gave her a few bars of 'Charlie is my darling.'

'Wheesht!' says she, and looked over her shoulder to the door.

'That's it,' said Alan.

'And him so young!' cries the lass.

'He's old enough to——' and Alan struck his forefinger on the back part of his neck, meaning that I was old enough to lose my head.

'It would be a black shame,' she cried, flushing high.

'It's what will be, though,' said Alan, 'unless we manage the better.'

At this the lass turned and ran out of that part of the house, leaving us alone together, Alan in high good humour at the furthering of his schemes, and I in bitter dudgeon at being called a Jacobite and treated like a child.

'Alan,' I cried, 'I can stand no more of this.'

'Ye'll have to sit it then, Davie,' said he. 'For if ye upset the pot now, ye may scrape your own life out of the fire, but Alan Breck is a dead man.'

This was so true I could only groan; and even my groan served Alan's purpose, for it was overheard by the lass as she came flying in again with a dish of white puddings and a bottle of strong ale.

'Poor lamb!' says she, and had no sooner set the meat before us, than she touched me on the shoulder with a little friendly touch, as much as to bid me cheer up. Then she told us to fall to, and there would be no more to pay; for the inn was her own, or at least her father's, and he was gone for the day to Pittencrieff. We waited for no second bidding, for bread and cheese is but cold comfort and the puddings smelt excellently well; and while we sat and ate, she took up the same place by the next table, looking on, and thinking, and frowning to herself, and drawing the string of her apron through her hand.

'I'm thinking ye have rather a long tongue,' she said at last to Alan.

'Ay,' said Alan; 'but ye see I ken the folk I speak to.'

'I would never betray ye,' said she, 'if ye mean that.'

'No,' said he, 'ye're not that kind. But I'll tell ye what ye would do, ye would help.'

'I couldnae,' said she, shaking her head. 'Na, I couldnae.'

'No,' said he, 'but if ye could?'

She answered him nothing.

'Look here, my lass,' said Alan, 'there are boats in the kingdom of Fife, for I saw two (no less) upon the beach, as I came in by your town's end. Now if we could have the use of a boat to pass under the cloud of night into Lothian, and some secret, decent kind of a man to bring that boat back again and keep his counsel, there would be two souls saved – mine to all likelihood – his to a dead sure. If we lack that boat, we have but three shillings left in this wide world; and where to go, and how to do, and what other place there is for us except the chains of a gibbet – I give you my naked word, I kenna! Shall we go wanting, lassie? Are ye to lie in your warm bed and think upon us, when the wind gowls in the chimney and the rain tirls on the roof? Are ye to lie in your warm bed and think upon this poor sick lad of mine, biting his finger-ends on blae muir for cauld and hunger? Sick or sound, he must aye be moving; with the death grapple at his throat he must aye be trailing in the rain on the lang roads; and when he gants his last on a rickle of cauld stanes, there will be nae friends near him but only me and God.'

At this appeal I could see the lass was in great trouble of mind, being tempted to help us, and yet in some fear she might be helping malefactors; and so now I determined to step in myself and allay her scruples with a portion of the truth.

'Did ever you hear,' said I 'of Mr. Rankeillor of the Ferry?'

'Rankeillor the writer?' said she 'I daursay that!'

'Well,' said I, 'it's to his door that I am bound, so you may judge by that if I am an ill-doer; and I will tell you more, that though I am indeed, by a dreadful error, in some peril of my life, King George has no truer friend in all Scotland than myself.'

Her face cleared up mightily at this, although Alan's darkened.

'That's more than I would ask,' said she. 'Mr. Rankeillor is a kennt man.' And she bade us finish our meat, get clear of the clachan as soon as might be, and lie close in the bit wood on the sea beach. 'And ye can trust me,' says she, 'I'll find some means to put you over.'

At this we waited for no more, but shook hands with her upon the bargain, made short work of the puddings, and set forth again from Limekilns as far as to the wood. It was a small piece of perhaps a score of elders and hawthorns and a few young ashes, not thick enough to veil us from passers-by upon the road or beach. Here we must lie, however, making the best of the brave warm weather and the good hopes we now had of a deliverance, and planning more particularly what remained for us to do.

We had but one trouble all day; when a strolling piper came and sat in the same wood with us; a red-nosed, blear-eyed, drunken dog, with a great bottle of whisky in his pocket, and a long story of wrongs that had been done him by all sorts of persons, from the Lord President of the Court of Session, who had denied him justice, down to the Bailies of Inverkeithing, who had given him more of it than he desired. It was impossible but he should conceive some suspicion of two men lying all day concealed in a thicket and having no business to allege. As long as he stayed there, he kept us in hot water with prying questions; and after he was gone, as he was a man not very likely to hold his tongue, we were in the great impatience to be gone ourselves.

The day came to an end with the same brightness; the night fell quiet and clear; lights came out in the houses and hamlets and then, one after another, began to be put out; but it was past eleven, and we were long since strangely tortured with anxieties, before we heard the grinding of oars upon the rowing pins. At that, we looked out and saw the lass herself coming rowing to us in a boat. She had trusted no one with our affairs, not even her sweetheart, if she had one; but as soon as her father was asleep, had left the house by a window, stolen a neighbour's boat, and come to our assistance single-handed.

I was abashed how to find expression for my thanks; but she was no less abashed at the thought of hearing them; begged us to lose no time and to hold our peace, saying (very properly) that the heart of the matter was in haste and silence; and so, what with one thing and another, she had set us on the Lothian shore not far from Carriden, had shaken hands with us, and was out again at sea and rowing for Limekilns, before there was one word said either of her service or our gratitude.

Even after she was gone we had nothing to say, as indeed nothing was enough for such a kindness. Only Alan stood a great while upon the shore shaking his head.

'It is a very fine lass,' he said at last. 'David, it is a very fine lass.' And a matter of an hour later, as we were lying in a den on the seashore and I had been already dozing, he broke out again in commendations of her character. For my part, I could say nothing, she was so simple a creature that my heart smote me both with remorse and fear; remorse because we had traded upon her ignorance; and fear lest we should have any way involved her in the dangers of our situation.

1 Hollow

27 I come to Mr. Rankeillor

The next day it was agreed that Alan should fend for himself till sunset; but as soon as it began to grow dark, he should lie in the fields by the roadside near to Newhalls, and stir for naught until he heard me whistling. At first I proposed I should give him for a signal the 'Bonnie House of Airlie,' which was a favourite of mine but he objected that as the piece was very commonly known, any ploughman might whistle it by accident; and taught me instead a little fragment of a Highland air, which has run in my head from that day to this, and will likely run in my head when I lie dying. Every time it comes to me, it takes me off to that last day of my uncertainty, with Alan sitting up in the bottom of the den, whistling and beating the measure with a finger, and the grey of the dawn coming on his face.

I was in the long street of Queensferry before the sun was up. It was a fairly built burgh, the houses of good stone, many slated; the town hall not so fine, I thought, as that of Peebles, nor yet the street so noble; but take it altogether, it put me to shame for my foul tatters.

As the morning went on, and the fires began to be kindled, and the windows to open, and the people to appear out of the houses, my concern and despondency grew ever the blacker. I saw now that I had no grounds to stand upon and no clear proof of my rights, nor so much as of my own identity. If it was all a bubble, I was indeed sorely cheated and left in a sore pass. Even if things were as I conceived, it would in all likelihood take time to establish my contentions; and what time had I to spare with less than three shillings in my pocket, and a condemned, hunted man upon my hands to ship out of the country? Truly, if my hope broke with me, it might come to the gallows yet for both of us. And as I continued to walk up and down, and saw people looking askance at me upon the street or out of windows, and nudging or speaking one to another with smiles, I began to take a fresh apprehension; that it might be no easy matter even to come to speech of the lawyer, far less to convince him of my story.

For the life of me I could not muster up the courage to address any of these reputable burghers; I thought shame even to speak with them in such a pickle of rags and dirt; and if I had asked for the house of such a man as Mr. Rankeillor, I supposed they would have burst out laughing in my face. So I went up and down and through the street, and down to the harbour-side, like a dog that has lost its master, with a strange gnawing in my inwards, and every now and then a movement of despair. It grew to be high day at last, perhaps nine in the forenoon; and I was worn with these wanderings, and chanced to have stopped in front of a very good house on the landward side, a house with beautiful, clear glass windowss, flowering knots upon the sills, the walls new-harled,[1] and a chase-dog sitting yawning on the step like one that was at home. Well, I was even envying this dumb brute, when the door fell open and there issued forth a shrewd, ruddy, kindly, consequential man in a well-powdered wig and spectacles. I was in such a plight that no one set eyes on me once but he looked at me again; and this gentleman, as it proved, was so much struck with my poor appearance, that he came straight up to me and asked me what I did.

I told him I was come to the Queensferry on business, and taking heart of grace, asked him to direct me to the house of Mr. Rankeillor.

'Why,' said he, 'that is his house that I have just come out of; and for a rather singular chance, I am that very man.'

'Then, sir,' said I, 'I have to beg the favour of an interview.'

'I do not know your name,' said he, 'nor yet your face.'

'My name is David Balfour,' said I.

'David Balfour?' he repeated, in rather a high tone, like one surprised. 'And where have you come from, Mr. David Balfour?' he asked, looking me pretty dryly in the face.

'I have come from a great many strange places, sir,' said I; 'but I think it would be as well to tell you where and how in a more private manner.'

He seemed to muse awhile, holding his lip in his hand, and looking now at me and now upon the causeway of the street.

'Yes,' says he, 'that will be the best, no doubt.' And he led me back with him into his house, cried out to someone whom I could not see that he would be engaged all morning, and brought me into a little dusty chamber full of books and documents. Here he sate down, and bade me be seated; though I thought he looked a little ruefully from his clean chair to my muddy rags. 'And now,' says he, 'if you have any business, pray be brief and come swiftly to the point. *Nec gemino bellum Trojanum orditur ab ovo*[2] – do you understand that?' says he, with a keen look.

'I will even do as Horace says, sir,' I answered, smiling, 'and carry you *in medias res*.'[3] He nodded as if he was well pleased, and indeed his scrap of Latin had been set to test me. For all that, and though I was somewhat encouraged, the blood came in my face when he added: 'I have reason to believe myself some rights on the estate of Shaws.'

He got a paper book out of a drawer and set it before him open. 'Well?' said he.

But I had shot my bolt and sat speechless.

'Come, come, Mr. Balfour,' said he, 'you must continue. Where were you born?'

'In Essendean, sir,' said I, 'the year 1734, the 12th of March.'

He seemed to follow this statement in his paper book; but what that meant I knew not. 'Your father and mother?' said he.

'My father was Alexander Balfour, schoolmaster of that place,' said I, 'and my mother Grace Pitarrow; I think her people were from Angus.'

'Have you any papers proving your identity?' asked Mr. Rankeillor.

'No, sir,' said I, 'but they are in the hands of Mr. Campbell, the minister, and could be readily produced. Mr. Campbell, too, would give me his word; and for that matter, I do not think my uncle would deny me.'

'Meaning Mr. Ebenezer Balfour?' says he.

'The same,' said I.

'Whom you have seen?' he asked.

'By whom I was received into his own house,' I answered.

'Did you ever meet a man of the name of Hoseason?' asked Mr. Rankeillor.

'I did so, sir, for my sins,' said I; 'for it was by his means and the procurement of my uncle that I was kidnapped within sight of this town, carried to sea, suffered shipwreck and a hundred other hardships, and stand before you to-day in this poor accoutrement.'

'You say you were shipwrecked,' said Rankeillor; 'where was that?'

'Off the south end of the Isle of Mull,' said I. 'The name of the isle on which I was cast up is the Island Earraid.'

'Ah!' says he, smiling, 'you are deeper than me in the geography. But so far, I may tell you, this agrees pretty exactly with other informations that I hold. But you say you were kidnapped; in what sense?'

'In the plain meaning of the word, sir,' said I. 'I was on my way to your house, when I was trepanned on board the brig, cruelly struck down, thrown below, and knew no more of anything till we were far at sea. I was destined for the plantations; a fate that, in God's providence, I have escaped.'

'The brig was lost on June the 27th,' says he, looking in his book, 'and we are now at August the 24th. Here is a considerable hiatus, Mr. Balfour, of near upon two months. It has already caused a vast amount of trouble to your friends; and I own I shall not be very well contented until it is set right.'

'Indeed, sir,' said I, 'these months are very easily filled up; but yet, before I told my story, I would be glad to know that I was talking to a friend.'

'This is to argue in a circle,' said the lawyer. 'I cannot be convinced till I have heard you. I cannot be your friend till I am properly informed. If you were more trustful, it would better befit your time of life. And you know, Mr. Balfour, we have a proverb in the country that evil-doers are aye evil-dreaders.'

'You are not to forget, sir,' said I, 'that I have already suffered by my trustfulness; and was shipped off to be a slave by the very man that (if I rightly understand) is your employer.'

All this while I had been gaining ground with Mr. Rankeillor, and in proportion as I gained ground, gaining confidence. But at this sally, which I made with something of a smile myself, he fairly laughed aloud.

'No, no,' said he, 'it is not so bad as that. *Fui non sum.*[4] I *was* indeed your uncle's man of business; but while you (*imberis juvenis custode remoto*[5]) were gallivanting in the west, a good deal of water has run under the bridges; and if your ears did not sing, it was not for lack of being talked about. On the very day of your sea disaster, Mr. Campbell stalked into my office, demanding you from all the winds. I had never heard of your existence; but I had known your father; and from matters in my competence (to be touched upon hereafter) I was disposed to fear the worst. Mr. Ebenezer admitted having seen you; declared (what seemed improbable) that he had given you considerable sums; and that you had started for the continent of Europe, intending to fulfil your education, which was probable and praiseworthy. Interrogated how you had come to send no word to Mr. Campbell, he deponed that you had expressed a great desire to break with your past life. Further interrogated where you now were, protested ignorance, but believed you were in Leyden. That is a close sum of his replies. I am not exactly sure that anyone believed him,' continued Mr. Rankeillor, with a smile; 'and in particular he so much disrelished some expressions of mine that (in a word) he showed me to the door. We were than at a full stand; for whateve shrewd suspicions we might entertain, we had no shadow of probation. In the very article, comes Captain Hoseason with the story of your drowning; whereupon all fell through; with no consequences but concern to Mr. Campbell, injury to my pocket, and another blot upon your uncle's character, which could very ill afford it. And now, Mr. Balfour,' said he, 'you understand the whole process of these matters and can judge for yourself to what extent I may be trusted.'

Indeed he was more pedantic than I can represent him, and placed more scraps of Latin in his speech; but it was all uttered with a fine geniality of eye and manner which went far to conquer my distrust. Moreover, I could see he now treated me as if I was myself beyond a doubt; so that first point of my identity seemed fully granted.

'Sir,' said I, 'if I tell you my story, I must commit a friend's life to your discretion. Pass me your word it shall be sacred; and for what touches myself I will ask no better guarantee than just your face.'

He passed me his word very seriously. 'But,' said he, 'these are rather alarming prolocutions; and if there are in your story any little jostles to the law, I would beg you to bear in mind that I am a lawyer, and pass lightly.'

Thereupon I told him my story from the first, he listening with his spectacles thrust up and his eyes closed, so that I sometimes feared he was asleep. But no such matter! he heard every word (as I found afterward) with such quickness of hearing and precision of memory as often surprised me. Even strange outlandish Gaelic names, heard for that time only, he remembered and would remind me of, years after. Yet when I called Alan Breck in full we had an odd scene. The name of Alan had of course rung through Scotland, with the news of the Appin murder and the offer of the reward; and it had no sooner escaped me than the lawyer moved in his seat and opened his eyes.

'I would name no unnecessary names, Mr. Balfour,' said he; 'above all of Highlanders, many of whom are obnoxious to the law.'

'Well, it might have been better not,' said I, 'but since I have let it slip, I may as well continue.'

'Not at all,' said Mr. Rankeillor. 'I am somewhat dull of hearing, as you may have remarked; and I am far from sure I caught the name exactly. We will call your friend, if you please Mr. Thomson – that there may be no reflections. And in future, I would take some such way with any Highlander that you may have to mention – dead or alive.'

By this, I saw he must have heard the name all too clearly, and had already guessed I might be coming to the murder. If he chose to play this part of ignorance, it was no matter of mine; so I smiled, said it was no very Highland-sounding name, and consented. Through all the rest of my story Alan was Mr. Thomson; which amused me the more, as it was a piece of policy after his own heart. James Stewart, in like manner, was mentioned under the style of Mr. Thomson's kinsman; Colin Campbell passed as a Mr. Glen; and to Cluny, when I came to that part of my tale, I gave the name of 'Mr. Jameson, a Highland chief.' It was truly the most open farce, and I wondered that the lawyer should care to keep it up; but, after all, it was quite in the taste of that age, when there were two parties in the State, and quiet persons, with no very high opinions of their own, sought out every cranny to avoid offence to either.

'Well, well,' said the lawyer, when I had quite done, 'this is a great epic, a great Odyssey of yours. You must tell it, sir, in a sound Latinity when your scholarship is riper; or in English if you please, though for my part I prefer the stronger tongue. You have rolled much; *quae regio in terris*[6] – what parish in Scotland (to make a homely translation) has not been filled with your wanderings? You have shown, besides, a singular aptitude for getting into false positions; and, yes, upon the whole, for behaving well in them. This Mr. Thomson seems to me a gentleman of some choice qualities, though perhaps a trifle bloody-minded. It would please me none the worse, if (with all his merits) he were soused in the North Sea, for the man, Mr. David, is a sore embarrassment. But you are doubtless quite right to adhere to him; indubitably, he adhered to you. *It comes* – we may say – he was your true companion; nor less *paribus curis vestigia figit*,[7] for I dare say you would both take an orra thought upon the gallows. Well, well, these days are fortunately by; and I think (speaking humanly) that you are near the end of your troubles.'

As he thus moralized on my adventures, he looked upon me with so much humour and benignity that I could scarce contain my satisfaction. I had been so long wandering with lawless people, and making my bed upon the hills, and under the barc sky, that to sit once more in a clean, covered house, and talk amicably with a gentleman in broadcloth, seemed mighty elevations. Even as I thought so, my eye fell on my unseemly tatters, and I was once more plunged in confusion. But the lawyer saw and understood me. He rose, called over the stair to lay another plate, for Mr. Balfour would stay to dinner, and led me into a bedroom in the upper part of the house. Here he set before me water and soap, and a comb; and laid out some clothes that belonged to his son; and here with another apposite tag, he left me to my toilet.

1 Newly rough-cast.
2 'Nor does he set forth the war of Troy from the twin eggs.' Horace, *Ars Poetica*, 147.
3 'Into the midst of things.' Ibid, 148.
4 I was but am not now.
5 'A beardless youth, freed from his guardian.' Horace, *Ars Poetica*, 161.
6 'What tract on earth.' Virgil, *Aeneid*, i. 460.
7 'His companion goes and plants his steps with a like load of care.' Ibid vi. 159.

28 I go in Quest of My Inheritance

I made what change I could in my appearance; and blithe was I to look in the glass and find the beggar-man a thing of the past, and David Balfour come to life again. And yet I was ashamed of the change too, and, above all, of the borrowed clothes. When I had done, Mr. Rankeillor caught me on the stair, made me his compliments, and had me again into the cabinet.

'Sit ye down, Mr. David,' said he, 'and now that you are looking a little more like yourself, let me see if I can find you any news. You will be wondering, no doubt, about your father and your uncle? To be sure it is a singular tale; and the explanation is one that I blush to have to offer you. For,' says he, really with embarrassment, 'the matter hinges on a love-affair.'

'Truly,' said I, 'I cannot very well join that notion with my uncle.'

'But your uncle, Mr. David, was not always old,' replied the lawyer, 'and what may perhaps surprise you more, not always ugly. He had a fine, gallant air; people stood in their doors to look after him, as he went by upon a mettle horse. I have seen it with these eyes, and I ingenuously confess, not altogether without envy; for I was a plain lad myself and a plain man's son; and in those days it was a case of *Odi te, qui bellus es, Sabelle.*[1]

'It sounds like a dream,' said I.

'Ay, ay,' said the lawyer, 'that is how it is with youth and age. Nor was that all, but he had a spirit of his own that seemed to promise great things in the future. In 1715, what must he do but run away to join the rebels? It was your father that pursued him, found him in a ditch, and brought him back *multum gementem*;[2] to the mirth of the whole county. However, *majora canamus*[3] – the two lads fell in love, and that with the same lady. Mr. Ebenezer, who was the admired and the beloved and the spoiled one, made, no doubt, mighty certain of the victory; and when he found he had deceived himself, screamed like a peacock. The whole county heard of it; now he lay sick at home, with his silly family standing round the bed in tears; now he rode from public house to public house, and shouted his sorrows into the lug of Tom, Dick, and Harry. Your father, Mr. David, was a kind gentleman; but he was weak, dolefully weak; took all this folly with a long countenance; and one day – by your leave! – resigned the lady. She was no such fool, however; it's from her you must inherit your excellent good sense; and she refused to be bandied from one to another. Both got upon their knees to her; and the upshot of the matter for that while was that she showed both of them the door. That was in August; dear me! the same year I came from college. The scene must have been highly farcical.'

I thought myself it was a silly business, but I could not forget my father had a hand in it. 'Surely, sir, it had some note of tragedy?' said I.

'Why, no, sir, not at all,' returned the lawyer. 'For tragedy implies some ponderable matter in dispute, some *dignus vindice nodus*;[4] and this piece of work was all about the petulance of a young ass that had been spoiled, and wanted nothing so much as to be tied up and soundly belted. However, that was not your father's view; and the end of it was, that from concession to concession on your father's part, and from one height to another of squalling, sentimental selfishness upon your uncle's, they came at last to drive a sort of bargain, from whose ill results you have recently been smarting. The one man took the lady, the other the estate. Now, Mr. David, they talk a great deal of charity and generosity; but in this disputable state of life, I often think the happiest consequences seem to flow when a gentleman consults his lawyer, and takes all the law allows him. Anyhow, this piece of Quixotry upon your father's part, as it was unjust in itself, has brought forth a monstrous family of injustices. Your father and mother lived and died poor folk; you were poorly reared; and in the meanwhile, what a time it has been for the tenants on the estate of Shaws! And I might add (if it was a matter I cared much about), what a time for Mr. Ebenezer!'

'And yet that is certainly the strangest part of all,' said I, 'that a man's nature should thus change.'

'True,' said Mr. Rankeillor. 'And yet I imagine it was natural enough. He could not think that he had played a handsome part. Those who knew the story gave him the cold shoulder; those who knew it not, seeing one brother disappear, and the other succeed in the estate, raised a cry of murder; so that upon all sides he found himself evited. Money was all he got by his bargain; well, he came to think the more of money. He was selfish when he was young, he is selfish now that he is old; and the latter end of all these pretty manners and fine feelings you have seen for yourself.'

'Well, sir,' said I, 'and in all this, what is my position?"

'The estate is yours beyond a doubt,' replied the lawyer. 'It matters nothing what your father signed, you are the heir of entail. But your uncle is a man to fight the indefensible; and it would be likely your identity that he would call in question. A lawsuit is always expensive, and a family lawsuit always scandalous; besides which, if any of your doings with your friend Mr. Thomson were to come out, we might find that we had burned our fingers. The kidnapping, to be sure, would be a court card upon our side, if we could only prove it. But it may be difficult to prove; and my advice (upon the whole) is to make a very easy bargain with your uncle, perhaps even leaving him at Shaws, where he has taken root for a quarter of a century, and contenting yourself in the meanwhile with a fair provision.'

I told him I was very willing to be easy, and that to carry family concerns before the public was a step from which I was naturally much averse. In the meantime (thinking to myself) I began to see the outlines of that scheme on which we afterwards acted.

'The great affair,' I asked, 'is to bring home to him the kidnapping.'

'Surely,' said Mr. Rankeillor, 'and if possible, out of court. For mark you here, Mr. David: we could no doubt find some men of the *Covenant* who would swear to your reclusion; but once they were in the box, we could no longer check their testimony, and some word of your friend Mr. Thomson must certainly crop out. Which (from what you have let fall) I cannot think to be desirable.'

'Well, sir,' said I, 'here is my way of it.' And I opened my plot to him.

'But this would seem to involve my meeting the man Thomson?' says he, when I had done.

'I think so, indeed, sir,' said I.

'Dear doctor!' cries he, rubbing his brow. 'Dear doctor! No, Mr. David, I am afraid your scheme is inadmissible. I say nothing against your friend, Mr. Thomson: I know nothing against him; and if I did – mark this, Mr. David! – it would be my duty to lay hands on him. Now I put it to you: is it wise to meet? He may have matters to his charge. He may not have told you all. His name may not be even Thomson!' cries the lawyer, twinkling; 'for some of these fellows will pick up names by the roadside as another would gather haws.'

'You must be the judge, sir,' said I.

But it was clear my plan had taken hold upon his fancy, for he kept musing to himself till we were called to dinner and the company of Mrs. Rankeillor; and that lady had scarce left us again to ourselves and a bottle of wine, ere he was back harping on my proposal. When and where was I to meet my friend Mr. Thomson? was I sure of Mr. T.'s discretion? supposing we could catch the old fox tripping, would I consent to such and such a term of an agreement? – these and the like questions he kept asking at long intervals, while he thoughtfully rolled his wine upon his tongue. When I had answered all of them, seemingly to his contentment, he fell into a still deeper muse, even the claret being now forgotten. Then he got a sheet of paper and a pencil, and set to work writing, and weighing every word; and at last touched a bell and had his clerk into the chamber.

'Torrance,' said he, 'I must have this written out fair against to-night; and when it is done, you will be so kind as to put on your hat and be ready to come along with this gentleman and me, for you will probably be wanted as a witness.'

'What, sir,' cried I, as soon as the clerk was gone, 'are you to venture it?'

'Why, so it would appear,' says he, filling his glass. 'But let us speak no more of business. The very sight of Torrance brings in my head a little droll matter of some years ago, when I had made a tryst with the poor oaf at the cross of Edinburgh. Each had gone his proper errand; and when it came four o'clock, Torrance had been taking a glass and did not know his master, and I, who had forgot my spectacles, was so blind without them that I give you my word I did not know my own clerk.' And thereupon he laughed heartily.

I said it was an odd chance, and smiled out of politeness; but what held me all the afternoon in wonder, he kept returning and dwelling on this story, and telling it again with fresh details and laughter; so that I began at last to be quite put out of countenance and feel ashamed for my friend's folly.

Towards the time I had appointed with Alan, we set out from the house, Mr. Rankeillor and I arm in arm, and Torrance following behind with the deed in his pocket and a covered basket in his hand. All through the town the lawyer was bowing right and left, and continually being buttonholed by gentlemen on matters of burgh or private business; and I could see he was one greatly looked up to in the county. At last we were clear of the houses, and began to go along the side of the haven and towards the Hawes Inn and the ferry pier, the scene of my misfortune. I could not look upon the place without emotion, recalling how many that had been there with me that day were now no more: Ransome taken, I could hope, from the evil to come; Shuan passed where I dared not follow him; and the poor souls that had gone down with the brig in her last plunge. All these, and the brig herself, I had outlived; and come through these hardships and fearful perils without scathe. My only thought should have been of gratitude; and yet I could not behold the place without sorrow for others and a chill of recollected fear.

I was so thinking when, upon a sudden, Mr. Rankeillor cried out, clapped his hand to his pockets, and began to laugh.

'Why,' he cries, 'if this be not a farcical adventure! After all that I said, I have forgot my glasses!'

At that, of course, I understood the purpose of his anecdote, and knew that if he had left his spectacles at home, it had been done on purpose, so that he might have the benefit of Alan's help without the awkwardness of recognizing him. And indeed it was well thought upon; for now (suppose things to go the very worst) how could Rankeillor swear to my friend's identity, or how be made to bear damaging evidence against myself? For all that, he had been a long while of finding out his want, and had spoken to and recognized a good few persons as we came through the town; and I had little doubt myself that he saw reasonably well.

As soon as we were past the Hawes (where I recognized the landlord smoking his pipe in the door, and was amazed to see him look no older) Mr. Rankeillor changed the order of march, walking behind with Torrance and sending me forward in the manner of a scout. I went up the hill, whistling from time to time my Gaelic air; and at length I had the pleasure to hear it answered and to see Alan rise from behind a bush. He was somewhat dashed in spirits, having passed a long day alone skulking in the county, and made but a poor meal in an ale-house near Dundas. But at the mere sight of my clothes he began to brighten up; and as soon as I had told him in what a forward state our matters were, and the part I looked to him to play in what remained, he sprang into a new man.

'And that is a very good notion of yours,' says he; 'and I dare to say that you could lay your hands upon no better man to put it through than Alan Breck. It is not a thing (mark ye) that anyone could do, but takes a gentleman of penetration. But it sticks in my head your lawyer-man will be somewhat wearying to see me,' says Alan.

Accordingly I cried and waved on Mr. Rankeillor, who came up alone and was presented to my friend, Mr. Thomson.

'Mr. Thomson, I am pleased to meet you,' said he. 'But I have forgotten my glasses; and our friend, Mr. David here' (clapping me on the shoulder), 'will tell you that I am little better than blind, and that you must not be surprised if I pass you by to-morrow.'

This he said, thinking that Alan would be pleased; but the Highlandman's vanity was ready to startle at a less matter than that.

'Why, sir,' says he stiffly, 'I would say it mattered the less as we are met here for a particular end, to see justice done to Mr. Balfour; and by what I can see, not very likely to have much else in common. But I accept your apology, which was a very proper one to make.'

'And that is more than I could look for, Mr. Thomson,' said Rankeillor heartily. 'And now as you and I are the chief actors in this enterprise, I think we should come into a nice agreement; to which end, I propose that you should lend me your arm, for (what with the dusk and the want of my glasses) I am not very clear as to the path; and as for you, Mr. David, you will find Torrance a pleasant kind of body to speak with. Only let me remind you it's quite needless he should hear more of your adventures or those of – ahem – Mr. Thomson.'

Accordingly these two went on ahead in very close talk, and Torrance and I brought up the rear.

Night was quite come when we came in view of the house of Shaws. Ten had been gone some time; it was dark and mild, with a pleasant, rustling wind in the south-west that covered the sound of our approach; and as we drew near we saw no glimmer of light in any portion of the building. It seemed my uncle was already in bed, which was indeed the best thing for our arrangements. We made our last whispered consultations some fifty yards away, and then the lawyer and Torrance and I crept quietly up and crouched down beside the corner of the house; and as soon as we were in our places, Alan strode to the door without concealment and began to knock.

1   I hate you, Sabellus, because you are handsome.
2   Groaning much.
3   'Let us sing of loftier things.' Virgil, *Eclogues*, iv. 1.
4   'A difficulty worthy of a deliverer.' Horace, *Aars Poetica*, 191.

29 I come into my Kingdom

For some time Alan volleyed upon the door, and his knocking only roused the echoes of the house and neighbourhood. At last, however, I could hear the noise of a window gently thrust up, and knew that my uncle had come to his observatory. By what light there was, he would see Alan standing, like a dark shadow, on the steps; the three witnesses were hidden quite out of his view; so that there was nothing to alarm an honest man in his own house. For all that, he studied his visitor awhile in silence, and when he spoke his voice had a quaver of misgiving.

'What's this?' says he. 'This is nae kind of time of night for decent folk; and I hae nae trokings¹ wi' nighthawks. What brings ye here? I have a blunderbush.'

'Is that yoursel', Mr. Balfour?' returned Alan, stepping back and looking up into the darkness. 'Have a care of that blunderbuss; they're nasty things to burst.'

'What brings ye here? and whae are ye?' says my uncle angrily.

'I have no manner of inclination to rowt out my name to the countryside,' said Alan; 'but what brings me here is another story, being more of your affairs than mine; and if ye're sure it's what ye would like, I'll set it to a tune and sing it to you.'

'And what is't?' asked my uncle.

'David,' says Alan.

'What was that?' cried my uncle, in a mighty changed voice.

'Shall I give ye the rest of the name, then?' said Alan.

There was a pause; and then, 'I'm thinking I'll better let ye in,' says my uncle doubtfully.

'I dare say that,' said Alan; 'but the point is, Would I go? Now I will tell you what I am thinking. I am thinking that it is here upon this doorstep that we must confer upon this business; and it shall be here or nowhere at all whatever; for I would have you to understand that I am as stiffnecked as yoursel', and a gentleman of better family.'

This change of note disconcerted Ebenezer; he was a little while digesting it, and then says he, 'Weel, weel, what must be must,' and shut the window. But it took him a long time to get downstairs, and a still longer to undo the fastenings, repenting (I dare say) and taken with fresh claps of fear at every second step and every bolt and bar. At last, however, we heard the creak of the hinges, and it seems my uncle slipped gingerly out and (seeing that Alan had stepped back a pace or two) sate him down on the top doorstep with the blunderbuss ready in his hands.

'And now,' says he, 'mind I have my blunderbush, and if ye take a step nearer ye're as good as deid.'

'And a very civil speech,' says Alan, 'to be sure.'

'Na,' says my uncle, 'but this is no a very chancy kind of a proceeding, and I'm bound to be prepared. And now that we understand each other, ye'll can name your business.'

'Why,' says Alan, 'you that are a man of so much understanding, will doubtless have perceived that I am a Hieland gentleman. My name has nae business in my story; but the county of my friends is no very far from the Isle of Mull, of which ye will have heard. It seems there was a ship lost in those parts; and the next day a gentleman of my family was seeking wreck-wood for his fire along the sands, when he came upon a lad that was half drowned. Well, he brought him to; and he and some other gentlemen took and clapped him in an auld, ruined castle, where from that day to this he has been a great expense to my friends. My friends are a wee wild-like, and not so particular about the law as some that I could name; and finding that the lad owned some decent folk, and was your born nephew, Mr. Balfour, they asked me to give ye a bit call and to confer upon the matter. And I may tell ye at the off-go, unless we can agree upon some terms, ye are little likely to set eyes upon him. For my friends,' added Alan, simply, 'are no very well off.'

My uncle cleared his throat. 'I'm no very caring,' says he. 'He wasnae a good lad at the best of it, and I've nae call to interfere.'

'Ay, ay,' said Alan, I see what ye would be at: pretending ye don't care, to make the ransom smaller.'

'Na,' said my uncle, 'it's the mere truth, I take nae manner of interest in the lad, and I'll pay nae ransom, and ye can make a kirk and a mill of him for what I care.'

'Hoot, sir,' says Alan. 'Blood's thicker than water, in the deil's

name! Ye cannae desert your brother's son for the fair shame of it; and
if ye did, and it came to be kennt, ye wouldnae be very popular in your
countryside, or I'm the more deceived.'

'I'm no just very popular the way it is,' returned Ebenezer; 'and I
dinnae see how it would come to be kennt. No by me, onyway; nor yet
by you or your friends. So that's idle talk, my buckie,' says he.

'Then it'll have to be David that tells it,' said Alan.

'How that?' says my uncle sharply.

'Ou, just this way,' says Alan. 'My friends would doubtless keep
your nephew as long as there was any likelihood of siller to be made of
it, but if there was nane, I am clearly of opinion they would let him
gang where he pleased, and be damned to him!'

'Ay, but I'm no very caring about that either,' said my uncle. 'I
couldnae be muckle made up with that.'

'I was thinking that,' said Alan.

'And what for why?' asked Ebenezer.

'Why, Mr. Balfour,' replied Alan, 'by all that I could hear, there
were two ways of it: either ye liked David and would pay to get him
back; or else ye had very good reasons for not wanting him, and would
pay for us to keep him. It seems it's not the first; well, then, it's the
second; and blithe am I to ken it, for it should be a pretty penny in my
pocket and the pockets of my friends.'

'I dinnae follow ye there,' said my uncle.

'No?' said Alan. 'Well, see here: you dinnae want the lad back;
well, what do ye want done with him, and how much will ye pay?'

My uncle made no answer, but shifted uneasily on his seat.

'Come, sir,' cried Alan. 'I would have ye to ken that I am a
gentleman; I bear a king's name; I am nae rider to kick my shanks at
your hall door. Either give me an answer in civility, and that out of
hand; or by the top of Glencoe, I will ram three feet of iron through
your vitals.'

'Eh, man,' cried my uncle, scrambling to his feet, 'give me a
meenit! What's like wrong with ye? I'm just a plain man and nae
dancing-master; and I'm trying to be as ceevil as it's morally possible.
As for that wild talk, it's fair disreputable. Vitals, says you! And where
would I be with my blunderbush?' he snarled.

'Powder and your auld hands are but as the snail to the swallow
against the bright steel in the hands of Alan,' said the other. 'Before
your jottering finger could find the trigger, the hilt would dirl on your
breast bane.'

'Eh, man, whae's denying it?' said my uncle. 'Pit it as ye please, hae't your ain way; I'll do naething to cross ye. Just tell me what like ye'll be wanting, and ye'll see that we'll can agree fine.'

'Troth, sir,' said Alan, 'I ask for nothing but plain dealing. In two words: do ye want the lad killed or kept?'

'Oh, sirs!' cried Ebenezer. 'Oh, sirs, me! that's no kind of language!'

'Killed or kept?' repeated Alan.

'Oh, keepit, keepit!' wailed my uncle. 'We'll have nae bloodshed, if you please.'

'Well,' says Alan, 'as ye please; that'll be the dearer.'

'The dearer?' cries Ebenezer. 'Would ye fyle your hands wi' crime?'

'Hoot!' said Alan, 'they're baith crime, whatever! And the killing's easier, and quicker, and surer. Keeping the lad'll be a fashious² job, a fashious, kittle business.'

'I'll have him keepit, though,' returned my uncle. 'I never had naething to do with onything morally wrong; and I'm no gaun to begin to pleasure a wild Hielandman.'

'Ye're unco scrupulous,' sneered Alan.

'I'm a man o' principle,' said Ebenezer simply; 'and if I have to pay for it, I'll have to pay for it. And besides,' says he, 'ye forget the lad's my brother's son.'

'Well, well,' said Alan, 'and now about the price. It's no very easy for me to set a name upon it; I would first have to ken some small matters. I would have to ken, for instance, what ye gave Hoseason at the first off-go?'

'Hoseason!' cries my uncle, struck aback. 'What for?'

'For kidnapping David,' says Alan.

'It's a lee, it's a black lee!' cried my uncle. 'He was never kidnapped. He leed in his throat that tauld ye that. Kidnapped? He never was!'

'That's no fault of mine nor yet of yours,' said Alan; 'nor yet of Hoseason's, if he's a man that can be trusted.'

'What do ye mean?' cried Ebenezer. 'Did Hoseason tell ye?'

'Why, ye donnered auld runt, how else would I ken?' cried Alan. 'Hoseason and I are partners; we gang shares; so ye can see for yoursel' what good ye can do leeing. And I must plainly say ye drove a fool's bargain when ye let a man like the sailorman so far forward in your private matters. But that's past praying for; and ye must lie on your bed the way ye made it. And the point in hand is just this; what did ye pay him?'

'Has he tauld ye himsel'?' asked my uncle.

'That's my concern,' said Alan.

'Weel,' said my uncle, 'I dinnae care what he said, he leed, and the solemn God's truth is this, that I gave him twenty pound. But I'll be perfec'ly honest with ye: forbye that, he was to have the selling of the lad in Caroliny, whilk would be as muckle mair, but no from my pocket, ye see.'

'Thank you, Mr. Thomson. That will do excellently well,' said the lawyer, stepping forward; and then mighty civilly, 'Good evening, Mr. Balfour,' said he.

And, 'Good evening, Uncle Ebenezer,' said I.

And, 'It's a braw nicht, Mr. Balfour,' added Torrance.

Never a word said my uncle, neither black nor white; but just sat where he was on the top doorstep and stared upon us like a man turned to stone. Alan filched away his blunderbuss; and the lawyer, taking him by the arm, plucked him up from the doorstep, led him into the kitchen, whither we all followed, and set him down in a chair beside the hearth, where the fire was out and only a rushlight burning.

There we all looked upon him for a while, exulting greatly in our success, but yet with a sort of pity for the man's shame.

'Come, come, Mr. Ebenezer,' said the lawyer, 'you must not be down-hearted, for I promise you we shall make easy terms. In the meanwhile give us the cellar key, and Torrance shall draw us a bottle of your father's wine in honour of the event.' Then, turning to me and taking me by the hand, 'Mr. David,' says he, 'I wish you all joy in your good fortune, which I believe to be deserved.' And then to Alan with a spice of drollery, 'Mr. Thomson, I pay you my compliment; it was most artfully conducted; but in one point you somewhat outran my comprehension. Do I understand your name to be James? or Charles? or is it George, perhaps?'

'And why should it be any of the three, sir?' quoth Alan, drawing himself up, like one who smelt an offence.

'Only, sir, that you mentioned a king's name,' replied Rankeillor; 'and as there has never been a King Thomson, or his fame at least has never come my way, I judged you must refer to that you had in baptism.'

'"Good evening, Uncle Ebenezer," said I'

This was just the stab that Alan would feel keenest, and I am free to confess he took it very ill. Not a word would he answer, but stepped off to the far end of the kitchen, and sat down and sulked; and it was not till I stepped after him, and gave him my hand, and thanked him by title as the chief spring of my success, that he began to smile a bit, and was at last prevailed upon to join our party.

By that time we had the fire lighted, and a bottle of wine uncorked; a good supper came out of the basket, to which Torrance and I and Alan set ourselves down; while the lawyer and my uncle passed into the next chamber to consult. They stayed there closeted about an hour; at the end of which period they had come to a good understanding, and my uncle and I set our hands to the agreement in a formal manner. By the terms of this, my uncle bound himself to satisfy Rankeillor as to his intromissions, and to pay me two clear thirds of the yearly income of Shaws.

So the beggar in the ballad had come home; and when I lay down that night on the kitchen chests, I was a man of means and had a name in the country. Alan and Torrance and Rankeillor slept and snored on their hard beds; but for me who had lain out under heaven and upon dirt and stones so many days and nights, and often with an empty belly, and in fear of death, this good change in my case unmanned me more than any of the former evil ones; and I lay till dawn, looking at the fire on the roof and planning the future.

1 Dealings.
2 Troublesome.

30 Good-bye!

So far as I was concerned myself, I had come to port; but I had still Alan, to whom I was so much beholden, on my hands; and I felt besides a heavy charge in the matter of the murder and James of the Glens. On both these heads I unbosomed to Rankeillor the next morning, walking to and fro about six of the clock before the house of Shaws, and with nothing in view but the fields and woods that had been my ancestors' and were now mine. Even as I spoke on these grave subjects, my eye would take a glad bit of a run over the prospect, and my heart jump with pride.

About my clear duty to my friend, the lawyer had no doubt; I must help him out of the country at whatever risk; but in the case of James, he was of a different mind.

'Mr. Thomson,' says he, 'is one thing, Mr. Thomson's kinsman quite another. I know little of the facts, but I gather that a great noble (whom we will call, if you like, the D. of A.)[1] has some concern in the matter. The D. of A. is doubtless an excellent nobleman; but, Mr. David, *timeo qui nocuere deos*.[2] If you interfere to baulk vengeance, you should remember there is one way to shut your testimony out; and that is to put you in the dock. There, you would be in the same pickle as Mr. Thomson's kinsman. You will object that you are innocent; well, but so is he. And to be tried for your life before a Highland jury, on a Highland quarrel, and with a Highland judge upon the bench, would be a brief transition to the gallows.'

Now I had made all these reasonings before and found no very good reply to them; so I put on all the simplicity I could. 'In that case, sir,' said I, 'I would just have to be hanged – would I not?'

'My dear boy,' cries he, 'go in God's name, and do what you think is right. It is a poor thought that at my time of life I should be advising you to choose the safe and shameful; and I take it back with an apology. Go and do your duty; and be hanged, if you must, like a gentleman.

There are worse things in the world than to be hanged.'

'Not many, sir,' said I, smiling.

'Why, yes, sir,' he cried, 'very many. And it would be ten times better for your uncle (to go no farther afield) if he were dangling upon a gibbet.'

Thereupon he turned into the house (still in a great fervour of mind, so that I saw I had pleased him heartily), and there he wrote me two letters, making his comments on them as he wrote.

'This,' says he, 'is to my bankers, the British Linen Company, placing a credit to your name. Consult Mr. Thomson, he will know of ways; and you, with this credit, can supply the means. I trust you will be a good husband of your money; but in the affair of a friend like Mr. Thomson, I would be even prodigal. Then for his kinsman, there is no better way than that you should seek the Advocate, tell him your tale, and offer testimony; whether he may take it or not, is quite another matter, and will turn on the D. of A. Now that you may reach the Lord Advocate well recommended, I give you here a letter to a namesake of your own, the learned Mr. Balfour of Pilrig, a man whom I esteem. It will look better that you should be presented by one of your name; and the laird of Pilrig is much looked up to in the Faculty and stands well with Lord Advocate Grant. I would not trouble him, if I were you, with any particulars; and (do you know?) I think it would be needless to refer to Mr. Thomson. Form yourself upon the laird, he's a good model; when you deal with the Advocate, be discreet; and in all these matters, may the Lord guide you, Mr. David!'

Thereupon he took his farewell, and set out with Torrance for the Ferry, while Alan and I turned our faces for the city of Edinburgh. As we went by the footpath and beside the gateposts and the unfinished lodge, we kept looking back at the house of my fathers. It stood there, bare and great and smokeless, like a place not lived in; only in one of the top windows there was the peak of a nightcap bobbing up and down and back and forward, like the head of a rabbit from a burrow. I had little welcome when I came, and less kindness while I stayed; but at least I was watched as I went away.

Alan and I went slowly forward upon our way, having little heart either to walk or speak. The same thought was uppermost in both, that we were near the time of our parting; and remembrance of all the bygone days sate upon us sorely. We talked indeed of what should be done; and it was resolved that Alan should keep to the country, biding now here, now there, but coming once in the day to a particular place where I might be able to communicate with him, either in my own person or by messenger. In the meanwhile, I was to seek out a lawyer, who was an Appin Stewart, and a man therefore to be wholly trusted; and it should be his part to find a ship and to arrange for Alan's safe embarkation. No sooner was this business done than the words seemed to leave us; and though I would seek to jest with Alan under the name of Mr. Thomson, and he with me on my new clothes and my estate, you could feel very well that we were nearer tears than laughter.

We came the by-way over the hill of Corstorphine; and when we got near to the place called Rest-and-be-Thankful, and looked down on Corstorphine bogs and over to the city and the castle on the hill, we both stopped, for we both knew without a word said that we had come to where our ways parted. Here he repeated to me once again what had been agreed upon between us; the address of the lawyer, the daily hour at which Alan might be found, and the signals that were to be made by any that came seeking him. Then I gave what money I had (a guinea or two of Rankeillor's) so that he should not starve in the meanwhile; and then we stood a space, and looked over at Edinburgh in silence.

'Well, good-bye,' said Alan, and held out his left hand.

'Good-bye,' said I, and gave the hand a little grasp, and went off down the hill.

Neither one of us looked the other in the face, nor so long as he was in my view did I take one back glance at the friend I was leaving. But as I went on my way to the city, I felt so lost and lonesome, that I could have found it in my heart to sit down by the dike and cry and weep like any baby.

It was coming near noon when I passed in by the West Kirk and the Grassmarket into the streets of the capital. The huge height of the buildings, running up to ten and fifteen storeys, the narrow arched entries that continually vomited passengers, the wares of the merchants in their windows, the hubbub and endless stir, the foul smells and the fine clothes, and a hundred other particulars too small to mention, struck me into a kind of stupor of surprise, so that I let the crowd carry me to and fro; and yet all the time what I was thinking of was Alan at Rest-and-be-Thankful; and all the time (although you would think I would not choose but be delighted with these braws and novelties) there was a cold gnawing in my inside like a remorse for something wrong.

The hand of Providence brought me in my drifting to the very doors of the British Linen Company's bank.

[Just there, with his hand upon his fortune, the present editor inclines for the time to say farewell to David. How Alan escaped, and what was done about the murder, with a variety of other delectable particulars, may be some day set forth. That is a thing, however, that hinges on the public fancy. The editor has a great kindness for both Alan and David, and would gladly spend much of his life in their society; but in this he may find himself to stand alone. In the fear of which, and lest anyone should complain of scurvy usage, he hastens to protest that all went well with both, in the limited and human sense of the word 'well'; that whatever befell them, it was not dishonour, and whatever failed them, they were not found wanting to themselves.[3]]

1   The Duke of Argyll.
2   I fear the gods who have injured me.
3   A sequel, *Catriona*, was subsequently published.

THE BLACK ARROW

THE BLACK ARROW

A Tale of the Two Roses

R. L. Stevenson

Contents

CRITIC ON THE HEARTH,

No one but myself knows what I have suffered, nor what my books have gained, by your unsleeping watchfulness and admirable pertinacity. And now here is a volume that goes into the world and lacks your *imprimatur*: a strange thing in our joint lives; and the reason of it stranger still! I have watched with interest, with pain, and at length with amusement, your unavailing attempts to peruse THE BLACK ARROW; and I think I should lack humour indeed, if I let the occasion slip and did not place your name in the fly-leaf of the only book of mine that you have never read – and never will read.

That others may display more constancy is still my hope. The tale was written years ago for a particular audience and (I may say) in rivalry with a particular author; I think I should do well to name him – Mr. Alfred R. Phillips. It was not without its reward at the time. I could not, indeed, displace Mr. Phillips from his well-won priority; but in the eyes of readers who thought less than nothing of TREASURE ISLAND, THE BLACK ARROW was supposed to mark a clear advance. Those who read volumes and those who read story papers belong to different worlds. The verdict on TREASURE ISLAND was reversed in the other court: I wonder, will it be the same with its successor?

R. L. S.

Saranac Lake
April 8, 1888.

List of Illustrations

John Amend-All

On a certain afternoon in the late spring time, the bell upon Tunstall Moat House was heard ringing at an unaccustomed hour. Far and near, in the forest and in the fields along the river, people began to desert their labours and hurry towards the sound; and in Tunstall hamlet a group of poor country-folk stood wondering at the summons.

Tunstall hamlet at that period, in the reign of old King Henry VI, wore much the same appearance that it wears to-day. A score or so of houses, heavily framed with oak, stood scattered in a long green valley ascending from the river. At the foot, the road crossed a bridge, and mounting on the other side, disappeared into the fringes of the forest on its way to the Moat House, and farther forth to Holywood Abbey. Half-way up the village the church stood among yews. On every side the slopes were crowned and the view bounded by the green elms and greening oak-trees of the forest.

Hard by the bridge there was a stone cross upon a knoll, and here the group had collected – half a dozen women and one tall fellow in a russet smock – discussing what the bell betided. An express had gone through the hamlet half an hour before, and drunk a pot of ale in the saddle, not daring to dismount for the hurry of his errand; but he had been ignorant himself of what was forward, and only bore sealed letters from Sir Daniel Brackley to Sir Oliver Oates, the parson, who kept the Moat House in the master's absence.

But now there was the noise of a horse; and soon, out of the edge of the wood and over the echoing bridge, there rode up young Master Richard Shelton, Sir Daniel's ward. He, at the least, would know, and they hailed him and begged him to explain. He drew bridle willingly enough – a young fellow not yet eighteen, sun-browned and grey-eyed, in a jacket of deer's leather, with a black velvet collar, a green hood upon his head, and a steel cross-bow at his back. The express, it appeared, had brought great news. A battle was impending. Sir Daniel had sent for every man that could draw a bow or carry a bill to go post-haste to Kettley, under pain of his severe displeasure; but for whom they were to fight, or of where the battle was expected, Dick knew nothing. Sir Oliver would come shortly himself, and Bennet Hatch was arming at that moment, for he it was who should lead the party.

'It is the ruin of this kind land,' a woman said. 'If the barons live at war, ploughfolk must eat roots.'

'Nay,' said Dick, 'every man that follows shall have sixpence a day, and archers twelve.'

'If they live,' returned the woman, 'that may very well be; but how if they die, my master?'

'They cannot better die than for their natural lord,' said Dick.

'No natural lord of mine,' said the man in the smock. 'I followed the Walsinghams; so we all did down Brierly way, till two years ago come Candlemas. And now I must side with Brackley! It was the law that did it; call ye that natural? But now, what with Sir Daniel and what with Sir Oliver – that knows more of law than honesty – I have no natural lord but poor King Harry the Sixt, God bless him! – the poor innocent that cannot tell his right hand from his left.'

'Ye speak with an ill tongue, friend,' answered Dick, 'to miscall your good master and my lord the king in the same libel. But King Harry praise be the saints! – has come again into his right mind, and will have all things peaceably ordained. And as for Sir Daniel, y' are very brave behind his back. But I will be no tale-bearer; and let that suffice.

'I say no harm of you, Master Richard, returned the peasant. 'Y' are a lad; but when ye come to a man's inches ye will find ye have an empty pocket. I say no more: the saints help Sir Daniel's neighbours, and the Blessed Maid protect his wards!'

'Clipsby,' said Richard, 'you speak what I cannot hear with honour. Sir Daniel is my good master and my guardian.'

'Come, now, will ye read me a riddle?' returned Clipsby. 'On whose side is Sir Daniel?'

'I know not,' said Dick, colouring a little; for his guardian had changed sides continually in the troubles of that period, and every change had brought him some increase of fortune.

'Ay,' returned Clipsby, 'you, nor no man. For, indeed, he is one that goes to bed Lancaster and gets up York.'

Just then the bridge rang under horse-shoe iron, and the party turned and saw Bennet Hatch come galloping – a brown-faced, grizzled fellow, heavy of hand and grim of mien, armed with sword and spear, a steel salet on his head, a leather jack upon his body. He was a great man in these parts; Sir Daniel's right hand in peace and war, and at that time, by his master's interest, bailiff of the hundred.

'Clipsby,' he shouted, 'off to the Moat House, and send all other laggards the same gate. Bowyer will give you jack and salet. We must ride before curfew. Look to it: he that is last at the lich-gate Sir Daniel shall reward. Look to it right well! I know you for a man of naught. Nance,' he added, to one of the women, 'is old Appleyard up town?'

'I'll warrant you,' replied the woman. 'In his field, for sure.'

So the group dispersed, and while Clipsby walked leisurely over the bridge, Bennet and young Shelton rode up the road together, through the village and past the church.

'Ye will see the old shrew,' said Bennet. 'He will waste more time grumbling and prating of Harry the Fift than would serve a man to shoe a horse. And all because he has been to the French wars!'

The house to which they were bound was the last in the village, standing alone among lilacs; and beyond it, on three sides, there was open meadow rising towards the borders of the wood.

Hatch dismounted, threw his rein over the fence, and walked down the field, Dick keeping close at his elbow, to where the old soldier was digging, knee-deep in his cabbages, and now and again, in a cracked voice, singing a snatch of song. He was all dressed in leather, only his hood and tippet were of black frieze, and tied with scarlet; his face was like a walnut-shell, both for colour and wrinkles; but his old grey eye was still clear enough, and his sight unabated. Perhaps he was deaf; perhaps he thought it unworthy of an old archer of Agincourt to pay any heed to such disturbances; but neither the surly notes of the alarm-bell, nor the near approach of Bennet and the lad, appeared at all to move him; and he continued obstinately digging, and piped up, very thin and shaky:

> 'Now, dear lady, if thy will be,
> I pray you that you will rue on me.'

'Nick Appleyard,' said Hatch, 'Sir Oliver commends him to you, and bids that ye shall come within this hour to the Moat House, there to take command.'

The old fellow looked up.

'Save you, my masters!' he said, grinning. 'And where goeth Master Hatch?'

'Master Hatch is off to Kettley, with every man that we can horse,' returned Bennet. 'There is a fight toward, it seems, and my lord stays as reinforcement.'

'Ay, verily,' returned Appleyard. 'And what will ye leave me to garrison withal?'

'I leave you six good men, and Sir Oliver to boot,' answered Hatch.

'It'll not hold the place,' said Appleyard; 'the number sufficeth not. It would take two-score to make it good.'

'Why, it's for that we came to you, old shrew!' replied the other. 'Who else is there but you that could do aught in such a house with such a garrison?'

'Ay, when the pinch comes, ye remember the old shoe,' returned Nick. 'There is not a man of you can back a horse or hold a bill; and as for archery – St Michael! if old Harry the Fift were back again, he would stand and let ye shoot at him for a farthing a shoot!'

'Nay, Nick, there's some can draw a good bow yet,' said Bennet.

'Draw a good Bow!' cried Appleyard. 'Yes! But who'll shoot me a good shot? It's there the eye comes in, and the head between your shoulders. Now, what might you call a long shoot, Bennet Hatch?'

'Well,' said Bennet, looking about him, 'it would be a long shoot from here into the forest.'

'Ay, it would be a longish shoot,' said the old fellow, turning to look over his shoulder; and then he put up his hand over his eyes, and stood staring.

'Why, what are you looking at?' asked Bennet, with a chuckle. 'Do you see Harry the Fift?'

The veteran continued looking up the hill in silence. The sun shone broadly over the shelving meadows; a few white sheep wandered browsing; all was still but the distant jangle of the bell.

'What is it, Appleyard?' asked Dick.

'Why, the birds,' said Appleyard.

And, sure enough, over the top of the forest, where it ran down in a tongue among the meadows, and ended in a pair of goodly green elms, about a bowshot from the field where they were standing, a flight of birds was skimming to and fro, in evident disorder.

'What of the birds?' said Bennet.

'Ay!' returned Appleyard, 'y' are a wise man to go to war, Master Bennet. Birds are a good sentry; in forest places they be the first line of battle. Look you, now, if we lay here in camp, there might be archers skulking down to get the wind of us; and here would you be, none the wiser!'

'Why, old shrew,' said Hatch, 'there be no men nearer us than Sir Daniel's, at Kettley; y' are as safe in London Tower; and ye raise scares upon a man for a few chaffinches and sparrows!'

'Hear him!' grinned Appleyard. 'How many a rogue would give his two crop ears to have a shoot at either of us! St Michael, man! they hate us like two polecats!'

'Well, sooth it is, they hate Sir Daniel,' answered Hatch, a little sobered.

'Ay, they hate Sir Daniel, and they hate every man that serves with him,' said Appleyard; 'and in the first order of hating, they hate Bennet Hatch and old Nicholas the bowman. See ye here: if there was a stout fellow yonder in the wood-edge, and you and I stood fair for him – as, by Saint George, we stand! – which, think ye, would he choose?'

'You, for a good wager,' answered Hatch.

'My surcoat to a leather belt, it would be you!' cried the old archer. 'Ye burned Grimstone, Bennet – they'll ne'er forgive you that, my master. And as for me I'll soon be in a good place, God grant, and out of bow-shot – ay, and cannon-shot – of all their malices. I am an old man, and draw fast to homeward, where the bed is ready. But for you, Bennet, y' are to remain behind here at your own peril, and if ye come to my years unhanged, the old true-blue English spirit will be dead.'

'Y' are, the shrewishest old dolt in Tunstall Forest,' returned Hatch, visibly ruffled by these threats. 'Get ye to your arms before Sir Oliver come, and leave prating for one good while. An ye had talked so much with Harry the Fift, his ears would ha' been richer than his pocket.'

An arrow sang in the air, like a huge hornet: it struck old Appleyard between the shoulder-blades, and pierced him clean through, and he fell forward on his face among the cabbages. Hatch, with a broken cry, leapt into the air; then, stooping double, he ran for the cover of the house. And in the meanwhile Dick Shelton had dropped behind a lilac, and had his cross-bow bent and shouldered, covering the point of the forest.

Not a leaf stirred. The sheep were patiently browsing; the birds had settled. But there lay the old man, with a clothyard arrow standing in his back; and there were Hatch holding to the gable, and Dick crouching and ready behind the lilac bush.

'D'ye see aught?' cried Hatch.

'Not a twig stirs,' cried Dick.

'I think shame to leave him lying,' said Bennet, coming forward once more with hesitating steps and a very pale countenance. 'Keep a good eye on the wood, Master Shelton – keep a clear eye on the wood. The saints assoil us! here was a good shoot!'

Bennet raised the old archer on his knee. He was not yet dead; his face worked, and his eyes shut and opened like machinery, and he had a most horrible, ugly look of one in pain.

'Can ye hear, old Nick?' asked Hatch. 'Have ye a last wish before ye wend, old brother?'

'Pluck out the shaft, and let me pass, a' Mary's name!' gasped Appleyard. 'I be done with old England. Pluck it out!'

'Master Dick,' said Bennet, 'come hither, and pull me a good pull upon the arrow. He would fain pass, the poor sinner.'

Dick laid down his cross-bow, and pulling hard upon the arrow, drew it forth. A gush of blood followed; the old archer scrambled half upon his feet, called once upon the name of God, and then fell dead. Hatch, upon his knees among the cabbages, prayed fervently for the welfare of the passing spirit. But even as he prayed, it was plain that his mind was still divided, and he kept ever an eye upon the corner of the wood from which the shot had come. When he had done, he got to his feet again, drew off one of his mailed gauntlets, and wiped his pale face, which was all wet with terror.

'Ay,' he said, 'it'll be my turn next.'

'Who hath done this, Bennet?' Richard asked, still holding the arrow in his hand.

'Nay, the saints know,' said Hatch. 'Here are a good two score Christian souls that we have hunted out of house and holding, he and I. He has paid his shot, poor shrew, nor will it be long, mayhap, ere I pay mine. Sir Daniel driveth over-hard.'

'This is a strange shaft,' said the lad, looking at the arrow in his hand.

'Ay, by my faith!' cried Bennet. 'Black, and black-feathered. Here is an ill-favoured shaft, by my sooth! for black, they say, bodes burial. And here be words written. Wipe the blood away. What read ye?'

'"*Appulyaird fro Jon Amend-All*,"' read Shelton. 'What should this betoken?'

'Nay, I like it not,' returned the retainer, shaking his head. 'John Amend-All! Here is a rogue's name for those that be up in the world! But why stand we here to make a mark? Take him by the knees, good Master Shelton, while I lift him by the shoulders, and let us lay him in his house. This will be a rare shog to poor Sir Oliver; he will turn paper-colour; he will pray like a windmill.'

They took up the old archer, and carried him between them into his house, where he had dwelt alone. And there they laid him on the floor, out of regard for the mattress, and sought, as best they might, to straighten and compose his limbs.

Appleyard's house was clean and bare. There was a bed, with a blue cover, a cupboard, a great chest, a pair of joint-stools, a hinged table in the chimney-corner, and hung upon the wall the old soldier's armoury of bows and defensive armour. Hatch began to look about him curiously.

'Nick had money,' he said. 'He may have had three score pounds put by. I would I could light upon 't! When ye lose an old friend, Master Richard, the best consolation is to heir him. See, now, this chest. I would go a mighty wager there is a bushel of gold therein. He had a strong hand to get, and a hard hand to keep withal, had Appleyard the archer. Now may God rest his spirit! Near eighty year he was afoot and about, and ever getting; but now he's on the broad of his back, poor shrew, and no more lacketh; and if his chattels came to a good friend, he would be merrier, methinks, in heaven.'

'Come, Hatch,' said Dick, 'respect his stone-blind eyes. Would ye rob the man before his body? Nay, he would walk!'

Hatch made several signs of the cross; but by this time his natural complexion had returned, and he was not easily to be dashed from any purpose. It would have gone hard with the chest had not the gate sounded, and presently after the door of the house opened and admitted a tall, portly, ruddy, black-eyed man of near fifty, in a surplice and black robe.

'Appleyard,' the newcomer was saying, as he entered, but he stopped dead. 'Ave Maria!' he cried. 'Saints be our shield! What cheer is this?'

'Cold cheer with Appleyard, sir parson,' answered Hatch, with perfect cheerfulness. 'Shot at his own door, and alighteth even now at purgatory gates. Ay! there, if tales be true, he shall lack neither coal nor candle.'

Sir Oliver groped his way to a joint-stool, and sat down upon it, sick and white.

'This is a judgment! O, a great stroke!' he sobbed, and rattled off a leash of prayers.

Hatch meanwhile reverently doffed his salet and knelt down.

'Ay, Bennet,' said the priest, somewhat recovering, 'and what may this be? What enemy hath done this?'

'Here, Sir Oliver, is the arrow. See, it is written upon with words,' said Dick.

'Nay,' cried the priest, 'this is a foul hearing! John Amend-All! A right Lollardy word. And black of hue, as for an omen! Sirs, this knave arrow likes me not. But it importeth rather to take counsel. Who should this be? Bethink you, Bennet. Of so many black ill-willers, which should he be that doth so hardily outface us? Simnel? I do much question it. The Walsinghams? Nay, they are not yet so broken; they still think to have the law over us, when times change. There was Simon Malmesbury, too. How think ye, Bennet?'

'What think ye, sir,' returned Hatch, 'of Ellis Duckworth?'

'Nay, Bennet, never. Nay, not he,' said the priest. 'There cometh never any rising, Bennet, from below – so all judicious chroniclers concord in their opinion; but rebellion travelleth ever downward from above; and when Dick, Tom, and Harry take them to their bills, look ever narrowly to see what lord is profited thereby. Now, Sir Daniel, having once more joined him to the Queen's party, is in ill odour with the Yorkist lords. Thence, Bennet, comes the blow – by what procuring, I yet seek; but therein lies the nerve of this discomfiture.'

'An't please you, Sir Oliver,' said Bennet, 'the axles are so hot in this country that I have long been smelling fire. So did this poor sinner, Appleyard. And, by your leave, men's spirits are so foully inclined to all of us, that it needs neither York nor Lancaster to spur them on. Hear my plain thoughts: You, that are a clerk, and Sir Daniel, that sails on any wind, ye have taken many men's goods, and beaten and hanged not a few. Y' are called to count for this; in the end, I wot not how, ye have ever the uppermost of law, and ye think all patched. But give me leave, Sir Oliver: the man that ye have dispossessed and beaten is but the angrier, and some day, when the black devil is by, he will up with his bow and clout me a yard of arrow through your inwards.'

'Nay, Bennet, y' are in the wrong. Bennet, ye should be glad to be corrected,' said Sir Oliver. 'Y' are a prater, Bennet, a talker, a babbler; your mouth is wider than your two ears. Mend it, Bennet, mend it.'

'Nay, I say no more. Have it as ye list,' said the retainer.

The priest now rose from the stool, and from the writing-case that hung about his neck took forth wax and a taper, and a flint and steel. With these he sealed up the chest and the cupboard with Sir Daniel's arms, Hatch looking on disconsolate; and then the whole party proceeded, somewhat timorously, to sally from the house and get to horse.

' 'Tis time we were on the road, Sir Oliver,' said Hatch, as he held the priest's stirrup while he mounted.

'Ay; but, Bennet, things are changed,' returned the parson. 'There is now no Appleyard – rest his soul! – to keep the garrison. I shall keep you, Bennet. I must have a good man to rest me on in this day of black arrows. "The arrow that flieth by day," saith the evangel; I have no mind of the context; nay, I am a sluggard priest, I am too deep in men's affairs. Well, let us ride forth, Master Hatch. The jackmen should be at the church by now.'

So they rode forward down the road with the wind after them, blowing the tails of the parson's cloak; and behind them, as they went, clouds began to rise and blot out the sinking sun. They had passed three of the scattered houses that make up Tunstall hamlet, when, coming to a turn, they saw the church before them. Ten or a dozen houses clustered immediately round it: but to the back the churchyard was next the meadows. At the lich-gate, near a score of men were gathered, some in the saddle, some standing by their horses' heads. They were variously armed and mounted: some with spears, some with bills, some with bows, and some bestriding plough-horses, still splashed with the mire of the furrow; for these were the very dregs of the country, and all the better men and the fair equipments were already with Sir Daniel in the field.

'We have not done amiss, praised be the cross of Holywood! Sir Daniel will be right well content,' observed the priest, inwardly numbering the troop.

'Who goes? Stand! if ye be true!' shouted Bennet.

A man was seen slipping through the churchyard among the yews; and at the sound of this summons he discarded all concealment, and fairly took to his heels for the forest. The men at the gate, who had been hitherto unaware of the stranger's presence, woke and scattered. Those who had dismounted began scrambling into the saddle: the rest rode in pursuit; but they had to make the circuit of the consecrated ground, and it was plain their quarry would escape them. Hatch, roaring an oath, put his horse at the hedge, to head him off; but the beast refused, and sent his rider sprawling in the dust. And though he was up again in a moment, and had caught the bridle, the time had gone by, and the fugitive had gained too great a lead for any hope of capture.

The wisest of all had been Dick Shelton. Instead of starting in a vain pursuit, he had whipped his cross-bow from his back, bent it, and set a quarrel to the string; and now, when the others had desisted, he turned to Bennet, and asked if he should shoot.

'Shoot! shoot!' cried the priest, with sanguinary violence.

'Cover him, Master Dick,' said Bennet. 'Bring me him down like a ripe apple.'

The fugitive was now within but a few leaps of safety; but this last part of the meadow ran very steeply uphill, and the man ran slower in proportion. What with the greyness of the falling night, and the uneven movements of the runner, it was no easy aim; and as Dick levelled his bow, he felt a kind of pity, and a half desire that he might miss. The quarrel sped.

The man stumbled and fell, and a great cheer arose from Hatch and the pursuers. But they were counting their corn before the harvest. The man fell lightly; he was lightly afoot again, turned and waved his cap in a bravado, and was out of sight next moment in the margin of the wood.

'And the plague go with him!' cried Bennet. 'He has thieves' heels: he can run, by St Banbury! But you touched him, Master Shelton; he has stolen your quarrel, may he never have good I grudge him less!'

'Nay, but what made he by the church?' asked Sir Oliver. 'I am shrewdly afeared there has been mischief here. Clipsby, good fellow, get ye down from your horse, and search thoroughly among the yews.'

Clipsby was gone but a little while ere he returned, carrying a paper.

'This writing was pinned to the church door,' he said, handing it to the parson. 'I found naught else, sir parson.'

'Now, by the power of Mother Church,' cried Sir Oliver, 'but this runs hard on sacrilege! For the king's good pleasure, or the lord of the manor — well! But that every run-the-hedge in a green jerkin should fasten papers to the chancel door — nay, it runs hard on sacrilege, hard; and men have burned for matters of less weight! But what have we here? The light falls apace. Good Master Richard, y' have young eyes. Read me, I pray, this libel.'

Dick Shelton took the paper in his hand and read it aloud. It contained some lines of a very rugged doggerel, hardly even rhyming, written in a gross character, and most uncouthly spelt. With the spelling somewhat bettered, this is how they ran:

> 'I had four blak arrows under my belt,
> Four for the greefs that I have felt,
> Four for the nomber of ill menne
> That have oppressid me now and then.

> 'One is gone; one is wele sped;
> Old Apulyaird is ded.

> 'One is for Maister Bennet Hatch,
> That burned Grimstone, walls and thatch.

> 'One for Sir Oliver Oates,
> That cut Sir Harry Shelton's throat.

> 'Sir Daniel, ye shull have the fourt;
> We shull think it fair sport.

> 'Ye shull each have your own part,
> A blak arrow in each blak heart.
> Get ye to your knees for to pray:
> Ye are ded theeves, by yea and nay!

> 'JON AMEND-ALL
>   of the Green Wood,
> And his jolly fellaweship.

'Item, we have mo arrowes and goode hempen cord for otheres of your following.'

'Now, well-a-day for charity and the Christian graces!' cried Sir Oliver lamentably. 'Sirs, this is an ill world, and groweth daily worse. I will swear upon the cross of Holywood I am as innocent of that good knight's hurt, whether in act or purpose, as the babe unchristened. Neither was his throat cut; for therein they are again in error, as there still live credible witnesses to show.'

'It boots not, sir parson,' said Bennet. 'Here is unseasonable talk.'

'Nay, Master Bennet, not so. Keep ye in your due place, good Bennet,' answered the priest. 'I shall make my innocence appear. I will upon no consideration lose my poor life in error. I take all men to witness that I am clear of this matter. I was not even in the Moat House. I was sent of an errand before nine upon the clock——'

'Sir Oliver,' said Hatch, interrupting, 'since it please you not to stop this sermon, I will take other means. Goffe, sound to horse.'

And while the tucket was sounding, Bennet moved close to the bewildered parson, and whispered violently in his ear.

Dick Shelton saw the priest's eye turned upon him for an instant in a startled glance. He had some cause for thought; for this Sir Harry Shelton was his own natural father. But he said never a word, and kept his countenance unmoved.

Hatch and Sir Oliver discussed together for a while their altered situation; ten men, it was decided between them, should be reserved, not only to garrison the Moat House, but to escort the priest across the wood. In the meantime, as Bennet was to remain behind, the command of the reinforcement was given to Master Shelton. Indeed, there was no choice; the men were loutish fellows, dull and unskilled in war, while Dick was not only popular, but resolute and grave beyond his age. Although his youth had been spent in these rough country places, the lad had been well taught in letters by Sir Oliver, and Hatch himself had shown him the management of arms and the first principles of command. Bennet had always been kind and helpful; he was one of those who are cruel as the grave to those they call their enemies, but ruggedly faithful and well-willing to their friends; and now, while Sir Oliver entered the next house to write, in his swift, exquisite penmanship, a memorandum of the last occurrences to his master, Sir Daniel Brackley, Bennet came up to his pupil to wish him god-speed upon his enterprise.

'Ye must go the long way about, Master Shelton,' he said; 'round by the bridge, for your life! Keep a sure man fifty paces afore you, to

'*Bennet moved close to the bewildered parson,*
and whispered violently in his ear'

draw shots; and go softly till y' are past the wood. If the rogues fall up on you, ride for 't; ye will do naught by standing. And keep ever forward, Master Shelton; turn me not back again, an ye love your life; there is no help in Tunstall, mind ye that. And now, since ye go to the great wars about the king, and I continue to dwell here in extreme jeopardy of my life, and the saints alone can certify if we shall meet again below, I give you my last counsels now at your riding. Keep an eye on Sir Daniel; he is unsure. Put not your trust in the jack-priest; he intendeth not amiss, but doth the will of others; it is a hand-gun for Sir Daniel! Get you good lordship where ye go; make you strong friends; look to it. And think ever a paternoster-while on Bennet Hatch. There are worse rogues afoot than Bennet. So, god-speed!'

'And Heaven be with you, Bennet!' returned Dick. 'Ye were a good friend to me-ward, and so I shall say ever.'

'And, look ye, master,' added Hatch, with a certain embarrassment, 'if this Amend-All should get a shaft into me, ye might, mayhap, lay out a gold mark or mayhap a pound for my poor soul; for it is like to go stiff with me in purgatory.'

'Ye shall have your will of it, Bennet,' answered Dick. 'But, what cheer, man! We shall meet again, where ye shall have more need of ale than masses.'

'The saints so grant it, Master Dick!' returned the other. 'But here comes Sir Oliver. An he were as quick with the long-bow as with the pen, he would be a brave man-at-arms.'

Sir Oliver gave Dick a sealed packet, with this superscription: 'To my ryght worchypful master, Sir Daniel Brackley, knyght, be thys delyvered in haste.'

And Dick, putting it in the bosom of his jacket, gave the word and set forth westward up the village.

PART I THE TWO LADS

1 At the Sign of the Sun in Kettley

Sir Daniel and his men lay in and about Kettley that night, warmly quartered and well patrolled. But the Knight of Tunstall was one who never rested from money-getting; and even now, when he was on the brink of an adventure which should make or mar him, he was up an hour after midnight to squeeze poor neighbours. He was one who trafficked greatly in disputed inheritances; it was his way to buy out the most unlikely claimant, and then, by the favour he curried with great lords about the king, procure unjust decisions in his favour; or, if that was too roundabout, to seize the disputed manor by force of arms, and rely on his influence and Sir Oliver's cunning in the law to hold what he had snatched. Kettley was one such place; it had come very lately into his clutches; he still met with opposition from the tenants; and it was to overawe discontent that he had led his troops that way.

By two in the morning, Sir Daniel sat in the inn room, close by the fireside, for it was cold at that hour among the fens of Kettley. By his elbow stood a pottle of spiced ale. He had taken off his visored headpiece, and sat with his bald head and thin, dark visage resting on one hand, wrapped in a sanguine-coloured cloak. At the lower end of the room about a dozen of his men stood sentry over the door or lay asleep on benches; and, somewhat nearer hand, a young lad, apparently of twelve or thirteen, was stretched in a mantle on the floor. The host of the Sun stood before the great man.

'Now, mark me, mine host,' Sir Daniel said, 'follow but mine orders, and I shall be your good lord ever. I must have good men for head-boroughs, and I will have Adam-a-More high constable; see to it narrowly. If other men be chosen, it shall avail you nothing; rather it shall be found to your sore cost. For those that have paid rent to Walsingham I shall take good measure – you among the rest, mine host.'

'Good knight,' said the host, 'I will swear upon the cross of

Holywood I did but pay to Walsingham upon compulsion. Nay, bully knight, I love not the rogue Walsinghams; they were as poor as thieves, bully knight. Give me a great lord like you. Nay; ask me among the neighbours, I am stout for Brackley.'

'It may be,' said Sir Daniel dryly. 'Ye shall then pay twice.'

The innkeeper made a horrid grimace; but this was a piece of bad luck that might readily befall a tenant in these unruly times, and he was perhaps glad to make his peace so easily.

'Bring up yon fellow, Selden!' cried the knight.

And one of his retainers led up a poor, cringing old man, as pale as a candle, and all shaking with the fen fever.

'Sirrah,' said Sir Daniel, 'your name?'

'An't please your worship,' replied the man, 'my name is Condall – Condall of Shoreby, at your good worship's pleasure.'

'I have heard you ill reported on,' returned the knight. 'Ye deal in treason, rogue; ye trudge the country leasing; y' are heavily suspicioned of the death of severals. How, fellow, are ye so bold? But I will bring you down.'

'Right honourable and my reverend lord,' the man cried, 'here is some hodge-podge, saving your good presence. I am but a poor private man, and have hurt none.'

'The under-sheriff did report of you most vilely,' said the knight. '"Seize me," saith he, "that Tyndal of Shoreby."'

'Condall, my good lord; Condall is my poor name,' said the unfortunate.

'Condall or Tyndal, it is all one,' replied Sir Daniel coolly. 'For, by my sooth, y' are here, and I do mightily suspect your honesty. If you would save your neck, write me swiftly an obligation for twenty pound.'

'For twenty pound, my good lord!' cried Condall. 'Here is midsummer madness! My whole estate amounteth not to seventy shillings.'

'Condall or Tyndal,' returned Sir Daniel, grinning. 'I will run my peril of that loss. Write me down twenty, and when I have recovered all I may, I will be good lord to you, and pardon you the rest.'

'Alas! my good lord, it may not be; I have no skill to write,' said Condall.

'Well-a-day!' returned the knight. 'Here, then, is no remedy. Yet I would fain have spared you, Tyndal, had my conscience suffered.

Selden, take me this old shrew softly to the nearest elm, and hang me him tenderly by the neck, where I may see him at my riding. Fare ye well, good Master Condall, dear Master Tyndal; y' are post-haste for Paradise; fare ye then well!'

'Nay, my right pleasant lord,' replied Condall, forcing an obsequious smile, 'an ye be so masterful, as doth right well become you, I will even, with all my poor skill, do your good bidding.'

'Friend,' quoth Sir Daniel, 'ye will now write two score. Go to! y' are too cunning for a livelihood of seventy shillings. Selden, see him write me this in good form, and have it duly witnessed.'

And Sir Daniel, who was a very merry knight, none merrier in England, took a drink of his mulled ale, and lay back, smiling.

Meanwhile, the boy upon the floor began to stir, and presently sat up and looked about him with a scare.

'Hither,' said Sir Daniel; and as the other rose at his command and came slowly towards him, he leaned back and laughed outright. 'By the rood!' he cried, 'a sturdy boy!'

The lad flashed crimson with anger, and darted a look of hate out of his dark eyes. Now that he was on his legs, it was more difficult to make certain of his age. His face looked somewhat older in expression, but it was as smooth as a young child's; and in bone and body he was unusually slender, and somewhat awkward of gait.

'Ye have called me, Sir Daniel,' he said. 'Was it to laugh at my poor plight?'

'Nay, now, let laugh,' said the knight. 'Good shrew, let laugh, I pray you. An ye could see yourself, I warrant ye would laugh the first.'

'Well,' cried the lad, flushing, 'ye shall answer this when ye answer for the other. Laugh while ye may!'

'Nay, now, good cousin,' replied Sir Daniel, with some earnestness, 'think not that I mock at you, except in mirth, as between kinsfolk and singular friends. I will make you a marriage of a thousand pounds, go to! and cherish you exceedingly. I took you, indeed, roughly, as the time demanded; but from henceforth I shall ungrudgingly maintain and cheerfully serve you. Ye shall be Mrs. Shelton – Lady Shelton, by my troth! for the lad promiseth bravely. Tut! ye will not shy for honest laughter; it purgeth melancholy. They are no rogues who laugh, good cousin. Good mine host, lay me a meal now for my cousin, Master John. Sit ye down, sweetheart, and eat.'

'Nay,' said Master John, 'I will break no bread. Since ye force me to this sin, I will fast for my soul's interest. But, good mine host, I pray you of courtesy give me a cup of fair water; I shall be much beholden to your courtesy indeed.'

'Ye shall have a dispensation, go to!' cried the knight. 'Shalt be well shriven, by my faith! Content you, then, and eat.'

But the lad was obstinate, drank a cup of water, and, once more wrapping himself closely in his mantle, sat in a far corner, brooding.

In an hour or two there rose a stir in the village of sentries challenging and the clatter of arms and horses; and then a troop drew up by the inn door, and Richard Shelton, splashed with mud, presented himself upon the threshold.

'Save you, Sir Daniel,' he said.

'How! Dickie Shelton!' cried the knight; and at the mention of Dick's name the other lad looked curiously across. 'What maketh Bennet Hatch?'

'Please you, sir knight, to take cognisance of this packet from Sir Oliver, wherein are all things fully stated,' answered Richard, presenting the priest's letter. 'And please you further, ye were best make all speed to Risingham; for on the way hither we encountered one riding furiously with letters, and by his report, my Lord of Risingham was sore bested, and lacked exceedingly your presence.'

'How say you? Sore bested?' returned the knight. 'Nay, then, we will make speed sitting down, good Richard. As the world goes in this poor realm of England, he that rides softliest rides surest. Delay, they say, begetteth peril; but it is rather this itch of doing that undoes men; mark it, Dick. But let me see, first, what cattle ye have brought. Selden, a link here at the door!'

And Sir Daniel strode forth into the village street, and, by the red glow of a torch, inspected his new troops. He was an unpopular neighbour and an unpopular master; but as a leader in war he was well beloved by those who rode behind his pennant. His dash, his proved courage, his forethought for the soldiers' comfort, even his rough gibes, were all to the taste of the bold blades in jack and salet.

'Nay, by the rood!' he cried, 'what poor dogs are these? Here be some as crooked as a bow, and some as lean as a spear. Friends, ye shall ride in the front of the battle; I can spare you, friends. Mark me this old villain on the piebald! A two-year mutton riding on a hog would look more soldierly! Ha! Clipsby, are ye there old rat? Y' are a man I could lose with a good heart; ye shall go in front of all, with a bull's-eye painted on your jack, to be the better butt for archery; sirrah, ye shall show me the way.'

'I will show you any way, Sir Daniel, but the way to change sides,' returned Clipsby sturdily.

Sir Daniel laughed a guffaw.

'Why, well said!' he cried. 'Hast a shrewd tongue in thy mouth, go to! I will forgive you for that merry word. Selden, see them fed, both man and brute.'

The knight re-entered the inn.

'Now, friend Dick,' he said, 'fall to. Here is good ale and bacon. Eat, while that I read.'

Sir Daniel opened the packet, and as he read his brow darkened. When he had done he sat a little, musing. Then he looked sharply at his ward.

'Dick,' said he, 'y' have seen this penny rhyme?'

The lad replied in the affirmative.

'It bears your father's name,' continued the knight; 'and our poor shrew of a parson is, by some mad soul, accused of slaying him.'

'He did most eagerly deny it,' answered Dick.

'He did?' cried the knight, very sharply. 'Heed him not. He has a loose tongue; he babbles like a jack-sparrow. Some day, when I may find the leisure, Dick, I will myself more fully inform you of these matters. There was one Duckworth shrewdly blamed for it; but the times were troubled, and there was no justice to be got.'

'It befell at the Moat House?' Dick ventured, with a beating at his heart.

'It befell between the Moat House and Holywood,' replied Sir Daniel calmly; but he shot a covert glance, black with suspicion, at Dick's face. 'And now,' added the knight, 'speed you with your meal; ye shall return to Tunstall with a line from me.'

Dick's face fell sorely.

'Prithee, Sir Daniel,' he cried, 'send one of the villains! I beseech you let me to the battle. I can strike a stroke, I promise you.'

'I misdoubt it not,' replied Sir Daniel, sitting down to write. 'But here, Dick, is no honour to be won. I lie in Kettley till I have sure tidings of the war, and then ride to join me with the conqueror. Cry not on cowardice; it is but wisdom, Dick; for this poor realm so tosseth with rebellion, and the king's name and custody so changeth hands, that no man may be certain of the morrow. Toss-pot and Shuttle-wit run in, but my Lord Good-Counsel sits o' one side, waiting.'

With that, Sir Daniel, turning his back to Dick, and quite at the farther end of the long table, began to write his letter, with his mouth on one side, for this business of the Black Arrow stuck sorely in his throat.

Meanwhile, young Shelton was going on heartily enough with his breakfast, when he felt a touch upon his arm, and a very soft voice whispering in his ear.

'Make not a sign, I do beseech you,' said the voice, 'but of your charity teach me the straight way to Holywood. Beseech you, now, good boy, comfort a poor soul in peril and extreme distress, and set me so far forth upon the way to my repose.'

'Take the path by the windmill,' answered Dick, in the same tone; 'it will bring you to Till Ferry; there inquire again.'

And without turning his head, he fell again to eating. But with the tail of his eye he caught a glimpse of the young lad called Master John stealthily creeping from the room.

'Why,' thought Dick, 'he is as young as I. "Good boy" doth he call me? An I had known, I should have seen the varlet hanged ere I had told him. Well, if he goes through the fen, I may come up with him and pull his ears.'

Half an hour later, Sir Daniel gave Dick the letter, and bade him speed to the Moat House. And again, some half an hour after Dick's departure, a messenger came, in hot haste, from my Lord of Risingham.

'Sir Daniel,' the messenger said, 'ye lose great honour, by my sooth! The fight began again this morning ere the dawn, and we have beaten their van and scattered their right wing. Only the main battle standeth fast. An we had your fresh men, we should tilt you them all into the river. What, sir knight! Will ye be the last? It stands not with your good credit.'

'Nay,' cried the knight, 'I was but now upon the march. Selden, sound me the tucket. Sir, I am with you on the instant. It is not two hours since the more part of my command came in, sir messenger. What would ye have? Spurring is good meat, but yet it killed the charger. Bustle, boys!'

By this time the tucket was sounding cheerily in the morning, and from all sides Sir Daniel's men poured into the main street and formed before the inn. They had slept upon their arms, with chargers saddled, and in ten minutes five-score men-at-arms and archers, cleanly equipped and briskly disciplined, stood ranked and ready. The chief part were in Sir Daniel's livery, murrey and blue, which gave the greater show to their array. The best armed rode first; and away out of sight, at the tail of the column, came the sorry reinforcement of the night before. Sir Daniel looked with pride along the linc.

'Here be the lads to serve you in a pinch,' he said.

'They are pretty men, indeed,' replied the messenger. 'It but augments my sorrow that ye had not marched the earlier.'

'Well,' said the knight, 'what would ye? The beginning of a feast and the end of a fray, sir messenger'; and he mounted into his saddle. 'Why! how now!' he cried. 'John! Joanna! Nay, by the sacred rood! where is she? Host, where is that girl?'

'Girl, Sir Daniel?' cried the landlord. 'Nay, sir, I saw no girl.'

'Boy, then, dotard!' cried the knight. 'Could ye not see it was a wench? She in the murrey-coloured mantle – she that broke her fast with water, rogue – where is she?'

'Nay, the saints bless us! Master John, ye called him,' said the host. 'Well, I thought none evil. He is gone. I saw him – her – I saw her in the stable a good hour agone; 'a was saddling a grey horse.'

'Now, by the rood!' cried Sir Daniel, 'the wench was worth five hundred pound to me and more.'

'Sir knight,' observed the messenger, with bitterness, 'while that ye are here, roaring for five hundred pounds, the realm of England is elsewhere being lost and won.'

'It is well said,' replied Sir Daniel. 'Selden, fall me out with six cross-bowmen; hunt mc her down. I care not what it cost; but at my returning, let me find her at the Moat House. Be it upon your head. And now, sir messenger, we march.'

And the troop broke into a good trot, and Selden and his six mcn were left behind upon the street of Kettley, with the staring villagers.

2 In the Fen

It was near six in the May morning when Dick began to ride down into the fen upon his homeward way. The sky was all blue; the jolly wind blew loud and steady; the windmill-sails were spinning; and the willows over all the fen rippling and whitening like a field of corn. He had been all night in the saddle, but his heart was good and his body sound, and he rode right merrily.

The path went down and down into the marsh, till he lost sight of all the neighbouring landmarks but Kettley windmill on the knoll behind him, and the extreme top of Tunstall Forest far before. On either hand there were great fields of blowing reeds and willows, pools of water shaking in the wind, and treacherous bogs, as green as emerald, to tempt and to betray the traveller. The path lay almost straight through the morass. It was already very ancient? its foundation had been laid by Roman soldiery; in the lapse of ages much of it had sunk, and every here and there, for a few hundred yards, it lay submerged below the stagnant waters of the fen.

About a mile from Kettley, Dick came to one such break in the plain line of the causeway, where the reeds and willows grew dispersedly like little islands and confused the eye. The gap besides, was more than unusually long; it was a place where any stranger might come readily to mischief; and Dick bethought him, with something like a pang, of the lad whom he had so imperfectly directed. As for himself, one look backward to where the windmill-sails were turning black against the blue of heaven – one look forward to the high ground of Tunstall Forest, and he was sufficiently directed and held straight on, the water washing to his horse's knees, as safe as on a highway.

Half-way across, and when he had already sighted the path rising high and dry upon the farther side, he was aware of a great splashing on his right, and saw a grey horse, sunk to its belly in the mud, and still spasmodically struggling. Instantly, as though it had divined the neighbourhood of help, the poor beast began to neigh most piercingly. It rolled, meanwhile, a bloodshot eye, insane with terror; and as it sprawled wallowing in the quag, clouds of stinging insects rose and buzzed about it in the air.

'Alack!' thought Dick, 'can the poor lad have perished? There is his horse, for certain – a brave grey! Nay, comrade, if thou criest to me so piteously, will do all man can to help thee. Shalt not lie there to drown by inches!'

And he made ready his cross-bow, and put a quarrel through the creature's head.

Dick rode on after this act of rugged mercy, somewhat sobered in spirit, and looking closely about him for any sign of his less happy predecessor in the way.

'I would I had dared to tell him further,' he thought; 'for I fear he had miscarried in the slough.'

And just as he was so thinking, a voice cried upon his name from the causeway side, and looking over his shoulders he saw the lad's face peering from a clump of reeds.

'Are ye there?' he said, reining in. 'Ye lay so close among the reeds that I had passed you by. I saw your horse bemired, and put him from his agony; which, by my sooth! an ye had been a more merciful rider, ye had done yourself. But come forth out of hiding. Here be none to trouble you.'

'Nay, good boy, I have no arms, nor skill to use them if had,' replied the other, stepping forth upon the pathway.

'Why call me "boy"?' cried Dick. 'Y' are not, I trow, the elder of us twain.'

'Good Master Shelton,' said the other, 'prithee forgive me. I have none the least intention to offend. Rather, I would in every way beseech your gentleness and favour, for I am now worse bested than ever, having lost my way, my cloak, and my poor horse. To have a riding-rod and spurs, and never a horse to sit upon! And before all,' he added, looking ruefully upon his clothes – 'before all, to be so sorrily besmirched!'

'Tut!' cried Dick. 'Would ye mind a ducking? Blood of wound or dust of travel – that's a man's adornment.'

'Nay, then, I like him better plain,' observed the lad. 'But, prithee, how shall I do? Prithee, good Master Richard, help me with your good counsel. If I come not safe to Holywood, I am undone.'

'Nay,' said Dick, dismounting, 'I will give more than counsel. Take my horse, and I will run awhile, and when I am weary we shall change again, that so, riding and running, both may go the speedier.'

So the change was made, and they went forward as briskly as they durst on the uneven causeway, Dick with his hand upon the other's knee.

'How call ye your name?' asked Dick.

'Call me John Matcham,' replied the lad.

'And what make ye to Holywood?' Dick continued.

'I seek sanctuary from a man that would oppress me,' was the answer. 'The good Abbot of Holywood is a strong pillar to the weak.'

'And how came ye with Sir Daniel, Master Matcham?' pursued Dick.

'Nay,' cried the other, 'by the abuse of force! He hath taken me by violence from my own place; dressed me in these weeds; ridden with me till my heart was sick; gibed me till I could 'a' wept; and when certain of my friends pursued, thinking to have me back, claps me in the rear to stand their shot! I was even grazed in the right foot, and walk but lamely. Nay, there shall come a day between us; he shall smart for all!'

'Would ye shoot at the moon with a hand-gun?' said Dick. ' 'Tis a valiant knight, and hath a hand of iron. An he guessed I had made or meddled with your flight, it would go sore with me.'

'Ay, poor boy,' returned the other, 'y' are his ward, I know it. By the same token, so am I, or so he saith; or else he hath bought my marriage – I wot not rightly which; but it is some handle to oppress me by.'

'Boy again!' said Dick.

'Nay, then, shall I call you girl, good Richard?' asked Matcham.

'Never a girl for me,' returned Dick. 'I do abjure the crew of them!'

'Ye speak boyishly,' said the other. 'Ye think more of them than ye pretend.'

'Not I,' said Dick stoutly. 'They come not in my mind. A plague of them, say I! Give me to hunt and to fight and to feast, and to live with jolly foresters. I never heard of a maid yet that was for any service, save one only; and she, poor shrew, was burned for a witch and the wearing of men's clothes in spite of nature.'

Master Matcham crossed himself with fervour, and appeared to pray.

'What make ye?' Dick inquired.

'I pray for her spirit,' answered the other, with somewhat troubled voice.

'For a witch's spirit?' Dick cried. 'But pray for her, an ye list; she was the best wench in Europe, was this Joan of Arc. Old Appleyard the archer ran from her, he said, as if she had been Mahoun. Nay, she was a brave wench.'

'Well, but, good Master Richard,' resumed Matcham, 'an ye like maids so little, y' are no true natural man; for God made them twain by intention, and brought true love into the world, to be man's hope and woman's comfort.'

'Faugh!' said Dick. 'Y' are a milk-sopping baby, so to harp on women. An ye think I be no true man, get down upon the path, and whether at fists, backsword, or bow and arrow, I will prove my manhood on your body.'

'Nay, I am no fighter,' said Matcham eagerly. 'I meant no tittle of offence. I meant but pleasantry. And if I talk of women, it is because I heard ye were to marry.'

'I to marry!' Dick exclaimed. 'Well, it is the first I hear of it. And with whom was I to marry?'

'One Joan Sedley,' replied Matcham, colouring. 'It was Sir Daniel's doing; he hath money to gain on both sides; and, indeed, I have heard the poor wench bemoaning herself pitifully of the match. It seems she is of your mind, or else distasted to the bridegroom.'

'Well! marriage is like death, it comes to all,' said Dick, with resignation. 'And she bemoaned herself? I pray ye now, see there how shuttle-witted are these girls: to bemoan herself before that she had seen me? Do I bemoan myself? Not I. An I be to marry, I will marry dry-eyed! But if ye know her, prithee, of what favour is she? fair or foul? And is she shrewish or pleasant?'

'Nay, what matters it?' said Matcham. 'An y' are to marry, ye can but marry. What matters foul or fair? These be but toys. Y' are no milksop, Master Richard; ye will wed with dry eyes, anyhow.'

'It is well said,' replied Shelton. 'Little I reck.'

'Your lady wife is like to have a pleasant lord,' said Matcham.

'She shall have the lord Heaven made her for,' returned Dick. 'I trow there be worse as well as better.'

'Ay, the poor wench!' cried the other.

'And why so poor?' asked Dick.

'To wed a man of wood,' replied his companion. 'O me, for a wooden husband!'

'I think I be a man of wood, indeed,' said Dick, 'to trudge afoot the while you ride my horse; but it is good wood, I trow.'

'Good Dick, forgive me,' cried the other. 'Nay, y' are the best heart in England; I but laughed. Forgive me now, sweet Dick.'

'Nay, no fool words,' returned Dick, a little embarrassed by his companion's warmth. 'No harm is done. I am not touchy, praise the saints.'

And at that moment the wind, which was blowing straight behind them as they went, brought them the rough flourish of Sir Daniel's trumpeter.

'Hark!' said Dick, 'the tucket soundeth.'

'Ay,' said Matcham, 'they have found my flight, and now I am unhorsed!' and he became pale as death.

'Nay, what cheer!' returned Dick. 'Y' have a start, and we are near the ferry. And it is I, methinks, that am unhorsed.'

'Alack, I shall be taken!' cried the fugitive. 'Dick, kind Dick, beseech ye help me but a little!'

'Why, now, what aileth thee?' said Dick. 'Methinks I help you very patently. But my heart is sorry for so spiritless a fellow! And see ye here, John Matcham – sith John Matcham is your name – I, Richard Shelton, tide what betideth, come what may, will see you safe in Holywood. The saints so do to me again if I default you. Come, pick me up a good heart, Sir Whiteface. The way betters here; spur me the horse. Go faster! faster! Nay, mind not for me; I can run like a deer.'

So, with the horse trotting hard, and Dick running easily alongside, they crossed the remainder of the fen, and came out upon the banks of the river by the ferryman's hut.

3 The Fen Ferry

The river Till was a wide, sluggish, clayey water, oozing out of the fens, and in this part of its course it strained among some score of willow-covered, marshy islets.

It was a dingy stream: but upon this bright, spirited morning everything was become beautiful. The wind and the martens broke it up into innumerable dimples; and the reflection of the sky was scattered over all the surface in crumbs of smiling blue.

A creek ran up to meet the path, and close under the bank the ferryman's hut lay snugly. It was of wattle and clay, and the grass grew green upon the roof.

Dick went to the door and opened it. Within, upon a foul old russet cloak, the ferryman lay stretched and shivering; a great hulk of a man, but lean and shaken by the country fever.

'Hey, Master Shelton,' he said, 'be ye for the ferry? Ill times, ill times! Look to yourself. There is a fellowship abroad. Ye were better turn round on your two heels and try the bridge.'

'Nay; time's in the saddle,' answered Dick. 'Time will ride, Hugh Ferryman. I am hot in haste.'

'A wilful man!' returned the ferryman, rising. 'An ye win safe to the Moat House, y' have done lucky; but I say no more.' And then catching sight of Matcham: 'Who be this?' he asked, as he paused, blinking, on the threshold of his cabin.

'It is my kinsman, Master Matcham,' answered Dick.

'Give ye good day, good ferryman,' said Matcham, who had dismounted, and now came forward, leading the horse. 'Launch me your boat, I prithee; we are sore in haste.'

The gaunt ferryman continued staring.

'By the mass!' he cried at length, and laughed with open throat.

Matcham coloured to his neck and winced; and Dick, with an angry countenance, put his hand on the lout's shoulder.

'How now, churl!' he cried. 'Fall to thy business, and leave mocking thy betters.'

Hugh Ferryman grumblingly undid his boat, and shoved it a little forth into the deep water. Then Dick led in the horse, and Matcham followed.

'Ye be mortal small made, master,' said Hugh, with a wide grin; 'something o' the wrong model, belike. Nay, Master Shelton, I am for you,' he added, getting to his oars. 'A cat may look at a king. I did but take a shot of the eye at Master Matcham.'

'Sirrah, no more words,' said Dick. 'Bend me your back.'

They were by that time at the mouth of the creek, and the view opened up and down the river. Everywhere it was enclosed with islands. Clay banks were falling in, willows nodding, reeds waving, martens dipping and piping. There was no sign of man in the labyrinth of waters.

'My master,' said the ferryman, keeping the boat steady with one oar, 'I have a shrewd guess that John-a-Fenne is on the island. He bears me a black grudge to all Sir Daniel's. How if I turned me up stream and landed you an arrow-flight above the path? Ye were best not meddle with John Fenne.'

'How, then? is he of this company?' asked Dick.

'Nay, mum is the word,' said Hugh. 'But I would go up water, Dick. How if Master Matcham came by an arrow?' and he laughed again.

'Be it so, Hugh,' answered Dick.

'Look ye then,' pursued Hugh. 'Sith it shall so be, unsling me your cross-bow – so: now make it ready – good; place me a quarrel. Ay, keep it so, and look upon me grimly.'

'What meaneth this?' asked Dick.

'Why, my master, if I steal you across, it must be under force or fear,' replied the ferryman; 'for else, if John Fenne got wind of it, he were like to prove my most distressful neighbour.'

'Do these churls ride so roughly?' Dick inquired. 'Do they command Sir Daniel's own ferry?'

'Nay,' whispered the ferryman, winking. 'Mark me! Sir Daniel shall down. His time is out. He shall down. Mum!' And he bent over his oars.

They pulled a long way up the river, turned the tail of an island, and came softly down a narrow channel next the opposite bank. Then

Hugh held water in mid stream.

'I must land you here among the willows,' he said.

'Here is no path but willow swamps and quagmires,' answered Dick.

'Master Shelton,' replied Hugh, 'I dare not take ye nearer down, for your own sake now. He watcheth me the ferry, lying on his bow. All that go by and owe Sir Daniel goodwill, he shooteth down like rabbits. heard him swear it by the rood. An I had not known you of old days – ay, and from so high upward – I would 'a' let you go on; but for old days' remembrance, and because ye had this toy with you that's not fit for wounds or warfare, I did risk my two poor ears to have you over whole. Content you; I can no more, on my salvation!'

Hugh was still speaking, lying on his oars, when there came a great shout from among the willows on the island, and sounds followed as of a strong man breasting roughly through the wood.

'A murrain!' cried Hugh. 'He was on the upper island all the while!' He pulled straight for shore. 'Threat me with your bow, good Dick; threat me with it plain,' he added. 'I have tried to save your skins, save you mine!'

The boat ran into a tough thicket of willows with a crash. Matcham, pale, but steady and alert, at a sign from Dick, ran along the thwarts and leaped ashore; Dick, taking the horse by the bridle, sought to follow, but what with the animal's bulk, and what with the closeness of the thicket, both stuck fast. The horse neighed and trampled; and the boat, which was swinging in an eddy, came on and off and pitched with violence.

'It may not be, Hugh; here is no landing,' cried Dick; but he still struggled valiantly with the obstinate thicket and the startled animal.

A tall man appeared upon the shore of the island, a long-bow in his hand. Dick saw him for an instant, with the corner of his eye, bending the bow with a great effort, his face crimson with hurry.

'Who goes?' he shouted. 'Hugh, who goes?'

''Tis Master Shelton, John,' replied the ferryman.

'Stand, Dick Shelton!' bawled the man upon the island. 'Ye shall have no hurt, upon the rood! Stand! Back out, Hugh Ferryman.'

Dick cried a taunting answer.

'Nay, then, ye shall go afoot,' returned the man; and he let drive an arrow.

The horse, struck by the shaft, lashed out in agony and terror; the boat capsized, and the next moment all were struggling in the eddies of the river.

When Dick came up, he was within a yard of the bank; and before his eyes were clear, his hand had closed on something firm and strong that instantly began to drag him forward. It was the riding-rod, that Matcham, crawling forth upon an overhanging willow, had opportunely thrust into his grasp.

'By the mass!' cried Dick, as he was helped ashore, 'that makes a life I owe you. I swim like a cannon-ball.' And he turned instantly towards the island.

Midway over, Hugh Ferryman was swimming with his upturned boat, while John-a-Fenne, furious at the ill-fortune of his shot, bawled to him to hurry.

'Come, Jack,' said Shelton, 'run for it! Ere Hugh can hale his barge across, or the pair of 'em can get it righted, we may be out of cry.'

And adding example to his words, he began to run, dodging among the willows, and in marshy places leaping from tussock to tussock. He had no time to look for his direction; all he could do was to turn back upon the river, and put all his heart to running.

Presently, however, the ground began to rise, which showed him he was still in the right way, and soon after they came forth upon a slope of solid turf, where elms began to mingle with willows.

But here Matcham, who had been dragging far into the rear, threw himself fairly down.

'Leave me, Dick!' he cried pantingly; 'I can no more.'

Dick turned, and came back to where his companion lay.

'Nay, Jack, leave thee!' he cried. 'That were a knave's trick, to be sure, when ye risked a shot and a ducking, ay, and a drowning too, to save my life. Drowning, in sooth; for why I did not pull you in along with me, the saints alone can tell!'

'Nay,' said Matcham, 'I would 'a' saved us both, good Dick, for I can swim.'

'Can ye so?' cried Dick, with open eyes. It was the one manly accomplishment of which he was himself incapable. In the order of the things that he admired, next to having killed a man in single fight came swimming. 'Well,' he said, 'here is a lesson to despise no man. I promised to care for you as far as Holywood, and, by the rood, Jack, y' are more capable to care for me.'

'Well, Dick, we're friends now,' said Matcham.

'Nay, I never was unfriends,' answered Dick. 'Y' are a brave lad in your way, albeit something of a milksop, too. I never met your like before this day. But, prithee, fetch back your breath, and let us on. Here is no place for chatter.'

'My foot hurts shrewdly,' said Matcham.

'Nay, I had forgot your foot,' returned Dick. 'Well, we must go the gentlier. I would I knew rightly where we were. I have clean lost the path; yet that may be for the better, too. An they watch the ferry, they watch the path, belike, as well. I would Sir Daniel were back with two-score men; he would sweep me these rascals as the wind sweeps leaves. Come, Jack, lean ye on my shoulder, ye poor shrew . Nay, y' are not tall enough. What age are ye, for a wager? – twelve?'

'Nay, I am sixteen,' said Matcham.

'Y' are poorly grown to height then,' answered Dick. 'But take my hand. We shall go softly, never fear. I owe you a life; I am a good repayer, Jack, of good or evil.'

They began to go forward up the slope.

'We must hit the road, early or late,' continued Dick; 'and then for a fresh start. By the mass! but y' 'ave a rickety hand, Jack. If I had a hand like that, I would think shame. I tell you,' he went on, with a sudden chuckle, 'I swear by the mass I believe Hugh Ferryman took you for a maid.'

'Nay, never!' cried the other, colouring high.

''A did, though, for a wager!' Dick exclaimed. 'Small blame to him. Ye look liker maid than man; and I tell ye more – y' are a strange-looking rogue for a boy; but for a hussy, Jack, ye would be fair right – ye would. Ye would be well-favoured for a wench.'

'Well,' said Matcham, 'ye know right well that I am none.'

'Nay, I know that; I do but jest,' said Dick. 'Ye'll be a man before your mother, Jack. What cheer, my bully? Ye shall strike shrewd strokes. Now, which, I marvel, of you or me, shall be first knighted, Jack? for knighted I shall be, or die for't. "Sir Richard Shelton, Knight": it soundeth bravely. But "Sir John Matcham" soundeth not amiss.'

'Prithee, Dick, stop till I drink,' said the other, pausing where a little clear spring welled out of the slope into a gravelled basin no bigger than a pocket. 'And O, Dick, if I might come by anything to eat! – my very heart aches with hunger.'

'Why, fool, did ye not eat at Kettley?' asked Dick.

'I had made a vow – it was a sin I had been led into,' stammered Matcham; 'but now, if it were but dry bread, I would eat it greedily.'

'Sit ye, then, and eat,' said Dick, 'while that I scout a little forward for the road.' And he took a wallet from his girdle, wherein were bread and pieces of dry bacon, and, while Matcham fell heartily to, struck farther forth among the trees.

A little beyond there was a dip in the ground, where a streamlet soaked among dead leaves; and beyond that, again, the trees were better grown and stood wider, and oak and beech began to take the place of willow and elm. The continued tossing and pouring of the wind among the leaves sufficiently concealed the sounds of his footsteps on the mast; it was for the ear what a moonless night is to the eye; but for all that Dick went cautiously, slipping from one big trunk to another, and looking sharply about him as he went. Suddenly a doe passed like a shadow through the underwood in front of him, and he paused, disgusted at the chance. This part of the wood had been certainly deserted, but now that the poor deer had run, she was like a messenger he should have sent before him to announce his coming; and instead of pushing further, he turned him to the nearest well-grown tree, and rapidly began to climb.

Luck had served him well. The oak on which he had mounted was one of the tallest in that quarter of the wood, and easily out-topped its neighbours by a fathom and a half; and when Dick had clambered into the topmost fork and clung there, swinging dizzily in the great wind, he saw behind him the whole fenny plain as far as Kettley, and the Till wandering among woody islets, and in front of him the white line of high-road winding through the forest. The boat had been righted – it was even now midway on the ferry. Beyond that there was no sign of man, nor aught moving but the wind. He was about to descend, when, taking a last view, his eye lit upon a string of moving points about the middle of the fen. Plainly a small troop was threading the causeway, and that at a good pace; and this gave him some concern as he shinned vigorously down the trunk and returned across the wood for his companion.

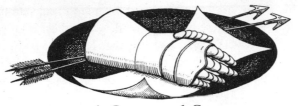

4 A Greenwood Company

Matcham was well rested and revived; and the two lads, winged by what Dick had seen, hurried through the remainder of the outwood, crossed the road in safety, and began to mount into the high ground of Tunstall Forest. The trees grew more and more in groves, with heathy places in between, sandy, gorsy, and dotted with old yews. The ground became more and more uneven, full of pits and hillocks. And with every step of the ascent the wind still blew the shriller, and the trees bent before the gusts like fishing-rods.

They had just entered one of the clearings, when Dick suddenly clapped down upon his face among the brambles, and began to crawl slowly backwards towards the shelter of the grove. Matcham, in great bewilderment, for he could see no reason for this flight, still imitated his companion's course; and it was not until they had gained the harbour of a thicket that he turned and begged him to explain.

For all reply, Dick pointed with his finger.

At the far end of the clearing, a fir grew high above the neighbouring wood, and planted its black shock of foliage clear against the sky. For about fifty feet above the ground the trunk grew straight and solid like a column. At that level, it split into two massive boughs; and in the fork, like a mast-headed seaman, there stood a man in a green tabard, spying far and wide. The sun glistened upon his hair; with one hand he shaded his eyes to look abroad, and he kept slowly rolling his head from side to side with the regularity of a machine.

The lads exchanged glances.

'Let us try to the left,' said Dick. 'We had near fallen foully, Jack.'

Ten minutes afterwards they struck into a beaten path.

'Here is a piece of forest that I know not,' Dick remarked. 'Where goeth me this track?'

'Let us even try,' said Matcham.

A few yards farther the path came to the top of a ridge and began to

'*Yet a little farther and they came forth before the ruins of the house*'

go down abruptly into a cup-shaped hollow. At the foot, out of a thick
wood of flowering hawthorn, two or three roofless gables, blackened as
if by fire, and a single tall chimney marked the ruins of a house.

'What may this be?' whispered Matcham

'Nay, by the mass, I know not,' answered Dick. 'I am all at sea. Let
us go warily.'

With beating hearts, they descended through the hawthorns. Here
and there they passed signs of recent cultivation: fruit-trees and pot-
herbs ran wild among the thicket; a sun-dial had fallen in the grass; it
seemed they were treading what once had been a garden. Yet a little
farther and they came forth before the ruins of the house.

'What may this be?' whispered Matcham.

It had been a pleasant mansion and a strong. A dry ditch was dug
deep about it; but it was now choked with masonry, and bridged by a
fallen rafter. The two farther walls still stood, the sun shining through
their empty windows; but the remainder of the building had collapsed,
and now lay in a great cairn of ruin, grimed with fire. Already in the
interior a few plants were springing green among the chinks.

'Now I bethink me,' whispered Dick, 'this must be Grimstone. It
was a hold of one Simon Malmesbury; Sir Daniel was his bane! 'Twas
Bennet Hatch that burned it, now five years agone. In sooth, 'twas
pity, for it was a fair house.'

Down in the hollow, where no wind blew, it was both warm and
still, and Matcham, laying one hand upon Dick's arm, held up a
warning finger.

'Hist!' he said.

Then came a strange sound, breaking on the quiet. It was twice
repeated ere they recognized its nature. It was the sound of a big man
clearing his throat; and just then a hoarse, untuneful voice broke into
singing:

'Then up and spake the master, the king of the outlaws:
  "What make ye here, my merry men, among the greenwood shaws?"
And Gamelyn made answer -- he looked never adown:
  "O, they must need to walk in wood that may not walk in town!" '

The singer paused, a faint clink of iron followed, and then silence.

The two lads stood looking at each other. Whoever he might be,
their invisible neighbour was just beyond the ruin. And suddenly the

colour came into Matcham's face, and next moment he had crossed the fallen rafter, and was climbing cautiously on the huge pile of lumber that filled the interior of the roofless house. Dick would have withheld him, had he been in time: as it was, he was fain to follow.

Right in the corner of the ruin, two rafters had fallen crosswise, and protected a clear space no larger than a pew in church. Into this the lads silently lowered themselves. There they were perfectly concealed, and through an arrow loophole commanded a view upon the farther side.

Peering through this, they were struck stiff with terror at their predicament. To retreat was impossible; they scarce dared to breathe. Upon the very margin of the ditch, not thirty feet from where they crouched, an iron cauldron bubbled and steamed above a glowing fire; and close by, in an attitude of listening, as though he had caught some sound of their clambering among the ruins, a tall, red-faced, battered-looking man stood poised, an iron spoon in his right hand, a horn and a formidable dagger at his belt. Plainly this was the singer; plainly he had been stirring the cauldron, when some incautious step among the lumber had fallen upon his ear. A little farther off another man lay slumbering, rolled in a brown cloak, with a butterfly hovering above his face. All this was in a clearing white with daisies; and at the extreme verge a bow, a sheaf of arrows, and part of a deer's carcass hung upon a flowering hawthorn.

Presently the fellow relaxed from his attitude of attention, raised the spoon to his mouth, tasted its contents, nodded and then fell again to stirring and singing.

'Oh, they must need to walk in wood that may not walk in town.'

he croaked, taking up his song where he had left it.

'O, sir, we walk not here at all an evil thing to do,
But if we meet with the good king's deer to shoot a shaft into.'

Still as he sang, he took from time to time another spoonful of the broth, blew upon it, and tasted it, with all the airs of an experienced cook. At length, apparently, he judged the mess was ready, for, taking the horn from his girdle, he blew three modulated calls.

The other fellow awoke, rolled over, brushed away the butterfly, and looked about him.

'How now, brother?' he said. 'Dinner?'

'Ay, sot,' replied the cook, 'dinner it is, and a dry dinner, too, with neither ale nor bread. But there is little pleasure in the greenwood now; time was when a good fellow could live here like a mitred abbot, set aside the rain and the white frosts; he had his heart's desire both of ale and wine. But now are men's spirits dead, and this John Amend-All, save us and guard us! but a stuffed booby to scare crows withal.'

'Nay,' returned the other, 'y' are too set on meat and drinking, Lawless. Bide ye a bit; the good time cometh.'

'Look ye,' returned the cook, 'I have even waited for this good time sith that I was so high. I have been a grey friar; I have been a king's archer; I have been a shipman, and sailed the salt seas; and I have been in greenwood before this, forsooth! and shot the king's deer. What cometh of it? Naught! I were better to have bided in the cloister. John Abbot availeth more than John Amend-All. By'r Lady! here they come.'

One after another, tall likely fellows began to stroll into the lawn. Each as he came produced a knife and a horn cup, helped himself from the cauldron, and sat down upon the grass to eat. They were very variously equipped and armed; some in rusty smocks, and with nothing but a knife and an old bow; others in the height of forest gallantry, all in Lincoln green, both hood and jerkin, with dainty peacock arrows in their belts, a horn upon a baldrick, and a sword and dagger at their sides. They came in the silence of hunger, and scarce growled a salutation, but fell instantly to meat.

There were, perhaps, a score of them already gathered, when a sound of suppressed cheering arose close by among the hawthorns, and immediately after five or six woodmen carrying a stretcher debouched upon the lawn. A tall, lusty fellow, somewhat grizzled, and as brown as a smoked ham, walked before them with an air of some authority, his bow at his back, a bright boar-spear in his hand.

'Lads!' he cried, 'good fellows all, and my right merry friends, y' have sung this while on a dry whistle and lived at little ease. But what said I ever? Abide Fortune constantly; she turneth, turneth swift. And lo! here is her little firstling – even that good creature, ale!'

There was a murmur of applause as the bearers set down the stretcher and displayed a goodly cask.

'And now haste ye, boys,' the man continued. 'There is work

toward. A handful of archers are but now come to the ferry; murrey and blue is their wear; they are our butts – they shall all taste arrows – no man of them shall struggle through this wood. For, lads, we are here some fifty strong, each man of us most foully wronged; for some they have lost lands, and some friends; and some they have been outlawed – all oppressed! Who, then, hath done this evil? Sir Daniel, by the rood! Shall he then profit? Shall he sit snug in our houses? shall he till our fields? shall he suck the bone he robbed us of? I trow not. He getteth him strength at law; he gaineth cases; nay, there is one case he shall not gain – I have a writ here at my belt that, please the saints, shall conquer him.'

Lawless the cook was by this time already at his second horn of ale. He raised it, as if to pledge the speaker.

'Master Ellis,' he said, 'y' are for vengeance – well it becometh you! – but your poor brother o' the greenwood, that had never lands to lose nor friends to think upon, looketh rather, for his poor part, to the profit of the thing. He had liever a gold noble and a pottle of canary wine than all the vengeances in purgatory.'

'Lawless,' replied the other, 'to reach the Moat House, Sir Daniel must pass the forest. We shall make that passage dearer, pardy, than any battle. Then, when he has got to earth with such ragged handful as escapeth us – all his great friends fallen and fled away, and none to give him aid – we shall beleaguer that old fox about, and great shall be the fall of him. 'Tis a fat buck; he will make a dinner for us all.'

'Ay,' returned Lawless, 'I have eaten many of these dinners beforehand; but the cooking of them is hot work, good Master Ellis. And meanwhile what do we? We make black arrows, we write rhymes, and we drink fair cold water, that discomfortable drink.'

'Y' are untrue, Will Lawless. Ye still smell of the Grey Friars' buttery; greed is your undoing,' answered Ellis. 'We took twenty pounds from Appleyard. We took seven marks from the messenger last night. A day ago we had fifty from the merchant.'

'And to-day,' said one of the men, 'I stopped a fat pardoner riding apace for Holywood. Here is his purse.'

Ellis counted the contents.

'Five-score shillings!' he grumbled. 'Fool, he had more in his sandal, or stitched into his tippet. Y' are but a child, Tom Cuckow; ye have lost the fish.'

But, for all that, Ellis pocketed the purse with nonchalance. He stood leaning on his boar-spear, and looked round upon the rest. They, in various attitudes, took greedily of the venison pottage, and liberally washed it down with ale. This was a good day; they were in luck; but business pressed, and they were speedy in their eating. The first comers had by this time even despatched their dinner. Some lay down upon the grass and fell instantly asleep, like boa-constrictors; others talked together, or overhauled their weapons; and one, whose humour was particularly gay, holding forth an ale-horn, began to sing:

> 'Here is no law in good green shaw,
>   Here is no lack of meat;
> 'Tis merry and quiet, with deer for our diet,
>   In summer, when all is sweet.
>
> 'Come winter again, with wind and rain –
>   Come winter, with snow and sleet,
> Get home to your places, with hoods on your faces,
>   And sit by the fire and eat.'

All this while the two lads had listened and lain close; only Richard had unslung his cross-bow, and held ready in one hand the windac, or grappling-iron, that he used to bend it. Otherwise they had not dared to stir; and this scene of forest life had gone on before their eyes like a scene upon a theatre. But now there came a strange interruption. The tall chimney which overtopped the remainder of the ruins rose right above their hiding-place. There came a whistle in the air, and then a sounding smack, and the fragments of a broken arrow fell about their ears. Someone from the upper quarters of the wood, perhaps the very sentinel they saw posted in the fir, had shot an arrow at the chimney-top.

Matcham could not restrain a little cry, which he instantly stifled, and even Dick started with surprise, and dropped the windac from his fingers. But to the fellows on the lawn, this shaft was an expected signal. They were all afoot together, tightening their belts, testing their bow-strings, loosening sword and dagger in the sheath. Ellis held up his hand; his face had suddenly assumed a look of savage energy; the white of his eyes shone in his sun-brown face.

'Lads,' he said, 'ye know your places. Let not one man's soul escape you. Appleyard was a whet before a meal; but now we go to table. I have three men whom I will bitterly avenge – Harry Shelton,

Simon Malmesbury, and' – striking his broad bosom – 'and Ellis Duckworth, by the mass!'

Another man came, red with hurry, through the thorns.

' 'Tis not Sir Daniel!' he panted. 'They are but seven. Is the arrow gone?'

'It struck but now,' replied Ellis.

'A murrain!' cried the messenger. 'Methought I heard it whistle. And I go dinnerless!'

In the space of a minute, some running, some walking sharply, according as their stations were nearer or farther away, the men of the Black Arrow had all disappeared from the neighbourhood of the ruined house; and the cauldron, and the fire, which was now burning low, and the dead deer's carcase on the hawthorn, remained alone to testify they had been there.

5 'Bloody as the Hunter'

The lads lay quiet till the last footstep had melted on the wind. Then they arose, and with many an ache, for they were weary with constraint, clambered through the ruins, and recrossed the ditch upon the rafter. Matcham had picked up the windac and went first, Dick following stiffly, with his cross-bow on his arm.

'And now,' said Matcham, 'forth to Holywood.'

'To Holywood!' cried Dick, 'when good fellows stand shot? Not I! I would see you hanged first, Jack!'

'Ye would leave me, would ye?' Matcham asked.

'Ay, by my sooth!' returned Dick. 'An I be not in time to warn these lads, I will go die with them. What! would ye have me leave my own men that I have lived among? I trow not! Give me my windac.'

But there was nothing further from Matcham's mind.

'Dick,' he said, 'ye sware before the saints that ye would see me safe to Holywood. Would ye be forsworn? Would you desert me – a perjurer?'

'Nay, I sware for the best,' returned Dick. 'I meant it too; but now! But look ye, Jack, turn again with me. Let me but warn these men, and if needs must, stand shot with them; then shall all be clear, and I will on again to Holywood and purge mine oath.'

'Ye but deride me,' answered Matcham. 'These men ye go to succour are the same that hunt me to my ruin.'

Dick scratched his head.

'I cannot help it, Jack,' he said. 'Here is no remedy. What would ye? Ye run no great peril, man; and these are in the way of death. Death!' he added. 'Think of it! What a murrain do ye keep me here for? Give me the windac. Saint George! shall they all die?'

'Richard Shelton,' said Matcham, looking him squarely in the face, 'would ye, then, join party with Sir Daniel? Have ye not ears? Heard ye not this Ellis, what he said? or have ye no heart for your own kindly blood and the father that men slew? "Harry Shelton," he said; and Sir Harry Shelton was your father, as the sun shines in heaven.'

'What would ye?' Dick cried again. 'Would ye have me credit thieves?'

'Nay, I have heard it before now,' returned Matcham. 'The fame goeth currently, it was Sir Daniel slew him. He slew him under oath; in his own house he shed the innocent blood. Heaven wearies for the avenging on 't; and you – the man's son – ye go about to comfort and defend the murderer!'

'Jack,' cried the lad, 'I know not. It may be; what know I? But, see here: This man hath bred me up and fostered me, and his men I have hunted with and played among; and to leave them in the hour of peril – O, man, if I did that, I were stark dead to honour! Nay, Jack, ye would not ask it; ye would not wish me to be base.'

'But your father, Dick?' said Matcham, somewhat wavering. 'Your father? and your oath to me? Ye took the saints to witness.'

'My father?' cried Shelton. 'Nay, he would have me go! If Sir Daniel slew him, when the hour comes this hand shall slay Sir Daniel; but neither him nor his will I desert in peril. And for mine oath, good Jack, ye shall absolve me of it here. For the lives' sake of many men that hurt you not, and for mine honour, ye shall set me free.'

'I, Dick? never!' returned Matcham. 'An ye leave me, y' are forsworn, and so I shall declare it.'

'My blood heats,' said Dick. 'Give me the windac! Give it me!'

'I'll not,' said Matcham. 'I'll save you in your teeth.'

'Not?' cried Dick. 'I'll make you!'

'Try it,' said the other.

They stood, looking in each other's eyes, each ready for a spring. Then Dick leaped; and though Matcham turned instantly and fled, in two bounds he was overtaken, the windac was twisted from his grasp; he was thrown roughly to the ground, and Dick stood across him, flushed and menacing, with doubled fist. Matcham lay where he had fallen, with his face in the grass, not thinking of resistance.

Dick bent his bow.

'I'll teach you!' he cried fiercely. 'Oath or no oath, ye may go hang for me!'

And he turned and began to run. Matcham was on his feet at once, and began running after him.

'What d'ye want?' cried Dick, stopping. 'What make ye after me? Stand off!'

'I will follow an I please,' said Matcham. 'This wood is free to me.'

'Stand back, by'r Lady!' returned Dick, raising his bow.

'Ah, y' are a brave boy!' retorted Matcham. 'Shoot!'

Dick lowered his weapon in some confusion.

'See here,' he said. 'Y' have done me ill enough. Go, then. Go your way in fair wise; or, whether I will or not, I must even drive you to it.'

'Well,' said Matcham doggedly, 'y' are the stronger. Do your worst. I shall not leave to follow thee, Dick, unless thou makest me,' he added.

Dick was almost beside himself. It went against his heart to beat a creature so defenceless; and, for the life of him, he knew no other way to rid himself of this unwelcome, and, as he began to think, perhaps untrue companion.

'Y' are mad, I think,' he cried. 'Fool-fellow, I am hasting to your foes; as fast as foot can carry me, go I thither.'

'I care not, Dick,' replied the lad. 'If y' are bound to die, Dick, I'll die too. I would liever go with you to prison than to go free without you.'

'Well,' returned the other, 'I may stand no longer prating. Follow me, if ye must; but if ye play me false, it shall but little advance you, mark ye that. Shalt have a quarrel in thine inwards, boy.'

So saying, Dick took once more to his heels, keeping in the margin of the thicket, and looking briskly about him as he went. At a good pace he rattled out of the dell, and came again into the more open quarters of the wood. To the left a little eminence appeared, spotted with golden gorse, and crowned with a black tuft of firs.

'I shall see from there,' he thought, and struck for it across a heathy clearing.

He had gone but a few yards, when Matcham touched him on the arm, and pointed. To the eastward of the summit there was a dip, and, as it were, a valley passing to the other side; the heath was not yet out; all the ground was rusty, like an unscoured buckler, and dotted sparingly with yews; and there, one following another, Dick saw half a score green jerkins mounting the ascent, and marching at their head, conspicuous by his boar-spear, Ellis Duckworth in person. One after another gained the top, showed for a moment against the sky, and then dipped upon the further side, until the last was gone.

Dick looked at Matcham with a kindlier eye.

'So y' are to be true to me, Jack?' he asked. 'I thought ye were of the other party.'

Matcham began to sob.

'What cheer!' cried Dick. 'Now the saints behold us! would ye snivel for a word?'

'Ye hurt me,' sobbed Matcham. 'Ye hurt me when ye threw me down. Y' are a coward to abuse your strength.'

'Nay, that is fool's talk,' said Dick roughly. 'Y' had no title to my windac, Master John. I would 'a' done right to have well basted you. If ye go with me, ye must obey me; and so, come.'

Matcham had half a thought to stay behind; but, seeing that Dick continued to scour full-tilt towards the eminence and not so much as looked across his shoulder, he soon thought better of that, and began to run in turn. But the ground was very difficult and steep; Dick had already a long start, and had, at any rate, the lighter heels, and he had long since come to the summit, crawled forward through the firs, and ensconced himself in a thick tuft of gorse, before Matcham, panting like a deer, rejoined him, and lay down in silence by his side.

Below, in the bottom of a considerable valley, the short cut from Tunstall hamlet wound downwards to the ferry. It was well beaten, and the eye followed it easily from point to point. Here it was bordered by open glades; there the forest closed upon it; every hundred yards it ran beside an ambush. Far down the path, the sun shone on seven steel salets, and from time to time, as the trees opened, Selden and his men could be seen riding briskly, still bent upon Sir Daniel's mission. The wind had somewhat fallen, but still tussled merrily with the trees, and, perhaps, had Appleyard been there, he would have drawn a warning from the troubled conduct of the birds.

'Now, mark,' Dick whispered. 'They be already well advanced into the wood; their safety lieth rather in continuing forward. But see ye where this wide glade runneth down before us, and in the midst of it, these two-score trees make like an island? There were their safety. An they but come sound as far as that, I will make shift to warn them. But my heart misgiveth me; they are but seven against so many, and they but carry cross-bows. The long-bow, Jack, will have the uppermost ever.'

Meanwhile, Selden and his men still wound up the path, ignorant of their danger, and momently drew nearer hand. Once, indeed, they paused, drew into a group, and seemed to point and listen. But it was something from far away across the plain that had arrested their attention – a hollow growl of cannon that came, from time to time, upon the wind, and told of the great battle. It was worth a thought, to be sure; for if the voice of the big guns were thus become audible in Tunstall Forest, the fight must have rolled ever eastward, and the day, by consequence, gone sore against Sir Daniel and the lords of the dark rose.

But presently the little troop began again to move forward, and came next to a very open, heathy portion of the way, where but a single tongue of forest ran down to join the road. They were but just abreast of this, when an arrow shone flying. One of the men threw up his arms, his horse reared, and both fell and struggled together in a mass. Even from where the boys lay they could hear the rumour of the men's voices crying out; they could see the startled horses prancing, and, presently, as the troop began to recover from their first surprise, one fellow beginning to dismount. A second arrow from somewhat farther off glanced in a wide arch; a second rider bit the dust. The man who was dismounting lost hold upon the rein, and his horse fled galloping, and dragged him by the foot along the road, bumping from stone to stone, and battered by the fleeing hoofs. The four who still kept the saddle instantly broke and scattered; one wheeled and rode, shrieking, towards the ferry; the other three, with loose rein and flying raiment, came galloping up the road from Tunstall. From every clump they passed an arrow sped. Soon a horse fell, but the rider found his feet and continued to pursue his comrades till a second shot dispatched him. Another man fell; then another horse; out of the whole troop there was but one fellow left, and he on foot; only, in different directions, the noise of the galloping of three riderless horses was dying fast into the distance.

All this time not one of the assailants had for a moment showed himself. Here and there along the path, horse or man rolled, undispatched, in his agony; but no merciful enemy broke cover to put them from their pain.

The solitary survivor stood bewildered in the road beside his fallen charger. He had come the length of that broad glade, with the island of timber, pointed out by Dick. He was not, perhaps, five hundred yards from where the boys lay hidden; and they could see him plainly, looking to and fro in deadly expectation. But nothing came; and the man began to pluck up his courage, and suddenly unslung and bent his bow. At the same time, by something in his action, Dick recognized Selden.

At this offer of resistance, from all about him in the covert of the woods there went up the sound of laughter. A score of men, at least, for this was the very thickest of the ambush, joined in this cruel and untimely mirth. Then an arrow glanced over Selden's shoulder; and he leaped and ran a little back. Another dart struck quivering at his heel. He made for the cover. A third shaft leaped out right in his face, and fell short in front of him. And then the laughter was repeated loudly, rising and re-echoing from different thickets.

It was plain that his assailants were but baiting him, as men, in those days, baited the poor bull, or as the cat still trifles with the mouse. The skirmish was well over; farther down the road, a fellow in green was already calmly gathering the arrows; and now, in the evil pleasure of their hearts, they gave themselves the spectacle of their poor fellow-sinner in his torture.

Selden began to understand; he uttered a roar of anger, shouldered his cross-bow, and sent a quarrel at a venture into the wood. Chance favoured him, for a slight cry responded. Then, throwing down his weapon, Selden began to run before him up the glade, and almost in a straight line for Dick and Matcham.

The companions of the Black Arrow now began to shoot in earnest. But they were properly served; their chance had passed; most of them had now to shoot against the sun; and Selden, as he ran, bounded from side to side to baffle and deceive their aim. Best of all, by turning up the glade he had defeated their preparations; there were no marksmen posted higher up than the one whom he had just killed or wounded; and the confusion of the foresters' counsels soon became apparent. A whistle sounded thrice, and then again twice. It was repeated from another quarter. The woods on either side became full of the sound of people bursting through the underwood; and a bewildered deer ran out into the open, stood for a second on three feet, with nose in air, and then plunged again into the thicket.

Selden still ran, bounding; ever and again an arrow followed him, but still would miss. It began to appear as if he might escape. Dick had his bow armed, ready to support him; even Matcham, forgetful of his interest, took sides at heart for the poor fugitive; and both lads glowed and trembled in the ardour of their hearts.

He was within fifty yards of them, when an arrow struck him, and he fell. He was up again, indeed, upon the instant; but now he ran staggering, and, like a blind man, turned aside from his direction.

Dick leaped to his feet and waved to him.

'Here!' he cried. 'This way! here is help! Nay, run, fellow – run!'

But just then a second arrow struck Selden in the shoulder between the plates of his brigandine, and, piercing through his jack, brought him, like a stone, to earth.

'Oh, the poor heart!' cried Matcham, with clasped hands.

And Dick stood petrified upon the hill, a mark for archery.

Ten to one he had speedily been shot – for the foresters were furious with themselves, and taken unawares by Dick's appearance in the rear of their position – but instantly out of a quarter of the wood surprisingly near to the two lads, a stentorian voice arose, the voice of Ellis Duckworth.

'Hold!' he roared. 'Shoot not! Take him alive! It is young Shelton – Harry's son.'

And immediately after a shrill whistle sounded several times, and was again taken up and repeated farther off. The whistle it appeared, was John Amend-All's battle trumpet, by which he published his directions.

'Ah, foul fortune!' cried Dick. 'We are undone. Swiftly, Jack, come swiftly!'

And the pair turned and ran back through the open pine clump that covered the summit of the hill.

6 To the Day's End

It was, indeed, high time for them to run. On every side the company of the Black Arrow was making for the hill. Some, being better runners, or having open ground to run upon, had far outstripped the others, and were already close upon the goal; some, following valleys, had spread out to right and left, and outflanked the lads on either side.

Dick plunged into the nearest cover. It was a tall grove of oaks, firm under foot and clear of underbrush, and as it lay down hill, they made good speed. There followed next a piece of open, which Dick avoided, holding to his left. Two minutes after, and the same obstacle arising, the lads followed the same course. Thus it followed that, while the lads, bending continually to the left, drew nearer and nearer to the high road and the river which they had crossed an hour or two before, the great bulk of their pursuers were leaning to the other hand, and running towards Tunstall.

The lads paused to breathe. There was no sound of pursuit. Dick put his ear to the ground, and still there was nothing; but the wind, to be sure, still made a turmoil in the trees, and it was hard to make certain.

'On again!' said Dick; and, tired as they were, and Matcham limping with his injured foot, they pulled themselves together, and once more pelted down the hill.

Three minutes later, they were breasting through a low thicket of evergreen. High overhead, the tall trees made a continuous roof of foliage. It was a pillared grove, as high as a cathedral, and, except for the hollies among which the lads were struggling, open and smoothly swarded.

On the other side, pushing through the last fringe of evergreen, they blundered forth again into the open twilight of the grove.

'Stand!' cried a voice.

And there, between the huge stems, not fifty feet before them, they beheld a stout fellow in green, sore blown with running, who instantly drew an arrow to the head and covered them. Matcham stopped with a cry; but Dick, without a pause, ran straight upon the forester, drawing his dagger as he went. The other, whether he was startled by the daring of the onslaught or whether he was hampered by his orders, did not shoot; he stood wavering; and before he had time to come to himself, Dick bounded at his throat, and sent him sprawling backward on the turf. The arrow went one way and the bow another with a sounding twang. The disarmed forester grappled his assailant; but the dagger shone and descended twice. Then came a couple of groans, and then Dick rose to his feet again, and the man lay motionless, stabbed to the heart.

'On!' said Dick; and he once more pelted forward, Matcham trailing in the rear. To say truth, they made but poor speed of it by now, labouring dismally as they ran, and catching for their breath like fish. Matcham had a cruel stitch, and his head swam; and as for Dick, his knees were like lead. But they kept up the form of running with undiminished courage.

Presently they came to the end of the grove. It stopped abruptly; and there, a few yards before them, was the high road from Risingham to Shoreby, lying, at this point, between two even walls of forest.

At the sight Dick paused; and as soon as he stopped running, he became aware of a confused noise, which rapidly grew louder. It was at first like the rush of a very high gust of wind, but it soon became more definite, and resolved itself into the galloping of horses; and then, in a flash, a whole company of men-at-arms came driving round the corner, swept before the lads, and were gone again upon the instant. They rode as for their lives, in complete disorder; some of them were wounded: riderless horses galloped at their side with bloody saddles. They were plainly fugitives from the great battle.

The noise of their passage had scarce begun to die away towards Shoreby, before fresh hoofs came echoing in their wake, and another deserter clattered down the road; this time a single rider, and, by his splendid armour, a man of high degree. Close after him there followed several baggage-wagons, fleeing at an ungainly canter, the drivers flailing at the horses as if for life. These must have run early in the day; but their cowardice was not to save them. For just before they came abreast of where the lads stood wondering, a man in hacked armour, and seemingly beside himself with fury, overtook the wagons, and with the truncheon of a sword began to cut the drivers down. Some leaped from their places and plunged into the wood; the others he sabred as they sat, cursing them the while for cowards in a voice that was scarce human.

All this time the noise in the distance had continued to increase; the rumble of carts, the clatter of horses, the cries of men, a great, confused rumour, came swelling on the wind; and it was plain that the rout of a whole army was pouring, like an inundation, down the road.

Dick stood sombre. He had meant to follow the highway till the turn for Holywood, and now he had to change his plan. But above all, he had recognized the colours of Earl Risingham, and he knew that the battle had gone finally against the rose of Lancaster. Had Sir Daniel joined, and was he now a fugitive and ruined? or had he deserted to the side of York, and was he forfeit to honour? It was an ugly choice.

'Come,' he said sternly; and, turning on his heel, he began to walk forward through the grove, with Matcham limping in his rear.

For some time they continued to thread the forest in silence. It was now growing late; the sun was setting in the plain beyond Kettley; the tree-tops overhead glowed golden; but the shadows had begun to grow darker and the chill of the night to fall.

'If there was anything to eat!' cried Dick suddenly, pausing as he spoke.

Matcham sat down and began to weep.

'Ye can weep for your own supper, but when it was to save men's lives, your heart was hard enough,' said Dick contemptuously. 'Y 'ave seven deaths upon your conscience, Master John; I'll ne'er forgive you that.'

'Conscience!' cried Matcham, looking fiercely up. 'Mine! And ye have the man's red blood upon your dagger! And wherefore did ye slay him, the poor soul? He drew his arrow, but he let not fly; he held you in his hand, and spared you! 'Tis as brave to kill a kitten as a man that not defends himself.'

Dick was struck dumb.

'I slew him fair. I ran me in upon his bow,' he cried.

'It was a coward blow,' returned Matcham. 'Y' are but a lout and bully, Master Dick; ye but abuse advantages; let there come a stronger, we will see you truckle at his boot! Ye care not for vengeance, neither – for your father's death that goes unpaid, and his poor ghost that clamoureth for justice. But if there come but a poor creature in your hands that lacketh skill and strength, and would befriend you, down she shall go!'

Dick was too furious to observe that 'she.'

'Marry!' he cried, 'and here is news! Of any two the one will still be stronger. The better man throweth the worse, and the worse is well served. Ye deserve a belting, Master Matcham, for your ill-guidance and unthankfulness to me-ward; and what ye deserve ye shall have.'

And Dick, who, even in his angriest temper, still preserved the appearance of composure, began to unbuckle his belt.

'Here shall be your supper,' he said grimly.

Matcham had stopped his tears; he was as white as a sheet, but he looked Dick steadily in the face, and never moved. Dick took a step, swinging the belt. Then he paused, embarrassed by the large eyes and the thin, weary face of his companion. His courage began to subside.

'Say ye were in the wrong, then,' he said lamely.

'Nay,' said Matcham, 'I was in the right. Come, cruel! I be lame; I be weary; I resist not; I ne'er did thee hurt; come, beat me – coward!'

Dick raised the belt at this last provocation, but Matcham winced, and drew himself together with so cruel an apprehension, that his heart failed him yet again. The strap fell by his side, and he stood irresolute, feeling like a fool.

'A plague upon thee, shrew!' he said. 'An ye be so feeble of hand, ye should keep the closer guard upon your tongue. But I'll be hanged before I beat you!' and he put on his belt again. 'Beat you I will not,' he continued; 'but forgive you? – never. I knew ye not; ye were my master's enemy; I lent you my horse; my dinner ye have eaten; y' 'ave called me a man o' wood, a coward, and a bully. Nay, by the mass! the measure is filled, and runneth over. 'Tis a great thing to be weak, I trow; ye can do your worst, yet shall none punish you; ye may steal a man's weapons in the hour of need, yet may the man not take his own again – y' are weak, forsooth! Nay, then, if one cometh charging at you with a lance, and crieth he is weak, ye must let him pierce your body through! Tut! fool words!'

'And yet ye beat me not,' returned Matcham.

'Let be,' said Dick, 'let be. I will instruct you. Y' 'ave been ill-nurtured, methinks, and yet ye have the makings of some good, and, beyond all question, saved me from the river. Nay, I had forgotten it; I am as thankless as thyself. But, come, let us on. An we be for Holywood this night, ay, or to-morrow early, we had best set forward speedily.'

But though Dick had talked himself back into his usual good humour, Matcham had forgiven him nothing. His violence, the recollection of the forester whom he had slain – above all, the vision of the upraised belt, were things not easily to be forgotten.

'I will thank you, for the form's sake,' said Matcham. 'But, in sooth, good Master Shelton, I had liever find my way alone. Here is a wide wood; prithee, let each choose his path; I owe you a dinner and a lesson. Fare ye well!'

'Nay,' cried Dick, 'if that be your tune, so be it, and a plague be with you!'

Each turned aside, and they began walking off severally, with no thought of the direction, intent solely on their quarrel. But Dick had not gone ten paces ere his name was called, and Matcham came running after.

'Dick,' he said, 'it were unmannerly to part so coldly. Here is my hand, and my heart with it. For all that wherein you have so excellently served and helped me – not for the form, but from the heart, I thank you. Fare ye right well.'

'Well, lad,' returned Dick, taking the hand which was offered him, 'good speed to you, if speed you may. But I misdoubt it shrewdly. Y' are too disputatious.'

So then they separated for the second time; and presently it was Dick who was running after Matcham.

'Here,' he said, 'take my cross-bow; shalt not go unarmed.'

'A cross-bow!' said Matcham. 'Nay, boy, I have neither the strength to bend nor yet the skill to aim with it. It were no help to me, good boy. But yet I thank you.'

The night had now fallen, and under the trees they could no longer read each other's face.

'I will go some little way with you,' said Dick, 'The night is dark. I would fain leave you on a path, at least. My mind misgiveth me, y' are likely to be lost.'

Without any more words, he began to walk forward, and the other once more followed him. The blackness grew thicker and thicker; only here and there, in open places, they saw the sky, dotted with small stars. In the distance, the noise of the rout of the Lancastrian army still continued to be faintly audible; but with every step they left it farther in the rear.

At the end of half an hour of silent progress they came forth upon a broad patch of heathy open. It glimmered in the light of the stars, shaggy with fern and islanded with clumps of yew. And here they paused and looked upon each other.

'Y' are weary?' Dick said.

'Nay, I am so weary,' answered Matcham, 'that methinks I could lie down and die.'

'I hear the chiding of a river,' returned Dick. 'Let us go so far forth, for I am sore athirst.'

The ground sloped down gently, and, sure enough, in the bottom, they found a little murmuring river, running among willows. Here they threw themselves down together by the brink; and putting their mouths to the level of a starry pool, they drank their fill.

'Dick,' said Matcham, 'it may not be. I can no more.'

'I saw a pit as we came down,' said Dick. 'Let us lie down therein and sleep.'

'Nay, but with all my heart!' cried Matcham.

The pit was sandy and dry; a shock of brambles hung upon one edge, and made a partial shelter; and there the two lads lay down, keeping close together for the sake of warmth, their quarrel all forgotten. And soon sleep fell upon them like a cloud, and under the dew and stars they rested peacefully.

7 The Hooded Face

They awoke in the grey of the morning; the birds were not yet in full song, but twittered here and there among the woods; the sun was not yet up, but the eastern sky was barred with solemn colours. Half-starved and over-weary as they were, they lay without moving, sunk in a delightful lassitude. And as they thus lay, the clang of a bell fell suddenly upon their ears.

'A bell!' said Dick, sitting up. 'Can we be, then, so near to Holywood?'

A little after, the bell clanged again, but this time somewhat nearer hand; and from that time forth, and still drawing nearer and nearer, it continued to sound brokenly abroad in the silence of the morning.

'Nay, what should this betoken?' said Dick, who was now broad awake.

'It is someone walking,' returned Matcham, 'and the bell tolleth ever as he moves.'

'I see that well,' said Dick. 'But wherefore? What maketh he in Tunstall Woods? Jack,' he added, 'laugh at me an ye will, but I like not the hollow sound of it.'

'Nay,' said Matcham, with a shiver, 'it hath a doleful note. An the day were not come——'

But just then the bell, quickening its pace, began to ring thick and hurried, and then it gave a single hammering jangle, and was silent for a space.

'It is as though the bearer had run for a paternoster-while, and then leaped the river,' Dick observed.

'And now beginneth he again to pace soberly forward,' added Matcham.

'Nay,' returned Dick, 'nay, not so soberly, Jack. 'Tis a man that walketh you right speedily. 'Tis a man in some fear of his life, or about some hurried business. See ye not how swift the beating draweth near?'

'It is now close by,' said Matcham.

They were now on the edge of the pit; and as the pit itself was on a certain eminence, they commanded a view over the greater proportion of the clearing, up to the thick woods that closed it in.

The daylight, which was very clear and grey, showed them a riband of white footpath wandering among the gorse. It passed some hundred yards from the pit, and ran the whole length of the clearing, east and west. By the line of its course, Dick judged it should lead more or less directly to the Moat House.

Upon this path, stepping forth from the margin of the wood, a white figure now appeared. It paused a little, and seemed to look about; and then, at a slow pace, and bent almost double, it began to draw near across the heath. At every step the bell clanked. Face it had none; a white hood, not even pierced with eyeholes, veiled the head; and as the creature moved, it seemed to feel its way with the tapping of a stick. Fear fell upon the lads, as cold as death.

'A leper!' said Dick, hoarsely.

'His touch is death,' said Matcham. 'Let us run.'

'Not so,' returned Dick. 'See ye not? – he is stone-blind. He guideth him with a staff. Let us lie still; the wind bloweth towards the path, and he will go by and hurt us not. Alas, poor soul, and we should rather pity him!'

'I will pity him when he is by,' replied Matcham.

The blind leper was now about half-way towards them, and just then the sun rose and shone full on his veiled face. He had been a tall man before he was bowed by his disgusting sickness, and even now he walked with a vigorous step. The dismal beating of his bell, the pattering of the stick, the eyeless screen before his countenance, and the knowledge that he was not only doomed to death and suffering, but shut out for ever from the touch of his fellow-men, filled the lads' bosoms with dismay; and at every step that brought him nearer, their courage and strength seemed to desert them.

As he came about level with the pit, he paused, and turned his face full upon the lads.

'Mary be my shield! He sees us!' said Matcham faintly.

'Hush!' whispered Dick. 'He doth but hearken. He is blind, fool!'

The leper looked or listened, whichever he was really doing, for some seconds. Then he began to move on again, but presently paused once more, and again turned and seemed to gaze upon the lads. Even

Dick became dead-white and closed his eyes, as if by the mere sight he might become infected. But soon the bell sounded, and this time, without any further hesitation, the leper crossed the remainder of the little heath and disappeared into the covert of the woods.

'He saw us,' said Matcham. 'I could swear it!'

'Tut!' returned Dick, recovering some sparks of courage. 'He but heard us. He was in fear, poor soul! An ye were blind, and walked in a perpetual night, ye would start yourself, if ever a twig rustled or a bird cried "Peep."'

'Dick, good Dick, he saw us,' repeated Matcham. 'When a man hearkeneth, he doth not as this man; he doth otherwise, Dick. This was seeing; it was not hearing. He means foully. Hark, else, if his bell be not stopped!'

Such was the case. The bell rang no longer.

'Nay,' said Dick, 'I like not that. Nay,' he cried again, 'I like that little. What may this betoken? Let us go, by the mass!'

'He hath gone east,' added Matcham. 'Good Dick, let us go westward straight. I shall not breathe till I have my back turned upon that leper.'

'Jack, y' are too cowardly,' replied Dick. 'We shall go fair for Holywood, or as fair, at least, as I can guide you, and that will be due north.'

They were afoot at once, passed the stream upon some stepping-stones, and began to mount on the other side, which was steeper, towards the margin of the wood. The ground became very uneven, full of knolls and hollows; trees grew scattered or in clumps; it became difficult to choose a path, and the lads somewhat wandered. They were weary, besides, with yesterday's exertions and the lack of food, and they moved but heavily and dragged their feet among the sand.

Presently, coming to the top of a knoll, they were aware of the leper, some hundred feet in front of them, crossing the line of their march by a hollow. His bell was silent, his staff no longer tapped the ground, and he went before him with the swift and assured footsteps of a man who sees. Next moment he had disappeared into a little thicket.

The lads, at the first glimpse, had crouched behind a tuft of gorse; there they lay, horror-struck.

'Certain, he pursueth us,' said Dick, 'certain. He held the clapper of his bell in one hand, saw ye? that it should not sound. Now may the saints aid and guide us, for I have no strength to combat pestilence!'

'What maketh he?' cried Matcham. 'What doth he want? Who ever heard the like, that a leper, out of mere malice, should pursue unfortunates? Hath he not his bell to that very end, that people may avoid him? Dick, there is below this something deeper.'

'Nay, I care not,' moaned Dick; 'the strength is gone out of me; my legs are like water. The saints be mine assistance!'

'Would ye lie there idle?' cried Matcham. 'Let us back into the open. We have the better chance; he cannot steal upon us unawares.'

'Not I,' said Dick. 'My time is come; and peradventure he may pass us by.'

'Bend me, then, your bow!' cried the other. 'What, will ye be a man?'

Dick crossed himself. 'Would ye have me shoot upon a leper?' he cried. 'The hand would fail me. Nay, now,' he added – 'nay, now, let be! With sound men I will fight, but not with ghosts and lepers. Which this is, I wot not. One or other, Heaven be our protection!'

'Now,' said Matcham, 'if this be man's courage, what a poor thing is man! But sith ye will do naught, let us lie close.'

Then came a single, broken jangle on the bell.

'He hath missed his hold upon the clapper,' whispered Matcham. 'Saints! how near he is!'

But Dick answered never a word; his teeth were near chattering.

Soon they saw a piece of the white robe between some bushes; then the leper's head was thrust forth from behind a trunk, and he seemed narrowly to scan the neighbourhood before he once again withdrew. To their stretched senses the whole bush appeared alive with rustlings and the creak of twigs; and they heard the beating of each other's heart.

Suddenly, with a cry, the leper sprang into the open close by, and ran straight upon the lads. They, shrieking aloud, separated and began to run different ways. But their horrible enemy fastened upon Matcham, ran him swiftly down, and had him almost instantly a prisoner. The lad gave one scream that echoed high and far over the forest, he had one spasm of struggling, and then all his limbs relaxed, and he fell limp into his captor's arms.

Dick heard the cry and turned. He saw Matcham fall; and on the instant his spirit and his strength revived. With a cry of pity and anger, he unslung and bent his arblast. But ere he had time to shoot the leper held up his hand.

'And then laying down Matcham on the turf, he undid
the hood from off his face'

'Hold your shot, Dickon!' cried a familiar voice. 'Hold your shot, mad wag! Know ye not a friend?'

And then laying down Matcham on the turf, he undid the hood from off his face, and disclosed the features of Sir Daniel Brackley.

'Sir Daniel!' cried Dick.

'Ay, by the mass, Sir Daniel!' returned the knight. 'Would ye shoot upon your guardian, rogue? But here is this——' And there he broke off, and pointing to Matcham, asked: 'How call ye him, Dick?'

'Nay,' said Dick. 'I call him Master Matcham. Know ye him not? He said ye knew him!'

'Ay,' replied Sir Daniel, 'I know the lad'; and he chuckled. 'But he has fainted; and, by my sooth, he might have had less to faint for. Hey, Dick? Did I put fear of death upon you?'

'Indeed, Sir Daniel, ye did that,' said Dick, and sighed again at the mere recollection. 'Nay, sir, saving your respect, I had as lief 'a' met the devil in person; and to speak truth, I am yet all a-quake. But what made ye, sir, in such a guise?'

Sir Daniel's brow grew suddenly black with anger.

'What made I?' he said. 'Ye do well to mind me of it! What? I skulked for my poor life in my own wood of Tunstall, Dick. We were ill sped at the battle; we but got there to be swept among the rout. Where be all my good men-at-arms? Dick, by the mass, I know not! We were swept down; the shot fell thick among us; I have not seen one man in my own colours since I saw three fall. For myself, I came sound to Shoreby, and being mindful of the Black Arrow, got me this gown and bell, and came softly by the path for the Moat House. There is no disguise to be compared with it, the jingle of this bell would scare me the stoutest outlaw in the forest; they would all turn pale to hear it. At length I came by you and Matcham. I could see but evilly through this same hood, and was not sure of you, being chiefly, and for many a good cause, astonished at the finding you together. Moreover, in the open, where I had to go slowly and tap with my staff, I feared to disclose myself. But see,' he added, 'this poor shrew begins a little to revive. A little good canary will comfort the heart of it.'

The knight, from under his long dress, produced a stout bottle, and began to rub the temples and wet the lips of the patient, who returned gradually to consciousness, and began to roll dim eyes from one to another.

'What cheer, Jack!' said Dick. 'It was no leper, after all; it was Sir Daniel! See!'

'Swallow me a good draught of this,' said the knight. 'This will give you manhood. Thereafter, I will give you both a meal, and we shall all three on to Tunstall. For, Dick,' he continued, laying forth bread and meat upon the grass, 'I will avow to you, in all good conscience, it irks me sorely to be safe between four walls. Not since I backed a horse have I been pressed so hard; peril of life, jeopardy of land and livelihood, and to sum up, all these losels in the wood to hunt me down. But I be not yet shent. Some of my lads will pick me their way home. Hatch hath ten fellows; Selden, he had six. Nay, we shall soon be strong again; and if I can but buy my peace with my right fortunate and undeserving Lord of York, why, Dick, we'll be a man again and go a-horseback!'

And so saying, the knight filled himself a horn of canary, and pledged his ward in dumb show.

'Selden——' Dick faltered, 'Selden——' And he paused again.

Sir Daniel put down the wine untasted.

'How!' he cried, in a changed voice. 'Selden? Speak! What of Selden?'

Dick stammered forth the tale of the ambush and the massacre.

The knight heard in silence; but as he listened, his countenance became convulsed with rage and grief.

'Now here,' he cried, 'on my right hand, I swear to avenge it! If that I fail, if that I spill not ten men's souls for each, may this hand wither from my body! I broke this Duckworth like a rush; I beggared him to his door; I burned the thatch above his head; I drove him from this country; and now, cometh he back to beard me? Nay, but, Duckworth, this time it shall go bitter hard!'

He was silent for some time, his face working.

'Eat!' he cried, suddenly. 'And you here,' he added to Matcham, 'swear me an oath to follow straight to the Moat House.'

'I will pledge mine honour,' replied Matcham.

'What make I with your honour?' cried the knight. 'Swear me upon your mother's welfare!'

Matcham gave the required oath; and Sir Daniel readjusted the hood over his face, and prepared his bell and staff. To see him once more in that appalling travesty somewhat revived the horror of his two companions. But the knight was soon upon his feet.

'Eat with dispatch,' he said, 'and follow me yarely to mine house.'

And with that he set forth again into the woods; and presently after the bell began to sound, numbering his steps, and the two lads sat by their untasted meal, and heard it die slowly away uphill into the distance.

'And so ye go to Tunstall!' Dick inquired.

'Yea, verily,' said Matcham, 'when needs must! I am braver behind Sir Daniel's back than to his face.'

They ate hastily, and set forth along the path through the airy upper levels of the forest, where great beeches stood apart among green lawns, and the birds and squirrels made merry on the boughs. Two hours later, they began to descend upon the other side, and already, among the tree-tops, saw before them the red walls and roofs of Tunstall House.

'Here,' said Matcham, pausing, 'ye shall take your leave of your friend Jack, whom y' are to see no more. Come, Dick, forgive him what he did amiss, as he, for his part, cheerfully and lovingly forgiveth you.'

'And wherefore so?' asked Dick. 'An we both go to Tunstall, I shall see you yet again, I trow, and that right often.'

'Ye'll never again see poor Jack Matcham,' replied the other, 'that was so fearful and burthensome, and yet plucked you from the river; ye'll not see him more, Dick, by mine honour!' He held his arms open, and the lads embraced and kissed. 'And Dick,' continued Matcham, 'my spirit bodeth ill. Y' are now to see a new Sir Daniel; for heretofore hath all prospered in his hands exceedingly, and fortune followed him; but now, methinks when his fate hath come upon him, and he runs the adventure of his life, he will prove but a foul lord to both of us. He may be brave in battle, but he hath the liar's eye; there is fear in his eye, Dick, and fear is as cruel as the wolf! We go down into that house, Saint Mary guide us forth again!'

And so they continued their descent in silence, and came out at last before Sir Daniel's forest stronghold, where it stood, low and shady, flanked with round towers and stained with moss and lichen, in the lilied waters of the moat. Even as they appeared, the doors were opened, the bridge lowered, and Sir Daniel himself, with Hatch and the parson at his side, stood ready to receive them.

1 Dick Asks Questions

The Moat House stood not far from the rough forest road. Externally it was a compact rectangle of red stone, flanked at each corner by a round tower, pierced for archery and battlemented at the top. Within, it enclosed a narrow court. The moat was perhaps twelve feet wide, crossed by a single drawbridge. It was supplied with water by a trench, leading to a forest pool, and commanded, through its whole length, from the battlements of the two southern towers. Except that one or two tall and thick trees had been suffered to remain within half a bowshot of the walls, the house was in a good posture for defence.

In the court, Dick found a part of the garrison, busy with preparations for defence, and gloomily discussing the chances of a siege. Some were making arrows, some sharpening swords that had long been disused; but even as they worked, they shook their heads.

Twelve of Sir Daniel's party had escaped the battle, run the gauntlet through the wood, and come alive to the Moat House. But out of this dozen, three had been gravely wounded: two at Risingham in the disorder of the rout, one by John Amend-All's marksmen as he crossed the forest. This raised the force of the garrison, counting Hatch, Sir Daniel, and young Shelton, to twenty-two effective men. And more might be continually expected to arrive. The danger lay not, therefore, in the lack of men.

It was the terror of the black arrow that oppressed the spirits of the garrison. For their open foes of the party of York, in these most changing times, they felt but a far-away concern. 'The world,' as people said in those days, 'might change again' before harm came. But for their neighbours in the wood they trembled. It was not Sir Daniel alone who was a mark for hatred. His men, conscious of impunity, had carried themselves cruelly through all the country. Harsh commands had been harshly executed; and of the little band that now sat talking in the court, there was not one but had been guilty of some act of oppression or barbarity. And now, by the fortune of war, Sir Daniel had become powerless to protect his instruments; now, by the issue of some hours of battle, at which many of them had not been present, they had all become punishable traitors to the State, outside the buckler of the law, a shrunken company in a poor fortress that was hardly tenable, and exposed upon all sides to the just resentment of their victims. Nor had there been lacking grisly advertisements of what they might expect.

At different periods of the evening and the night, no fewer than seven riderless horses had come neighing in terror to the gate. Two were from Selden's troop; five belonged to men who had ridden with Sir Daniel to the field. Lastly, a little before dawn, a spearman had come staggering to the moat-side, pierced by three arrows; even as they carried him in, his spirit had departed; but by the words that he uttered in his agony, he must have been the last survivor of a considerable company of men.

Hatch himself showed, under his sun-brown, the pallor of anxiety; and when he had taken Dick aside and learned the fate of Selden, he fell on a stone bench and fairly wept. The others, from where they sat on stools or doorsteps in the sunny angle of the court, looked at him with wonder and alarm, but none ventured to inquire the cause of his emotion.

'Nay, Master Shelton,' said Hatch at last, 'nay, but what said I? We shall all go. Selden was a man of his hands; he was like a brother to me. Well, he has gone second; well, we shall all follow! For what said their knave rhyme? – "A black arrow in each black heart." Was it not so it went? Appleyard, Selden, Smith, old Humphrey gone; and there lieth poor John Carter, crying, poor sinner, for the priest.'

Dick gave ear. Out of a low window, hard by where they were talking, groans and murmurs came to his ear.

'Lieth he there?' he asked.

'Ay, in the second porter's chamber,' answered Hatch. 'We could not bear him farther, soul and body were so bitterly at odds. At every step we lifted him, he thought to wend. But now, methinks, it is the soul that suffereth. Ever for the priest he crieth, and Sir Oliver, I wot not why still cometh not. 'Twill be a long shrift; but poor Appleyard and poor Selden, they had none.'

Dick stooped to the window and looked in. The little cell was low and dark, but he could make out the wounded soldier lying moaning on his pallet.

'Carter, poor friend, how goeth it?' he asked.

'Master Shelton,' returned the man, in an excited whisper, 'for the dear light of heaven, bring the priest. Alack, I am sped: I am brought very low down; my hurt is to the death. Ye may do me no more service; this shall be the last. Now, for my poor soul's interest, and as a loyal gentleman, bestir you; for I have that matter on my conscience that shall drag me deep.'

He groaned, and Dick heard the grating of his teeth, whether in pain or terror.

Just then Sir Daniel appeared upon the threshold of the hall. He had a letter in one hand.

'Lads,' he said, 'we have had a shog, we have had a tumble; wherefore, then, deny it? Rather it imputeth to get speedily again to saddle. This old Harry the Sixt has had the undermost. Wash, we, then, our hands of him. I have a good friend that rideth next the duke, the Lord of Wensleydale. Well, I have writ a letter to my friend, praying his good lordship, and offering large satisfaction for the past and reasonable surety for the future. Doubt not but he will lend a favourable ear. A prayer without gifts is like a song without music; I surfeit him with promises, boys – I spare not to promise. What, then, is lacking? Nay, a great thing – wherefore should I deceive you? – a great thing and a difficult: a messenger to bear it. The woods – y' are not ignorant of that – lie thick with our ill-willers. Haste is most needful; but without sleight and caution all is nought. Which, then, of this company will take me this letter, bear it to my Lord of Wensleydale, and bring me the answer back?'

One man instantly rose.

'I will, an't like you,' said he. 'I will even risk my carcass.'

'Nay, Dicky Bowyer, not so,' returned the knight. 'It likes me not. Y' are sly, indeed, but not speedy. Ye were a laggard ever.'

'An't be so, Sir Daniel, here am I,' cried another.

'The saints forfend!' said the knight. 'Y' are speedy, but not sly. Ye would blunder me headforemost into John Amend-All's camp. I thank you both for your good courage; but, in sooth, it may not be.'

Then Hatch offered himself, and he also was refused.

'I want you here, good Bennet; y' are my right hand, indeed,' returned the knight; and then several coming forward in a group, Sir Daniel at length selected one and gave him the letter.

'Now,' he said, 'upon your good speed and better discretion we do all depend. Bring me a good answer back, and before three weeks I will have purged my forest of these vagabonds, that brave us to our faces. But mark it well, Throgmorton: the matter is not easy. Ye must steal forth under night, and go like a fox; and how ye are to cross Till I know not, neither by the bridge nor ferry.'

'I can swim,' returned Throgmorton. 'I will come soundly, fear not.'

'Well, friend, get ye to the buttery,' replied Sir Daniel. 'Ye shall swim first of all in nut-brown ale.' And with that he turned back into the hall.

'Sir Daniel hath a wise tongue,' said Hatch, aside, to Dick. 'See, now, where many a lesser man had glossed the matter over, he speaketh it out plainly to his company. Here is a danger, 'a saith, and here difficulty: and jesteth in the very saying. Nay, by Saint Barbary, he is a born captain! Not a man but he is some deal heartened up! See how they fall again to work.'

This praise of Sir Daniel put a thought in the lad's head.

'Bennet,' he said, 'how came my father by his end?'

'Ask me not that,' replied Hatch. 'I had no hand nor knowledge in it; furthermore, I will even be silent, Master Dick. For look you, in a man's own business, there he may speak; but of hearsay matters and of common talk, not so. Ask me Sir Oliver – ay, or Carter, if ye will; not me.'

And Hatch set off to make the rounds, leaving Dick in a muse.

'Wherefore would he not tell me?' thought the lad. 'And wherefore named he Carter? Carter – nay, then Carter had a hand in it, perchance.'

He entered the house, and passing some little way along a flagged and vaulted passage, came to the door of the cell where the hurt man lay groaning. At his entrance Carter started eagerly.

'Have ye brought the priest?' he cried.

'Not yet awhile,' returned Dick. 'Y' 'ave a word to tell me first. How came my father, Harry Shelton, by his death?'

The man's face altered instantly.

'I know not,' he replied doggedly.

'Nay, ye know well,' returned Dick. 'Seek not to put me by.'

'I tell you I know not,' repeated Carter.

'Then,' said Dick, 'ye shall die unshriven. Here am I, and here shall stay. There shall no priest come near you, rest assured. For of what avail is penitence, an ye have no mind to right those wrongs ye had a hand in? and without penitence, confession is but mockery.'

'Ye say what ye mean not, Master Dick,' said Carter composedly. 'It is ill threatening the dying, and becometh you (to speak truth) little. And for as little as it commends you, it shall serve you less. Stay, an ye please. Ye will condemn my soul – ye shall learn nothing! There is my last word to you.' And the wounded man turned upon the other side.

Now Dick, to say truth, had spoken hastily and was ashamed of his threat. But he made one more effort.

'Carter,' he said, 'mistake me not. I know ye were but an instrument in the hands of others; a churl must obey his lord; I would not bear heavily on such an one. But I begin to learn upon many sides that this great duty lieth on my youth and ignorance, to avenge my father. Prithee, then, good Carter, set aside the memory of my threatenings, and in pure good-will and honest penitence, give me a word of help.'

The wounded man lay silent; nor, say what Dick pleased, could he extract another word from him.

'Well,' said Dick, 'I will go call the priest to you as ye desired; for howsoever ye be in fault to me or mine, I would not willingly in fault to any, least of all to one upon the last change.'

Again the old soldier heard him without speech or motion; even his groans he had suppressed; and as Dick turned and left the room, he was filled with admiration for that rugged fortitude.

'And yet,' he thought, 'of what use is courage without wit? Had his hands been clean, he would have spoken; his silence did confess the secret louder than words. Nay, upon all sides, proof floweth on me. Sir Daniel, he or his men, hath done this thing.'

Dick paused in the stone passage with a heavy heart. At that hour, in the ebb of Sir Daniel's fortune, when he was beleaguered by the archers of the Black Arrow, and proscribed by the victorious Yorkists, was Dick, also, to turn upon the man who had nourished and taught him, who had severely punished indeed, but yet unweariyingly protected his youth? The necessity, if it should prove to be one, was cruel.

'Pray Heaven he be innocent!' he said.

And then steps sounded on the flagging, and Sir Oliver came gravely towards the lad.

'One seeketh you earnestly,' said Dick.

'I am upon the way, good Richard,' said the priest. 'It is this poor Carter. Alack, he is beyond cure.'

'And yet his soul is sicker than his body,' answered Dick.

'Have ye seen him?' asked Sir Oliver, with a manifest start.

'I do but come from him,' replied Dick.

'What said he – what said he?' snapped the priest, with extraordinary eagerness.

'He but cried for you the more piteously, Sir Oliver. It were well done to go the faster, for his hurt is grievous,' returned the lad.

'I am straight for him,' was the reply. 'Well, we have all our sins. We must all come to our latter day, good Richard.'

'Ay, sir; and it were well if we all came fairly,' answered Dick.

The priest dropped his eyes, and with an inaudible benediction hurried on.

'He, too!' thought Dick, 'he, that taught me in piety! Nay, then, what a world is this, if all that care for me be blood-guilty of my father's death! Vengeance! Alas! what a sore fate is mine, if I must be avenged upon my friends!'

The thought put Matcham in his head. He smiled at the remembrance of his strange companion, and then wondered where he was. Ever since they had come together to the doors of the Moat House the younger lad had disappeared, and Dick began to weary for a word with him.

About an hour after, mass being somewhat hastily run through by Sir Oliver, the company gathered in the hall for dinner. It was a long, low apartment, strewn with green rushes, and the walls hung with arras in a design of savage men questing bloodhounds; here and there hung spears and bows and bucklers; a fire blazed in the big chimney; there were arras-covered benches round the wall, and in the midst the table, fairly spread awaited the arrival of the diners. Neither Sir Daniel nor his lady made their appearance. Sir Oliver himself was absent, and here again there was no word of Matcham. Dick began to grow alarmed, to recall his companion's melancholy forebodings, and to wonder to himself if any foul play had befallen him in that house.

After dinner he found Goody Hatch, who was hurrying to my lady Brackley.

'Goody,' he said, 'where is Master Matcham, I prithee? I saw ye go in with him when we arrived.'

The old woman laughed aloud.

'Ah, Master Dick,' she said, 'y' have a famous bright eye in your head, to be sure!' and laughed again.

'Nay, but where is he, indeed?' persisted Dick.

'Ye will never see him more,' she returned; 'never. It is sure.'

'An I do not,' returned the lad, 'I will know the reason why. He came not hither of his full free will; such as I am, I am his best protector, and I will see him justly used. There be too many mysteries; I do begin to weary of the game!'

But as Dick was speaking, a heavy hand fell on his shoulder. It was Bennet Hatch that had come unperceived behind him. With a jerk of his thumb the retainer dismissed his wife.

'Friend Dick,' he said, as soon as they were alone, 'are ye a moonstruck natural? An ye leave not certain things in peace, ye were better in the salt sea than here in Tunstall Moat House. Y' have questioned me; y' have baited Carter; y' have frighted the jack-priest with hints. Bear ye more wisely, fool; and even now when Sir Daniel calleth you, show me a smooth face, for the love of wisdom. Y' are to be sharply questioned. Look to your answers.'

'Hatch,' returned Dick, 'in all this I smell a guilty conscience.'

'An ye go not the wiser, ye will soon smell blood,' replied Bennet. 'I do but warn you. And here cometh one to call you.'

And indeed, at that very moment, a messenger came across the court to summon Dick into the presence of Sir Daniel.

2 The Two Oaths

Sir Daniel was in the hall; there he paced angrily before the fire, awaiting Dick's arrival. None was by except Sir Oliver, and he sat discreetly backward, thumbing and muttering over his breviary.

'Y' have sent for me, Sir Daniel?' said young Shelton.

'I have sent for you, indeed,' replied the knight. 'For what cometh to mine ears? Have I been to you so heavy a guardian that ye make haste to credit ill of me? Or sith that ye see me, for the nonce, some worsted, do ye think to quit my party? By the mass, your father was not so! Those he was near, those he stood by, come wind or weather. But you, Dick, y' are a fair-day friend, it seemeth, and now seek to clear yourself of your allegiance.'

'An 't please you, Sir Daniel, not so,' returned Dick firmly. 'I am grateful and faithful, where gratitude and faith are due. And before more is said, I thank you, and I thank Sir Oliver; y' have great claims upon me, both – none can have more; I were a hound if I forgot them.'

'It is well, said Sir Daniel; and then; rising into anger: 'Gratitude and faith are words, Dick Shelton,' he continued; 'but I look to deeds. In this hour of my peril, when my name is attainted, when my lands are forfeit, when this wood is full of men that hunger and thirst for my destruction, what doth gratitude? what doth faith? I have but a little company remaining; is it grateful or faithful to poison me their hearts with your insidious whisperings? Save me from such gratitude! But, come, now, what is it ye wish? Speak; we're here to answer. If ye have aught against me, stand forth and say it.'

'Sir,' replied Dick, 'my father fell when I was yet a child. It hath come to mine ears that he was foully done by. It hath come to mine ears – for I will not dissemble – that ye had a hand in his undoing. And in all verity, I shall not be at peace in mine own mind, nor very clear to help you, till I have certain resolution of these doubts.'

Sir Daniel sat down in a deep settle. He took his chin in his hand

and looked at Dick fixedly.

'And ye think I would be guardian to the man's son that I had murdered?' he asked.

'Nay,' said Dick, 'pardon me if I answer churlishly; but indeed ye know right well a wardship is most profitable. All these years have ye not enjoyed my revenues, and led my men? Have ye not still my marriage? I wot not what it may be worth – it is worth something. Pardon me again; but if ye were base enough to slay a man under trust, here were, perhaps, reasons enough to move you to the lesser baseness.'

'When I was a lad of your years,' returned Sir Daniel sternly, 'my mind had not so turned upon suspicions. And Sir Oliver here,' he added, 'why should he, a priest, be guilty of this act?'

'Nay, Sir Daniel,' said Dick, 'but where the master biddeth, there will the dog go. It is well known this priest is but your instrument. I speak very freely; the time is not for courtesies. Even as I speak, so would I be answered. And answer get I none! Ye but put more questions. I rede ye beware, Sir Daniel; for in this way ye will but nourish and not satisfy my doubts.'

'I will answer you fairly, Master Richard,' said the knight. 'Were I to pretend ye have not stirred my wrath, I were no honest man. But I will be just even in anger. Come to me with these words when y' are grown and come to man's estate, and I am no longer your guardian, and so helpless to resent them. Come to me then, and I will answer you as ye merit, with a buffet in the mouth. Till then ye have two courses: either swallow me down these insults, keep a silent tongue, and fight in the meanwhile for the man that fed and fought for your infancy; or else – the door standeth open, the woods are full of mine enemies – go.'

The spirit with which these words were uttered, the looks with which they were accompanied, staggered Dick; and yet he could not but observe that he had got no answer.

'I desire nothing more earnestly, Sir Daniel, than to believe you,' he replied. 'Assure me ye are free from this.'

'Will ye take my word of honour, Dick?' inquired the knight.

'That would I,' answered the lad.

'I give it you,' returned Sir Daniel. 'Upon my word of honour, upon the eternal welfare of my spirit, and as I shall answer for my deeds hereafter, I had no hand nor portion in your father's death.'

He extended his hand, and Dick took it eagerly. Neither of them observed the priest, who, at the pronunciation of that solemn and false oath, had half arisen from his seat in an agony of horror and remorse.

'Ah,' cried Dick, 'ye must find it in your great-heartedness to pardon me! I was a churl indeed to doubt of you. But ye have my hand upon it; I will doubt no more.'

'Nay, Dick' replied Sir Daniel, 'y' are forgiven. Ye know not the world and its calumnious nature.'

'I was the more to blame,' added Dick, 'in that the rogues pointed, not directly at yourself, but at Sir Oliver.'

As he spoke, he turned towards the priest, and paused in the middle of the last word. This tall, ruddy, corpulent, high-stepping man had fallen, you might say, to pieces; his colour was gone, his limbs were relaxed, his lips stammered prayers; and now, when Dick's eyes were fixed upon him suddenly, he cried out aloud, like some wild animal, and buried his face in his hands.

Sir Daniel was by him in two strides, and shook him fiercely by the shoulder. At the same moment Dick's suspicions reawakened.

'Nay,' he said, 'Sir Oliver may swear also. 'Twas him they accused.'

'He shall swear,' said the knight.

Sir Oliver speechlessly waved his arms.

'Ay, by the mass! but ye shall swear,' cried Sir Daniel, beside himself with fury. 'Here, upon this book, ye shall swear,' he continued, picking up the breviary, which had fallen to the ground. 'What! Ye make me doubt you! Swear, I say; swear.'

But the priest was still incapable of speech. His terror of Sir Daniel, his terror of perjury, risen to about an equal height, strangled him.

And just then, through the high stained-glass window of the hall, a black arrow crashed, and struck, and stuck quivering in the midst of the long table.

Sir Oliver, with a loud scream, fell fainting on the rushes; while the knight, followed by Dick, dashed into the court and up the nearest corkscrew stair to the battlements. The sentries were all on the alert. The sun shone quietly on the green lawns dotted with trees, and on the wooded hills of the forest which enclosed the view. There was no sign of a besieger.

'Whence came that shot?' asked the knight.

'From yonder clump, Sir Daniel,' returned the sentinel.

The knight stood a little, musing. Then he turned to Dick. 'Dick,' he said, 'keep me an eye upon these men; I leave you in charge here. As for the priest, he shall clear himself, or I will know the reason why. I do almost begin to share in your suspicions. He shall swear, trust me, or we shall prove him guilty.'

Dick answered somewhat coldly, and the knight, giving him a piercing glance, hurriedly returned to the hall. His first glance was for the arrow. It was the first of these missiles he had seen, and as he turned it to and fro, the dark hue of it touched him with some fear. Again there was some writing: one word – 'Earthed.'

'Ay,' he broke out, 'they know I am home, then. Earthed! Ay, but there is not a dog among them fit to dig me out.'

Sir Oliver had come to himself, and now scrambled to his feet.

'Alack, Sir Daniel!' he moaned. 'y' 'ave sworn a dread oath; y' are doomed to the end of time.'

'Ay,' returned the knight, 'I have sworn an oath, indeed, thou chuckle-head; but thyself shalt swear a greater. It shall be on the blessed cross of Holywood. Look to it; get the words ready. It shall be sworn to-night.'

'Now, may Heaven lighten you!' replied the priest; 'may Heaven incline your heart from this iniquity!'

'Look you, my good father,' said Sir Daniel, 'if y' are for piety, I say no more; ye begin late, that is all. But if y' are in any sense bent upon wisdom, hear me. This lad beginneth to irk me like a wasp. I have a need for him, for I would sell his marriage. But I tell you, in all plainness, if that he continue to weary me, he shall go join his father. I give orders now to change him to the chamber above the chapel. If that ye can swear your innocency with a good solid oath and an assured countenance, it is well: the lad will be at peace a little, and I will spare him. If that ye stammer or blench, or anyways boggle at the swearing, he will not believe you; and by the mass, he shall die. There is for your thinking on.'

'The chamber above the chapel!' gasped the priest.

'That same,' replied the knight. 'So if ye desire to save him, save him; and if ye desire not, prithee, go to, and let me be at peace! for an I had been a hasty man, I would already have put my sword through you, for your intolerable cowardice and folly. Have ye chosen? Say!'

'I have chosen,' said the priest. 'Heaven pardon me, I will do evil for good. I will swear for the lad's sake.'

'So is it best!' said Sir Daniel. 'Send for him, then, speedily. Ye shall see him alone. Yet I shall have an eye on you. I shall be here in the panel room.'

The knight raised the arras and let it fall again behind him. There was the sound of a spring opening; then followed the creaking of trod stairs.

Sir Oliver, left alone, cast a timorous glance upward at the arras-covered wall, and crossed himself with every appearance of terror and contrition.

'Nay, if he is in the chapel room,' the priest murmured, 'were it at my soul's cost, I must save him.'

Three minutes later, Dick, who had been summoned by another messenger, found Sir Oliver standing by the hall table, resolute and pale.

'Richard Shelton,' he said, 'ye have required an oath from me. I might complain, I might deny you; but my heart is moved toward you for the past, and I will even content you as ye choose. By the true cross of Holywood, I did not slay your father.'

'Sir Oliver,' returned Dick, 'when first we read John Amend-All's paper, I was convinced of so much. But suffer me to put two questions. Ye did not slay him; granted. But had ye no hand in it?'

'None,' said Sir Oliver. And at the same time he began to contort his face, and signal with his mouth and eyebrows, like one who desired to convey a warning, yet dared not utter a sound.

Dick regarded him in wonder; then he turned and looked all about him at the empty hall.

'What make ye?' he inquired.

'Why, naught,' returned the priest, hastily smoothing his countenance. 'I make naught; I do but suffer; I am sick. I – I – I – prithee, Dick, I must be gone. On the true cross of Holywood, I am clean innocent alike of violence or treachery. Content ye, good lad. Farewell!'

And he made his escape from the apartment with unusual alacrity.

Dick remained rooted to the spot, his eyes wandering about the room, his face a changing picture of various emotions – wonder, doubt, suspicion, and amusement. Gradually, as his mind grew clearer, suspicion took the upper hand, and was succeeded by certainty of the worst. He raised his head, and as he did so, violently started. High upon the wall there was the figure of a savage hunter woven in the tapestry. With one hand he held a horn to his mouth; in the other he brandished a stout spear. His face was dark, for he was meant to represent an African.

Now here was what had startled Richard Shelton. The sun had moved away from the hall windows, and at the same time the fire had blazed up high on the wide hearth, and shed a changeful glow upon the roof and hangings. In this light the figure of the black hunter had winked at him with a white eyelid.

He continued staring at the eye. The light shone upon it like a gem; it was liquid, it was alive. Again the white eyelid closed upon it for a fraction of a second, and the next moment it was gone.

There could be no mistake. The live eye that had been watching him through a hole in the tapestry was gone. The light no longer shone on a reflecting surface.

And instantly Dick awoke to the terrors of his position. Hatch's warning, the mute signals of the priest, this eye that had observed him from the wall, ran together in his mind. He saw he had been put upon his trial, that he had once more betrayed his suspicions, and that, short of some miracle, he was lost.

'If I cannot get me forth out of this house,' he thought, 'I am a dead man! And this poor Matcham, too – to what a cockatrice's nest have I not led him!'

Here was still so thinking, when there came one in haste, to bid him help in changing his arms, his clothing, and his two or three books, to a new chamber.

'A new chamber?' he repeated. 'Wherefore so? What chamber?'

' 'Tis one above the chapel,' answered the messenger.

'It hath stood long empty,' said Dick, musing. 'What manner of room is it?'

'Nay, a brave room,' returned the man. 'But yet' – lowering his voice – 'they call it haunted.'

'Haunted?' repeated Dick, with a chill. 'I have not heard of it. Nay, then, and by whom?'

The messenger looked about him; and then, in a low whisper, 'By the sacrist of St John's,' he said. 'They had him there to sleep one night, and in the morning – whew! – he was gone. The devil had taken him, they said; the more betoken, he had drunk late the night before.'

Dick followed the man with black forebodings.

3 The Room Over the Chapel

From the battlements nothing further was observed. The sun journeyed westward and at last went down; but to the eyes of all these eager sentinels, no living thing appeared in the neighbourhood of Tunstall House.

When the night was at length fairly come, Throgmorton was led to a room overlooking an angle of the moat. Thence he was lowered with every precaution; the ripple of his swimming was audible for a brief period; then a black figure was observed to land by the branches of a willow and crawl away among the grass. For some half-hour Sir Daniel and Hatch stood eagerly giving ear; but all remained quiet. The messenger had got away in safety.

Sir Daniel's brow grew clearer. He turned to Hatch.

'Bennet,' said he, 'this John Amend-All is no more than a man ye see. He sleepeth. We will make a good end of him Go to!'

All the afternoon and evening Dick had been ordered hither and thither, one command following another, till he was bewildered with the number and the hurry of commissions. All that time he had seen no more of Sir Oliver, and nothing of Matcham; and yet both the priest and the young lad ran continually in his mind. It was now his chief purpose to escape from Tunstall Moat House as speedily as might be; and yet, before he went, he desired a word with both of these.

At length, with a lamp in one hand, he mounted to his new apartment. It was large, low, and somewhat dark. The window looked upon the moat, and although it was so high up, it was heavily barred. The bed was luxurious, with one pillow of down, and one of lavender, and a red coverlet, worked in a pattern of roses. All about the walls were cupboards, locked and padlocked, and concealed from view by hangings of dark-coloured arras. Dick made the round, lifting the arras, sounding the panels, seeking vainly to open the cupboards. He assured himself that the door was strong, and the bolt solid; then he set down his lamp upon a bracket, and once more looked all round.

For what reason had he been given this chamber? It was larger and finer than his own. Could it conceal a snare? Was there a secret entrance? Was it indeed haunted? His blood ran a little chilly in his veins.

Immediately over him the heavy foot of a sentry trod the leads. Below him, he knew, was the arched roof of the chapel; and next to the chapel was the hall. Certainly there was a secret passage in the hall; the eye that had watched him from the arras gave him proof of that. Was it not more than probable that the passage extended to the chapel, and if so, that it had an opening in his room?

To sleep in such a place, he felt, would be foolhardy. He made his weapons ready, and took his position in a corner of the room behind the door. If ill was intended he would sell his life dear.

The sound of many feet, the challenge, and the password sounded overhead along the battlements; the watch was being changed.

And just then there came a scratching at the door of the chamber; it grew a little louder; then a whisper:

'Dick, Dick, it is I!'

Dick ran to the door, drew the bolt, and admitted Matcham. He was very pale, and carried a lamp in one hand and a drawn dagger in the other.

'Shut me the door,' he whispered. 'Swift, Dick! This house is full of spies; I hear their feet follow me in the corridors; I hear them breathe behind the arras.'

'Well, content you,' returned Dick, 'it is closed. We are safe for this while, if there be safety anywhere within these walls. But my heart is glad to see you. By the mass, lad, I thought ye were sped. Where hid ye?'

'It matters not,' returned Matcham. 'Since we be met, it matters not. But, Dick, are your eyes open? Have they told ye of to-morrow's doings?'

'Not they,' replied Dick. 'What make they to-morrow?'

'To-morrow, or to-night, I know not,' said the other; 'but one time or other, Dick, they do intend upon your life. I had the proof of it: I have heard them whisper; nay, they as good as told me.'

'Ay,' returned Dick, 'is it so? I had thought as much.'

And he told him the day's occurrences at length.

When it was done, Matcham arose and began, in turn, to examine the apartment.

'No,' he said, 'there is no entrance visible. Yet 'tis a pure certainty there is one. Dick, I will stay by you. An y' are to die, I will die with you. And I can help – look! I have stolen a dagger – I will do my best! And meanwhile, an ye know of any issue, any sally-port we could get opened, or any window that we might descend by, I will most joyfully face any jeopardy to flee with you.'

'Jack,' said Dick, 'by the mass, Jack, y' are the best soul, and the truest, and the bravest in all England! Give me your hand, Jack.'

And he grasped the other's hand in silence.

'I will tell you,' he resumed. 'There is a window out of which the messenger descended; the rope should still be in the chamber. 'Tis a hope.'

'Hist!' said Matcham.

Both gave ear. There was a sound below the floor; then it paused, and then began again.

'Someone walketh in the room below,' whispered Matcham.

'Nay,' returned Dick, 'there is no room below; we are above the chapel. It is my murderer in the secret passage. Well, let him come; it shall go hard with him!' And he ground his teeth.

'Blow me the lights out,' said the other. 'Perchance he will betray himself.'

They blew out both the lamps and lay still as death. The footfalls underneath were very soft, but they were clearly audible. Several times they came and went; and then there was a loud jar of a key turning in a lock, followed by a considerable silence.

Presently the steps began again, and then, all of a sudden, a chink of light appeared in the planking of the room in a far corner. It widened; a trap-door was being opened, letting in a gush of light. They could see the strong hand pushing it up; and Dick raised his cross-bow, waiting for the head to follow.

But now there came an interruption. From a distant corner of the Moat House shouts began to be heard, and first one voice, and then several, crying aloud upon a name. This noise had plainly disconcerted the murderer, for the trap-door was silently lowered to its place, and the steps hurriedly returned, passed once more close below the lads, and died away in the distance.

Here was a moment's respite. Dick breathed deep, and then, and not till then, he gave ear to the disturbance which had interrupted the attack, and which was now rather increasing than diminishing. All about the Moat House feet were running, doors were opening and slamming, and still the voice of Sir Daniel towered above all this bustle, shouting for 'Joanna.'

'Joanna!' repeated Dick. 'Why, who the murrain should this be? Here is no Joanna, nor ever hath been. What meaneth it?'

Matcham was silent. He seemed to have drawn further away. But only a little faint starlight entered by the window, and at the far end of the apartment, where the pair were, the darkness was complete.

'Jack,' said Dick, 'I wot not where ye were all day. Saw ye this Joanna?'

'Nay,' returned Matcham, 'I saw her not.'

'Nor heard tell of her?' he pursued.

The steps drew nearer. Sir Daniel was still roaring the name of Joanna from the courtyard.

'Did ye hear of her?' repeated Dick.

'I heard of her,' said Matcham.

'How your voice twitters! What aileth you?' said Dick. ''Tis a most excellent good fortune, this Joanna; it will take their minds from us.'

'Dick,' cried Matcham, 'I am lost; we are both lost! Let us flee if there be yet time. They will not rest till they have found me. Or, see! let me go forth; when they have found me, ye may flee. Let me forth, Dick – good Dick, let me away!'

She was groping for the bolt, when Dick at last comprehended.

'By the mass!' he cried, 'y' are no Jack; y' are Joanna Sedley; y' are the maid that would not marry me!'

The girl paused, and stood silent and motionless. Dick, too, was silent for a little; then he spoke again.

'Joanna,' he said, 'y' 'ave saved my life, and I have saved yours; and we have seen blood flow, and been friends and enemies – ay, and I took my belt to thrash you; and all that time I thought ye were a boy. But now death has me, and my time's out, and before I die I must say this: Y' are the best maid and the bravest under heaven, and, if only I could live, I would marry you blithely: and, live or die, I love you!'

She answered nothing.

'Come,' he said, 'speak up, Jack. Come, be a good maid, and say ye love me!'

'Why, Dick,' she cried, 'would I be here?'

'Well, see ye here,' continued Dick, 'an we but escape whole, we'll marry; and an we're to die, we die, and there's an end on't. But now that I think, how found ye my chamber?'

'I asked it of Dame Hatch,' she answered.

'Well, the dame's staunch,' he answered; 'she'll not tell upon you. We have time before us.'

And just then, as if to contradict his words, feet came down the corridor, and a fist beat roughly on the door.

'Here!' cried a voice. 'Open, Master Dick; open!'

Dick neither moved nor answered.

'It is all over,' said the girl; and she put her arms about Dick's neck.

One after another, men came trooping to the door. Then Sir Daniel arrived himself, and there was a sudden cessation of the noise.

'Dick,' cried the knight, 'be not an ass. The Seven Sleepers had been awake ere now. We know she is within there. Open, then, the door, man.'

Dick was silent again.

'Down with it,' said Sir Daniel. And immediately his followers fell savagely upon the door with foot and fist. Solid as it was, and strongly bolted, it would soon have given way, but once more fortune interfered. Over the thunderstorm of blows the cry of a sentinel was heard; it was followed by another; shouts ran along the battlements, shouts answered out of the wood. In the first moment of alarm it sounded as if the foresters were carrying the Moat House by assault. And Sir Daniel and his men, desisting instantly from their attack upon Dick's chamber, hurried to defend the walls.

'Now,' cried Dick, 'we are saved.'

He seized the great old bedstead with both hands, and bent himself in vain to move it.

'Help me, Jack. For your life's sake, help me stoutly!' he cried.

Between them, with a huge effort, they dragged the big frame of oak across the room, and thrust it endwise to the chamber door.

'Ye do but make things worse,' said Joanna sadly. 'He will then enter by the trap.'

'Not so,' replied Dick. 'He durst not tell his secret to so many. It is by the trap that we shall flee. Hark! The attack is over. Nay, it was none!'

It had, indeed, been no attack; it was the arrival of another party of

'The trap moved, gaped a little, and at length came widely open'

stragglers from the defeat of Risingham that had disturbed Sir Daniel. They had run the gauntlet under cover of the darkness; they had been admitted by the great gate; and now with a great stamping of hoofs and jingle of accoutrements and arms, they were dismounting in the court.

'He will return anon,' said Dick. 'To the trap!'

He lighted a lamp, and they went together into the corner of the room. The open chink through which some light still glittered was easily discovered, and, taking a stout sword from his small armoury, Dick thrust it deep into the seam, and weighed strenuously on the hilt. The trap moved, gaped a little, and at length came widely open. Seizing it with their hands, the two young folk threw it back. It disclosed a few steps descending, and at the foot of them, where the would-be murderer had left it, a burning lamp.

'Now,' said Dick, 'go first and take the lamp. I will follow to close the trap.'

So they descended one after the other, and, as Dick lowered the trap, the blows began once again to thunder on the panels of the door.

4 The Passage

The passage in which Dick and Joanna now found themselves was narrow, dirty, and short. At the other end of it a door stood partly open; the same door, without doubt, that they had heard the man unlocking. Heavy cobwebs hung from the roof, and the paved flooring echoed hollow under the lightest tread.

Beyond the door there were two branches, at right angles. Dick chose one of them at random, and the pair hurried, with echoing footsteps, along the hollow of the chapel roof. The top of the arched ceiling rose like a whale's back in the dim glimmer of the lamp. Here and there were spy-holes, concealed, on the other side, by the carving of the cornice; and looking down through one of these, Dick saw the paved floor of the chapel – the altar, with its burning tapers – and stretched before it on the steps, the figure of Sir Oliver praying with uplifted hands.

At the other end, they descended a few steps. The passage grew narrower; the wall upon one hand was now of wood; the noise of people talking, and a faint flickering of lights, came through the interstices; and presently they came to a round hole about the size of a man's eye, and Dick, looking down through it, beheld the interior of the hall, and some half a dozen men sitting, in their jacks, about the table, drinking deep and demolishing a venison pie. These were certainly some of the late arrivals.

'Here is no help,' said Dick. 'Let us try back.'

'Nay,' said Joanna; 'maybe the passage goeth farther.'

And she pushed on. But a few yards farther the passage ended at the top of a short flight of steps; and it became plain that, as long as the soldiers occupied the hall, escape was impossible upon that side.

They retraced their steps with all imaginable speed, and set forward to explore the other branch. It was exceedingly narrow, scarce wide enough for a large man; and it led then continually up and down by little breakneck stairs, until even Dick had lost all notion of his whereabouts.

At length it grew both narrower and lower; the stairs continued to descend; the walls on either hand became damp and slimy to the touch; and far in front of them they heard the squeaking and scuttling of the rats.

'We must be in the dungeons,' Dick remarked.

'And still there is no outlet,' added Joanna.

'Nay, but an outlet there must be!' Dick answered.

Presently, sure enough, they came to a sharp angle, and then the passage ended in a flight of steps. On the top of that there was a solid flag of stone by way of trap, and to this they both set their backs. It was immovable.

'Someone holdeth it,' suggested Joanna.

'Not so,' said Dick; 'for were a man as strong as ten he must still yield a little. But this resisteth like dead rock. There is a weight upon the trap. Here is no issue; by my sooth, good Jack, we are here as fairly prisoners as though the gyves were on our ankle-bones. Sit ye then down, and let us talk. After a while we shall return, when perchance they shall be less carefully upon their guard; and, who knoweth? we may break out and stand a chance. But, in my poor opinion, we are as good as shent.'

'Dick!' she cried, 'alas the day that ever ye should have seen me! For like a most unhappy and unthankful maid, it is I have led you hither.'

'What cheer!' returned Dick. 'It was all written, and that which is written, willy-nilly, cometh still to pass. But tell me a little what manner of a maid ye are, and how ye came into Sir Daniel's hands; that will do better than to bemoan yourself, whether for your sake or mine.'

'I am an orphan, like yourself, of father and mother,' said Joanna; 'and for my great misfortune, Dick, and hitherto for yours, I am a rich marriage. My Lord Foxham had me to ward; yet it appears Sir Daniel bought the marriage of me from the king, and a right dear price he paid for it. So here was I, poor babe, with two great and rich men fighting which should marry me, and I still at nurse! Well, then the world changed, and there was a new Chancellor, and Sir Daniel bought the warding of me over the Lord Foxham's head. And then the world changed again, and Lord Foxham bought my marriage over Sir Daniel's; and from then to now it went on ill betwixt the two of them.

But still Lord Foxham kept me in his hands, and was a good lord to me. And at last I was to be married – or sold, if ye like it better. Five hundred pounds Lord Foxham was to get for me. Hamley was the groom's name, and to-morrow, Dick, of all days in the year, was I to be betrothed. Had it not come to Sir Daniel, I had been wedded, sure – and never seen thee, Dick – dear Dick!'

And here she took his hand, and kissed it with the prettiest grace; and Dick drew her hand to him and did the like.

'Well,' she went on, 'Sir Daniel took me unawares in the garden, and made me dress in these men's clothes, which is a deadly sin for a woman; and, besides, they fit me not. He rode with me to Kettley, as ye saw, telling me I was to marry you; but I, in my heart, made sure I would marry Hamley in his teeth.'

'Ay!' cried Dick, 'and so ye loved this Hamley?'

'Nay,' replied Joanna, 'not I. I did but hate Sir Daniel. And then, Dick, ye helped me, and ye were right kind, and very bold, and my heart turned towards you in mine own despite; and now, if we can in any way compass it, I would marry you with right goodwill. And if, by cruel destiny, it may not be, still ye'll be dear to me. While my heart beats, it'll be true to you.'

'And I,' said Dick, 'that never cared a straw for any manner of woman until now, I took to you when I thought ye were a boy. I had a pity to you, and knew not why. When I would have belted you, the hand failed me. But when ye owned ye were a maid, Jack – for still I will call you Jack – I made sure ye were the maid for me. Hark!' he said, breaking off – 'one cometh.'

And indeed a heavy tread was now audible in the echoing passage, and the rats again fled in armies.

Dick reconnoitred his position. The sudden turn gave him a post of vantage. He could thus shoot in safety from the cover of the wall. But it was plain the light was too near him, and, running some way forward, he set down the lamp in the middle of the passage, and then returned to watch.

Presently, at the far end of the passage, Bennet hove in sight. He seemed to be alone, and he carried in his hand a burning torch, which made him the better mark.

'Stand, Bennet!' cried Dick. 'Another step and y' are dead.'

'So here ye are,' returned Hatch, peering forward into the darkness. 'I see you not. Aha! y' 'ave done wisely, Dick; y' 'ave put your lamp before you. By my sooth, but, though it was done to shoot my own knave body, I do rejoice to see ye profit of my lessons! And now, what make ye? what seek ye here? Why would ye shoot upon an old, kind friend? And have ye the young gentlewoman there?'

'Nay, Bennet, it is I should question and you answer,' replied Dick. 'Why am I in this jeopardy of my life? Why do men come privily to slay me in my bed? Why am I now fleeing in mine own guardian's strong house, and from the friends that I have lived among and never injured?'

'Master Dick, Master Dick,' said Bennet, 'what told I you? Y' are brave, but the most uncrafty lad that I can think upon!'

'Well,' returned Dick, 'I see ye know all, and that I am doomed indeed. It is well. Here, where I am, I stay. Let Sir Daniel get me out if he be able!'

Hatch was silent for a space.

'Hark ye,' he began, 'I return to Sir Daniel, to tell him where ye are, and how posted; for, in truth, it was to that end he sent me. But you, if ye are no fool, had best be gone ere I return.'

'Begone!' repeated Dick. 'I would begone already, an I wist how. I cannot move the trap.'

'Put me your hand into the corner, and see what ye find there,' replied Bennet. 'Throgmorton's rope is still in the brown chamber. Fare ye well.'

And Hatch, turning upon his heel, disappeared again into the windings of the passage.

Dick instantly returned for his lamp, and proceeded to act upon the hint. At one corner of the trap there was a deep cavity in the wall. Pushing his arm into the aperture, Dick found an iron bar, which he thrust vigorously upwards. There followed a snapping noise, and the slab of stone instantly started in its bed.

They were free of the passage. A little exercise of strength easily raised the trap; and they came forth into a vaulted chamber, opening on one hand upon the court, where one or two fellows, with bare arms, were rubbing down the horses of the last arrivals. A torch or two, each stuck in an iron ring against the wall, changefully lit up the scene.

5　How Dick Changed Sides

Dick, blowing out his lamp lest it should attract attention, led the way upstairs and along the corridor. In the brown chamber the rope had been made fast to the frame of an exceedingly heavy and ancient bed. It had not been detached, and Dick, taking the coil to the window, began to lower it slowly and cautiously into the darkness of the night. Joan stood by; but as the rope lengthened, and still Dick continued to pay it out, extreme fear began to conquer her resolution.

'Dick,' she said, 'is it so deep? I may not essay it. I should infallibly fall, good Dick.'

It was just at the delicate moment of the operations that she spoke. Dick started; the remainder of the coil slipped from his grasp, and the end fell with a splash into the moat. Instantly, from the battlement above, the voice of a sentinel cried, 'Who goes?'

'A murrain!' cried Dick. 'We are paid now? Down with you – take the rope.'

'I cannot,' she cried, recoiling.

'An ye cannot, no more can I,' said Shelton. 'How can I swim the moat without you? Do ye desert me, then?'

'Dick,' she gasped, 'I cannot. The strength is gone from me.'

'By the mass, then, we are all shent!' he shouted, stamping with his foot; and then, hearing steps, he ran to the room door and sought to close it.

Before he could shoot the bolt, strong arms were thrusting it back upon him from the other side. He struggled for a second; then, feeling himself overpowered, ran back to the window. The girl had fallen against the wall in the embrasure of the window; she was more than half insensible; and when he tried to raise her in his arms, her body was limp and unresponsive.

At the same moment the men who had forced the door against him laid hold upon him. The first he poniarded at a blow, and the others falling back for a second in some disorder, he profited by the chance, bestrode the window-sill, seized the cord in both hands, and let his body slip.

The cord was knotted, which made it the easier to descend; but so furious was Dick's hurry, and so small his experience of such gymnastics, that he span round and round in mid air like a criminal upon a gibbet, and now beat his head, and now bruised his hands, against the rugged stonework of the wall. The air roared in his ears; he saw the stars overhead, and the reflected stars below him in the moat, whirling like dead leaves before the tempest. And then he lost hold and fell, and soused head over ears into the icy water.

When he came to the surface his hand encountered the rope, which, newly lightened of his weight, was swinging wildly to and fro. There was a red glow overhead, and looking up, he saw, by the light of several torches and a cresset full of burning coals, the battlements lined with faces. He saw the men's eyes turning hither and thither in quest of him; but he was too far below, the light reached him not, and they looked in vain.

And now he perceived that the rope was considerably too long, and he began to struggle as well as he could towards the other side of the moat, still keeping his head above water. In this way he got much more then half-way over; indeed, the bank was almost within reach before the rope began to draw him back by its own weight. Taking his courage in both hands, he left go and made a leap for the trailing sprays of willow that had already, that same evening, helped Sir Daniel's messenger to land. He went down, rose again, sank a second time, and then his hand caught a branch, and with the speed of thought he had dragged himself into the thick of the tree and clung there, dripping and panting, and still half uncertain of his escape.

But all this had not been done without a considerable splashing, which had so far indicated his position to the men along the battlements. Arrows and quarrels fell thick around him in the darkness, thick like driving hail; and suddenly a torch was thrown down – flared through the air in its swift passage – stuck for a moment on the edge of the bank, where it burned high and lit up its whole surroundings like a bonfire – and then, in a good hour for Dick, slipped off, plumped into the moat, and was instantly extinguished.

It had served its purpose. The marksmen had had time to see the willow, and Dick ensconced among its boughs; and though the lad instantly sprang higher up the bank and ran for his life, he was yet not quick enough to escape a shot. An arrow struck him in the shoulder, another grazed his head.

The pain of his wounds lent him wings; and he had no sooner got upon the level than he took to his heels and ran straight before him in the dark, without a thought for the direction of his flight.

For a few steps missiles followed him, but these soon ceased; and when at length he came to a halt and looked behind, he was already a good way from the Moat House, though he could still see the torches moving to and fro along its battlements.

He leaned against a tree, streaming with blood and water, bruised, wounded, and alone. For all that, he had saved his life for that bout; and though Joanna remained behind in the power of Sir Daniel, he neither blamed himself for an accident that it had been beyond his power to prevent, nor did he augur any fatal consequences to the girl herself. Sir Daniel was cruel, but he was not likely to be cruel to a young gentlewoman who had other protectors, willing and able to bring him to account. It was more probable he would make haste to marry her to some friend of his own.

'Well,' thought Dick, 'between then and now I will find the means to bring that traitor under; for I think, by the mass, that I be now absolved from any gratitude or obligation; and when war is open, there is a fair chance for all.'

In the meanwhile, here he was in a sore plight.

For some little way farther he struggled forward through the forest; but what with the pain of his wounds, the darkness of the night, and the extreme uneasiness and confusion of his mind, he soon became equally unable to guide himself or to continue to push through the close undergrowth, and he was fain at length to sit down and lean his back against a tree.

When he awoke from something betwixt sleep and swooning, the grey of the morning had begun to take the place of night. A little chilly breeze was bustling among the trees, and as he still sat staring before him, only half awake, he became aware of something dark that swung to and fro among the branches, some hundred yards in front of him. The progressive brightening of the day and the return of his own senses at last enabled him to recognize the object. It was a man hanging from the bough of a tall oak. His head had fallen forward on his breast; but at every stronger puff of wind his body span round and round, and his legs and arms tossed, like some ridiculous plaything.

Dick clambered to his feet, and, staggering and leaning on the tree-trunks as he went, drew near to this grim object.

The bough was perhaps twenty feet above the ground, and the poor fellow had been drawn up so high by his executioners that his boots swung clear above Dick's reach; and as his hood had been drawn over his face, it was impossible to recognize the man.

Dick looked about him right and left; and at last he perceived that the other end of the cord had been made fast to the trunk of a little hawthorn which grew, thick with blossom, under the lofty arcade of the oak. With his dagger, which alone remained to him of all his arms, young Shelton severed the rope, and instantly, with a dead thump, the corpse fell in a heap upon the ground.

Dick raised the hood; it was Throgmorton, Sir Daniel's messenger. He had not gone far upon his errand. A paper, which had apparently escaped the notice of the men of the Black Arrow, stuck from the bosom of his doublet, and Dick, pulling it forth, found it was Sir Daniel's letter to Lord Wensleydale.

'Come,' thought he, 'if the world changes yet again, I may have here the wherewithal to shame Sir Daniel – nay, and perchance to bring him to the block.'

And he put the paper in his own bosom, said a prayer over the dead man, and set forth again through the woods.

His fatigue and weakness increased; his ears sang, his steps faltered, his mind at intervals failed him, so low had he been brought by loss of blood. Doubtless he made many deviations from his true path, but at last he came out upon the high-road, not very far from Tunstall hamlet.

A rough voice bid him stand.

'Stand?' repeated Dick. 'By the mass, but I am nearer falling.'

And he suited the action to the word, and fell all his length upon the road.

Two men came forth out of the thicket, each in green forest jerkin, each with long-bow and quiver and short sword.

'Why, Lawless,' said the younger of the two, 'it is young Shelton.'

'Ay, this will be as good as bread to John Amend-All,' returned the other. 'Though, faith, he hath been to the wars. Here is a tear in his scalp that must 'a' cost him many a good ounce of blood.'

'And here,' added Greensheve, 'is a hole in his shoulder that must have pricked him well. Who hath done this, think ye? If it be one of ours, he may all to prayer; Ellis will give him a short shrift and a long rope.'

'Up with the cub,' said Lawless. 'Clap him on my back.'

And then, when Dick had been hoisted to his shoulders, and he had taken the lad's arms about his neck, and got a firm hold of him, the ex-Grey Friar added:

'Keep ye the post, brother Greensheve. I will on with him by myself.'

So Greensheve returned to his ambush on the wayside, and Lawless trudged down the hill, whistling as he went with Dick, still in a dead faint, comfortably settled on his shoulders.

The sun rose as he came out of the skirts of the wood and saw Tunstall hamlet straggling up the opposite hill. All seemed quiet, but a strong post of some half a score of archers lay close by the bridge on either side of the road, and, as soon as they perceived Lawless with his burden, began to bestir themselves and set arrow to string like vigilant sentries.

'Who goes?' cried the man in command.

'Will Lawless, by the rood – ye know me as well as your own hand,' returned the outlaw contemptuously.

'Give the word, Lawless,' returned the other.

'Now, Heaven lighten thee, thou great fool,' replied Lawless. 'Did I not tell it thee myself? But ye are all mad for this playing at soldiers. When I am in the greenwood, give me greenwood ways; and my word for this tide is, "A fig for all mock soldiery!"'

'Lawless, ye but show an ill example; give us the word, fool jester,' said the commander of the post.

'And if I had forgotten it?' asked the other.

'An ye had forgotten it – as I know y' 'ave not – by the mass, I would clap an arrow into your big body,' returned the first.

'Nay, an y' are so ill a jester,' said Lawless, 'ye shall have your word for me. "Duckworth and Shelton" is the word; and here, to the illustration, is Shelton on my shoulders, and to Duckworth do I carry him.'

'Pass, Lawless,' said the sentry.

'And where is John?' asked the Grey Friar.

'He holdeth a court, by the mass, and taketh rents as to the manner born!' cried another of the company.

So it proved. When Lawless got as far up the village as the little inn, he found Ellis Duckworth surrounded by Sir Daniel's tenants, and, by the right of his good company of archers, coolly taking rents, and giving written receipts in return for them. By the faces of the tenants, it was plain how little this proceeding pleased them; for they argued very rightly that they would simply have to pay them twice.

As soon as he knew what had brought Lawless, Ellis dismissed the remainder of the tenants, and, with every mark of interest and apprehension, conducted Dick into an inner chamber of the inn. There the lad's hurts were looked to; and he was recalled, by simple remedies, to consciousness.

'Dear lad,' said Ellis, pressing his hand, 'y' are in a friend's hands that loved your father, and loves you for his sake. Rest ye a little quietly, for ye are somewhat out of case. Then shall ye tell me your story, and betwixt the two of us we shall find a remedy for all.'

A little later in the day, and after Dick had awakened from a confortable slumber to find himself still very weak, but clearer in mind and easier in body, Ellis returned, and sitting down by the bedside, begged him, in the name of his father, to relate the circumstances of his escape from Tunstall Moat House. There was something in the strength of Duckworth's frame, in the honesty of his brown face, in the clearness and shrewdness of his eyes, that moved Dick to obey him; and from first to last the lad told him the story of his two days' adventures.

'Well,' said Ellis, when he had done, 'see what the kind saints have done for you, Dick Shelton, not alone to save your body in so numerous and deadly perils, but to bring you into my hands that have no dearer wish than to assist your father's son. Be but true to me – and I see y' are true – and betwixt you and me, we shall bring that false-heart traitor to the death.'

'Will ye assault the house?' asked Dick.

'I were mad, indeed, to think of it,' returned Ellis. 'He hath too much power; his men gather to him; those that gave me the slip last night, and by the mass came in so handily for you – those have made him safe. Nay, Dick, to the contrary, thou and I and my brave bowmen, we must all slip from this forest speedily, and leave Sir Daniel free.'

'My mind misgiveth me for Jack,' said the lad.

'For Jack!' repeated Duckworth. 'Oh, I see, for the wench! Nay,

Dick, I promise you if there come talk of any marriage we shall act at once; till then, or till the time is ripe, we shall all disappear, even like shadows at morning; Sir Daniel shall look east and west, and see none enemies; he shall think, by the mass, that he hath dreamed awhile, and hath now awakened in his bed. But our four eyes, Dick, shall follow him right close, and our four hands – so help us all the army of the saints! – shall bring that traitor low!'

Two days later Sir Daniel's garrison had grown to such a strength that he ventured on a sally, and at the head of some two-score horsemen pushed without opposition as far as Tunstall hamlet. Not an arrow flew, not a man stirred in the thicket; the bridge was no longer guarded, but stood open to all comers; and as Sir Daniel crossed it, he saw the villagers looking timidly from their doors.

Presently one of them, taking heart of grace, came forward, and with the lowliest salutations, presented a letter to the knight.

His face darkened as he read the contents. It ran thus:

To the most untrue and cruel gentylman, Sir Daniel Brackley, Knyght, These:

I fynde ye were untrue and unkynd fro the first. Ye have my father's blood upon your hands? let be, it will not wasshe. Some day ye shall perish by my procurement, so much I let you to wytte? and I let you to wytte farther, that if ye seek to wed to any other the gentylwoman, Mistresse Joan Sedley, whom that I am bound upon a great oath to wed myself, the blow will be very swift. The first step therinne will be thy first step to the grave.

RIC SHELTON.

PART 3 MY LORD FOXHAM

1 The House by the Shore

Months had passed away since Richard Shelton made his escape from the hands of his guardian. These months had been eventful for England. The party of Lancaster, which was then in the very article of death, had once more raised its head. The Yorkists defeated and dispersed, their leader butchered on the field, it seemed, for a very brief season in the winter following upon the events already recorded, as if the House of Lancaster had finally triumphed over its foes.

The small town of Shoreby-on-the-Till was full of the Lancastrian nobles of the neighbourhood. Earl Risingham was there, with three hundred men-at-arms; Lord Shoreby, with two hundred; Sir Daniel himself, high in favour and once more growing rich on confiscations, lay in a house of his own, on the main street, with three-score men. The world had changed indeed.

It was a black, bitter cold evening in the first week of January, with a hard frost, a high wind, and every likelihood of snow before the morning.

In an obscure ale-house in a by-street near the harbour three or four men sat drinking ale and eating a hasty mess of eggs. They were all likely, lusty, weather-beaten fellows, hard of hand, bold of eye; and though they wore plain tabards, like country ploughmen, even a drunken soldier might have looked twice before he sought a quarrel in such company.

A little apart before the huge fire sat a younger man, almost a boy, dressed in much the same fashion, though it was easy to see by his looks that he was better born, and might have worn a sword, had the time suited.

'Nay,' said one of the men at the table, 'I like it not. Ill will come of it. This is no place for jolly fellows. A jolly fellow loveth open country, good cover, and scarce foes; but here we are shut in a town, girt about with enemies; and, for the bull's-eye of misfortune, see if it snow not ere the morning.'

' 'Tis for Master Shelton there,' said another, nodding his head towards the lad before the fire.

'I will do much for Master Shelton,' returned the first; 'but to come to the gallows for any man – nay, brothers, not that!'

The door of the inn opened, and another man entered hastily and approached the youth before the fire.

'Master Shelton,' he said, 'Sir Daniel goeth forth with a pair of links and four archers.'

Dick (for this was our young friend) rose instantly to his feet.

'Lawless,' he said, 'ye will take John Capper's watch. Greensheve, follow with me. Capper, lead forward. We will follow him this time, an he go to York.'

The next moment they were outside in the dark street, and Capper, the man who had just come, pointed to where two torches flared in the wind at a little distance.

The town was already sound asleep; no one moved upon the streets, and there was nothing easier than to follow the party without observation. The two link-bearers went first; next followed a single man, whose long cloak blew about him in the wind; and the rear was brought up by the four archers, each with his bow upon his arm. They moved at a brisk walk, threading the intricate lanes and drawing nearer to the shore.

'He hath gone each night in this direction?' asked Dick, in a whisper.

'This is the third night running, Master Shelton,' returned Capper, 'and still at the same hour and with the same small following, as though his end were secret.'

Sir Daniel and his six men were now come to the outskirts of the country. Shoreby was an open town, and though the Lancastrian lords who lay there kept a strong guard on the main roads, it was still possible to enter or depart unseen by any of the lesser streets or across the open country.

The lane which Sir Daniel had been following came to an abrupt end. Before him there was a stretch of rough down, and the noise of the sea-surf was audible upon one hand. There were no guards in the neighbourhood, nor any light in that quarter of the town.

Dick and his two outlaws drew a little closer to the object of their chase, and presently, as they came forth from between the houses and could see a little farther upon either hand, they were aware of another torch drawing near from another direction.

'Hey,' said Dick, 'I smell treason.'

Meanwhile Sir Daniel had come to a full halt. The torches were stuck into the sand, and the men lay down, as if to await the arrival of the other party.

This drew near at a good rate. It consisted of four men only – a pair of archers, a varlet with a link, and a cloaked gentleman walking in their midst.

'Is it you, my lord?' cried Sir Daniel.

'It is I, indeed; and if ever true knight gave proof, I am that man,' replied the leader of the second troop; 'for who would not rather face giants, sorcerers, or pagans, than this pinching cold?'

'My lord,' returned Sir Daniel, 'beauty will be the more beholden, misdoubt it not. But shall we forth? for the sooner ye have seen my merchandise, the sooner shall we both get home.'

'But why keep ye her here, good knight?' inquired the other. 'An she be so young, and so fair, and so wealthy, why do ye not bring her forth among her mates? Ye would soon make her a good marriage, and no need to freeze your fingers and risk arrow-shots by going abroad at such untimely seasons in the dark.'

'I have told you, my lord,' replied Sir Daniel, 'the reason thereof concerneth me only. Neither do I purpose to explain it farther. Suffice it that if ye be weary of your old gossip, Daniel Brackley, publish it abroad that y' are to wed Joanna Sedley, and I give you my word ye will be quit of him right soon. Ye will find him with an arrow in his back.'

Meantime the two gentlemen were walking briskly forward over the down; the three torches going before them, stooping against the wind and scattering clouds of smoke and tufts of flame, and the rear brought up by the six archers.

Close upon the heels of these, Dick followed. He had, of course, heard no word of this conversation; but he had recognized in the second of the speakers old Lord Shoreby himself, a man of an infamous reputation, whom even Sir Daniel affected, in public, to condemn.

Presently they came close down upon the beach. The air smelt salt; the noise of the surf increased; and here, in a large walled garden, there stood a small house of two storeys, with stables and other offices.

The foremost torch-bearer unlocked a door in the wall, and after the whole party had passed into the garden, again closed and locked it on the other side.

Dick and his men were thus excluded from any further following, unless they should scale the wall and thus put their necks in a trap.

They sat down in a tuft of furze and waited. The red glow of the torches moved up and down and to and fro within the enclosure, as if the link-bearers steadily patrolled the garden.

Twenty minutes passed, and then the whole party issued forth again upon the down; and Sir Daniel and the baron, after an elaborate salutation, separated and turned severally homeward, each with his own following of men and lights.

As soon as the sound of their steps had been swallowed by the wind, Dick got to his feet as briskly as he was able, for he was stiff and aching with the cold.

'Capper, ye will give me a back up,' he said.

They advanced, all three, to the wall; Capper stooped, and Dick, getting upon his shoulders, clambered on to the cope-stone.

'Now, Greensheve,' whispered Dick, 'follow me up here; lie flat upon your face, that ye may be the less seen; and be ever ready to give me a hand if I fall foully on the other side.'

And so saying he dropped into the garden.

It was all pitch dark; there was no light in the house. The wind whistled shrill among the poor shrubs, and the surf beat upon the beach; there was no other sound. Cautiously Dick footed it forth, stumbling among bushes, and groping with his hands; and presently the crisp noise of gravel underfoot told him that he had struck upon an alley.

Here he paused, and taking his cross-bow from where he kept it concealed under his long tabard, he prepared it for instant action, and went forward once more with greater resolution and assurance. The path led him straight to the group of buildings.

All seemed to be sorely dilapidated: the windows of the house were secured by crazy shutters; the stables were open and empty; there was no hay in the hay-loft, no corn in the corn-box. Anyone would have supposed the place to be deserted; but Dick had good reason to think otherwise. He continued his inspection, visiting the offices, trying all the windows. At length he came round to the sea side of the house, and there, sure enough, there burned a pale light in one of the upper windows.

He stepped back a little way, till he thought he could see the movement of a shadow on the wall of the apartment. Then he remembered that in the stable his groping hand had rested for a moment on a ladder, and he returned with all dispatch to bring it. The ladder was very short, but yet, by standing on the topmost round, he could bring his hands as high as the iron bars of the window; and seizing these, he raised his body by main force until his eyes commanded the interior of the room.

Two persons were within: the first he readily knew to be Dame Hatch; the second, a tall and beautiful and grave young lady, in a long embroidered dress – could that be Joanna Sedley? his old wood-companion, Jack, whom he had thought to punish with a belt?

He dropped back again to the top round of the ladder in a kind of amazement. He had never thought of his sweetheart as of so superior a being, and he was instantly taken with a feeling of diffidence. But he had little opportunity for thought. A low 'Hist!' sounded from close by, and he hastened to descend the ladder.

'Who goes?' he whispered.

'Greensheve,' came the reply, in tones similarly guarded.

'What want ye?' asked Dick.

'The house is watched, Master Shelton,' returned the outlaw. 'We are not alone to watch it; for even as I lay on my belly on the wall I saw men prowling in the dark, and heard them whistle softly one to the other.'

'By my sooth,' said Dick, 'but this is passing strange! Were they not men of Sir Daniel's?'

'Nay, sir, that they were not,' returned Greensheve, 'for if I have eyes in my head, every man-Jack of them weareth me a white badge in his bonnet, something chequered with dark.'

'White, chequered with dark?' repeated Dick. 'Faith, 'tis a badge I know not. It is none of this country's badges. Well, an that be so, let us slip as quietly forth from this garden as we may; for here we are in an evil posture for defence. Beyond all question there are men of Sir Daniel's in that house, and to be taken between two shots is a beggarman's position. Take me this ladder; I must leave it where I found it.'

They returned the ladder to the stable, and groped their way to the place where they had entered.

Capper had taken Greensheve's position on the cope, and now he leaned down his hand, and, first one and then the other, pulled them up.

Cautiously and silently they dropped again upon the other side; nor did they dare to speak until they had returned to their old ambush in the gorse.

'Now, John Capper,' said Dick, 'back with you to Shoreby, even as for your life. Bring me instantly what men ye can collect. Here shall be the rendezvous; or if the men be scattered and the day be near at hand before they muster, let the place be something farther back, and by the entering in of the town. Greensheve and I lie here to watch. Speed ye, John Capper, and the saints aid you to dispatch! And now, Greensheve,' he continued, as soon as Capper had departed, 'let thou and I go round about the garden in a wide circuit. I would fain see whether thine eyes betrayed thee.'

Keeping well outwards from the wall, and profiting by every height and hollow, they passed about two sides, beholding nothing. On the third side the garden wall was built close upon the beach, and to preserve the distance necessary to their purpose, they had to go some way down upon the sands. Although the tide was still pretty far out, the surf was so high, and the sands so flat, that at each breaker a great sheet of froth and water came careering over the expanse, and Dick and Greensheve made this part of their inspection wading, now to the ankles, and now as deep as to the knees, in the salt and icy waters of the German Ocean.

Suddenly, against the comparative whiteness of the garden wall, the figure of a man was seen, like a faint Chinese shadow, violently signalling with both arms. As he dropped again to the earth, another arose a little farther on and repeated the same performance. And so, like a silent watchword, these gesticulations made the round of the beleaguered garden.

'They keep good watch,' Dick whispered.

'Let us back to land, good master,' answered Greensheve. 'We stand here too open; for, look ye, when the seas break heavy and white out there behind us, they shall see us plainly against the foam.'

'Ye speak sooth,' returned Dick. 'Ashore with us, right speedily.'

2 A Skirmish in the Dark

Thoroughly drenched and chilled, the two adventurers returned to their position in the gorse.

'I pray Heaven that Capper make good speed!' said Dick. 'I vow a candle to St Mary of Shoreby if he come before the hour!'

'Y' are in a hurry, Master Dick?' asked Greensheve.

'Ay, good fellow,' answered Dick; 'for in that house lieth my lady, whom I love, and who should these be that lie about her secretly by night? Unfriends for sure!'

'Well,' returned Greensheve, 'an John come speedily, we shall give a good account of them. They are not two-score at the outside – I judge so by the spacing of their sentries – and, taken where they are, lying so widely, one score would scatter them like sparrows. And yet, Master Dick, an she be in Sir Daniel's power already, it will little hurt that she should change into another's. Who should these be?'

'I do suspect the Lord of Shoreby,' Dick replied. 'When came they?'

'They began to come, Master Dick,' said Greensheve, 'about the time ye crossed the wall. I had not lain there the space of a minute ere I marked the first of the knaves crawling round the corner.'

The last light had been already extinguished in the little house when they were wading in the wash of the breakers, and it was impossible to predict at what moment the lurking men about the garden wall might make their onslaught. Of two evils, Dick preferred the least. He preferred that Joanna should remain under the guardianship of Sir Daniel rather than pass into the clutches of Lord Shoreby; and his mind was made up, if the house should be assaulted, to come at once to the relief of the besieged.

But the time passed, and still there was no movement. From quarter of an hour to quarter of an hour the same signal passed about the garden wall, as if the leader desired to assure himself of the vigilance of his scattered followers; but in every other particular the neighbourhood of the little house lay undisturbed.

Presently Dick's reinforcements began to arrive. The night was not yet old before nearly a score of men crouched beside him in the gorse.

Separating these into two bodies, he took the command of the smaller himself, and entrusted the larger to the leadership of Greensheve.

'Now, Kit,' said he to this last, 'take me your men to the near angle of the garden wall upon the beach. Post them strongly, and wait till that ye hear me falling on upon the other side. It is those upon the sea-front that I would fain make certain of, for there will be the leader. The rest will run; even let them. And now, lads, let no man draw an arrow; ye will but hurt friends. Take to the steel, and keep to the steel; and if we have the uppermost, I promise every man of you a gold noble when I come to mine estate.'

Out of the odd collection of broken men, thieves, murderers, and ruined peasantry whom Duckworth had gathered together to serve the purpose of his revenge, some of the boldest and the most experienced in war had volunteered to follow Richard Shelton. The service of watching Sir Daniel's movements in the town of Shoreby had from the first been irksome to their temper, and they had of late begun to grumble loudly and threaten to disperse. The prospect of a sharp encounter and possible spoils restored them to good humour, and they joyfully prepared for battle.

Their long tabards thrown aside, they appeared, some in plain green jerkins, and some in stout leathern jacks; under their hoods many wore bonnets strengthened by iron plates; and for offensive armour, swords, daggers, a few stout boar-spears, and a dozen of bright bills, put them in a posture to engage even regular feudal troops. The bows, quivers, and tabards were concealed among the gorse, and the two bands set resolutely forward.

Dick, when he had reached the other side of the house, posted his six men in a line, about twenty yards from the garden wall, and took position himself a few paces in front. Then they all shouted with one voice, and closed upon the enemy.

These, lying widely scattered, stiff with cold, and taken at unawares, sprang stupidly to their feet, and stood undecided. Before they had time to get their courage about them, or even to form an idea of the number and mettle of their assailants, a similar shout of onslaught sounded in their ears from the far side of the enclosure. Thereupon they gave themselves up for lost and ran.

In this way the two small troops of the men of the Black Arrow closed upon the sea-front of the garden wall, and took a part of the strangers, as it were, between two fires; while the whole of the remainder ran for their lives in different directions, and were soon scattered in the darkness.

For all that the fight was but beginning. Dick's outlaws, although they had the advantage of the surprise, were still considerably outnumbered by the men they had surrounded. The tide had flowed in the meanwhile; the beach was narrowed to a strip; and on this wet field, between the surf and the garden wall, there began, in the darkness, a doubtful, furious, and deadly contest.

The strangers were well armed; they fell in silence upon their assailants; and the affray became a series of single combats. Dick, who had come first into the mellay, was engaged by three; the first he cut down at the first blow, but the other two coming upon him hotly he was fain to give ground before their onset. One of these two was a huge fellow, almost a giant for stature, and armed with a two-handed sword, which he brandished like a switch. Against this opponent, with his reach of arm and the length and weight of his weapon, Dick and his bill were quite defenceless; and had the other continued to join vigorously in the attack, the lad must have indubitably fallen. This second man, however, less in stature and slower in his movements, paused for a moment to peer about him in the darkness, and to give ear to the sounds of the battle.

The giant still pursued his advantage, and still Dick fled before him, spying for his chance. Then the huge blade flashed and descended, and the lad, leaping on one side and running in, slashed sideways and upwards with his bill. A roar of agony responded, and before the wounded man could raise his formidable weapon, Dick, twice repeating his blow, had brought him to the ground.

The next moment he was engaged upon more equal terms with his second pursuer. Here there was no great difference in size, and though the man, fighting with sword and dagger against a bill, and being wary and quick of fence, had a certain superiority of arms, Dick more than made it up by his greater agility on foot. Neither at first gained any obvious advantage; but the older man was still insensibly profiting by the ardour of the younger to lead him where he would; and presently Dick found that they had crossed the whole width of the beach, and were now fighting above the knees in the spume and bubble of the breakers. Here his own superior activity was rendered useless; he found himself more or less at the discretion of his foe; yet a little, and he had his back turned upon his own men, and saw that this adroit and skilful adversary was bent upon drawing him farther and farther away.

Dick ground his teeth. He determined to decide the combat instantly; and when the wash of the next wave had ebbed and left them dry, he rushed in, caught a blow upon his bill, and leaped right at the throat of his opponent. The man went down backwards, with Dick still upon the top of him; and the next wave, speedily succeeding the last, buried him below a rush of water.

While he was still submerged, Dick forced his dagger from his grasp, and rose to his feet victorious.

'Yield ye!' he said. 'I give you life.'

'I yield me,' said the other, getting to his knees. 'Ye fight like a young man, ignorantly and foolhardily; but, by the array of the saints, ye fight bravely!'

Dick turned to the beach. The combat was still raging doubtfully in the night; over the hoarse roar of the breakers steel clanged upon steel, and cries of pain and the shout of battle resounded.

'Lead me to your captain, youth,' said the conquered knight. 'It is fit this butchery should cease.'

'Sir,' replied Dick, 'so far as these brave fellows have a captain, the poor gentleman who here addresses you is he.'

'Call off your dogs, then, and I will bid my villains hold,' returned the other.

There was something noble both in the voice and manner of his late opponent, and Dick instantly dismissed all fears of treachery.

'Lay down your arms, men!' cried the stranger knight. 'I have yielded me, upon promise of life.'

The tone of the stranger was one of absolute command, and almost instantly the din and confusion of the mellay ceased.

'Lawless,' cried Dick, 'are ye safe?'

'Ay,' cried Lawless, 'safe and hearty,'

'Light me the lantern,' said Dick.

'Is not Sir Daniel here?' inquired the knight.

'Sir Daniel?' echoed Dick. 'Now, by the rood, I pray not. It would go ill with me if he were.'

'Ill with *you*, fair sir?' inquired the other. 'Nay, then, if ye be not of Sir Daniel's party, I profess I comprehend no longer. Wherefore, then, fell ye upon mine ambush? in what quarrel, my young and very fiery friend? to what earthly purpose? and, to make a clear end of questioning, to what good gentleman have I surrendered?'

But before Dick could answer, a voice spoke in the darkness from close by. Dick could see the speaker's black and white badge, and the respectful salute which he addressed to his superior.

'My lord,' said he, 'if these gentlemen be unfriends to Sir Daniel, it is a pity, indeed, we should have been at blows with them; but it were tenfold greater that either they or we should linger here. The watchers in the house – unless they all be dead or deaf – have heard our hammering this quarter-hour agone; instantly they will have signalled to the town; and unless we be the livelier in our departure, we are like to be taken, both of us, by a fresh foe.'

'Hawksley is in the right,' added the lord. 'How please ye, sir? Whither shall we march?'

'Nay, my lord,' said Dick, 'go where you will for me. I do begin to suspect we have some ground of friendship, and if, indeed, I began our acquaintance somewhat ruggedly, I would not churlishly continue. Let us, then, separate, my lord, you laying your right hand in mine; and at the hour and place that ye shall name, let us encounter and agree.'

'Y' are too trustful, boy,' said the other; 'but this time your trust is not misplaced. I will meet you at the point of day at St Bride's Cross. Come, lads, follow!'

The strangers disappeared from the scene with a rapidity that seemed suspicious; and, while the outlaws fell to the congenial task of rifling the dead bodies, Dick made once more the circuit of the garden wall to examine the front of the house. In a little upper loophole of the roof he beheld a light set; and as it would certainly be visible in town from the back windows of Sir Daniel's mansion, he doubted not that this was the signal feared by Hawksley, and that ere long the lances of the Knight of Tunstall would arrive upon the scene.

He put his ear to the ground, and it seemed to him as if he heard a jarring and hollow noise from townward. Back to the beach he went hurrying. But the work was already done; the last body was disarmed and stripped to the skin, and four fellows were already wading seaward to commit it to the mercies of the deep.

A few minutes later, when there debouched out of the nearest lanes of Shoreby some two-score horsemen, hastily arrayed and moving at the gallop of their steeds, the neighbourhood of the house beside the sea was entirely silent and deserted.

Meanwhile, Dick and his men had returned to the ale-house of the Goat and Bagpipes to snatch some hours of sleep before the morning tryst.

3　St Bride's Cross

St Bride's Cross stood a little way back from Shoreby, on the skirts of Tunstall Forest. Two roads met: one, from Holywood across the forest; one, that road from Risingham down which we saw the wrecks of a Lancastrian army fleeing in disorder. Here the two joined issue, and went on together down the hill to Shoreby; and a little back from the point of the junction, the summit of a little knoll was crowned by the ancient and weather-beaten cross.

Here, then, about seven in the morning, Dick arrived. It was as cold as ever; the earth was all grey and silver with hoar-frost, and the day began to break in the east with many colours of purple and orange.

Dick set him down upon the lowest step of the cross, wrapped himself well in his tabard, and looked vigilantly upon all sides. He had not long to wait. Down the road from Holywood a gentleman in very rich and bright armour, and wearing over that a surcoat of the rarest furs, came pacing on a splendid charger. Twenty yards behind him followed a clump of lancers; but these halted as soon as they came in view of the trysting-place, while the gentleman in the fur surcoat continued to advance alone.

His visor was raised, and showed a countenance of great command and dignity, answerable to the richness of his attire and arms. And it was with some confusion of manner that Dick arose from the cross and stepped down the bank to meet his prisoner.

'I thank you, my lord, for your exactitude,' he said, louting very low. 'Will it please your lordship to set foot to earth?'

'Are ye here alone, young man?' inquired the other.

'I was not so simple,' answered Dick; 'and, to be plain with your lordship, the woods upon either hand of this cross lie full of mine honest fellows lying on their weapons.'

'Y' 'ave done wisely,' said the lord. 'It pleaseth me the rather, since last night ye fought foolhardily, and more like a savage Saracen

*'His visor was raised, and showed a countenance
of great command and dignity'*

lunatic than any Christian warrior. But it becomes not me to complain that had the undermost.'

'Ye had the undermost indeed, my lord, since ye so fell,' returned Dick; 'but had the waves not holpen me, it was I that should have had the worst. Ye were pleased to make me yours with several dagger marks, which I still carry. And in fine, my lord, methinks I had all the danger, as well as all the profit, of that little blind-man's medley on the beach.'

'Y' are shrewd enough to make light of it, I see,' returned the stranger.

'Nay my lord, not shrewd,' replied Dick, 'in that I shoot at no advantage to myself. But when, by the light of this new day, I see how stout a knight hath yielded, not to my arms alone, but to fortune, and the darkness, and the surf – and how easily the battle had gone otherwise, with a soldier so untried and rustic as myself – think it not strange, my lord, if I feel confounded with my victory.'

'Ye speak well,' said the stranger. 'Your name?'

'My name, an't like you, is Shelton,' answered Dick.

'Men call me the Lord Foxham,' added the other.

'Then, my lord, and under your good favour, ye are guardian to the sweetest maid in England,' replied Dick; 'and for your ransom, and the ransom of such as were taken with you on the beach, there will be no uncertainty of terms. I pray you, my lord, of your goodwill and charity, yield me the hand of my mistress, Joan Sedley; and take ye, upon the other part, your liberty, the liberty of these your followers, and (if ye will have it) my gratitude and service till I die.'

'But are ye not ward to Sir Daniel? Methought, if y' are Harry Shelton's son, that I had heard it so reported,' said Lord Foxham.

'Will it please you, my lord, to alight? I would fain tell you fully who I am, how situate, and why so bold in my demands. Beseech you, my lord, take place upon these steps, hear me to a full end, and judge me with allowance.'

And so saying, Dick lent a hand to Lord Foxham to dismount; led him up the knoll to the cross; installed him in the place where he had himself been sitting; and standing respectfully before his noble prisoner, related the story of his fortunes up to the events of the evening before.

Lord Foxham listened gravely, and, when Dick had done, 'Master Shelton,' he said, 'ye are a most fortunate-unfortunate young gentleman; but what fortune y' 'ave had, that you have amply merited; and what unfortune, ye have noways deserved. Be of good cheer; for ye have made a friend who is devoid neither of power nor favour. For yourself, although it fits not for a person of your birth to herd with outlaws, I must own ye are both brave and honourable; very dangerous in battle, right courteous in peace; a youth of excellent disposition and brave bearing. For your estates, ye will never see them till the world shall change again; so long as Lancaster hath the strong hand, so long shall Sir Daniel enjoy them for his own. For my ward, it is another matter; I had promised her before to a gentleman, a kinsman of my house, one Hamley; the promise is old——'

'Ay, my lord, and now Sir Daniel hath promised her to my Lord Shoreby,' interrupted Dick. 'And his promise, for all it is but young, is still the likelier to be made good.'

' 'Tis the plain truth,' returned his lordship. 'And considering, moreover, that I am your prisoner, upon no better composition than my bare life, and over and above that, that the maiden is unhappily in other hands, I will so far consent. Aid me with your good fellows——'

'My lord,' cried Dick, 'they are these same outlaws that ye blame me for consorting with,'

'Let them be what they will, they can fight,' returned Lord Foxham. 'Help me, then; and if between us we regain the maid, upon my knightly honour, she shall marry you!'

Dick bent his knee before his prisoner; but he; leaping up lightly from the cross, caught the lad up and embraced him like a son.

'Come,' he said, 'an y' are to marry Joan, we must be early friends.'

4　The Good Hope

An hour thereafter, Dick was back at the Goat and Bagpipes, breaking his fast, and receiving the report of his messengers and sentries. Duckworth was still absent from Shoreby; and this was frequently the case, for he played many parts in the world, shared many different interests, and conducted many various affairs. He had founded that fellowship of the Black Arrow, as a ruined man longing for vengeance and money; and yet among those who knew him best, he was thought to be the agent and emissary of the great King-maker of England, Richard, Earl of Warwick.

In his absence, at any rate, it fell upon Richard Shelton to command affairs in Shoreby; and, as he sat at meat, his mind was full of care, and his face heavy with consideration. It had been determined, between him and the Lord Foxham, to make one bold strike that evening, and, by brute force, to set Joanna free. The obstacles, however, were many; and as one after another of his scouts arrived, each brought him more discomfortable news.

Sir Daniel was alarmed by the skirmish of the night before. He had increased the garrison of the house in the garden; but not content with that, he had stationed horsemen in all the neighbouring lanes, so that he might have instant word of any movement. Meanwhile, in the court of his mansion, steeds stood saddled, and the riders, armed at every point, awaited but the signal to ride.

The adventure of the night appeared more and more difficult of execution, till suddenly Dick's countenance lightened.

'Lawless!' he cried, 'you that were a shipman, can ye steal me a ship?'

'Master Dick,' replied Lawless, 'if ye would back me, I would agree to steal York Minster.'

Presently after, these two set forth and descended to the harbour. It was a considerable basin, lying among sandhills, and surrounded with patches of down, ancient ruinous lumber, and tumbledown slums of the town. Many decked ships and many open boats either lay there at anchor, or had been drawn up on the beach. A long duration of bad weather had driven them from the high seas into the shelter of the port; and the great trooping of black clouds, and the cold squalls that followed one another, now with a sprinkling of dry snow, now in a mere swoop of wind, promised no improvement, but rather threatened a more serious storm in the immediate future.

The seamen, in view of the cold and the wind, had for the most part slunk ashore, and were now roaring and singing in the shoreside taverns. Many of the ships already rode unguarded at their anchors; and as the day wore on, and the weather offered no appearance of improvement, the number was continually being augmented. It was to these deserted ships, and, above all, to those of them that lay far out, that Lawless directed his attention; while Dick, seated upon an anchor that was half embedded in the sand, and giving ear, now to the rude, potent, and boding voices of the gale, and now to the hoarse singing of the shipmen in a neighbouring tavern, soon forgot his immediate surroundings and concerns in the agreeable recollection of Lord Foxham's promise.

He was disturbed by a touch upon his shoulder. It was Lawless, pointing to a small ship that lay somewhat by itself, and within but a little of the harbour mouth, where it heaved regularly and smoothly on the entering swell. A pale gleam of winter sunshine fell at that moment on the vessel's deck, relieving her against a bank of scowling cloud; and in this momentary glitter Dick could see a couple of men hauling the skiff alongside.

'There, sir,' said Lawless, 'mark ye it well! There is the ship for to-night.'

Presently the skiff put out from the vessel's side, and the two men, keeping her head well to the wind, pulled lustily for shore. Lawless turned to a loiterer.

'How call ye her?' he asked, pointing to the little vessel.

'They call her the *Good Hope*, of Dartmouth,' replied the loiterer. 'Her captain, Arblaster by name. He pulleth the bow oar in yon skiff.'

This was all that Lawless wanted. Hurriedly, thanking the man, he moved round the shore to a certain sandy creek, for which the skiff was heading. There he took up his position, and as soon as they were within earshot, opened fire on the sailors of the *Good Hope*.

· 'What! Gossip Arblaster!' he cried. 'Why, ye be well met; nay, gossip, ye be right well met, upon the road! And is that the *Good Hope*? Ay, I would know her among ten thousand! – a sweet shear, a sweet boat! But marry come up, my gossip, will ye drink! I have come into mine estate, which doubtless ye remember to have heard on. I am now rich; I have left to sail upon the sea; I do sail now, for the most part, upon spiced ale. Come, fellow, thy hand upon't! Come, drink with an old shipfellow!'

Skipper Arblaster, a long-faced, elderly, weather-beaten man, with a knife hanging about his neck by a plaited cord, and for all the world like any modern seaman in his gait and bearing, had hung back in obvious amazement and distrust. But the name of an estate, and a certain air of tipsified simplicity and good-fellowship which Lawless very well affected, combined to conquer his suspicious jealousy; his countenance relaxed, and he at once extended his open hand and squeezed that of the outlaw in a formidable grasp.

'Nay,' he said, 'I cannot mind you. But what o' that? I would drink with any man, gossip, and so would my man Tom. Man Tom,' he added, addressing his follower, 'here is my gossip, whose name I cannot mind, but no doubt a very good seaman. Let's go drink with him and his shore friend.'

Lawless led the way, and they were soon seated in an ale-house, which, as it was very new, and stood in an exposed and solitary station, was less crowded than those nearer to the centre of the port. It was but a shed of timber, much like a block-house in the backwoods of to-day, and was coarsely furnished with a press or two, a number of naked benches, and boards set upon barrels to play the part of tables. In the middle, and besieged by half a hundred violent draughts, a fire of wreck-wood blazed and vomited thick smoke.

'Ay, now,' said Lawless, 'here is a shipman's joy – a good fire and a good stiff cup ashore, with foul weather without and an off-sea gale a-snoring in the roof! Here's to the *Good Hope*! May she ride easy!'

'Ay,' said Skipper Arblaster, ' 'tis good weather to be ashore in, that is sooth. Man Tom, how say ye to that? Gossip, ye speak well, though I can never think upon your name; but ye speak very well. May the *Good Hope* ride easy! Amen.'

'Friend Dickon,' resumed Lawless, addressing his commander, 'ye have certain matters on hand, unless I err? Well, prithee be about them incontinently. For here I be with the choice of all good company, two tough old shipmen; and till that ye return I will go warrant these brave fellows will bide here and drink me cup for cup. We are not like shoremen, we old, tough tarry-Johns!'

'It is well meant,' returned the skipper. 'Ye can go, boy; for I will keep your good friend and my good gossip company till curfew – ay, and by St Mary, till the sun get up again! For, look ye, when a man hath been long enough at sea, the salt getteth me into the clay upon his bones; and let him drink a draw-well, he will never be quenched.'

Thus encouraged upon all hands, Dick rose, saluted his company, and going forth again into the gusty afternoon, got him as speedily as he might to the Goat and Bagpipes. Thence he sent word to my Lord Foxham that, so soon as ever the evening closed, they would have a stout boat to keep the sea in. And then leading along with him a couple of outlaws who had some experience of the sea, he returned himself to the harbour and the little sandy creek.

The skiff of the *Good Hope* lay among many others, from which it was easily distinguished by its extreme smallness and fragility. Indeed, when Dick and his two men had taken their places, and begun to put forth out of the creek into the open harbour, the little cockle dipped into the swell and staggered under every gust of wind, like a thing upon the point of sinking.

The *Good Hope*, as we have said, was anchored far out, where the swell was heaviest. No other vessel lay nearer than several cables' length; those that were the nearest were themselves entirely deserted; and as the skiff approached, a thick flurry of snow and a sudden darkening of the weather further concealed the movements of the outlaws from all possible espial. In a trice they had leaped upon the heaving deck, and the skiff was dancing at the stern. The *Good Hope* was captured.

She was a good stout boat, decked in the bows and amidships, but open in the stern. She carried one mast, and was rigged between a felucca and a lugger. It would seem that Skipper Arblaster had made an excellent venture, for the hold was full of pieces of French wine; and in the little cabin, besides the Virgin Mary in the bulkhead which proved the captain's piety, there were many lockfast chests and cupboards, which showed him to be rich and careful.

A dog, who was the sole occupant of the vessel, furiously barked and bit the heels of the boarders; but he was soon kicked into the cabin, and the door shut upon his just resentment. A lamp was lit and fixed in the shrouds to mark the vessel clearly from the shore; one of the wine-pieces in the hold was broached, and a cup of excellent Gascony emptied to the adventure of the evening; and then, while one of the outlaws began to get ready his bow and arrows and prepare to hold the ship against all comers, the other hauled in the skiff and got overboard, where he held on, waiting for Dick.

'Well, Jack, keep me a good watch,' said the young commander, preparing to follow his subordinate. 'Ye will do right well.'

'Why,' returned Jack, 'I shall do excellent well indeed, so long as we lie here; but once we put the nose of this poor ship outside the harbour—— See, there she trembles! Nay, the poor shrew heard the words, and the heart misgave her in her oak-tree ribs. But look, Master Dick! how black the weather gathers!'

The darkness ahead was, indeed, astonishing. Great billows heaved up out of the blackness, one after another; and one after another the *Good Hope* buoyantly climbed, and giddily plunged upon the further side. A thin sprinkle of snow and thin flakes of foam came flying, and powdered the deck; and the wind harped dismally among the rigging.

'In sooth, it looketh evilly,' said Dick. 'But what cheer! 'Tis but a squall, and presently it will blow over.' But, in spite of his words, he was depressingly affected by the bleak disorder of the sky and the wailing and fluting of the wind; and as as he got over the side of the *Good Hope* and made once more for the landing-creek with the best speed of oars, he crossed himself devoutly, and recommended to Heaven the lives of all who should adventure on the sea.

At the landing-creek there had already gathered about a dozen of the outlaws. To these the skiff was left, and they were bidden embark without delay.

A little farther up the beach Dick found Lord Foxham hurrying in quest of him, his face concealed with a dark hood, and his bright armour covered by a long russet mantle of a poor appearance.

'Young Shelton,' he said, 'are ye for sea, then, truly?'

'My lord,' replied Richard, 'they lie about the house with horsemen; it may not be reached from the land side without alarum; and, Sir Daniel once advertised of our adventure, we can no more carry it to a good end than, saving your presence, we could ride upon the wind. Now, in going round by sea, we do run some peril by the elements; but, what much outweigheth all, we have a chance to make good our purpose and bear off the maid.'

'Well,' returned Lord Foxham, 'lead on. I will, in some sort, follow you for shame's sake; but I own I would I were in bed.'

'Here, then,' said Dick. 'Hither we go to fetch our pilot.'

And he led the way to the rude ale-house where he had given rendezvous to a portion of his men. Some of these he found lingering round the door outside; others had pushed more boldly in, and, choosing places as near as possible to where they saw their comrade, gathered close about Lawless and the two shipmen. These, to judge by the distempered countenance and cloudy eye, had long since gone beyond the boundaries of moderation; and as Richard entered, closely followed by Lord Foxham, they were all three tuning up an old, pitiful sea-ditty, to the chorus of the wailing of the gale.

The young leader cast a rapid glance about the shed. The fire had just been replenished, and gave forth volumes of black smoke, so that it was difficult to see clearly in the farther corners. It was plain, however, that the outlaws very largely outnumbered the remainder of the guests. Satisfied upon this point, in case of any failure in the operation of his plan, Dick strode up to the table and resumed his place upon the bench.

'Hey?' cried the skipper, tipsily, 'who are ye, hey?'

'I want a word with you without, Master Arblaster,' returned Dick; 'and here is what we shall talk of.' And he showed him a gold noble in the glimmer of the firelight.

The shipman's eyes burned, although he still failed to recognize our hero.

'Ay, boy,' he said, 'I am with you. Gossip, I will be back anon. Drink fair, gossip'; and, taking Dick's arm to steady his uneven steps, he walked to the door of the ale-house.

As soon as he was over the threshold, ten strong arms had seized and bound him; and in two minutes more, with his limbs trussed one to another, and a good gag in his mouth, he had been tumbled neck and crop into a neighbouring hay-barn. Presently, his man Tom, similarly secured, was tossed beside him, and the pair were left to their uncouth reflections for the night.

And now, as the time for concealment had gone by, Lord Foxham's followers were summoned by a preconcerted signal, and the party, boldly taking possession of as many boats as their numbers required, pulled in a flotilla for the light in the rigging of the ship.

Long before the last man had climbed to the deck of the *Good Hope*, the sound of furious shouting from the shore showed that a part, at least, of the seamen had discovered the loss of their skiffs.

But it was now too late, whether for recovery or revenge,. Out of some forty fighting men now mustered in the stolen ship, eight had been to sea, and could play the part of mariners. With the aid of these, a slice of sail was got upon her. The cable was cut. Lawless, vacillating on his feet, and still shouting the chorus of sea-ballads, took the long tiller in his hands; and the *Good Hope* began to flit forward into the darkness of the night, and to face the great waves beyond the harbour-bar.

Richard took his place beside the weather rigging. Except for the ship's own lantern, and for some lights in Shoreby town, that were already fading to leeward, the whole world of air was as black as in a pit. Only from time to time, as the *Good Hope* swooped dizzily down into the valley of the rollers, a crest would break – a great cataract of snowy foam would leap in one instant into being – and, in an instant more, would stream into the wake and vanish.

Many of the men lay holding on and praying aloud; many more were sick, and had crept into the bottom, where they sprawled among the cargo. And what with the extreme violence of the motion, and the continued drunken bravado of Lawless, still shouting and singing at the helm, the stoutest heart on board may have nourished a shrewd misgiving as to the result.

But Lawless, as if guided by an instinct, steered the ship across the breakers, struck the lee of a great sand-bank, where they sailed for a while in smooth water, and presently after laid her alongside a rude, stone pier, where she was hastily made fast, and lay ducking and grinding in the dark.

5 The Good Hope (continued)

The pier was not far distant from the house in which Joanna lay; it now only remained to get the men on shore, to surround the house with a strong party, burst in the door, and carry off the captive. They might then regard themselves as done with the *Good Hope*; it had placed them on the rear of their enemies; and the retreat, whether they should succeed or fail in the main enterprise, would be directed with a greater measure of hope in the direction of the forest and my Lord Foxham's reserve.

To get the men on shore, however, was no easy task; many had been sick, all were pierced with cold; the promiscuity and disorder on board had shaken their discipline; the movement of the ship and the darkness of the night had cowed their spirits. They made a rush upon the pier; my lord, with his sword drawn on his own retainers, must throw himself in front; and this impulse of rabblement was not restrained without a certain clamour of voices, highly to be regretted in the case.

When some degree of order had been restored, Dick, with a few chosen men, set forth in advance. The darkness on shore, by contrast with the flashing of the surf, appeared before him like a solid body; and the howling and whistling of the gale drowned any lesser noise.

He had scarce reached the end of the pier, however, when there fell a lull of the wind; and in this he seemed to hear on shore the hollow footing of horses and the clash of arms. Checking his immediate followers, he passed forward a step or two alone, even setting foot upon the down; and here he made sure he could detect the shape of men and horses moving. A strong discouragement assailed him. If their enemies were really on the watch, if they had beleaguered the shoreward end of the pier, he and Lord Foxham were taken in a posture of very poor defence – the sea behind, the men jostled in the dark upon a narrow causeway. He gave a cautious whistle, the signal previously agreed upon.

It proved to be a signal for more than he desired. Instantly there fell, through the black night, a shower of arrows sent at a venture; and so close were the men huddled on the pier that more than one was hit, and the arrows were answered with cries of both fear and pain. In this first discharge, Lord Foxham was struck down, Hawksley had him carried on board again at once; and his men, during the brief remainder of the skirmish, fought (when they fought at all) without guidance. That was, perhaps, the chief cause of the disaster which made haste to follow.

At the shore end of the pier, for perhaps a minute, held his own with a handful; one or two were wounded upon either side; steel crossed steel; nor had there been the least signal of advantage, when, in the twinkling of an eye, the tide turned against the party from the ship. Someone cried out that all was lost; the men were in the very humour to lend an ear to a discomfortable counsel; the cry was taken up. 'On board, lads, for your lives!' cried another. A third, with the true instinct of the coward, raised that inevitable report on all retreats: 'We are betrayed!' And in a moment the whole mass of men went surging and jostling backward down the pier, turning their defenceless backs on their pursuers and piercing the night with craven outcry.

One coward thrust off the ship's stern, while another still held her by the bows. The fugitives leaped, screaming, and were hauled on board, or fell back and perished in the sea. Some were cut down upon the pier by the pursuers. Many were injured on the ship's deck in the blind haste and terror of the moment, one man leaping upon another, and a third on both. At last, and whether by design or accident, the bows of the *Good Hope* were liberated; and the ever-ready Lawless, who had maintained his place at the helm through all the hurly-burly by sheer strength of body and a liberal use of the cold steel, instantly clapped her on the proper tack. The ship began to move once more forward on the stormy sea, its scuppers running blood, its deck heaped with fallen men, sprawling and struggling in the dark.

Thereupon, Lawless sheathed his dagger, and turning to his next neighbour. 'I have left my mark on them, gossip,' said he, 'the yelping, coward hounds.'

Now, while they were all leaping and struggling for their lives, the men had not appeared to observe the rough shoves and cutting stabs with which Lawless had held his post in the confusion. But perhaps they had already begun to understand somewhat more clearly, or perhaps another ear had overheard the helmsman's speech.

Panic-stricken troops recover slowly, and men who have just disgraced themselves by cowardice, as if to wipe out the memory of their fault, will sometimes run straight into the opposite extreme of insubordination. So it was now; and the same men who had thrown away their weapons and been hauled, feet foremost, into the *Good Hope*, began to cry out upon their leaders, and demand that someone should be punished.

This growing ill-feeling turned upon Lawless.

In order to get a proper offing, the old outlaw had put the head of the *Good Hope* to seaward.

'What!' bawled one of the grumblers, 'he carrieth us to seaward!'

''Tis sooth,' cried another. 'Nay, we are betrayed for sure.'

And they all began to cry out in chorus that they were betrayed, and in shrill tones and with abominable oaths bade Lawless go about-ship and bring them speedily ashore. Lawless, grinding his teeth, continued in silence to steer the true course, guiding the *Good Hope* among the formidable billows. To their empty terrors, as to their dishonourable threats, between drink and dignity he scorned to make reply. The malcontents drew together a little abaft the mast, and it was plain they were like barnyard cocks, 'crowing for courage.' Presently they would be fit for any extremity of injustice or ingratitude. Dick began to mount by the ladder, eager to interpose, but one of the outlaws, who was also something of a seaman, got beforehand.

'Lads,' he began, 'ye' are right wooden heads, I think. For to get back, by the mass, we must have an offing, must we not? And this old Lawless——'

Someone struck the speaker on the mouth, and the next moment, as a fire springs among dry straw, he was felled upon the deck, trampled under feet, and despatched by the daggers of his cowardly companions. At this the wrath of Lawless rose and broke.

'Steer yourselves,' he bellowed, with a curse; and, careless of the result, he left the helm.

The *Good Hope* was, at that moment, trembling on the summit of a swell. She subsided, with sickening velocity, upon the further side. A wave, like a great black bulwark, hove immediately in front of her; and, with a staggering blow, she plunged headforemost through that liquid hill. The green water passed right over her from stem to stern, as high as a man's knees; the sprays ran higher than the mast; and she rose again upon the other side, with an appalling tremulous indecision, like a beast that has been deadly wounded.

Six or seven of the malcontents had been carried bodily overboard; and as for the remainder, when they found their tongues again it was to bellow to the saints and wail upon Lawless to come back and take the tiller.

Nor did Lawless wait to be twice bidden. The terrible result of his fling of just resentment sobered him completely. He knew, better than anyone on board, how nearly the *Good Hope* had gone bodily down below their feet; and he could tell, by the laziness with which she met the sea, that the peril was by no means over.

Dick, who had been thrown down by the concussion and half drowned, rose wading to his knees in the swamped well of the stern, and crept to the old helmsman's side.

'Lawless,' he said, 'we do all depend on you; y' are a brave, steady man, indeed, and crafty in the management of ships; I shall put three sure men to nwatch upon your safety.'

'Bootless, my master, bootless,' said the steersman, peering forward through the dark. 'We come every moment somewhat clearer of these sand-banks; with every moment, then, the sea packeth upon us heavier, and for all these whimperers, they will presently be on their backs. For, my master, 'tis a right mystery, but true, there never yet was a bad man that was a good shipman. None but the honest and the bold can endure me this tossing of a ship.'

'Nay, Lawless,' said Dick, laughing, 'that is a right shipman's byword, and hath no more of sense than the whistle of wind. But, prithee, how we go! Do we lie well? Are we in good case?'

'Master Shelton,' replied Lawless, 'I have been a Grey Friar – I praise fortune – an archer, a thief, and a shipman. Of all these coats, I had the best fancy to die in the Grey Friar's, as ye may readily conceive, and the least fancy to die in John Shipman's tarry jacket; and that for two excellent good reasons: first, that the death might take a man suddenly; and second, for the horror of that great salt smother and welter under my foot here' – and Lawless stamped with his foot. 'Howbeit,' he went on, 'an I die not a sailor's death, and that this night, I shall owe a tall candle to our Lady.'

'Is it so?' asked Dick.'

'It is right so,' replied the outlaw. 'Do ye not feel how heavy and dull she moves upon the waves? Do ye not hear the water washing in her hold? She will scarce mind the rudder even now. Bide till she has settled a bit lower; and she will either go down below your boots like a stone image, or drive ashore here, under our lee, and come all to pieces like a twist of string.'

'Ye speak with a good courage,' returned Dick. 'Ye are not then appalled?'

'Why, master,' answered Lawless, 'if ever a man had an ill crew to come to port with, it is I – a renegade friar, a thief, and all the rest on 't. Well, ye may wonder, but I keep a good hope in my wallet; and if that I be to drown, I will drown with a bright eye, Master Shelton, and a steady hand.'

Dick returned no answer, but he was surprised to find the old vagabond of so resolute a temper, and fearing some fresh violence or treachery, set forth upon his quest for three sure men. The great bulk of the men had now deserted the deck, which was continually wetted with the flying sprays, and where they lay exposed to the shrewdness of the winter wind. They had gathered, instead, into the hold of the merchandise, among the butts of wine, and lighted by two swinging lanterns.

Here a few kept up the form of revelry, and toasted each other deep in Arblaster's Gascony wine. But as the *Good Hope* continued to tear through the smoking waves, and toss her stem and stern alternately high in air and deep into white foam, the number of these jolly companions diminished with every moment and with every lurch. Many sat apart, tending their hurts, but the majority were already prostrated with sickness, and lay moaning in the bilge.

Greensheve, Cuckow, and a young fellow of Lord Foxham's whom Dick had already remarked for his intelligence and spirit, were still, however, both fit to understand and willing to obey. These Dick set as a bodyguard about the person of the steersman, and then, with a last look at the black sky and sea, he turned and went below into the cabin, whither Lord Foxham had been carried by his servants.

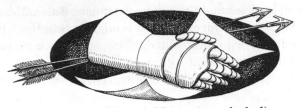

6 The Good Hope (concluded)

The moans of the wounded baron blended with the wailing of the ship's dog. The poor animal, whether he was merely sick at heart to be separated from his friends, or whether he indeed recognized some peril in the labouring of the ship, raised his cries, like minute-guns, above the roar of wave and weather; and the more superstitious of the men heard, in these sounds, the knell of the *Good Hope*.

Lord Foxham had been laid in a berth, upon a fur cloak. A little lamp burned dim before the Virgin in the bulkhead, and by its glimmer Dick could see the pale countenance and hollow eyes of the hurt man.

'I am sore hurt,' said he. 'Come near to my side, young Shelton; let there be one by me who, at least, is gentle born; for after having lived nobly and richly all the days of my life, this is a sad pass that I should get my hurt in a little ferreting skirmish, and die here, in a foul, cold ship upon the sea, among broken men and churls.'

'Nay, my lord,' said Dick, 'I pray rather to the saints that ye will recover you of your hurt, and come soon and sound ashore.'

'How?' demanded his lordship. 'Come sound ashore? There is, then, a question of it?'

'The ship laboureth – the sea is grievous and contrary,' replied the lad; 'and by what I can learn of my fellow that steereth us, we shall do well, indeed, if we come dryshod to land.'

'Ha!' said the baron gloomily, 'thus shall every terror attend upon the passage of my soul! Sir, pray rather to live hard, that ye may die easy, than to be fooled and fluted all through life, as to pipe and tabor, and, in the last hour, be plunged among misfortunes! Howbeit, I have that upon my mind that must not be delayed. We have no priest aboard?'

'None,' replied Dick.

'Here, then, to my secular interests,' resumed Lord Foxham; 'ye must be as good a friend to me dead as I found you a gallant enemy when I was living. I fall in an evil hour for me, for England, and for them that trusted me. My men are being brought by Hamley – he that was your rival; they will rendezvous in the long room at Holywood; this ring from off my finger will accredit you to represent mine orders; and I shall write, besides, two words upon this paper, bidding Hamley yield to you the damsel. Will ye obey? I know not.'

'But, my lord, what orders?' inquired Dick.

'Ay,' quoth the baron, 'ay – the orders'; and he looked upon Dick with hesitation. 'Are ye Lancaster or York?' he asked, at length.

'I shame to say it,' answered Dick, 'I can scarce clearly answer. But so much I think is certain: since I serve with Ellis Duckworth, I serve the House of York. Well, if that be so, I declare for York.'

'It is well,' returned the other; 'it is exceeding well. For, truly, had ye said Lancaster, I wot not for the world what I had done. But sith ye are for York, follow me. I came hither but to watch these lords at Shoreby, while mine excellent young lord, Richard of Gloucester,[1] prepareth a sufficient force to fall upon and scatter them. I have made me notes of their strength, what watch they keep, and how they lie; and these I was to deliver to my young lord on Sunday, an hour before noon, at St Bride's Cross beside the forest. This tryst I am not like to keep, but I pray you, of courtesy, to keep it in my stead; and see that not pleasure, nor pain, tempest, wound, not pestilence withhold you from the hour and place, for the welfare of England lieth upon this cast.'

'I do soberly take this upon me,' said Dick. 'In so far as in me lieth, your purpose shall be done.'

'It is good,' said the wounded man. 'My lord Duke shall order you farther, and if ye obey him with spirit and goodwill, then is your fortune made. Give me the lamp a little nearer to mine eyes, till I write these words for you.'

He wrote a note, 'to his worshipful kinsman, Sir John Hamley'; and then a second, which he left without external superscription.

'This is for the Duke,' he said. 'The word is "England and Edward," and the counter, "England and York."'

'And Joanna, my lord?' asked Dick.

'Nay, ye must get Joanna how ye can,' replied the baron. 'I have named you for my choice in both these letters; but ye must get her for yourself, boy. I have tried, as ye see here before you, and have lost my life. More could no man do.'

By this time the wounded man began to be very weary; and Dick, putting the precious papers in his bosom, bade him be of good cheer, and left him to repose.

The day was beginning to break, cold and blue, with flying squalls of snow. Close under the lee of the *Good Hope*, the coast lay in alternate rocky headlands and sandy bays; and further inland the wooded hill-tops of Tunstall showed along the sky. Both the wind and the sea had gone down; but the vessel wallowed deep, and scarce rose upon the waves.

Lawless was still fixed at the rudder; and by this time nearly all the men had crawled on deck, and were now gazing, with blank faces, upon the inhospitable coast.

'Are we going ashore?' asked Dick.

'Ay,' said Lawless, 'unless we get first to the bottom.'

And just then the ship rose so languidly to meet a sea, and the water weltered so loudly in her hold, that Dick involuntarily seized the steersman by the arm.

'By the mass!' cried Dick, as the bows of the *Good Hope* reappeared above the foam, 'I thought we had foundered, indeed; my heart was at my throat.'

In the waist, Greensheve, Hawksley, and the better men of both companies were busy breaking up the deck to build a raft: and to these Dick joined himself, working the harder to drown the memory of his predicament. But, even as he worked, every sea that struck the poor ship, and every one of her dull lurches, as she tumbled wallowing among the waves, recalled him with a horrid pang to the immediate proximity of death.

Presently, looking up from his work, he saw that they were close in below a promontory; a piece of ruinous cliff against the base of which the sea broke white and heavy, almost over-plumbed the deck; and, above that again, a house appeared, crowning a down.

Inside the bay, the seas ran gaily, raised the *Good Hope* upon their foam-flecked shoulders, carried her beyond the control of the steersman, and in a moment dropped her with a great concussion on the sand, and began to break over her, half-mast high, and roll her to and fro. Another great wave followed, raised her again, and carried her yet farther in; and then a third succeeded, and left her far inshore of the more dangerous breakers, wedged upon a bank.

'Now, boys,' cried Lawless, 'the saints have had a care of us, indeed. The tide ebbs; let us but sit down and drink a cup of wine, and before half an hour ye may all march me ashore as safe as on a bridge.'

A barrel was broached, and, sitting in what shelter they could find from the flying snow and spray, the shipwrecked company handed the cup around, and sought to warm their bodies and restore their spirits.

Dick, meanwhile, returned to Lord Foxham, who lay in great perplexity and fear, the floor of his cabin washing knee-deep in water, and the lamp, which had been his only light, broken and extinguished by the violence of the blow.

'My lord,' said young Shelton, 'fear not at all; the saints are plainly for us; the seas have cast us high upon a shoal, and as soon as the tide hath somewhat ebbed, we may walk ashore upon our feet.'

It was nearly an hour before the vessel was sufficiently deserted by the ebbing sea, and they could set forth for the land, which appeared dimly before them through a veil of driving snow.

Upon a hillock on one side of their way a party of men lay huddled together, suspiciously observing the movements of the new arrivals.

'They might draw near and offer us some comfort,' Dick remarked.

'Well, an they come not to us, let us even turn aside to them,' said Hawksley. 'The sooner we come to a good fire and a dry bed, the better for my poor lord.'

But they had not moved far in the direction of the hillock before the men, with one consent, rose suddenly to their feet, and poured a flight of well-directed arrows on the shipwrecked company.

'Back! back!' cried his lordship. 'Beware, in Heaven's name, that ye reply not!'

'Nay,' cried Greensheve, pulling an arrow from his leather jack. 'We are in no posture to fight, it is certain, being drenching wet, dog-weary, and three-parts frozen; but, for the love of old England, what aileth them to shoot thus cruelly on their poor country people in distress?'

'They take us to be French pirates,' answered Lord Foxham. 'In these most troublesome and degenerate days we cannot keep our own shores of England; but our old enemies whom we once chased on sea and land, do now range at pleasure, robbing and slaughtering and burning. It is the pity and reproach of this poor land.'

The men upon the hillock lay, closely observing them, while they trailed upward from the beach, and wound inland among desolate sand-hills; for a mile or so they even hung upon the rear of the march, ready, at a sign, to pour another volley on the weary and dispirited fugitives; and it was only when, striking at length upon a firm high-road, Dick began to call his men to some more martial order, that these jealous guardians of the coast of England silently disappeared among the snow. They had done what they desired; they had protected their own homes and farms, their own families and cattle; and their private interest being thus secured, it mattered not the weight of a straw to any one of them although the Frenchmen should carry blood and fire to every other parish in the realm of England.

1 At the date of this story, Richard Crookback could not have been created Duke of Gloucester; but for clearness, with the reader's leave, he shall so be called.

PART 4 THE DISGUISE

1 The Den

The place where Dick had struck the line of a high-road was not far from Holywood, and within nine or ten miles of Shoreby-on-the-Till; and here, after making sure that they were pursued no longer, the two bodies separated. Lord Foxham's followers departed, carrying their wounded master towards the comfort and security of the great abbey; and Dick, as he saw them wind away and disappear in the thick curtain of the falling snow, was left alone with near upon a dozen outlaws, the last remainder of his troop of volunteers.

Some were wounded; one and all were furious at their ill-success and long exposure; and though they were now too cold and hungry to do more, they grumbled and cast sullen looks upon their leaders. Dick emptied his purse among them, leaving himself nothing; thanked them for the courage they had displayed, though he could have found it more readily in his heart to rate them for poltroonery; and having thus somewhat softened the effect of his prolonged misfortune, dispatched them to find their way, either severally or in pairs, to Shoreby and the Goat and Bagpipes.

For his own part, influenced by what he had seen on board of the *Good Hope*, he chose Lawless to be his companion on the walk. The snow was falling, without pause or variation, in one even, blinding cloud; the wind had been strangled, and now blew no longer; and the whole world was blotted out and sheeted down below that silent inundation. There was great danger of wandering by the way and perishing in drifts; and Lawless, keeping half a step in front of his companion, and holding his head forward like a hunting dog upon the scent, inquired his way of every tree, and studied out their path as though he were conning a ship among dangers.

About a mile into the forest they came to a place where several ways met, under a grove of lofty and contorted oaks. Even in the narrow horizon of the falling snow, it was a spot that could not fail to be recognized; and Lawless evidently recognized it with particular delight.

'Now, Master Richard,' said he, 'an y' are not too proud to be the guest of a man who is neither a gentleman by birth nor so much as a good Christian, I can offer you a cup of wine and a good fire to melt the marrow in your frozen bones.'

'Lead on, Will,' answered Dick. 'A cup of wine and a good fire! Nay, I would go a far way round to see them.'

Lawless turned aside under the bare branches of the grove, and, walking resolutely forward for some time, came to a steepish hollow or den, that had now drifted a quarter full of snow. On the verge a great beech-tree hung, precariously rooted; and here the old outlaw, pulling aside some bushy underwood, bodily disappeared into the earth.

The beech had, in some violent gale, been half uprooted, and had torn up a considerable stretch of turf; and it was under this that old Lawless had dug out his forest hiding-place. The roots served him for rafters, the turf was his thatch, for walls and floor he had his mother the earth. Rude as it was, the hearth in one corner, blackened by fire, and the presence in another of a large oaken chest well fortified with iron, showed it at one glance to be the den of a man, and not the burrow of a digging beast.

Though the snow had drifted at the mouth and sifted in upon the floor of this earth-cavern, yet was the air much warmer than without; and when Lawless had struck a spark, and the dry furze bushes had begun to blaze and crackle on the hearth, the place assumed, even to the eye, an air of comfort and of home.

With a sigh of great contentment Lawless spread his broad hands before the fire, and seemed to breathe the smoke.

'Here, then,' he said, 'is this old Lawless's rabbit-hole; pray Heaven there come no terrier! Far have I rolled hither and thither, and here and about, since that I was fourteen years of mine age and first ran away from mine abbey, with the sacrist's gold chain and a mass-book that I sold for four marks. I have been in England and France and Burgundy, and in Spain, too, on a pilgrimage for my poor soul; and upon the sea, which is no man's country. But here is my place, Master Shelton. This is my native land, this burrow in the earth. Come rain or wind – and whether it's April, and the birds all sing, and the blossoms fall about my bed, or whether it's winter, and I sit alone with my good gossip the fire, and robin redbreast twitters in the woods – here is my church and market, my wife and child. It's here I come back to, and it's here, so please the saints, that I would like to die.'

' 'Tis a warm corner, to be sure,' replied Dick, 'and a pleasant, and a well hid.'

'It had need to be,' returned Lawless, 'for an they found it, Master Shelton, it would break my heart. But here,' he added, burrowing with his stout fingers in the sandy floor, 'here is my wine cellar, and ye shall have a flask of excellent strong stingo.'

Sure enough, after but a little digging, he produced a big leathern bottle of about a gallon, nearly three parts full of a very heady and sweet wine; and when they had drunk to each other comradely, and the fire had been replenished and blazed up again, the pair lay at full length, thawing and steaming, and divinely warm.

'Master Shelton,' observed the outlaw, 'y' 'ave had two mischances this last while, and y' are like to lose the maid – do I take it aright?'

'Aright,' returned Dick, nodding his head.

'Well, now,' continued Lawless, 'hear an old fool that hath been nigh-hand everything, and seen nigh-hand all. Ye go too much on other people's errands, Master Dick. Ye go on Ellis's; but he desireth rather the death of Sir Daniel. Ye go on Lord Foxham's; well – the saints preserve him! – doubtless he meaneth well. But go ye upon your own, good Dick. Come right to the maid's side. Court her, lest that she forget you. Be ready; and when the chance shall come, off with her at the saddlebow.'

'Ay, but, Lawless, beyond doubt she is now in Sir Daniel's own mansion,' answered Dick.

'Thither, then, go we,' replied the outlaw.

Dick stared at him.

'Nay, I mean it,' nodded Lawless. 'And if y' are of so little faith, and stumble at a word, see here!'

And the outlaw, taking a key from about his neck, opened the oak chest, and dipping and groping deep among its contents, produced first a friar's robe, and next a girdle of rope; and then a huge rosary of wood, heavy enough to be counted as a weapon.

'Here,' he said, 'is for you. On with them!'

And then, when Dick had clothed himself in this clerical disguise, Lawless produced some colours and a pencil, and proceeded, with the greatest cunning, to disguise his face. The eyebrows he thickened and produced; to the moustache, which was yet hardly visible, he rendered a like service; while, by a few lines around his eye, he changed the expression and increased the apparent age of this young monk.

'Now,' he resumed, 'when I have done the like, we shall make as bonny a pair of friars as the eye could wish. Boldly to Sir Daniel's we shall go, and there be hospitably welcomed for the love of Mother Church.'

'And how, dear Lawless,' cried the lad, 'shall I repay you?'

'Tut, brother,' replied the outlaw, 'I do naught but for my pleasure. Mind not for me. I am one, by the mass, that mindeth for himself. When that I lack, I have a long tongue and a voice like the monastery bell – I do ask, my son; and where asking faileth, I do most usually take.'

The old rogue made a humorous grimace; and although Dick was displeased to lie under so great favours to so equivocal a personage, he was yet unable to restrain his mirth.

With that, Lawless returned to the big chest, and was soon similarly disguised; but below his gown, Dick wondered to observe him conceal a sheaf of black arrows.

'Wherefore do ye that?' asked the lad. 'Wherefore arrows, when ye take no bow?'

'Nay,' replied Lawless lightly, ' 'tis like there will be heads broke – not to say backs – ere you and I win sound from where we're going to; and if any fall, I would our fellowship should come by the credit on't. A black arrow, Master Dick, is the seal of our abbey; it showeth you who writ the bill.'

'An ye prepare so carefully,' said Dick, 'I have here some papers that, for mine own sake, and the interest of those that trusted me, were better left behind than found upon my body. Where shall I conceal them, Will?'

'Nay,' replied Lawless, 'I will go forth into the wood and whistle me three verses of a song; meanwhile, do you bury them where ye please, and smooth the sand upon the place.'

'Never!' cried Richard. 'I trust you, man. I were base indeed if I trusted you not.'

'Brother, y' are but a child,' replied the old outlaw, pausing and turning his face upon Dick from the threshold of the den. 'I am a kind old Christian, and no traitor to men's blood, and no sparer of mine own in a friend's jeopardy. But fool, child, I am a thief by trade and birth and habit. If my bottle were empty and my mouth dry, I would rob you, dear child, as sure as I love, honour, and admire your parts and person! Can it be clearer spoken? No.'

And he stumped forth through the bushes with a snap of his big fingers.

Dick, thus left alone, after a wondering thought upon the inconsistencies of his companion's character, hastily produced, reviewed, and buried his papers. One only he reserved to carry along with him, since it in nowise compromised his friends, and yet might serve him, in a pinch, against Sir Daniel. That was the knight's own letter to Lord Wensleydale, sent by Throgmorton, on the morrow of the defeat at Risingham, and found next day by Dick upon the body of the messenger.

Then, treading down the embers of the fire, Dick left the den, and rejoined the old outlaw, who stood awaiting him under the leafless oaks, and was already beginning to be powdered by the falling snow. Each looked upon the other, and each laughed, so thorough and so droll was the disguise.

'Yet I would it were but summer and a clear day,' grumbled the outlaw, 'that I might see myself in the mirror of a pool. There be many of Sir Daniel's men that know me and if we fell to be recognized, there might be two words for you, my brother, but as for me, in a paternoster-while, I should be kicking in a rope's-end.'

Thus they set forth together along the road to Shoreby, which, in this part of its course, kept near along the margin of the forest, coming forth from time to time in the open country, and passing beside poor folks' houses and small farms.

Presently, at sight of one of these, Lawless pulled up.

'Brother Martin,' he said, in a voice capitally disguised, and suited to his monkish robe, 'let us enter and seek alms, from these poor sinners. *Pax vobiscum!* Ah,' he added, in his own voice, ' 'tis as I feared; I have somewhat lost the whine of it; and by your leave, good Master Shelton, ye must suffer me to practise in these country places, before that I risk my fat neck by entering Sir Daniel's. But look ye a little, what an excellent thing it is to be a Jack-of-all-trades! An I had not been a shipman, ye had infallibly gone down in the *Good Hope*; an I had not been a thief, I could not have painted me your face; and but that I had been a Grey Friar, and sung loud in the choir, and ate hearty at the board, I could not have carried this disguise, but the very dogs would have spied us out and barked at us for shams.'

He was by this time close to the window of the farm, and he rose on his tiptoes and peeped in.

'Nay,' he cried, 'better and better. We shall here try our false faces with a vengeance, and have a merry jest on Brother Capper to boot.'

And so saying he opened the door and led the way into the house.

Three of their own company sat at the table, greedily eating. Their daggers, stuck beside them in the board, and the black and menacing looks which they continued to shower upon the people of the house, proved that they owed their entertainment rather to force than to favour. On the two monks, who now, with a sort of humble dignity, entered the kitchen of the farm, they seemed to turn with a particular resentment; and one – it was John Capper in person – who seemed to play the leading part, instantly and rudely ordered them away.

'We want no beggars here!' he cried.

But another – although he was as far from recognizing Dick and Lawless – inclined to more moderate counsels.

'Not so,' he cried. 'We be strong men, and take; these be weak, and crave; but in the latter end these shall be uppermost and we below. Mind him not, my father; but come, drink of my cup, and give me a benediction.'

'Y' are men of a light mind, carnal and accursed,' said the monk. 'Now, may the saints forbid that ever I should drink with such companions! But here, for the pity I bear to sinners, here I do leave you a blessed relic, the which, for your soul's interest, I bid you kiss and cherish.'

So far Lawless thundered upon them like a preaching friar; but with these words he drew from under his robe a black arrow, tossed it on the board in front of the three startled outlaws, turned in the same instant, and, taking Dick along with him, was out of the room and out of sight among the falling snow before they had time to utter a word or move a finger.

'So,' he said, 'we have proved our false faces, Master Shelton. I will now adventure my poor carcass where ye please.'

'Good!' returned Richard. 'It irks me to be doing. Set we on for Shoreby!'

2 'In Mine Enemies' House'

Sir Daniel's residence in Shoreby was a tall, commodious plastered mansion, framed in carven oak, and covered by a low-pitched roof of thatch. To the back there stretched a garden, full of fruit-trees, alleys, and thick arbours, and overlooked from the far end by the tower of the abbey church.

The house might contain, upon a pinch, the retinue of a greater person than Sir Daniel; but even now it was filled with hubbub. The court rang with arms and horse-shoe iron; the kitchen roared with cookery like a bees'-hive; minstrels, and the players of instruments, and the cries of tumblers, sounded from the hall. Sir Daniel, in his profusion, in the gaiety and gallantry of his establishment, rivalled with Lord Shoreby, and eclipsed Lord Risingham.

All guests were made welcome. Minstrels, tumblers, players of chess, the sellers of relics, medicines, perfumes, and enchantments, and along with these every sort of priest, friar or pilgrim, were made welcome to the lower table, and slept together in the ample lofts, or on the bare boards of the long dining-hall.

On the afternoon following the wreck of the *Good Hope*, the buttery, the kitchens, the stables, the covered cart-shed that surrounded two sides of the court, were all crowded by idle people, partly belonging to Sir Daniel's establishment, and attired in his livery of murrey and blue, partly nondescript strangers attracted to the town by greed, and received by the knight through policy, and because it was the fashion of the time.

The snow, which still fell without interruption, the extreme chill of the air, and the approach of night, combined to keep them under shelter. Wine, ale, and money were all plentiful; many sprawled gambling in the straw of the barn, many were still drunken from the noontide meal. To the eye of a modern it would have looked like the sack of a city; to the eye of a contemporary it was like any other rich and noble household at a festive season.

Two monks – a young and an old – had arrived late, and were now warming themselves at a bonfire in a corner of the shed. A mixed crowd surrounded them – jugglers, mountebanks, and soldiers; and with these the elder of the two had soon engaged so brisk a conversation, and exchanged so many loud guffaws and country witticisms, that the group momentarily increased in number.

The younger companion, in whom the reader has already recognized Dick Shelton, sat from the first somewhat backward, and gradually drew himself away. He listened, indeed, closely, but he opened not his mouth; and by the grave expression of his countenance, he made but little account of his companion's pleasantries.

At last his eye, which travelled continually to and fro, and kept a guard upon all the entrances of the house, lit upon a little procession entering by the main gate and crossing the court in an oblique direction. Two ladies, muffled in thick furs, led the way, and were followed by a pair of waiting-women and four stout men-at-arms. The next moment they had disappeared within the house; and Dick, slipping through the crowd of loiterers in the shed, was already giving hot pursuit.

'The taller of these twain was Lady Brackley,' he thought; 'and where Lady Brackley is, Joan will not be far.'

At the door of the house the four men-at-arms had ceased to follow, and the ladies were now mounting the stairway of polished oak, under no better escort than that of the two waiting-women. Dick followed close behind. It was already the dusk of the day; and in the house the darkness of the night had almost come. On the stair-landings torches flared in iron holders; down the long tapestried corridors a lamp burned by every door. And where the door stood open, Dick could look in upon arras-covered walls, and rush bescattered floors, glowing in the light of the wood-fires.

Two floors were passed, and at every landing the younger and shorter of the two ladies had looked back keenly at the monk. He, keeping his eyes lowered, and affecting the demure manners that suited his disguise, had but seen her once, and was unaware that he had attracted her attention. And now, on the third floor, the party separated, the younger lady continuing to ascend alone, the other, followed by the waiting-maids, descending the corridor to the right.

Dick mounted with a swift foot, and holding to the corner, thrust forth his head and followed the three women with his eyes. Without turning or looking behind them, they continued to descend the corridor.

'It is right well,' thought Dick. 'Let me but know my Lady Brackley's chamber, and it will go hard an I find not Dame Hatch upon an errand.'

And just then a hand was laid upon his shoulder, and, with a bound and a choked cry, he turned to grapple his assailant.

He was somewhat abashed to find, in the person whom he had so roughly seized, the short young lady in the furs. She, on her part, was shocked and terrified beyond expression and hung trembling in his grasp.

'Madam,' said Dick, releasing her, 'I cry you a thousand pardons; but I have no eyes behind, and, by the mass, I could not tell ye were a maid.'

The girl continued to look at him, but, by this time, terror began to be succeeded by surprise, and surprise by suspicion. Dick, who could read these changes on her face, became alarmed for his own safety in that hostile house.

'Fair maid,' he said, affecting easiness, 'suffer me to kiss your hand, in token ye forgive my roughness, and I will even go.'

'Y' are a strange monk, young sir,' returned the young lady, looking him both boldly and shrewdly in the face; 'and now that my first astonishment hath somewhat passed away, I can spy the layman in each word you utter. What do ye here? Why are ye thus sacrilegiously tricked out? Come ye in peace or war? And why spy ye after Lady Brackley like a thief?'

'Madam,' quoth Dick, 'of one thing I pray ye to be very sure: I am no thief. And even if I come here in war, as in some degree I do, I make no war upon fair maids, and I hereby entreat them to copy me so far, and to leave me be. For, indeed, fair mistress, cry out – if such be your pleasure – cry but once, and say what ye have seen, and the poor gentleman before you is merely a dead man. I cannot think ye would be cruel,' added Dick; and taking the girl's hand gently in both of his, he looked at her with courteous admiration.

'Are ye then a spy – a Yorkist?' asked the maid.

'Madam,' he replied, 'I am indeed a Yorkist, and in some sort, a spy. But that which bringeth me into this house, the same which will win for me the pity and interest of your kind heart, is neither of York

nor Lancaster. I will wholly put my life in your discretion. I am a
lover, and my name——'

But here the young lady clapped her hand suddenly upon Dick's
mouth, looked hastily up and down and east and west, and, seeing the
coast clear, began to drag the young man, with great strength and
vehemence, upstairs.

'Hush!' she said, 'and come. 'Shalt talk hereafter.'

Somewhat bewildered, Dick suffered himself to be pulled
upstairs, bustled along a corridor, and thrust suddenly into a chamber,
lit, like so many of the others, by a blazing log upon the hearth.

'Now,' said the young lady, forcing him down upon a stool, 'sit ye
there and attend my sovereign good pleasure. I have life and death
over you, and I will not scruple to abuse my power. Look to yourself;
y' 'ave cruelly mauled my arm. He knew not I was a maid, quoth he!
Had he known I was a maid, he had ta'en his belt to me, forsooth!'

And with these words she whipped out of the room, and left Dick
gaping with wonder, and not very sure if he were dreaming or awake.

'Ta'en my belt to her!' he repeated. 'Ta'en my belt to her!' And
the recollection of that evening in the forest flowed back upon his
mind, and he once more saw Matcham's wincing body and beseeching
eyes.

And then he was recalled to the dangers of the present. In the next
room he heard a stir, as of a person moving; then followed a sigh,
which sounded strangely near; and then the rustle of skirts and tap of
feet once more began. As he stood hearkening, he saw the arras wave
along the hall; there was the sound of a door being opened, the
hangings divided, and, lamp in hand, Joanna Sedley entered the
apartment.

She was attired in costly stuffs of deep and warm colours, such as
befit the winter and the snow. Upon her head, her hair had been
gathered together and became her as a crown. And she, who had
seemed so little and so awkward in the attire of Matcham, was now tall
like a young willow, and swam across the floor as though she scorned
the drudgery of walking.

Without a start, without a tremor, she raised her lamp and looked
at the young monk.

'What make ye here, good brother?' she inquired. 'Ye are
doubtless ill-directed. Whom do ye require?' And she set her lamp
upon the bracket.

'. . . Joanna Sedley entered the apartment'

'Joanna,' said Dick; and then his voice failed him. 'Joanna,' he began again, 'ye said ye loved me; and the more fool I, but I believed it!'

'Dick!' she cried. 'Dick!'

And then, to the wonder of the lad, this beautiful and tall young lady made but one step of it, and threw her arms about his neck, and gave him a hundred kisses all in one.

'Oh, the fool fellow!' she cried. 'Oh, dear Dick! Oh, if ye could see yourself! Alack!' she added, pausing, 'I have spoilt you, Dick! I have knocked some of the paint off. But that can be mended. What cannot be mended, Dick – or I much fear it cannot! – is my marriage with Lord Shoreby.'

'Is it decided, then?' asked the lad.

'To-morrow before noon, Dick, in the abbey church,' she answered, 'John Matcham and Joanna Sedley both shall come to a right miserable end. There is no help in tears, or I could weep mine eyes out. I have not spared myself to pray, but Heaven frowns on my petition. And, dear Dick – good Dick – but that ye can get me forth of this house before the morning, we must even kiss and say good-bye.'

'Nay,' said Dick, 'not I; I will never say that word. 'Tis like despair; but while there's life, Joanna, there is hope. Yet will I hope. Ay, by the mass, and triumph! Look ye, now, when ye were but a name to me, did I not follow – did I not rouse good men – did I not stake my life upon the quarrel? And now that I have seen you for what ye are – the fairest maid and stateliest of England – think ye I would turn? – if the deep sea were there, I would straight through it; if the way were full of lions, I would scatter them like mice.'

'Ay,' she said dryly, 'ye make a great ado about a sky-blue robe!'

'Nay, Joan,' protested Dick, ''tis not alone the robe. But, lass, ye were disguised. Here am I disguised; and, to the proof, do I not cut a figure of fun – a right fool's figure?'

'Ay, Dick, an' that ye do!' she answered, smiling.

'Well, then!' he returned, triumphant. 'So was it with you, poor Matcham, in the forest. In sooth, ye were a wench to laugh at. But now!'

So they ran on, holding each other by both hands, exchanging smiles and lovely looks, and melting minutes into seconds; and so they might have continued all night long. But presently there was a noise behind them; and they were aware of the short young lady, with her finger on her lips.

'Saints!' she cried, 'but what a noise ye keep! Can ye not speak in compass? And now, Joanna, my fair maid of the woods, what will ye give your gossip for bringing you your sweetheart?'

Joanna ran to her, by way of answer, and embraced her fierily.

'And you, sir,' added the young lady, 'what do ye give me?'

'Madam,' said Dick, 'I would fain offer to pay you in the same money.'

'Come, then,' said the lady, 'it is permitted you.'

But Dick, blushing like a peony, only kissed her hand.

'What ails ye at my face, fair sir?' she inquired, curtsying to the very ground; and, then, when Dick had at length and most tepidly embraced her, 'Joanna,' she added, 'your sweetheart is very backward under your eyes; but I warrant you, when first we met, he was more ready, I am all black and blue, wench; trust me never, if I be not black and blue! And now,' she continued, 'have ye said your sayings? for I must speedily dismiss the paladin.'

But at this they both cried out that they had said nothing, that the night was still very young, and that they would not be separated so early.

'And supper?' asked the young lady. 'Must we not go down to supper?'

'Nay, to be sure!' cried Joan. 'I had forgotten.'

'Hide me, then,' said Dick, 'put me behind the arras, shut me in a chest, or what ye will, so that I may be here on your return. Indeed, fair lady,' he added, 'bear this in mind, that we are sore bested, and may never look upon each other's face from this night forward till we die.'

At this the young lady melted; and when, a little after, the bell summoned Sir Daniel's household to the board, Dick was planted very stiffly against the wall, at a place where a division in the tapestry permitted him to breathe the more freely, and even to see into the room.

He had not been long in this position when he was somewhat strangely disturbed. The silence in that upper storey of the house was only broken by the flickering of the flames and the hissing of a green log in the chimney; but presently, to Dick's strained hearing, there came the sound of someone walking with extreme precaution; and soon after the door opened, and a little black-faced, dwarfish fellow, in

Lord Shoreby's colours, pushed first his head and then his crooked body into the chamber. His mouth was open, as though to hear the better; and his eyes, which were very bright, flitted restlessly and swiftly to and fro. He went round and round the room, striking here and there upon the hangings; but Dick, by a miracle, escaped his notice. Then he looked below the furniture, and examined the lamp; and at last, with an air of cruel disappointment, was preparing to go away as silently as he had come, when down he dropped upon his knees, picked up something from among the rushes on the floor, examined it, and with every signal of delight, concealed it in the wallet at his belt.

Dick's heart sank, for the object in question was a tassel from his own girdle; and it was plain to him that this dwarfish spy, who took a malign delight in his employment, would lose no time in bearing it to his master, the baron. He was half tempted to throw aside the arras, fall upon the scoundrel, and, at the risk of his life, remove the telltale token. And while he was still hesitating, a new cause of concern was added. A voice, hoarse and broken by drink, began to be audible from the stair; and presently after uneven, wandering, and heavy footsteps sounded without along the passage.

'What make ye here, my merry men, among the greenwood shaws?' sang the voice. 'What make ye here? Hey! sots, what make ye here!' it added, with a rattle of drunken laughter; and then once more breaking into song:

> 'If ye should drink the clary wine,
>   Fat Friar John, ye friend o' mine——
>   If I should eat, and ye should drink,
>   Who shall sing the mass, d'ye think?'

Lawless, alas! rolling drunk, was wandering the house, seeking for a corner wherein to slumber off the effects of his potations. Dick inwardly raged. The spy, at first terrified, had grown reassured as he found he had to deal with an intoxicated man, and now, with a movement of cat-like rapidity, slipped from the chamber, and was gone from Richard's eyes.

What was to be done? If he lost touch of Lawless for the night he was left impotent, whether to plan or carry forth Joanna's rescue. If, on the other hand, he dared to address the drunken outlaw, the spy might still be lingering within sight, and the most fatal consequences ensue.

It was, nevertheless, upon this last hazard that Dick decided. Slipping from behind the tapestry, he stood ready in the doorway of the chamber, with a warning hand upraised. Lawless, flushed crimson, with his eyes injected, vacillating on his feet, drew still unsteadily nearer. At last he hazily caught sight of his commander, and, in despite of Dick's imperious signals, hailed him instantly and loudly by his name.

Dick leaped upon and shook the drunkard furiously.

'Beast!' he hissed, 'beast, and no man! It is worse than treachery to be so witless. We may all be shent for thy sotting.'

But Lawless only laughed and staggered, and tried to clap young Shelton on the back.

And just then Dick's quick ear caught a rapid brushing in the arras. He leaped towards the sound, and the next moment a piece of the wall-hanging had been torn down, and Dick and the spy were sprawling together in its folds. Over and over they rolled, grappling for each other's throat, and still baffled by the arras, and still silent in their deadly fury. But Dick was by much the stronger, and soon the spy lay prostrate under his knee, and, with a single stroke of the long poniard, ceased to breathe.

3 The Dead Spy

Throughout this furious and rapid passage, Lawless had looked on helplessly, and even when all was over, and Dick, already re-arisen to his feet, was listening with the most passionate attention to the distant bustle in the lower storeys of the house, the old outlaw was still wavering on his legs like a shrub in a breeze of wind, and still stupidly staring on the face of the dead man.

'It is well,' said Dick, at length; 'they have not heard us, praise the saints! But, now, what shall I do with this poor spy? At least, I will take my tassel from his wallet.'

So saying, Dick opened the wallet; within he found a few pieces of money, the tassel, and a letter addressed to Lord Wensleydale, and sealed with my Lord Shoreby's seal. The name awoke Dick's recollection; and he instantly broke the wax and read the contents of the letter. It was short, but, to Dick's delight, it gave evident proof that Lord Shoreby was treacherously corresponding with the House of York.

The young fellow usually carried his ink-horn and implements about him, and so now, bending a knee beside the body of the dead spy, he was able to write these words upon a corner of the paper:

My Lord of Shoreby, ye that writt the letter, wot ye why your man is ded! But let me rede you, marry not.

JON AMEND-ALL.

He laid this paper on the breast of the corpse; and then Lawless, who had been looking on upon these last manoeuvres with some flickering returns of intelligence, suddenly drew a black arrow from below his robe, and therewith pinned the paper in its place. The sight of this disrespect, or, as it almost seemed, cruelty to the dead, drew a cry of horror from young Shelton, but the old outlaw only laughed.

'Nay, I will have the credit for mine order,' he hiccupped. 'My jolly boys must have the credit on't – the credit, brother'; and then, shutting his eyes tight, and opening his mouth like a precentor, he began to thunder, in a formidable voice:

'If ye should drink the clary wine——'

'Peace, sot!' cried Dick, and thrust him hard against the wall. 'In two words – if so be that such a man can understand me who hath more wine than wit in him – in two words, and, a-Mary's name, begone out of this house, where, if ye continue to abide, ye will not only hang yourself, but me also! Faith, then, up foot! be yare, or, by the mass, I may forget that I am in some sort your captain, and in some your debtor! Go!'

The sham monk was now, in some degree, recovering the use of his intelligence; and the ring in Dick's voice, and the glitter in Dick's eye, stamped home the meaning of his words.

'By the mass,' cried Lawless, 'an I be not wanted, I can go'; and he turned tipsily along the corridor and proceeded to flounder downstairs, lurching against the wall.

So soon as he was out of sight, Dick returned to his hiding-place, resolutely fixed to see the matter out. Wisdom, indeed, moved him to be gone; but love and curiosity were stronger.

Time passed slowly for the young man, bolt upright behind the arras. The fire in the room began to die down, and the lamp to burn low and to smoke. And still there was no word of the return of anyone to these upper quarters of the house; still the faint hum and clatter of the supper party sounded from far below; and still, under the thick fall of the snow, Shoreby town lay silent upon every side.

At length, however, feet and voices began to draw near upon the stair; and presently after several of Sir Daniel's guests arrived upon the landing, and, turning down the corridor, beheld the torn arras and the body of the spy.

Some ran forward and some back, and all together began to cry aloud.

At the sound of their cries, guests, men-at-arms, ladies, servants, and, in a word, all the inhabitants of that great house, came flying from every direction, and began to join their voices to the tumult.

Soon a way was cleared, and Sir Daniel came forth in person, followed by the bridegroom of the morrow, my Lord Shoreby.

'My lord,' said Sir Daniel, 'have I not told you of this knave Black Arrow? To the proof, behold it! There it stands, and, by the rood, my gossip, in a man of yours, or one that stole your colours?'

'In good sooth, it was a man of mine,' replied Lord Shoreby, hanging back. 'I would I had more such. He was keen as a beagle and secret as a mole.'

'Ay, gossip, truly?' asked Sir Daniel keenly. 'And what came he smelling up so many stairs in my poor mansion? But he will smell no more.'

'An 't please you, Sir Daniel,' said one, 'here is a paper written upon with some matter, pinned upon his breast.'

'Give it me, arrow and all,' said the knight. And when he had taken into his hand the shaft, he continued for some time to gaze upon it in a sullen musing. 'Ay,' he said, addressing Lord Shoreby, 'here is a hate that followeth hard and close upon my heels. This black stick, or its just likeness, shall yet bring me down. And, gossip, suffer a plain knight to counsel you; and if these hounds begin to wind you, flee! 'Tis like a sickness – it still hangeth, hangeth upon the limbs. But let us see what they have written. It is as I thought, my lord; y' are marked, like an old oak, by the woodman; to-morrow or next day, by will come the axe. But what wrote ye in a letter?'

Lord Shoreby snatched the paper from the arrow, read it, crumpled it between his hands, and, overcoming the reluctance which had hitherto withheld him from approaching, threw himself on his knees beside the body and eagerly groped in the wallet.

He rose to his feet with a somewhat unsettled countenance.

'Gossip,' he said, 'I have indeed lost a letter here that much imported; and could I lay my hand upon the knave that took it, he should incontinently grace a halter. But let us, first of all, secure the issues of the house. Here is enough harm already, by St George!'

Sentinels were posted close around the house and garden; a sentinel on every landing of the stair, a whole troop in the main entrance-hall, and yet another about the bonfire in the shed. Sir Daniel's followers were supplemented by Lord Shoreby's; there was thus no lack of men or weapons to make the house secure, or to entrap a lurking enemy, should one be there.

Meanwhile, the body of the spy was carried out through the falling snow and deposited in the abbey church.

It was not until these dispositions had been taken, and all had returned to a decorous silence, that the two girls drew Richard Shelton from his place of concealment, and made a full report to him of what had passed. He, upon his side, recounted the visit of the spy, his dangerous discovery and speedy end.

Joanna leaned back very faint against the curtained wall.

'It will avail but little,' she said. 'I shall be wed to-morrow, in the morning, after all!'

'What!' cried her friend. 'And here is our paladin that driveth lions like mice! Ye have little faith, of a surety. But come, friend lion-driver, give us some comfort; speak and let us hear bold counsels.'

Dick was confounded to be thus outfaced with his own exaggerated words; but though he coloured, he still spoke stoutly.

'Truly,' said he, 'we are in straits. Yet, could I but win out of this house for half an hour, I do honestly tell myself that all might still go well; and for the marriage, it should be prevented.'

'And for the lions,' mimicked the girl, 'they shall be driven.'

'I crave your excuse,' said Dick. 'I speak not now in any boasting humour, but rather as one inquiring after help or counsel; for if I get not forth of this house through these sentinels, I can do less than naught. Take me, I pray you, rightly.'

'Why said ye he was rustic, Joan?' the girl inquired. 'I warrant he hath a tongue in his head; ready, soft, and bold is his speech at pleasure. What would ye more?'

'Nay,' sighed Joanna, with a smile, 'they have changed me my friend Dick, 'tis sure enough. When I beheld him, he was rough indeed. But it matters little; there is no help for my hard case, and I must still be Lady Shoreby!'

'Nay, then,' said Dick, 'I will even make the adventure. A friar is not much regarded; and if I found a good fairy to lead me up, I may find another belike to carry me down. How call they the name of this spy?'

'Rutter,' said the young lady; 'and an excellent good name to call him by. But how mean ye, lion-driver? What is in your mind to do?'

'To offer boldly to go forth,' returned Dick; 'and, if any stop me, to keep an unchanged countenance, and say I go to pray for Rutter. They will be praying over his poor clay even now.'

'The device is somewhat simple,' replied the girl, 'yet it may hold.'

'Nay,' said young Shelton, 'it is no device, but mere boldness, which serveth often better in great straits.'

'Ye say true,' she said. 'Well, go, a-Mary's name. And may Heaven speed you! Ye leave here a poor maid that loves you entirely, and another that is most heartily your friend. Be wary, for their sakes, and make not shipwreck of your safety.'

'Ay,' added Joanna, 'go, Dick. Ye run no more peril, whether ye go or stay. Go, ye take my heart with you; the saints defcnd you!'

Dick passed the first sentry with so assured a countenance that the fellow merely fidgeted and stared; but at the second landing the man carried his spear across and bade him name his business.

'*Pax vobiscum*,' answered Dick. 'I go to pray over the body of this poor Rutter.'

'Like enough,' returned the sentry; 'but to go alone is not permitted you.' He leaned over the oaken balusters and whistled shrill. 'One cometh,' he cried; and then motioned Dick to pass.

At the foot of the stair he found the guard afoot and awaiting his arrival; and when he had once more repeated his story, the commander of the post ordered four men out to accompany him to the church.

'Let him not slip, my lads,' he said. 'Bring him to Sir Oliver, on your lives!'

The door was then opened; one of the men took Dick by either arm, another marched ahead with a link, and the fourth, with bent bow and the arrow on the string, brought up the rear. In this order they proceeded through the garden, under the thick darkness of the night and the scattering snow, and drew near to the dimly illuminated windows of the abbey church.

At the western portal a picket of archers stood, taking what shelter they could find in the hollow of the arched doorways, and all powdered with the snow; and it was not until Dick's conductors had exchanged a word with these, that they were suffered to pass forth and enter the nave of the sacred edifice.

The church was doubtfully lighted by the tapers upon the great altar, and by a lamp or two that swung from the arched roof before the private chapels of illustrious families. In the midst of the choir the dead spy lay, his limbs piously composed, upon a bier.

A hurried mutter of prayer sounded along the arches; cowled figures knelt in the stalls of the choir, and on the steps of the high altar a priest in pontifical vestments celebrated mass.

Upon this fresh entrance, one of the cowled figures arose, and, coming down the steps which elevated the level of the choir above that of the nave, demanded from the leader of the four men what business brought him to the church. Out of respect for the service and the dead, they spoke in guarded tones; but the echoes of that huge, empty building caught up their words, and hollowly repeated and repeated them along the aisles.

'A monk!' returned Sir Oliver (for he it was), when he had heard the report of the archer. 'My brother, I looked not for your coming,' he added, turning to young Shelton. 'In all civility, who are ye? and at whose instance do ye join your supplications to ours?'

Dick, keeping his cowl about his face, signed to Sir Oliver to move a pace or two aside from the archers; and, so soon as the priest had done so, 'I cannot hope to deceive you, sir,' he said. 'My life is in your hands.'

Sir Oliver violently started; his stout cheeks grew pale, and for a space he was silent.

'Richard,' he said, 'what brings you here, I know not; but I much misdoubt it to be evil. Nevertheless, for the kindness that was, I would not willingly deliver you to harm. Ye shall sit all night beside me in the stalls: ye shall sit there till my Lord of Shoreby be married, and the party gone safe home; and if all goeth well, and ye have planned no evil, in the end ye shall go whither ye will. But if your purpose be bloody, it shall return upon your head. Amen!'

And the priest devoutly crossed himself, and turned and louted to the altar.

With that, he spoke a few words more to the soldiers, and taking Dick by the hand, led him up to the choir, and placed him in the stall beside his own, where, for mere decency, the lad had instantly to kneel and appear to be busy with his devotions.

His mind and his eyes, however, were continually wandering. Three of the soldiers, he observed, instead of returning to the house, had got them quietly into a point of vantage in the aisle; and he could not doubt that they had done so by Sir Oliver's command. Here, then, he was trapped. Here he must spend the night in the ghostly glimmer and shadow of the church, and looking on the pale face of him he slew; and here, in the morning he must see his sweetheart married to another man before his eyes.

But, for all that, he obtained a command upon his mind, built himself up in patience to await the issue.

4 In the Abbey Church

In Shoreby Abbey Church the prayers were kept up all night without cessation, now with the singing of psalms, now with a note or two upon the bell.

Rutter, the spy, was nobly waked. There he lay, meanwhile, as they had arranged him, his dead hands crossed upon his bosom, his dead eyes staring on the roof; and hard by, in the stall, the lad who had slain him waited, in sore disquietude, the coming of the morning.

Once only, in the course of the hours, Sir Oliver leaned across to his captive.

'Richard,' he whispered, 'my son, if ye mean me evil, I will certify, on my soul's welfare, ye design upon an innocent man. Sinful in the eye of Heaven I do declare myself, but sinful as against you I am not, neither have been ever.'

'My father,' returned Dick, in the same tone of voice, 'trust me, I design nothing; but as for your innocence, I may not forget that ye cleared yourself but lamely.'

'A man may be innocently guilty,' replied the priest. 'He may be set blindfolded upon a mission, ignorant of its true scope. So it was with me. I did decoy your father to his death; but as Heaven sees us in this sacred place, I knew not what I did.'

'It may be,' returned Dick, 'but see what a strange web ye have woven, that I should be, at this hour, at once your prisoner and your judge; that ye should both threaten my days and deprecate my anger. Methinks, if ye had been all your life a true man and good priest, ye would neither thus fear nor thus detest me. And now to your prayers. I do obey you, since needs must; but I will not be burthened with your company.'

The priest uttered a sigh so heavy that it had almost touched the lad into some sentiment of pity, and he bowed his head upon his hands like a man borne down below a weight of care. He joined no longer in the psalms; but Dick could hear the beads rattle through his fingers and the prayers a-pattering between his teeth.

Yet a little, and the grey of the morning began to struggle through the painted casements of the church, and to put to shame the glimmer of the tapers. The light slowly broadened and brightened, and presently through the south eastern clerestories a flush of rosy sunlight flickered on the walls. The storm was over; the great clouds had disburdened their snow and fled farther on, and the new day was breaking on a merry winter landscape sheathed in white.

A bustle of church officers followed; the bier was carried forth to the dead-house, and the stains of blood were cleansed from off the tiles, that no such ill-omened spectacle should disgrace the marriage of Lord Shoreby. At the same time, the very ecclesiastics who had been so dismally engaged all night began to put on morning faces, to do honour to the merrier ceremony which was about to follow. And further to announce the coming of the day, the pious of the town began to assemble and fall to prayer before their favourite shrines, or wait their turn at the confessionals.

Favoured by this stir, it was of course easily possible for any man to avoid the vigilance of Sir Daniel's sentries at the door; and presently Dick, looking about him warily, caught the eye of no less a person than Will Lawless, still in his monk's habit.

The outlaw, at the same moment, recognized his leader, and privily signed to him with hand and eye.

Now Dick was far from having forgiven the old rogue his most untimely drunkenness, but he had no desire to involve him in his own predicament; and he signalled back to him, as plain as he was able, to begone.

Lawless, as though he had understood, disappeared at once behind a pillar, and Dick breathed again.

What, then, was his dismay to feel himself plucked by the sleeve and to find the old robber installed beside him, upon the next seat, and, to all appearance, plunged in his devotions!

Instantly Sir Oliver arose from his place, and, gliding behind the stalls, made for the soldiers in the aisle. If the priest's suspicions had been so lightly wakened, the harm was already done, and Lawless a prisoner in the church.

'Move not,' whispered Dick. 'We are in the plaguiest pass, thanks, before all things, to thy swinishness of yestereven. When ye saw me here, so strangely seated, where I have neither right nor interest, what a murrain! could ye not smell harm and get ye gone from evil?'

'Nay,' returned Lawless, 'I thought ye had heard from Ellis, and were here on duty.'

'Ellis!' echoed Dick. 'Is Ellis then returned?'

'For sure,' replied the outlaw. 'He came last night, and belted me sore for being in wine – so there ye are avenged, my master. A furious man is Ellis Duckworth! He hath ridden me hot-spur from Craven to prevent this marriage; and, Master Dick, ye know the way of him – do so he will!'

'Nay, then,' returned Dick, with composure, 'you and I, my poor brother, are dead men; for I sit here a prisoner upon suspicion, and my neck was to answer for this very marriage that he purposeth to mar. I had a fair choice, by the rood! to lose my sweetheart or else lose my life! Well, the cast is thrown – it is to be my life.'

'By the mass,' cried Lawless, half rising, 'I am gone!'

But Dick had his hand upon his shoulder.

'Friend Lawless, sit ye still,' he said. 'An ye have eyes, look yonder at the corner by the chancel arch; see ye not that, even upon the motion of your rising, yon armed men are up and ready to intercept you? Yield ye, friend. Ye were bold aboard ship, when ye thought to die a sea-death; be bold again, now that y' are to die presently upon the gallows.'

'Master Dick,' gasped Lawless, 'the thing hath come upon me somewhat of the suddenest. But give me a moment till I fetch my breath again; and, by the mass, I will be as stout-hearted as yourself.'

'Here is my bold fellow!' returned Dick. 'And yet, Lawless, it goes hard against the grain with me to die; but where whining mendeth nothing, wherefore whine?'

'Nay, that indeed!' chimed Lawless. 'And a fig for death at worst! It has to be done, my master, soon or late. And hanging in a good quarrel is an easy death, they say, though I could never hear of any that came back to say so.'

And so saying the stout old rascal leaned back in his stall, folded his arms, and began to look about him with the greatest air of insolence and unconcern.

'And for the matter of that,' Dick added, 'it is yet our best chance to keep quiet. We wot not yet what Duckworth purposes; and when all is said, and if the worst befall, we may yet clear our feet of it.'

Now that they ceased talking, they were aware of a very distant and thin strain of mirthful music which steadily drew nearer, louder, and merrier. The bells in the tower began to break forth into a doubling peal, and a greater and greater concourse of people to crowd into the church, shuffling the snow from off their feet, and clapping and blowing in their hands. The western door was flung wide open, showing a glimpse of sunlight, snowy street, and admitting in a great gust the shrewd air of the morning; and in short, it became plain by every sign that Lord Shoreby desired to be married very early in the day, and that the wedding-train was drawing near.

Some of Lord Shoreby's men now cleared a passage down the middle of the aisle, forcing the people back with lance-stocks; and just then, outside the portal, the secular musicians could be descried drawing near over the frozen snow, the fifers and trumpeters scarlet in the face with lusty blowing, the drummers and the cymbalists beating as for a wager.

These, as they drew near the door of the sacred building, filed off on either side, and marking time to their own vigorous music, stood stamping in the snow. As they thus opened their ranks, the leaders of this noble bridal train appeared behind and between them; and such was the variety and gaiety of their attire, such the display of silks and velvet, fur and satin, embroidery and lace, that the procession showed forth upon the snow like a flower-bed in a path or a painted window in a wall.

First came the bride, a sorry sight, as pale as winter, clinging to Sir Daniel's arm, and attended, as bridesmaid, by the short young lady who had befriended Dick the night before. Close behind, in the most radiant toilet, followed the bridegroom, halting on a gouty foot, and as he passed the threshold of the sacred building, and doffed his hat, his bald head was seen to be rosy with emotion.

And now came the hour of Ellis Duckworth.

Dick, who sat stunned among contrary emotions, grasping the desk in front of him, beheld a movement in the crowd, people jostling backward, and eyes and arms uplifted. Following these signs, he beheld three or four men with bent bows, leaning from the clerestory gallery. At the same instant they delivered their discharge, and before the clamour and cries of the astonished populace had time to swell fully upon the ear, they had flitted from their perch and disappeared.

The nave was full of swaying heads and voices screaming; the ecclesiastics thronged in terror from their places; the music ceased, and though the bells overhead continued for some seconds to clang upon the air, some wind of the disaster seemed to find its way at last even to the chamber where the ringers were leaping on their ropes, and they also desisted from their merry labours.

Right in the midst of the nave the bridegroom lay stone-dead, pierced by two black arrows. The bride had fainted. Sir Daniel stood, towering above the crowd in his surprise and anger, a clothyard shaft quivering in his left forearm, and his face streaming blood from another which had grazed his brow.

Long before any search could be made for them, the authors of this tragic interruption had clattered down a turnpike stair and decamped by a postern door.

But Dick and Lawless still remained in pawn; they had indeed arisen on the first alarm and pushed manfully to gain the door; but what with the narrowness of the stalls, and the crowding of terrified priests and choristers, the attempt had been in vain, and they had stoically resumed their places.

And now, pale with horror, Sir Oliver rose to his feet and called upon Sir Daniel, pointing with one hand at Dick.

'Here,' he cried, 'is Richard Shelton – alas the hour! – blood guilty! Seize him! – bid him be seized! For all our lives' sakes, take him and bind him surely! He hath sworn our fall.'

Sir Daniel was blinded by anger – blinded by the hot blood that still streamed across his face.

'Where?' he bellowed. 'Hale him forth! By the cross of Holywood but he shall rue this hour.'

The crowd fell back, and a party of archers invaded the choir, laid rough hands on Dick, dragged him head foremost from the stall, and thrust him by the shoulders down the chancel steps. Lawless, on his part, sat still as a mouse.

Sir Daniel, brushing the blood out of his eyes, stared blinkingly upon his captive.

'Ay,' he said, 'treacherous and insolent, I have thee fast; and by all potent oaths, for every drop of blood that now trickles in mine eyes, I will wring a groan out of thy carcass. Away with him!' he added. 'Here is no place. Off with him to my house. I will number every joint of thy body with a torture.'

But Dick, putting off his captors, uplifted his voice.

'Sanctuary!' he shouted. 'Sanctuary! Ho, there, my fathers! They

'*The bridegroom lay stone-dead, pierced by two black arrows*'

would drag me from the church!'

'From the church thou hast defiled with murder, boy,' added a tall man, magnificently dressed.

'On what probation?' cried Dick. 'They do accuse me, indeed, of some complicity, but have not proved one tittle. I was, in truth, a suitor for this damsel's hand; and she, I will be bold to say, repaid my suit with favour. But what then? To love a maid is no offence, I trow — nay, nor to gain her love. In all else, I stand here free from guiltiness.'

There was a murmur of approval among the bystanders, so boldly Dick declared his innocence; but at the same time a throng of accusers arose upon the other side, crying how he had been found last night in Sir Daniel's house, how he wore a sacrilegious disguise; and in the midst of the babel, Sir Oliver indicated Lawless, both by voice and gesture, as accomplice to the fact. He, in his turn, was dragged from his seat and set beside his leader. The feelings of the crowd rose high on either side, and while some dragged the prisoners to and fro to favour their escape, others cursed and struck them with their fists. Dick's ears rang and his brain swam dizzily, like a man struggling in the eddies of a furious river.

But the tall man who had already answered Dick, by a prodigious exercise of voice restored silence and order in the mob.

'Search them,' he said, 'for arms. We may so judge of their intentions.'

Upon Dick, they found no weapon but his poniard, and this told in his favour, until one man officiously drew it from its sheath, and found it still uncleansed of the blood of Rutter. At this there was a great shout among Sir Daniel's followers, which the tall man suppressed by a gesture and an imperious glance. But when it came to the turn of Lawless, there was found under his gown a sheaf of arrows identical with those that had been shot.

'How say ye now?' asked the tall man, frowningly, of Dick.

'Sir,' replied Dick, 'I am here in sanctuary, is it not so? Well sir, I see by your bearing that ye are high in station, and I read in your countenance the marks of piety and justice. To you, then, I will yield me prisoner, and that blithely, foregoing the advantage of this holy place. But rather than to be yielded into the discretion of that man — whom I do here accuse with a loud voice to be the murderer of my natural father and the unjust detainer of my lands and revenues — rather than that, I would beseech you, under favour, with your own gentle hand, to dispatch me on the spot. Your own ears have heard him, how before that I was proven guilty he did threaten me with torments. It standeth not with your own honour to deliver me to my sworn enemy and old oppressor, but to try me fairly by the way of law, and, if that I be guilty indeed, to slay me mercifully.'

'My lord,' cried Sir Daniel, 'ye will not hearken to this wolf? His bloody dagger reeks him the lie into his face.'

'Nay, but suffer me, good knight,' returned the tall stranger; 'your own vehemence doth somewhat tell against yourself.'

And here the bride, who had come to herself some minute past and looked wildly on upon this scene, broke loose from those that held her, and fell upon her knees before the last speaker.

'My Lord of Risingham,' she cried, 'hear me, in justice. I am here in this man's custody by mere force, reft from mine own people. Since that day I had never pity, countenance, nor comfort from the face of man – but from him only – Richard Shelton – whom they now accuse and labour to undo. My lord, if he was yesternight in Sir Daniel's mansion, it was I that brought him there; he came but at my prayer, and thought to do no hurt. While yet Sir Daniel was a good lord to him, he fought with them of the Black Arrow loyally; but when his foul guardian sought his life by practices, and he fled by night, for his soul's sake, out of that bloody house, whither was he to turn – he, helpless and penniless? Or if he be fallen among ill company, whom should ye blame – the lad that was unjustly handled, or the guardian that did abuse his trust?'

And then the short young lady fell on her knees by Joanna's side.

'And I, my good lord and natural uncle,' she added, 'I can bear testimony, on my conscience and before the face of all, that what this maiden saith is true. It was I, unworthy, that did lead the young man in.'

Earl Risingham had heard in silence, and when the voices ceased, he still stood silent for a space. Then he gave Joanna his hand to arise, though it was to be observed that he did not offer the like courtesy to her who had called herself his niece.

'Sir Daniel,' he said, 'here is a right intricate affair, the which, with your good leave, it shall be mine to examine and adjust. Content ye, then; your business is in careful hands; justice shall be done you; and in the meanwhile, get ye incontinently home, and have your hurts attended. The air is shrewd, and I would not ye took cold upon these scratches.'

He made a sign with his hand; it was passed down the nave by obsequious servants, who waited there upon his smallest gesture. Instantly, without the church, a tucket sounded shrill, and through the open portal archers and men-at-arms, uniformly arrayed in the colours and wearing the badge of Lord Risingham, began to file into the church, took Dick and Lawless from those who still detained them, and, closing their files about the prisoners, marched forth again and disappeared.

As they were passing, Joanna held both her hands to Dick and cried him her farewell; and the bridesmaid, nothing downcast by her uncle's evident displeasure, blew him a kiss, with a 'Keep your heart up, lion-driver!' that for the first time since the accident called up a smile to the faces of the crowd.

5 Earl Risingham

Earl Risingham, although by far the most important person then in Shoreby, was poorly lodged in the house of a private gentleman upon the extreme outskirts of the town. Nothing but the armed men at the doors, and the mounted messengers that kept arriving and departing, announced the temporary residence of a great lord.

Thus it was that, from lack of space, Dick and Lawless were clapped into the same apartment.

'Well spoken, Master Richard,' said the outlaw; 'it was excellently well spoken, and, for my part, I thank you cordially. Here we are in good hands; we shall be justly tried, and some time this evening decently hanged on the same tree.'

'Indeed, my poor friend, I do believe it,' answered Dick.

'Yet we have a string to our bow,' returned Lawless. 'Ellis Duckworth is a man out of ten thousand; he holdeth you right near his heart, both for your own and for your father's sake; and knowing you guiltless of this fact, he will stir earth and heaven to bear you clear.'

'It may not be,' said Dick. 'What can he do? He hath but a handful. Alack, if it were but to-morrow – could I but keep a certain tryst an hour before noon to-morrow – all were, I think, otherwise. But now there is no help.'

'Well,' concluded Lawless, 'an ye will stand to it for my innocence, I will stand to it for yours, and that stoutly. It shall naught avail us; but an I be to hang, it shall not be for lack of swearing.'

And then, while Dick gave himself over to his reflections, the old rogue curled himself down into a corner, pulled his monkish hood about his face, and composed himself to sleep. Soon he was loudly snoring, so utterly had his long life of hardship and adventure blunted the sense of apprehension.

It was long after noon, and the day was already failing, before the door was opened and Dick taken forth and led upstairs to where, in a warm cabinet, Earl Risingham sat musing over the fire.

On his captive's entrance he looked up.

'Sir,' he said, 'I knew your father, who was a man of honour, and this inclineth me to be the more lenient; but I may not hide from you that heavy charges lie against your character. Ye do consort with murderers and robbers; upon a clear probation ye have carried war against the king's peace; ye are suspected to have piratically seized upon a ship; ye are found skulking with a counterfeit presentment in your enemy's house; a man is slain that very evening——'

'An it like you, my lord,' Dick interposed, 'I will at once avow my guilt, such as it is. I slew this fellow Rutter; and to the proof' – searching in his bosom – 'here is a letter from his wallet.'

Lord Risingham took the letter, and opened and read it twice.

'Ye have read this?' he inquired.

'I have read it,' answered Dick.

'Are ye for York or Lancaster?' the earl demanded.

'My lord, it was but a little while back that I was asked that question, and knew not how to answer it,' said Dick; 'but having answered once, I will not vary. My lord, I am for York.'

The earl nodded approvingly.

'Honestly replied,' he said. 'But wherefore, then, deliver me this letter?'

'Nay, but against traitors, my lord, are not all sides arrayed?' cried Dick.

'I would they were, young gentleman,' returned the earl; 'and I do at least approve your saying. There is more youth than guile in you, I do perceive; and were not Sir Daniel a mighty man upon our side, I were half tempted to espouse your quarrel. For I have inquired, and it appears that you have been hardly dealt with, and have much excuse. But look ye, sir, I am, before all else, a leader in the Queen's interest; and though by nature a just man, as I believe, and leaning even to the excess of mercy, yet must I order my goings for my party's interest, and, to keep Sir Daniel, I would go far about.'

'My lord,' returned Dick, 'ye will think me very bold to counsel you; but do ye count upon Sir Daniel's faith? Methought he had changed sides intolerably often.'

'Nay, it is the way of England. What would ye have?' the earl demanded. 'But ye are unjust to the knight of Tunstall, and as faith goes, in this unfaithful generation, he hath of late been honourably true to us of Lancaster. Even in our last reverses he stood firm.'

'An it please you, then,' said Dick, 'to cast your eye upon this letter, ye might somewhat change your thought of him,' and he handed to the earl Sir Daniel's letter to Lord Wensleydale.

The effect upon the earl's countenance was instant; he lowered like an angry lion, and his hand, with a sudden movement, clutched at his dagger.

'Ye have read this also?' he asked.

'Even so,' said Dick. 'It is your lordship's own estate he offers to Lord Wensleydale.'

'It is my own estate, even as ye say!' returned the earl. 'I am your bedesman for this letter. It hath shown me a fox's hole. Command me, Master Shelton; I will not be backward in gratitude, and to begin with, York or Lancaster, true man or thief, I do now set you at freedom. Go, a–Mary's name! But judge it right that I retain and hang your fellow Lawless. The crime hath been most open, and it were fitting that some open punishment should follow.'

'My lord, I make it first suit to you to spare him also,' pleaded Dick.

'It is an old condemned rogue, thief, and vagabond, Master Shelton,' said the earl. 'He hath been gallows-ripe this score of years. And, whether for one thing or another, whether to-morrow or the day after, where is the great choice?'

'Yet, my lord, it was through love to me that he came hither,' answered Dick, 'and I were churlish and thankless to desert him.'

'Master Shelton, ye are troublesome,' replied the earl, severely. 'It is an evil way to prosper in this world. Howbeit, and to be quit of your importunity, I will once more humour you. Go, then, together; but go warily, and get swiftly out of Shoreby town. For this Sir Daniel (whom may the saints confound!) thirsteth most greedily to have your blood.'

'My lord, I do now offer you in words my gratitude, trusting at some brief date to pay you some of it in service,' replied Dick, as he turned from the apartment.

6 Arblaster Again

When Dick and Lawless were suffered to steal, by a back way, out of the house where Lord Risingham held his garrison, the evening had already come.

They paused in shelter of the garden wall to consult on their best course. The danger was extreme. If one of Sir Daniel's men caught sight of them and raised the view-hallo, they would be run down and butchered instantly. And not only was the town of Shoreby a mere net of peril for their lives, but to make for the open country was to run the risk of the patrols.

A little way off, upon some open ground, they spied a windmill standing; and hard by that, a very large granary with open doors.

'How if we lay there until the night fall?' Dick proposed.

And Lawless having no better suggestion to offer, they made a straight push for the granary at a run, and concealed themselves behind the door among some straw. The daylight rapidly departed; and presently the moon was silvering the frozen snow. Now or never was their opportunity to gain the Goat and Bagpipes unobserved and change their telltale garments. Yet even then it was advisable to go round by the outskirts, and not run the gauntlet of the market-place, where, in the concourse of people, they stood the more imminent peril to be recognized and slain.

This course was a long one. It took them not far from the house by the beach, now lying dark and silent, and brought them forth at last by the margin of the harbour. Many of the ships, as they could see by the clear moonshine, had weighed anchor, and, profiting by the calm sky, proceeded for more distant parts; answerable to this, the rude ale-houses along the beach (although, in defiance of the curfew law, they still shone with fire and candle) were no longer thronged with customers, and no longer echoed to the chorus of sea songs.

Hastily, half running, with their monkish raiment kilted to the knee, they plunged through the deep snow, and threaded the labyrinth of marine lumber; and they were already more than half-way round the harbour when, as they were passing close before an ale-house, the door suddenly opened and let out a gush of light upon their fleeting figures.

Instantly they stopped, and made believe to be engaged in earnest conversation.

Three men, one after another, came out of the ale-house, and the last closed the door behind him. All three were unsteady upon their feet, as if they had passed the day in deep potations, and they now stood wavering in the moonlight, like men who knew not what they would be after. The tallest of the three was talking in a loud, lamentable voice.

'Seven pieces of as good Gascony as ever a tapster broached,' he was saying, 'the best ship o' the port o' Dartmouth, a Virgin Mary parcel-gilt, thirteen pounds of good gold money——'

'I have had losses, too,' interrupted one of the others. 'I have had losses of mine own, gossip Arblaster. I was robbed at Martinmas of five shillings and a leather wallet well worth ninepence farthing.'

Dick's heart smote him at what he heard. Until that moment he had not perhaps thought twice of the poor skipper who had been ruined by the loss of the *Good Hope*; so careless, in those days, were men who wore arms of the goods and interests of their inferiors. But this sudden encounter reminded him sharply of the high-handed manner and ill ending of his enterprise; and both he and Lawless turned their heads the other way, to avoid the chance of recognition.

The ship's dog had, however, made his escape from the wreck and found his way back again to Shoreby. He was now at Arblaster's heels, and suddenly sniffing and pricking his ears, he darted forward and began to bark furiously at the two sham friars.

His master unsteadily followed him.

'Hey, shipmates!' he cried. 'Have ye ever a penny piece for a poor old shipman, clean destroyed by pirates? I am a man that would have paid for you both o' Thursday morning; and now here I be o' Saturday night, begging for a flagon of ale! Ask my man Tom, if ye misdoubt me. Seven pieces of good Gascon wine, a ship that was mine own, and was my father's before me, a Blessed Mary of plane-tree wood and parcel-gilt, and thirteen pounds of gold and silver. Hey; what say ye? A man that fought the French, too; for I have fought the French; I have cut more French throats upon the high seas than ever a man that sails out of Dartmouth. Come, a penny piece.'

Neither Dick nor Lawless durst answer him a word, lest he should recognize their voices; and they stood there as helpless as a ship ashore, not knowing where to turn nor what to hope.

'Are ye dumb, boy?' inquired the skipper. 'Mates,' he added, with a hiccup, 'they be dumb. I like not this manner of discourtesy; for an a man be dumb, so be as he's courteous, he will still speak when he was spoken to, methinks.'

By this time the sailor, Tom, who was a man of great personal strength, seemed to have conceived some suspicion of these two speechless figures; and being soberer than his captain, stepped suddenly before him, took Lawless roughly by the shoulder, and asked him, with an oath, what ailed him that he held his tongue. To this the outlaw, thinking all was over, made answer by a wrestling feint that stretched the sailor on the sand, and, calling upon Dick to follow him, took to his heels among the lumber.

The affair passed in a second. Before Dick could run at all, Arblaster had him in his arms; Tom, crawling on his face, had caught him by one foot, and the third man had a drawn cutlass brandishing above his head.

It was not so much the danger, it was not so much the annoyance, that now bowed down the spirits of young Shelton; it was the profound humiliation to have escaped Sir Daniel, convinced Lord Risingham, and now fall helpless in the hands of this old drunken sailor; and not merely helpless, but, as his conscience loudly told him when it was too late, actually guilty – actually the bankrupt debtor of the man whose ship he had stolen and lost.

'Bring me him back into the ale-house, till I see his face,' said Arblaster.

'Nay, nay,' returned Tom; 'but let us first unload his wallet, lest the other lads cry share.'

But though he was searched from head to foot, not a penny was found upon him; nothing but Lord Foxham's signet, which they plucked savagely from his finger.

'Turn me him to the moon,' said the skipper; and taking Dick by the chin, he cruelly jerked his head into the air. 'Blessed Virgin!' he cried, 'it is the pirate.'

'Hey!' cried Tom.

'By the Virgin of Bordeaux, it is the man himself!' repeated Arblaster. 'What, sea-thief, do I hold you?' he cried. 'Where is my ship? Where is my wine? Hey! have I you in my hands? Tom, give me one end of a cord here; I will so truss me this sea-thief, hand and foot together, like a basting turkey – marry, I will so bind him up – and thereafter I will so beat – so beat him!'

And so he ran on, winding the cord meanwhile about Dick's limbs with the dexterity peculiar to seamen, and at every turn and cross securing it with a knot, and tightening the whole fabric with a savage pull.

When he had done, the lad was a mere package in his hands – as helpless as the dead. The skipper held him at arm's length, and laughed aloud. Then he fetched him a stunning buffet on the ear; and then turned him about, and furiously kicked and kicked him. Anger rose up in Dick's bosom like a storm; anger strangled him, and he thought to have died; but when the sailor, tired of his cruel play, dropped him all his length upon the sand and turned to consult with his companions, he instantly regained command of his temper. Here was a momentary respite; ere they began again to torture him, he might have found some method to escape from this degrading and fatal misadventure.

Presently, sure enough, and while his captors were still discussing what to do with him, he took heart of grace, and, with a pretty steady voice, addressed them.

'My masters,' he began, 'are ye gone clean foolish? Here hath Heaven put into your hands as pretty an occasion to grow rich as ever shipman had – such as ye might make thirty oversea adventures and not find again – and, by the mass! what do ye? Beat me? – nay; so would an angry child. But for long-headed tarry-Johns, that fear not fire nor water, and that love gold as they love beef, methinks ye are not wise.'

'Ay,' said Tom, 'now y' are trussed ye would cozen us.'

'Cozen you!' repeated Dick. 'Nay, if ye be fools, it would be easy. But if ye be shrewd fellows, as I trow ye are, ye can see plainly where your interest lies. When I took your ship from you, we were many, we were well clad and armed: but now, bethink you a little, who mustered that array? One incontestably that hath made much gold. And if he, being already rich, continueth to hunt after more even in the face of storms – bethink you once more – shall there not be a treasure somewhere hidden?'

'What meaneth he?' asked one of the men.

'Why, if ye have lost an old skiff and a few jugs of vinegary wine,' continued Dick, 'forget them, for the trash they are; and do ye rather buckle to an adventure worth the name, that shall, in twelve hours, make or mar you for ever. But take me up from where I lie, and let us go somewhere near at hand and talk across a flagon, for I am sore and frozen, and my mouth is half among the snow.'

'He seeks but to cozen us,' said Tom contemptuously.

'Cozen! cozen!' cried the third man. 'I would I could see the man that could cozen me! He were a cozener indeed! Nay, I was not born yesterday. I can see a church when it hath a steeple on it; and for my part, gossip Arblaster, methinks there is some sense in this young man. Shall we go hear him, indeed? Say, shall we go hear him?'

'I would look gladly on a pottle of strong ale, good Master Pirret,' returned Arblaster. 'How say ye, Tom? But then the wallet is empty.'

'I will pay,' said the other, 'I will pay. I would fain see this matter out; I do believe, upon my conscience, there is gold in it.'

'Nay, if ye get again to drinking, all is lost!' cried Tom.

'Gossip Arblaster, ye suffer your fellow to have too much liberty,' returned Master Pirret. 'Would ye be led by a hired man? Fy, fy!'

'Peace, fellow!' said Arblaster, addressing Tom. 'Will ye put your oar in! Truly a fine pass, when the crew is to correct the skipper!'

'Well, then, go your way,' said Tom; 'I wash my hands of you.'

'Set him, then, upon his feet,' said Master Pirret. 'I know a privy place where we may drink and discourse.'

'If I am to walk, my friends, ye must set my feet at liberty,' said Dick, when he had been once more planted upright like a post.

'He saith true,' laughed Pirret. 'Truly, he could not walk accoutred as he is. Give it a slit – out with your knife and slit it, gossip.'

Even Arblaster paused at this proposal; but as his companion continued to insist, and Dick had the sense to keep the merest wooden indifference of expression, and only shrugged his shoulders over the delay, the skipper consented at last, and cut the cords which tied his prisoner's feet and legs. Not only did this enable Dick to walk, but the whole network of his bonds being proportionately loosened, he felt the arm behind his back begin to move more freely, and could hope, with time and trouble, to entirely disengage it. So much he owed already to the owlish silliness and greed of Master Pirret.

That worthy now assumed the lead, and conducted them to the

very same rude ale-house where Lawless had taken Arblaster on the day of the gale. It was now quite deserted; the fire was a pile of red embers, radiating the most ardent heat; and when they had chosen their places, and the landlord had set before them a measure of mulled ale, both Pirret and Arblaster stretched forth their legs and squared their elbows like men bent upon a pleasant hour.

The table at which they sat, like all the others in the ale-house, consisted of a heavy, square board, set on a pair of barrels; and each of the four curiously assorted cronies sat at one side of the square, Pirret facing Arblaster, and Dick opposite to the common sailor.

'And now, young man,' said Pirret, 'to your tale. It doth appear, indeed, that ye have somewhat abused our gossip Arblaster; but what then? Make it up to him – show him but this chance to become wealthy – and I will go pledge he will forgive you.'

So far Dick had spoken pretty much at random; but it was now necessary, under the supervision of six eyes, to invent and tell some marvellous story, and, if it were possible, get back into his hands the all-important signet. To squander time was the first necessity. The longer his stay lasted, the more would his captors drink, and the surer should he be when he attempted his escape.

Well, Dick was not much of an inventor, and what he told was pretty much the tale of Ali Baba, with Shoreby and Tunstall Forest substituted for the East, and the treasures of the cavern rather exaggerated than diminished. As the reader is aware, it is an excellent story, and has but one drawback – that it is not true; and so as these three simple shipmen now heard it for the first time, their eyes stood out of their faces, and their mouths gaped like codfish at a fishmonger's.

Pretty soon a second measure of mulled ale was called for; and while Dick was still artfully spinning out the incidents a third followed the second.

Here was the position of the parties towards the end:

Arblaster, three-parts drunk and one-half asleep, hung helpless on his stool. Even Tom had been much delighted with the tale, and his vigilance had abated in proportion. Meanwhile, Dick had gradually wormed his right arm clear of its bonds, and was ready to risk all.

'And so,' said Pirret, 'y' are one of these?'

'I was made so,' replied Dick, 'against my will; but an I could but get a sack or two of gold coin to my share, I should be a fool indeed to continue dwelling in a filthy cave, and standing shot and buffet like a soldier. Here be we four; good! Let us, then, go forth into the forest to-morrow ere the sun be up. Could we come honestly by a donkey, it were better; but an we cannot, we have our four strong backs, and I warrant me we shall come home staggering.'

Pirret licked his lips.

'And this magic,' he said – 'this password, whereby the cave is opened – how call ye it, friend?'

'Nay, none know the word but the three chiefs,' returned Dick; 'but here is your great good fortune, that, on this very evening, I should be the bearer of a spell to open it. It is a thing not trusted twice a year beyond the captain's wallet.'

'A spell!' said Arblaster, half awakening, and squinting upon Dick with one eye. 'Aroint thee! no spells! I be a good Christian. Ask my man Tom, else.'

'Nay, but this is white magic,' said Dick. 'It doth naught with the devil; only the powers of numbers, herbs, and planets.'

'Ay, ay,' said Pirret; ' 'tis but white magic, gossip. There is no sin therein, I do assure you. But proceed, good youth. This spell – in what should it consist?'

'Nay, that I will incontinently show you,' answered Dick. 'Have ye there the ring ye took from my finger? Good! Now hold it forth before you by the extreme finger-ends, at the arm's length, and over against the shining of these embers. 'Tis so exactly. Thus, then, is the spell.'

With a haggard glance, Dick saw the coast was clear between him and the door. He put up an internal prayer. Then whipping forth his arm, he made but one snatch of the ring, and at the same instant, levering up the table, he sent it bodily over upon the seaman Tom. He, poor soul, went down bawling under the ruins; and before Arblaster understood that anything was wrong, or Pirret could collect his dazzled wits, Dick had run to the door and escaped into the moonlit night.

The moon, which now rode in the mid heavens, and the extreme whiteness of the snow, made the open ground about the harbour bright as day; and young Shelton leaping, with kilted robe, among the lumber was a conspicuous figure from afar.

Tom and Pirret followed him with shouts; from every drinking-shop they were joined by others whom their cries aroused; and presently a whole fleet of sailors was in full pursuit. But Jack ashore was a bad runner, even in the fifteenth century, and Dick, besides, had a start, which he rapidly improved, until, as he drew near the entrance of a narrow lane, he even paused and looked laughingly behind him.

Upon the white floor of snow, all the shipmen of Shoreby came clustering in an inky mass, and tailing out rearward in isolated clumps. Every man was shouting or screaming; every man was gesticulating with both arms in air; someone was continually falling; and to complete the picture, when one fell, a dozen would fall upon the top of him.

The confused mass of sound which they rolled up as high as to the moon was partly comical and partly terrifying to the fugitive whom they were hunting. In itself, it was impotent, for he made sure no seaman in the port could run him down. But the mere volume of noise, in so far as it must awake all the sleepers in Shoreby, and bring all the skulking sentries to the street, did really threaten him with danger in the front. So, spying a dark doorway at a corner, he whipped briskly into it, and let the uncouth hunt go by him, still shouting and gesticulating, and all red with hurry, and white with tumbles in the snow.

It was a long while, indeed, before this great invasion of the town by the harbour came to an end, and it was long before silence was restored. For long, lost sailors were still to be heard pounding and shouting through the streets in all directions and in every quarter of the town. Quarrels followed, sometimes among themselves, sometimes with the men of the patrols; knives were drawn, blows given and received, and more than one dead body remained behind upon the snow.

When, a full hour later, the last seaman returned grumblingly to the harbour side and his particular tavern, it may fairly be questioned if he had ever known what manner of man he was pursuing, but it was absolutely sure that he had now forgotten. By next morning there were many strange stories flying; and a little while after, the legend of the devil's nocturnal visit was an article of faith with all the lads of Shoreby.

But the return of the last seaman did not, even yet, set free young Shelton from his cold imprisonment in the doorway.

For some time after there was a great activity of patrols; and special parties came forth to make the round of the place and report to one or other of the great lords, whose slumbers had been thus unusually broken.

The night was already well spent before Dick ventured from his hiding-place and came, safe and sound, but aching with cold and bruises, to the door of the Goat and Bagpipes. As the law required, there was neither fire nor candle in the house; but he groped his way into a corner of the icy guest-room, found an end of the blanket, which he hitched around his shoulders, and creeping close to the nearest sleeper, was soon lost in slumber.

PART 4 CROOKBACK

1 The Shrill Trumpet

Very early the next morning, before the first peep of the day, Dick arose, changed his garments, armed himself once more like a gentleman, and set forth for Lawless's den in the forest. There, it will be remembered, he had left Lord Foxham's papers; and to get these and be back in time for the tryst with the young Duke of Gloucester could only be managed by an early start, and the most vigorous walking.

The frost was more rigorous than ever; the air windless and dry, and stinging to the nostril. The moon had gone down, but the stars were still bright and numerous, and the reflection from the snow was clear and cheerful. There was no need for a lamp to walk by; nor, in that still but ringing air, the least temptation to delay.

Dick had crossed the greater part of the open ground between Shoreby and the forest, and had reached the bottom of the little hill, some hundred yards below the Cross of St Bride, when, through the stillness of the black morn, there rang forth the note of a trumpet, so shrill, clear and piercing, that he thought he had never heard the match of it for audibility. It was blown once, and then hurriedly a second time; and then the clash of steel succeeded.

At this young Shelton pricked up his ears, and drawing his sword, ran forward up the hill.

Presently he came in sight of the cross, and was aware of a most fierce encounter raging on the road before it. There were seven or eight assailants, and but one to keep head against them; but so active and dexterous was this one, so desperately did he charge and scatter his opponents, so deftly keep his footing on the ice, that already, before Dick could intervene, he had slain one, wounded another, and kept the whole in check.

Still, it was by a miracle that he continued his defence, and at any moment, any accident, the least slip of foot or error of hand, his life would be a forfeit.

'Hold ye well sir! Here is help!' cried Richard; and forgetting that he was alone, and that the cry was somewhat irregular, 'To the Arrow! to the Arrow!' he shouted, as he fell upon the rear of the assailants.

These were stout fellows also, for they gave not an inch at this surprise, but faced about, and fell with astonishing fury upon Dick. Four against one, the steel flashed about him in the starlight: the sparks flew fiercely; one of the men opposed to him fell – in the stir of the fight he hardly knew why; then he himself was struck across the head, and though the steel cap below his hood protected him, the blow beat him down upon one knee, with a brain whirling like a windmill sail.

Meanwhile the man whom he had come to rescue, instead of joining in the conflict, had, on the first sign of intervention, leaped aback and blown again, and yet more urgently and loudly, on that same shrill-voiced trumpet that began the alarm. Next moment, indeed, his foes were on him, and he was once more charging and fleeing, leaping, stabbing, dropping to his knee, and using indifferently sword and dagger, foot and hand, with the same unshaken courage and feverish energy and speed.

But that ear-piercing summons had been heard at last. There was a muffled rushing in the snow; and, in a good hour for Dick, who saw the sword-points glitter already at his throat, there poured forth out of the wood upon both sides a disorderly torrent of mounted men-at-arms, each cased in iron, and with visor lowered, each bearing his lance in rest, or his sword bared and raised and each carrying, so to speak, a passenger, in the shape of an archer or page, who leaped one after another from their perches, and had presently doubled the array.

The original assailants, seeing themselves outnumbered and surrounded, threw down their arms without a word.

'Seize me these fellows!' said the hero of the trumpet; and when his order had been obeyed, he drew near to Dick and looked him in the face.

Dick, returning this scrutiny, was surprised to find in one who had displayed such strength, skill, and energy, a lad no older than himself – slightly deformed, with one shoulder higher than the other, and a pale, painful, and distorted countenance.[1] The eyes, however, were very clear and bold.

'Sir,' said this lad, 'ye came in good time for me, and none too early.'

'My lord,' returned Dick, with a faint sense that he was in the presence of a great personage, 'ye are yourself so marvellous a good swordsman that I believe ye had managed them single-handed. Howbeit, it was certainly well for me that your men delayed no longer than they did.'

'How knew ye who I was?' demanded the stranger.

'Even now, my lord,' Dick answered, 'I am ignorant of whom I speak with.'

'Is it so?' asked the other. 'And yet ye threw yourself head first into this unequal battle.'

'I saw one man valiantly contending against many,' replied Dick, 'and I had thought myself dishonoured not to bear him aid.'

A singular sneer played about the young nobleman's mouth as he made answer:

'These are very brave words. But to the more essential – are ye Lancaster or York?'

'My lord, I make no secret; I am clear for York,' Dick answered.

'By the mass!' replied the other, 'it is well for you.'

And so saying, he turned towards one of his followers.

'Let me see,' he continued, in the same sneering and cruel tones, 'let me see a clean end of these brave gentlemen. Truss me them up.'

There were but five survivors of the attacking party. Archers seized them by the arms; they were hurried to the borders of the wood, and each placed below a tree of suitable dimensions; the rope was adjusted; an archer, carrying the end of it, hastily clambered overhead, and before a minute was over, and without a word passing upon either hand, the five men were swinging by the neck.

'And now,' cried the deformed leader, 'back to your posts, and when I summon you next, be readier to attend.'

'My lord duke,' said one man, 'beseech you, tarry not here alone. Keep but a handful of lances at your hand.'

'Fellow,' said the duke, 'I have forborne to chide you for your slowness. Cross me not, therefore, I trust my hand and arm, for all that I be crooked. Ye were backward when the trumpet sounded: and ye are now too forward with your counsels. But it is ever so; last with the lance and first with tongue. Let it be reversed.'

And with a gesture that was not without a sort of dangerous nobility, he waved them off.

The footmen climbed again to their seats behind the men-at-arms, and the whole party moved slowly away and disappeared in twenty different directions, under the cover of the forest.

The day was by this time beginning to break, and the stars to fade. The first grey glimmer of dawn shone upon the countenances of the two young men, who now turned once more to face each other.

'Here,' said the duke, 'ye have seen my vengeance, which is, like my blade, both sharp and ready. But I would not have you, for all Christendom, suppose me thankless. You that came to my aid with a good sword and a better courage – unless that ye recoil from my misshapenness – come to my heart.'

And so saying the young leader held out his arms for an embrace.

In the bottom of his heart Dick already entertained a great terror and some hatred for the man whom he had rescued; but the invitation was so worded that it would not have been merely discourteous, but cruel, to refuse or hesitate, and he hastened to comply.

'And now, my lord duke,' he said, when he had regained his freedom, 'do I suppose right? Are ye my Lord Duke of Gloucester?'

'I am Richard of Gloucester,' returned the other. 'And you – how call they you?'

Dick told him his name, and presented Lord Foxham's signet, which the duke immediately recognized.

'Ye come too soon,' he said, 'but why should I complain? Ye are like me, that was here at watch two hours before the day. But this is the first sally of mine arms; upon this adventure, Master Shelton, shall I make or mar the quality of my renown. There lie mine enemies, under two old, skilled captains, Risingham and Brackley, well posted for strength, I do believe, but yet upon two sides without retreat, enclosed betwixt the sea, the harbour, and the river. Methinks, Shelton, here were a great blow to be stricken, an we could strike it silently and suddenly.'

'I do think so, indeed,' cried Dick, warming.

'Have ye my Lord Foxham's notes?' inquired the duke.

And then Dick, having explained how he was without them for the moment, made himself bold to offer information every jot as good, of his own knowledge.

'And for mine own part, my lord duke,' he added, 'an ye had men enough, I would fall on even at this present. For, look ye, at the peep of day the watches of the night are over; but by day they keep neither watch nor ward – only scour the outskirts with horsemen. Now, then, when the night-watch is already unarmed, and the rest are at their morning cup – now were the time to break them.'

'How many do ye count?' asked Gloucester.

'They number not two thousand,' Dick replied.

'I have seven hundred in the woods behind us,' said the duke; 'seven hundred follow from Kettley, and will be here anon; behind these, and farther, are four hundred more; and my Lord Foxham hath five hundred half a day from here, at Holywood. Shall we attend their coming, or fall on?'

'My lord,' said Dick, 'when ye hanged these five poor rogues ye did decide the question. Churls although they were, in these uneasy times they will be lacked and looked for, and the alarm be given. Therefore, my lord, if ye do count upon the advantage of a surprise, ye have not, in my poor opinion, one whole hour in front of you.'

'I do think so indeed,' returned Crookback. 'Well, before an hour, ye shall be in the thick on't, winning spurs. A swift man to Holywood, carrying Lord Foxham's signet; another along the road to speed my laggards! Nay, Shelton, by the rood, it may be done!'

Therewith he once more set his trumpet to his lips and blew.

This time he was not long kept waiting. In a moment the open space about the cross was filled with horse and foot. Richard of Gloucester took his place upon the steps, and dispatched messenger after messenger to hasten the concentration of the seven hundred men that lay hidden in the immediate neighbourhood among the woods; and before a quarter of an hour had passed, all his dispositions being taken, he put himself at their head, and began to move down the hill towards Shoreby.

His plan was simple. He was to seize a quarter of the town of Shoreby lying on the right hand of the high-road, and make his position good there in the narrow lanes until his reinforcements followed.

If Lord Risingham chose to retreat, Richard would follow upon his rear, and take him between two fires; or, if he preferred to hold the town, he would be shut in a trap, there to be gradually overwhelmed by force of numbers.

There was but one danger, but that was imminent and great – Gloucester's seven hundred might be rolled up and cut to pieces in the first encounter, and, to avoid this, it was needful to make the surprise of their arrival as complete as possible.

The footmen, therefore, were all once more taken up behind the riders, and Dick had the signal honour meted out to him of mounting behind Gloucester himself. For as far as there was any cover the troops moved slowly, and when they came near the end of the trees that lined the highway, stopped to breathe and reconnoitre.

The sun was now well up, shining with a frosty brightness out of a yellow halo, and right over against the luminary, Shoreby, a field of snowy roofs and ruddy gables, was rolling up its columns of morning smoke.

Gloucester turned round to Dick.

'In that poor place,' he said, 'where people are cooking breakfast, either you shall gain your spurs and I begin a life of mighty honour and glory in the world's eye, or both of us, as I conceive it, shall fall dead and be unheard of. Two Richards are we. Well then, Richard Shelton, they shall be heard about, these two! Their swords shall not ring more loudly on men's helmets than their names shall ring in people's ears.'

Dick was astonished at so great a hunger after fame, expressed with so great vehemence of voice and language; and he answered very sensibly and quietly that, for his part, he promised he would do his duty, and doubted not of victory if everyone did the like.

By this time the horses were well breathed, and the leader holding up his sword and giving rein, the whole troop of chargers broke into the gallop and thundered, with their double load of fighting men, down the remainder of the hill and across the snow-covered plain that still divided them from Shoreby.

---

1 Richard Crookback would have been really far younger at this date.

2 The Battle of Shoreby

The whole distance to be crossed was not above a quarter of a mile. But they had no sooner debouched beyond the cover of the trees than they were aware of people fleeing and screaming in the snowy meadows upon either hand. Almost at the same moment a great rumour began to arise, and spread and grow continually louder in the town; and they were not yet half-way to the nearest house before the bells began to ring backward from the steeple.

The young duke ground his teeth together. By these so early signals of alarm he feared to find his enemies prepared; and if he failed to gain a footing in the town, he knew that his small party would soon be broken and exterminated in the open.

In the town, however, the Lancastrians were far from being in so good a posture. It was as Dick had said. The night-guard had already doffed their harness; the rest were still hanging – unlatched, unbraced, all unprepared for battle – about their quarters; and in the whole of Shoreby there were not, perhaps, fifty men full armed, or fifty chargers ready to be mounted.

The beating of the bells, the terrifying summons of men who ran about the streets crying and beating upon the doors, aroused in an incredibly short space at least two-score out of that half-hundred. These got speedily to horse, and, the alarm still flying wild and contrary, galloped in different directions.

Thus it befell that, when Richard of Gloucester reached the first house of Shoreby, he was met in the mouth of the street by a mere handful of lances, whom he swept before his onset as the storm chases the bark.

A hundred paces into the town, Dick Shelton touched the duke's arm; the duke, in answer, gathered his reins, put the shrill trumpet to his mouth, and blowing a concerted point, turned to the right hand out of the direct advance. Swerving like a single rider, his whole command turned after him, and, still at the full gallop of the chargers, swept up the narrow by-street. Only the last score of riders drew rein and faced about in the entrance; the footmen, whom they carried behind them, leapt at the same instant to the earth, and began, some to bend their bows, and others to break into and secure the houses upon either hand.

Surprised at this sudden change of direction, and daunted by the firm front of the rear-guard, the few Lancastrians, after a momentary consultation, turned and rode farther into town to seek for reinforcements.

The quarter of the town upon which, by the advice of Dick, Richard of Gloucester had now seized, consisted of five small streets of poor and ill-inhabited houses, occupying a very gentle eminence, and lying open towards the back.

The five streets being each secured by a good guard, the reserve would thus occupy the centre, out of shot, and yet ready to carry aid wherever it was needed.

Such was the poorness of the neighbourhood that none of the Lancastrian lords, and but few of their retainers, had been lodged therein; and the inhabitants, with one accord, deserted their houses and fled, squalling, along the streets or over garden walls.

In the centre, where the five ways all met, a somewhat ill-favoured ale-house displayed the sign of the Chequers; and here the Duke of Gloucester chose his headquarters for the day.

To Dick he assigned the guard of one of the five streets.

'Go,' he said, 'win your spurs. Win glory for me; one Richard for another. I tell you, if I rise, ye shall rise by the same ladder. Go,' he added, shaking him by the hand.

But, as soon as Dick was gone, he turned to a little shabby archer at his elbow.

'Go, Dutton, and that right speedily,' he added. 'Follow that lad. If ye find him faithful, ye answer for his safety, a head for a head. Woe unto you, if ye return without him! But if he be faithless – or, for one instant, ye misdoubt him – stab him from behind.'

In the meanwhile Dick hastened to secure his post. The street he had to guard was very narrow, and closely lined with houses, which projected and overhung the roadway; but narrow and dark as it was, since it opened upon the market-place of the town, the main issue of the battle would probably fall to be decided on that spot.

The market-place was full of townspeople fleeing in disorder; but there was as yet no sign of any foeman ready to attack, and Dick judged he had some time before him to make ready his defence.

The two houses at the end stood deserted, with open doors, as the inhabitants had left them in their flight, and from these he had the furniture hastily tossed forth and piled into a barrier in the entry of the lane. A hundred men were placed at his disposal, and of these he threw the more part into the houses, where they might lie in shelter and deliver their arrows from the windows. With the rest, under his own immediate eye, he lined the barricade.

Meanwhile the utmost uproar and confusion had continued to prevail throughout the town; and what with the hurried clashing of bells, the sounding of trumpets, the swift movement of bodies of horse, the cries of the commanders, and the shrieks of women, the noise was almost deafening to the ear. Presently, little by little, the tumult began to subside; and soon after, files of men in armour and bodies of archers began to assemble and form in line of battle in the market-place.

A large portion of this body were in murrey and blue, and in the mounted knight who ordered their array Dick recognized Sir Daniel Brackley.

Then there befell a long pause, which was followed by the almost simultaneous sounding of four trumpets from four different quarters of the town. A fifth rang in answer from the market-place, and at the same moment the files began to move, and a shower of arrows rattled about the barricade, and sounded like blows upon the walls of the two flanking houses.

The attack had begun, by a common signal, on all the five issues of the quarter. Gloucester was beleaguered upon every side; and Dick judged, if he would make good his post, he must rely entirely on the hundred men at his command.

Seven volleys of arrows followed one upon the other, and in the very thick of the discharges Dick was touched from behind upon the arm, and found a page holding out to him a leathern jack, strengthened with bright plates of mail.

'It is from my Lord of Gloucester,' said the page. 'He hath observed, Sir Richard, that ye went unarmed.'

Dick, with a glow at his heart at being so addressed, got to his feet and, with the assistance of the page, donned the defensive coat. Even as he did so, two arrows rattled harmlessly upon the plates, and a third struck down the page, mortally wounded, at his feet.

Meanwhile the whole body of the enemy had been steadily drawing nearer across the market-place; and by this time were so close at hand that Dick gave the order to return their shot. Immediately, from behind the barrier and from the windows of the houses, a counterblast of arrows sped, carrying death. But the Lancastrians, as if they had but waited for a signal, shouted loudly in answer; and began to close at a run upon the barrier, the horsemen still hanging back, with visors lowered.

Then followed an obstinate and deadly struggle, hand to hand. The assailants, wielding their falchions with one hand, strove with the other to drag down the structure of the barricade. On the other side, the parts were reversed; and the defenders exposed themselves like madmen to protect their rampart. So for some minutes the contest raged almost in silence, friend and foe falling one upon another. But it is always the easier to destroy; and when a single note upon the tucket recalled the attacking party from this desperate service, much of the barricade had been removed piecemeal, and the whole fabric had sunk to half its height, and tottered to a general fall.

And now the footmen in the market-place fell back, at a run, on every side. The horsemen, who had been standing in a line two deep, wheeled suddenly, and made their flank into their front; and as swift as a striking adder, the long, steel-clad column was launched upon the ruinous barricade.

Of the first two horsemen, one fell, rider and steed, and was ridden down by his companions. The second leaped clean upon the summit of the rampart, transpiercing an archer with his lance. Almost in the same instant he was dragged from the saddle and his horse dispatched.

And then the full weight and impetus of the charge burst upon and scattered the defenders. The men-at-arms, surmounting their onslaught, dashed through Dick's broken line and poured thundering up the lane beyond, as a stream bestrides and pours across a broken dam.

Yet was the fight not over. Still, in the narrow jaws of the entrance, Dick and a few survivors plied their bills like woodmen; and already, across the width of the passage, there had been formed a second, a higher, and a more effectual rampart of fallen men and disembowelled horses, lashing in the agonies of death.

Baffled by this fresh obstacle, the remainder of the cavalry fell back; and as, at the sight of this movement, the flight of arrows redoubled from the casements of the houses, their retreat had, for a moment, almost degenerated into flight.

Almost at the same time, those who had crossed the barricade and charged farther up the street, being met before the door of the Chequers by the formidable hunchback and the whole reserve of the Yorkists, began to come scattering backward, in the excess of disarray and terror.

Dick and his fellows faced about, fresh men poured out of the houses; a cruel blast of arrows met the fugitives full in the face, while Gloucester was already riding down their rear; in the inside of a minute and a half there was no living Lancastrian in the street.

Then, and not till then, did Dick hold up his reeking blade and give the word to cheer.

Meanwhile Gloucester dismounted from his horse and came forward to inspect the post. His face was as pale as linen; but his eyes shone in his head like some strange jewel, and his voice, when he spoke, was hoarse and broken with the exultation of battle and success. He looked at the rampart, which neither friend nor foe could now approach without precaution, so fiercely did the horses struggle in the throes of death, and at the sight of that great carnage he smiled upon one side.

'Dispatch these horses,' he said; 'they keep you from your vantage. Richard Shelton,' he added, 'ye have pleased me. Kneel.'

The Lancastrians had already resumed their archery, and the shafts fell thick in the mouth of the street; but the duke, minding them not at all, deliberately drew his sword and dubbed Richard a knight upon the spot.

'And now, Sir Richard,' he continued, 'if that ye see Lord Risingham, send me an express upon the instant. Were it your last man, let me hear of it incontinently. I had rather venture the post than lose my stroke at him. For mark me, all of ye,' he added, raising his voice, 'if Earl Risingham fall by another hand than mine, I shall count this victory a defeat.'

'My lord duke,' said one of his attendants, 'is your grace not weary of exposing his dear life unneedfully? Why tarry we here?'

'Catesby,' returned the duke, 'here is the battle, not elsewhere. The rest are but feigned onslaughts. Here must we vanquish. And for the exposure – if ye were an ugly hunchback, and the children gecked at you upon the street, ye would count your body cheaper, and an hour of glory worth a life. Howbeit, if ye will, let us ride on and visit the other posts. Sir Richard here, my namesake, he shall still hold this entry, where he wadeth to the ankles in hot blood. Him can we trust. But mark it, Sir Richard, ye are not yet done. The worst is yet toward. Sleep not.'

He came right up to young Shelton, looking him hard in the eyes, and taking his hand in both of his, gave it so extreme a squeeze that the blood had nearly spurted. Dick quailed before his eyes. The insane excitement, the courage, and the cruelty that he read therein, filled him with dismay about the future. This young duke's was indeed a gallant spirit, to ride foremost in the ranks of war; but after the battle, in the days of peace and in the circle of his trusted friends, that mind, it was to be dreaded, would continue to bring forth the fruits of death.

3 The Battle of Shoreby (concluded)

Dick, once more left to his own counsels, began to look about him. The arrow-shot had somewhat slackened. On all sides the enemy were falling back, and the greater part of the market-place was now left empty, the snow here trampled into orange mud, there splashed with gore, scattered all over with dead men and horses, and bristling thick with feathered arrows.

On his own side the loss had been cruel. The jaws of the little street and the ruins of the barricade were heaped with the dead and dying; and out of the hundred men with whom he had begun the battle, there were not seventy left who could still stand to arms.

At the same time the day was passing. The first reinforcements might be looked for to arrive at any moment; and the Lancastrians, already shaken by the result of their desperate but unsuccessful onslaught, were in an ill temper to support a fresh invader.

There was a dial in the wall of one of the two flanking houses; and this, in the frosty, winter sunshine, indicated ten of the forenoon.

Dick turned to the man who was at his elbow, a little insignificant archer, binding a cut in his arm.

'It was well fought,' he said, 'and, by my sooth, they will not charge us twice.'

'Sir,' said the little archer, 'ye have fought right well for York, and better for yourself. Never hath man in so brief space prevailed so greatly on the duke's affections. That he should have entrusted such a post to one he knew not is a marvel. But look to your head, Sir Richard! If ye be vanquished – ay, if ye give way one foot's breadth – axe or cord shall punish it; and I am set if ye do aught doubtful, I will tell you honestly, here to stab you from behind!'

Dick looked at the little man in amaze.

'You!' he cried. 'And from behind!'

'It is right so,' returned the archer; 'and because I like not the affair I tell it you. Ye must make the post good, Sir Richard, at your peril. O, our Crookback is a bold blade and a good warrior; but whether in cold blood or in hot, he will have all things done exact to his commandment. If any fail or hinder, they shall die the death.'

'Now, by the saints!' cried Richard, 'is this so? And will men follow such a leader?'

'Nay, they follow him gleefully,' replied the other; 'for if he be exact to punish, he is most open-handed to reward. And if he spare not the blood and sweat of others, he is ever liberal of his own, still in the first front of battle, still the last sleep. He will go far, will Crookback Dick o' Gloucester!'

The young knight, if he had before been brave and vigilant, was now all the more inclined to watchfulness and courage. His sudden favour, he began to perceive, had brought perils in its train. And he turned from the archer, and once more scanned anxiously the market-place. It lay empty as before.

'I like not this quietude,' he said. 'Doubtless they prepare us some surprise.'

And, as if in answer to his remark, the archers began once more to advance against the barricade, and the arrows to fall thick. But there was something hesitating in the attack. They came not on roundly, but seemed rather to await a further signal.

Dick looked uneasily about him, spying for a hidden danger. And sure enough, about half-way up the little street a door was suddenly opened from within, and the house continued, for some seconds, and both by door and window, to disgorge a torrent of Lancastrian archers. These, as they leaped down, hurriedly stood to their ranks, bent their bows, and proceeded to pour upon Dick's rear a flight of arrows.

At the same time, the assailants in the market-place redoubled their shot, and began to close in stoutly upon the barricade.

Dick called down his whole command out of the houses, and facing them both ways, and encouraging their valour both by word and gesture, returned as best he could the double shower of shafts that fell about his post.

Meanwhile house after house was opened in the street, and the Lancastrians continued to pour out of the doors and leap down from the windows, shouting victory, until the number of enemies upon Dick's rear was almost equal to the number in his face. It was plain that he could hold the post no longer; what was worse, even if he could

'*They cleared the street in a triumphant style*'

have held it, it had now become useless; and the whole Yorkist army lay in a posture of helplessness upon the brink of a complete disaster.

The men behind him formed the vital flaw in the general defence; and it was upon these that Dick turned, charging at the head of his men. So vigorous was the attack, that the Lancastrian archers gave ground and staggered, and, at last, breaking their ranks, began to crowd back into the houses from which they had so recently and so vaingloriously sallied.

Meanwhile the men from the market-place had swarmed across the undefended barricade, and fell on hotly upon the other side; and Dick must once again face about, and proceed to drive them back. Once again the spirit of his men prevailed; they cleared the street in a triumphant style, but even as they did so the others issued again out of the houses, and took them, a third time, upon the rear.

The Yorkists began to be scattered; several times Dick found himself alone among his foes and plying his bright sword for life; several times he was conscious of a hurt. And meanwhile the fight swayed to and fro in the street without determinate result.

Suddenly Dick was aware of a great trumpeting about the outskirts of the town. The war-cry of York began to be rolled up to heaven, as by many and triumphant voices. And at the same time the men in front of him began to give ground rapidly, streaming out of the street, and back upon the market-place. Someone gave the word to fly. Trumpets were blown distractedly, some for a rally, some to charge. It was plain that a great blow had been struck, and the Lancastrians were thrown, at least for the moment, into full disorder, and some degree of panic.

And then, like a theatre trick, there followed the last act of Shoreby battle. The men in front of Richard turned tail, like a dog that has been whistled home, and fled like the wind. At the same moment there came through the market place a storm of horsemen, fleeing and pursuing, the Lancastrians turning back to strike with the sword, the Yorkists riding them down at the point of the lance.

Conspicuous in the mellay, Dick beheld the Crookback. He was already giving a foretaste of that furious valour and skill to cut his way across the ranks of war, which, years afterwards upon the field of Bosworth, and when he was stained with crimes, almost sufficed to change the fortunes of the day and the destiny of the English throne. Evading, striking, riding down, he so forced and so manoeuvred his strong horse, so aptly defended himself, and so liberally scattered death to his opponents, that he was now far ahead of the foremost of his knights, hewing his way, with the truncheon of a bloody sword, to where Lord Risingham was rallying the bravest. A moment more and they had met; the tall, splendid, and famous warrior against the deformed and sickly boy.

Yet Shelton had never a doubt as to the result; and when the fight next opened for a moment, the figure of the earl had disappeared; but still, in the first of the danger, Crookback Dick was launching his big horse and plying the truncheon of his sword.

Thus, by Shelton's courage in holding the mouth of the street against the first attack, and by the opportune arrival of his seven hundred reinforcements, the lad, who was afterwards to be handed down to the execration of posterity under the name of Richard III, had won his first considerable fight.

4 The Sack of Shoreby

There was not a foe left within striking distance; and Dick, as he looked ruefully about him on the remainder of his gallant force, began to count the cost of victory. He was himself, now that the danger was ended, so stiff and sore, so bruised and cut and broken, and, above all, so utterly exhausted by his desperate and unremitting labours in the fight, that he seemed incapable of any fresh exertion.

But this was not yet the hour for repose. Shoreby had been taken by assault; and though an open town, and not in any manner to be charged with the resistance, it was plain that these rough fighters would be not less rough now that the fight was over, and that the more horrid part of war would fall to be enacted. Richard of Gloucester was not the captain to protect the citizens from his infuriated soldiery; and even if he had the will, it might be questioned if he had the power.

It was therefore Dick's business to find and to protect Joanna; and with that end he looked about him at the faces of his men. The three or four who seemed likeliest to be obedient and to keep sober he drew aside; and promising them a rich reward and a special recommendation to the duke, led them across the market-place now empty of horsemen, and into the streets upon the farther side.

Every here and there small combats of from two to a dozen still raged upon the open street; here and there a house was being besieged, the defenders throwing out stools and tables on the heads of the assailants. The snow was strewn with arms and corpses; but except for these partial combats the streets were deserted, and the houses, some standing open, and some shuttered and barricaded, had for the most part ceased to give out smoke.

Dick, threading the skirts of these skirmishers, led his followers briskly in the direction of the abbey church; but when he came the length of the main street, a cry of horror broke from his lips. Sir Daniel's great house had been carried by assault. The gates hung in splinters from the hinges, and a double throng kept pouring in and out through the entrance, seeking and carrying booty. Meanwhile, in the upper storeys, some resistance was still being offered to the pillagers; for just as Dick came within eyeshot of the building, a casement was burst open from within, and a poor wretch in murrey and blue, screaming and resisting, was forced through the embrasure and tossed into the street below.

The most sickening apprehension fell upon Dick. He ran forward like one possessed, forced his way into the house among the foremost, and mounted without pause to the chamber on the third floor where he had last parted from Joanna. It was a mere wreck; the furniture had been overthrown, the cupboards broken open, and in one place a trailing corner of the arras lay smouldering on the embers of the fire.

Dick, almost without thinking, trod out the incipient conflagration, and then stood bewildered. Sir Daniel, Sir Oliver, Joanna, all were gone; but whether butchered in the rout or safe escaped from Shoreby, who should say?

He caught a passing archer by the tabard.

'Fellow,' he asked, 'were ye here when this house was taken?'

'Let be,' said the archer. 'A murrain! let be, or I strike.'

'Hark ye,' returned Richard, 'two can play at that. Stand and be plain.'

But the man, flushed with drink and battle, struck Dick upon the shoulder with one hand, while with the other he twitched away his garment. Thereupon the full wrath of the young leader burst from his control. He seized the fellow in his strong embrace, and crushed him on the plates of his mailed bosom like a child; then, holding him at arm's length, he bid him speak as he valued life.

'I pray you mercy!' gasped the archer. 'An I had thought ye were so angry I would 'a' been charier of crossing you. I was here indeed.'

'Know ye Sir Daniel?' pursued Dick.

'Well do I know him,' returned the man.

'Was he in the mansion?'

'Ay, sir, he was,' answered the archer; 'but even as we entered by the yard gate he rode forth by the garden.'

'Alone?' cried Dick.

'He may 'a' had a score of lances with him,' said the man.

'Lances! No women, then?' asked Shelton.

'Troth, I saw not,' said the archer. 'But there were none in the house, if that be your quest.'

'I thank you,' said Dick. 'Here is a piece for your pains.' But groping in his wallet, Dick found nothing. 'Inquire for me to-morrow,' he added – 'Richard Shel—— Sir Richard Shelton,' he corrected, 'and I will see you handsomely rewarded.'

And then an idea struck Dick. He hastily descended to the courtyard, ran with all his might across the garden, and came to the great door of the church. It stood wide open; within, every corner of the pavement was crowded with fugitive burghers, surrounded by their families and laden with the most precious of their possessions, while, at the high altar, priests in full canonicals were imploring the mercy of God. Even as Dick entered, the loud chorus began to thunder in the vaulted roofs.

He hurried through the groups of refugees, and came to the door of the stair that led into the steeple. And here a tall churchman stepped before him and arrested his advance.

'Whither, my son?' he asked severely.

'My father,' answered Dick, 'I am here upon an errand of expedition. Stay me not. I command here for my Lord of Gloucester.'

'For my Lord of Gloucester?' repeated the priest. 'Hath, then, the battle gone so sore?'

'The battle, father, is at an end, Lancaster clean sped, my Lord of Risingham – Heaven rest him! – left upon the field. And now, with your good leave, I follow mine affairs.' And thrusting on one side the priest, who seemed stupefied at the news, Dick pushed open the door and rattled up the stairs four at a bound, and without pause or stumble, till he stepped upon the open platform at the top.

Shoreby church tower not only commanded the town, as in a map, but looked far, on both sides, over sea and land. It was now near upon noon, the day exceeding bright, the snow dazzling. And as Dick looked around him, he could measure the consequences of the battle.

A confused, growling uproar reached him from the streets, and now and then, but very rarely, the clash of steel. Not a ship, not so much as a skiff remained in harbour; but the sea was dotted with sails and row-boats laden with fugitives. On shore, too, the surface of the snowy meadows was broken up with bands of horsemen, some cutting their way towards the borders of the forest, others, who were doubtless of the Yorkist side, stoutly interposing and beating them back upon the town. Over all the open ground there lay a prodigious quantity of fallen men and horses, clearly defined upon the snow.

To complete the picture, those of the foot soldiers as had not found place upon a ship still kept up an archery combat on the borders of the port, and from the cover of the shoreside taverns. In that quarter, also, one or two houses had been fired, and the smoke towered high in the frosty sunlight, and blew off to sea in voluminous folds.

Already close upon the margin of the woods, and somewhat in the line of Holywood, one particular clump of fleeing horsemen riveted the attention of the young watcher on the tower. It was fairly numerous; in no other quarter of the field did so many Lancastrians still hold together; thus they had left a wide, discoloured wake upon the snow, and Dick was able to trace them step by step from where they had left the town.

While Dick stood watching them, they had gained unopposed the first fringe of the leafless forest, and turning a little from their direction, the sun fell for a moment full on their array, as it was relieved against the dusky wood.

'Murrey and blue!' cried Dick. 'I swear it – murrey and blue!'

The next moment he was descending the stairway.

It was now his business to seek out the Duke of Gloucester, who, alone, in the disorder of the forces, might be able to supply him with a sufficiency of men. The fighting in the main town was now practically at an end; and as Dick ran hither and thither, seeking the commander, the streets were thick with wandering soldiers, some laden with more booty than they could well stagger under, others shouting drunk. None of them, when questioned, had the least notion of the duke's whereabouts; and, at last, it was by sheer good fortune that Dick found him, where he sat in the saddle directing operations to dislodge the archers from the harbour side.

'Sir Richard Shelton, ye are well found,' he said. 'I owe you one thing that I value little, my life; and one that I can never pay you for, this victory. Catesby, if I had ten such captains as Sir Richard, I would march forthright on London. But now, sir, claim your reward.'

'Freely, my lord,' said Dick, 'freely and loudly. One hath escaped to whom I owe some grudges, and taken with him one whom I owe love and service. Give me, then, fifty lances, that I may pursue; and for any obligation that your graciousness is pleased to allow, it shall be clean discharged.'

'How call ye him?' inquired the duke.

'Sir Daniel Brackley,' answered Richard.

'Out upon him, double-face!' cried Gloucester. 'Here is no reward, Sir Richard; here is fresh service offered, and, if that ye bring his head to me, a fresh debt upon my conscience. Catesby, get him these lances; and you, sir, bethink ye, in the meanwhile, what pleasure, honour, or profit it shall be mine to give you.'

Just then the Yorkist skirmishers carried one of the shoreside taverns, swarming in upon it on three sides, and driving out or taking its defenders. Crookback Dick was pleased to cheer the exploit, and pushing his horse a little nearer, called to see the prisoners.

There were four or five of them – two men of my Lord Shoreby's and one of Lord Risingham's among the number, and last, but in Dick's eyes not least, a tall, shambling, grizzled old shipman, between drunk and sober, and with a dog whimpering and jumping at his heels.

The young duke passed them for a moment under a severe review.

'Good,' he said. 'Hang them.'

And he turned the other way to watch the progress of the fight.

'My lord,' said Dick, 'so please you, I have found my reward. Grant me the life and liberty of yon old shipman.'

Gloucester turned and looked the speaker in the face.

'Sir Richard,' he said, 'I make not war with peacock's feathers, but steel shafts. Those that are mine enemies I slay, and that without excuse or favour. For, bethink ye, in this realm of England, that is so torn in pieces, there is not a man of mine but hath a brother or a friend upon the other party. If, then, I did begin to grant these pardons, I might sheathe my sword.'

'It may be so, my lord; and yet I will be over-bold, and, at the risk of your disfavour, recall your lordship's promise,' replied Dick.

Richard of Gloucester flushed.

'Mark it right well,' he said harshly. 'I love not mercy, nor yet mercy-mongers. Ye have this day laid the foundations of high fortune. If ye oppose to me my word, which I have plighted, I will yield. But, by the glory of heaven, there your favour dies!'

'Mine is the loss,' said Dick.

'Give him his sailor,' said the duke; and wheeling his horse, he turned his back upon young Shelton.

Dick was not glad nor sorry. He had seen too much of the young duke to set great store on his affection; and the origin and growth of his own favour had been too flimsy and too rapid to inspire much confidence. One thing alone he feared – that the vindictive leader might revoke the offer of the lances. But here he did justice neither to Gloucester's honour (such as it was) nor, above all, to his decision. If he had once judged Dick to be the right man to pursue Sir Daniel, he was not one to change; and he soon proved it by shouting after Catesby to be speedy, for the paladin was waiting.

In the meanwhile, Dick turned to the old shipman, who had seemed equally indifferent to his condemnation and to his subsequent release.

'Arblaster,' said Dick, 'I have done you ill; but now, by the rood, I think I have cleared the score.'

But the old skipper only looked upon him dully and held his peace.

'Come,' continued Dick, 'a life is a life, old shrew, and it is more than ships or liquor. Say ye forgive me; for if your life is worth nothing to you, it hath cost me the beginnings of my fortune. Come, I have paid for it dearly; be not so churlish.'

'An I had had my ship,' said Arblaster, 'I would 'a' been forth and safe on the high seas – I and my man Tom. But ye took my ship, gossip, and I'm a beggar; and for my man Tom, a knave fellow in russet shot him down. "Murrain!" quoth he, and spake never again. "Murrain" was the last of his words, and the poor spirit of him passed. 'A will never sail no more, will my Tom.'

Dick was seized with unavailing penitence and pity; he sought to take the skipper's hand, but Arblaster avoided his touch.

'Nay,' said he, 'let be. Y' have played the devil with me, and let that content you.'

The words died in Richard's throat. He saw, through tears, the poor old man, bemused with liquor and sorrow, go shambling away, with bowed head, across the snow, and the unnoticed dog whimpering at his heels; and for the first time began to understand the desperate game that we play in life, and how a thing once done is not to be changed or remedied by any penitence.

But there was no time left to him for vain regret. Catesby had now collected the horsemen, and riding up to Dick he dismounted, and offered him his own horse.

'This morning,' he said, 'I was somewhat jealous of your favour; it hath not been of a long growth; and now, Sir Richard, it is with a very good heart that I offer you this horse – to ride away with.'

'Suffer me yet a moment,' replied Dick. 'This favour of mine –

whereupon was it founded?'

'Upon your name,' answered Catesby. 'It is my lord's chief superstition. Were my name Richard, I should be an earl to-morrow.'

'Well, sir, I thank you,' returned Dick; 'and since I am little likely to follow these great fortunes, I will even say farewell. I will not pretend I was displeased to think myself upon the road to fortune; but I will not pretend, neither, that I am over-sorry to be done with it. Command and riches, they are brave things, to be sure; but a word in your ear — yon duke of yours, he is a fearsome lad.'

Catesby laughed.

'Nay,' said he, 'of a verity he that rides with Crooked Dick will ride deep. Well, God keep us all from evil! Speed ye well.'

Thereupon Dick put himself at the head of his men, and giving the word of command, rode off.

He made straight across the town, following what he supposed to be the route of Sir Daniel, and spying around for any signs that might decide if he were right.

The streets were strewn with the dead and the wounded, whose fate, in the bitter frost, was far the more pitiable. Gangs of the victors went from house to house, pillaging and stabbing, and sometimes singing together as they went.

From different quarters, as he rode on, the sounds of violence and outrage came to young Shelton's ears; now the blows of the sledge-hammer on some barricaded door, and now the miserable shrieks of women.

Dick's heart had just been awakened. He had just seen cruel consequences of his own behaviour; and the thought of the sum of misery that was now acting in the whole of Shoreby filled him with despair.

At length he reached the outskirts, and there, sure enough, he saw straight before him the same broad, beaten track across the snow that he had marked from the summit of the church. Here, then, he went the faster on; but still, as he rode, he kept a bright eye upon the fallen men and horses that lay beside the track. Many of these, he was relieved to see, wore Sir Daniel's colours, and the faces of some, who lay upon their backs, he even recognized.

About half-way between the town and the forest, those whom he was following had plainly been assailed by archers; for the corpses lay pretty closely scattered, each pierced by an arrow. And here Dick spied among the rest the body of a very young lad, whose face was somehow hauntingly familiar to him.

He halted his troop, dismounted, and raised the lad's head. As he did so, the hood fell back, and a profusion of long brown hair unrolled itself. At the same time the eyes opened. 'Ah! lion-driver!' said a feeble voice. 'She is farther on. Ride – ride fast!'

And then the poor young lady fainted once again.

One of Dick's men carried a flask of some strong cordial, and with this Dick succeeded in reviving consciousness. Then he took Joanna's friend upon his saddle-bow, and once more pushed toward the forest.

'Why do ye take me?' said the girl. 'Ye but delay your speed.'

'Nay, Mistress Risingham,' replied Dick. 'Shoreby is full of blood and drunkenness and riot. Here ye are safe; content ye.'

'I will not be beholden to any of your faction,' she cried; 'set me down.'

'Madam, ye know not what ye say,' returned Dick. 'Y' are hurt——'

'I am not,' she said. 'It was my horse was slain.'

'It matters not one jot,' replied Richard. 'Ye are here in the midst of open snow, and compassed about with enemies. Whether ye will or not, I carry you with me. Glad am I to have the occasion; for thus shall I repay some portion of our debt.'

For a little while she was silent. Then, very suddenly, she asked: 'My uncle?'

'My Lord Risingham?' returned Dick. 'I would I had good news to give you, madam; but I have none. I saw him once in the battle and once only. Let us hope the best.'

5 Night in the Woods: Alicia Risingham

It was almost certain that Sir Daniel had made for the Moat House; but, considering the heavy snow, the lateness of the hour, and the necessity under which he would lie of avoiding the few roads and striking across the wood, it was equally certain that he could not hope to reach it ere the morrow.

There were two courses open to Dick; either to continue to follow in the knight's trail, and, if he were able, to fall upon him that very night in camp; or to strike out a path of his own, and seek to place himself between Sir Daniel and his destination.

Either scheme was open to serious objection, and Dick, who feared to expose Joanna to the hazards of a fight, had not yet decided between them when he reached the borders of the wood.

At this point Sir Daniel had turned a little to his left, and then plunged straight under a grove of very lofty timber. His party had then formed to a narrower front, in order to pass between the trees, and the track was trod proportionately deeper in the snow. The eye followed it, under the leafless tracery of the oaks, running direct and narrow; the trees stood over it, with knotty joints and the great, uplifted forest of their boughs; there was no sound, whether of man or beast – not so much as the stirring of a robin; and over the field of snow the winter sun lay golden among netted shadows.

'How say ye,' asked Dick of one of the men, 'to follow straight on, or strike across for Tunstall?'

'Sir Richard,' replied the man-at-arms, 'I would follow the line until they scatter.'

'Ye are, doubtless, right,' returned Dick; 'but we came right hastily upon the errand, even as the time commanded. Here are no houses, neither for food nor shelter, and by the morrow's dawn we shall know both cold fingers and an empty belly. How say ye, lads? Will ye stand a pinch for expedition's sake, or shall we turn by

Holywood and sup with Mother Church? The case being somewhat doubtful, I will drive no man; yet if ye would suffer me to lead you, ye would choose the first.'

The men answered, almost with one voice, that they would follow Sir Richard where he would.

And Dick, setting spur to his horse, began once more to go forward.

The snow in the trail had been trodden very hard, and the pursuers had thus a great advantage over the pursued. They pushed on, indeed, at a round trot, two hundred hoofs beating alternately on the dull pavement of the snow, and the jingle of weapons and the snorting of horses raising a warlike noise along the arches of the silent wood.

Presently, the wide slot of the pursued came out upon the high-road from Holywood; it was there, for a moment, indistinguishable; and, where it once more plunged into the unbeaten snow upon the farther side, Dick was surprised to see it narrower and lighter trod. Plainly, profiting by the road, Sir Daniel had begun already to scatter his command.

At all hazards, one chance being equal to another, Dick continued to pursue the straight trail; and that, after an hour's riding, in which it led into the very depths of the forest, suddenly split, like a bursting shell, into two dozen others, leading to every point of the compass.

Dick drew bridle in despair. The short winter's day was near an end; the sun, a dull red orange, shorn of rays, swam low among the leafless thickets; the shadows were a mile long upon the snow; the frost bit cruelly at the finger-nails; and the breath and steam of the horses mounted in a cloud.

'Well, we are outwitted,' Dick confessed. 'Strike we for Holywood, after all. It is still nearer us than Tunstall – or should be by the station of the sun.'

So they wheeled to their left, turning their backs on the red shield of sun, and made across country for the abbey. But now times were changed with them; they could no longer spank forth briskly on a path beaten firm by the passage of their foes, and for a goal to which that path itself conducted them. Now they must plough at a dull pace through the encumbering snow, continually pausing to decide their course, continually floundering in drifts. The sun soon left them; the glow of the west decayed; and presently they were wandering in a shadow of blackness, under frosty stars.

Presently, indeed, the moon would clear the hill-tops, and they might resume their march. But till then, every random step might carry them wider of their march. There was nothing for it but to camp and wait.

Sentries were posted; a spot of ground was cleared of snow, and after some failures, a good fire blazed in the midst. The men-at-arms sat close about this forest hearth, sharing such provisions as they had, and passing about the flask; and Dick, having collected the most delicate of the rough and scanty fare, brought it to Lord Risingham's niece, where she sat apart from the soldiery against a tree.

She sat upon one horse-cloth, wrapped in another, and stared straight before her at the firelit scene. At the offer of food she started, like one wakened from a dream, and then silently refused.

'Madam,' said Dick, 'let me beseech you, punish me not so cruelly. Wherein I have offended you, I know not; I have, indeed, carried you away, but with a friendly violence; I have, indeed, exposed you to the inclemency of night, but the hurry that lies upon me hath for its end the preservation of another, who is no less frail and no less unfriended than yourself. At least, madam, punish not yourself; and eat, if not for hunger, then for strength.'

'I will eat nothing at the hands that slew my kinsman,' she replied.

'Dear madam,' Dick cried, 'I swear to you upon the rood I touched him not.'

'Swear to me that he still lives,' she returned.

'I will not palter with you,' answered Dick. 'Pity bids me to wound you. In my heart I do believe him dead.'

'And ye ask me to eat!' she cried. 'Ay, and they call you "sir"! Y' have won your spurs by my good kinsman's murder. And had I not been fool and traitor both, and saved you in your enemy's house, ye should have died the death, and he — he that was worth twelve of you — were living.'

'I did but my man's best, even as your kinsman did upon the other party,' answered Dick. 'Were he still living – as I vow to Heaven I wish it! – he would praise, not blame me.'

'Sir Daniel hath told me,' she replied. 'He marked you at the barricade. Upon you, he saith, their party foundered; it was you that won the battle. Well, then, it was you that killed my good Lord Risingham, as sure as though ye had strangled him. And ye would have me eat with you – and your hands not washed from killing? But Sir Daniel hath sworn your downfall. He 'tis that will avenge me!'

The unfortunate Dick was plunged in gloom. Old Arblaster returned upon his mind, and he groaned aloud.

'Do ye hóld me so guilty?' he said; 'you that defended me – you that are Joanna's friend?'

'What made ye in the battle?' she retorted. 'Y' are of no party; y' are but a lad – but legs and body, without government of wit or counsel! Wherefore did ye fight? For the love of hurt, pardy!'

'Nay,' cried Dick, 'I know not. But as the realm of England goes, if that a poor gentleman fight not upon the one side, perforce he must fight upon the other. He may not stand alone, 'tis not in nature.'

'They that have no judgment should not draw the sword,' replied the young lady. 'Ye that fight but for a hazard, what are ye but a butcher? War is but noble by the cause, and y' have disgraced it.'

'Madam,' said the miserable Dick, 'I do partly see mine error. I have made too much haste; I have been busy before my time. Already I stole a ship – thinking, I do swear it, to do well – and thereby brought about the death of many innocent, and the grief and ruin of a poor old man whose face this very day hath stabbed me like a dagger. And for this morning, I did but design to do myself credit, and get fame to marry with, and, behold! I have brought about the death of your dear kinsman that was good to me. And what besides, I know not. For, alas! I may have set York upon the throne, and that may be the worser cause, and may do hurt to England. O! madam, I do see my sin. I am unfit for life. I will, for penance sake and to avoid worse evil, once I have finished this adventure, get me to a cloister. I will forswear Joanna and the trade of arms. I will be a friar, and pray for your good kinsman's spirit all my days.'

It appeared to Dick, in this extremity of his humiliation and repentance, that the young lady had laughed.

Raising his countenance, he found her looking down upon him, in the firelight, with a somewhat peculiar but not unkind expression.

'Madam,' he cried, thinking the laughter to have been an illusion of his hearing, but still, from her changed looks, hoping to have touched her heart – 'madam, will not this content you? I give up all to undo what I have done amiss; I make heaven certain for Lord Risingham. And all this upon the very day that I have won my spurs, and thought myself the happiest young gentleman on ground.'

'O, boy,' she said, 'good boy!'

And then, to the extreme surprise of Dick, she first very tenderly wiped the tears away from his cheeks, and then, as if yielding to a sudden impulse, threw both her arms about his neck, drew up his face, and kissed him. A pitiful bewilderment came over simple-minded Dick.

'But come,' she said, with great cheerfulness, 'you that are a captain, ye must eat. Why sup ye not?'

'Dear Mistress Risingham,' replied Dick, 'I did but wait first upon my prisoner; but, to say truth, penitence will no longer suffer me to endure the sight of food. I were better to fast, dear lady, and to pray.'

'Call me Alicia,' she said; 'are we not old friends? And now, come, I will eat with you, bit for bit and sup for sup; so if ye eat not, neither will I; but if ye eat hearty, I will dine like a ploughman.'

So there and then she fell to; and Dick, who had an excellent stomach, proceeded to bear her company, at first with great reluctance, but gradually, as he entered into the spirit, with more and more vigour and devotion; until, at last, he forgot even to watch his model, and most heartily repaired the expenses of his day of labour and excitement.

'Lion-driver,' she said, at length, 'ye do not admire a maid in a man's jerkin?'

The moon was now up; and they were only waiting to repose the wearied horses. By the moon's light, the still penitent but now well-fed Richard beheld her looking somewhat coquettishly down upon him.

'Madam——' he stammered, surprised at this new turn in her manners.

'Nay,' she interrupted, 'it skills not to deny; Joanna hath told me; but come, Sir Lion-driver, look at me – am I so homely? – come!'

And she made bright eyes at him.

'Ye are something smallish, indeed——' began Dick.

And here again she interrupted him, this time with a ringing peal of laughter that completed his confusion and surprise.

'Smallish!' she cried. 'Nay, now, be honest as ye are bold; I am a dwarf, or little better; but for all that – come, tell me! – for all that, passably fair to look upon; is't not so?'

'Nay, madam, exceedingly fair,' said the distressed knight, pitifully trying to seem easy.

'And a man would be right glad to wed me?' she pursued.

'O, madam, right glad!' agreed Dick.

'Call me Alicia,' said she.

'Alicia,' quoth Sir Richard.

'Well, then, Lion-driver,' she continued, 'sith that ye slew my kinsman, and left me without stay, ye owe me, in honour, every reparation; do ye not?'

'I do, madam,' said Dick. 'Although, upon my heart, I do hold me but partially guilty of that brave knight's blood.'

'Would ye evade me?' she cried.

'Madam, not so. I have told you; at your bidding, I will even turn me a monk,' said Richard.

'Then, in honour, ye belong to me?' she concluded.

'In honour, madam, I suppose——' began the young man.

'Go to!' she interrupted; 'ye are too full of catches. In honour do ye belong to me, till ye have paid the evil?'

'In honour I do,' said Dick.

'Hear, then,' she continued. 'Ye would make but a sad friar, methinks; and since I am to dispose of you at pleasure, I will even take you for my husband. Nay, now, no words!' cried she. 'They will avail you nothing. For see how just it is, that you who deprived me of one home, should supply me with another. And as for Joanna, she will be the first, believe me, to commend the change; for, after all, as we be dear friends, what matter it with which of us ye wed? Not one whit!'

'Madam,' said Dick, 'I will go into a cloister, an ye please to bid me; but to wed with anyone in this big world besides Joanna Sedley is what I will consent to neither for man's force nor yet for lady's pleasure. Pardon me if I speak my plain thoughts plainly; but where a maid is very bold, a poor man must be even the bolder.'

'Dick,' she said, 'ye sweet boy, ye must come and kiss me for that word. Nay, fear not, ye shall kiss me for Joanna, and when we meet I shall give it back to her, and say I stole it. And as for what ye owe me, why, dear simpleton, methinks ye were not alone in that great battle; and even if York be on the throne, it was not you that set him there. But for a good, sweet, honest heart, Dick, y' are all that; and if I could find it in my soul to envy your Joanna anything, I would even envy her your love.'

6 Night in the Woods (concluded): Dick and Joan

The horses had by this time finished the small store of provender, and fully breathed from their fatigues. At Dick's command the fire was smothered in snow; and while his men got once more wearily to saddle, he himself, remembering, somewhat late, true woodland caution, chose a tall oak, and nimbly clambered to the topmost fork. Hence he could look far abroad on the moonlit and snow-paven forest. On the south-west, dark against the horizon, stood those upland heathy quarters where he and Joanna had met with the terrifying misadventure of the leper. And there his eye was caught by a spot of ruddy brightness no bigger than a needle's eye.

He blamed himself sharply for his previous neglect. Were that, as it appeared to be, the shining of Sir Daniel's camp-fire, he should long ago have seen and marched for it; above all, he should, for no consideration, have announced his neighbourhood by lighting a fire of his own. But now he must no longer squander valuable hours. The direct way to the uplands was about two miles in length: but it was crossed by a very deep, precipitous dingle, impassable to mounted men; for the sake of speed, it seemed to Dick advisable to desert the horses and attempt the adventure on foot.

Ten men were left to guard the horses; signals were agreed upon by which they could communicate in case of need; and Dick set forth at the head of the remainder, Alicia Risingham walking stoutly by his side.

The men had freed themselves of heavy armour, and left behind their lances; and they now marched with a very good spirit in the frozen snow, and under the exhilarating lustre of the moon. The descent into the dingle, where a stream strained sobbing through the snow and ice, was effected with silence and order; and on the further side, being then within a short half mile of where Dick had seen the glimmer of the fire, the party halted to breathe before the attack.

In the vast silence of the wood, the lightest sounds were audible from far; and Alicia, who was keen of hearing, held up her finger warningly, and stooped to listen. All followed her example; but besides the groans of the choked brook in the dingle close behind, and the barking of a fox at a distance of many miles among the forest, to Dick's acutest hearkening not a breath was audible.

'But yet, for sure, I heard the clash of harness,' whispered Alicia.

'Madam,' returned Dick, who was more afraid of that young lady than of ten stout warriors, 'I would not hint ye were mistaken; but it might well have come from either of the camps.'

'It came not thence. It came from westward,' she declared.

'It may be what it will,' returned Dick; 'and it must be as Heaven please. Reck we not a jot, but push on the livelier, and put it to the touch. Up, friends – enough breathed.'

As they advanced, the snow became more and more trampled with hoof-marks, and it was plain that they were drawing near to the encampment of a considerable force of mounted men. Presently they could see the smoke pouring from among the trees, ruddily coloured on its lower edge and scattering bright sparks.

And here, pursuant to Dick's orders, his men began to open out, creeping stealthily in the covert, to surround on every side the camp of their opponents. He himself, placing Alicia in the shelter of a bulky oak, stole straight forth in the direction of the fire.

At last, through an opening of the wood, his eye embraced the scene of the encampment. The fire had been built upon a heathy hummock of the ground, surrounded on three sides by thicket, and it now burned very strong, roaring aloud and brandishing flames. Around it there sat not quite a dozen people, warmly cloaked; but though the neighbouring snow was trampled down as by a regiment, Dick looked in vain for any horse. He began to have a terrible misgiving that he was outmanœuvred. At the same time, in a tall man with a steel salet, who was spreading his hands before the blaze, he recognized his old friend and still kindly enemy, Bennet Hatch; and in two others, sitting a little back, he made out, even in their male disguise, Joanna Sedley and Sir Daniel's wife.

'Well,' thought he to himself, 'even if I lose my horses, let me get my Joanna, and why should I complain?'

And then, from the farther side of the encampment, there came a little whistle, announcing that his men had joined, and the investment was complete.

'Bennet, at the sound, started to his feet; but ere he had time to spring upon his arms, Dick hailed him.

'Bennet,' he said, 'Bennet, old friend, yield ye. Ye will but spill men's lives in vain if ye resist.'

''Tis Master Shelton, by St Barbary!' cried Hatch. 'Yield me? Ye ask much. What force have ye?'

'I tell you Bennet, ye are outnumbered and begirt,' said Dick. 'Caesar and Charlemagne would cry for quarter. I have two-score men at my whistle, and with one shoot of arrows I could answer for you all.'

'Master Dick,' said Bennet, 'it goes against my heart; but I must do my duty. The saints help you!' And therewith he raised a little tucket to his mouth and wound a rousing call.

Then followed a moment of confusion; for while Dick, fearing for the ladies, still hesitated to give the word to shoot, Hatch's little band sprang to their weapons and formed back to back as for a fierce resistance. In the hurry of their change of place, Joanna sprang from her seat and ran like an arrow to her lover's side.

'Here, Dick!' she cried, as she clasped his hand in hers.

But Dick still stood irresolute; he was yet young to the more deplorable necessities of war, and the thought of old Lady Brackley checked the command upon his tongue. His own men became restive. Some of them cried on him by name; others, of their own accord, began to shoot; and at the first discharge poor Bennet bit the dust. Then Dick awoke.

'On!' he cried. 'Shoot, boys, and keep to cover. England and York!'

But just then the dull beat of many horses on the snow suddenly arose in the hollow ear of the night, and, with incredible swiftness, drew nearer and swelled louder. At the same time, answering tuckets repeated and repeated Hatch's call.

'Rally, rally!' cried Dick. 'Rally upon me! Rally for your lives!'

But his men – afoot, scattered, taken in the hour when they had counted on an easy triumph – began, instead, to give ground severally, and either stood wavering or dispersed into the thickets. And when the first of the horsemen came charging through the open avenues and fiercely riding their steeds into the underwood, a few stragglers were overthrown or speared among the brush, but the bulk of Dick's command had simply melted at the rumour of their coming.

Dick stood for a moment, bitterly recognizing the fruits of his precipitate and unwise valour. Sir Daniel had seen the fire; he had moved out with his main force, whether to attack his pursuers or to take them in the rear if they should venture the assault. His had been throughout the part of a sagacious captain; Dick's the conduct of an eager boy. And here was the young knight, his sweetheart, indeed, holding him tightly by the hand, but otherwise alone, his whole command of men and horses dispersed in the night and the wide forest, like a paper of pins in a hay barn.

'The saints enlighten me!' he thought. 'It is well I was knighted for this morning's matter; this doth me little honour.'

And thereupon, still holding Joanna, he began to run.

The silence of the night was now shattered by the shouts of the men of Tunstall, as they galloped hither and thither, hunting fugitives; and Dick broke boldly through the underwood and ran straight before him like a deer. The silver clearness of the moon upon the open snow increased, by contrast, the obscurity of the thickets; and the extreme dispersion of the vanquished led the pursuers into widely divergent paths. Hence, in but a little while, Dick and Joanna paused, in a close covert, and heard the sounds of the pursuit, scattering abroad, indeed, in all directions, but yet fainting already in the distance.

'An I had but kept a reserve of them together,' Dick cried bitterly, 'I could have turned the tables yet! Well, we live and learn; next time it shall go better, by the rood.'

'Nay, Dick,' said Joanna, 'what matters it? Here we are together once again.'

He looked at her, and there she was – John Matcham, as of yore, in hose and doublet. But now he knew her; now, even in that ungainly dress, she smiled upon him, bright with love; and his heart was transported with joy.

'Sweetheart,' he said, 'if ye forgive this blunderer, what care I? Make we direct for Holywood; there lieth your good guardian and my better friend, Lord Foxham. There shall we be wed; and whether poor or wealthy, famous or unknown, what matters it? This day, dear love, I won my spurs; I was commended by great men for my valour; I thought myself the goodliest man of war in all broad England. Then, first, I fell out of my favour with the great; and now have I been well thrashed, and clean lost my soldiers. There was a downfall for conceit! But, dear, I care not – dear, if ye still love me and will wed, I would have my knighthood done away, and mind it not a jot.'

'My Dick!' she cried. 'And did they knight you?'

'Ay, dear, ye are my lady now,' he answered fondly; 'or ye shall, ere noon to-morrow – will ye not?'

'That will I, Dick, with a glad heart,' she answered.

'Ay, sir? Methought ye were to be a monk!' said a voice in their ears.

'Alicia!' cried Joanna.

'Even so,' replied the young lady, coming forward. 'Alicia, whom ye left for dead, and whom your lion-driver found, and brought to life again, and, by my sooth, made love to, if ye want to know.'

'I'll not believe it,' cried Joanna. 'Dick!'

'Dick!' mimicked Alicia. 'Dick, indeed! Ay, fair sir, and ye desert poor damsels in distress,' she continued, turning to the young knight. 'Ye leave them planted behind oaks. But they say true, the age of chivalry is dead.'

'Madam,' cried Dick, in despair, 'upon my soul I had forgotten you outright. Madam, ye must try to pardon me. Ye see, I had new found Joanna!'

'I did not suppose that ye had done it o' purpose,' she retorted. 'But I will be cruelly avenged. I will tell a secret to my Lady Shelton – she that is to be,' she added, curtsying. 'Joanna,' she continued, 'I believe, upon my soul, your sweetheart is a bold fellow in a fight, but he is, let me tell you plainly, the softest-hearted simpleton in England. Go to – ye may do your pleasure with him! And now, fool children, first kiss me, either one of you, for luck and kindness; and then kiss each other just one minute by the glass, and not one second longer; and then let us all three set forth for Holywood as fast as we can stir; for these woods, methinks, are full of peril and exceeding cold.'

'But did my Dick make love to you?' asked Joanna, clinging to her sweetheart's side.

'Nay, fool girl,' returned Alicia, 'it was I made love to him. I offered to marry him, indeed; but he bade me go marry with my likes. These were his words. Nay, that I will say: he is more plain than pleasant. But now, children, for the sake of sense set forward. Shall we go once more over the dingle, or push straight for Holywood?'

'Why,' said Dick, 'I would like dearly to get upon a horse; for I have been sore mauled and beaten, one way and another, these last days, and my poor body is one bruise. But how think ye? If the men, upon the alarm of the fighting, had fled away, we should have gone about for nothing. 'Tis but some three short miles to Holywood direct; the bell hath not beat nine; the snow is pretty firm to walk upon, the moon clear; how if we went even as we are?'

'Agreed,' cried Alicia; but Joanna only pressed upon Dick's arm.

Forth, then, they went, through open leafless groves and down snow-clad alleys, under the white face of the winter moon; Dick and Joanna walking hand in hand and in a heaven of pleasure; and their light-minded companion, her own bereavements heartily forgotten, followed a pace or two behind, now rallying them upon their silence, and now drawing happy pictures of their future and united lives.

Still, indeed, in the distance of the wood, the riders of Tunstall might be heard urging their pursuit; and from time to time cries or the clash of steel announced the shock of enemies. But in these young folk, bred among the alarms of war, and fresh from such a multiplicity of dangers, neither fear nor pity could be lightly wakened. Content to find the sounds still drawing farther and farther away, they gave up their hearts to the enjoyment of the hour, walking already, as Alicia put it, in a wedding procession; and neither the rude solitude of the forest, nor the cold of the freezing night had any force to shadow or distract their happiness.

At length, from a rising hill, they looked below them on the dell of Holywood. The great windows of the forest abbey shone with torch and candle; its high pinnacles and spires arose very clear and silent, and the gold rood upon the topmost summit glittered brightly in the moon. All about it, in the open glade, camp-fires were burning, and the ground was thick with huts; and across the midst of the picture the frozen river curved.

'By the mass,' said Richard, 'there are Lord Foxham's fellows still encamped. The messenger hath certainly miscarried. Well, then, so better. We have power at hand to face Sir Daniel.'

But if Lord Foxham's men still lay encamped in the long holm at Holywood, it was from a different reason from the one supposed by Dick. They had marched, indeed, for Shoreby; but ere they were half-way thither, a second messenger met them, and bade them return to their morning's camp, to bar the road against Lancastrian fugitives, and to be so much nearer to the main army of York. For Richard of Gloucester, having finished the battle and stamped out his foes in that district, was already on the march to rejoin his brother; and not long after the return of my Lord Foxham's retainers, Crookback himself drew rein before the abbey door. It was in honour of this august visitor that the windows shone with lights; and at the hour of Dick's arrival with his sweetheart and her friend, the whole ducal party was being entertained in the refectory with the splendour of that powerful and luxurious monastery.

Dick, not quite with his good will, was brought before them. Gloucester, sick with fatigue, sat leaning upon one hand his white and terrifying countenance; Lord Foxham, half recovered from his wound, was in a place of honour on his left.

'How, sir?' asked Richard. 'Have ye brought me Sir Daniel's head?'

'My lord duke,' replied Dick, stoutly enough, but with a qualm at heart, 'I have not even the good fortune to return with my command. I have been, so please your grace, well beaten.'

Gloucester looked upon him with a formidable frown.

'I gave you fifty lances,[1] sir,' he said.

'My lord duke, I had but fifty men-at-arms,' replied the young knight.

'How is this?' said Gloucester. 'He did ask me fifty lances.'

'May it please your grace,' replied Catesby smoothly, 'for a pursuit we gave him but the horsemen.'

'It is well,' replied Richard, adding, 'Shelton, ye may go.'

'Stay!' said Lord Foxham. 'This young man likewise had a charge from me. It may be he hath better sped. Say, Master Shelton, have ye found the maid?'

'I praise the saints, my lord,' said Dick, 'she is in this house.'

'Is it even so? Well, then, my lord duke,' resumed Lord Foxham, 'with your good will, to-morrow, before the army march, I do propose a marriage. This young squire——'

'Young knight,' interrupted Catesby.

'Say ye so, Sir William?' cried Lord Foxham.

'I did myself, and for good service, dub him knight,' said Gloucester. 'He hath twice manfully served me. It is not valour of hands, it is a man's mind of iron, that he lacks. He will not rise, Lord Foxham. 'Tis a fellow that will fight indeed bravely in a mellay, but hath a capon's heart. How-be-it, if he is to marry, marry him in the name of Mary, and be done!'

'Nay, he is a brave lad – I know it,' said Lord Foxham. 'Content yc, then, Sir Richard. I have compounded this affair with Master Hamley, and to-morrow ye shall wed.'

Whereupon Dick judged it prudent to withdraw; but he was not yet clear of the refectory, when a man, but newly alighted at the gate, came running four stairs at a bound, and brushing through the abbey servants, threw himself on one knee before the duke.

'Victory, my lord,' he cried.

And before Dick had got to the chamber set apart for him as Lord Foxham's guest, the troops on the holm were cheering around their fires; for upon that same day, not twenty miles away, a second crushing blow had been dealt to the power of Lancaster.

---

1 Technically, the term 'lance' included a not quite certain number of foot soldiers attached to the man-at-arms.

7 Dick's Revenge

The next morning Dick was afoot before the sun, and having dressed himself to the best advantage with the aid of the Lord Foxham's baggage, and got good reports of Joan, he set forth on foot to walk away his impatience.

For some while he made rounds among the soldiery, who were getting to arms in the wintry twilight of the dawn and by the red glow of torches; but gradually he strolled farther afield, and at length passed clean beyond the outpost, and walked alone in the frozen forest, waiting for the sun.

His thoughts were both quiet and happy. His brief favour with the duke he could not find it in his heart to mourn; with Joan to wife, and my Lord Foxham for a faithful patron, he looked most happily upon the future; and in the past he found but little to regret.

As he thus strolled and pondered, the solemn light of the morning grew more clear, the east was already coloured by the sun, and a little scathing wind blew upon the frozen snow. He turned to go home; but even as he turned, his eye lit upon a figure behind a tree.

'Stand!' he cried. 'Who goes?'

The figure stepped forth and waved its hand like a dumb person. It was arrayed like a pilgrim, the hood lowered over the face, but Dick, in an instant, recognized Sir Daniel.

He strode up to him, drawing his sword; and the knight, putting his hand in his bosom, as if to seize a hidden weapon, steadfastly awaited his approach.

'Well, Dickon,' said Sir Daniel, 'how is it to be? Do ye make war upon the fallen?'

'I made no war upon your life,' replied the lad; 'I was your true friend until ye sought for mine; but ye have sought for it greedily.'

'Nay – self defence,' replied the knight. 'And now, boy, the news of this battle, and the presence of yon crooked devil here in mine own wood, have broken me beyond all help. I go to Holywood for sanctuary; thence overseas, with what I can carry, and to begin life again in Burgundy or France.'

'Ye may not go to Holywood,' said Dick.

'How! May not?' asked the knight.

'Look ye, Sir Daniel, this is my marriage morn,' said Dick; 'and yon sun that is to rise will make the brightest day that ever shone for me. Your life is forfeit – doubly forfeit, for my father's death and your own practices to me-ward. But I myself have done amiss; I have brought about men's death's; and upon this glad day I will be neither judge nor hangman. An ye were the devil, I would not lay a hand on you. An ye were the devil, ye might go where ye will for me. Seek God's forgiveness; mine ye have freely. But to go on to Holywood is different. I carry arms for York, and I will suffer no spy within their lines. Hold it, then, for certain, if ye set one foot before another, I will uplift my voice and call the nearest post to seize you.'

'Ye mock me,' said Sir Daniel. 'I have no safety out of Holywood.'

'I care no more,' returned Richard. 'I let you go east, west, or south; north I will not. Holywood is shut against you. Go, and seek not to return. For, once ye are gone, I will warn every post about this army, and there will be so shrewd a watch upon all pilgrims that, once again, were ye the very devil, ye would find it ruin to make the essay.'

'Ye doom me,' said Sir Daniel gloomily.

'I doom you not,' returned Richard. 'If it so please you to set your valour against mine, come on; and though I fear it be disloyal to my party, I will take the challenge openly and fully, fight you with mine own single strength, and call for none to help me. So shall I avenge my father, with a perfect conscience.'

'Ay,' said Sir Daniel, 'y' have a long sword against my dagger.'

'I rely upon Heaven only,' answered Dick, casting his sword some way behind him on the snow. 'Now, if your ill fate bids you, come; and, under the pleasure of the Almighty, I make myself bold to feed your bones to foxes.'

'I did but try you, Dickon,' returned the knight, with an uneasy semblance of a laugh. 'I would not spill your blood.'

'Go then, ere it be too late,' replied Shelton. 'In five minutes I will call the post. I do perceive that I am too long-suffering. Had but our places been reversed, I should have been bound hand and foot some minutes past.'

'Well, Dickon, I will go,' replied Sir Daniel. 'When we next meet, it shall repent you that ye were so harsh.'

And with these words, the knight turned and began to move off under the trees. Dick watched him with strangely mingled feelings, as he went swiftly and warily, and ever and again turning a wicked eye upon the lad who had spared him, and whom he still suspected.

There was upon one side of where he went a thicket, strongly matted with green ivy, and, even in its winter state, impervious to the eye. Herein, all of a sudden, a bow sounded like a note of music. An arrow flew, and with a great choked cry of agony and anger, the Knight of Tunstall threw up his hands and fell forward in the snow.

Dick bounded to his side and raised him. His face desperately worked; his whole body was shaken by contorting spasms.

'Is the arrow black?' he gasped.

'It is black,' replied Dick gravely.

And then, before he could add one word, a desperate seizure of pain shook the wounded man from head to foot, so that his body leaped in Dick's supporting arms, and with the extremity of that pang his spirit fled in silence.

The young man laid him back gently on the snow and prayed for that unprepared and guilty spirit, and as he prayed the sun came up at a bound, and the robins began chirping in the ivy.

When he rose to his feet, he found another man upon his knees but a few steps behind him, and, still with uncovered head, he waited until that prayer also should be over. It took long; the man, with his head bowed and his face covered with his hands, prayed like one in a great disorder or distress of mind; and by the bow that lay beside him, Dick judged that he was no other than the archer who had laid Sir Daniel low.

At length he also rose, and showed the countenance of Ellis Duckworth.

'Richard,' he said very gravely, 'I heard you. Ye took the better part and pardoned; I took the worse and there lies the clay of mine enemy. Pray for me.'

And he wrung him by the hand.

'Sir,' said Richard, 'I will pray for you indeed; though how I may prevail I wot not. But if ye have so long pursued revenge, and find it now of such a sorry flavour, bethink ye, were it not well to pardon others? Hatch – he is dead, poor shrew! I would have spared a better;

and for Sir Daniel, here lies his body. But for the priest, if I might anywise prevail, I would have you let him go.'

A flash came into the eyes of Ellis Duckworth.

'Nay,' he said, 'the devil is still strong within me. But be at rest; the Black Arrow flieth nevermore – the fellowship is broken. They that still live shall come to their quiet and ripe end, in Heaven's good time, for me; and for yourself, go where your better fortune calls you, and think no more of Ellis.'

8 Conclusion

About nine in the morning, Lord Foxham was leading his ward, once more dressed as befitted her sex, and followed by Alicia Risingham, to the church of Holywood, when Richard Crookback, his brow already heavy with cares, crossed their path and paused.

'Is this the maid?' he asked; and when Lord Foxham had replied in the affirmative, 'Minion,' he added, 'hold up your face until I see its favour.'

He looked upon her sourly for a little.

'Ye are fair,' he said at last, 'and, as they tell me, dowered. How if I offered you a brave marriage, as became your face and parentage?'

'My lord duke,' replied Joanna, 'may it please your grace, I had rather wed Sir Richard.'

'How so?' he asked harshly. 'Marry but the man I name to you, and he shall be my lord, and you my lady, before night. For Sir Richard, let me tell you plainly, he will die Sir Richard.'

'I ask no more of Heaven, my lord, than but to die Sir Richard's wife,' returned Joanna.

'Look ye at that, my lord,' said Gloucester, turning to Lord Foxham. 'Here be a pair for you. The lad, when for good services I gave him his choice of my favour, chose but the grace of an old, drunken shipman. I did warn him freely, but he was stout in his besottedness. "Here dieth your favour," said I; and he, my lord, with a most assured impertinence, "Mine be the loss," quoth he. It shall be so, by the rood!'

'Said he so?' cried Alicia. 'Then well said, lion-driver!'

'Who is this?' asked the duke.

'A prisoner of Sir Richard's,' answered Lord Foxham; 'Mistress Alicia Risingham.'

'See that she be married to a sure man,' said the duke.

'I had thought of my kinsman, Hamley, an it like your grace,' returned Lord Foxham. 'He hath well served the cause.'

'It likes me well,' said Richard. 'Let them be wedded speedily. Say, fair maid, will you wed?'

'My lord duke,' said Alicia, 'so as the man is straight——' And there, in a perfect consternation, the voice died on her tongue.

'He is straight, my mistress,' replied Richard calmly. 'I am the only crookback of my party; we are else passably well shapen. Ladies, and you, my lord,' he added, with a sudden change to grave courtesy, 'judge me not too churlish if I leave you. A captain, in the time of war, hath not the ordering of his hours.'

And with a very handsome salutation he passed on, followed by his officers.

'Alack,' cried Alicia, 'I am shent!'

'Ye know him not,' replied Lord Foxham. 'It is but a trifle; he hath already clean forgot your words.'

'He is, then, the very flower of knighthood,' said Alicia.

'Nay, he but mindeth other things,' returned Lord Foxham. 'Tarry we no more.'

In the chancel they found Dick waiting, attended by a few young men; and there were he and Joan united. When they came forth again, happy and yet serious, into the frosty air and sunlight, the long files of the army were already winding forward up the road; already the Duke of Gloucester's banner was unfolded and began to move from before the abbey in a clump of spears; and behind it, girt by steel-clad knights, the bold, black-hearted, and ambitious hunchback moved on towards his brief kingdom and his lasting infamy. But the wedding party turned upon the other side, and sat down, with sober merriment, to breakfast. The father cellarer attended on their wants, and sat with them at table. Hamley, all jealousy forgotten, began to ply the nowise loth Alicia with courtship. And there, amid the sounding of tuckets and the clash of armoured soldiery and horses continually moving forth, Dick and Joan sat side by side, tenderly held hands, and looked, with ever-growing affection, in each other's eyes.

Thenceforth the dust and blood of that unruly epoch passed them by. They dwelt apart from alarms in the green forest where their love began.

Two old men in the meanwhile enjoyed pensions in great prosperity and peace, and with perhaps a superfluity of ale and wine, in Tunstall hamlet. One had been all his life a shipman, and continued to the last to lament his man Tom. The other, who had been a bit of everything, turned in the end towards piety, and made a most religious death under the name of Brother Honestus in the neighbouring abbey. So Lawless had his will, and died a friar.